JOHN CALDIGATE

ANTHONY TROLLOPE

Born in London, April 24th, 1815
Died in London, December 6th, 1882

JOHN CALDIGATE

ANTHONY TROLLOPE

1972

THE ZODIAC PRESS

LONDON

Published by
Chatto & Windus Ltd
40 William IV Street
London W.C.2

*

Clarke, Irwin & Co. Ltd
Toronto

ISBN 0 7011 1715 x

Printed in Great Britain by
Redwood Press Limited,
Trowbridge & London

CONTENTS

I.	*Folking*	9
II.	*Puritan Grange*	16
III.	*Daniel Caldigate*	23
IV.	*The Shands*	30
V.	*The Goldfinder*	37
VI.	*Mrs. Smith*	44
VII.	*The Three Attempts*	52
VIII.	*Reaching Melbourne*	60
IX.	*Nobble*	67
X.	*Polyeuka Hall*	74
XI.	*Ahalala*	81
XII.	*Mademoiselle Cettini*	88
XIII.	*Coming Back*	95
XIV.	*Again at Home*	102
XV.	*Again at Pollington*	109
XVI.	*Again at Babington*	116
XVII.	*Again at Puritan Grange*	123
XVIII.	*Robert Bolton*	130
XIX.	*Men are so wicked*	138
XX.	*Hester's Courage*	145
XXI.	*The Wedding*	152
XXII.	*As to touching Pitch*	159
XXIII.	*The New Heir*	166
XXIV.	*News from the Gold Mines*	173
XXV.	*The Baby's Sponsors*	181
XXVI.	*A Stranger in Cambridge*	189
XXVII.	*The Christening*	196
XXVIII.	*Tom Crinkett at Folking*	203
XXIX.	*'Just by telling me that I am'*	211
XXX.	*The Conclave at Puritan Grange*	218
XXXI.	*Hester is Lured Back*	226
XXXII.	*The Babington Wedding*	234

CONTENTS

XXXIII.	*Persuasion*	242
XXXIV.	*Violence*	250
XXXV.	*In Prison*	257
XXXVI.	*The Escape*	264
XXXVII.	*Again at Folking*	271
XXXVIII.	*Bollum*	278
XXXIX.	*Restitution*	285
XL.	*Waiting for the Trial*	292
XLI.	*The First Day*	299
XLII.	*The Second Day*	306
XLIII.	*The Last Day*	313
XLIV.	*After the Verdict*	321
XLV.	*The Boltons are much Troubled*	328
XLVI.	*Burning Words*	335
XLVII.	*Curlydown and Bagwax*	343
XLVIII.	*Sir John Joram's Chambers*	350
XLIX.	*All the Shands*	358
L.	*Again at Sir John's Chambers*	365
LI.	*Dick Shand goes to Cambridgeshire*	373
LII.	*The Fortunes of Bagwax*	380
LIII.	*Sir John backs his Opinion*	388
LIV.	*Judge Bramber*	395
LV.	*How the Conspirators Throve*	402
LVI.	*The Boltons are very Firm*	409
LVII.	*Squire Caldigate at the Home Office*	416
LVIII.	*Mr. Smirkie is Ill-used*	423
LIX.	*How the Big-Wigs doubted*	430
LX.	*How Mrs. Bolton was nearly conquered*	437
LXI.	*The News reaches Cambridge*	444
LXII.	*John Caldigate's Return*	451
LXIII.	*How Mrs. Bolton was quite conquered*	458
LXIV.	*Conclusion*	465

JOHN CALDIGATE

CHAPTER I

Folking

PERHAPS it was more the fault of Daniel Caldigate the father than of his son John Caldigate, that they two could not live together in comfort in the days of the young man's early youth. And yet it would have been much for both of them that such comfortable association should have been possible to them. Wherever the fault lay, or the chief fault —for probably there was some on both sides—the misfortune was so great as to bring crushing troubles upon each of them.

There were but the two of which to make a household. When John was fifteen, and had been about a year at Harrow, he lost his mother and his two little sisters almost at a blow. The two girls went first, and the poor mother, who had kept herself alive to see them die, followed them almost instantly. Then Daniel Caldigate had been alone.

And he was a man who knew how to live alone,—a just, hard, unsympathetic man,—of whom his neighbours said, with something of implied reproach, that he bore up strangely when he lost his wife and girls. This they said, because he was to be seen riding about the country, and because he was to be heard talking to the farmers and labourers as though nothing special had happened to him. It was rumoured of him, too, that he was as constant with his books as before; and he had been a man always constant with his books; and also that he had never been seen to shed a tear, or been heard to speak of those who had been taken from him.

He was, in truth, a stout, self-constraining man, silent unless when he had something to say. Then he could become loud enough, or perhaps it might be said, eloquent. To his wife he had been inwardly affectionate, but outwardly almost stern. To his daughters he had been the same,—always anxious for every good thing on their behalf, but never able to make the children conscious of this anxiety. When they were taken from him, he suffered in silence, as such men do suffer; and he suffered the more because he knew well how little of gentleness there had been in his manners with them.

But he had hoped, as he sat alone in his desolate house, that it would be different with him and his only son,—with his son who was now the only thing left to him. But the son was a boy, and he had to look forward to what years might bring him rather than to present happiness from that source. When the boy came home for his holidays, the father would sometimes walk with him, and discourse on certain chosen subjects,—on the politics of the day, in regard to which Mr. Caldigate was an advanced Liberal, on the abomination of the Game Laws, on the folly of Protection, on the antiquated absurdity of a State Church;—as to all which matters his son John lent him a very inattentive ear. Then the lad would escape and kill rabbits, or rats, or even take birds' nests, with a zest for such pursuits which was disgusting to the father, though he would not absolutely forbid them. Then John would be allured to go to his uncle Babington's house, where there was a pony on which he could hunt, and fishing-rods, and a lake with a boat, and three fine bouncing girl-cousins, who made much of him, and called him Jack; so that he soon preferred his uncle Babington's house, and would spend much of his holidays at Babington House.

Mr. Caldigate was a country squire with a moderate income, living in a moderate house called Folking, in the parish of Utterden, about ten miles from Cambridge. Here he owned nearly the entire parish, and some portion of Netherden, which lay next to it, having the reputation of an income of £3,000 a-year. It probably amounted to about two-thirds of that. Early in life he had been a very poor man, owing to the improvidence of his father; but he had soon quarrelled with his father,—as he had with almost everyone else,—and had for some ten years earned his own bread in the metropolis among the magazines and newspapers. Then, when his father died, the property was his own, with such encumbrances as the old squire had been able to impose upon it. Daniel Caldigate had married when he was a poor man, but did not go to Folking to live till the estate was clear, at which time he was forty years old. When he was endeavouring to inculcate good Liberal principles into that son of his, who was burning the while to get off to a battle of rats among the corn-stacks, he was not yet fifty. There might therefore be some time left to him for the promised joys of companionship if he could only convince the boy that politics were better than rats.

But he did not long make himself any such promise. It seemed to him that his son's mind was of a nature very different from his own; and much like to that of his grandfather. The lad could be awakened to no enthusiasm in the abuse of Conservative leaders. And those Babingtons were such fools! He despised the whole race of them,—especially those thick-legged, romping, cherry-cheeked damsels, of whom, no doubt, his son would marry one. They were all of the earth earthy, without an idea among them. And yet he did not dare to forbid his son to go to the house, lest people should say of him that his sternness was unendurable.

Folking is not a place having many attractions of its own, beyond the rats. It lies in the middle of the Cambridgeshire fens, between St. Ives, Cambridge, and Ely. In the two parishes of Utterden and Netherden there is no rise of ground which can by any stretch of complaisance be called a hill. The property is bisected by an immense straight dike, which is called the Middle Wash, and which is so sluggish, so straight, so ugly, and so deep, as to impress the mind of a stranger with the ideas of suicide. And there are straight roads and straight dikes, with ugly names on all sides, and passages through the country called droves, also with ugly appellations of their own, which certainly are not worthy of the name of roads. The Folking Causeway possesses a bridge across the Wash, and is said to be the remains of an old Roman Way which ran in a perfectly direct line from St. Neots to Ely. When you have crossed the bridge going northward,—or north-westward,— there is a lodge at your right hand, and a private road running, as straight as a line can be drawn, through pollard poplars, up to Mr. Caldigate's house. Round the house there are meadows, and a large old-fashioned kitchen garden, and a small dark flower-garden, with clipt hedges and straight walks, quite in the old fashion. The house itself is dark, picturesque, well-built, low, and uncomfortable. Part of it is as old as the time of Charles II, and part dates from Queen Anne. Something was added at a later date,—perhaps early in the Georges; but it was all done with good materials, and no stint of labour. Shoddy had not been received among building materials when any portion of Folking was erected. But then neither had modern ideas of comfort become in vogue. Just behind the kitchen-garden a great cross ditch, called Foul-water Drain, runs, or rather creeps, down to the Wash, looking on that side as though it had been made to act as a moat to the house; and on the other side of the drain there is Twopenny Drove, at the end of which Twopenny Ferry leads to Twopenny Hall, a farmhouse across the Wash belonging to Mr. Caldigate. The fields around are all square and all flat, all mostly arable, and are often so deep in mud that a stranger wonders that a plough should be able to be dragged through the soil. The farming is, however, good of its kind, and the ploughing is mostly done by steam.

Such is and has been for some years the house at Folking in which Mr. Caldigate has lived quite alone. For five years after his wife's death he had only on rare occasions received visitors there. Twice his brother had come to Folking, and had brought a son with him. The brother had been a fellow of a college at Cambridge, and had taken a living, and married late in life. The living was far away in Dorsetshire, and the son, at the time of these visits, was being educated at a private school. Twice they had both been at Folking together, and the uncle had, in his silent way, liked the boy. The lad had preferred, or had pretended to prefer, books to rats; had understood, or seemed to understand, something of the advantages of cheap food for the people, and had been commended by the father for general good conduct. But when they had last taken their departure from Folking, no one had entertained any idea of any peculiar relations between the nephew and the uncle. It was not till a year or two more had run by, that Mr. Daniel Caldigate thought of making his nephew George the heir to the property.

The property indeed was entailed upon John, as it had been entailed upon John's father. There were many institutions of his country which Mr. Caldigate hated with almost an inhuman hatred; but there were none more odious to him than that of entails, which institution he was wont to prove by many arguments to be the source of all the ignorance and all the poverty and all the troubles by which his country was inflicted. He had got his own property by an entail, and certainly never would have had an acre had his father been able to consume more than a life-interest. But he had denied that the property had done him any good, and was loud in declaring that the entail had done the property and those who lived on it very much harm. In his heart of hearts he did feel a desire that when he was gone the acres should still belong to Caldigate. There was so much in him of the leaven of a the old English squirarchic aristocracy as to create a pride in the fact that the Caldigates had been at Folking for three hundred years, and a wish that they might remain there; and no doubt he knew that without repeated entails they would not have remained there. But still he had hated the thing, and as years rolled on he came to think that the entail now existing would do an especial evil.

His son on leaving school spent almost the whole four months between that time and the beginning of his first term at Cambridge with the Babingtons. This period included the month of September, and afforded therefore much partridge shooting,—than which nothing was meaner in the opinion of the Squire of Folking. When a short visit was made to Folking, the father was sarcastic and disagreeable; and then, for the first time, John Caldigate showed himself to be possessed of a power of reply which was peculiarly disagreeable to the old man. This had the effect of cutting down the intended allowance of £250 to £220 per annum, for which sum the father had been told that his son could live like a gentleman at the University. This parsimony so disgusted uncle Babington, who lived on the other side of the county, within the borders of Suffolk, that he insisted on giving his nephew a hunter, and an undertaking to bear the expense of the animal as long as John should remain at the University. No arrangement could have been more foolish. And that last visit made by John to Babington House for the two days previous to his Cambridge career was in itself most indiscreet. The angry father would not take upon himself to forbid it, but was worked up by it to perilous jealousy. He did not scruple to declare aloud that old Humphrey Babington was a thick-headed fool; nor did Humphrey Babington, who, with his ten or twelve thousand a-year, was considerably involved, scruple to say that he hated such cheese-paring ways. John Caldigate felt more distaste to the cheese-paring ways than he did to his uncle's want of literature.

Such was the beginning of the rupture which took place before the time had come for John to take his degree. When that time came he had a couple of hunters at Cambridge, played in the Cambridge eleven, and rowed in one of the Trinity boats. He also owed something over £800 to the regular tradesmen of the University, and a good deal more to other creditors who were not 'regular.' During the whole of this time his visits to Folking had been short and few. The old squire had become more and more angry, and not the less so because he was sensible of a non-performance of duty on his own part. Though he was close to Cambridge he never went to see his son; nor would even press the lad to come out to Folking. Nor when, on rare occasions, a visit was made, did he endeavour to make the house pleasant. He was jealous, jealous to hot anger, at being neglected, but could not bring himself to make advances to his own son. Then when he heard from his son's tutor that his son could not pass his degree without the payment of £800 for recognised debts,—then his anger boiled over, and he told John Caldigate that he was expelled from his father's heart and his father's house.

The money was paid and the degree was taken: and there arose the question as to what was to be done. John, of course, took himself to Babington House, and was condoled with by his uncle and cousins. His troubles at this time were numerous enough. That £800 by no means summed up his whole indebtedness;—covered indeed but a small part of it. He had been at Newmarket; and there was a pleasant gentleman, named Davis, who frequented that place and Cambridge, who had been very civil to him when he lost a little money, and who now held his acceptances for, alas! much more than £800. Even uncle Babington knew nothing of this when the degree was taken. And then there came a terrible blow to him. Aunt Babington,—aunt Polly as she was called,—got him into her own closet upstairs, where she kept her linen and her jams and favourite liqueurs, and told him that his cousin Julia was dying in love for him. After all that had passed, of course it was expected he would engage himself to his cousin Julia. Now Julia was the eldest, the thickest-ankled, and the cherry-cheekedest of the lot. To him up to that time the Babington folk had always been a unit. No one else had been so good-natured to him, had so petted him, and so freely administered to all his wants. He would kiss them all round whenever he went to Babington; but he had not kissed Julia more than her sisters. There were three sons, whom he never specially liked, and who certainly were fools. One was the heir, and, of course, did nothing; the second was struggling for a degree at Oxford with an eye to the family living; the third was in a fair way to become the family gamekeeper. He certainly did not wish to marry into the family;—and yet they had all been so kind to him!

'I should have nothing to marry on, aunt Polly,' he said.

Then he was reminded that he was his father's heir, and that his father's house was sadly in want of a mistress. They could live at Babington till Folking should be ready. The prospect was awful!

What is a young man to say in such a position? 'I do not love the young lady after that fashion, and therefore I must decline.' It requires a hero, and a cold-blooded hero, to do that. And aunt Polly was very much in earnest, for she brought Julia into the room, and absolutely delivered her up into the young man's arms.

'I am so much in debt,' he said, 'that I don't care to think of it.'

Aunt Polly declared that such debts did not signify in the least. Folking was not embarrassed. Folking did not owe a shilling. Every one knew that. And there was Julia in his arms! He never said that he would marry her; but when he left the linen-closet the two ladies understood that the thing was arranged.

Luckily for him aunt Polly had postponed this scene till the moment before his departure from the house. He was at this time going to Cambridge, where he was to be the guest, for one night, of a certain Mr. Bolton, who was one of the very few friends to whom his father was still attached. Mr. Bolton was a banker, living close to Cambridge, an old man now, with four sons and one daughter; and to his house John Caldigate was going in order that he might there discuss with Mr. Bolton certain propositions which had been made between him and his father respecting the Folking property. The father had now realised the idea of buying his son out; and John himself, who had all the world and all his life before him, and was terribly conscious of the obligations which he owed to his friend Davis, had got into his head a notion that he would prefer to face his fortune with a sum of ready money, than to wait in absolute poverty for the reversion of the family estate. He had his own ideas, and in furtherance of them he had made certain inquiries. There was gold being found at this moment among the mountains of New South Wales, in quantities which captivated his imagination. And this was being done in a most lovely spot, among circumstances which were in all respects romantic. His friend, Richard Shand, who was also a Trinity man, was quite resolved to go out, and he was minded to accompany his friend. In this way, and, as he thought, in this way only, could a final settlement be made with that most assiduous of attendants, Mr. Davis. His mind was fully set upon New South Wales, and his little interview with his cousin Julia did not tend to bind him more closely to his own country, or to Babington, or to Folking.

CHAPTER II

Puritan Grange

PERHAPS there had been a little treachery on the part of Mr. Davis, for he had, in a gently insinuating way, made known to the Squire the fact of those acceptances, and the additional fact that he was, through unforeseen circumstances, lamentably in want of ready money. The Squire became eloquent, and assured Mr. Davis that he would not pay a penny to save either Mr. Davis or his son from instant imprisonment,— or even from absolute starvation. Then Mr. Davis shrugged his shoulders, and whispered the word, 'Post-obits.' The Squire, thereupon, threatened to kick him out of the house, and, on the next day, paid a visit to his friend Mr. Bolton. There had, after that, been a long correspondence between the father, the son, and Mr. Bolton, as to which John Caldigate said not a word to the Babingtons. Had he been more communicative, he might have perhaps saved himself from that scene in the linen-closet. As it was, when he started for Cambridge, nothing was known at Babington either of Mr. Davis or of the New South Wales scheme.

Mr. Bolton lived in a large red-brick house, in the village of Chesterton, near to Cambridge, which, with a large garden, was surrounded by an old, high, dark-coloured brick-wall. He rarely saw any company; and there were probably not many of the more recently imported inhabitants of the town who had ever been inside the elaborate iron gates by which the place was to be approached. He had been a banker all his life, and was still reported to be the senior partner in Bolton's bank. But the management of the concern had, in truth, been given up to his two elder sons. His third son was a barrister in London, and a fourth was settled in Cambridge as a solicitor. These men were all married, and were doing well in the world, living in houses better than their father's, and spending a great deal more money. Mr. Bolton had the name of being a hard man, because, having begun life in small circumstances, he had never learned to chuck his shillings about easily; but he had, in a most liberal manner, made over the bulk of his fortune to his sons; and though he himself could rarely be got to sit at their tables, he took delight in hearing that they lived bounteously with their friends. He had been twice married, and there now lived with him his second wife and a daughter, Hester,—a girl about sixteen years of age at the period of John Caldigate's visit to Puritan Grange, as

16

Mr. Bolton's house was called. At this time Puritan Grange was not badly named; for Mrs. Bolton was a lady of stern life, and Hester Bolton was brought up with more of seclusion and religious observances than are now common in our houses.

Mr. Bolton was probably ten years older than the Squire of Folking; but circumstances had, in early life, made them fast friends. The old Squire had owed a large sum of money to the bank, and Mr. Bolton had then been attracted by the manner in which the son had set himself to work, so that he might not be a burden on the estate. They had been fast friends for a quarter of a century, and now the arrangement of terms between the present Squire and his son had been left to Mr. Bolton.

Mr. Bolton had, no doubt, received a very unfavourable account of the young man. Men, such as was Mr. Bolton, who make their money by lending it out at recognised rates of interest,—and who are generally very keen in looking after their principal,—have no mercy whatsoever for the Davises of creation, and very little for their customers. To have had dealings with a Davis is condemnation in their eyes. Mr. Bolton would not, therefore, have opened his gates to this spendthrift had not his feelings for the father been very strong. He had thought much upon the matter, and had tried hard to dissuade the Squire. He, the banker, was not particularly attached to the theory of primogeniture. He had divided his wealth equally between his own sons. But he had a strong idea as to property and its rights. The young man's claim to Folking after his father's death was as valid as the father's claim during his life. No doubt, the severance of the entail, if made at all, would be made in accordance with the young man's wishes, and on certain terms which should be declared to be just by persons able to compute the value of such rights. No doubt, also,—so Mr. Bolton thought,—the property would be utterly squandered if left in its present condition. It would be ruined by incumbrances in the shape of post-obits. All this had been deeply considered, and at last Mr. Bolton had consented to act between the father and the son.

When John Caldigate was driven up through the iron gates to Mr. Bolton's door, his mind was not quite at ease within him. He had seen Mr. Bolton on two or three occasions during his University career, and had called at the house; but he had never entered it, and had never seen the ladies; and now it was necessary that he should discuss his own follies, and own all his faults. Of course, that which he was going to do would, in the eyes of the British world, be considered very unwise. The British world regards the position of heirship to acres as the most desirable which a young man could hold. That he was about to

17

abandon. But, as he told himself, without abandoning it he could not rid himself from the horror of Davis. He was quite prepared to acknowledge his own vice and childish stupidity in regard to Davis. He had looked all round that now, and was sure that he would do nothing of the kind again. But how could he get rid of Davis in any other way than this? And then Folking had no charms for him. He hated Folking. He was certain that any life would suit him better than a life to be passed as squire of Folking. And he was quite alive to the fact that, though there was at home the prospect of future position and future income, for the present there would be nothing. Were he to submit himself humbly to his father, he might probably be allowed to vegetate at the old family home. But there was no career for him. No profession had as yet been even proposed. His father was fifty-five, a very healthy man,—likely to live for the next twenty years. And then it would be impossible that he should dwell in peace under the same roof with his father. And Davis! Life would be miserable to him if he could not free himself from that thraldom. The sum of money which was to be offered to him, and which was to be raised on the Folking property, would enable him to pay Davis, and to start upon his career with plentiful means in his pocket. He would, too, be wise, and not risk all his capital. Shand had a couple of thousand pounds, and he would start with a like sum of his own. Should he fail in New South Wales, there would still be something on which to begin again. With his mind thus fixed, he entered Mr. Bolton's gates.

He was to stay one night at Puritan Grange; and then, if the matter were arranged, he would go over to Folking for a day or two, and endeavour to part from his father on friendly terms. In that case he would be able to pay Davis himself, and there need be no ground for quarrelling on that score.

Before dinner the matter was settled at the Grange. The stern old man bade his visitor sit down, and then explained to him at full length that which it was proposed to do. So much money the Squire had himself put by; so much more Mr. Bolton himself would advance; the value had been properly computed; and, should the arrangement be completed, he, John Caldigate, would sell his inheritance at its proper price. Over and over again the young man endeavoured to interrupt the speaker, but was told to postpone his words till the other should have done. Such interruptions came from the too evident fact that Mr. Bolton thoroughly despised his guest. Caldigate, though he had been very foolish, though he had loved to slaughter rats and rabbits, and to romp with the girls at Babington, was by no means a fool. He was possessed of good natural abilities, of great activity, and of a high

18

spirit. His appreciation was quicker than that of the old banker, who, as he soon saw, had altogether failed to understand him. In every word that the banker spoke, it was evident that he thought that these thousands would be squandered instantly. The banker spoke as though this terrible severance was to be made because the natural heir had shown himself to be irrevocably bad. What could be expected from a youth who was deep in the books of a Davis before he had left his college? 'I do not recommend this,' he said at last. 'I have never recommended it. The disruption is so great as to be awful. But when your father has asked what better step he could take, I have been unable to advise him.' It was as though the old man were telling the young one that he was too bad for hope, and that, therefore, he must be consigned for ever to perdition.

Caldigate, conscious of the mistake which the banker was making, full of hope as to himself, intending to acknowledge the follies of which he had been guilty, and, at the same time, not to promise,—for he would not condescend so far,—but to profess that they were things of the past, and impatient of the judgment expressed against him, endeavoured to stop the old man in his severity, so that the tone in which the business was being done might be altered. But when he found that he could not do this without offence, he leaned back in his chair, and heard the indictment to the end. 'Now, Mr. Bolton,' he said, when at length his time came, 'you shall hear my view of the matter.' And Mr. Bolton did hear him, listening very patiently. Caldigate first asserted, that in coming there, to Puritan Grange, his object had been to learn what were the terms proposed,—as to which he was now willing to give his assent. He had already quite made up his mind to sell what property he had on the estate, and therefore, though he was much indebted to Mr. Bolton for his disinterested and kind friendship, he was hardly in want of counsel on that matter. Mr. Bolton raised his eyebrows, but still listened patiently. Caldigate then went on to explain his views as to life, declaring that under no circum-stances—had there been no Davis—would he have consented to remain at Folking as a deputy-squire, waiting to take up his position some twenty years hence at his father's death. Nor, even were Folking his own at this moment, would he live there! He must do something; and, upon the whole, he thought that gold-mining in the colonies was the most congenial pursuit to which he could put his hand. Then he made a frank acknowledgment as to Davis and his gambling follies, and ended by saying that the matter might be regarded as settled.

He had certainly been successful in changing the old man's opinion. Mr. Bolton did not say as much, nor was he a man likely to make such acknowledgment; but when he led John Caldigate away to be introduced to his wife in the drawing-room, he felt less of disdain for his guest than he had done half an hour before. Mr. Bolton was a silent, cautious man, even in his own family, and had said nothing of this business to his wife, and nothing, of course, to his daughter. Mrs. Bolton asked after the Squire, and expressed a hope that her guest would not find the house very dull for one night. She had heard that John Caldigate was a fast young man, and of course regarded him as a lost sinner. Hester, who was with her mother, looked at him with all her young big eyes, but did not speak a word. It was very seldom that she saw any young man, or indeed young people of either sex. But when this stranger spoke freely to her mother about this subject and the other, she listened to him and was interested.

John Caldigate, without being absolutely handsome, was a youth sure to find favour in a woman's eyes. He was about five feet ten in height, strong and very active, with bright dark eyes which were full of life and intelligence. His forehead was square and showed the angles of his brow; his hair was dark and thick and cut somewhat short; his mouth was large, but full of expression and generally, also, of good-humour. His nose would have been well formed, but that it was a little snubbed at the end. Altogether his face gave you the idea of will, intellect, and a kindly nature; but there was in it a promise, too, of occasional anger, and a physiognomist might perhaps have expected from it that vacillation in conduct which had hitherto led him from better things into wretched faults.

As he was talking to Mrs. Bolton he had observed the girl, who sat apart, with her fingers busy on her work, and who had hardly spoken a word since his entrance. She was, he thought, the most lovely human being that he had ever beheld; and yet she was hardly more than a child. But how different from those girls at Babington! Her bright brown hair was simply brushed from off her forehead and tied in a knot behind her head. Her dress was as plain as a child's, —as though it was intended that she should still be regarded as a child. Her face was very fair, with large, grey, thoughtful eyes, and a mouth which, though as Caldigate watched her it was never opened, seemed always as if it was just about to pour forth words. And he could see that though her eyes were intent upon her work, from time to time she looked across at him; and he thought that if only they two were alone together, he could teach her to speak.

But no such opportunity was given to him now, or during his short sojourn at the Grange. After a while the old man returned to the room and took him up to his bed-chamber. It was then about half-past four, and he was told that they were to dine at six. It was early in November,—not cold enough for bedroom fires among thrifty people, and there he was left, apparently to spend an hour with nothing to do. Rebelling against this, declaring that even at Puritan Grange he would be master of his own actions, he rushed down into the hall, took his hat, and walked off into the town. He would go and take one last look at the old college.

He went in through the great gate and across the yard, and passing by the well-known buttery-hatches, looked into the old hall for the last time. The men were all seated at dinner, and he could see the fellows up at the high table. Three years ago it had been his fixed resolve to earn for himself the right to sit upon that dais. He had then been sure of himself,—that he would do well, and take honours, and win a fellowship. There had been moments in which he had thought that a college life would suit him till he came into his own property. But how had all that faded away! Everybody had congratulated him on the ease with which he did his work,—and the result had been Newmarket, Davis, and a long score in the ephemeral records of a cricket match. As he stood there, with his slouched hat over his eyes, one of the college servants recognised him, and called him by his name. Then he passed on quickly, and made his way out to the gravel-walk by the river-side. It was not yet closed for the night, and he went on, that he might take one last turn up and down the old avenue.

He had certainly made a failure of his life so far. He did acknowledge to himself that there was something nobler in these classic shades than in the ore-laden dirt of an Australian gold-gully. He knew as much of the world as that. He had not hitherto chosen the better part, and now something of regret, even as to Folking,—poor old Folking,—came upon him. He was, as it were, being kicked out and repudiated by his own family as worthless. And what was he to do about Julia Babington? After that scene in the linen-closet, he could not leave his country without a word either to Julia or to aunt Polly. But the idea of Julia was doubly distasteful to him since that lovely vision of young female simplicity had shone upon him from the corner of Mrs. Bolton's drawing-room. Romping with the Babington girls was all very well; but if he could only feel the tips of that girl's fingers come within the grasp of his hand! Then he thought that it would lend a fine romance to his life if he could resolve to come back, when he should be laden with gold, and make Hester Bolton his wife. It should be his romance, and he swore that he would cling to it.

He turned back, and came down to dinner five minutes after the time. At ten minutes before dinner-time Mr. Bolton heard that he was gone out and was offended,—thinking it quite possible that he would not return at all. What might not be expected from a young man who could so easily abandon his inheritance! But he was there, only five minutes after the time, and the dinner was eaten almost in silence. In the evening there was tea, and the coldest shivering attempt at conversation for half an hour, during which he could still at moments catch the glance of Hester's eyes, and see the moving curve of her lips. Then there was a reading of the Bible, and prayer, and before ten he was in his bed-room.

On the next morning as he took his departure, Mr. Bolton said a word intended to be gracious. 'I hope you may succeed in your enterprise, Mr. Caldigate.'

'Why should I not as well as another?' said John, cheerily.

'If you are steady, sober, industrious, self-denying and honest, you probably will,' replied the banker.

'To promise all that would be to promise too much,' said John. 'But I mean to make an effort.' Then at that moment he made one effort which was successful. For an instant he held Hester's fingers within his hand.

CHAPTER III

Daniel Caldigate

THAT piece of business was done. It was one of the disagreeable things which he had had to do before he could get away to the gold-diggings, and it was done. Now he had to say farewell to his father, and that would be a harder task. As the moment was coming in which he must bid adieu to his father, perhaps for ever, and bid adieu to the old place which, though he despised it, he still loved, his heart was heavy within him. He felt sure that his father had no special regard for him;—in which he was, of course, altogether wrong, and the old man was equally wrong in supposing that his son was unnaturally deficient in filial affection. But they had never known each other, and were so different that neither had understood the other. The son, however, was ready to confess to himself that the chief fault had been with himself. It was natural, he thought, that a father's regard should be deadened by such conduct as his had been, and natural that an old man should not believe in the quick repentance and improvement of a young one.

He hired a gig and drove himself over from Cambridge to Folking. As he got near to the place, passed along the dikes, and looked to the right and left down the droves, and trotted at last over the Folking bridge across the Middle Wash, the country did not seem to him to be so unattractive as of yore; and when he recognised the faces of the neighbours, when one of the tenants spoke to him kindly, and the girls dropped a curtsey as he passed, certain soft regrets began to crop up in his mind. After all, there is a comfort in the feeling of property—not simply its money comfort, but in the stability and reputation of a recognised home. Six months ago there had seemed to him to be some-thing ridiculous in the idea of a permanent connection between the names of Caldigate and Folking. It was absurd that, with so wild and beautiful a world around him, he should be called upon to live in a washy fen because his father and grandfather had been unfortunate enough to do so. And then, at that time, all sympathy with bricks and mortar, any affection for special trees or well-known home-haunts, was absurd in his eyes. And as his father had been harsh to him, and did not like him, would it not be better that they should be far apart? It was thus that he had reasoned. But now all that was changed. An unwonted tenderness had come upon his spirit. The very sallows by

23

the brook seemed to appeal to him. As he saw the house chimneys through the trees, he remembered that they had carried smoke from the hearths of many generations of Caldigates. He remembered, too, that his father would soon be old, and would be alone. It seemed to himself that his very mind and spirit were altered.

But all that was too late. He had agreed to the terms proposed; and even were he now to repudiate them, what could he do with Davis, and how could he live for the present? Not for a moment did he entertain such an idea, but he had lost that alacrity of spirit which had been his when he first found the way out of his difficulties.

His father did not come forth to meet him. He went in across the hall and through the library, into a little closet beyond, in which Mr. Caldigate was wont to sit. 'Well, John,' said the old man, 'how have you and Mr. Bolton got on together?'

There seemed to be something terribly cold in this. It might be better that they should part,—better, even, though the parting should be for ever. It might be right;—nay, he knew that it was right that he should be thrust out of the inheritance. He had spent money that was not his own, and, of course, he must pay the debt. But that his father should sit there in his chair on his entrance, not even rising to greet him, and should refer at once to Mr. Bolton and that business arrangement, as though that, and that alone, need now be discussed, did seem to him to be almost cruel. Of all that his father had suffered in constraining himself to this conduct, he understood nothing. 'Mr. Bolton made himself very plain, sir.'

'He would be sure to do so. He is a man of business, and intelligent. But as to the terms proposed, were they what you had expected?'

'Quite as good as I had expected.'

'Whether good or bad, of course you will understand that I have had nothing to do with them. The matter has been referred to two gentlemen conversant with such subjects; and, after due inquiry, they told Mr. Bolton what was the money value of your rights. It is a question to be settled as easily as the price of a ton of coals or a joint of beef. But you must understand that I have not interfered.'

'I am quite aware of that, sir.'

'As for the money, something over a third of it is in my own hands. I have not been extravagant myself, and have saved so much. The remainder will come out of Mr. Bolton's bank, and will be lent on mortgage. I certainly shall not have cause for extravagance now, living here alone; and shall endeavour to free the estate from the burden by degrees. When I die, it will, in accordance with my present purpose, go to your cousin George.' As this was said, John thought he perceived

24

something live a quiver in his father's voice, which, up to that point, had been hard, clear, and unshaken. 'As to that, however, I do not intend to pledge myself,' he continued. 'The estate will now be my own, subject to the claim from Messrs. Bolton's bank. I don't know that there is anything else to be said.'

'Not about business, sir.'

'And it is business, I suppose, that has brought you here,—and to Cambridge. I do not know what little things you have of your own in the house.'

'Not much, sir.'

'If there be anything that you wish to take, take it. But with you now, I suppose, money is the only possession that has any value.'

'I should like to have the small portrait of you,—the miniature.'

'The miniature of me,' said the father, almost scoffingly, looking up at his son's face, suspiciously. And yet, though he would not show it, he was touched. Only if this were a ruse on the part of the young man, a mock sentiment, a little got-up theatrical pretence,—then,—then how disgraced he would be in his own estimation at having been moved by such mockery!

The son stood square before his father, disdaining any attempt to evince a supplicating tenderness either by his voice or by his features. 'But, perhaps, you have a special value for it,' he said.

'No, indeed. It is others, not oneself, that ought to have such trifles, —that is, if they are of value at all.'

'There is none but myself that can care much for it.'

'There is no one to care at all. No one else that is,' he added, wishing to avoid any further declaration. 'Take that or anything else you want in the house. There will be things left, I suppose,—clothes and books and suchlike.'

'Hardly anything, sir. Going so far, I had better give them away. A few books I shall take.' Then the conversation was over; and in a few minutes John Caldigate found himself roaming alone about the place.

It was so probable that he might never see it again! Indeed it seemed to him now that were he to return to England with a fortune made, he would hardly come to Folking. Years and years must roll by before that could be done. If he could only come back to Cambridge and fetch that wife away with him, then he thought it would be better for him to live far from England, whether he were rich or whether he were poor. It was quite evident that his father's heart was turned from him altogether. Of course he had himself to blame,—himself only; but still it was strange to him that a father should feel no tenderness at parting with an only son. While he had been in the room he had constrained

25

himself manfully; not a drop of moisture had glittered in his eye; not a tone of feeling had thrilled in his voice; his features had never failed him. There had always been that look of audacity on his brow joined to a certain manliness of good-humour in his mouth, as though he had been thoroughly master of himself and the situation. But now, as he pushed his hat from off his forehead, he rubbed his hand across his eyes to dash away the tears. He felt almost inclined to rush back to the house and fall on his knees before his father, and kiss the old man's hands, and beg the old man's blessing. But though he was potent for much he was not potent for that. Such expression of tenderness would have been true; but he knew that he would so break down in the attempt as to make it seem to be false.

He got out upon Twopenny Drove and passed over the ferry, meaning to walk across the farm and so out on to the Causeway, and round home by the bridge. But on the other side of the Wash he encountered Mr. Ralph Holt, the occupier of Twopenny farm, whose father also and grandfather had lived upon the same acres. 'And so thou be'est going away from us, Mr. John,' said the farmer, with real tenderness, almost with solemnity, in his voice, although there was at the same time something ridiculous in the far-fetched sadness of his tone and gait.

'Yes, indeed, Holt, I want to travel and see the world at a distance from here.'

'If it was no more than that, Mr. John, there would be nothing about it. Zeeing the world! You young collegers allays does that. But be'est thou to come back and be Squoire o' Foulking?'

'I think not, Holt, I think not. My father, I hope, will be Squire for many a year.'

'Like enough. And we all hope that, for there aren't nowhere a juster man nor the Squoire, and he's hale and hearty. But in course of things his time'll run out. And it be so, Mr. John, that thou be'est going for ever and allays?'

'I rather think I am.'

'It's wrong, Mr. John. Though maybe I'm making over-free to talk of what don't concern me. Yet I say it's wrong. Sons should come arter fathers, specially where there's land. We don't none of us like it;—none of us! It's worse nor going, any one of ourselves. For what's a lease? But when a man has a freehold he should stick to it for ever and aye. It's just as though the old place was a-tumbling about all our ears.' Caldigate was good-natured with the man, trying to make him understand that everything was being done for the best. And at last he bade him good-bye affectionately, shaking hands with him, and going into the farmhouse to perform the same ceremony with his wife and daughters. But to the last Ralph Holt was uncomfortable and dismal, foretelling miseries. It was clear that, to his thinking, the stability of this world was undermined and destroyed by the very contemplation of such a proceeding as this.

Caldigate pursued his walk, and in the course of it bade farewell to more than one old friend. None of them were so expressive as Holt, but he could perceive that he was regarded by all of them as a person who, by his conduct, was bringing misfortune, not only on himself, but on the whole parishes of Utterden and Netherden.

At dinner the Squire conversed upon various subjects, if not easily to himself, at least with affected ease. Had he applied himself to subjects altogether indifferent,—to the state of politics, or the Game Laws, or the absurdities of a State Church, the unfitness of such matters for the occasion would have been too apparent. Both he and his son would have broken down in the attempt. But he could talk about Babington,—abusing the old family,—and even about himself, and about New South Wales, and gold, and the coming voyage, without touching points which had been, and would be, specially painful. Not a word had ever been spoken between them as to Davis. There had, of course, been letters, very angry letters; but the usurer's name had never been mentioned. Nor was there any need that it should be mentioned now. It was John's affair,—not in any way his. So he asked and listened to much about Richard Shand, and the mode of gold-finding practised among the diggings in New South Wales.

When the old butler had gone he was even more free, speaking of things that were past, not only without anger, but, as far as possible, without chagrin,—treating his son as a person altogether free from any control of his. 'I dare say it is all for the best,' he said.

'It is well at any rate to try to think so, sir,' replied John, conscience-stricken as to his own faults.

'I doubt whether there would have been anything for you to do here,—or at least anything that you would have done. You would have had too much ambition to manage this little estate under me, and not enough of industry, I fear, to carry you to the front in any of the professions. I used to think of the bar.'

'And so did I.'

'But when I found that the Babingtons had got hold of you, and that you liked horses and guns, better than words and arguments—'

'I never did, sir.'

'It seemed so.'

'Of course I have been weak.'

'Do not suppose for a moment that I am finding fault. It would be of no avail, and I would not thus embitter our last hours together. But when I saw how your tastes seemed to lead you, I began to fear that there could be no career for you here. On such a property as Babington an eldest son may vegetate like his father before him, and may succeed to it in due time, before he has wasted everything, and may die as he had lived, useless, but having to the end all the enjoyments of a swine.'

'You are severe upon my cousins, sir.'

'I say what I think. But you would not have done that. And though you are not industrious, you are far too active and too clever for such a life. Now you are probably in earnest as to the future.'

'Yes, I am certainly in earnest.'

'And though you are going to risk your capital in a precarious business, you will only be doing what is done daily by enterprising men. I could wish that your position were more secure;—but that now cannot be helped.'

'My bed is as I have made it. I quite understand that, sir.'

'Thinking of all this, I have endeavoured to reconcile myself to your going.' Then he paused a moment, considering what he should next say. And his son was silent, knowing that something further was to come. 'Had you remained in England we could hardly have lived together as father and son should live. You would have been dependent on me, and would have rebelled against that submission which a state of dependence demands. There would have been nothing for you but to have waited,—and almost to have wished, for my death.'

'No, sir; never; never that.'

'It would have been no more than natural. I shall hear from you sometimes?'

'Certainly, sir.'

'It will give an interest to my life if you will write occasionally. Whither do you go to-morrow?'

It had certainly been presumed, though never said, that this last visit to the old home was to be only for one day. The hired gig had been kept; and in his letter the son had asked whether he could be taken in for Thursday night. But now the proposition that he should go so soon seemed to imply a cold-blooded want of feeling on his part. 'I need not be in such a hurry, sir,' he said.

'Of course, it shall be as you please, but I do not know that you will do any good by staying. A last month may be pleasant enough, or even a last week, but a last day is purgatory. The melancholy of the occasion cannot be shaken off. It is only the prolonged wail of a last farewell.' All this was said in the old man's ordinary voice, but it seemed to betoken, if not feeling itself, a recognition of feeling which the son had not expected.

'It is very sad,' said the son.

'Therefore, why prolong it? Stand not upon the order of your going but go at once,—seeing that it is necessary that you should go. Will you take any more wine? No? Then let us go into the other room. As they are making company of you and have lighted another fire, we will do as they would have us.' Then for the rest of the evening there was some talk about books, and the father, who was greatly given to reading, explained to his son what kind of literature would, as he thought, fit in best with the life of a gold-digger.

After what had passed, Caldigate, of course, took his departure on the following morning. 'Good-bye,' said the old man, as the son grasped his hand, 'Good-bye.' He made no overture to come even as far as the hall in making this his final adieu.

'I trust I may return to see you in health.'

'It may be so. As to that we can say nothing. Good-bye.' Then, when the son had turned his back, the father recalled him, by a murmur rather than by a word,—but in that moment he had resolved to give way a little to the demands of nature. 'Good-bye, my son,' he said, in a low voice, very solemnly; 'May God bless you and preserve you.' Then he turned back at once to his own closet.

CHAPTER IV

The Shands

JOHN CALDIGATE had promised to go direct from Folking to the house of his friend Richard Shand, or rather, to the house in which lived Richard Shand's father and family. The two young men had much to arrange together, and this had been thought to be expedient. When Caldigate, remembering how affairs were at his own home, had suggested that at so sad a moment he might be found to be in the way, Shand had assured him that there would be no sadness at all. 'We are not a sentimental race,' he had said. 'There are a dozen of us, and the sooner some of us disperse ourselves, the more room will there be in the nest for the others.'

Shand had been Caldigate's most intimate friend at college through the whole period of their residence, and now he was to be his companion in a still more intimate alliance. And yet, though he liked the man, he did not altogether approve of him. Shand had also got into debt at Cambridge, but had not paid his debts; and had dealings also with Davis, as to which he was now quite indifferent. He had left the University without taking a degree, and had seemed to bear all these adversities with perfect equanimity. There had not been hitherto much of veneration in Caldigate's character, but even he had, on occasions, been almost shocked at the want of respect evinced by his friend for conventional rules. All college discipline, all college authorities, all university traditions, had been despised by Shand, who even in his dress had departed as far from recognised customs and fashions among the men as from the requisitions of the statutes and the milder requirements of the dignitaries of the day. Now, though he could not pay his debts,—and intended, indeed, to run away from them,—he was going to try his fortune with a certain small capital which his father had agreed to give him as his share of what there might be of the good things of the world among the Shands generally. As Shand himself said of both of them, he was about to go forth as a prodigal son, with a perfect assurance that, should he come back empty-handed, no calf would be killed for him. But he was an active man, with a dash of fun, and perhaps a sprinkling of wit, quick and brave, to whom life was apparently a joke, and who boasted of himself that, though he was very fond of beef and beer, he could live on bread and water, if put to it, without complaining. Caldigate almost feared that the man was a dangerous companion, but still there was a certain fitness about him for the thing contemplated; and, for such a venture, where could he find any other companion who would be fit?

Dr. Shand, the father, was a physician enjoying a considerable amount of provincial eminence in a small town in Essex. Here he had certainly been a succesful man; for, with all the weight of such a family on his back, he had managed to save some money. There had been small legacies from other Shands, and trifles of portion had come to them from the Potters, of whom Mrs. Shand had been one,—Shand and Potter having been wholesale druggists in Smithfield. The young Shands had generally lived a pleasant life; had gone to school,—the eldest son, as we have seen, to the university also,—and had had governesses, and ponies to ride, and had been great at dancing, and had shot arrows, and played Badminton, and been subject to but little domestic discipline. They had lived crowded together in a great red-brick house, plenteously, roughly, quarrelling continually, but very fond of each other in their own way, and were known throughout that side of the country as a happy family. The girls had always gloves and shoes for dancing, and the boys had enjoyed a considerable amount of shooting and hunting without owning either guns or horses of their own. Now Dick was to go in quest of a fortune, and all the girls were stitching shirts for him, and were as happy as possible. Not a word was said about his debts, and no one threw it in his teeth that he had failed to take a degree. It was known of the Shands that they always made the best of everything.

When Caldigate got out of the railway carriage at Pollington; he was still melancholy with the remembrance of all that he had done and all that he had lost, and he expected to find something of the same feeling at his friend's house. But before he had been there an hour he was laughing with the girls as though such an enterprise as theirs was the best joke in the world. And when a day and a night had passed, Mrs. Shand was deep among his shirts and socks, and had already given him much advice about flannel and soft soap. 'I know Maria would like to go out with you,' said the youngest daughter on the third day, a girl of twelve years old, who ought to have known better, and who, nevertheless, knew more than she ought to have done.

'Indeed Maria would like nothing of the kind,' said the young lady in question.

'Only, Mr. Caldigate, of course you would have to marry her.' Then· the child was cuffed, and Maria declared that the proposed arrangement would suit neither her nor Mr. Caldigate in the least. The eldest daughter, Harriet, was engaged to marry a young clergyman in the neighbourhood, which event, however, was to be postponed till he had got a living; and the second, Matilda, was under a cloud because she would persist in being in love with Lieutenant Postlethwaite, of the Dragoons, whose regiment was quartered in the town. Maria was the third. All these family secrets were told to him quite openly as well as the fact that Josh, the third son, was to become a farmer because he could not be got to learn the multiplication table.

Between Pollington and London, Caldigate remained for six weeks, during which time he fitted himself out, took his passage, and executed the necessary deeds as to the estate. It might have been pleasant enough, —this little interval before his voyage,—as the Shands, though rough and coarse, were kind to him and good-humoured, had it not been that a great trouble befell him through over conscientiousness as to a certain matter. After what had passed at Babington House, it was expedient that he should, before he started for New South Wales, give some notice to his relatives there, so that Julia might know that destiny did not intend her to become Mrs. Caldigate of Folking. Aunt Polly had, no doubt, been too forward in that matter, and in wishing to dispose of her daughter had put herself in the way of merited rebuke and disappointment. It was, however, not the less necessary that she should be told of the altered circumstances of her wished-for son-in-law. But, had he been wise, he would so have written his letter that no answer should reach him before he had left the shores of England. His conscience, however, pinched him, and before he had even settled the day on which he would start, he wrote to his aunt a long letter in which he told her everything,—how he had disposed of his inheritance,— how he had become so indebted to Davis as to have to seek a new fortune out of England,—how he had bade farewell to Folking for ever, — and how impossible it was under all these circumstances that he should aspire to the hand of his cousin Julia.

It was as though a thunderbolt had fallen among them at Babington. Mr. Babington himself was certainly not a clever man, but he knew enough of his own position, as an owner of acres, to be very proud of it, and he was affectionate enough towards his nephew to feel the full weight of this terrible disruption. It seemed to him that his brother-in-law, Daniel Caldigate, was doing a very wicked thing, and he hurried across the country, to Folking, that he might say so. 'You have not sense enough to understand the matter,' said Daniel Caldigate. 'You have no heart in your bowels if you can disinherit an only son,' said the big squire. 'Never mind where I carry my heart,' said the smaller squire; 'but it is a pity you should carry so small an amount of brain.' No good could be done by such a meeting as that, nor by the journey which aunt Polly took to Pollington. The Caldigates, both father and son, were gifted with too strong a will to be turned from their purpose by such interference. But a great deal of confusion was occasioned; and aunt Polly among the Shands was regarded as a very wonderful woman indeed. 'Oh, my son, my darling son!' she said, weeping on John Caldigate's shoulder. Now John Caldigate was certainly not her son, in the usual acceptation of the word, nor did Maria Shand believe that he was so even in that limited sense in which a daughter's husband may be so designated. It was altogether very disagreeable, and made our hero almost resolve to get on board the ship a week before it started from the Thames instead of going down to Plymouth and catching it at the last moment. Of course it would have been necessary that the Babingtons should know all about it sooner or later, but John very much regretted that he had not delayed his letter till the day before his departure.

There is something jovial when you are young in preparing for a long voyage and for totally altered circumstances in life, especially when the surroundings are in themselves not melancholy. A mother weeping over a banished child may be sad enough,—going as an exile when there is no hope of a return. But here among the Shands, with whom sons and daughters were plentiful, and with whom the feelings were of a useful kind, and likely to wear well, rather than of a romantic nature, the bustle, the purchasings, the arrangements, and the packings generally had in them a pleasantness of activity with no disagreeable accompaniments.

'I do hope you will wear them, Dick,' the mother said with something like a sob in her voice; but the tenderness came not from the approaching departure, but from her fear that the thick woollen drawers on which she was re-sewing all the buttons, should be neglected,—after Dick's usual fashion. 'Mr. Caldigate, I hope you will see that he wears them. He looks strong, but indeed he is not.' Our hero who had always regarded his friend as a bull for strength of constitution generally, promised that he would be attentive to Dick's drawers.

'You may be sure that I shall wear them,' said Dick; 'but the time will come when I shall probably wear nothing else, so you had better make the buttons firm.'

Everything was to be done with strict economy, but yet there was plenty of money for purchases. There always is at such occasions. The quantity of clothes got together seemed to be more than any two men could ever wear; and among it all there were no dress-coats and no dress-trousers: or, if either of them had such articles, they were smuggled. The two young men were going out as miners, and took a delight in preparing themselves to be rough. Caldigate was at first somewhat modest in submitting his own belongings to the females of the establishment; but that feeling soon wore off, and the markings and mendings, and buttonings and hemmings went on in a strictly impartial manner as though he himself were a chick out of the same brood.

'What will you do?' said the doctor, 'if you spend your capital and make nothing?'

'Work for wages,' said Dick. 'We shall have got, at any rate, enough experience out of our money to be able to do that. Men are getting 10s. a-day.'

'But you'd have to go on doing that always,' said the mother.

'Not at all. Of course it's a life of ups and downs. A man working for wages can put half what he earns into a claim, so that when a thing does come up trumps at last, he will have his chance. I have read a good deal about it now. There is plenty to be got if a man only knows how to keep it.'

'Drinking is the worst,' said the doctor.

'I think I can trust myself for that,' said Dick, whose hand at the moment was on a bottle of whisky, and who had been by no means averse to jollifications at Cambridge. 'A miner when he's at work should never drink.'

'Nor when he's not at work, if he wants to keep what he earns.'

'I'm not going to take the pledge, or anything of that kind,' continued the son, 'but I think I know enough of it all, not to fall into that pit.' During this discussion, Caldigate sat silent, for he had already had various conversations on this subject with his friend. He had entertained some fears, which were not, perhaps, quite removed by Dick's manly assurances.

A cabin had been taken for the joint use of the young men on board the Goldfinder, a large steamer which was running at the time from London to Melbourne, doing the voyage generally in about two months. But they were going as second-class passengers and their accommodation therefore was limited. Dick had insisted on this economy, which was hardly necessary to Caldigate, and which was not absolutely pressed upon the other. But Dick had insisted. 'Let us begin as we mean to go on,' he had said; 'of course we've got to rough it. We shall come across something a good deal harder than second-class fare before we have made our fortunes, and worked probably with mates more uncouth than second-class passengers.' It was impossible to oppose counsel such as this, and therefore second-class tickets were taken on board the Goldfinder.

A terrible struggle was made during the last fortnight to prevent the going of John Caldigate. Mr. Babington was so shocked that he did not cease to stir himself. Allow a son to disinherit himself, merely because he had fallen into the hands of a money-lending Jew before he had left college! To have the whole condition of a property changed by such a simple accident! It was shocking to him; and he moved himself in the matter with much more energy than old Mr. Caldigate had expected from him. He wrote heartrending letters to Folking, in spite of the hard words which had been said to him there. He made a second journey to Cambridge, and endeavoured to frighten Mr. Bolton. Descent of acres from father to son was to him so holy a thing, that he was roused to unexpected energies. He was so far successful that Mr. Daniel Caldigate did write a long letter to his son, in which he offered to annul the whole proceeding. 'Your uncle accuses me of injustice,' he said. 'I have not been unjust. But there is no reason whatever why the arrangement should stand. Even if the money has been paid to Davis I will bear that loss rather than you should think that I have taken advantage of you in your troubles.' But John Caldigate was too firm and too determined for such retrogression. The money had been paid to Davis, and other monies had been used in other directions. He was quite contented with the bargain, and would certainly adhere to it.

Then came the last night before their departure; the evening before the day on which they were to go from Pollington to London, and from London to Plymouth. All the heavy packages, and all the clothes had, of course, been put on board the Goldfinder in the London docks. The pleasant task of preparation was at an end, and they were now to go forth upon their hard labours. Caldigate had become so intimate with the family, that it seemed as though a new life had sprung up for him, and that as he had parted from all that he then had of a family at Folking, he was now to break away from new ties under the doctor's roof. They had dined early, and at ten o'clock there was what Mrs. Shand called a little bit of supper. They were all of them high in heart, and very happy,—testifying their affection to the departing ones by helping them to the nicest bits, and by filling their tumblers the fullest. How it happened, no one could have said, but it did happen that, before the evening was over, Maria and Caldigate were together in a little room behind the front parlour. What still remained of their luggage was collected there, and this last visit had probably been made in order that the packages might be once more counted.

'It does seem so odd that you should be going,' she said.

'It is so odd to me that I should ever have come.'

'We had always heard of you since Dick went to Cambridge.'

35

'I knew that there were so many of you, and that was all. Brothers never talk of their sisters, I suppose. But I seem to know you now so well! You have been so kind to me!'

'Because you are Dick's friend.'

'I didn't suppose that it was anything else.'

'That's not nice of you, Mr. Caldigate. You know that we are all very fond of you. We shall be so anxious to hear. You will be good to him, won't you?'

'And he to me, I hope.'

'I think you are steadier than he is, and can do more for him than he can for you. I wonder, shall we ever see each other again, Mr. Caldigate?'

'Why not?'

'New South Wales is so far, and you will both marry there, and then you will not want to come back. I hope I may live to see dear Dick again some day.'

'But only Dick?'

'And you too, if you would care about it.'

'Of course I should care about it,' he said. And as he said so, of course he put his arm round her waist and kissed her. It did not mean much. She did not think it meant much. But it gave a little colouring of romance to that special moment of her life. He, when he went up to his bed, declared to himself that it meant nothing at all. He still had those large eyes clear before him, and was still fixed in his resolution to come back for them when some undefined point in his life should have passed by.

'Now,' said Dick Shand, as they were seated together in a third-class railway carriage on the following morning, 'now I feel that I am beginning life.'

'With proper resolutions, I hope, as to honesty, sobriety, and industry.'

'With a fixed determination to make a fortune, and come back, and be *facile princeps* among all the Shands. I have already made up my mind as to the sum I will give each of the girls, and the way I will start the two younger boys in business. In the meantime let us light a pipe.'

CHAPTER V

The Goldfinder

THERE is no peculiar life more thoroughly apart from life in general, more unlike our usual life, more completely a life of itself, governed by its own rules and having its own roughnesses and amenities, than life on board ship. What tender friendship it produces, and what bitter enmities! How completely the society has formed itself into separate sets after the three or four first days! How thoroughly it is acknowledged that this is the aristocratic set, and that the plebeian! How determined are the aristocrats to admit no intrusion, and how anxious are the plebeians to intrude! Then there arises the great demagogue, who heads a party, having probably been disappointed in early life,— that is, in his first endeavours on board the ship. And the women have to acknowledge all their weaknesses, and to exercise all their strength. It is a bad time for them on board ship if they cannot secure the attention of the men,—as it is in the other world; but in order that they may secure it, they assume indifference. They assume indifference, but are hard at work with their usual weapons. The men can do very well by themselves. For them there is drinking, smoking, cards, and various games; but the potency of female spells soon works upon them, and all who are worth anything are more or less in love by the end of the first week. Of course it must all come to an end when the port is reached. That is understood, though there may sometimes be mistakes. Most pathetic secrets are told with the consciousness that they will be forgotten as soon as the ship is left. And there is the whole day for these occupations. No work is required from any one. The lawyer does not go to his court, nor the merchant to his desk. Pater-familias receives no bills; mater-familias orders no dinners. The daughter has no household linen to disturb her. The son is never recalled to his books. There is no parliament, no municipality, no vestry. There are neither rates nor taxes nor rents to be paid. The government is the softest despotism under which subjects were ever allowed to do almost just as they please. That the captain has a power is known, but hardly felt. He smiles on all, is responsible for everything, really rules the world submitted to him, from the setting of the sails down to the frying of the chops, and makes one fancy that there must be something wrong with men on shore because first-class nations cannot be governed like first-class ships.

The Goldfinder had on board her over a hundred first-class passengers, and nearly as many of the second class. The life among them was much of the same kind, though in the second class there was less of idleness, less of pleasure, and something more of an attempt to continue the ordinary industry of life. The women worked more and the men read more than their richer neighbours. But the love-making, and the fashion, and the mutiny against the fashion, were the same in one set as in the other. Our friends were at first subjected to an inconvenience which is always felt in such a position. They were known to have had saloon rather than second-class antecedents. Everybody had heard that they had been at Cambridge, and therefore they were at first avoided. And as they themselves were determined not to seek associates among their more aristocratic neighbours, they were left to themselves and solitary for some few days. But this was a condition not at all suited to Dick Shand's temperament, and it was not long before he had made both male and female acquaintances.

'Have you observed that woman in the brown straw hat?' Dick said to Caldigate, one morning, as they were leaning together on the forepart of the vessel against one of the pens in which the fowls were kept. They were both dressed according to the parts they were acting, and which they intended to act, as second-class passengers and future working miners. Any one knowing in such matters would have seen that they were over-dressed; for the real miner, when he is away from his work, puts on his best clothes, and endeavours to look as little rough as possible. And all this had no doubt been seen and felt, and discounted among our friends' fellow-passengers.

'I have seen her every day, of course,' said Caldigate, 'and have been looking at her for the last half hour.'

'She is looking at us now.'

'She seems to me to be very attentive to the stocking she is mending.'

'Just a woman's wiles. At this moment she can't hear us, but she knows pretty nearly what we are saying by the way our lips are going. Have you spoken to her?'

'I did say a word or two to her yesterday.'

'What did she say?'

'I don't recollect especially. She struck me as talking better than her gown, if you know what I mean.'

'She talks a great deal better than her gown,' said Dick. 'I don't quite know what to make of her. She says that she is going out to earn her bread; but when I asked her how, she either couldn't or wouldn't answer me. She is a mystery, and mysteries are always worth unravelling. I shall go to work and unravel her.'

At that moment the female of whom they were speaking got up from her seat on one of the spars which was bound upon the deck, folded up her work, and walked away. She was a remarkable woman, and certainly looked to be better than her gown, which was old and common enough. Caldigate had observed her frequently, and had been much struck by the word or two she had spoken to him on the preceding day. 'I should like ship-life well enough,' she had said, in answer to some ordinary question, 'if it led to nothing else.'

'You would not remain here for ever?'

'Certainly, if I could. There is plenty to eat, and a bed to sleep on, and no one to be afraid of. And though nobody knows me, everybody knows enough of me not to think that I ought to be taken to a police office because I have not gloves to my hands.'

'Don't you think it wearisome?' he had asked.

'Everything is wearisome; but here I have a proud feeling of having paid my way. To have settled in advance for your dinner for six weeks to come is a magnificent thing. If I get too tired of it I can throw myself overboard. You can't even do that in London without the police being down upon you. The only horror to me here is that there will so soon be an end to it.'

At that time he had not even heard her name, or known whether she were alone or joined to others. Then he had inquired, and a female fellow-passenger had informed him that she was a Mrs. Smith,—that she had seen better days, but had been married to a ne'er-do-well husband, who had drank himself to death within a year of their marriage, and that she was now going out to the colony, probably,— so the old lady said who was the informant,—in search of a second husband. She was to some extent, the old lady said, in charge of a distant relative, who was then on board, with a respectable husband and children, and who was very much ashamed of her poor connection. So much John Caldigate had heard.

Though he had heard this he did not feel inclined to tell it all to Dick Shand. Dick had professed his intention of unravelling the mystery, but Caldigate almost thought that he would like to unravel it himself. The woman was so constantly alone! And then, though she was ill-dressed, untidy, almost unkempt on occasions, still, through it all, there was something attractive about her. There was a brightness in her eye, and a courage about her mouth, which had made him think that, in spite of her appearance, she would be worth his attention—just for the voyage. When he had been speaking to herself they had been on the deck together, and it had been dusk and he had not been able to look her in the face; but while Shand had been speaking to him he had observed that she was very comely. And this was the more remarkable because it seemed to him to be so evident that she made the worst rather than the best of herself. She was quite a young woman;—probably, he thought, not more than three or four and twenty; and she was there, with many young men round her, and yet she made no effort to attract attention. When his eye had fallen upon her she had generally been quite alone, doing some piece of coarse and ordinary work.

'I have had another conversation with her,' said Shand to him that night.

'Have you unravelled the mystery?'

'Not quite; but I have got the fact that there is a mystery. She told me that you and I and she herself ought not to be here. When I asked her why, she said that you and I ought to be gentlemen and that she ought to be a lady. I told her that you and I were gentlemen, in spite of our trousers. "Ah," she said, "there comes the difference; I'm not a lady any longer!" When I contradicted her she snubbed me, and said that I hadn't seen enough of the world to know anything about it. But I'll have it all out of her before I've done.'

For some days after that Caldigate kept himself aloof from Mrs. Smith, not at all because he had ceased to notice her or to think about her, but from a feeling of dislike to exhibit rivalry with his friend. Shand was making himself very particular, and he thought that Shand was a fool for his pains. He was becoming angry with Shand, and had serious thoughts of speaking to him with solemn severity. What could such a woman be to him? But at the bottom of all this there was something akin to jealousy. The woman was good-looking, and certainly clever, and was very interesting. Shand, for two or three evenings running, related his success; how Mrs. Smith had communicated to him the fact that she utterly despised those Cromptons, who were distant cousins of her late husband's, and with whom she had come on board; how she preferred to be alone to having aught to do with them; how she had one or two books with her, and passed some hours in reading; and how she was poor, very poor, but still had something on which to live for a few weeks after landing. But Caldigate fancied that there must be a betrayal of trust in these revelations, and though he was in truth interested about the woman, did not give much encouragement to his friend.

'Upon my word,' he said, 'I don't seem to care so very much about Mrs. Smith's affairs.'

'I do,' said Shand, who was thick-skinned and irrepressible. 'I declared my intention of unravelling the mystery, and I mean to do it.'

'I hope you are not too inquisitive?'

'Of course she likes to have some one to whom she can talk. And what can people talk about on board ship except themselves? A woman who has a mystery always likes to have it unravelled. What else is the good of a mystery?'

He was thick-skinned and irrepressible, but Caldigate endeavoured to show his displeasure. He felt that the poor woman was in coarse hands; and he thought that, had matters gone otherwise, he might have accepted, in a more delicate manner, so much confidence as she chose to vouchsafe.

So it was when they had been a fortnight at sea. They had left home in mid-winter; but now they were in the tropics, near the line, and everything was sultry, sleepy, and warm. Flying-fishes were jumping from the waves on to the deck, and when the dusk of night was come, the passengers would stand by the hour together watching the phosphorus on the water. The Southern Cross had shown itself plainly, and possessed the heavens in conjunction with the Bear. The thick woollen drawers which had been so carefully prepared, were no longer in use, and men were going about in light pantaloons and linen jackets,—those on the quarter-deck at first beautifully clean and white, while our friends of the second cabin were less careful. The women, too, had got quit of their wraps, and lounged about the deck in light attire. During the bright hours of the day the aristocrats, in the stern, were shrouded from the sun by a delightful awning; but, forward, the passengers sought the shade of the loose idle sails, or screened themselves from the fierce rays as best they might among the hatchways and woodwork. But it was when the burning sun had hidden himself, when the short twilight had disappeared, and the heavens were alive and alight with stars, that all the world of the ship would be crowded on the upper deck. There they would remain, long after the lamps below had been extinguished, some of them sleeping through the whole night in the comparative coolness of the air. But it was from eight, when tea would be over, till midnight, that the hum of voices would be thickest, and the tread of those who walked for their exercise the most frequent.

At such times Caldigate would be often alone; for though he had made acquaintances, and had become indeed intimate with some of those around him, he had never thrust himself into the life of the ship as Shand had done. Charades were acted in the second cabin, in which Shand always took part,—and there were penny readings, at which Shand was often the reader. And he smoked much and drank somewhat with those who smoked and drank. The awe at first inspired by his university superiority and supposed rank in the world had faded almost into nothing, but by Caldigate, unconsciously, much of this had been preserved. I am not sure that he did not envy his friend, but at any rate he stood aloof. And, in regard to Mrs. Smith, when he saw her walking one evening with Shand in the sweetly dim light of the evening, with her hand upon Shand's arm, he made up his mind that he would think no more about her.

They had been at sea just a fortnight when this happened. And in about a quarter of an hour after this resolve had been formed Mrs. Smith was standing by him and talking to him. A ball was being held on the quarter-deck, or rather, as there was in truth no quarter-deck to the Goldfinder, on that clean, large, luxurious expanse devoted to the aristocracy in the after-part of the vessel. From among the second-class passengers, two fiddlers and a flute player had been procured, who formed the band. At sea you have always to look for your musicians among the second-class passengers. And now under the awning young and old were standing up, and making themselves happy beneath the starlight and the glimmer of the dozen ship-lamps which had been hung around. On board ship there are many sources of joy of which the land knows nothing. You may flirt and dance at sixty; and if you are awkward in the turn of a valse, you may put it down to the motion of the ship. You need wear no gloves, and may drink your soda-and-brandy without being ashamed of it.

It was not for John Caldigate to join the mazes of that dance, though he would have liked it well, and was well fitted by skill and taste for such exercise. But the ground was hallowed on which they trod, and forbidden to him; and though there was probably not a girl or a dancing married woman there who would not have been proud to stand up with Mr. Caldigate of Folking, there was not one who would have dared to take the hand of a second-class passenger. So he stood, just within his own boundary, and looked and longed. Then there was a voice in his ear. 'Do you dance, Mr. Caldigate?'

It was a very pleasant voice, low, but distinct and silvery, infinitely better again than the gown; a voice so distinct and well-managed that it would have been noticed for its peculiar sweetness if coming from any high-bred lady. He turned round and found her face close to his. Why had she come to speak to him when she must have perceived that he had intentionally avoided her.

'I used to be very fond of dancing,' he said, 'but it is one of the things that have gone away.'

'I, too, was fond of dancing; but, as you say, it has gone away. It will come back to you, in half-a-dozen years, perhaps. It can never come back to me. Things do come back to men.'

'Why more than to women?'

'You have a resurrection;—I mean here upon earth. We never have. Though we live as long as you, the pleasure-seeking years of our lives are much shorter. We burst out into full flowering early in our spring, but long before the summer is over, we are no more than huddled leaves and thick stalks.'

'Are you a thick stalk, Mrs. Smith?'

'Unfortunately, not. My flowers are gone while my stalk is still thin and sensitive. And then women can't recuperate.'

'I don't quite know what that means.'

'Yes, you do. It is good English enough even for Cambridge by this time. If you had made a false step, got into debt and ran away, or mistaken another man's wife for your own, or disappeared altogether under a cloud for a while, you could retrieve your honour, and, sinking at twenty-five or thirty, could come up from out of the waters at thirty-five as capable of enjoyment and almost as fresh as ever. But a woman does not bear submersion. She is draggled ever afterwards. She must hide everything by a life of lies, or she will get no admittance anywhere. The man is rather the better liked because he has sown his wild oats broadly. Of all these ladies dancing there, which dances the best? There is not one who really knows how to dance.'

CHAPTER VI

Mrs. Smith

S HE had changed the conversation so suddenly, rushing off from that great question as to the condition of women generally to the very unimportant matter of the dancing powers of the ladies who were manoeuvring before them, that Caldigate hardly knew how to travel with her so quickly. 'They all dance well enough for ship dancing,' he replied; 'but as to what you were saying about women—'

'No, Mr. Caldigate; they don't dance well enough for ship dancing. Dancing, wherever it be done, should be graceful. A woman may at any rate move her feet in accordance with time, and she need not skip, nor prance, nor jump, even on board ship. Look at that stout lady.'

'Mrs. Callander?'

Everybody by this time knew everybody's name.

'If she is Mrs. Callander?'

Mrs. Smith, no doubt, knew very well that it was Mrs. Callander.

'Does not your ear catch separately the thud of her footfall every time she comes to the ground?'

'She is fat, fair, and forty.'

'Fat enough;—and what she lacks in fairness may be added on to the forty; but if she were less ambitious and had a glimmer of taste, she might do better than that. You see that girl with the green scarf round her? She is young and good-looking. Why should she spring about like a bear on a hot iron?'

'You should go and teach them.'

'It is just what I should like; only they would not be taught; and I should be stern, and tell them the truth.'

'Why don't you go and dance with them yourself?'

'I!'

'Why not? There is one second-class lady there?' This was true. For though none of the men would have been admitted from the inferior rank to join the superior, the rule of demarcation had so far been broken that a pretty girl who was known to some of the first-class passengers had been invited to come over the line and join the amusements of the evening. 'She dances about as well as any of them.'

'If you were among them would you dare to come out and ask me to join them? That is a question which you won't even dare to answer.'

44

'It is a little personal.'

' "No," you ought to say. "I could not do that because your clothes are so poor, and because of your ragged old hat, and I am not quite sure that your shoes are fit to be seen." Is not that what you would say, if you said what you thought?'

'Perhaps it is.'

'And if you said all that you thought, perhaps you would remind me that a woman of whom nobody knows anything is always held to be disreputable. That girl, no doubt, has her decent belongings. I have nobody.'

'You have your friends on board.'

'No, I have not. I have not a single friend on board. Those Cromptons were very unwillingly persuaded to take a sort of interest in me, though they really know nothing about me. And I have already lost any good which might come from their protection. She told me yesterday, that I ought not to walk about with Mr. Shand.'

'And what did you say?'

'Of course I told her to mind her own business. I had no alternative. A woman has to show a little spirit or she will be trodden absolutely into the dirt. It was something to have a woman to speak to, even though I had not a thought in common with her;—though she was to my feeling as inferior to myself as I no doubt am thought to be by that fat prancing woman to herself. Even Mrs. Crompton's countenance was of value. But if I had yielded she would have taken it out in tyranny. So now we don't speak.'

'That is a pity.'

'It is a pity. You watch them all and see how they look at me,—the women, I mean. They know that Mr. Shand speaks to me, and that you and Mr. Shand are the two gentlemen we have among us. There are, no doubt, a dozen of them watching me now, somewhere, and denouncing me for the impropriety of my behaviour.'

'Is it improper?'

'What do you think?'

'Why may we not talk as well as others?'

'Exactly. But there are people who are tabooed. Look at that Miss Green and the ship doctor.' At that moment the ship's doctor and the young lady in question came close to them in the dance. 'There is no harm in Miss Green talking by the hour together with the doctor, because she is comfortably placed. She has got an old father and mother on board who don't look after her, and everything is respectable. But if I show any of the same propensities, I ought almost to be put into irons.'

45

'Has anybody else been harsh to you?'

'The Captain has been making inquiries,—no doubt with the idea that he may at last be driven to harsh measures. Have you got a sister?'

'No.'

'Or a mother?'

'No.'

'Or a housemaid?'

'Not even a housemaid. I have no female belongings whatever.'

'Don't you know that if you had a sister, and a mother, and a housemaid, your mother would quite expect that your sister should in time have a lover, but that she would be horrified at the idea of the housemaid having a follower?'

'I did not know that. I thought housemaids got married sometimes.'

'Human nature is stronger than tyranny.'

'But what does all this mean? You are not a housemaid, and you have not got a mistress?'

'Not exactly. But at present;—if I say my outward woman you'll know what I mean perhaps.'

'I think I shall.'

'Well; my present outward woman stands to me in lieu of the housemaid's broom, and the united authority of the Captain and Mrs. Crompton make up the mistress between them. And the worst of it all is, that though I have to endure the tyranny, I have not got the follower. It is as hard upon Mr. Shand as it is upon me.'

'Shand, I suppose, can take care of himself.'

'No doubt;—and so in real truth can I. I can stand apart and defy them all; and as I look at them looking at me, and almost know with what words they are maligning me, I can tell myself that they are beneath me, and that I care nothing for them. I shall do nothing which will enable any one to interfere with me. But it seems hard that all this should be so because I am a widow,—and because I am alone,—and because I am poorly clothed.'

As she said this there were tears in her eyes, true ones, and something of the sound of a broken sob in her voice. And Caldigate was moved. The woman's condition was to be pitied, whether it had been produced with or without fault on her own part. To be alone is always sad,—even for a man; but for a woman, and for a young woman, it is doubly melancholy. Of a sudden the dancing was done and the lamps were taken away.

'If you do not want to go to bed,' he said, 'let us take a turn.'

'I never go to bed. I mean here, on board ship. I linger up on deck, half hiding myself about the place, till I see some quartermaster eyeing me suspiciously, and then I creep down into the little hole which I occupy with three of Mrs. Crompton's children, and then I cry myself to sleep. But I don't call that going to bed.'

'Take a turn now.'

'I shall feel like the housemaid talking to her follower through the area-gate. But she is brave, and why should I be a coward?' Then she put her hand upon his arm. 'And you,' she said, 'why are not you dancing in the other part of the ship with Mrs. Callander and Miss Green, instead of picking your way among the hencoops here with me?'

'This suited my pocket best,—and my future prospects.'

'You are making a delightful experiment in roughing it,—as people eat pic-nic dinners out in the woods occasionally, so that there may be a break in the monotony of chairs and tables.'

While Shand had been unravelling her mystery, she, perhaps, had been more successful in unravelling his.

'We intend to be miners.'

'And to return home before long with some vast treasure. I hope you may be successful.'

'You seem to doubt it.'

'Of course it is doubtful. If not, the thing would be common and hardly worth the doing. Will Mr. Shand be very persistent as a working miner?'

'I hope so.'

'He seems to me to have great gifts of idleness, which on board ship are a blessing. How I do envy men when I see them smoking! It seems to me that nothing is wanting to them. Women have their needlework; but though they hate it less than idleness, they do hate it. But you really like your tobacco.'

'I don't like being idle. I read a good deal. Do you read?'

'I have but few books here. I have read more perhaps than most young women of my age. I came away in such a hurry that I have almost nothing with me.'

'Can I lend you books?'

'If you will. I will promise to take care of them.'

'I have "The Heartbroken One," by Spratt, you know. It is very absurd, but full of life from beginning to end. All that Spratt writes is very lively.'

'I don't think I care for Spratt. He may be lively, but he's not life-like.'

'And "Michael Bamfold." It is hard work, perhaps, but very thoughtful, if you can digest that sort of thing.'

'I hate thought.'

'What do you say to Miss Bouverie's last;—"Ridden to a Standstill;" a little loud, perhaps, but very interesting? Or "Green Grow the Rushes O," by Mrs. Tremaine? None of Mrs. Tremaine's people do anything that anybody would do, but they all talk well.'

'I hate novels written by women. Their girls are so unlovely, and their men such absurdly fine fellows!'

'I have William Coxe's "Lock picked at Last," of which I will defy you to find the secret till you have got to the end of it.'

'I am a great deal too impatient.'

'And Thompson's "Four Marquises." That won't give you any trouble, because you will know it all from the first chapter.'

'And never have a moment of excitement from the beginning to the end. I don't think I care very much for novels. Have you nothing else?'

Caldigate had many other books, a Shakespeare, some lighter poetry, and sundry heavier works of which he did not wish specially to speak, lest he should seem to be boasting of his own literary taste; but at last it was settled that on the next morning he should supply her with what choice he had among the poets. Then at about midnight they parted, and Caldigate, as he found his way down to his cabin, saw the quarter-master with his eye fixed upon Mrs. Smith. There is no so stern guardian of morality and propriety as your old quartermaster on board a first-class ship.

'You have been having a grand time of it with Mrs. Smith,' said Shand as soon as Caldigate was in their cabin.

'Pretty well,—as far as fine times go on board ship. Is there anything against it?'

'Oh, no, not that I know of. I started the hare; if you choose to run it I have no right to complain, I suppose.'

'I don't know anything about the hare, but you certainly have no right to complain because I have been talking to Mrs. Smith;—unless indeed you tell me that you are going to make her Mrs. Shand.'

'You are much more likely to make her Mrs. Caldigate.'

'I don't know that I should have any objection;—that is, if I wanted a wife. She is good-looking, clever, well-educated, and would be well-mannered were it not that she bristles up against the ill-usage of the world too roughly.'

'I didn't know it had gone so far as that,' said Shand, angrily.

'Nor did I, till you suggested it to me. Now I think I'll go to sleep, if you please, and dream about it.'

He did not go to sleep, but lay awake half thinking and half dreaming. He certainly liked Mrs. Smith; but then, as he had begun to find out of himself, he liked women's society generally. He was almost jealous of the doctor, because the doctor was allowed to talk to Miss Green and waltz with Miss Green, whereas he could not approach her. Then he thought of Maria Shand and that kiss in the little back parlour, —the kiss which had not meant much, but which had meant something; and then of Julia Babington, to whom he was not quite sure that he ought not to feel himself engaged. But the face that was clearest to him of all,—and which became the dearer the nearer that he approached to a state of dozing,—was that of Hester Bolton, whose voice he had hardly heard, who had barely spoken to him;—the tips of whose fingers he had only just touched. If there was any one thing fixed on his mind it was that, as soon as he had put together a large lump of gold, he would go back to Cambridge and win Hester Bolton to be his wife. But yet what a singular woman was this Mrs. Smith! As to marrying her, that of course had been a joke produced by the petulance of his snoring friend. He began to dislike Shand, because he did snore so loudly, and drank so much bottled ale, and smelt so strongly of cavendish tobacco. Mrs. Smith was at any rate much too good for Shand. Surely she must have been a lady, or her voice would not have been sweet and silvery? And though she did bristle roughly against the ill-usage of the world, and say strong things, she was never absolutely indelicate or even loud. And she was certainly very interesting. How did it come to pass that she was so completely alone, so poor, so unfriended, and yet possessed of such gifts? There certainly was a mystery, and it would certainly be his fate, and not the fate of Dick Shand, to unravel it. The puzzle was much too delicate and too intricate for Dick Shand's rough hands. Then, giving his last waking thoughts for a moment to Hester Bolton, he went to sleep in spite of the snoring.

On the next morning, as soon as he was out of bed, he opened a small portmanteau in which he had put up some volumes the day before he left Pollington, and to which he had not yet had recourse since the beginning of the voyage. From these he would select one or two for the use of his new friend. So he dragged out the valise from beneath the berth, while Shand abused him for the disturbance he made. On the top, lying on the other volumes, which were as he had placed them, was a little book, prettily bound, by no means new, which he was sure had never been placed there by himself. He took it up, and, standing in the centre of the cabin, between the light of the porthole and Dick's bed, he examined it. It was a copy of Thomson's 'Seasons', and on the flyleaf was written in a girl's hand the name of its late owner,—Maria Shand. The truth flashed upon him at once. She must have gone down on the last night after he was in bed, and thus have made her little offering in silence, knowing that it would be hidden from him till he was far away from her.

'What book is that?' said Shand suddenly, emerging with his head and shoulders from the low berth.

'A book of mine,' said Caldigate, disconcerted for the moment.

'What are you going to do with it?'

'I am looking for something to lend to Mrs. Smith.'

'That is Molly's Thomson's "Seasons," ' said the brother, remembering, as we are so apt to remember, the old thing that had met his eye so often in the old house. 'Where did you get it?'

'I didn't steal it, Dick.'

'I don't suppose you did; but I'm sure it's the book I say.'

'No doubt it is. If you think it is in bad hands, shall I give it back to you?'

'I don't want it. If she gave it you, she was a fool for her pains.'

'I don't see that.'

'I would rather, at any rate, that you would not lend a book with my sister's name in it to Mrs. Smith.'

'I was not thinking of doing so. She wants a Shakespeare that I have got here, and a volume of Tennyson.' Then Dick retreated back into his berth, and snored again, while Caldigate dressed himself. When that operation was completed,—which, including his lavations, occupied about five minutes,—he went up on the deck with the books for Mrs. Smith in his hand, and with Thomson's 'Seasons' in his pocket. So the poor girl had absolutely stolen down-stairs in the middle of the cold night, and had opened the case and re-fastened it, in order that he, when in strange lands, might find himself in possession of something that had been hers!

He had not been alone a minute or two, and was looking about to see if Mrs. Smith was there, when he was accosted by the Captain. The Captain was a pleasant-looking, handsome man, about forty-five years of age, who had the good word of almost everybody on board, but who had not before spoken specially to Caldigate.

'Good morning, Mr. Caldigate. I hope you find yourself fairly comfortable where you are.'

'Pretty well, thank you, Captain.'

'If there is anything I can do.'

'We have all that we have a right to expect.'

'I wish, Mr. Caldigate, I could invite you and your friends to come astern among us sometimes, but it would be contrary to rule.'

'I can quite understand that, Captain.'

'You are doing a bit of roughing,—no doubt for the sake of

experience. If you only knew the sort of roughing I've had in my time!'

'I dare say.'

'Salt pork and hard biscuit, and only half enough of that. You find yourself among some queer fellow-passengers, I dare say, Mr. Caldigate.'

'Everybody is very civil.'

'They're sure to be that to a gentleman. But one has to be careful. The women are the most dangerous.' Then the Captain laughed, as though it had only been a joke,—this allusion to the women. But Caldigate knew that there was more than a joke in it. The Captain had intended to warn him against Mrs. Smith.

CHAPTER VII

The Three Attempts

SOMETHING more than a month had gone by, and John Caldigate and Mrs. Smith were very close companions. This had not been effected without considerable opposition, partly on the part of Shand, and partly by the ship's inhabitants generally. The inhabitants of the ship were inimical to Mrs. Smith. She was a woman who had no friends; and the very female who had first appeared as a friend was now the readiest to say hard things of her. And Caldigate was a handsome well-mannered young man. By this time all the ladies in the first-class knew very well who he was, and some of them had spoken to him. On one or two occasions the stern law of the vessel had been broken; and he had been absolutely invited to sit on those august after-benches. He was known to be a gentleman, and believed, on the evidence of Dick Shand, to be possessed of considerable means. It was therefore a thing horrible to all of them, and particularly to Miss Green, that he should allow himself to be enticed into difficulties by such a creature as that Mrs. Smith. Miss Green had already been a little cold to the doctor in consequence of a pleasant half-hour spent by her in Caldigate's company, as they looked over the side of the vessel at the flying-fish. Mrs. Callander had been with them, and everything had been quite proper. But what a pity it was that he should devote so much of his time to that woman! 'Fancy his condition if he should be induced to marry her!' said Miss Green, holding up her hands in horror. The idea was so terrible that Mrs. Callander declared that she would speak to him. 'Nobody ever disliked interfering so much as I do,' said Mrs. Callander; 'but sometimes a word from a lady will go so far with a young man!' Mrs. Callander was a most respectable woman, whose father had begun life as a cattle drover in the colonies, but had succeeded in amassing a considerable fortune. 'Oh, I do wish that something may be done to save him!' said Miss Green.

Among the second-class passengers the same feeling existed quite as strongly. The woman herself had not only been able but had been foolish enough to show that in spite of her gown she considered herself superior to them all. When it was found that she was, in truth, handsome to look upon,—that her words were soft and well chosen,—that she could sit apart and read,—and that she could trample upon Mrs. Crompton in her scorn,—then, for a while, there were some who made little efforts to get into her good graces. She might even have made an ally of good-natured Mrs. Bones, the wife of the butcher who was going out with his large family to try his fortune at Melbourne. Mrs. Bones had been injured, after some ship fashion, by Mrs. Crompton, and would have made herself pleasant. But Mrs. Smith had despised them all, and had shown her contempt, and was now as deeply suspected by Mrs. Bones as by Mrs. Crompton or Mrs. Callander.

But of all the foes to this intimacy Dick Shand was for a time the most bitter and the most determined. No doubt this arose at first from jealousy. He had declared his purpose of unravelling the mystery; but the task had been taken out of his hands, and the unravelling was being done by another. And the more that the woman was abused, and the more intent were all the people in regard to her wicked determination to be intimate with Caldigate, the more interesting she became. Dick, who was himself the very imp of imprudence,—who had never been deterred from doing anything he fancied by any glimmer of control,—would have been delighted to be the hero of all the little stories that were being told. But as that morsel of bread had been taken, as it were, from between his very teeth by the unjustifiable interference of his friend, he had become more alive than any one else to the danger of the whole proceeding. He acknowledged to the Captain that his friend was making a fool of himself; and, though he was a little afraid of Caldigate, he resolved upon interfering.

'Don't you think you are making an ass of yourself about this woman?' he said.

'I daresay I am.'

'Well!'

'All the wise men, from David downwards, have made asses of themselves about women; and why should I be wiser than the rest?'

'That's nonsense, you know.'

'Very likely.'

'I am trying to talk to you in earnest.'

'You make such a failure of it, old boy, that I am compelled to talk nonsense in return. The idea of your preaching! Here I am with nothing special to do, and I like to amuse myself. Ought not that to be enough for you?'

'But what is to be the end of it?' Dick Shand asked, very solemnly.

'How can I tell? But the absurdity is that such a man as you should talk about the end of anything. Did you ever look before you leaped in your life?'

'We are to be together, you know, and it won't do for us to

53

be hampered with that woman.'

'Won't it? Then let me tell you that, if I choose to hamper myself with that woman, or with a whole harem of women, and am not deterred by any consideration for myself, I certainly shall not be deterred by any consideration for you. Do you understand me?'

'That is not being a true partner,' said Shand.

'I'm quite sure of this,—that I'm likely to be as true as you are. I'm not aware that I have entered into any terms with you by which I have bound myself to any special mode of living. I have left England. as I fancy you have done also, because I desired more conventional freedom than one can find among the folk at home. And now, on the first outset, I am to be cautioned and threatened by you because I have made acquaintance with a young woman. Of all the moral pastors and masters that one might come across in the world, you, Dick Shand, appear to me to be the most absurd. But you are so far right as this, that if my conduct is shocking to you, you had better leave me to my wickedness.'

'You are always so d——upsetting,' said Dick, 'that no one can speak to you.' Then Dick turned away, and there was nothing more said about Mrs. Smith on that occasion.

The next to try her hand was Mrs. Callander. By this time the passengers had become familiar with the ship, and knew what they might and what they might not do. The second-class passengers were not often found intruding across the bar, but the first-class frequently made visits to their friends amidship. In this way Mrs. Callander had become acquainted with our two gold-seekers, and often found herself in conversation with one or the other. Even Miss Green, as has been stated before, would come and gaze upon the waves from the inferior part of the deck.

'What a very nice voyage we are having, Mr. Caldigate,' Mrs. Callander said one afternoon.

'Yes, indeed. It is getting a little cold now, but we shall enjoy that after all the heat.'

'Quite so; only I suppose it will be very cold when we get quite south. You still find yourself tolerably comfortable.'

'I shall be glad to have it over,' said Caldigate, who had in truth become disgusted with Dick's snoring.

'I daresay,—I am sure we shall. My young people are getting very tired of it. Children, when they are accustomed to every comfort on shore, of course feel it grievously. I suppose you are rather crowded?'

'Of course we are crowded. One can't have a twenty-foot square room on board ship.'

'No, indeed. But then you are with your friend, and that is much pleasanter than a stranger.'

'That would depend on whether the stranger snored, Mrs. Callander.'

'Don't talk of snoring, Mr. Caldigate. If you only heard Mr. Callander! But, as I was saying, you must have some very queer characters down there.' She had not been saying anything of the kind, but she found a difficulty in introducing her subjects.

'Take them altogether, they are a very decent, pleasant, well-mannered set of people, and all of them in earnest about their future lives.'

'Poor creatures! But I dare say they're very good.' Then she paused a moment, and looked into his face. She had undertaken a duty, and she was not the woman to shrink from it. So she told herself at that moment. And yet she was very much afraid of him as she saw the squareness of his forehead, and the set of his mouth. And there was a frown across his brow, as though he were preparing himself to fight. 'You must have found it hard to accommodate yourselves to them, Mr. Caldigate?'

'Not at all.'

'Of course we all know that you are a gentleman.'

'I am much obliged to you; but I do not know any word that requires a definition so much as that. I am going to work hard to earn my bread; and I suppose these people are going to do the same.'

'There always will be some danger in such society,' said Mrs. Callander.

'I hope I may escape any great evil.'

'I hope so too, Mr. Caldigate. You probably have had a long roll of ancestors before you?'

'We all have that;—back to Adam.'

'Ah! but I mean a family roll, of which you ought to be proud;—all ladies and gentlemen.'

'Upon my word I don't know.'

'So I hear, and I have no doubt it is true.' Then she paused, looking again into his face. It was very square, and his lips were hard, and there was a gleam of anger in his eyes. She wished herself back again in her own part of the ship; but she had boasted to Miss Green that she was not the woman to give up a duty when she had undertaken it. Though she was frightened, still she must go on. 'I hope you will excuse me, Mr. Caldigate.'

'I am sure you will not say anything that I cannot excuse.'

'Don't you think—' Then she paused. She had looked into his face again, and was so little satisfied that she did not dare to go on. He

55

would not help her in the least, but stood there looking at her, with something of a smile stealing over the hardness of his face, but with such an expression that the smile was even worse than the hardness.

'Were you going to speak to me about another lady, Mrs. Callender?'

'I was. That is what I was going to speak of——' She was anxious to remonstrate against that word lady, but her courage failed her.

'Then don't you think that perhaps you had better leave it alone. I am very much obliged to you, and all that kind of thing; and as to myself, I really shouldn't care what you said. Any good advice would be taken most gratefully,—if it didn't affect any one else. But you might say things of the lady in question which I shouldn't bear patiently.'

'She can't be your equal.'

'I won't hear even that patiently. You know nothing about her, except that she is a second-class passenger,—in which matter she is exactly my equal. If you come to that, don't you think that you are degrading yourself in coming here and talking to me? I am not your equal.'

'But you are.'

'And so is she, then. We shan't arrive at anything, Mrs. Callander, and so you had better give it up.' Whereupon she did give it up and retreat to her own part of the ship, but not with a very good grace.

They had certainly become very intimate,—John Caldigate and Mrs. Smith; and there could be no doubt that, in the ordinary language of the world, he was making a fool of himself. He did in fact know nothing about her but what she told herself, and this amounted to little more than three statements, which might or might not be true,— that she had gone on the stage in opposition to her friends,—that she had married an actor, who had treated her with great cruelty,—and that he had died of drink. And with each of these stories there had been an accompaniment of mystery. She had not told him her maiden name, nor what had been the condition of her parents, nor whether they were living, nor at what theatres she and her husband had acted, nor when he had died. She had expressed a hope that she might get an engagement in the colonies, but she had not spoken of any recommendation or letters of introduction. He simply knew of her that her name was Euphemia Smith.

In that matter of her clothes there had been a great improvement, but made very gradually. She had laughed at her own precautions, saying, that in her poverty she had wished to save everything that could be saved, and that she had only intended to make herself look like others in the same class. 'And I had wanted to avoid all attention,—

at first,' she said, smiling, as she looked up at him.

'In which you have been altogether unsuccessful,' he replied, 'as you are certainly more talked about than any one in the ship.'

'Has it been my fault?' she asked.

Then he comforted her, saying that it certainly had not been her fault; that she had been reticent and reserved till she had been either provoked or invited to come forth; and, in fact, that her conduct had been in all respects feminine, pretty, and decorous;—as to all which he was not perhaps the best judge in the world.

But she was certainly much pleasanter to look at, and even to talk to, now that she had put on a small, clean, black felt hat instead of the broken straw, and had got out from her trunks a pretty warm shawl, and placed a ribbon or two about her in some indescribable manner, and was no longer ashamed of showing her shoes as she sat about upon the deck. There could be no doubt, as she was seen now, that she was the most attractive female on board the ship; but it may be doubted whether the anger of the Mrs. Cromptons, Mrs Callanders, and Miss Greens was mitigated by the change. The battle against her became stronger, and the duty of rescuing that infatuated young man from her sorceries was more clear than ever;—if only anything could be done to rescue him!

What could be done? Mrs. Smith could not be locked up. No one,—not even the Captain,—could send her down to her own wretched little cabin because she would talk with a gentleman. Talking is allowed on board ship, and even flirting, to a certain extent. Mrs. Smith's conduct with Mr. Caldigate was not more peculiar than that of Miss Green and the doctor. Only it pleased certain people to think that Miss Green might be fond of the doctor if she chose, and that Mrs. Smith had no right to be fond of any man. There was a stubbornness about both the sinners which resolved to set public opinion at defiance. The very fact that others wished to interfere with him made Caldigate determined to resent all interference; and the woman, with perhaps a deeper insight into her own advantages, was brave enough to be able to set opposition at defiance.

They were about a week from their port when the captain,—Captain Munday,—was induced to take the matter into his own hands, It is hardly too much to say that he was pressed to do so by the united efforts of the first-class passengers. It was dreadful to think that this unfortunate young man should go on shore merely to become the prey of such a woman as that. So Captain Munday, who at heart was not afraid of his passenger,—but who persisted in saying that no good could be done, and who had, as may be remembered, already made a slight attempt,—was induced to take the matter in hand. He came up to Caldigate on the deck one afternoon, and without any preface began his business. 'Mr. Caldigate,' he said, 'I am afraid you are getting into a scrape with one of your fellow-passengers.'

'What do you call a scrape, Captain Munday?'

'I should call it a scrape if a young gentleman of your position and your prospects were to find himself engaged on board ship to marry a woman he knew nothing about.'

'Do you know anything about my position and prospects, Captain Munday?'

'I know you are a gentleman.'

'And I think you know less about the lady.'

'I know nothing;—but I will tell you what I hear.'

'I really would rather that you did not. Of course, Captain Munday, on board your own ship you are a despot, and I must say that you have made everything very pleasant for us. But I don't think even your position entitles you to talk to me about my private affairs,—or about hers. You say you know nothing. Is it manly to repeat what one hears about a poor forlorn woman?' Then the Captain retreated without another word, owning to himself that he was beaten. If this foolish young man chose to make for himself a bed of that kind he must lie upon it. Captain Munday went away shrugging his shoulders, and spoke no further word to John Caldigate on that or any other subject during the voyage.

Caldigate had driven off his persecutors valiantly, and had taught them all to think that he was resolute in his purposes in regard to Mrs. Smith, let those purposes be what they might; but nothing could be further from the truth; for he had no purposes; and was, within his own mind, conscious of his lack of all purpose, and very conscious of his folly. And though he could repel Mrs. Callander and the Captain,— as he had always repelled those who had attempted to control him,— still he knew that they had been right. Such an intimacy as this could not be wise, and its want of wisdom became the more strongly impressed upon him the nearer he got to shore, and the more he felt that when he had got ashore he should not know how to act in regard to her.

The intimacy had certainly become very close. He had expressed his great admiration, and she had replied that, 'had things not been as they were,' she could have returned the feeling. But she did not say what the things were which might have been otherwise. Nor did she seem to attempt to lead him on to further and more definite proposals. And she never spoke of any joint action between them when on shore, though she gave herself up to his society here on board the ship. She seemed to think that they were then to part, as though one would be going one way, and one the other;—but he felt that after so close an intimacy they could not part like that.

CHAPTER VIII

Reaching Melbourne

THINGS went on in the same way till the night before the morning on which they were to enter Hobson's Bay. Hobson's Bay, as every one knows, is the inlet of the sea into which the little river runs on which Melbourne is built. After leaving the tropics they had gone down south, and had encountered showers and wind, and cold weather, but now they had come up again into warm latitudes and fine autumn weather,— for it was the beginning of March, and the world out there is upside down. Before that evening nothing had been said between Mrs. Smith and John Caldigate as to any future; not a word to indicate that when the journey should be over, there would or that there would not be further intercourse between them. She had purposely avoided any reference to a world after this world of the ship, even refusing, in her half-sad but half-joking manner, to discuss matters so far ahead. But he felt that he could not leave her on board, as he would the other passengers, without a word spoken as to some future meeting. There will arrive on occasions a certain pitch of intimacy,—which cannot be defined as may a degree of cousinship, but which is perfectly under-stood by the persons concerned,—so close as to forbid such mere shaking of the hands. There are many men, and perhaps more women, cautious enough and wise enough to think of this beforehand, and, thinking of it, to guard themselves from the dangerous attractions of casual companions by a composed manner and unenthusiastic con-versation. Who does not know the sagacious lady who, after sitting at table with the same gentleman for a month, can say, 'Good-bye, Mr. Jones,' just as though Mr. Jones had been a stranger under her notice but for a day. But others gush out, and when Mr. Jones takes his departure, hardly know how not to throw themselves into his arms, The intercourse between our hero and Mrs. Smith had been such that, as a gentleman, he could not leave her without some allusion to future meetings. That was all up to the evening before their arrival. The whole ship's company, captain, officers, quartermasters, passengers, and all, were quite sure that she had succeeded in getting a promise of marriage from him. But there had been nothing of the kind.

Among others, Dick Shand was sure that there was some entangle-ment. Entanglement was the word he always used in discussing the matter with Mrs. Callander. Between Dick and his friend there had been very little confidential communication of late. Caldigate had forbidden Shand to talk to him about Mrs. Smith, and thus had naturally closed the man's mouth on other matters. And then they had fallen into different sets. Dick, at least, had fallen into a set, while Caldigate had hardly associated with any but the one dangerous friend. Dick had lived much with a bevy of noisy young men who had been given to games and smoking, and to a good deal of drink. Caldigate had said not a word, even when on one occasion Dick had stumbled down into the cabin very much the worse for what he had taken. How could he find fault with Dick's folly when he would not allow Dick to say a word to him as to his own? But on this last day at sea it became necessary that they should understand each other.

'What do you mean to do when you land?' Caldigate asked.

All that had been settled between them very exactly long since. At a town called Nobble, about three hundred miles west of Sydney, there lived a man, supposed to be knowing in gold, named Crinkett, with whom they had corresponded, and to whom they intended, in the first instance, to apply. And about twenty miles beyond Nobble were the new and now much reputed Ahalala diggings, at which they purposed to make their first debut. It had been decided that they would go direct from Melbourne to Nobble,—not round by Sydney so as to see more of the world, and thus spend more money,—but by the direct route, taking the railway to Albury, and the coaches, which they were informed were running between Albury and Nobble. And it had also been determined that they would spend but two nights in Melbourne,—'just to get their things washed,'—so keen had they been in their determination to begin their work. But on all these matters there had been no discussion now for a month, nor even an allusion to them.

'What do you mean to do when we land?' Caldigate asked on that last day.

'I thought all that was settled. But I suppose you are going to change everything?'

'I am going to change nothing. Only you seem to have got into such a way of life that I didn't know whether you would be prepared for serious work.'

'I shall be as well prepared as you are, I don't doubt,' said Dick. 'I have no impediment of any kind.'

'I certainly have none. Then we will start by the first train on Wednesday morning for Albury. We must have our heavy things sent round by sea to Sydney, and get them from there as best we can. When we are a little fixed, one of us can run down to Sydney.'

And so it was settled, without any real confidence between them, but in conformity with their previous arrangements.

It was on the evening of the same day, after they had sighted Cape Otway, that Mrs. Smith and Caldigate began their last conversation on board the Goldfinder,—a conversation which lasted, with one or two interruptions, late into the night.

'So we have come to the end of it,' she said.

'To the end of what?'

'To the end of all that is pleasant and easy and safe. Don't you remember my telling you how I dreaded the finish? Here I have been fairly comfortable, and have in many respects enjoyed it. I have had you to talk to; and there has been a flavour of old days about it. What shall I be doing this time to-morrow?'

'I don't know your plans.'

'Exactly;—and I have not told you, because I would not have you bothered with me when I land. You have enough on your own hands; and if I were to be a burden to you now it might be a serious trouble. I am afraid poor Mr. Shand objects to me.'

'You don't think that would stand in my way?'

'It stands in mine. Of course, with your pride and your obstinacy you would tell Mr. Shand to go to—the devil if he ventured to object to any little delay that might be occasioned by looking after me. Then Mr. Shand would go—there, or elsewhere; and all your plans would be broken up, and you would be without a companion.'

'Unless I had you.' Of all the words which he could have spoken in such an emergency these were the most foolish; and yet, at so tender a moment, how were they to be repressed?

'I do think that Dick Shand is dangerous,' she answered, laughing; 'but I should be worse. I am afraid Dick Shand will—drink.'

'If so, we must part. And what would you do?'

'What would I do? What could I do?' Then there was a pause. 'Perhaps I should want you to—marry me, which would be worse than Dick Shand's drinking. Eh?'

There is an obligation on a man to persevere when a woman has encouraged him in love-making. It is like riding at a fence. When once you have set your horse at it you must go on, however impracticable it may appear as you draw close to it. If you have never looked at the fence at all,—if you have ridden quite the other way, making for some safe gate or clinging to the dull lane,—then there will be no excitement, but also there will be no danger and no disgrace. Caldigate had ridden hard at the fence, and could not crane it at now that it was so close to him. He could only trust to his good fortune to carry him safe over. 'I don't suppose you would want it,' he said, 'but I might.'

'You would want me, but you would not want me for always. I should be a burden less easy to shake off than Dick Shand.'

'Is that the way a man is always to look at a woman?'

'It is the way in which they do, I think. I often wonder that any man is ever fool enough to marry. A poor man may want some one to serve him, and may be able to get service in no other way; or a man, poor in another way, may find an heiress convenient;—but otherwise I think men only marry when they are caught. Women are prehensile things, which have to cling to something for nourishment and support. When I come across such a one as you I naturally put out my feelers.'

'I have not been aware of it.'

'Yes, you are; and I do not doubt that your mind is vacillating about me. I am sure you like me.'

'Certainly, I like you.'

'And you know that I love you.'

'I did not know it.'

'Yes, you did. You are not the man to be diffident of yourself in such a matter. You must either think that I love you, or that I have been a great hypocrite in pretending to do so. Love you!' They were sitting together on a large spar which was lashed on to the deck, and which had served throughout all the voyage for a seat for second-class passengers. There were others now on the farther end of it; but there was a feeling that when Caldigate and Mrs. Smith were together it would not be civil to intrude upon their privacy. At this time it was dark; but their eyes had become used to the gloom, and each could see the other's face. 'Love you!' she repeated, looking up at him, speaking in a very low voice, but yet, oh so clearly, so that not a fraction of a sound was lost to his ears, with no special emotion in her face, with no contortion, no grimace, but with her eyes fixed upon his. 'How should it be possible that I should not love you? For two months we have been together as people seldom are in the world,—as they never can be without hating each other or loving each other thoroughly. You have been very good to me who am all alone and desolate. And you are clever, educated,—and a man. How should I not love you? And I know from the touch of your hand, from your breath when I feel it on my face, from the fire in your eye, and from the tenderness of your mouth, that you, too, love me.'

'I do,' he said.

'But as there may be marriage without love, so there may be love without marriage. You cannot but feel how little you know of me, and ignorant as you are of so much, that to marry me might be—

63

ruin.' It was just what he had told himself over and over again, when he had been trying to resolve what he would do in regard to her. 'Don't you know that?'

'I know that it might have been so among the connections of home life.'

'And to you the connections of home life may all come back. That woman talked about your "roll of ancestors." Coming from her it was absurd. But there was some truth in it. You know that were you to marry me, say to-morrow, in Melbourne, it would shut you out from—well, not the possibility but the probability of return.'

'I do not want to go back.'

'Nor do I want to hinder you from doing so. If we were alike desolate, alike alone, alike cast out, oh then, what a heaven of happiness I should think had been opened to me by the idea of joining myself to you! There is nothing I could not do for you. But I will not be a millstone round your neck.'

She had taken so much the more prominent part in all this that he felt himself compelled by his manliness to say something in contradiction to it—something that should have the same flavour about it as had her self-abnegation and declared passion. He also must be unselfish and enthusiastic. 'I do not deny that there is truth in what you say.'

'It is true.'

'Of course I love you.'

'It ought to be of course,—now.'

'And of course I do not mean to part from you now, as though we were never to see each other again.'

'I hope not quite that.'

'Certainly not. I shall therefore hold you as engaged to me, and myself as engaged to you,—unless something should occur to separate us.' It was a foolish thing to say, but he did not know how to speak without being foolish. It is not usual that a gentleman should ask a lady to be engaged to him '—unless something should occur to separate them!' 'You will consent to that,' he said.

'What I will consent to is this, that I will be yours, all yours, whenever you may choose to send for me. At any moment I will be your wife for the asking. But you shall go away first, and shall think of it, and reflect upon it,—so that I may not have to reproach myself with having caught you.'

'Caught me?'

'Well, yes, caught you. I do feel that I have caught you,—almost. I do feel,—almost,—that I ought to have had nothing to do with you. From the beginning of it all I knew that I ought to have nothing to say to you. You are too good for me.' Then she rose from her place as though to leave him. 'I will go down now,' she said, 'because I know you will have many things to do. To-morrow, when we get up, we shall be in the harbour, and you will be on shore quite early. There will be no time for a word of farewell then. I will meet you again here just before we go to bed,—say at half-past ten. Then we will arrange, if we can arrange, how we may meet again.'

And so she glided away from him, and he was left alone, sitting on the spar. Now, at any rate, he had engaged himself. There could not be any doubt about that. He certainly could not be justified in regarding himself as free because she had told him that she would give him time to think of it. Of course he was engaged to marry her. When a man has been successful in his wooing he is supposed to be happy. He asked himself whether he was proud of the result of this intimacy. She had told him,—she herself,—that she had 'caught him', meaning thereby that he had been taken as a rabbit with a snare or a fish with a baited hook. If it had been so, surely she would not herself have said so. And yet he was aware how common it is for a delinquent to cover his own delinquency by declaring it. 'Of course I am idle,' says the idle one, escaping the disgrace of his idleness by his honesty. 'I have caught you!' There is something soothing to the vanity in such a declaration from a pretty woman. That she should have wished to catch you is something;—something that the net should itself be so pleasant, with its silken meshes! But the declaration may not the less be true and the fact unpleasant. In the matter of matrimony a man does not wish to be caught; and Caldigate, fond as he was of her, acknowledged that what she said was true.

He leant back in a corner that was made by the hatchway, and endeavoured to think over his life and prospects. If this were a true engagement, then must he cease altogether to think of Hester Bolton. Then must that dream be abandoned. It is of no use to the most fervid imagination to have a castle projected in Spain from which all possible foundation has been taken away. In his dreams of life a man should never dream that which is altogether impossible. There had been something in the thought of Hester Bolton which had taken him back from the roughnesses of his new life, from the doubtful respectability of Mrs. Smith, from the squalor of the second-class, from the whisky-laden snores of Dick Shand, to a sweeter, brighter, cleaner world. Till this engagement had been absolutely spoken he could still indulge in that romance, distant and unreal as it was. But now,—now it seemed to be brought in upon him very forcibly that he must rid his thoughts of Hester Bolton,—or else rid his life of Mrs. Smith.

But he was engaged to marry Mrs. Smith. Then he got up, and walked backwards and forwards along the deck, asking himself whether this could really be the truth. Was he bound to this woman for his life? And if so, had he done a thing of which he already repented himself? He tried to persuade himself that she was admirably fitted for the life which he was fated to lead. She was handsome, intellectual, a most delightful companion, and yet capable of enduring the hardships of an adventurous uncertain career. Ought he not to think himself peculiarly lucky in having found for himself so eligible a companion? But there is something so solemn, so sacred, in the name of wife. A man brought up among soft things is so imbued with the feeling that his wife should be something better, cleaner, sweeter, holier than himself, that he could not but be awe-struck when he thought that he was bound to marry this all but nameless widow of some drunken player,--this woman who, among other women, had been thought unfit for all companionship!

But things arrange themselves. How probable it was that he would never be married to her. After all, this might be but an incident, and not an unpleasant incident, in his life. He had had his amusement out of it, and she had had hers. Perhaps they would part to meet no more. But when he thought that there might be comfort in this direction, he felt that he was a scoundrel for thinking so.

'And this is to say good-bye?' 'Twas thus she greeted him again that night. 'Good-bye—'

'Good-bye, my love.'

'My love! my love! And now remember this; my address will be, Post-office, Melbourne. It will be for you to write to me. You will not hear from me unless you do. Indeed I shall know nothing of you. Let me have a line before a month is over.' This he promised, and then they parted.

At break of day on the following morning the Goldfinder rode over the Rip into Hobson's Bay. There were still four hours before the ship lay at her moorings; but during all that time Mrs. Smith was not seen by Caldigate. As he got into the boat which took him and Shand from the ship to the pier at Sandridge she kissed her hand to him over the side of the vessel. Before eleven o'clock Dick Shand and his companion were comfortably put up at the Miners' Home in Flinders Lane.

CHAPTER IX

Nobble

DURING the two days which Dick and Caldigate spent together in Melbourne Mrs. Smith's name was not mentioned between them. They were particularly civil each to the other and went to work together, making arrangements at a bank as to their money, taking their places, despatching their luggage, and sorting their belongings as though there had been no such woman as Mrs. Smith on board the Goldfinder. Dick, though he had been inclined to grumble when his mystery had been taken out of his hands,—who had, of course, been jealous when he saw that the lady had discarded her old hat and put on new ribbons, not for him, but for another,—was too conscious of the desolation to which he would be subjected by quarrelling with his friend. He felt himself unable to go alone, and was therefore willing that the bygones of the ship should be bygones. Caldigate, on the other hand, acknow-ledged to himself that he owed some reparation to his companion. Of course he had not bound himself to any special mode of life;—but had he, in his present condition, allied himself more closely to Mrs. Smith, he would, to some extent, have thrown Dick over. And then, as soon as he was on shore, he did feel somewhat ashamed of himself in regard to Mrs. Smith. Was it not manifest that any closer alliance, let the alliance be what it might, must be ruinous to him? As it was, had he not made an absolute fool of himself with Mrs. Smith? Had he not got himself already into a mess from which there was no escape? Of course he must write to her when the month was over. The very weight of his thoughts on this matter made him tamer with Dick and more observant than he would otherwise have been.

They were during those two days frequently about the town, looking at the various streets and buildings, at the banks and churches and gardens,—as is usual with young men when they visit a new town; but, during it all, Caldigate's mind was more intent on Mrs. Smith than he was on the sights of the place. Melbourne is not so big but that she might easily have thrown herself in his way had she pleased. Strangers residing in such a town are almost sure to see each other before twenty-four hours are gone. But Mrs. Smith was not seen. Two or three times he went up and down Collins Street alone, without his friend, not wishing to see her,—aware that he had better not see her,—but made restless by a nervous feeling that he ought to wish to see her, that he should, at any rate, not keep out of her way. But Mrs. Smith did not show herself. Whatever might be her future views, she did not now take steps to present herself to him. 'I shall be so much the more bound to present myself to her,' he said to himself. 'But perhaps she knows all that,' he added in the same soliloquy.

On the Wednesday morning they left Melbourne by the 6 A.M. train for Albury, which latter place they reached the same day, about 2 P.M., having then crossed the Murray river, and passed into the colony of New South Wales. Here they stayed but a few hours and then went on by coach on their journey to Nobble. From one wretched vehicle they were handed on to another, never stopping anywhere long enough to go to bed,—three hours at one wretched place and five at another,—travelling at the rate of six miles an hour, bumping through the mud and slush of the bush roads, and still going on for three days and three nights. This was roughing it indeed. Even Dick complained, and said that, of all the torments prepared for wicked mortals on earth, this Australian coaching was the worst. They went through Wagga-Wagga and Murrumburra, and other places with similar names, till at last they were told that they had reached Nobble. Nobble they thought was the foulest place which they had ever seen. It was a gold-digging town, as such places are called, and had been built with great rapidity to supply the necessities of adjacent miners. It was constructed altogether of wood, but no two houses had been constructed alike. They generally had gable ends opening on to the street, but were so different in breadth, altitude, and form, that it was easy to see that each enterprising proprietor had been his own architect. But they were all alike in having enormous advertisement-boards, some high, some broad, some sloping, on which were declared the merits of the tradesmen who administered within to the wants of mining humanity. And they had generally assumed most singular names for themselves: 'The Old Stick-in-the-Mud Soft Goods Store.' 'The Polyeuka Stout Depot,' 'Number Nine Flour Mills,' and so on,— all of which were very unintelligible to our friends till they learned that these were the names belonging to certain gold-mining claims which had been opened in the neighbourhood of Nobble. The street itself was almost more perilous to vehicles than the slush of the forest-tracks, so deep were the holes and so uncertain the surface. When Caldigate informed the driver that they wanted to be taken as far as Henniker's hotel, the man said that he had given up going so far as that for the last two months, the journey being too perilous. So they shouldered their portmanteaus and struggled forth down the street. Here and there a short bit of wooden causeway, perhaps for the length of three houses, would assist them; and then, again, they would have to descend into the roadway and plunge along through the mud.

'It is not quite as nice walking as the old Quad at Trinity,' said Caldigate.

'It is the beastliest hole I ever put my foot in since I was born,' said Dick, who had just stumbled and nearly came to the ground with his burden. 'They told us that Nobble was a fine town.'

Henniker's hotel was a long, low wooden shanty, divided into various very small partitions by thin planks, in most of which two or more dirty-looking beds had been packed very closely. But between these little compartments there was a long chamber containing a long and very dirty table, and two long benches. Here were sitting a crowd of miners, drinking, when our friends were ushered in through the bar or counter which faced to the street. At the bar they were received by a dirty old woman who said that she was Mrs. Henniker. Then they were told, while the convivial crowd were looking on and listening, that they could have the use of one of the partitions and their 'grub' for 7s. 6d. a-day each. When they asked for a partition apiece, they were told that if they didn't like what was offered to them they might go elsewhere. Upon that they agreed to Mrs. Henniker's terms, and sitting down on one of the benches looked desolately into each other's faces.

Yes;—it was different from Trinity College, different from Babington, very different even from the less luxurious comfort of the house at Pollington. The deck, even the second-class cabin, of the Goldfinder had been better than this. And then they had no friend, not even an acquaintance, within some hundred miles. The men around them were not uncivil. Australian miners never are so. But they were inquisitive, familiar, and with their half-drunken good-humour, almost repulsive. It was about noon when our friends reached Henniker's, and they were told that there would be dinner at one. There was always 'grub' at one, and 'grub' at seven, and 'grub' at eight in the morning. So one of the men informed them. The same gentleman hoped that the strangers were not very particular, as the 'grub', though plentiful, was apt to be rough of its kind.

'You'll have it a deal worse before you've done if you're going on to Ahalala,' said another. Then Caldigate said that they did intend to go on to Ahalala. 'We're going to have a spell at gold-digging,' said he. What was the use of making any secret of the matter? 'We knowed that ready enough,' said one of the men. 'Chaps like you don't come much to Nobble for nothing else. Have you got any money to start with?'

'A few half-crowns,' said Dick, cautiously.

'Half-crowns don't go very far here, my mate. If you can spend four or five pounds a-week each for the next month, so as to get help till you know where you are, it may be you'll turn up gold at Ahalala;—but if not, you'd better go elsewhere. You needn't be afraid. We ain't a-going to rob you of nothing.'

'Nor yet we don't want nothing to drink,' said another.

'Speak for yourself, Jack,' said a third. 'But come;—as these are regular new chums, I don't care if I shout for the lot myself.' Then the dirty old woman was summoned, and everybody had whisky all round. When that was done, another generous man came to the front, and there was more whisky, till Caldigate was frightened as to the result.

Evil might have come from it, had not the old woman opportunely brought the 'grub' into the room. This she chucked down on the table in such a way that the grease out of the dish spattered itself all around. There was no tablecloth, nor had any preparation been made; but in the middle of the table there was a heap of dirty knives and forks, with which the men at once armed themselves; and each took a plate out of a heap that had been placed on a shelf against the wall. Caldigate and Shand, when they saw how the matter was to be arranged, did as the other men. The 'grub' consisted of an enormous lump of boiled beef, and a bowl of potatoes, which was moderate enough in size considering that there were in all about a dozen men to be fed. But there was meat enough for double the number, and bread in plenty, but so ill-made as to be rejected by most of the men. The potatoes were evidently the luxury; and guided by that feeling, the man who had told the strangers that they need not be afraid of being robbed, at once selected six out of the bowl, and deposited three each before Dick and Caldigate. He helped the others all round to one each, and then was left without any for himself. 'I don't care a damn for that sort of tucker,' he said, as though he despised potatoes from the bottom of his heart. Of all the crew he was the dirtiest, and was certainly half drunk. Another man holloaed to 'Mother Henniker' for pickles; but Mother Henniker, without leaving her seat at the bar, told them to 'pickle themselves.' Whereupon one of the party, making some allusion to Jack Brien's swag,—Jack Brien being absent at the moment,—rose from his seat and undid a great roll lying in one of the corners. Every miner has his swag,—consisting of a large blanket which is rolled up, and contains all his personal luggage. Out of Jack Brien's swag were extracted two large square bottles of pickles. These were straightway divided among the men, care being taken that Dick and Caldigate should have ample shares. Then every man helped himself to beef, as much as he would, passing the dish round from one to the other.

When the meal was half finished, Mrs. Henniker brought in an enormous jorum of tea, which she served out to all the guests in tin pannikins, giving to every man a fixed and ample allowance of brown sugar, without at all consulting his taste. Milk there was none. In the midst of this Jack Brien came in, and with a clamour of mirth the empty pickle jars were shown him. Jack, who was a silent man, and somewhat melancholy, merely shook his head and ate his beef. It may be presumed that he was fond of pickles, having taken so much trouble to provide them; but he said not a word of the injury to which he had been subjected.

'Them's a-going to Ahalala, Jack,' said the distributor of the potatoes, nodding his head to indicate the two new adventurers.

'Then they're a-going to the most infernal, mean,—, —breakheartedest place as God Almighty ever put on this 'arth for the perplexment of poor unfortunate — — miners.' This was Jack Brien's eloquence, and his description of Ahalala. Before this he had not spoken a word, nor did he speak again till he had consumed three or four pounds of beef, and had swallowed two pannikins of tea. Then he repeated his speech: 'There isn't so — — an infernal, mean, breakhearted a place as Ahalala,–not nowhere; no, not nowhere. And so them chums'll find for theirselves if they go there.' Then his neighbour whispered into Caldigate's ear that Jack had gone to Ahalala with fifty sovereigns in his pocket, and that he wasn't now worth a red cent.

'But there is gold there?' asked Caldigate.

'It's my belief there's gold pretty much everywhere, and you may find it, or you mayn't. That's where it is;–and the mayn'ts are a deal oftener turning up than the mays.'

'A man can get work for wages,' suggested Dick.

'Wages! What's the use of that? A man as knows mining can earn wages. But Ahalala ain't a place for wages. If you want wages, go to one of the old-fashioned places,–Bendigo, or the like of that. I've worked for wages, but what comes of it? A man goes to Ahalala because he wants to run his chance, and get a big haul. It's every one on his own bottom pretty much at Ahalala.'

'Wages be —!' said Jack Brien, rising from the seat and hitching up his trousers as he left the room. It was very evident that Jack Brien was a gambler.

After dinner there was a smoke, and after the smoke Dick Shand 'shouted' for the company. Dick had quite learned by this time the mystery of shouting. When one man 'stands' drinks all round, he shouts; and then it is no more than reciprocal that another man should do the same. And, in this way, when the reciprocal feeling is spread over a good many drinkers, a good deal of liquor is consumed.

While Dick Shand's 'shout' was being consumed, Caldigate asked one of his new friends where Mr. Crinkett lived. Was Mr. Crinkett known in Nobble? It seemed that Crinkett was very well known in Nobble indeed. If anybody had done well at Nobble, Mr. Crinkett had done well. He was the 'swell' of the place. This informant did not think that Mr. Crinkett had himself gone very deep at Ahalala. Mr. Crinkett had risen high enough in his profession to be able to achieve more certainty than could be found at such a place as Ahalala. By this time they were on the road to Mr. Crinkett's house, this new friend having undertaken to show them the way.

'He can put you up to a thing or two, if he likes,' said the new friend. 'Perhaps he's a pal of yourn?'

Caldigate explained that he had never seen Mr. Crinkett, but that he had come to Nobble armed with a letter from a gentleman in England who had once been concerned in gold-digging.

'He's a civil enough gent, is Crinkett,' said the miner;—'but he do like making money. They say of him there's nothing he wouldn't sell,—not even his grandmother's bones. I like trade, myself,' added the miner; 'but some of 'em's too sharp. That's where Crinkett lives. He's a swell; ain't he?'

They had walked about half a mile from the town, turning down a lane at the back of the house, and had made their way through yawning pit-holes and heaps of dirt and pools of yellow water,—where everything was disorderly and apparently deserted,—till they came to a cluster of heaps so large as to look like little hills; and here there were signs of mining vitality. On their way they had not come across a single shred of vegetation, though here and there stood the bare trunks of a few dead and headless trees, the ghosts of the forest which had occupied the place six or seven years previously. On the tops of these artificial hills there were sundry rickety-looking erections, and around them were troughs and sheds and rude water-works. These, as the miner explained, were the outward and visible signs of the world-famous 'Old Stick-in-the-Mud' claim, which was now giving two ounces of gold to the ton of quartz, and which was at present the exclusive property of Mr. Crinkett, who had bought out the tribute share-holders and was working the thing altogether on his own bottom. As they ascended one of those mounds of upcast stones and rubble, they could see on the other side the crushing-mills, and the engine-house, and could hear the thud, thud, thud of the great iron hammers as they fell on the quartz,—and then, close beyond, but still among the hillocks, and surrounded on all sides by the dirt and filth of the mining operations, was Mr. Crinkett's mansion. 'And there's his very self a-standing at the gate a-counting how many times the hammer falls a minute, and how much gold is a-coming from every blow as it falls.' With this little observation as to Mr. Crinkett's personal character, the miner made his way back to his companions.

CHAPTER X

Polyeuka Hall

THE house which they saw certainly surprised them much, and seemed to justify the assertion just before made to them that Mr. Crinkett was a swell. It was marvellous that any man should have contemplated the building of such a mansion in a place so little attractive, with so many houses within view. The house and little attempted garden, together with the stables and appurtenances, may have occupied half an acre. All around it were those hideous signs of mining operations which make a country rich in metals look as though the devil had walked over it, dragging behind him an enormous rake. There was not a blade of grass to be seen. As far as the eye could reach there stood those ghost-like skeletons of trees in all spots where the soil had not been turned up; but on none of them was there a leaf left, or even a branch. Everywhere the ground was thrown about in hideous uncovered hillocks, all of which seemed to have been deserted except those in the immediate neighbourhood of Mr. Crinkett's house. But close around him one could see wheels turning and long ropes moving, and water running in little wooden conduits, all of which were signs of the activity going on under ground. And then there was the never-ceasing thud, thud, thud of the crushing-mill, which from twelve o'clock on Sunday night to twelve o'clock on Saturday night, never paused for a moment, having the effect, on that vacant day, of creating a painful strain of silence upon the ears of those who were compelled to remain on the spot during the unoccupied time. It was said that in Mr. Crinkett's mansion every sleeper would wake from his sleep as soon as the engine was stopped, disturbed by the unwonted quiescence.

But the house which had been built in this unpromising spot was quite entitled to be called a mansion. It was of red brick, three storeys high, with white stone facings to all the windows and all the corners, which glittered uncomfortably in the hot sun. There was a sweep up to it, the road having been made from the débris of the stone out of which the gold had been crushed; but though there was the sweep up to the door carefully made for the length of a few dozen yards, there was nothing that could be called a road outside, though there were tracks here and there through the hillocks, along which the waggons employed about the place struggled through the mud. The house itself was built with a large hall in the middle, and three large windows

74

on each side. On the floor there were four large rooms, with kitchens opening out behind, and above there were, of course, chambers in proportion; and in the little garden there was a pond and a big bath-house, and there were coach-houses and stables;—so that it was quite a mansion. It was called Polyeuka Hall, because while it was being built Mr. Crinkett was drawing large gains from the Polyeuka mine, about three miles distant on the other side of Nobble. For the building of his mansion on this special site, no one could imagine any other reason than that love which a brave man has of overcoming difficulties. To endeavour to create a paradise in such a Pandemonium required all the energies of a Crinkett. Whether or not he had been successful depended of course on his own idiosyncrasies. He had a wife who, it is to be hoped, liked her residence. They had no children, and he spent the greater part of his time away in other mining districts in which he had ventures. When thus absent, he would live as Jack Brien and his friends were living at Mrs. Henniker's, and was supposed to enjoy the ease of his inn more thoroughly than he did the constraint of his grand establishment.

At the present moment he was at home, and was standing at the gate of his domain all alone, with a pipe in his mouth,—perhaps listening, as the man had said, to the noise of his own crushing-machine. He was dressed in black, with a chimney-pot on his head,—and certainly did not look like a miner, though he looked as little like a gentleman. Our friends were in what they conceived to be proper miners' costume, but Mr. Crinkett knew at a glance that there was something uncommon about them. As they approached he did not attempt to open the gate, but awaited them, looking over the top of it from the inside. 'Well, my mates, what can I do for you?' he said, still remaining on his side, and apparently intending that they should remain on theirs. Then Caldigate brought forth his letter, and handed it to the owner of the place across the top of the gate. 'I think Mr. Jones wrote to you about us before,' said Caldigate.

Crinkett read the letter very deliberately. Perhaps he required time to meditate what his conduct should be. Perhaps he was not quick at reading written letters. But at last he got to the end of the very few words which the note contained. 'Jones!' he said, 'Jones wasn't much account when he was out here.'

'We don't know a great deal about him,' said Dick.

'But when he heard that we were coming, he offered us a letter to you,' said Caldigate. 'I believe him to be an honest man.'

'Honest! Well, yes; I daresay he's honest enough. He never robbed me of nothing. And shall I tell you why? Because I know how to take care that he don't, nor yet nobody else.' As he said this, he looked at them as though he intended that they were included among the numbers against whom he was perfectly on his guard.

'That's the way to live,' said Dick.

'That's the way I live, my friend. He did write before. I remember saying to myself what a pair of simpletons you must be if you was thinking of going to Ahalala.'

'We do think of going there,' said Caldigate.

'The road's open to you. Nobody won't prevent you. You can get beef and mutton there, and damper, and tea no doubt, and what they call brandy, as long as you've got the money to pay for it. One won't say anything about what price they'll charge you. Have you got any money?' Then Caldigate made a lengthened speech, in which he explained so much of their circumstances as seemed necessary. He did not name the exact sum which had been left at the bank in Melbourne, but he did make Mr. Crinkett understand that they were not paupers. They were anxious to do something in the way of mining, and particularly anxious to make money. But they did not quite know how to begin. Could he give them a hint? They meant to work with their own hands, but perhaps it might be well for them at first to hire the services of some one to set them a-going.

Crinkett listened very patiently, still maintaining his position on his own side of the gate. Then he spoke words of such wisdom as was in him. 'Ahalala is just the place to ease you of a little money. Mind I tell you. Gold! of course there's been gold to be got there. But what's been the cost of it? What's been the return? If sixteen hundred men, among 'em, can sell fifteen hundred pounds' worth of gold a week, how is each man to have twenty shillings on Saturday night? That's about what it is at Ahalala. Of course there's gold. And where there's gold chucked about in that way, just on the surface, one gets it and ten don't. Who is to say you mayn't be the one. As to hiring a man to show you the way,—you can hire a dozen. As long as you'll pay 'em ten shillings a-day to loaf about, you may have men enough. But whether they'll show you the way to anything except the liquor store, that's another thing. Now shall I tell you what you two gents had better do?' Dick declared that the two gents would be very much obliged to him if he would take that trouble. 'Of course you've heard of the "Old Stick-in-the-Mud"?' Dick told him that they had heard of that very successful mining enterprise since their arrival at Nobble. 'You ask on the veranda at Melbourne, or at Ballarat, or at Sydney. If they don't tell you about it, my name's not Crinkett. You put your money, what you've got, into ten-shilling shares. I'll accommodate you, as you're friends of Jones, with any reasonable number. We're getting two ounces to the ton. The books'll show you that.'

'We thought you'd purchased out all the shareholders,' said Caldigate.

'So I did, and now I'm redividing it. I'd rather have a company. It's pleasanter. If you can put in a couple of thousand pounds or so between you, you can travel about and see the country, and your money'll be working for you all the time. Did you ever see a gold mine?'

They owned that they never yet had been a yard below ground. Then he opened his gate preparatory to taking them down the 'Old Stick-in-the-Mud,' and brought them with him into one of the front rooms. It was a large parlour, only half furnished, not yet papered, without a carpet, in which it appeared that Mr. Crinkett kept his own belongings. Here he divested himself of his black clothes and put on a suit of miner's garments,—real miner's garments, very dirty, with a slouch hat, on the top of which there was a lump of mud in which to stick a candle-end. Any one learned in the matter would immediately have known the real miner. 'Now if you like to see a mine we will go down, and then you can do as you like about your money.'

They started forth, Crinkett leading the way, and entered the engine-house. As they went he said not a word, being aware that gold, gold that they could see with their eyes in its raw condition, would tempt them more surely than all his eloquence. In the engine-house the three of them got into a box or truck that was suspended over the mouth of a deep shaft, and soon found themselves descending through the bowels of the earth. They went down about four hundred feet, and as they were reaching the bottom Crinkett remarked that it was 'a goodish deep hole all to belong to one man.' 'Yes,' he added as Caldigate extricated himself from the truck, 'and there's a precious lot more gold to come out of it yet, I can tell you.'

In all the sights to be seen about the world there is no sight in which there is less to be seen than in a gold-mine. The two young men were made to follow their conductor along a very dirty under-ground gallery for about a quarter of a mile, and then they came to four men working with picks in a rough sort of chamber, and four others driving holes in the walls. They were simply picking down the rock, in doing which they were assisted by gun-powder. With keen eyes Crinkett searched along the roof and sides, and at last showed to his companions one or two little specks which he pronounced to be gold. 'When it shows itself like that all about, you may guess whether it's a paying concern! Two ounces to the ton, my boys!' As Dick and

77

Caldigate hitherto knew nothing about ounces and tons in reference to gold, and as they had heard of nuggets, and lumps of gold nearly as big as their fist, they were not much exalted by what they saw down the 'Old Stick-in-the-Mud.' Nor did they like the darkness and damp-ness and dirt and dreariness of the place. They had both resolved to work, as they had often said, with their own hands;–but in thinking over it their imagination had not pictured to them so uncomfortable a workshop as this. When they had returned to the light, the owner of the place took them through the crushing-mill attached, showed them the stone or mulloch, as it was thrust into the jaws of the devouring animal, and then brought them in triumph round to the place where the gold was eliminated from the débris of mud and water. The gold did not seem to them to be very much; but still there it was. 'Two ounces to the ton, my boys!' said Crinkett, as he brought them back to his house. 'You'll find that a 10s. share'll give you about 6d. a month. That's about 60 per cent, I guess. You can have your money monthly. What comes out of that there mine in a March, you can have in a April, and so on. There ain't nothing like it anywhere else,–not as I knows on. And instead of working your hearts out, you can be just amusing yourselves about the country. Don't go to Ahalala;–unless it is for dropping your money. If that's what you want, I won't say but Ahalala is as good a place as you'll find in the colony.' Then he brought a bottle of whisky out of a cupboard, and treated them to a glass of grog apiece. Beyond that his hospitality did not go.

Dick looked as though he liked the idea of having a venture in the 'Old Stick-in-the-Mud.' Caldigate, without actually disbelieving all that had been said to him, did not relish the proposal. It was not the kind of thing which they had intended. After they had learned their trade as miners it might be very well for them to have shares in some estab-lished concern;–but in that case he would wish to be one of the managers himself, and not to trust everything to any Crinkett, how-ever honest. That suggestion of travelling about and amusing them-selves, did not commend itself to him. New South Wales might, he thought, be a good country for work, but did not seem to offer much amusement beyond sheer idleness, and brandy-and-water.

'I rather think we should like to do a little in the rough first,' he said.

'A very little'll go a long way with you, I'm thinking.'

'I don't see that at all,' said Dick, stoutly.

'You go down there and take one of them picks in your hand for a week,–eight hours at a time, with five minutes' spell allowed for a smoke, and see how you'll feel at the end of the week.'

'We'll try it on, if you give us 10s. a-day for the week,' said Caldigate rubbing his hands together.

'I wouldn't give you half-a-crown for the whole time between you, and you wouldn't earn it. Ten shillings a day! I suppose you think a man has only just to say the word and become a miner out of hand. You've a deal to learn before you'll be worth half the money. I never knew chaps like you to come to any good at working. If you've got a little money, you know, I've shown you what you can do with it. But perhaps you haven't.'

The conversation was ended by a declaration on the part of Caldigate that they would take a week to think over Mr. Crinkett's kind proposition, and that they might as well occupy the time by taking a look at Ahalala. A place that had been so much praised and so much abused must be worth seeing. 'Who's been a-praising it,' asked Crinkett, angrily, 'unless it's that fool Jones? And as for waiting, I don't say that you'll have the shares at that price next week.' In this way he waxed angry; but, nevertheless, he condescended to recommend a man to them, when Caldigate declared that they would like to hire some practical miner to accompany them. 'There's Mick Maggott,' said he, 'knows mining a'most as well as anybody. You'll hear of him, may be, up at Henniker's. He's honest; and if you can keep him off the drink he'll do as well as anybody. But neither Mick nor nobody else can do you no good at Ahalala.' With that he led them out of the gate, and nodding his head at them by way of farewell, left them to go back to Mrs. Henniker's.

To Mrs. Henniker's they went, and there, stretched out at length on the wooden veranda before the house, they found the hero of the potatoes,—the man who had taken them down to Crinkett's house. He seemed to be fast asleep, but as they came up on the boards, he turned himself on his elbow, and looked at them. 'Well, mates,' he said, 'what do you think of Tom Crinkett now you've seen him?'

'He doesn't seem to approve of Ahalala,' said Dick.

'In course he don't. When a new rush is opened like that, and takes away half the hands a man has about him, and raises the wages of them who remain, in course he don't like it. You see the difference. The Old Stick-in-the-Mud is an established kind of thing.'

'It's a paying concern, I suppose,' said Caldigate.

'It has paid;—not a doubt about it. Whether it's played out or not, I'm not so sure. But Ahalala is a working-man's diggings, not a master's, such as Crinkett is now. Of course Crinkett has a down on Ahalala.'

'Your friend Jack Brien didn't seem to think much of the place,' said Dick.

79

'Poor Jack is one of them who never has a stroke of luck. He's a sort of chum who, when he has a bottle of pickles, somebody else is sure to eat 'em. Ahalala isn't so bad. It's one of them chancy places, of course. You may and you mayn't, as I was a-saying before. When the great rush was on, I did uncommon well at Ahalala. I never was the man I was then.'

'What became of it?' asked Caldigate with a smile.

'Mother Henniker can tell you that, or any other publican round the country. It never will stick to me. I don't know why, but it never will. I've had my luck, too. Oh, laws! I might have had my house, just as grand as Polly Hooker this moment, only I never could stick to it like Tom Crinkett. I've drank cham—paign out of buckets;—I have.'

'I'd rather have a pot of beer out of the pewter,' said Caldigate.

'Very like. One doesn't drink cham—paign because it's better nor anything else. A nobbler of brandy's worth ten of it. It's the glory of out-facing the swells at their own game. There was a chap over in the other colony shod his horse with gold,—and he had to go shepherding afterwards for thirty pounds a-year and his grub. But it's something for him to have ridden a horse with gold shoes. You've never seen a bucketful of cham—paign in the old country?'

When both Dick and Caldigate had owned that they had never encountered luxury so superabundant, and had discussed the matter in various shapes,—asking whether the bucket had been emptied, and other questions of the same nature,—Caldigate inquired of his friend whether he knew Mick Maggott?

'Mick Maggott!' said the man, jumping up to his feet. 'Who wants Mick Maggott?' Then Caldigate explained the recommendation which Mr. Crinkett had made. 'Well;—I'm darned;—Mick Maggott? I'm Mick Maggott, myself.'

Before the evening was over an arrangement had been made between the parties, and had even been written on paper and signed by all the three. Mick on the morrow was to proceed to Ahalala with his new comrades, and was to remain with them for a month, assisting them in all their views; and for this he was to receive ten shillings a-day. But, in the event of his getting drunk, he was to be liable to dismissal at once. Mick pleaded hard for one bout of drinking during the month; —but when Dick explained that one bout might last for the entire time, he acknowledged that the objection was reasonable and assented to the terms proposed.

CHAPTER XI

Ahalala

I T was all settled that night, and some necessary purchases made. Ahalala was twenty-three miles from Nobble, and a coach had been established through the bush for the benefit of miners going to the diggings;—but Mick was of opinion that miners ought to walk, with their swag on their backs, when the distance was not more than forty miles. 'You look so foolish getting out of one of them rattletrap coaches,' he said, 'and everybody axing whether you're going to pick for yourself or buy a share in a claim. I'm all for walking,—if it ain't beneath you.' They declared themselves quite ready to walk, and under Mick's guidance they went out and bought two large red blankets and two pannikins. Mick declared that if they went without swags on their backs and pannikins attached to their swags, they would be regarded with evil eyes by all who saw them. There were some words about the portmanteaus. Mick proposed that they should be left for the entire month in the charge of Mrs. Henniker, and, when this was pronounced impossible, he was for a while disposed to be off the bargain. Caldigate declared that, with all his ambition to be a miner, he must have a change of shirts. Then Mick pointed to the swag. Couldn't he put another shirt into the swag? It was at last settled that one portmanteau should be sent by the coach, and one left in the charge of Mrs. Henniker. 'Them sort of traps ain't never any good, in my mind,' said Mick. 'It's unmanly, having all them togs. I like a wash as well as any man,—trousers, jersey, drawers, and all. I'm always at 'em when I get a place for a rinse by the side of a creek. But when my things are so gone that they won't hang on comfortable any longer, I chucks 'em away and buys more. Two jerseys is good, and two drawers is good, because of wet. Boots is awkward, and I allays does with one pair. Some have two, and ties 'em on with the pannikin. But it ain't ship-shape. Them's my ideas, and I've been at it these nine years. You'll come to the same.'

The three started the next morning at six, duly invested with their swags. Before they went they found Mrs. Henniker up, with hot tea, boiled beef, and damper. 'Just one drop at starting,—for the good of the house,' said Mick, apologetically. Whereupon the whisky was brought, and Mick insisted on 'shouting' for it out of his own pocket.

They had hardly gone a mile out of Nobble before Maggott started a little difficulty,—merely for the purpose of solving it with a master's hand. 'There ain't to be no misters among us, you know.'

'Certainly not,' said Caldigate.

'My name's Mick. This chap's name's Dick. I didn't exactly catch your'n. I suppose you've been kursened.'

'Yes;—they christened me John.'

'Ain't it never been Jack with you?'

'I don't think it ever was.'

'John! It do sound lackadaisical. What I call womanish. But perhaps it's for the better. We have such a lot of Jacks. There's dirty Jack, and Jack the nigger, and Jack Misery,—that's poor Jack Brien;—and a lot more. Perhaps you wouldn't like not another name of that sort.'

'Well; no,—unless it's necessary.'

'There ain't another John about the place, as I know. I never knew a John down a mine,—never. We'll try it, anyhow.'

And so that was settled. As it happened, though Dick Shand had always been Dick to his friend, Caldigate had never, as yet, been either John or Jack to Dick Shand. There are men who fall into the way of being called by their Christian names, and others who never hear them except from their own family. But before the day was out, Caldigate had become John to both his companions. 'It don't sound as it ought to do;—not yet,' said Mick, after he had tried it about a dozen times in five minutes.

Before the day was over it was clear that Mick Maggott had assumed the mastery. When three men start on an enterprise together, one man must be 'boss.' Let the republic be as few as it may one man must be president. And as Mick knew what he was about, he assumed the situation easily. The fact that he was to receive wages from the others had no bearing on the subject at all. Before they got to Ahalala, Caldigate had begun to appreciate all this, and to understand in part what they would have to do during this month, and how they would have to live. It was proposed that they should at once fix on a spot,—'peg out a claim,' on some unoccupied piece of ground, buy for themselves a small tent,—of which they were assured that they would find many for sale,—and then begin to sink a hole. When they entered Ahalala, Caldigate was surprised to find that Mick was the most tired of the three. It is always so. The man who has laboured from his youth upwards can endure with his arms. It is he who has had leisure to shoot, to play cricket, to climb up mountains, and to handle a racket, that can walk. 'Darned if you ain't better stuff than I took you for,' said Mick, as the three let the swags down from their backs on the veranda of Ridley's hotel at Ahalala.

Ahalala was a very different place from Nobble,—made Nobble seem to be almost a compact and prosperous city. At Nobble there was at any rate a street. But at Ahalala everything was straggling. The houses, such as they were, stood here and there about the place, while a great part of the population lived under canvas. And then Ahalala was decidedly in the forest. The trees around had not yet been altogether killed, nor had they been cut down in sufficient numbers to divest the place of its forest appearance. Ahalala was leafy, and therefore, though much less regular, also less hideous than Nobble. When Dick first made tender inquiry as to the comforts of an hotel, he was assured that there were at least a couple of dozen. But the place was bewildering. There seemed to be no beginning to it and no end. There were many tracks about here and there,—but nothing which could be called a road. The number of holes was infinite,—each hole covered by a rough windlass used for taking out the dirt, which was thrown loosely anywhere round the aperture. Here and there were to be seen little red flags stuck upon the end of poles. These indicated, as Mick informed them, those fortunate adventures in which gold had been found. At those very much more numerous hillocks which showed no red flag, the labourers were hitherto labouring in vain. There was a little tent generally near to each hillock in which the miners slept, packed nearly as close as sheep in a fold. As our party made its way through the midst of this new world to Ridley's hotel, our friend observed many a miner sitting at his evening meal. Each generally had a frying-pan between his legs, out of which he was helping himself to meat which he had cooked on the ashes just behind him. Sometimes two or three were sharing their provisions out of the same frying-pan; but as a rule each miner had his own, and each had it between his legs.

Before they had been at Ahalala twenty-four hours they also had their tent and their frying-pan and their fire, and had pegged out their claim, and were ready to commence operations on the morrow. It was soon manifest to Caldigate and Dick Shand that they would have been very much astray without a 'boss' to direct them. Three or four hours had been passed in forming a judgment as to the spot on which they should commence to dig. And in making his choice Mick had been guided by many matters as to which our two adventurers were altogether ignorant. It might be that Mick was equally so; but he at any rate assumed some knowledge. He looked to the fall of the ground, the line in which the red flags were to be traced,—if any such line could be found,—and was possessed of a considerable amount of jargon as to topographical mining secrets. At last they found a spot, near a creek, surrounded by forest-trees, perhaps three hundred yards from the nearest adjacent claim, and, as Mick declared, in a direct line with three red flags. Here they determined to commence their operations. 'I don't suppose we shall do any good,' said Caldigate to Dick, 'but we must make a beginning, if only for the sake of hardening our hands. We shall be learning something at the time even though we only shovel up so much mud.'

For a fortnight they shovelled up the soil continuously without any golden effects, and, so far, without any feeling of disappointment. Mick had told them that if they found a speck at the end of three weeks they would be very fortunate. They had their windlass, and they worked in relays; one man at the bottom, one man at the wheel, and one man idle. In this way they kept up their work during eighteen hours of the day. Each man in this way worked twelve hours, and had twelve for sleeping, and cooking, and eating. Other occupation they had none. During the fortnight neither of them went any further distance from their claim than to the neighbouring shop. Mick often expressed his admiration at their continued industry, not understanding the spirit which will induce such young men as them to work, even when the work is agonising. And they were equally charmed with Mick's sobriety and loyalty. Not a word had been said as to hours of work,— and yet he was as constant to their long hours as though the venture was his own,—as though there was no question of wages.

'We ain't had a drop o' drink yet,' said Mick one night. 'Ain't we a holding off like Britons?' There was a great triumph in his voice as he said this;—very great triumph, but, also, as Caldigate thought, a sound of longing also. They were now in their third week, and the word whisky had never been pronounced between them. At this moment, when Mick's triumphant ejaculation was uttered, they were all lying—in bed. It shall be called bed by way of compliment. They had bought a truss of straw, which Mick had declared to be altogether unnecessary and womanish, and over that was laid a white india-rubber sheet which Caldigate had brought with him from England. This, too, had roused the miner's wrath. Nevertheless he condescended to lie upon it. This was their bed; and here they lay, each wrapped up in his blanket, Mick in the middle, with our two friends at the sides. Now it was not only on Mick's account, but quite as much in reference to Dick Shand, that Caldigate deprecated any reference to drink. The abstention hitherto had been marvellous. He himself would have gone daily to the store for a bottle of beer, but that he recognised the expediency of keeping them away from the place. He had heard that it was a peculiarity of the country that all labour was done without drink, even when it was done by determined drunkards. The drunkard would work for a month, and then drink for a month,—and then, after a time, would die. The drink almost always consisted of spirits of the worst description. It seemed to be recognised by the men that work and drink must be kept separate. But Mick's mind travelled away on this occasion from the little tent to the delights of Ridley's bar. 'We haven't had a drop of drink yet,' he said.

'We'll push through the month without it;—eh, old boy?' said Caldigate.

'What wouldn't I give for a pint of bitter beer?' said Shand.

'Or a bottle of Battleaxe between the three of us!' said Mick;— Battleaxe being the name for a certain brand of brandy.

'Not a drop till the month is over,' said Caldigate, turning himself round in his blanket. Then there were whisperings between the other two men, of which he could only hear the hum.

On the next morning at six Caldigate and Dick Shand were at the hole together. It was Caldigate's turn to work till noon, whereas Dick went off at nine, and Mick would come on from nine till three. At nine Mick did not make his appearance, and Dick declared his purpose of looking after him. Caldigate also threw down his tools, as he could not work alone, and went in search. The upshot of it was, that he did not see either of his companions again till he found them both very drunk at a drinking-shop about two miles away from their claim, just before dusk!

This was terrible. He did at last succeed in bringing back his own friend to the tent, having, however, a sad task in doing so. But Mick Maggott would not be moved. He had his wits about him enough to swear that he cared for nothing. He was going to have a spree. Nobody had ever known him to be talked out of it when he had once set his mind upon it. He had set his mind upon it now, and he meant to have his whack. This was what he said of himself: 'It ain't no good, John. It ain't no good at all, John. Don't you trouble yourself, John. I'm going to have it out, John, so I tell you.' This he said, nodding his head about in a maudlin sort of way, and refusing to allow himself to be moved.

On the next day Dick Shand was sick, repentant, and idle. On the third, he returned to his work,—working, however, with difficulty. After that, he fairly recovered himself, and the two Cambridge men went on resolutely at their hole. They soon found how hard it was not to go astray without their instructed mate. The sides of the shaft became crooked and uneven, and the windlass sometimes could not be made to work. But still they persevered, and went on by themselves for an

entire week without a sign of gold. During this time various fruitless
expeditions were made by both the men in search of Maggott. He was
still at the same drinking-shop, but could not be induced to leave it.
At last they found him with the incipient horrors of delirium tremens,
and yet they could not get him away. The man who kept the place
was quite used to delirium tremens, and thought nothing of it. When
Caldigate tried a high moral tone everybody around him laughed at
him.

They had been digging for a month, and still without a speck of
gold, when, one morning early, Mick appeared in front of the tent. It
was then about eight, and our friends had stopped their work to eat
their breakfast. The poor man, without saying a word, came and
crouched down before them;—not in shame,—not at all that; but
apparently in an agony of sickness,—'I've had my bout,' he said.

'I don't suppose you're much the better for it,' replied Caldigate.

'No; I ain't none the better. I thought it was all up with me yesterday.
Oh, laws! I've had it heavy this time.'

'Why are you such a fool?'

'Well;—you see, John, some of us is born fools. I'm one of 'em. You
needn't tell me, 'cause I know all about it without any sermoning.
Nobody don't know it so well as I do! How should they? If you had
my inside now,—and my head! Oh, laws!'

'Give it up, man.'

'That's easy said;—as if I wouldn't if I could. I haven't got a
blessed coin left to buy a bite of bread with,—and I couldn't touch a
morsel if I had ever so much. I'll take my blanket and be off as soon as
I can move.' All this time he had been crouching, but now he threw
himself at length upon the ground.

Of course they did what they could for the poor wretch. They got
him into the tent, and they made him swallow some tea. Then he
slept; and in the course of the afternoon he had so far recovered as to
be able to eat a bit of meat. The, when his companions were at their
work, he carefully packed up his swag, and fastening it on to his
back, appeared by the side of the hole. 'I'm come to bid you good-
bye,' he said.

'Where are you going, Mick?' asked Caldigate, climbing up out of the
hole by the rope.

'I'm blessed if I know, but I'm off. You are getting that hole tar-
nation crooked.'

The man was going without any allusion to the wages he had earned,
or to the work that he had done. But then, in truth, he had not earned
his wages, as he had broken his contract. He made no complaint,

however, and no apology, but was prepared to start.

'That's all nonsense,' said Dick, catching hold of him.

'You put your swag down,' said Caldigate, also catching hold of the other shoulder.

'What am I to put my swag down for? I'm a-going back to Nobble. Crinkett'll give me work.'

'You're not going to leave us in that way,' said Dick.

'Stop and make the shaft straight,' said Caldigate. The man looked irresolute. 'Friends are not to part like that.'

'Friends!' said the poor fellow. 'Who'll be friends to such a beast as I be? But I'll stay out the month if you'll find me my grub.'

'You shall have your grub and your money, too. Do you think we've forgotten the potatoes?'

'—the potatoes,' said the man, bursting into tears. Then he chucked away his swag, and threw himself under the tent upon the straw. The next day he was making things as straight as he could down the shaft.

When they had been at work about five weeks there was a pole stuck into their heap of dirt, and on the top of the pole there was a little red flag flying. At about thirty feet from the surface, when they had already been obliged to insert transverse logs in the shaft to prevent the sides from falling in, they had come upon a kind of soil altogether different from the ordinary clay through which they had been working. There was a stratum of loose shingle or gravelly earth, running apparently in a sloping direction, taking the decline of the very slight hill on which their claim was situated. Mick, as soon as this was brought to light, became an altered man. The first bucket of this stuff that was pulled up was deposited by him separately, and he at once sat down to wash it. This he did in an open tin pan. Handful after handful he washed, shifting and teasing it about in the pan, and then he cast it out, always leaving some very small residuum. He was intent upon his business to a degree that Caldigate would have thought to be beyond the man's nature. With extreme patience he went on washing handful after handful all the day, while the other two pulled up fresh buckets of the same stuff. He would not pause to eat, or hardly to talk. At last there came a loud exclamation. 'By —, we've got it!' Then Dick and Caldigate, stooping down, were shown four or five little specks in the angle of the pan's bottom. Before the sun had set they had stuck up their little red flag, and a crowd of neighbours was standing round them asking questions as to their success.

CHAPTER XII

Mademoiselle Cettini

AFTER three days of successful washing, when it became apparent that a shed must be built, and that, if possible, some further labour must be hired, Mick said that he must go. 'I ain't earned nothing,' he said, 'because of that bout, and I ain't going to ask for nothing, but I can't stand this any longer. I hope you'll make your fortins.' Then came the explanation. It was not possible, he said, that a regular miner, such as he was, should be a party to such a grand success without owning a share in it. He was quite aware that nothing belonged to him. He was working for wages and he had forfeited them. But he couldn't see the gold coming out under his hands in pailfuls and feel that none of it belonged to him. Then it was agreed that there should be no more talk of wages, and that each should have a third share in the concern. Very much was said on the matter of drink, in all of which Caldigate was clever enough to impose on his friend Dick the heavy responsibility of a mentor. A man who has once been induced to preach to another against a fault will feel himself somewhat constrained by his own sermons. Mick would make no promises; but declared his intention of trying very hard. 'If anybody 'd knock me down as soon as I goes a yard off the claim, that 'd be best.' And so they renewed their work, and at the end of six weeks from the commencement of their operations sold nine ounces of gold to the manager of the little branch bank which had already established itself at Ahalala. These were hardly 'pailfuls'; but gold is an article which adds fervour to the imagination and almost creates a power for romance.

Other matters, however, were not running smoothly with John Caldigate at this eventful time. To have found gold so soon after their arrival was no doubt a great triumph, and justified him in writing a long letter to his father, in which he explained what he had done, and declared that he looked forward to success with confidence. But still he was far from being at ease. He could not suffer himself to remain hidden at Ahalala without saying something of his whereabouts to Mrs. Smith. After what had happened between them he would be odious to himself if he omitted to keep the promise which he had made to her. And yet he would so fain have forgotten her,—or rather have wiped away from the reality of his past life that one episode, had it been possible. A month's separation had taught him to see how very silly he had been in regard to this woman,—and had also detracted much from those charms which had delighted him on board ship. She was pretty, she was clever, she had the knack of being a pleasant companion. But how much more than all these was wanted in a wife? And then he knew nothing about her. She might be, or have been, all that was disreputable. If he could not shake himself free from her, she would be a millstone round his neck. He was aware of all that, and as he thought of it he would think also of the face of Hester Bolton, and remember her form as she sat silent in the big house at Chesterton. But nevertheless it was necessary that he should write to Mrs. Smith. He had promised that he would do so, and he must keep his word.

The name of the woman had not been mentioned between him and Dick Shand since they left the ship. Dick had been curious, but had been afraid to inquire, and had in his heart applauded the courage of the man who had thus been able to shake off at once a woman with whom he had amused himself. Caldigate himself was continually meditating as he worked with the windlass in his hand, or with his pick at the bottom of the hole, whether in conformity with the usages of the world he could not simply—drop her. Then he remembered the words which had passed between them on the subject, and he could not do it. He was as yet too young to be at the same time so wise and so hard. 'I shall hold you as engaged to me,' he had said, 'and myself as engaged to you.' And he remembered the tones of her voice as, with her last words, she had said to him, 'My love, my love!' They had been very pleasant to him then, but now they were most unfortunate. They were unfortunate because there had been a power in them from which he was now unable to extricate himself.

Therefore, during one of those leisure periods in which Mick and Dick were at work, he wrote his letter, with the paper on his knees, squatting down just within his tent on a deal case which had contained boxes of sardines, bottles of pickles, and cans of jam. For now, in their prosperity, they had advanced somewhat beyond the simple plenty of the frying-pan. It was a difficult letter to write. Should it be ecstatic and loving, or cold and severe,—or light, and therefore false? 'My own one, here I am. I have struck gold. Come to me and share it.' That would have been ecstatic and loving. ' 'Tis a hard life this, and not fit for a woman's weakness. But it must be my life—and therefore let there be an end of all between us.' That would have been cold and severe. 'How are you, and what are you doing? Dick and I are shoving along. It isn't half as nice as on board ship. Hope to see you before long, and am yours,—just the same as ever.' That would have been light and false,—keeping the word of promise to the ear but breaking it to the heart. He could not write either of these. He began by describing what they had done, and had completed two pages before he had said a word of their peculiar circumstances in regard to each other. He felt that his letter was running into mere gossip, and was not such as she would have a right to expect. If any letter were sent at all, there must be something more in it than all this. And so, after much thinking of it, he at last rushed, as it were, into hot words, and ended it as follows: 'I have put off to the last what I have really got to say. Let me know what you are doing and what you wish,—and whether you love me. I have not as yet the power of offering you a home, but I trust that the time may come.' These last words were false. He knew that they were false. But the falseness was not of a nature to cause him to be ashamed. It shames no man to swear that he loves a woman when he has ceased to love her;—but it does shame him to drop off from the love which he has promised. He balanced the matter in his mind for a while before he would send his letter. Then getting up quickly, he rushed forth, and dropped it into the post-office box.

The very next day chance brought to Ahalala one who had been a passenger on board the Goldfinder; and the man, hearing of the success of Shand and Caldigate, came to see them. 'Of course you know,' said the man, 'what your fellow-passenger is doing down at Sydney?' Dick Shand, who was present, replied that they had heard nothing of any fellow-passenger. Caldigate understood at once to whom the allusion was made, and was silent. 'Look here,' said the man, bringing the newspaper out of his pocket, and pointing to a special advertisement. 'Who do you think that is?' The advertisement declared that Mademoiselle Cettini would, on such and such a night, sing a certain number of songs, and dance a certain number of dances, and perform a certain number of tableaux, at a certain theatre in Sydney. 'That's your Mrs. Smith,' said the man, turning to Caldigate.

'I am very glad she has got employment,' said Caldigate; 'but she is not my Mrs. Smith.'

'We all thought that you and she were very thick.'

'All the same I beg you to understand that she is not my Mrs. Smith,' repeated Caldigate, endeavouring to appear unconcerned, but hardly able to conceal his anger.

Dancing dances, singing songs, and acting tableaux;—and all under the name of Mademoiselle Cettini! Nothing could be worse,—unless, indeed, it might be of service to him to know that she was earning her bread, and therefore not in distress, and earning it after a fashion of which he would be at liberty to express his disapproval. Nothing more

90

was said at the time about Mrs. Smith, and the man went his way.

Ten days afterwards Caldigate, in the presence both of Mick and Dick, declared his purpose of going down to Sydney. 'Our luggage must be looked after,' said he;—'and I have a friend whom I want to see,' he added, not choosing to lie. At this time all was going successfully with them. Mick Maggott lived in such a manner that no one near him would have thought that he knew what whisky meant. His self-respect had returned to him, and he was manifestly 'boss'. There had come to be necessity for complicated woodwork below the surface, and he had shown himself to be a skilled miner. And it had come to pass that our two friends were as well assured of his honesty as of their own. He had been a veritable godsend to them,—and would remain so, could he be kept away from the drinking-shops.

'If you go away don't you think he'll break out?' Dick asked when they were alone together.

'I hope not. He seems to have been steadied by success. At any rate I must go.'

'Is it to see—Mrs. Smith?' Dick as he asked the question put on his most serious face. He did not utter the name as though he were finding fault. The time that had passed had been sufficient to quench the unpleasantness of their difference on board ship. He was justified in asking his friend such a question, and Caldigate felt that it was so.

'I am.'

'Don't you think, upon the whole, —. I don't like to interfere, but upon my word the thing is so important.'

'You think I had better not see her?'

'I do.'

'And lie to her?'

'All is fair in love and war.'

'That means that no faith is due to a woman. I cannot live by such a doctrine. I do not mind owning to you that I wish I could do as you bid me. I can't. I cannot be so false. I must go, old fellow; but I know all that you would say to me, and I will endeavour to escape honestly from this trouble.' And so he went.

Yes;—to escape honestly from that trouble! But how? It is just that trouble from which there is no honest escape,—unless a man may honestly break his word. He had engaged himself to her. After that, simply to ignore her would be cowardly as well as false. There was but one thing that he could do, but one step that he could take, by which his security and his self-respect might both be maintained. He would tell her the exact truth, and put it to her whether, looking at their joint circumstances, it would not be better that they should—part.

Reflecting on this during his three days' journey down to Sydney, it was thus that he resolved,—forgetting altogether in his meditations the renewed force of the woman's charms upon himself.

As he went from the railway station at Sydney to the third-class inn at which he located himself, he saw the hoardings on all sides placarded with the name of Mademoiselle Cettini. And there was a picture on some of these placards of a wonderful female, without much clothes, which was supposed to represent some tragic figure in a tableau. There was the woman whom he was to make his wife. He had travelled all night, and had intended to seek Mrs. Smith immediately after his breakfast. But so unhappy was he, so much disgusted by the tragic figure in the picture, that he postponed his visit and went after his luggage. His luggage was all right in the warehouse, and he arranged that it should be sent down to Nobble. Waggons with stores did make their way to Nobble from the nearest railway station, and hopes were held out that the packages might be there in six weeks' time. He would have been willing to postpone their arrival for twelve months, for twenty-four months, could he, as compensation, have been enabled to postpone, with honour, his visit to Mrs. Smith for the same time.

Soon after noon, however, his time was vacant, and he rushed to his fate. She had sent him her address, and he found her living in very decent lodgings overlooking the public park. He was at once shown up to her room, where he found her at breakfast. 'So you have come,' she said. Then, when the door was shut, she flung herself into his arms.

He was dressed as a miner might be dressed who was off work and out for a holiday;—clean, rough, and arranged with a studied intention to look as little like a gentleman as possible. The main figure and manner were so completely those of a gentleman, that the disguise was not perfect; but yet he was rough. She was dressed with all the pretty care which a woman can use when she expects her lover to see her in morning costume. Anything more unlike the Mrs. Smith of the ship could not be imagined. If she had been attractive then, what was she now? If her woman's charms sufficed to overcome his prudence while they were so clouded, what effect would they have upon him now? And she was in his arms! Here there was no quartermaster to look after the proprieties;—no Mrs. Crompton, no Mrs. Callander, no Miss Green to watch with a hundred eyes for the exchange of a chance kiss in some moment of bliss. 'So you have come! Oh, my darling; oh, my love!' No doubt it was all just as it should be. If a lady may not call the man to whom she is engaged her love and her darling, what proper use can there be for such words? And into whose arms is she to jump, if not into his? As he pressed her to his heart, and pressed his lips to hers, he told himself that he ought to have arranged it all by letter.

'Why Cettini?' he asked. But he smiled as he put the question. It was intended to be serious, but still he could not be hard upon her all at once.

'Why fifty thousand fools?'

'I don't understand.'

'Supposing there to be fifty thousand people in Sydney,—as to which I know nothing. Or why ever so many million fools in London? If I called myself Mrs. Smith nobody would come and see me. If I called myself Madame Cettini, not nearly so many would come. You have got to inculcate into the minds of the people an idea that a pure young girl is going to jump about for their diversion. They know it isn't so. But there must be a flavour of the idea. It isn't nice, but one has to live.'

'Were you ever Cettini before?'

'Yes,—when I was on the stage as a girl.' Then he thought he remembered that she had once told him some particular in regard to her early life, which was incompatible with this, unless indeed she had gone under more than one name before she was married. 'I used as a child to dance and sing under that name.'

'Was it your father's name?'

She smiled as she answered, 'You want to discover all the little mean secrets of my life at once, and do not reflect that, in so far as they were mean, they are disagreeable as subjects of conversation. I was not mean myself.'

'I am sure of that.'

'If you are sure of it, is not that enough? Of course I have been among low people. If not, why should I have been a singer on the stage at so early an age, why a dancer, why should I have married such a one as Mr. Smith?'

'I do not know of what sort he was,' said Caldigate.

'This is not the time to ask, when you have just come to see me;— when I am so delighted to see you! Oh, it is such a pleasure! I have not had a nice word spoken to me since I left the Goldfinder. Come and take a walk in the gardens? Nobody knows me off the stage yet, and nobody knows you. So we can do just as we like. Come and tell me about the gold.'

He did go, and did tell her about the gold, and before he had been with her an hour, sitting about on the benches in that loveliest of all places, the public gardens at Sydney, he was almost happy with her.

It was now late in the autumn, in May; but the end of the autumn in Sydney is the most charming time of the year. He spent the whole day with her, dining with her in her lodgings at five in order that he might take her to the theatre at seven. She had said a great deal to him about her performances, declaring that he would find them to be neither vulgar nor disagreeable. She told him that she had no friend in Sydney, but that she had been able to get an engagement for a fortnight at Melbourne, and had been very shortly afterwards pressed to come on to Sydney. She listened not only with patience, but apparently with the greatest pleasure to all that he could tell her of Dick Shand, and Mr. Crinkett, and Mick Maggott, arousing herself quite to enthusiasm when he came to the finding of the gold. But there was not a word said the whole day as to their future combined prospects. Nor was there any more outspoken allusion to loves and darlings, or any repetition of that throwing herself into his arms. For once it was natural. If she were wanted thus again, the action must be his,—not hers. She was clever enough to know that.

'What do you think of it?' she said, when he waited to take her home.

'It is the only good dancing I ever saw in my life. But—'

'Well!'

'I will tell you to-morrow,'

'Tell me whatever you think and you will see that I will attend to you. Come about eleven,—not sooner, as I shall not be dressed. Now goodnight.'

CHAPTER XIII

Coming Back

THE letter which Caldigate wrote to his father from Ahalala, telling him of the discovery of gold upon their claim, contained the first tidings which reached Folking of the wanderer, and that was not received till seven or eight months had passed by since he left the place. The old Squire, during that time, had lived a very solitary life. In regard to his nephew, whom he had declared his purpose of partially adopting, he had expressed himself willing to pay for his education, but had not proposed to receive him at Folking. And as to that matter of heirship, he gave his brother to understand that it was not to be regarded as a settled thing. Folking was now his own to do what he liked with it, and as such it was to remain. But he would treat his nephew as a son while the nephew seemed to him to merit such treatment. As for the estate, he was not at all sure whether it would not be better for the community at large, and for the Caldigate family in particular, that it should be cut up and sold in small parcels. There was a long correspondence between him and his brother, which was ended by his declaring that he did not wish to see any of the family just at present at Folking. He was low in spirits, and would prefer to be alone.

He was very low in spirits and completely alone. All those who knew anything about him,—and they were very few, the tenants, perhaps, and servants, and old Mr. Bolton,—were of opinion that he had torn his son out from all place in his heart, had so thoroughly dis-inherited the sinner, not only from his house and acres, but from his love, that they did not believe him capable of suffering from regret. But even they knew very little of the man. As he wandered about alone among the dikes, as he sat alone among his books, even as he pored over the volumes which were always in his hand, he was ever mourning and moaning over his desolation. His wife and daughters had been taken from him by the hand of God;—but how had it come to pass that he had also lost his son, that son who was all that was left to him? When he had first heard of those dealings with Davis, while John was amusing himself with the frivolities of Babington, he had been full of wrath, and had declared to himself that the young man must be expelled, if not from all affection, yet from all esteem. And he had gone on to tell himself that it would be unprofitable for him to live with a son whom he did not esteem. Then it had come to pass that, arguing it out in his own mind, rationally, as he had thought, but still under the impulse of hot anger, he had determined that it was better that they should part, even though the parting should be for ever. But now he had almost forgotten Davis,—had turned the matter over in his mind till he had taught himself to think that the disruption had been altogether his son's work, and in no degree his own. His son had not loved him. He had not been able to inspire his son with love. He was solitary and wretched because he had been harsh and unforgiving. That was his own judgment as to himself. But he never said a word of his feelings to any human being.

John had promised to write. The promise had not been very enthusiastically given; but still, as the months went by it was constantly remembered. The young man, after leaving Cambridgeshire, had remained some weeks at the Shands' house before he had started;—and from thence he had not written. The request had been that he should write from Australia, and the correspondence between him and his father had always been so slight, that it had not occurred to him to write from Pollington. But Mr. Caldigate had,—not expected, but hoped that a letter might come at the last moment. He knew to a day, to an hour, when the vessel would sail from Plymouth. There might have been a letter from Plymouth, but no letter came. And then the months went by slowly. The son did not write from Melbourne, nor from Nobble,—nor from Ahalala till gold had been found. So it came to pass that nearly eight months had passed, and that the father had told himself again and again that his son had torn himself altogether away from all remembrance of his home, before the letter came.

It was not a long letter, but it was very satisfactory. The finding of the gold was in itself, of course, a great thing; but the manner in which it was told, without triumph or exultation, but with an air of sober, industrious determination, was much more; and then there was a word or two at the end: 'Dear father,—I think of you every day, and am already looking forward to the time when I may return and see you again.' As he read it, the tears rolled down his cheeks, and unluckily the old housekeeper came into the room at the same time.

'Is is from Mr. John, sir?'

He had to recover himself, and to get rid of his tears, and to answer the old woman in an unconcerned tone, all in a moment, and it disconcerted him.

'Yes,—yes,' he said. 'I'll tell you all about it another time.'

'Is he well, sir?'

'I daresay he is. He doesn't say. It's about business. Didn't you hear

me say that I'd tell you another time?' And so the old woman was
turned out of the room, having seen the tear and heard the little
gurgle in the throat.

'He seems to be doing well,' the Squire said to Mr. Holt. 'He has got
a couple of partners, and they have succeeded in finding gold. He may
probably come back some day; but I don't suppose it will be for the
next twenty years.'

After that he marked the posts, which he knew came from that
part of the world by San Francisco, and had resolved not to expect
anything by that of the next month,—when there came, a day before
its time, a much longer letter than the last. In this there was a given
detailed description of the 'claim' at Ahalala, which had already been
named Folking. Much was said of Mick, and much was said of Dick,
both of whom were working 'as steady as rocks.' The number of
ounces extracted were stated, with the amount of profits which had
been divided. And something was said as to the nature of their life at
Ahalala. They were still living under their original tent, but were
meditating the erection of a wooden shanty. Ahalala, the writer said,
was not a place at which a prosperous miner could expect to locate
himself for many years; but the prospects were good enough to
justify some present attention to personal comforts. All this was
rational, pleasant, and straightforward. And in the letter there was no
tone or touch of the old quarrel. It was full and cordial,—such as any
son might write to any father. It need hardly be said that there was no
mention made in it of Mrs. Smith. It was written after the return of
John Caldigate from Sydney to Ahalala, but contained no reference to
any matrimonial projects.

Letters then came regularly, month by month, and were always
regularly answered,—till a chance reader would have thought that no
father and no son stood on better terms with each other. There had
been misfortunes; but the misfortunes did not seem to touch John
Caldigate himself. After three months of hard work and steady conduct
Mick Maggott had broken out and had again taken to drinking
champagne out of buckets. Efforts were made, with infinite trouble,
to reclaim him, which would be successful for a time,—and then again
he would slip away into the mud. And then Shand would sometimes
go into the mud with him; and Shand, when drunk, would be more
unmanageable even than Mick. And this went on till Mick had—killed
himself, and Dick Shand had disappeared. 'I grieve for the man as for a
dear friend,' he said in one of his father's letters; 'for he has been as true
to me as steel in all things, save drink; and I feel that I have learned
under him the practical work of a goldminer, as it cannot be learned

97

except by the unwearied attention of the teacher. Could he have kept from spirits, this man would have made a large fortune, and would have deserved it; for he was indefatigable and never-ending in resources.' Such was the history of poor Mick Maggott.

And Shand's history was told also. Shand strayed away to Queensland, and then returning was again admitted to a certain degree of partnership, and then again fell into drink, and at last, deserting the trade of a miner, tried his hand at various kinds of work, till at last he became a simple shepherd. From time to time Caldigate sent him money when he was in want of it, but they had not again come together as associates in their work.

All this was told in his monthly letters which came to be expected at Folking, till each letter was regarded as the rising of a new sun. There is a style of letter-writing which seems to indicate strength of purpose and a general healthy condition on the part of the writer. In all his letters, the son spoke of himself and his doings with confidence and serenity, somewhat surprising his father after a while by always desiring to be remembered to Mr., Mrs., and Miss Bolton. This went on not only from month to month, but from year to year, till at the end of three years from the date at which the son had left Folking, there had come to be a complete confidence between him and his father. John Caldigate had gone into partnership with Crinkett,—who had indeed tried to cheat him wretchedly but had failed,—and at that time was the manager of the Polyeuka mine. The claim at Ahalala had been sold, and he had deserted the flashy insecurity of alluvial searchings for the fundamental security of rock-gold. He was deep in the crushing of quartz, and understood well the meaning of two ounces to the ton,—that glittering boast by which Crinkett had at first thought to allure him. From time to time he sent money home, paying back to his father and to Bolton's bank what had been borrowed on the estate. For there had passed between them many communications respecting Folking. The extravagances of the son became almost the delight of the father, when the father had become certain of the son's reform. There had been even jocular reference to Davis, and a complete understanding as to the amount of money to be given to the nephew in compensation for the blighted hopes as to the reversion of the property.

Why it should have been that these years of absence should have endeared to John Caldigate a place which, while it was his home, had always been distasteful to him, I cannot perhaps explain to those readers who have never strayed far from their original nests;—and to those who have been wanderers I certainly need not explain it. As soon as he felt that he could base the expression of his desires as to

Folking on the foundation of substantial remittances, he was not slow to say that he should like to keep the place. He knew that he had no right to the reversion, but perhaps his father would sympathise with his desire to buy back his right. His father, with all his political tenets as to land, with his often-expressed admiration as to the French system, with his loud denunciations of the absurdity of binding a special family to a special fraction of the earth's surface, did sympathise with him so strongly, that he at once accepted the arrangement. 'I think that his conduct has given him a right to demand it,' he said to Mr. Bolton.

'I don't quite see that. Money certainly gives a man great powers. If he has money enough he can buy the succession to Folking if you choose to sell it to him.'

'I mean as my son,' said the father somewhat proudly. 'He was the heir.'

'But he ceased to be so,—by his own doing. I advised you to think longer over it before you allowed him to dispossess himself.'

'It certainly has been all for the best.'

'I hope so. But when you talk of his right, I am bound to say that he has none. Folking is now yours, without encumbrance, and you can give it to whom you please.'

'It was he who paid off the mortgage.'

'You have told me that he sent you part of the money;—but that's between you and him. I am very glad, Caldigate, that your son has done so well;—and the more so perhaps because the early promise was not good. But it may be doubted whether a successful gold-digger will settle down quietly as an English country gentleman.'

There can be no doubt that old Mr. Bolton was a little jealous, and, perhaps, in some degree incredulous, as to the success of John Caldigate. His sons had worked hard from the very beginning of their lives. With them there had been no period of Newmarket, Davis, and disreputation. On the basis of capital, combined with conduct, they had gradually risen to high success. But here was a young man, who, having by his self-indulgence thrown away all the prospects of his youth, had re-habilitated himself by the luck of finding gold in a gully. To Mr. Bolton it was no better than had he found a box of treasure at the bottom of a well. Mr. Bolton had himself been a seeker of money all his life, but he had his prejudices as to the way in which money was to be sought. It should be done in a gradual, industrious manner, and in accordance with recognised forms. A digger who might by chance find a lump of gold as big as his head, or might work for three months without finding any, was to him only one degree better than Davis, and therefore he did not receive his old friend's statements as to the young

99

man's success with all the encouragement which his old friend would have liked.

But his father was very enthusiastic in his return letter to the miner. The matter as to the estate had been arranged. The nephew, who, after all, had not shown himself to be very praiseworthy, had already been—compensated. His own will had already been made,—of course in his son's favour. As there had been so much success,—and as continued success must always be doubtful,—would it not be well that he should come back as soon as possible? There would be enough now for them all. Then he expressed an opinion that such a place as Nobble could not be very nice for a permanent residence.

Nobble was not very nice. Over and beside his professional success, there was not much in his present life which endeared itself to John Caldigate. But the acquisition of gold is a difficult thing to leave. There is a curse about it, or a blessing,—it is hard to decide which,—that makes it almost impossible for a man to tear himself away from its pursuit when it is coming in freely. And the absolute gold,—not the money, not the balance at one's banker's, not the plentiful so much per annum,—but the absolute metal clinging about the palm of one's hands like small gravel, or welded together in a lump too heavy to be lifted, has a peculiar charm of its own. I have heard of a man who, having his pocket full of diamonds, declared, as he let them run through his fingers, that human bliss could not go beyond that sensation. John Caldigate did not shoe his horse with gold; but he liked to feel that he had enough gold by him to shoe a whole team. He could not return home quite as yet. His affairs were too complicated to be left quite at a moment's notice. If, as he hoped, he should find himself able to leave the colony within four years of the day on which he had begun work, and could then do so with an adequate fortune, he believed that he should have done better than any other Englishman who had set himself to the task of gold-finding. In none of his letters did he say anything special about Hester Bolton; but his inquiries about the family generally were so frequent as to make his father wonder why such questions should be asked. The squire himself, who was living hardly a dozen miles from Mr. Bolton's house, did not see the old banker above once a quarter perhaps, and the ladies of the family certainly not oftener than once a year. Very little was said in answer to any of John's inquiries. 'Mr. and Mrs. and Miss Bolton are, I believe, quite well.' So much was declared in one of the old squire's letters; and even that little served to make known that at any rate, so far, no tidings as to marriage on the part of Hester had reached the ear of her father's old friend. Perhaps this was all that John Caldigate wanted to learn.

At last there came word that John intended to come home with the next month's mail. This letter arrived about midsummer, when the miner had been absent three years and a half. He had not settled all his affairs so completely but that it might be necessary that he should return; but he thought that he would be able to remain at least twelve months in England. And in England he intended to make his home. Gold, he said, was certainly very attractive; but he did not like New South Wales as a country in which to live. He had now contracted his ventures to the one enterprise of the Polyeuka mine, from which he was receiving large monthly dividends. If that went on prosperously, perhaps he need not return to the colony at all. 'Poor Dick Shand!' he said. 'He is a shepherd far away in the west, hardly earning better wages than an English ploughman, and I am coming home with a pocket full of money! A few glasses of whisky have made all the difference!'

The squire when he received this felt more of exultation than he had ever known in his life. It seemed as though something of those throbbings of delight which are common to most of us when we are young, had come to him for the first time in his old age. He could not bring himself to care in the least for Dick Shand. At last,—at last,—he was going to have near him a companion that he could love.

'Well, yes; I suppose he has put together a little money,' he said to Farmer Holt, when that worthy tenant asked enthusiastically as to the truth of the rumours which were spread about as to the young squire's success. 'I rather think he'll settle down and live in the old place after all.'

'That's what he ought to do, squoire—that's what he ought to do,' said Mr. Holt, almost choked by the energy of his own utterances.

CHAPTER XIV

Again At Home

ON his arrival in England John Caldigate went instantly down to Folking. He had come back quite fortified in his resolution of making Hester Bolton his wife, if he should find Hester Bolton willing, and if she should have grown at all into that form and manner, into those ways of look, of speech, and of gait, which he had pictured to himself when thinking of her. Away at Nobble the females by whom he had been surrounded had not been attractive to him. In all our colonies the women are beautiful; and in the large towns a society is soon created, of which the fastidious traveller has very little ground to complain; but in the small distant bush-towns, as they are called, the rougher elements must predominate. Our hero, though he had worn moleskin trousers and jersey shirts, and had worked down a pit twelve hours a-day with a pickaxe, had never reconciled himself to female rough-nesses. He had condescended to do so occasionally,—telling himself that it was his destiny to pass his life among such surroundings; but his imagination had ever been at work with them, and he possessed a certain aptitude for romance which told him continually that Hester Bolton was the dream of his life, and ought to become, if possible, the reality; and now he came back resolved to attempt the reality,—unless he should find that the Hester Bolton of Chesterton was altogether different from the Hester Bolton of his dreams.

The fatted calf was killed for him in a very simple but full-hearted way. There was no other guest to witness the meeting. 'And here you are,' said the father.

'Yes, sir, here I am;—all that's left of me.'

'There is quite plenty,' said the father, looking at the large propor-tions of his son. 'It seems but a day or two since you went;—and yet they have been long days. I hardly expected to see you again, John,—certainly not so soon as this; certainly not in such circumstances. If ever a man was welcome to a house, you are welcome to this. And now, —what do you mean to do with yourself?'

'By nine o'clock to-morrow morning you will probably find a pit opened on the lawn, and I shall be down to the middle, looking for gold. Ah, sir, I wish you could have known poor Mick Maggott.'

'If he would have made holes in my lawn I am glad he did not come home with you.' This was the first conversation, but both the father and son felt that there was a tone about it which had never before been heard between them.

John Caldigate at this time was so altered in appearance, that they who had not known him well might possibly have mistaken him. He was now nearly thirty, but looked older than his age. The squareness of his brow was squarer, and here and there through his dark brown hair there was to be seen an early tinge of coming grey; and about his mouth was all the decision of purpose which comes to a man when he is called upon to act quickly on his own judgment in matters of importance; and there was that look of self-confidence which success gives. He had thriven in all that he had undertaken. In that gold-finding business of his he had made no mistakes. Men who had been at it when a boy had tried to cheat him, but had failed. He had seen into such mysteries as the business possessed with quick glances, and had soon learned to know his way. And he had neither gambled nor drank,—which are the two rocks on which gold-miners are apt to wreck their vessels. All this gave him an air of power and self-assertion which might, perhaps, have been distasteful to an indifferent acquaintance, but which at this first meeting was very pleasing to the father. His son was somebody,—had done something, that son of whom he had been so thoroughly ashamed when the dealings with Davis had first been brought to light. He had kept up his reading too; had strong opinions of his own respecting politics; regarded the colonies generally from a politico-economical point of view; had ideas on social, religious, and literary subjects sufficiently alike to his father's not to be made disagreeable by the obstinacy with which he maintained them. He had become much darker in colour, having been, as it seemed, bronzed through and through by colonial suns and colonial labour. Altogether he was a son of whom any father might be proud, as long as the father managed not to quarrel with him. Mr. Caldigate, who during the last four years had thought very much on the subject, was determined not to quarrel with his son.

'You asked, sir, the other day what I meant to do?'

'What are we to find to amuse you?'

'As for amusement, I could kill rats as I used to do; or slaughter a hecatomb of pheasants at Babington,'—here the old man winced, though the word hecatomb reconciled him a little to the disagreeable allusion. 'But it has come to me now that I want so much more than amusement. What do you say to a farm?'

'On the estate?'—and the landlord at once began to think whether there was any tenant who could be induced to go without injustice.

'About three times as big as the estate if I could find it. A man can farm five thousand acres as well as fifty, I take it, if he have the capital. I should like to cut a broad sward, or, better still, to roam among many herds. I suppose a man should have ten pounds an acre to begin with. The difficulty would be in getting the land.' But all this was said half in joke; for he was still of opinion that he would, after his year's holiday, be forced to return for a time to New South Wales. He had fixed a price for which, up to a certain date, he would sell his interest in the Polyeuka mine. But the price was high, and he doubted whether he could get it; and if not, then he must return.

He had not been long at Folking,—not as yet long enough to have made his way into the house at Chesterton,—before annoyance arose. Mrs. Shand was most anxious that he should go to Pollington and 'tell them anything about poor Dick.' They did, in truth, know everything about poor Dick; that poor Dick's money was all gone, and that poor Dick was earning his bread, or rather his damper, mutton, and tea, wretchedly, in the wilderness of a sheep-run in Queensland. The mother's letter was not very piteous, did not contain much of complaint,—alluded to poor Dick as one whose poverty was almost natural, but still it was very pressing. The girls were so anxious to hear all the details,—particularly Maria! The details of the life of a drunken sot are not pleasant tidings to be poured into a mother's ear, or a sister's. And then, as they two had gone away equal, and as he, John Caldigate, had returned rich, whereas poor Dick was a wretched menial creature, he felt that his very presence in England would carry with it some reproach against himself. He had in truth been both loyal and generous to Dick; but still,—there was the truth. He had come back as a rich man to his own country, while Dick was a miserable Queensland shepherd. It was very well for him to tell his father that a few glasses of whisky had made all the difference; but it would be difficult to explain this to the large circle at Pollington, and very disagreeable even to him to allude to it. And he did not feel disposed to discuss the subject with Maria, with that closer confidence of which full sympathy is capable. And yet he did not know how to refuse to pay the visit. He wrote a line to say that as soon as he was at liberty he would run up to Pollington, but that at present business incidental to his return made such a journey impossible.

But the letter, or letters, which he received from Babington were more difficult to answer even than the Shand despatch. There were three of them,—from his uncle, from Aunt Polly, and from—not Julia—but Julia's second sister; whereby it was signified that Julia's heart was much too heavily laden to allow her to write a simple, cousinly note. The Babington girls were still Babington girls,—would still romp, row boats, and play cricket; but their condition was becoming a care to their parents. Here was this cousin come back, unmarried, with gold at command,—not only once again his father's heir, but with means at command which were not at all diminished by the Babington imagination. After all that had passed in the linen-closet, what escape would there be for him? That he should come to Babington would be a matter of course. The real kindness which had been shown to him there as a child would make it impossible that he should refuse.

Caldigate did feel it to be impossible to refuse. Though Aunt Polly had on that last occasion been somewhat hard upon him, had laid snares for him, and endeavoured to catch him as a fowler catches a bird, still there had been the fact that she had been as a mother to him when he had no other mother. His uncle, too, had supplied him with hunting and shooting and fishing, when hunting and shooting and fishing were the great joys of his life. It was incumbent on him to go to Babington,—probably would be incumbent on him to pay a prolonged visit there. But he certainly would not marry Julia. As to that his mind was so fixed that even though he should have to declare his purpose with some rudeness, still he would declare it. 'My aunt wants me to go over to Babington,' he said to his father.

'Of course she does.'

'And I must go?'

'You know best what your own feelings are as to that. After you went, they made all manner of absurd accusations against me. But I don't wish to force a quarrel upon you on that account.'

'I should be sorry to quarrel with them, because they were kind to me when I was a boy. They are not very wise.'

'I don't think I ever knew such a houseful of fools.' There was no relationship by blood between the Squire of Folking and the Squire of Babington; but they had married two sisters, and therefore Mrs. Babington was Aunt Polly to John Caldigate.

'But fools may be very worthy, sir. I should say that a great many people are fools to you.'

'Not to me especially,' said the squire, almost angrily.

'People who read no books are always fools to those who do read.'

'I deny it. Our neighbour over the water'—the middle wash was always called the water at Folking—'never looks at a book, as far as I know, and he is not a fool. He thoroughly understands his own business. But your uncle Babington doesn't know how to manage his own property,—and yet he knows nothing else. That's what I call being a fool.'

'Now, I'm going to tell you a secret, sir.'

'A secret!'

'You must promise to keep it.'

'Of course I will keep it, if it ought to be kept.'

'They want me to marry Julia.'

'What!'

'My cousin Julia. It's an old affair. Perhaps it was not Davis only that made me run away five years ago.'

'Do you mean they asked you;—or did you ask her?'

'Well; I did not ask her. I do not know that I can be more explicit. Nevertheless it is expected; and as I do not mean to do it, you can see that there is a difficulty.'

'I would not go near the place, John.'

'I must.'

'Then you'll have to marry her.'

'I won't.'

'Then there'll be a quarrel.'

'It may be so, but I will avoid it if possible. I must go. I could not stay away without laying myself open to a charge of ingratitude. They were very kind to me in the old days.' Then the subject was dropped; and on the next morning, John wrote to his aunt saying that he would go over to Babington after his return from London. He was going to London on business, and would come back from London to Babington on a day which he named. Then he resolved that he would take Pollington on his way down, knowing that a disagreeable thing to be done is a lion in one's path which should be encountered and conquered as soon as possible.

But there was one visit which he must pay before he went up to London. 'I think I shall ride over to-morrow, and call on the Boltons,' he said to his father.

'Of course; you can do that if you please.'

'He was a little rough to me, but he was kind. I stayed a night at his house, and he advanced me the money.'

'As for the money, that was a matter of business. He had his security, and, in truth, his interest. He is an honest man, and a very old friend of mine. But perhaps I may as well tell you that he has always been a little hard about you.'

'He didn't approve of Davis,' said the son, laughing.

'He is too prejudiced a man to forget Davis.'

'The more he thinks of Davis, the better he'll think of me if I can make him believe that I am not likely to want a Davis again.'

'You'll find him probably at the bank about half-past two.'

'I shall go to the house. It wouldn't be civil if I didn't call on Mrs. Bolton.'

As the squire was never in the habit of going to the house at Chesterton himself, and as Mrs. Bolton was a lady who kept up none of the outward ceremonies of social life, he did not quite understand this; but he made no further objection.

On the following day, about five in the afternoon, he rode through the iron gates, which he with difficulty caused to be opened for him, and asked for Mrs. Bolton. When he had been here before, the winter had commenced, and everything around had been dull and ugly; but now it was July, and the patch before the house was bright with flowers. The roses were in full bloom, and every morsel of available soil was bedded out with geraniums. As he stood holding his horse by the rein while he rang the bell, a side-door leading through the high brick wall from the garden, which stretched away behind the house, was suddenly opened, and a lady came through with a garden hat on, and garden gloves, and a basket full of rose leaves in her hand. It was the lady of whom he had never ceased to think from the day on which he had been allowed just to touch her fingers, now five years ago.

It was she, of course, whom he had come to see, and there she was to be seen. It was of her that he had come to form a judgment,—to tell himself whether she was or was not such as he had dreamed her to be. He had not been so foolishly romantic as to have been unaware that in all probability she might have grown up to be something very different from that which his fancy had depicted. It might or it might not come to pass that that promise of loveliness,—of loveliness combined with innocence and full intelligence,—should be kept. How often it is that Nature is unkind to a girl as she grows into womanhood, and robs the attractive child of her charms! How often will the sparkle of early youth get itself quenched utterly by the dampness and clouds of the opening world. He knew all that,—and knew too that he had only just seen her, had barely heard the voice which had sounded so silvery sweet in his ears.

But there she was,—to be seen again, to be heard, if possible, and to receive his judgment. 'Miss Bolton,' he said, coming down the stone steps which he had ascended, that he might ring the bell, and offering her his hand.

'Mr. Caldigate!'

'You remember me, then?'

'Oh yes, I remember you very well. I do not see people often enough to forget them. And papa said that you were coming home.'

'I have come at once to call upon your mother and your father,—

and upon you. I have to thank him for great kindness to me before I went.'

'Poor mamma is not quite well,' said the daughter. 'She has headaches so often, and she has one now. And papa has not come back from the bank. I have been gardening and am all——.' Then she stopped and blushed, as though ashamed of herself for saying so much.

'I am sorry Mrs. Bolton is unwell. I will not go through the ceremony of leaving a card, as I hope to be able to come again to thank her for her kindness before I went on my travels. Will you tell your father that I called?' Then he mounted his horse, feeling, as he did so, that he was throwing away an opportunity which kind fortune had given him. There they were together, he and this girl of whom he had dreamed;—and now he was leaving her, because he did not know how to hold her in conversation for ten minutes! But it was true, and he had to leave her. He could not instantly tell her how he admired her, how he loved her, how he had thought of her, and how completely she had realised all his fondest dreams. When on his horse, he turned round, and, lifting his hat to her, took a last glance. It could not have been otherwise, he said to himself. He had been sure that she would grow up to be exactly that which he had found her. To have supposed that Nature could have been untrue to such promises as had been made then, would have been to suppose Nature a liar.

Just outside the gate he met the old banker, who, according to his daily custom, had walked back from the town. 'Yes,' said Mr. Bolton, 'I remember you,—I remember you very well. So you found a lot of gold?'

'I got some.'

'You have been one of the few fortunate, I hear. I hope you will be able to keep it, and to make a good use of it. My compliments to your father. Good evening.'

'I shall take an early opportunity of paying my respects again to Mrs. Bolton, who, I am sorry to hear, is not well enough to see me,' said Caldigate, preventing the old curmudgeon from escaping with his intended rapidity.

'She is unfortunately often an invalid, sir,—and feels therefore that she has no right to exact from any one the ceremony of morning visits. Good evening, sir.'

But he cared not much for this coldness. Having found where the gold lay at this second Ahalala,—that the gold was real gold,— he did not doubt but that he would be able to make good his mining operations.

CHAPTER XV

Again At Pollington

ON his arrival at Pollington, all the Shands welcomed him as though he had been the successful son or successful brother who had gone out from among them; and spoke of 'Poor Dick' as being the unsuccessful son or unsuccessful brother,—as indeed he was. There did not seem to be the slightest anger against him, in that he had thriven and had left Dick behind him in such wretched poverty. There was no just ground for anger, indeed. He was well aware of that. He had done his duty by Dick to the best of his ability. But fathers and mothers are sometimes apt to think that more should be done for their own children than a friend's best ability can afford. These people, however, were reasonable. 'Poor Dick!' 'Isn't it sad?' 'I suppose when he's quite far away in the bush like that he can't get it,'—by which last miserable shred of security the poor mother allowed herself to be in some degree comforted.

'Now I want you to tell me,' said the father, when they were alone together on the first evening, 'what is really his condition?'

'He was a shepherd when I last heard about him.'

'He wrote to his mother by the last mail, asking whether something cannot be done for him. He was a shepherd then. What is a shepherd?'

'A man who goes about with the sheep all day, and brings them up to a camp at night. He may probably be a week without seeing a human being. That is the worst of it.'

'How is he fed?'

'Food is brought out to his hut,—perhaps once a week, perhaps once a fortnight,—so much meat, so much flour, so much tea, and so much sugar. And he has thirty or thirty-five pounds a-year besides.'

'Paid weekly?'

'No;—perhaps quarterly, perhaps half-yearly. He can do nothing with his money as long as he is there. If he wants a pair of boots or a new shirt, they send it out to him from the store, and his employer charges him with the price. It is a poor life, sir.'

'Very poor. Now tell me, what can we do for him?'

'It is an affair of money.'

'But is it an affair of money, Mr. Caldigate? Is it not rather an affair of drink? He has had his money,—more than his share; more

109

than he ought to have had. But even though I were able to send him more, what good would it do him?'

This was a question very difficult to answer. Caldigate had been forced to answer it to himself in reference to his own conduct. He had sent money to his former friend, and could without much damage to himself have sent more. Latterly he had been in that condition as to money in which a man thinks nothing of fifty pounds,—that condition which induces one man to shoe his horse with gold, and another to chuck his bank-notes about like half-crowns. The condition is altogether opposed to the regulated prudence of confirmed wealth. Caldigate had stayed his hand in regard to Dick Shand simply because the affair had been one not of money but of drink. 'I suppose a man may be cured by the absence of liquor?'

'By the enforced absence?'

'No doubt, they often break out again. I hardly know what to say, sir. If you think that money will do good,—money, that is, in moderation,—I will advance it. He and I started together, and I am sometimes aghast with myself when I think of the small matter which, like the point on a railway, sent me running rapidly on to prosperity,—while the same point, turned wrong, hurried him to ruin. I have taken my glass of grog, too, my two glasses,—or perhaps more. But that which would elate him into some fury of action would not move me. It was something nature did for me rather than virtue. I am a rich man, and he is a shepherd, because something was put into my stomach capable of digesting bad brandy, which was not put into his.'

'A man has more than one chance. When he found how it was with him, he should have abstained. A man must pay the fine of his own weakness.'

'Oh, yes. It is all understood somewhere, I suppose, though we don't understand it. I tell you what it is, Dr. Shand. If you think that five hundred pounds left with you can be of any assistance, you can have it.'

But the doctor seemed to doubt whether the money would do any good, and refused to take it, at any rate for the present. What could he do with it, if he did take it? 'I fear that he must lie upon his bed as he has made it,' said the doctor sorrowfully. 'It is a complaint which money cannot cure, but can always exaggerate. If, without costing myself or my family a shilling, I could put a thousand pounds into his hands to-morrow, I do not know whether I ought to do it.'

'You will remember my offer.'

The doctor thanked him, and said that he would remember. So the conversation was ended, and the doctor went about the ordinary occupation of his life apparently without any settled grief at his heart. He had done his duty by his son, and that sufficed,—or almost sufficed, for him.

Then came the mother's turn. Could anything be sent to the poor lost one,—to poor Dick? Clothes ran chiefly in her mind. If among them they could make up a dozen of shirts, would there by any assured means of getting them conveyed safely to Dick's shepherd-hut out in the Queensland bush? In answer to this Caldigate would fain have explained, had it been possible, that Dick would not care much for a dozen new shirts,—that they would be to him, even if received, almost as little a source of comfort as would be a ton of Newcastle coals. He had sunk below shirts by the dozen; almost below single shirts, such as Mrs. Shand and her daughters would be able to fabricate. Some upper flannel garment, and something in the nature of trousers, with a belt round his middle, and an old straw-hat would be all the wardrobe required by him. Men by dint of misery rise above the need of super-fluities. The poor wretch whom you see rolling himself, as it were, at the corner of the street within his old tattered filthy coat, trying to extract something more of life and warmth out of the last glass of gin which he has swallowed, is by no means discomposed because he has no clean linen for the morrow. All this Caldigate understood thoroughly; —but there was a difficulty in explaining it to Dick Shand's mother. 'I think there would be some trouble about the address,' he said.

'But you must know so many people out there.'

'I have never been in Queensland myself, and have no acquaintance with squatters. But that is not all, Mrs. Shand.'

'What else? You can tell me. Of course I know what it is that he has come to. I don't blind myself to it, Mr. Caldigate, even though I am his mother. But I am his mother; and if I could comfort him, just a little—'

'Clothes are not what he wants;—of clothes he can get what is necessary, poor as he is.'

'What is it he wants most?'

'Somebody to speak to;—some one to be kind to him.'

'My poor boy!'

'As he has fallen to what he is now, so can he rise again if he can find courage to give his mind to it. I think that if you write to him and tell him so, that will be better than sending him shirts. The doctor has been talking to me about money for him.'

'But, Mr. Caldigate, he couldn't drink the shirts out there in the bush. Here, where there is a pawnbroker at all the corners, they drink everything.'

He had promised to stay two days at Pollington and was of course aware of the dangers among which he walked. Maria had been by no means the first to welcome him. All the other girls had presented themselves before her. And when at last she did come forward she was very shy. The eldest daughter had married her clergyman though he was still only a curate; and the second had been equally successful with Lieutenant Postlethwaite though the lieutenant had been obliged in consequence to leave the army and to earn his bread by becoming agent to a soap-making company. Maria Shand was still Maria Shand, and was it not too probable that she had remained so for the sake of that companion who had gone away with her darling brother Dick? 'Maria has been thinking so much about your coming,' said the youngest,– not the girl who had been impertinent and ill-behaved before, for she had since become a grown-up Miss Shand, and had a young attorney of her own on hand, and was supposed to be the one of the family most likely to carry her pigs to a good market,–but the youngest of them all who had been no more than a child when he had been at Pollington before. 'I hope she is at home,' said Caldigate. 'At home! Of course she's at home. She wouldn't be away when you're coming!'

The Shands were demonstrative, always;–and never hypocritical. Here it was; told at once,–the whole story. He was to atone for having left Dick in the lurch by marrying Maria. There did seem to him to be a certain amount of justice in the idea; but then, unfortunately, it could not be carried out. If there were nothing else against it but the existence of the young lady at Chesterton, that alone would have been sufficient. And then, though Maria Shand was very well, though, no doubt, she would make a true and loving wife to any husband, though there had been a pretty touch of feeling about the Thomson's 'Seasons,'–still, still, she was not all that he fancied that a wife should be. He was quite willing to give £500 for Dick; but after that he thought that he would have had almost enough of the Shands. He could not marry Maria, and so he must say plainly if called upon to declare himself in the matter. There was an easiness about the family generally which enabled him to hope that the difficulty would be light. It would be as nothing compared with that coming scene between himself and aunt Polly, perhaps between himself and his uncle Babington, or perhaps,–worse again,–between himself and Julia!

When he found himself alone with Maria in the drawing-room on the following morning, he almost thought that it must have been arranged by the family. 'Doesn't it seem almost no time since you went away,' said the young lady.

'It has gone quickly;– but a great deal has been done.'

'I suppose so. Poor Dick!'

'Yes, indeed! Poor fellow! We can only hope about Dick. I have been speaking to your father about him.'

'Of course we all know that you did your very best for him. He has said so himself when he has written. But you;—you have been fortunate.'

'Yes, I have done very well. There is so much chance at it that there is nothing to be proud of.'

'I am sure there is a great deal;—cleverness, and steadiness, and courage, and all that. We were delighted to hear it, though poor Dick could not share it with you. You have made an immense fortune.'

'Oh dear no,—not that. I have been able to get over the little difficulties which I left behind me when I went away, and have got something in hand to live upon.'

'And now—?'

'I suppose I shall go back again,' said Caldigate, with an air of indifference.

'Go back again!' said Maria, who had not imagined this. But still a man going back to Australia might take a wife with him. She would not object to the voyage. Her remembrance of the evening on which she had crept down and put the little book into his valise was so strong that she felt herself to be justified in being in love with him. 'But not for always?'

'Certainly not;—but just to wind up affairs.'

It would be no more than a pleasant wedding-tour,—and, perhaps, she could do something for poor Dick. She could take the shirts so far on their destination.

'Oh, Mr. Caldigate, how well I remember that last night!'

'So indeed, do I,—and the book.' The hardship upon the moth is that though he has already scorched himself terribly in the flame, and burned up all the tender fibre of his wings, yet he can't help returning to the seductions of the tallow-candle till his whole body has become a wretched cinder. Why should he have been the first to speak of the book?

Of course she blushed, and of course she stammered. But in spite of her stammering she could say a word. 'I dare say you never looked at it.'

'Indeed I did,—very often. Once when Dick saw it in my hands, he wanted to take it away from me.'

'Poor Dick!'

'But I have never parted with it for an hour!'

'Where is it now?' she asked.

'Here,' said Caldigate, pulling it out of the breast-pocket of his coat. If he had had the presence of mind to say that he had lent the book to another young lady, and that she had never returned it, there might probably have been an end of this little trouble at once. But when the little volume appeared, just as though it had been kept close to his heart during all these four years, of course she was entitled to hope. He had never opened the book since that morning in his cabin, not caring for the academic beauties of Thomson's 'Seasons';—had never looked at it till it had occurred to him as proper that he should take it with him to Pollington. Now he brought it out of his pocket, and she put out her hand to receive it from him. 'You are not going to take it back again?'

'Certainly not if it be of any value to you?'

'Do you not value the presents which your friends make you?'

'If I care for the friends, I do.'

'As I care very much for this friend I shall keep the book.'

'I don't think that can be true, Mr. Caldigate?'

He was painfully near the blaze;—determined not to be burned, and yet with no powers of flying away from the candle into the farthest corner of the room. 'Why not true? I have kept it hitherto. It has been with me in many very strange places.'

Then there was a pause,—while he thought of escaping, and she of utilising the occasion. And yet it was not in her nature to be unmaidenly or aggressive. Only if he did like her it would be so very nice, and it is so often the case that men want a little encouragement! 'I dare say you thought more of the book than the donor.'

'That is intended to be unkind.'

'No;—certainly not. I can never be unkind to a friend who has been so very good as you were to poor Dick. Whatever else may happen, I shall,—never,—forget—that.' By this time there was a faint sound of sobbing to be heard, and then she turned away her face that she might wipe a tear from her eyes. It was a real tear, and a real sob, and she really thought that she was in love with him.

'I know I ought not to have come here,' he said.

'Why not?' she asked energetically.

'Because my coming would give rise to so much sadness about your brother.'

'I am so glad you have come,—so very glad. Of course we wanted to hear. And besides—'

'What besides?'

'Papa and mamma, and all of them, are so glad to see you. We never forget old friends.' Then again there was silence. 'Never,' she repeated, as she rose from her chair slowly and went out of the room.

114

Though he had fluttered flamewards now and again, though he had shown some moth-like aptitudes, he had not shown himself to be a downright, foolish, blind-eyed moth, determined to burn himself to a cinder as a moth should do. And she;—she was weak. Having her opportunity at command, she went away and left him, because she did not know what more to say. She went away to her own bedroom, and cried, and had a headache, during the remainder of the day. And yet there was no other day!

Late that evening, just at the hour when, on the previous night, he was closeted with the father, he found himself closeted with the mother. 'She has never forgotten you for one moment since you left us,' said the mother. Mrs. Shand had rushed into the subject so quickly that these were almost the first words she said to him. He remained quite quiet, looking out from the open window into the moonlight. When a distinct proposition was made to him like this, he certainly would not be a moth. 'I don't know whether you have thought of her too, Mr. Caldigate.' He only shook his head. 'That is so?'

'I hope you do not think that I have been to blame in any way,' he said, with a conscience somewhat stricken;—for he remembered well that he had kissed the young lady on that evening four years ago.

'Oh no. I have no complaint to make. My poor child! It is a pity. But I have nothing more to say. It must be so then?'

'I am the least settled man in all the world, Mrs. Shand.'

'But at some future time?'

'I fear not. My mind is intent on other things.' So it was;—intent on Hester Bolton! But the statement, as he made it, was certainly false, for it was intended to deceive. Mrs. Shand shook hands with him kindly, however, as she sent him away to bed, telling him that breakfast should be ready for him at eight the next morning.

His train left Pollington at nine, and at eight the doctor with all his family were there to greet him at the breakfast-table,—with all the family except Maria. The mother, in the most natural tone in the world, said that poor Maria had a headache and could not come down. They filled his plate with eggs and bacon and toast, and were as good to him as though he had blighted no hopes and broken no heart. He whispered one word at going to the doctor. 'Pray remember that whenever you think the money can be of use, it is there. I consider that I owe him quite as much as that.' The father grasped his hand, and all of them blessed him as he went.

'If I can only get away from Babington as easily!' he said to himself, as he took his place in the railway carriage.

CHAPTER XVI

Again At Babington

THE affair of Julia Babington had been made to him in set terms, and had, if not accepted, not been at once refused. No doubt this had occurred four years ago, and, if either of them had married since, they would have met each other without an unpleasant reminiscence. But they had not done so, and there was no reason why the original proposition should not hold good. After escaping from Babington he had, indeed, given various reasons why such a marriage was impossible. He had sold his inheritance. He was a ruined man. He was going out to Australia as a simple miner. It was only necessary for him to state all this, and it became at once evident that he was below the notice of Julia Babington. But everything had been altered since that. He had regained his inheritance, he had come back a rich man, and he was more than ever indebted to the family because of the violent fight they had made on his behalf, just as he was going. As he journeyed to Babington all this was clear to him; and it was clear to him also that, from his first entrance into the house, he must put on an air of settled purpose, he must gird up his loins seriously, he must let it be understood that he was not as he used to be, ready for worldly lectures from his aunt, or for romping with his female cousins, or for rats, or rabbits, or partridges, with the male members of the family. The cares of the world must be seen to sit heavy on him, and at the very first mention of a British wife he must declare himself to be wedded to Polyeuka.

At Babington he was received with many fatted calves. The whole family were there to welcome him, springing out upon him and dragging him out of the fly as soon as he had entered the park gates. Aunt Polly almost fainted as she was embracing him under an oak tree; and tears, real tears, ran down the squire's face as he shook both his nephew's hands at once. 'By George,' said the Babington heir, 'you're the luckiest fellow I ever heard of! We all thought Folking was gone for good.' As though the possessions of Folking were the summit of human bliss! Caldigate with all the girls around him could not remonstrate with words, but his spirit did remonstrate. 'Oh, John, we are so very, very, very, very glad to have you back again,' said Julia, sobbing and laughing at the same time. He had kissed them all of course, and now Julia was close to his elbow as he walked up to the house.

In the midst of all this there was hardly opportunity for that deportment which he meant to exercise. When fatted calves are being killed for you by the dozen, it is very difficult to repudiate the good nature of the slaughterers. Little efforts he did make even before he got to the house. 'I hardly know how I stand just yet,' he had said, in answer to his uncle's congratulations as to his wealth. 'I must go out again at any rate.'

'Back to Australia?' asked his aunt.

'I fear so. It is a kind of business,—gold-mining,—in which it is very hard for a man to know what he's worth. A claim that has been giving you a thousand pounds net every month for two years past, comes all of sudden a great deal worse than valueless. You can't give it up, and you have to throw back your thousands in profitless work.'

'I wouldn't do that,' said the squire.

'I'd stick to what I'd got,' said the Babington heir.

'It is a very difficult business,' said Caldigate, with a considerable amount of deportment, and an assumed look of age,—as though the cares of gold-seeking had made him indifferent to all the lighter joys of existence.

'But you mean to live at Folking?' asked Aunt Polly.

'I should think probably not. But a man situated as I am, never can say where he means to live.'

'But you are to have Folking?' whispered the squire,—whispered it so that all the party heard the words;—whispering not from reticence but excitement.

'That's the idea at present,' said the Folking heir. 'But Polyeuka is so much more to me than Folking! A gold mine with fifty or sixty thousand pounds' worth of plant about it, Aunt Polly, is an imperious mistress.' In all this our hero was calumniating himself. Polyeuka and the plant he was willing to abandon on very moderate terms, and had arranged to wipe his hands of the whole concern if those moderate terms were accepted. But cousin Julia and aunt Polly were enemies against whom it was necessary to assume whatever weapons might come to his hand.

He had arranged to stay a week at Babington. He had considered it all very deeply, and had felt that as two days was the least fraction of time which he could with propriety devote to the Shands, so must he give at least a week to Babington. There was, therefore, no necessity for any immediate violence on the part of the ladies. The whole week might probably have been allowed to pass without absolute violence, had he not shown by various ways that he did not intend to make many visits to the old haunts of his childhood before his return to Australia.

When he said that he should not hunt in the coming winter; that he feared his hand was out for shooting; that he had an idea of travelling on the Continent during the autumn; and that there was no knowing when he might be summoned back to Polyeuka, of course there came across Aunt Polly's mind,—and probably also across Julia's mind,—an idea that he meant to give them the slip again. On the former occasion he had behaved badly. This was their opinion. But, as it had turned out, his circumstances at the moment were such as to make his conduct pardonable. He had been harassed by the importunities both of his father and of Davis; and that, under such circumstances, he should have run away from his affianced bride, was almost excusable. But now——! It was very different now. Something must be settled. It was very well to talk about Polyeuka. A man who has engaged himself in business must, no doubt, attend to it. But married men can attend to business quite as well as they who are single. At any rate, there could be no reason why the previous engagement should not be consolidated and made a family affair. There was felt to be something almost approaching to resistance in what he had said and done already. Therefore Aunt Polly flew to her weapons, and summoned Julia also to take up arms. He must be bound at once with chains, but the chains were made as soft as love and flattery could make them. Aunt Polly was almost angry,—was prepared to be very angry;—but not the less did she go on killing fatted calves.

There were archery meetings at this time through the country, the period of the year being unfitted for other sports. It seemed to Caldigate as though all the bows and all the arrows had been kept specially for him,—as though he was the great toxophilite of the age,—whereas no man could have cared less for the amusement than he. He was carried here and was carried there; and then there was a great gathering in their own park at home. But it always came to pass that he and Julia were shooting together,—as though it were necessary that she should teach him,—that she should make up by her dexterity for what was lost by his awkwardness,—that she by her peculiar sweetness should reconcile him to his new employment. Before the week was over, there was a feeling among all the dependants at Babington, and among many of the neighbours, that everything was settled, and that Miss Julia was to be the new mistress of Folking.

Caldigate knew that it was so. He perceived the growth of the feeling from day to day. He could not say that he would not go to the meetings, all of which had been arranged beforehand. Nor could he refuse to stand up beside his cousin Julia and shoot his arrows directly after she had shot hers. Nor could he refrain from acknowledging that though she was awkward in a drawing-room, she was a buxom young woman dressed in green with a feather in her hat and a bow in her hand; and then she could always shoot her arrows straight into the bull's-eye. But he was well aware that the new hat had been bought specially for him, and that the sharpest arrow from her quiver was intended to be lodged in his heart. He was quite determined that any such shooting as that should be unsuccessful.

'Has he said anything?' the mother asked the daughter. 'Not a word.' This occurred on the Sunday night. He had reached Babington on the previous Tuesday, and was to go to Folking on next Tuesday. 'Not a word.' The reply was made in a tone almost of anger. Julia did believe that her cousin had been engaged to her, and that she actually had a right to him, now that he had come back, no longer ruined.

'Some men never do,' said Aunt Polly, not wishing to encourage her daughter's anger just at present. 'Some men are never left alone with a girl for half a moment, but what they are talking stuff and nonsense. Others never seem to think about it in the least. But whether it's the one or whether it's the other, it makes no difference afterwards. He never had much talk of that kind. I'll just say a word to him, Julia.'

The saying of the word was put off till late on Sunday evening. Sunday was rather a trying day at Babington. If hunting, shooting, fishing, croquet, lawn-billiards, bow and arrows, battledore and shuttle-cock, with every other game, as games come up and go, constitute a worldly kind of life, the Babingtons were worldly. There surely never was a family in which any kind of work was so wholly out of the question, and every amusement so much a matter of course. But if worldliness and religion are terms opposed to each other, then they were not worldly. There were always prayers for the whole household morning and evening. There were two services on Sunday, at the first of which the males, and at both of which the females, were expected to attend. But the great struggle came after dinner at nine o'clock, when Aunt Polly always read a sermon out loud to the assembled household. Aunt Polly had a certain power of her own, and no one dared to be absent except the single servant who was left in the kitchen to look after the fire.

The squire himself was always there, but a peculiar chair was placed for him, supposed to be invisible to the reader, in which he slept during the whole time, subject to correction from a neighbouring daughter in the event of his snoring. An extra bottle of port after dinner was another Sunday observance which added to the irritability of the occasion,—so that the squire, when the reading and prayers were over, would generally be very cross, and would take himself up to bed almost without a word, and the brothers would rush away almost with indecent haste to their smoking. As the novels had all been put away into a cupboard, and the good books which were kept for the purpose strewed about in place of them, and as knitting, and even music, were tabooed, the girls, having nothing to do, would also go away at an early hour.

'John, would you mind staying a few moments with me?' said Aunt Polly, in her softest voice when Caldigate was hurrying after his male cousins. He knew that the hour had come, and he girded up his loins.

'Come nearer, John,' she said,—and he came nearer, so that she could put her hand upon his. 'Do you remember, John, when you and I and Julia were together in that little room up-stairs?' There was so much pathos in her voice, she did her acting so well, that his respect for her was greatly augmented,—as was also his fear. 'She remembers it very well.'

'Of course I remember it, Aunt Polly. It's one of those things that a man doesn't forget.'

'A man ought not to forget such a scene as that,' she said, shaking her head. 'A man would be very hard of heart if he could forget it.'

Now must be the moment for his exertion! She had spoken so plainly as to leave no doubt of her meaning, and she was pausing for an answer; yet he hesitated,—not in his purpose, but doubting as to his own manner of declaring it. He must be very decided. Upon that he was resolved. He would be decided, though they should drag him in pieces with wild horses for it afterwards. But he would fain be gentle with his aunt if it were possible. 'My dear Aunt Polly, it won't do; I'm not going to be caught, and so you may as well give it over.' That was what he wished her to understand;—but he would not say it in such language. Much was due to her, though she was struggling to catch him in a trap. 'When I had made such a fool of myself before I went—about money,' he said, 'I thought that was all over.'

'But you have made anything but a fool of yourself since,' she replied triumphantly; 'you have gone out into the world like a man, and have made your fortune, and have so returned that everybody is proud of you. Now you can take a wife to yourself and settle down, and be a happy goodman.'

It was exactly his view of life;—only there was a difference about the wife to be taken. He certainly had never said a word to his cousin which could justify this attack upon him. The girl had been brought to him in a cupboard, and he had been told that he was to marry her! And that when he had been young and drowned with difficulties.

How is a man ever to escape if he must submit under such circumstances as these? 'My dear Aunt Polly, I had better tell you at once that I cannot marry my cousin Julia.' Those were the words which he did speak, and as he spoke there was a look about his eyes and his mouth which ought to have made her know that there was no hope.

'And why not? John Caldigate, is this you that I hear?'

'Why should I?'

'Because you promised it.'

'I never did, Aunt Polly.'

'And because she loves you.'

'Even if it were so, am I to be bound by that? But, indeed, indeed, I never even suggested it,—never thought of it. I am very fond of my cousin, very fond of all my cousins. But marriage is a different thing. I am inclined to think that cousins had better not marry.'

'You should have said that before. But it is nonsense. Cousins marry every day. There is nothing about it either in the Bible or the Prayer-book. She will die.'

Aunt Polly said this in a tone of voice which made it a matter of regret that she should not have been educated for Drury Lane. But as she said it, he could not avoid thinking of Julia's large ankles, and red cheeks, and of the new green hat and feather. A girl with large ankles is, one may suppose, as liable to die for love as though she were as fine about her feet as a thorough-bred filly; and there is surely no reason why a true heart and a pair of cherry cheeks should not go together. But our imagination has created ideas in such matters so fixed, that it is useless to contend against them. In our endeavours to produce effects, these ideas should be remembered and obeyed. 'I hope not on that account,' said Caldigate, and as he uttered the words some slightest suspicion of a smile crossed his face.

Then Aunt Polly blazed forth in wrath. 'And at such a moment as this you can laugh!'

'Indeed, I did not laugh;—I am very far from laughing, Aunt Polly.'

'Because I am anxious for my child, my child whom you have deceived, you make yourself merry with me!'

'I am not merry. I am miserably unhappy because of all this. But I cannot admit that I have deceived my cousin. All that was settled, I thought, when I went away. But coming back at the end of four years, of four such long years, with very different ideas of life—'

'What ideas?'

'Well,—at any rate, with ideas of having my own way,—I cannot submit myself to this plan of yours, which, though it would have given me so much—'

'It would give you everything, sir.'

'Granted! But I cannot take everything. It is better that we should understand each other, so that my cousin, for whom I have the most sincere regard, should not be annoyed.'

'Much you care!'

'What shall I say?'

'It signifies nothing what you say. You are a false man. You have inveigled your cousin's affections, and now you say that you can do nothing for her. This comes from the sort of society you have kept out at Botany Bay! I suppose a man's word there is worth nothing, and that the women are of such a kind they don't mind it. It is not the way with gentlemen here in England; let me tell you that!' Then she stalked out of the room, leaving him either to go to bed, or join the smokers or to sit still and repent at his leisure, as he might please. His mind, however, was chiefly occupied for the next half-hour with thinking whether it would be possible for him to escape from Babington on the following morning.

Before the morning he had resolved that, let the torment of the day be what it might, he would bear it,—unless by chance he might be turned out of the house. But no tragedy such as that came to relieve him. Aunt Polly gave him his tea at breakfast with a sternly forbidding look,—and Julia was as cherry-cheeked as ever, though very silent. The killing of calves was over, and he was left to do what he pleased during the whole day. One spark of comfort came to him. 'John, my boy,' said his uncle in a whisper, 'what's the matter between you and Madame?' Mr. Babington would sometimes call his wife Madame when he was half inclined to laugh at her. Caldigate of course declared that there was nothing wrong. The squire shook his head and went away. But from this it appeared to Caldigate that the young lady's father was not one of the conspirators,—by ascertaining which his mind was somewhat relieved.

On the next morning the fly came for him, and he went away without any kisses. Upon the whole he was contented with both his visits, and was inclined to assure himself that a man has only to look a difficulty in the face, and that the difficulty will be difficult no longer.

CHAPTER XVII

Again At Puritan Grange

AS Caldigate travelled home to Folking he turned many things in his mind. In the first place he had escaped, and that to him was a matter of self-congratulation. He had declared his purpose in reference to his cousin Julia very clearly;—and though he had done so he had not quarrelled utterly with the family. As far as the young lady's father was concerned, or her brothers, there had been no quarrel at all. The ill-will against him was confined to the women. But as he thought of it all, he was not proud of himself. He had received great kindness from their hands, and certainly owed them much in return. When he had been a boy he had been treated almost as one of the family;—but as he had not been quite one of them, would it not have been natural that he should be absorbed in the manner proposed? And then he could not but admit to himself that he had been deficient in proper courage when he had been first caught and taken into the cupboard. On that occasion he had neither accepted nor rejected the young lady; and in such a matter as this silence certainly may be supposed to give consent. Though he rejoiced in his escape he was not altogether proud of his conduct in reference to his friends at Babington.

Would it not have been better that he should have told his aunt frankly that his heart was engaged elsewhere? The lady's name would have been asked, and the lady's name could not have been given. But he might in this way have prepared the way for the tidings which would have to be communicated should he finally be successful with Hester Bolton. Now such news would reach them as an aggravation of the injury. For that, however, there could be no remedy. The task at present before him was that of obtaining a footing in the house at Chesterton, and the more he thought of it the more he was at a loss to know how to set about it. They could not intend to shut such a girl up, through all her young years, as in a convent. There must be present to the minds of both of them an idea that marriage would be good for her, or, at any rate, that she should herself have some choice in the matter. And if there were to be any son-in-law why should not he have as good a chance as any other? When they should learn how constantly the girl's image had been present to his mind, so far away, during so many years, under such hard circumstances, would not that recommend him to them? Had he not proved himself to be steady, industrious, and a good man of business? In regard to position and fortune was he not such as a father would desire for his daughter? Having lost his claim to Folking, had he not regained it;—and in doing so had he not shown himself to be something much more than merely the heir to Folking? An immediate income would, of course, be necessary;—but there was money enough. He would ask the old man for nothing. Reports said that though the old man had been generous to his own sons, still he was fond of money. He should have the opportunity of bestowing his daughter in marriage without being asked for a shilling. And then John Caldigate bethought himself with some pride that he could make a proper settlement on his wife without burdening the estate at Folking with any dowers. But of what use would be all this if he could not get at the girl to tell her that he loved her?

He might, indeed, get at the father and tell his purpose plainly and honestly. But he thought that his chance of prevailing with the girl might be better than with the father. In such cases it is so often the daughter who prevails with her own parents after she has surrendered her own heart. The old man had looked at him sternly, had seemed even in that moment of time to disapprove of him. But the girl——. Well; in such an interview as that there had not been much scope for approval. Nor was he a man likely to flatter himself that any girl could fall in love with him at first sight. But she had not looked sternly at him. In the few words which she had spoken her voice had been very sweet. Both of them had said they remembered him after the long interval that had passed;—but the manner of saying so had been very different. He was almost sure that the old man would be averse to him, though he could tell himself personally that there was no just cause for such aversion. But if this were so, he could not forward his cause by making his offer through the father.

'Well, John, how has it gone with you at Babington?' his father asked almost as soon as they were together.

It had not been difficult to tell his father of the danger before he made his visit, but now he hesitated before he could avow that the young lady's hand had again been offered to him. 'Pretty well, sir. We had a good deal of archery and that kind of thing. It was rather slow.'

'I should think so. Was there nothing besides the archery?'

'Not much.'

'The young lady was not troublesome?'

'Perhaps the less we say about it the better, sir. They were very kind to me when I was a boy.'

'I have nothing to say at all, unless I am to be called on to welcome her as a daughter-in-law.'

'You will not have to do that, sir.'

'I suppose, John, you mean to marry some day,' said the father after a pause. Then it occurred to the son that he must have some one whom he could trust in this matter which now occupied his mind, and that no one probably might be so able to assist him as his father. 'I wish I knew what your idea of life is,' continued Mr. Caldigate. 'I fear you will be growing tired of this place, and that when you get back to your gold-mines you will stay there.'

'There is no fear of that. I do not love the place well enough.'

'If you were settled here, I should feel more comfortable. I sometimes think, John, that if you would fix yourself I would give the property up to you altogether and go away with my books into some town. Cambridge, perhaps, would do as well as any other.'

'You must never do that, sir. You must not leave Folking. But as for myself,—I have ideas about my own life.'

'Are they such that you can tell them?'

'Yes;—you shall hear them all. But I shall expect you to help me;—or at least not turn against me?'

'Turn against you, John! I hope I may never have to do that again. What is that you mean?' This he said very seriously. There was usually in his voice something of a tone of banter,—a subdued cynicism,—which had caused everybody near him to be afraid of him, and which even yet was habitual to him. But now that was all gone. Was there to be any new source of trouble betwixt him and his son?

'I intend to ask Hester Bolton to be my wife,' said John Caldigate.

The father, who was standing in the library, slapped both his hands down upon the table. 'Hester Bolton!'

'Is there any objection?'

'What do you know about her? Why;—she's a child.'

'She is nearly twenty, sir.'

'Have you ever seen her?'

'Yes, I have seen her,—twice. I daresay you'll think it very absurd, but I have made up my mind about it. If I say that I was thinking about it all the time I was in Australia, of course you will laugh at me.'

'I will not laugh at you at all, John.'

'If any one else were to say so to me, I should laugh at them. But yet it was so. Have you ever seen her?'

'I suppose I have. I think I remember a little girl.'

'For beauty I have never seen anybody equal to her,' said the lover. 'I wish you'd go over to Chesterton and judge for yourself.'

'They wouldn't know what such a thing meant. It is years since I have been in the house. I believe that Mrs. Bolton devotes herself to religious exercises, and that she regards me as a pagan.'

'That's just the difficulty, sir. How am I to get at her? But you may be sure of this, I mean to do it. If I were beat I do think that then I should go back and bury myself in the gold-mines. You asked me what I meant to do about my future life. That is my purpose. If she were my wife I should consult her. We might travel part of the time, and I might have a farm. I should always look upon Folking as my home. But till that is settled, when you ask me what I mean to do with my life, I can only say that I mean to marry Hester Bolton.'

'Did you tell them at Babington?'

'I have told nobody but you. How am I to set about it?'

Then Mr. Caldigate sat down and began to scratch his head and to consider. 'I don't suppose they ever go out anywhere.'

'I don't think they do;—except to church.'

'You can't very well ask her there. You can always knock at the house-door.'

'I can call once again;—but what if I am refused then? It is of no use knocking if a man does not get in.' After a little more conversation the squire was so far persuaded that he assented to the proposed marriage as far as his assent was required; but he did not see his way to give any assistance. He could only suggest that his son should go direct to the father and make his proposition in the old-fashioned legitimate fashion. But when it was put to him whether Mr. Bolton would not certainly reject the offer unless it were supported by some goodwill on the part of his own daughter, he acknowledged that it might probably be so. 'You see,' said the squire, 'he believes in gold, but he doesn't believe in gold-mines.'

'It is that accursed Davis that stands against me,' said the son.

John Caldigate, no doubt, had many things to trouble him. Before he had resolved on making his second visit to Chesterton, he received a most heartrending epistle from Aunt Polly in which he was assured that he was quite as dear to her as ever, quite as dear as her own children, and in which he was implored to return to the haunts of his childhood where everybody loved him and admired him. After what had passed, he was determined not to revisit the haunts till he was married, or, at any rate, engaged to be married. But there was a difficulty in explaining this to Aunt Polly without an appearance of ingratitude. And then there were affairs in Australia which annoyed him. Tom Crinkett was taking advantage of his absence in reference to Polyeuka,—so that his presence would soon be required there;—and other things were not going quite smoothly. He had much to trouble him;—but still he was determined to carry out his purpose with

Hester Bolton. Since the day on which he had roused himself to the necessity of an active life he had ever called upon himself 'not to let the grass grow under his feet.' And he had taught himself to think that there were few things a man could not achieve if he would only live up to that motto. Therefore, though he was perplexed by letters from Australia, and though his Aunt Polly was a great nuisance, he determined to persevere at once. If he allowed himself to revisit Nobble before he had settled this matter with Hester Bolton, would it not be natural that Hester Bolton should be the wife of some other man before he returned?

With all this on his mind he started off one day on horseback to Cambridge. When he left Folking he had not quite made up his mind whether he would go direct to the bank and ask for old Mr. Bolton, or make a first attempt at that fortified castle at Chesterton. But on entering the town he put his horse up at an inn just where the road turns off to Chesterton, and proceeded on foot to the house. This was about a mile distant from the stable, and as he walked that mile he resolved that if he could get into the house at all he would declare his purpose to some one before he left it. What was the use of shilly-shallying? 'Who ever did anything by letting the grass grow under his feet?' So he knocked boldly at the door and asked for Mrs. Bolton. After a considerable time, the maid came and told him, apparently with much hesitation, that Mrs. Bolton was at home. He was quite determined to ask for Miss Bolton if Mrs. Bolton were denied to him. But the girl said that Mrs. Bolton was at home, seeming by her manner to say at the same time, 'I cannot tell a lie about it, because of the sin; but I don't know what business you can have here, and I'm sure that my mistress does not want to see any such a one as you.' Nevertheless she showed him into the big sitting-room on the left hand of the hall, and as he entered he saw the skirts of a lady's dress vanishing through another door. Had there been a moment allowed him he would boldly have called the lady back, for he was sure that the lady was Hester;—but the lady was gone and the door closed before he could open his mouth.

Then he waited for full ten minutes, which, of course, seemed to him to be very much more than an hour. At last the door opened and Mrs. Bolton appeared. The reader is not to suppose that she was an ugly, cross-looking old woman. She was neither ugly, nor old, nor cross. When she had married Mr. Bolton, she had been quite young, and now she was not much past forty. And she was handsome too, with a fine oval face which suited well with the peculiar simplicity of her dress and the sober seriousness of her gait and manner. It might, perhaps, be said of her that she tried to look old and ugly,—and cross too, but that she did not succeed. She now greeted her visitor very coldly, and having asked after old Mr. Caldigate, sat silent looking at John Caldigate as though there were nothing more possible for her to say.

'I could not but come to see you and thank you for your kindness before I went,' said John.

'I remember your coming about some business. We have very few visitors here.'

'I went out, you know, as a miner.'

'I think I heard Mr. Bolton say so.'

'And I have succeeded very well.'

'Oh, indeed!'

'So well that I have been able to come back; and though I may perhaps be obliged to revisit the colony to settle my affairs there, I am going to live here at home.'

'I hope that will be comfortable to you.' At every word she spoke, her voice took more and more plainly that tone of wonder which we are all of us apt to express when called on to speak on matters which we are at the moment astonished to have introduced to us.

'Yes; Mrs. Bolton, I hope it will. And now I have got something particular to say.'

'Perhaps you had better see—Mr. Bolton—at the bank.'

'I hope I may be able to do so. I quite intend it. But as I am here, if you will allow me, I will say a word to you first. In all matters there is nothing so good as being explicit.' She looked at him as though she was altogether afraid of him. And indeed she was. Her husband's opinion of the young man had been very bad five years ago,—and she had not heard that it had been altered since. Young men who went out to the colonies because they were ruined, were, to her thinking, the worst among the bad,—men who drank and gambled and indulged in strange lives, mere castaways, the adopted of Satan. And, to her thinking, among men, none were so rough as miners,—and among miners none were so godless, so unrestrained, so wild as the seekers after gold. She had read, perhaps, something of the Spaniards in Central America, and regarded such adventurers as she would pirates and freebooters generally. And then with regard to the Caldigates generally,—the elder of whom she knew to have been one of her husband's intimate friends in his less regenerated days,—she believed them to be infidel free-thinkers. She was not, therefore, by any means predisposed in favour of this young man; and when he spoke of his desire to be explicit, she thought that he had better be explicit anywhere rather than in her

128

drawing-room. 'You may remember,' he said, 'that I had the pleasure of meeting your daughter here before I left the country five years ago.' Then she listened with all her ears. There were not many things in this empty, vain, hard unattractive world which excited her. But the one thing in regard to which she had hopes and fears, doubts and resolutions,—the one matter as to which she knew that she must ever be on her guard, and yet as to which she hardly knew how she was to exercise her care,—was her child. 'And once I have seen her since I have been back, though only for a moment.' Then he paused as though expecting that she should say something;—but what was it possible that she should say? She only looked at him with all her eyes, and retreated a little from him with her body, as anxious to get away from a man of his class who should dare even to speak to her of her girl. 'The truth is, Mrs. Bolton, that her image has been present to me through all my wanderings, and I am here to ask her to be my wife.' She rose from her chair as though to fly from him,—and then sitting down again stared at him with her mouth open and her eyes fixed upon him. His wife! Her Hester to become the wife of such a one as that! Her girl, as to whom, when thinking of the future life of her darling, she had come to tell herself that there could be no man good enough, true enough, firm enough in his faith and life, to have so tender, so inestimable a treasure committed to his charge!

CHAPTER XVIII

Robert Bolton

CALDIGATE felt at the moment that he had been very abrupt,—so abrupt as to have caused infinite dismay. But then it had been necessary that he should be abrupt in order that he might get the matter understood. The ordinary approaches were not open to him, and unless he had taken a more than usually rapid advantage of the occasion which he had made for himself, he would have had to leave the house without having been able to give any of its inmates the least idea of his purpose. And then,—as he said to himself,—matrimony is honest. He was in all worldly respects a fit match for the young lady. To his own thinking there was nothing preposterous in the nature of his request, though it might have been made with some precipitate informality. He did not regard himself exactly as the lady regarded him, and therefore, though he saw her surprise, he still hoped that he might be able to convince her that in all that he was doing he was as anxious for the welfare of her child as she could be herself.

She sat there so long without saying a word that he found himself obliged to renew his suit. 'Of course, Mrs. Bolton, I am aware how very little you know of me.'

'Nothing at all,' she answered, hurriedly;—'or rather too much.'

He blushed up to his eyes, perfectly understanding the meaning of her words; and, knowing that he had not deserved them, he was almost angry. 'If you will make inquiry I think you will find that I have so far succeeded as to justify you in hoping that I may be able to marry and settle myself in my own country.'

'You don't know my daughter at all.'

'Very little.'

'It is quite out of the question. She is very young, and such a thing has never occurred to her. And we are not the same sort of people.'

'Why not, Mrs. Bolton? Your husband and my father have been intimate friends for a great many years. It is not as though I had taken up the idea only yesterday. It has been present with me, comforting me, during all my work, for the last five years. I know all your daughter's features as though she had been my constant companion.' The lady shivered and almost trembled at this profanation of her child's name. It was trouble to her that one so holy should ever

130

have been thought about by one so unholy. 'Of course I do not ask for anything at present;–but will you not consult your husband as to the propriety of allowing her to make my acquaintance?'

'I shall tell my husband, of course.'

'And will repeat to him what I say?'

'I shall tell him,–as I should any other most wild proposition that might be made to me. But I am quite sure that he will be very angry.'

'Angry! why should he be angry?'

'Because——' Then she stopped.

'I do not think, Mrs. Bolton, that there can be any cause for anger. If I were a beggar, if I were below her in position, if I had not means to keep a wife,–even if I were a stranger to his name, he might be angry. But I do not think he can be angry with me, now, because, in the most straightforward way, I come to the young lady's parents and tell them that I love their child. Is it a disgrace to me that of all whom I have seen I think her to be the loveliest and best? Her father may reject me; but he will be very unreasonable if he is angry with me.'

She could not tell him about the dove and the kite, or the lamb and the wolf. She could not explain to him that he was a sinner, unre-generated, a wild man in her estimation, a being of quite another kind than herself, and therefore altogether unfitted to be the husband of her girl! Her husband, no doubt, could do all this–if he would. But then she too had her own skeleton in her own cupboard. She was not quite assured of her own husband's regeneration. He went to church regularly, and read his Bible, and said his prayers. But she feared,– she was almost sure,–that he liked the bank-books better than his Bible. That he would reject this offer from John Caldigate, she did not doubt. She had always heard her husband speak of the man with disapprobation and scorn. She had heard the whole story of Davis and the Newmarket debts. She had heard, too, the man's subsequent pros-perity spoken of as a thing of chance,–as having come from gambling on an extensive scale. She herself regarded money acquired in so unholy a way as likely to turn to slate-stones, or to fly away and become worse than nothing. She knew that Mr. Bolton, whether regenerate or not, regarded young Caldigate as an adventurer, and that therefore, the idea of such a marriage would be as unpalatable to him as to herself. But she did not dare to tell her visitor that he was an unregenerate kite, lest her husband would not support her.

'Whatever more you have got to say, you had better say it to him,' she replied to the lover when he had come to the end of his defence. At that moment the door opened, and a gentleman entered the room. This was Mr. Robert Bolton, the attorney. Now of all her husband's sons,—who were, of course, not her sons,—Mrs. Bolton saw this one the most frequently and perhaps liked him the least. Or it might be juster to say that she was more afraid of him than of the others. The two eldest, who were both in the bank, were quiet, sober men, who lived affluently and were married to religious wives, and brought up their children plentifully and piously. She did not see very much of them, because her life was not a social life. But among her friends they were the most intimate. But Robert's wife was given to gaiety and dinner-parties, and had been seen even at balls. And Robert himself was much oftener at the Grange than either of the other brothers. He managed his father's private affairs, and was, perhaps, of all his sons the best liked by the father. He was prosperous in his business, and was reported to be the leading lawyer in the town. In the old Cambridge days he had entertained John Caldigate at his house; and though they had not met since the miner's return from Australia, each at once knew the other, and their greeting was friendly. 'Where's Hess?' said Robert, asking at once after his sister.

'She is engaged, Robert,' said Mrs. Bolton, very seriously, and very firmly.

'She gave me a commission about some silk, and Margaret says that it can't be executed in Cambridge. She must write to Fanny.' Margaret was Mrs. Robert Bolton, and Fanny was the wife of the barrister brother who lived in London.

'I will tell her, Robert.'

'All the same I should have liked to have seen her.'

'She is engaged, Robert.' This was said almost more seriously and more firmly than before.

'Well, Caldigate,' said the attorney, turning to the visitor, 'so you are the one man who has not only gone to the gold country and found gold, but has brought his gold home with him.'

'I have brought a little home;—but I hope others have done so before.'

'I have never heard of any. You seem to have been uncommonly lucky. Hard work, wasn't it?'

'Hard enough at first.'

'And a good deal of chance?'

'If a man will work steadily, and has backbone enough to stand up against reverses without consoling himself with drink; and if, when the gold comes, he can refrain from throwing it about as though it were endless, I think a man may be tolerably sure to earn something.' Then he told the story of the horse with the golden shoes.

'Shoes of gold upon a horse!' said Mrs. Bolton, holding up both her hands. The man who could even tell such a story must be an adventurer. But, nevertheless, the story had interested her so that she had been enticed into taking some part in the conversation.

When Caldigate got up to take his leave, Robert Bolton offered to walk back to the town with him. He had expected to find his father, but would now look for him at the bank. They started together; and as they went Caldigate told his story to the young lady's half-brother. It occurred to him that of all the family Robert Bolton would be the most reasonable in such a matter; and that of all the family he might perhaps be the best able to give assistance. When Robert Bolton had heard it all, at first he whistled. Then he asked the following question. 'What did she say to you?'

'She did not give me much encouragement.'

'I should think not. Though I say it who shouldn't, Hester is the sweetest girl in Cambridgeshire. But her mother thinks her much too good to be given in marriage to any man. This kind of thing was bound to come about some day.'

'But Mrs. Bolton seems to have some personal objection to me.'

'That's probable.'

'I don't know why she should.'

'She has got one treasure of her own, in enjoying which she is shut out from all the rest of the world. Is it unnatural that she should be a little suspicious about a man who proposes to take her treasure away from her?'

'She must surrender her treasure to some one,—some day.'

'If it be so, she will hope to do so to a man of whose antecedents she may know more than she does of yours. What she does know of you is of a nature to frighten her. You will excuse me.'

'Oh, of course.'

'She has heard that you went away under a cloud, having surrendered your estate. That was against you. Well;—you have come back, and she hears that you have brought some money with you. She does not care very much about money; but she does care about regularity and fixed habits. If Hess is to be married at all she would especially wish that her husband should be a religious man. Perhaps you are.'

'I am neither the one thing nor the other,—especially.'

'And therefore peculiarly dangerous in her eyes. It is natural that she should oppose you.'

'What am I to do, then?'

'Ah! How am I to answer that? The whole story is very romantic, and I do not know that we are a romantic family. My father is autocratic in his own house.'

133

This last assurance seemed to contain some comfort. As Mrs. Bolton would be his enemy in the matter, it was well that the power of deciding should be in other hands. 'I do not mean to give it up,' said he.

'I suppose you must if they won't open their doors to you.'

'I think they ought to allow me to have the chance of seeing her.'

'I don't see why they should. Mind I am not saying anything of this for myself. If I were my sister's guardian, I should take the trouble to make many inquiries before I either asked you into my house or declined to do so. I should not give access to you, or to any other gentleman merely because he asked it.'

'Let them make inquiry.'

'Mrs. Bolton probably thinks that she already knows enough. What my father may say I cannot even surmise.'

'Will you tell him?'

'If you wish it.'

'Tell him also that I will wait upon him at once if he desires it. He shall know everything about my affairs,—which indeed require no concealment. I can settle enough upon her for her comfort. If she is to have anything of her own, that will be over and above. As far as I am concerned myself, I ask no question about that. I think that a man ought to earn enough for himself and for his wife too. As to religion—'

'If I were you, I would leave that alone,' said the lawyer.

'Perhaps so.'

'I will tell my father. That is all I can say. Good-bye.'

So they parted; and Caldigate, getting on his horse, rode back to Folking. Looking back at what he had done that day, he was almost disposed to be contented with it. The lady's too evident hostility was, of course, to be deprecated;—but then he had expected it. As Robert Bolton had explained to him very clearly, it was almost impossible that he should, at the first, be regarded by her with favourable eyes. But he thought that the brother had been quite as favourable to him as he could have expected, and the ice was broken. The Bolton family generally would know what he was about. Hester would not be told, of course;—at any rate, not at once. But the first steps had been taken, and it must be for him now so to press the matter that the ultimate decision should be made to rest in her hands as soon as possible.

'What did Mr. Bolton say to you?' asked the squire.

'I did not see him.'

'And what did the young lady say?'

'I did not see her.'

'Or the mamma?'

'I did see her, and told her my project.'

'I should think she would be startled?'

'She was not very propitious, sir; but that was not to be expected.'

'She is a poor melancholy half-crazed creature, I take it,' said the squire; 'at least, that is what I hear. The girl, I should think, would be glad to get away from such a home. But I am afraid you will find a good many obstacles.' After that nothing more was said about the matter at Folking for some days.

But there was a great deal said upon the matter both in Cambridge and Chesterton. Robert Bolton found his father at the bank on the same afternoon, and performed his promise. 'Did he see your step-mother?' asked the old man.

'Oh yes; and as far as I can understand, did not receive very much at her hands.'

'But he did not see Hester?'

'Certainly not to-day.'

Then the old man looked up into his son's face, as though seeking some expression there from which he might take some counsel. His own nature had ever been imperious; but he was old now, and, in certain difficulties which environed him, he was apt to lean on his son Robert. It was Robert who encouraged him still to keep in his hands some share of the management of the bank; and it was to Robert that he could look for counsel when the ceremonious strictness of his wife at home became almost too hard even for him.

'It is natural to suppose that Hester should be married some day,' said the lawyer.

'Her mother will never wish it.'

'She will never wish it at any given moment, but she would probably assent to the proposition generally. Why not Hester as well as another girl? It is the happiest life for women.'

'I am not sure. I am not sure.'

'Women think so themselves, and Hester will probably be the same as the others. She will, of course, have an opinion of her own.'

'She will be guided by her mother.'

'Not altogether. It will only be fair that she should be consulted on a matter of such importance to herself.'

'You would not tell her what this man has been saying?'

'Not necessarily. I say that she should be consulted generally as to her future life. In regard to this man, I see no objection to him if he be a good man.'

'He was here at college. You know what he did then?'

'Yes; and I know, too, something of what he has done since. He

135

went away disinherited and almost degraded. He has come back, as I hear, comparatively a rich man. He has got back his inheritance, which might probably be settled on his children if he were to be married. And all this he has done off his own bat. Where other men stumble so frequently, he has stood on his legs. No doubt, he has lived with rough people, but still he seems to be a gentleman. Hester will be well off, no doubt, some day.'

'She will have something,—something,' said the old man.

'But this suitor asks for nothing. It is not as though he were coming to you to prop him up in the world. It does not look like that at least. Of course, we ought to make inquiry as to his means.'

'The mortgage has been paid off.'

'So much we know, and the rest may be found out. I do not mean at all to say that he should be allowed to have his own way. I think too much of my sister for that. But, in this matter, we ought to regard simply her happiness and her welfare;—and in considering that you ought to be prepared for her coming marriage. You may take it for granted that she will choose to give herself, sooner or later, to some man. Give a girl good looks, and good sense, and good health, and she is sure to wish to be some man's wife,—unless she be deterred by some conventual superstition.'

If there were any words capable of conveying horror to the mind of the old banker, they were convents, priests and, papacy,— of which the lawyer was well aware when speaking thus of his sister. Mrs. Bolton was certainly not addicted to papistical observances, nor was she at all likely to recommend the seclusion of her daughter in a convent. All her religious doctrines were those of the Low Church. But she had a tendency to arrive at similar results by other means. She was so afraid of the world, the flesh, and the devil, that she would fain shut up her child so as to keep her from the reach of all evil. Vowed celibacy was abominable to her, because it was the resource of the Roman Catholics; and because she had been taught to believe that convent-walls were screens for hiding unheard-of-wickedness. But yet, on behalf of her child, she desired seclusion from the world, fancying that so and so only might security be ensured. Superstition was as strong with her as with any self-flagellated nun. Fasting, under that name, she held in abhorrence. But all sensual gratifications were wicked in her sight. She would allow all home indulgences to her daughter, each under some separate plea,—constrained to do so by excessive

136

love; but she did so always in fear and trembling, lest she was giving some foothold to Satan. All of which Robert Bolton understood better even than did his father when he gave the above advice in reference to this lover.

CHAPTER XIX

Men Are So Wicked

A MONTH had passed by since Caldigate's interview with Mrs. Bolton, and nothing had as yet been decided either for him or against him at Chesterton. And the fact that no absolute decision had been made against him may be taken as having been very much in his favour. But of those who doubted, and doubting, had come to no decision, Mrs. Bolton herself was by no means one. She was as firm as ever in her intention that the idea should not even be suggested to her daughter. Nor, up to this time, had our hero's name been even mentioned to Hester Bolton.

About a week after Caldigate's visit to Chesterton, in the early days of August, he wrote to Robert Bolton saying that he was going into Scotland for a month, and that he trusted that during that time his proposition might be considered. On his return he would take the liberty of calling on Mr. Bolton at the bank. In the meantime he hoped that inquiries might be made as to his position in the world, and in order that such inquiries might be effectual he gave a reference to his man of business in London. To this letter Robert Bolton sent no answer; but he went up to London, and did make the inquiries as suggested, and consulted his brother the barrister, and his sister-in-law the barrister's wife. They were both of opinion that John Caldigate was behaving well, and were of opinion also that something should be done to liberate Hester from the thraldom of her mother. 'I knew how it would be when she grew up and became a woman,' said Mrs. William Bolton. 'Nobody will be allowed to see her, and she won't have a chance of settling herself. When we asked her to come up here for a couple of months in the season, Mrs. Bolton sent me word that London is a terrible place for young girls,—though, of course, she knew that our own girls were being brought up here.' Then the ways of Mrs. Bolton at Chesterton and Hester's future life generally were discussed in a spirit that was by no means unfriendly to our hero.

The suggested inquiries were made in the city, and were all favourable. Everyone connected with the mining interests of the Australian colonies knew the name of John Caldigate. All of that class of people were well aware of his prosperity and confirmed good-fortune. He had brought with him or sent home nobody quite knew how much money. But it was very well known that he had left his interest in the Polyeuka mine to be sold for £60,000, and now there had come word that a company had created itself for the sake of making the purchase, and that the money would be forthcoming. The gentleman in the city connected with mining matters did not think that Mr. Caldigate would be called upon to go out to the colony again, unless he chose to do so for his own pleasure. All this Robert Bolton learned in the City, and he learned also that the man as to whom he was making inquiry was held in high esteem for honesty, perseverance, and capacity. The result of all this was that he returned to Cambridge with a feeling that his sister ought to be allowed to make the man's acquaintance. He and his brother had agreed that something should be done to liberate their sister from her present condition. Love on the part of a mother may be as injurious as cruelty, if the mother be both tyrannical and superstitious. While Hester had been a child, no interference had been possible or perhaps expedient,— but the time had now come when something ought to be done. Such having been the decision in Harley Street, where the William Boltons lived, Robert Bolton went back home with the intention of carrying it out.

This could only be done through the old man, and even with him not without great care. He was devotedly attached to his young wife;— but was very averse to having it thought that he was ruled by her. Indeed, in all matters affecting his establishment, his means, and his business, he would hardly admit of interference from her at all. His worldly matters he kept between himself and his sons. But in regard to his soul he could not restrain her, and sometimes would hardly oppose her. The prolonged evening prayers, the sermons twice a-week, the two long church services on Sundays,—indulgence as to the third being allowed to him only on the score of his age,—he endured at her command. And in regard to Hester, he had hitherto been ruled by his wife, thinking it proper that a daughter should be left in the hands of her mother. But now, when he was told that if he did not interfere, his girl would be constrained by the harsh bonds of an unnatural life, stern as he was himself and inclined to be gloomy, little as he was disposed to admit ideas of recreation and delight, he did acknowledge that something should be done to relieve her. 'But when I die she must be left in her mother's hands,' said the old banker.

'It is to be hoped that she may' be in other hands before that,' replied his son. 'I do not mean to say anything against my stepmother;— but for a young woman it is generally best that she should be married. And in Hester's peculiar position, she ought to have the chance of choosing for herself.'

In this way something almost like a conspiracy was made on behalf of Caldigate. And yet the old man did not as yet abandon his prejudices against the miner. A man who had at so early an age done so much to ruin himself, and had then sprung so suddenly from ruin to prosperity, could not, he thought, be regarded as a steady well-to-do man of business. He did agree that, as regarded Hester, the prison-bars should be removed; but he did not think that she should be invited to walk forth with Mr. John Caldigate. Robert declared that his sister was quite able to form an opinion of her own, and boldly suggested that Hester should be allowed to come and dine at his house. 'To meet the man?' asked the banker in dismay. 'Yes,' said Robert. 'He isn't an ogre. You needn't be afraid of him. I shall be there,—and Margaret. Bring her yourself if you are afraid of anything. No plant ever becomes strong by being kept always away from the winds of heaven.' To this he could not assent at the time. He knew that it was impossible to assent without consulting his wife. But he was brought so far round as to think that if nothing but his own consent were wanting, his girl would be allowed to go and meet the ogre.

'I suppose we ought to wish that Hester should be married some day,' he said to his wife about this time. She shuddered and dashed her hands together as though deprecating some evil,—some event which she could hardly hope to avoid but which was certainly an evil. 'Do you not wish that yourself?' She shook her head. 'Is it not the safest condition in which a woman can live?'

'How shall any one be safe among the dangers of this world, Nicholas?' She habitually called her husband by his Christian name, but she was the only living being who did so.

'More safe then?' said he. 'It is the natural condition of a woman.'

'I do not know. Sin is natural.'

'Very likely. No doubt. But marriage is not sinful.'

'Men are so wicked.'

'Some of them are.'

'Where is there one that is not steeped in sin over his head?'

'That applies to women also; doesn't it?' said the banker petulantly. He was almost angry because she was introducing a commonplace as to the world's condition into a particular argument as to their daughter's future life,—which he felt to be unfair and illogical.

'Of course it does, Nicholas. We are all black and grimed with sin, men and women too; and perhaps something more may be forgiven to men because they have to go out into the world and do their work. But neither one nor the other can be anything but foul with sin;—except,—except——'

140

He was quite accustomed to the religious truth which was coming, and, in an ordinary way, did not object to the doctrine which she was apt to preach to him often. But it had no reference whatever to the matter now under discussion. The general condition of things produced by the fall of Adam could not be used as an argument against matrimony generally. Wicked as men and women are it is so evidently intended that they should marry and multiply, that even she would not deny the general propriety of such an arrangement. Therefore when he was talking to her about their daughter, she was ill-treating him when on that occasion she flew away to her much-accustomed discourse.

'What's the use, then, of saying that men are wicked?'

'They are. They are!'

'Not a doubt about it. And so are the women. But they've got to have husbands and wives. They wouldn't be any the better if there were no marrying. We have to suppose that Hester will do the same as other girls.'

'I hope not, Nicholas.'

'But why not?'

'They are vain, and they adorn themselves, not in modest apparel, as St. Paul says in First Timothy, chapter second, nor with shame-facedness and sobriety; but with braided hair and gold and pearls and costly array.'

'What has that to do with it?'

'Oh, Nicholas!'

'She might be married without all those things.'

'You said you wanted her to be like other girls.'

'No, I didn't. I said she would have to get married like other girls. You don't want to make a nun of her.'

'A nun! I would sooner sit by her bedside and watch her die! My Hester a nun!'

'Very well, then. Let her go out into the world——'

'The world, Nicholas! The world, the flesh, and the devil! Do they not always go together?'

He was much harassed and very angry. He knew how unreasonable she was, and yet he did not know how to answer her. And she was dishonest with him. Because she felt herself unable to advocate in plain terms a thorough shutting up of her daughter,—a protecting of her from the temptation of sin by absolute and prolonged sequestra-tion,—therefore she equivocated with him, pretending to think that he was desirous of sending his girl out to have her hair braided and herself arrayed in gold and pearls. It was thoroughly dishonest, and he under-stood the dishonesty. 'She must go somewhere,' he said, rising from his chair and closing the conversation. At this time a month had passed since Caldigate had been at Chesterton, and he had now returned from Scotland to Folking.

On the following day Hester was taken out to dinner at The Nurseries, as Robert Bolton's house was called,—was taken out by her father. This was quite a new experiment, as she had never dined with any of her aunts and cousins except at an early dinner almost as a child,—and even as a child not at her brother Robert's. But the banker, after having declared that she must go somewhere, had persisted. It is not to be supposed that Caldigate was on this occasion invited to meet her;—nor that the father had as yet agreed that any such meeting should be allowed. But as William Bolton,—the London brother,—and Mrs. William, and one of their girls were down at Cambridge, it was arranged that Hester should meet her relatives. Even so much as this was not settled without much opposition on the part of Hester's mother.

There was nobody at the house but members of the family. The old banker's oldest son Nicholas was not there as his wife and Mrs. Robert Bolton did not get on well together. Mrs. Nicholas was almost as strict as Mrs. Bolton herself, and, having no children of her own, would not have sympathised at all in any desire to procure for Hester the wicked luxury of a lover. The second son Daniel joined the party with his wife, but he had married too late to have grown-up children. His wife was strict too,—but of a medium strictness. Teas, concerts, and occasional dinner parties were with her permissible;—as were also ribbons and a certain amount of costly array. Mrs. Nicholas was in the habit of telling Mrs. Daniel that you cannot touch pitch and not be defiled,—generally intending to imply that Mrs. Robert was the pitch; and would harp on the impossibility of serving both God and mammon, thinking perhaps that her brother-in-law Robert and mammon were one and the same. But Daniel, who could go to church as often as any man on Sundays, and had thoroughly acquired for himself the reputation of a religious man of business, had his own ideas as to proprieties and expediencies, and would neither quarrel with his brother Robert, or allow his wife to quarrel with Mrs. Robert. So that the Nicholases lived very much alone. Mrs. Nicholas and Mrs. Bolton might have suited each other, might have been congenial and a comfort each to the other, but the elder son and the elder son's wife had endeavoured to prevent the old man's second marriage, and there had never been a thorough reconciliation since. There are people who can never forgive. Mrs. Nicholas had never forgiven the young girl for marrying the old man, and the young girl had never forgiven the opposition of her elder

142

step-daughter-in-law to her own marriage. Hence it had come to pass
that the Nicholases were extruded from the family conclaves, which
generally consisted of the Daniels and the Roberts. The Williams were
away in London, not often having much to do with these matters.
But they too allied themselves with the dominant party, it being quite
understood that as long as the old man lived Robert was and would be
the most potent member of the family.

When the father and the three sons were in the dining-room together,
after the six or seven ladies had left them, the propriety of allowing
John Caldigate to make Hester's acquaintance was fully discussed. 'I
would not for the world interfere,' said Robert, 'if I did not think it
unfair to the dear girl that she should be shut up there altogether.'

'Do you suppose that the young man is in earnest?' asked Daniel.

As to this they all agreed that there could be no doubt. He was,
too, an old family friend, well-to-do in the world, able to make proper
settlements, and not at all greedy as to a fortune with his wife. Even
Daniel Bolton thought that the young man should have a chance,—by
saying which he was supposed to declare that the question ought to be
left to the arbitrament of the young lady. The old banker was unhappy
and ill at ease. He could not reconcile himself at once to so great a
change. Though he felt that the excessive fears of his wife, if indulged,
would be prejudicial to their girl, still he did not wish to thrust her out
into the world all at once. Could there not be some middle course?
Could there not be a day named, some four years hence, at which she
might be allowed to begin to judge for herself? But his three sons were
against him, and he could not resist their joint influence. It was therefore absolutely decided that steps should be taken for enabling John
Caldigate to meet Hester at Robert Bolton's house.

'I suppose it will end in a marriage,' William Bolton said to his
brother Robert when they were alone.

'Of course it will. She is the dearest creature in the world;—so good
to her mother; but no fool, and quite aware that the kind of restraint
to which she has been subjected is an injustice. Of course she will be
gratified when a man like that tells her that he loves her. He is a good-
looking fellow, with a fine spirit and plenty of means. How on earth
can she do better?'

'But Mrs. B.?' said William, who would sometimes thus disrespect-
fully allude to his stepmother.

'Mrs. B. will do all she can to prevent it,' said Robert; 'but I think
we shall find that Hester has a will of her own.'

On the following day John Caldigate called at the bank, where the
banker had a small wainscoted back-parlour appropriated to himself.

He had already promised that he would see the young man, and Caldigate was shown into the little room. He soon told his story, and was soon clever enough to perceive that the telling of his story was at any rate permitted. The old father did not receive him with astonishment and displeasure combined, as the young mother had done. Of course he made difficulties, and spoke of the thing as being beyond the bounds of probability. But objection no stronger than that may be taken as amounting almost to encouragement in such circumstances. And he paid evident attention to all that Caldigate said about his own pecuniary affairs,—going so far as to say that he was not in a condition to declare whether he would give his daughter any fortune at all on her marriage.

'It is quite unnecessary.' said Caldigate.

'She will probably have something at my death,' rejoined the old man.

'And when may I see her?' asked Caldigate.

In answer to that Mr. Bolton would not at first make any suggestion whatsoever,—falling back upon his old fears, and declaring that there could be no such meetings at all, but at last allowing that the lover should discuss the matter with his son Robert.

'Perhaps I may have been mistaken about the young man Caldigate,' the banker said to his wife that night.

'Oh, Nicholas!'

'I only say that perhaps I may have been mistaken.'

'You are not thinking of Hester?'

'I said nothing about Hester then;—but perhaps I may have been mistaken in my opinion about that young man John Caldigate.'

John Caldigate, as he rode home after his interview at the bank, almost felt that he had cleared away many difficulties, and that, by his perseverance, he might probably be enabled to carry out the dream of his earlier youth.

CHAPTER XX

Hester's Courage

AFTER that Caldigate did not allow the grass to grow under his feet, and before the end of November the two young people were engaged. As Robert Bolton had said, Hester was of course flattered and of course delighted with this new joy. John Caldigate was just the man to recommend himself to such a girl, not too light, not too prone to pleasure, not contenting himself with bicycles, cricket matches, or billiards, and yet not wholly given to serious matters as had been those among whom she had hitherto passed her days. And he was one who could speak of his love with soft winning words, neither roughly nor yet with too much of shamefaced diffidence. And when he told her how he had sworn to himself after seeing her that once,—that once when all before him in life was enveloped in doubt and difficulty,— that he would come home and make her his wife, she thought that the manly constancy of his heart was almost divine. Of course she loved him with all her heart. He was in all respects one made to be loved by a woman;—and then what else had she ever had to love? When once it was arranged that he should be allowed to speak to her, the thing was done. She did not at once tell him that it was done. She took some few short halcyon weeks to dally with the vow which her heart was ready to make; but those around her knew that the vow had been in- wardly made; and those who were anxious on her behalf with a new anxiety, with a new responsibility, redoubled their inquiries as to John Caldigate. How would Robert Bolton or Mrs. Robert excuse themselves to that frightened miserable mother if at last it should turn out that John Caldigate was not such as they had represented him to be?

But no one could pick a hole in him although many attempts to pick holes were made. The question of his money was put quite at rest by the transference of all his securities, balances, and documents to the Boltons' bank, and the £60,000 for Polyeuka was accepted, so that there was no longer any need that he should go again to the colony. This was sweet news to Hester when she first heard it;—for it had come to pass that it had been agreed that the marriage should be postponed till his return, that having been the one concession made to Mrs. Bolton. There had been many arguments about it;—but Hester at last told him that she had promised so much to her mother and that she would of course keep her promise. Then the arrangement took

145

such a form that the journey was not necessary,—or perhaps the objection to the journey became so strong in Caldigate's mind that he determined to dispense with it at any price. And thus, very greatly to the dismay of Mrs. Bolton, suddenly there came to be no reason why they should not be married almost at once.

But there was an attempt made at the picking of holes,—or rather many attempts. It would be unfair to say that this was carried on by Mrs. Bolton herself;—but she was always ready to listen to what evil things were said to her. Mrs. Nicholas, in her horror at the general wickedness of the Caldigates almost reconciled herself to her step-mother, and even Mrs. Daniel began to fear that a rash thing was being done. In the first place there was the old story of Davis and Newmarket. Robert Bolton, who had necessarily become the advocate and defender of our hero generally, did not care much for Davis and Newmarket. All young men sow their wild oats. Of course he had been extravagant. Since his extravagance he had shown himself to be an industrious, sensible, steady member of society;—and there was the money that he had earned! What young man had earned more in a shorter time, or had ever been more prudent in keeping it? Davis and Newmarket were easily answered by a reference to the bank account. Did he ever go to Newmarket now, though he was living so close to it? On that matter Robert Bolton was very strong.

But Mrs. Nicholas had found out that Caldigate had spent certainly two Sundays running at Folking without going to church at all; and, as far as she could learn, he was altogether indifferent about public worship. Mrs. Bolton, who could never bring herself to treat him as a son-in-law, but who was still obliged to receive him, taxed him to his face with his paganism. 'Have you no religion, Mr. Caldigate?' He assured her that he had, and fell into a long discussion in which he thoroughly confused her, though he by no means convinced her that he was what he ought to be. But he went with her to church twice on one Sunday, and showed her that he was perfectly familiar with the ways of the place.

But perhaps the loudest complaint came from the side of Babington; and here two sets of enemies joined their forces together who were thoroughly hostile to each other. Mrs. Babington declared loudly that old Bolton had been an errand-boy in his youth, and that his father had been a porter and his mother a washerwoman. This could do no real harm, as Caldigate would not have been deterred by any such rumours, even had they been true; but they tended to show animosity, and enabled Mrs. Nicholas to find out the cause of the Babington opposition. When she learned that John Caldigate had been engaged to his cousin Julia, of course she made the most of it; and so did Mrs. Bolton. And in this way it came to be reported not only that the young man had been engaged to Miss Babington before he went to Australia,—but also that he had renewed his engagement since his return. 'You do not love her, do you?' Hester asked him. Then he told her the whole story, as nearly as he could tell it with some respect for his cousin, laughing the while at his aunt's solicitude, and saying, perhaps, something not quite respectful as to Julia's red cheeks and green hat, all of which certainly had not the effect of hardening Hester's heart against him. 'The poor young lady can't help it if her feet are big,' said Hester, who was quite alive to the grace of a well-made pair of boots, although she had been taught to eschew braided hair and pearls and gold.

Mrs. Babington, however, pushed her remonstrances so far that she boldly declared that the man was engaged to her daughter, and wrote to him more than once declaring that this was so. She wrote, indeed, very often, sometimes abusing him for his perfidy, and then, again, imploring him to return to them, and not to defile the true old English blood of the Caldigates with the suds of a washerwoman and the swept-up refuse of a porter's shovel. She became quite eloquent in her denunciation, but always saying that if he would only come back to Babington all would be forgiven him. But in these days he made no visits to Babington.

Then there came a plaintive little note from Mrs. Shand. Of course they wished him joy if it were true. But could it be true? Men were very fickle, certainly; but this change seemed to have been very, very sudden! And there was a word or two, prettily written in another hand, on a small slip of paper—'Perhaps you had better send back the book'; and Caldigate, as he read it, thought that he could discern the almost-obliterated smudge of a wiped-up tear. He wrote a cheerful letter to Mrs. Shand, in which he told her that though he had not been absolutely engaged to marry Hester Bolton before he started for Australia,—and consequently before he had ever been at Pollington,—yet his mind had been quite made up to do so; and that therefore he regarded himself as being abnormally constant rather than fickle. 'And tell your daughter, with my kindest regards,' he added, 'that I hope I may be allowed to keep the book.'

The Babington objections certainly made their way in Cambridge and out at Chesterton further than any others, and for a time did give a hope to Mrs. Bolton and Mrs. Nicholas,—and made Robert Bolton shrug his shoulders uneasily when he heard all the details of the engagement in the linen-closet. But there came at one moment a rumour, which did not count for much among the Boltons, but which disturbed Caldigate himself more than any of the other causes adduced for breaking off his intended marriage. Word came that he had been very intimate with a certain woman on his way out to Melbourne,— a woman supposed to be a foreigner and an actress; and the name of Cettini was whispered. He did not know whence the rumour came;— but on one morning Robert Bolton, half-laughing, but still with a tone of voice that was half-earnest, taxed him with having as many loves as Lothario. 'Who is Cettini?' asked Robert Bolton.

'Cettini?' said Caldigate, with a struggle to prevent a blush.

'Did you travel with such a woman?'

'Yes;—at least, if that was her name. I did not hear it till afterwards. A very agreeable woman she was.'

'They say that you promised to marry her when on board.'

'Then they lie. But that is a matter of course. There are so many lies going about that I almost feel myself to be famous.'

'You did not see her after the journey?'

'Yes, I did. I saw her act at Sydney; and very well she acted. Have you anything else to ask?' Robert Bolton said that he had nothing else to ask,—and seemed, at the moment, to turn his half-serious mood into one that was altogether jocular. But the mention of the name had been a wound; and when an anonymous letter a few days afterwards reached Hester herself he was really unhappy. Hester made nothing of the letter— did not even show it to her mother. At that time a day had been fixed for their marriage; and she already regarded her lover as nearer to her than either father or mother. The letter purported to be from some one who had travelled with her lover and this woman on board ship, and declared that everybody on board the ship had thought that Caldigate meant to marry the woman,—who then, so said the letter, called herself Mrs. Smith. Hester showed the letter to Caldigate, and then Caldigate told his story. There had been such a woman, who had been much ill-treated because of her poverty. He had certainly taken the woman's part. She had been clever and, as he had thought, well-behaved. And, no doubt, there had been a certain amount of friendship. He had seen her again in Sydney, where he had found her exercising her profession as an actress. That had been all. 'I cannot imagine, dear,' he said, 'that you should be jealous of any woman; but certainly not of such a one as she.' 'Nor can I imagine,' said Hester, stoutly, 'that I could possibly be jealous of any woman.' And then there was nothing more said about the woman Smith-Cettini.

During all this time there were many family meetings. Those between Mr. Caldigate, the father, and old Mr. Bolton were pleasant enough, though not peculiarly cordial. The banker, though he had been brought to agree to the marriage had not been quite reconciled to it. His younger son had been able to convince him that it was his duty to liberate his daughter from the oppression of her mother's over-vigilance, and all the rest had followed very quickly,—overwhelming him, as it were, by stern necessity. When once the girl had come to understand that she could have her own way, if she chose to have a way of her own, she very quickly took the matter into her own manage-ment. And in this way the engagement became a thing settled before the banker had realised the facts of the position. Though he could not be cordial he endeavoured to be gracious to his old friend. But Mrs. Bolton spoke words which made all friendship impossible. She asked old Mr. Caldigate after his soul, and when he replied to her less seriously than she thought becoming, she told him that he was in the bad way. And then she said things about the marriage which implied that she would sooner see her daughter in her grave than married to a man who was no more than a professing Christian. The conversation ended in a quarrel, after which the squire would not go again to Puritan Grange.

There was indeed a time, an entire week, during which the mother and daughter hardly spoke to each other. In these days Mrs. Bolton continually demanded of her husband that he should break off the match, always giving as a reason the alleged fact that John Caldigate was not a true believer. It had been acknowledged between them that if such were the fact the man would be an unfit husband for their daughter. But they differed as to the fact. The son had over and over again declared himself to be a faithful member of the Church of England,—not very scrupulous perhaps in the performance of her cere-monies,—but still a believing member. That his father was not so every one knew, but he was not responsible for his father. Mr. Bolton seemed to think that the argument was good;—but Mrs. Bolton was of opinion that to become willingly the daughter-in-law of an infidel, would be to throw oneself with one's eyes open in the way of perdition. Hester through all this declared that nothing should now turn her from the man she loved, 'Not though he were an infidel himself?' said the terror-stricken mother. 'Nothing!' said Hester, bravely. 'Of course I should try to change him.' A more wretched woman than Mrs. Bolton might not probably then have been found. She suddenly perceived her-self to be quite powerless with the child over whom her dominion had hitherto been supreme. And she felt herself compelled to give way to people whom, with all her heart, she hated. She determined that nothing,—nothing should induce her to soften her feelings to this son-in-law who was forced upon her. The man had come and had stolen from her her treasure, her one treasure. And that other man whom she had always feared and always hated, Robert Bolton, the man whose craft and worldliness had ever prevented her from emancipating her husband from the flesh and the devil, had brought all this about. Then she reconciled herself to her child, and wept over her, and implored heaven to save her. Hester tried to argue with her,—spoke of her own love,—appealed to her mother, asking whether, as she had now declared her love, it could be right that she should abandon a man who was so good and so fondly attached to her. Then Mrs. Bolton would hide her face, and sob, and put up renewed prayers to heaven that her daughter might not by means of this unhappy marriage become lost to all sense of grace.

It was very miserable, but still the prospect of the marriage was never abandoned nor postponed. A day had been settled a little before Christmas, and the Robert Boltons would allow of no postponement. The old man was so tormented by the misery of his own home that he himself was averse to delay. There could be no comfort for him till the thing should have been done. Mrs. Bolton had suggested that it should be put off till the spring;—but he had gloomily replied that as the thing had to be done, the sooner it was done the better.

It had been settled almost from the first that the marriage festival should be held, not at Puritan Grange, but at The Nurseries; and gradually it came to be understood that Mrs. Bolton herself would not be present, either at the church or at the breakfast. It was in vain that Hester implored her mother to yield to her in something, to stand with her at any rate on the steps before the altar. 'Would you wish me to go and lie before my God?' said the unhappy woman. 'When I would give all that I have in the world except my soul,—my life, my name, even my child herself, to prevent this, am I to go and smile and be congratulated, and to look as though I were happy?' There was, therefore, very much unhappiness at the Grange, and an absence of all triumph even at The Nurseries. At the old bank-house in the town where the Nicholases lived, the marriage was openly denounced; and even the Daniels, though they were pledged to be present, were in doubt.

'I suppose it is all right,' said Mrs. Robert to her husband.

'Of course it is all right. Why not?'

'It seems sad that such an event as a marriage should give rise to so much ill-feeling. I almost wish we had not meddled, Robert.'

'I don't think there is anything to regret. Remember what Hester's position would have been if my father had died, leaving her simply to her mother's guardianship! We were bound to free her from that, and we have done it.' This was all very well;—but still there was no triumph, no ringing of those inward marriage bells the sound of whose music ought to be so pleasant to both the families concerned.

There were, however, two persons quite firm to their purpose, and these were the bride and bridegroom. With him firmness was comparatively easy. When his father suggested that the whole Bolton family was making itself disagreeable, he could with much satisfaction reply that he did not intend to marry the whole Bolton family. Having answered the first letter or two he could ignore the Babington remonstrances. And when he was cross-examined as to points of doctrine, he could with sincerity profess himself to be of the same creed with his examiners. If he went to church less often than old Mr. Bolton, so did old Mr. Bolton go less often than his wife. It was a matter as to which there was no rule. Thus his troubles were comparatively light, and his firmness might be regarded as a thing of course. But she was firm too, and firm amidst very different circumstances. Though her mother prayed and sobbed, implored her, and almost cursed her, still she was firm. She had given her word to the man, and her heart, and she would not go back. 'Yes, papa. It is too late now,' she said, when her father coming from his wife, once suggested to her that even yet it was not too late. 'Of course I shall marry him,' she said to Mrs. Robert, almost with indignation, when Mrs. Robert on one occasion almost broke down in her purpose.

'Dear aunt, indeed, indeed, you need not interfere,' she said to Mrs. Nicholas. 'If he were all that they have called him, still I would marry him,' she said to her other aunt,—'because I love him.' And so they all became astonished at the young girl whom they had reared up among them, and to understand that whatever might now be their opinions, she would have her way.

And so it was decided that they should be married on a certain Tuesday in the middle of December. Early in the morning she was to be brought down to her aunt's house, there to be decked in her bridal robes, thence to be taken to the church, then to return for the bridal feast, and from thence to be taken off by her husband,—to go whither they might list.

CHAPTER XXI

The Wedding

IT was a sad wedding, though everything within the power of Mr. Robert Bolton was done to make it gay. There was a great breakfast, and all the Boltons were at last persuaded to be present except Mrs. Bolton and Mrs. Nicholas. As to Mrs. Nicholas she was hardly even asked. 'Of course we would be delighted to see Mrs. Nicholas, if she would come,' Mrs. Robert said to Nicholas himself. But there had been such long-continued and absolute hostility between the ladies that this was known to be impossible. In regard to Mrs. Bolton herself, great efforts were made. Her husband condescended to beg her to consent on this one occasion to appear among the Philistines. But as the time came nearer she became more and more firm in her resolution. 'You shall not touch pitch and not be defiled,' she said. 'You cannot serve God and Mammon.' When the old man tried to show her that there was no question of Mammon here, she evaded him, as she always did on such occasions, either by a real or simulated deficiency of consequent intelligence. She regarded John Caldigate as being altogether unregenerate, and therefore a man of the world,—and therefore a disciple of Mammon. She asked him whether he wanted her to do what she thought to be sinful. 'It is very sinful hating people as you hate my sons' families,' he said in his wrath. 'No, Nicholas, I do not hate their families. I certainly do not hate Margaret, nor yet Fanny;—but I think that they live in opposition to the Gospel. Am I to belie my own belief?' Now the old man was quite certain that his wife did hate both Robert's wife and William's and would not admit in her own mind this distinction between the conduct of persons and the persons themselves. But he altogether failed in his attempts to induce her to go to the breakfast.

The great contest was between the mother and the daughter; but in all that passed between them no reference was even made to the banquet. As to that Hester was indifferent. She thought, on the whole, that her mother would do best to be absent. After all, what is a breakfast;—or what the significance of any merry-meeting, even for a wedding? There would no doubt be much said and much done on such an occasion at variance with her mother's feelings. Even the enforced gaiety of the dresses would be distasteful to her, and there would hardly be sufficient cause for pressing her to be present on such an occasion. But in reference to the church, the question, to Hester's thinking, was very different, 'Mamma,' she said, 'if you are not there, it will be a lasting misery to me.'

'How can I go there when I would give so much to save you from going there yourself?' This was a terrible thing for a mother to say to her own child on the eve of her wedding, but it had been now said so often as to have lost something of its sting. It had come to be understood that Mrs. Bolton would not allow herself to give any assent to the marriage, but that the marriage was to go on without such assent. All that had been settled. But still she might go to the church with them and pray for good results. She feared that evil would come, but still she might wish for good,—wish for it and pray for it.

'You don't want me to be unhappy, mamma?'

'Want!' said the mother. 'Who can want her child to be unhappy? But there is an unhappiness harder to be borne, more to be dreaded, enduring so much longer than that which we may suffer here.'

'Will you not come and pray that I may be delivered also from that? As I am going from you, will you not let me know that you are there with me at the last moment. Though you do not love him, you do not wish to quarrel with me. Oh, mamma, let me feel at any rate that you are there.' Then the mother promised that she would be there, in the church, though unknown to or at least unrecognised by any one else. When the morning came, and when Hester was dropped at The Nurseries, in order that she might go up and be invested in her finery amidst her bridesmaids, who were all her cousins, the carriage went on and took Mrs. Bolton to the church. It was represented to her that, by this arrangement, she would be forced to remain an hour alone in the cold building. But she was one of those who regarded all discomfort as meritorious, as in some way adding something to her claim for heaven. Self-scourging with rods as a penance, was to her thinking a papistical ordinance most abominable and damnatory; but the essence of the self-scourging was as comfortable to her as ever was a hairshirt to a Roman Catholic enthusiast. So she went and sat apart in a dark distant pew, dressed in black and deeply veiled, praying, not it is to be feared, that John Caldigate might be a good husband to her girl, but that he, as he made his way downward to things below, might not drag her darling with him. That only a few can be saved was the fact in all her religion with which she was most thoroughly conversant. The strait way and the narrow gate, through which only a few can pass! Were they not known to all believers, to all who had a glimmering of belief, as an established part of the Christian faith, as a part so established that to dream even that the gate would be made broad and the way open would be to dream against the Gospel, against the very plainest of God's words? If so,—and she would tell herself at all hours that certainly, certainly, certainly so it was,—then why should she trouble herself for one so little likely to come in the way of salvation as this man who was now robbing her of her daughter? If it was the will of the Almighty,—as it clearly was the will of the Almighty,—that, out of every hundred, ninety and nine should perish, could she dare now to pray more than for one? Or if her prayers were wider must they not be inefficacious? Yes;—there had been the thief upon the cross! It was all possible. But this man was a thief, not upon the cross. And, therefore, as she prayed that morning, she said not a prayer for him.

In the meantime the carriage had gone back for the bride, who in very simple raiment, but yet in bridal-white array, was taken up to the church. These Boltons were prosperous people, who had all their carriages, so that there was no lack of vehicles. Two of the girls from London and two from The Nurseries made up the bevy of bridesmaids, who were as bright and fair as though the bride had come from some worldlier stock. Mrs. Robert, indeed, had done all she could to give to the whole concern a becoming bridal brightness, till even Mrs. Daniel had been tempted to remonstrate. 'I don't see why you shouldn't wear pretty things if you've got the money to pay for them,' said Mrs. Robert. Mrs. Daniel shook her head, but on the afternoon before the wedding she bought an additional ribbon.

Caldigate came over from Folking that morning attended by one John Jones, an old college friend, as his best man. The squire was not at the wedding, but on the day before he was with Hester at The Nurseries, telling her that she should be his dear daughter, and at the same time giving her a whole set of wicked but very pretty worldly gauds. 'Upon my word, my dear, he has been very gracious,' said Mrs. Robert, when she saw them. 'I quite envy the girls being married nowadays, because they get such pretty things.'

'They are very pretty,' said Hester.

'And must have cost, I'm afraid to say how much money.'

'I suppose it means to say that he will love me, and therefore I am glad to have them!' But the squire, though he did mean to say that he would love her, did not come to the wedding. He was, he said, unaccustomed to such things, and hoped that he might be excused.

Therefore, from the Folking side there was no one but John Caldigate himself and John Jones. Of the Babingtons, of course, there was not one. As long as there was a possibility of success Mrs. Babington had kept up her remonstrances;—but when there was no longer a possibility she announced that there was to be an everlasting quarrel between the houses. Babington and Folking were for the future to know nothing of each other. Caldigate had hoped that though the ladies would for a time be unforgiving, his uncle and his male cousins would not take up the quarrel. But aunt Polly was too strong for that; and he was declared to be a viper who had been warmed in all their bosoms and had then stung them all round. 'If you will look into your dictionary of natural history you will see that vipers have no stings. Yours truly, D. Caldigate.' This letter was supposed to add much to the already existing offence.

But the marriage ceremony was performed in spite of all this quarrelling, and the mother standing up in the dark corner of her pew heard her daughter's silver-clear voice as she vowed to devote herself to her husband. As she heard it, she also devoted herself. When sorrow should come as sorrow certainly would come, then she would be ready once again to be a mother to her child. But till that time should come the wife of John Caldigate would be nothing to her.

She was not content with thinking and resolving that it should be so, but she declared her intention in so many words to her daughter. For poor Hester, though she was proud of her husband, this was in truth a miserable day. Could she have been induced to separate herself altogether from her mother on the previous night, or even on that morning, it would have been better, but there was with her that customary longing for a last word of farewell which has often made so many of us wretched. And then there was a feeling that, as she was giving herself away in marriage altogether in opposition to her mother's counsels, on that very account she owed to her more attacned and increased observance. Therefore, she had arranged with her husband that when she returned from the banquet to prepare herself for her journey, a longer absence than usual should be allowed to her;—so that she might be taken back to Chesterton, and might thus see her mother the last after saying farewell to all the others. Then the carriage should return to The Nurseries and he would be ready to step in, and she need not show herself again, worn out as she would be with the tears and sobbings which she anticipated.

It all went as it was arranged, but it would have been much better to arrange it otherwise. The journey to the Grange and back, together with the time spent in the interview, took an hour,—and the time went very slowly with the marriage guests. There always comes a period beyond which it is impossible to be festive. When the bride left the room, the bridesmaids and other ladies went with her. Then the gentlemen who remained hardly knew what to do with each other.

155

Old Mr. Bolton was not jovial on the occasion, and the four brothers hardly knew how to find subjects for conversation on such an occasion. The bridegroom felt the hour to be very long, although he consented to play billiards with the boys; and John Jones, although he did at last escape and find his way up among the girls, thought that his friend had married himself into a very sombre family. But all this was pleasant pastime indeed compared with that which poor Hester endured in her mother's bedroom. 'So it has been done,' said Mrs. Bolton, sitting in a comfortless little chair, which she was accustomed to use when secluded, with her Bible, from all the household. She spoke in a voice that might have been fit had a son of hers been just executed on the gallows.

'Oh, mamma, do not speak of it like that!'

'My darling, my own one; would you have me pretend what I do not feel?' 'Why, yes. Even that would be better than treatment such as this.' That would have been Hester's reply could she have spoken her mind; but she could not speak it, and therefore she stood silent. 'I will not pretend. You and your father have done this thing against my wishes and against my advice.'

'It is I that have done it, mamma.'

'You would not have persevered had he been firm,—as firm as I have been. But he has vacillated, turning hither and thither, serving God and Mammon. And he has allowed himself to be ruled by his own son. I will never, never speak to Robert Bolton again.'

'Oh mamma, do not say that.'

'I do say it. I swear it. You shall not touch pitch and not be defiled. If there be pitch on earth he is pitch. If your eye offend you, pluck it out. He is my stepson, I know; but I will pluck him out like an eye that has offended. It is he that has robbed me of my child.'

'Am I not still your child?' said Hester, going down on her knees with her hands in her mother's lap and her eyes turned up to her mother's face.

'No. You are not mine any longer. You are his. You are that man's wife. When he bids you do that which is evil in the sight of the Lord, you must do it. And he will bid you. You are not my child now. As days run on and sins grow black I cannot warn you now against the wrath to come. But though you are not my child, though you are this man's wife, I will pray for you.'

'And for him?'

'I do not know. I cannot say. Who am I that I should venture to pray specially for a stranger? That His way may be shown to all sinners;—thus will I pray for him. And it will be shown. Though whether he will walk in it,—who can say that?' So much was true of John

Caldigate, no doubt, and is true of all; but there was a tone in her voice which implied that in regard to this special sinner there could be very little hope indeed.

'Why should you think that he is bad, mamma?'

'We are all bad. There is no doubt about his being bad. There is not one among us fit to sweep the lowest step of God's throne. But they who are His people shall be made bright enough to sit round His feet. May the time come when you, my darling, shall be restored to the fold.' The poor young wife by this time had acknowledged to herself the mistake she had made in thus coming to her mother after her marriage. She now was of course in that ecstatic phase of existence which makes one's own self altogether subordinate to the self of another person. That her husband should be happy constituted her hope of happiness; that he should be comfortable, her comfort. If he were thought worthy, that would be her worthiness; or if he were good, that would be her goodness. And even as to those higher, more distant aspirations, amidst which her mother was always dwelling, she would take no joy for herself which did not include him. The denunciations against him which were so plainly included even in her mother's blessings and prayers for herself, did not frighten her on behalf of the man to whom she had devoted herself. She could see the fanaticism and fury of her mother's creed. But she could not escape from the curse of the moment. When that last imprecation was made by the woman, with her hands folded and her eyes turned up to heaven, Hester could only bury her face on her mother's knees and weep. 'When that time comes, and I know it will come, you shall return to me, and once more be my child,' said the mother.

'You do not mean that I shall leave my husband?'

'Who can tell? If you do, and I am living, you shall be my child. Till then we must be apart. How can it be otherwise? Can I give my cheek to a man to be kissed, and call him my son, when I think that he has robbed me of my only treasure?'

This was so terrible that the daughter could only hang around her mother's neck, sobbing and kissing her at the same time, and then go without another word. She was sure of this,—that if she must lose one or the other, her mother or her husband, then she would lose her mother. When she returned to The Nurseries, her husband, according to agreement, came out to her at once. She had bidden adieu to all the others; but at the last moment her father put his hand into the carriage, so that she could take it and kiss it. 'Mamma is so sad,' she said to him; 'go home and comfort her.' Of course the old man did go home, but he was aware that there would for some time be little

157

comfort there either for him or for his wife. He and his sons had been too powerful for her in arranging the marriage; but now, now that it was done, nothing could stop her reproaches. He had been made to think it wrong on one side to shut his girl up, and now from the other side he was being made to think that he had done very wrong in allowing her to escape.

It had been arranged that they should be driven out of Cambridge to the railway station at Audley End on their way to London; so that they might avoid the crowd of people who would know them at the Cambridge station. As soon as they had got away from the door of Robert Bolton's house, the husband attempted to comfort his young wife. 'At any rate it is over,' he said, alluding of course to the tedium of their wedding festivities.

'So much is over,' she replied.

'You do not regret anything?'

She shook her head slowly as she leaned lovingly against his shoulder. 'You are not sorry, Hester, that you have become my wife?'

'I had to be your wife,—because I love you.'

'Is that a sorrow?'

'I had been all my mother's;—and now I am all yours. She has thrown me off because I have disobeyed her. I hope you will never throw me off.'

'Is it likely?'

'I think not. I know that I shall never throw you off. They have tried to make me believe that you are not all that you ought to be—in religion. But now your religion shall be my religion, and your life my life. I shall be of your colour—altogether. But, John, a limb cannot be wrenched out of a socket, as I have been torn away from my mother, without pain.'

'She will forgive it all when we come back.'

'I fear—I fear. I never knew her to forgive anything yet.' This was very bad; but nevertheless it was plain to him as it had been plain to Robert and William Bolton, that not because of the violence of the woman's character should the life of her daughter have been sacrificed to her. His duty to make her new life bright for her was all the more plain and all the more sound,—and as they made their first journey together he explained to her how sacred that duty should always be to him.

CHAPTER XXII

As To Touching Pitch

BEFORE the wedding old Mr. Caldigate arranged with his son that he would give up to the young married people the house at Folking, and indeed the entire management of the property. 'I have made up my mind about it,' said the squire, who at this time was living with his son on happy terms. 'I have never been adapted for the life of a country gentleman,' he continued, 'though I have endeavoured to make the best of it, and have in a certain way come to love the old place. But I don't care about wheat nor yet about bullocks;—and a country house should always have a mistress.' And so it was settled. Mr. Caldigate took for himself a house in Cambridge, whither he proposed to remove nothing but himself and his books, and promised to have Folking ready for his son and his son's bride on their return from their wedding tour. In all this Robert Bolton and the old squire acted together, the brother thinking that the position would suit his sister well. But others among the Boltons,—Mrs. Daniel, the London people, and even Mrs. Robert herself,—had thought that the 'young people' had better be further away from the influences or annoyances of Puritan Grange. Robert, however, had declared that it would be absurd to yield to the temper, and prejudice, and fury—as he called it—of his father's wife. When this discussion was going on she had absolutely quarrelled with the attorney, and the attorney had made up his mind that she should be—ignored. And then, too, as Robert explained, it must be for the husband and not for the wife to choose where they would live. Folking was, or at any rate would be, his own, by right of inheritance, and it was not to be thought of that a man should be driven away from his natural duties and from the enjoyment of his natural privileges by the mad humours of a fanatic female. In all this old Mr. Bolton was hardly consulted; but there was no reason why he should express an opinion. He was giving his daughter absolutely no fortune; nor had he even vouchsafed to declare what money should be coming to her at his death. John Caldigate had positively refused to say a word on the subject;—had refused even when instigated to do so by Hester's brother; 'It shall be just as he pleases,' Caldigate had said. 'I told your father that I was not looking after his daughter with any view to money, and I will be as good as my word.' Robert had told her father that something should be arranged;—but the old man had put it off from day to day, and nothing had been arranged. And so it came to pass that he was excluded almost from having an opinion as to his daughter's future life.

It was understood that the marriage trip should be continued for some months. Caldigate was fettered by no business that required an early return. He had worked hard for five years, and felt that he had earned a holiday. And Hester naturally was well disposed to be absent for as long a time as would suit her husband. Time, and time alone, might perhaps soften her mother's heart. They went to Italy, and stayed during the winter months in Rome, and then, when the fine weather came, they returned across the Alps, and lingered about among the playgrounds of Europe, visiting Switzerland, the Tyrol, and the Pyrenees, and returning home to Cambridgeshire at the close of the following September.

And then there was a reason for the return. It would be well that the coming heir to the Folking estate should be born at Folking. Whether an heir, or only an insignificant girl, it would be well that the child should be born amidst the comforts of home; and so they came back. When they reached the station at Cambridge the squire was there to receive them, as were also Robert Bolton and his wife. 'I am already in my new house,' said the old man,—'but I mean to go out with you for to-day and to-morrow, and just stay till you are comfortably fixed.'

'I never see her myself,' said Robert, in answer to a whispered inquiry from his sister. 'Or it would be more correct to say she will never see me. But I hear from the others that she speaks of you constantly.'

'She has written to me of course. But she never mentions John. In writing back I have always sent his love, and have endeavoured to show that I would not recognise any quarrel.'

'If I were you,' said Robert, 'I would not take him with me when I went.' Then the three Caldigates were taken off to Folking.

A week passed by and then arrived the day on which it had been arranged that Hester was to go to Chesterton and see her mother. There had been numerous letters, and at last the matter was settled between Caldigate and old Mr. Bolton at the bank. 'I think you had better let her come alone,' the old man had said when Caldigate asked whether he might be allowed to accompany his wife. 'Mrs. Bolton has not been well since her daughter's marriage, and has felt the desolation of her position very much. She is weak and nervous, and I think you had better let Hester come alone.' Had Caldigate known his mother-in-law better he would not have suggested a visit from himself. No one who did know her would have looked forward to see her old hatred eradicated by an absence of nine months. Hester therefore went into Cambridge alone, and was taken up to the house by her father. As she entered the iron gates she felt almost as though she were going into the presence of one who was an enemy to herself. And yet when she saw her mother, she rushed at once into the poor woman's arms. 'Oh, mamma, dear mamma, dearest mamma! My own, own, own mamma!'

Mrs. Bolton was sitting by the open window of a small breakfast parlour which looked into the garden, and had before her on her little table her knitting and a volume of sermons. 'So you have come back, Hester,' she said after a short pause. She had risen at first to receive her daughter, and had returned her child's caresses, but had then reseated herself quickly, as though anxious not to evince any strong feeling on the occasion.

'Yes, mamma, I have come back. We have been so happy!'

'I am glad you have been happy. Such joys are short-lived; but still—'

'He has been so good to me, mamma!'

Good! What was the meaning of the word good? She doubted the goodness of such goodness as his. Do not they who are tempted by the pleasures of the world always praise the good-nature and kindness of them by whom they are tempted? There are meanings to the word good which are so opposed one to another! 'A husband is, I suppose, generally kind to his wife, at any rate for a little time,' she said.

'Oh, mamma, I do so wish you knew him!' The woman turned her face round, away from her daughter, and assumed that look of hard, determined, impregnable obstinacy with which Hester had been well acquainted all her life. But the young wife had come there with a purpose, not strong, perhaps, in actual hope, but resolute even against hope to do her best. There must be an enduring misery to her unless she could bring her mother into some friendly relation with her husband, and she had calculated that the softness produced by her return would give a better chance for this than she might find at any more protracted time. But Mrs. Bolton had also made her calculations and had come to her determination. She turned her head away therefore, and sat quite silent, with the old stubborn look of resolved purpose.

'Mamma, you will let him come to you now?'

'No.'

'Not your own Hester's husband?'

'No.'

'Are we to be divided for ever?'

'Did I not tell you before,—when you were going? Shall I lie, and say that I love him? I will not touch pitch, lest I be defiled.'

'Mamma, he is my husband. You shall not call him pitch. He is my very own. Mamma, mamma!—recall the word that you have said.'

The woman felt that it had to be recalled in some degree. 'I said nothing of him, Hester. I call that pitch which I believe to be wrong, and if I swerve but a hair's-breadth willingly towards what I believe to be evil, then I shall be touching pitch and then I shall be defiled. I did not say that he was pitch. Judge not and ye shall not be judged.' But if ever judgment was pronounced, and a verdict given, and penalties awarded, such was done now in regard to John Caldigate.

'But, mamma, why will it be doing evil to be gracious to your daughter's husband?'

The woman had an answer to this appeal very clearly set forth in her mind though she was unable to produce it clearly in words. When the marriage had been first discussed she had opposed it with all her power, because she had believed the man to be wicked. He was unregenerate;—and when she had put it to her husband and to the Nicholases and to the Daniels to see whether such was not the case, they had not contradicted her. It was acknowledged that he was such a one as Robert,—a worldly man all round. And then he was worse than Robert, having been a spendthrift, a gambler, and, if the rumours which had reached them were true, given to the company of loose women. She had striven with all her might that such a one should not be allowed to take her daughter from her, and had striven in vain. He had succeeded;—but his character was not changed by his success. Did she not know him to be chaff that must be separated by the wind from the corn and then consumed in the fire? His character was not altered because that human being whom she loved the best in all the world had fallen into his power. He was not the less chaff,—the less likely to be burned. That her daughter should become chaff also,—ah, there was the agony of it! If instead of taking the husband and wife together, she could even now separate them,—would it not be her duty to do so? Of all duties would it not be the first? Let the misery here be what it might, what was that to eternal misery or to eternal bliss? When therefore she was asked whether she would be going evil were she to be gracious to her own son-in-law, she was quite, quite sure that any such civility would be a sin. The man was pitch,—though she had been coerced by the exigencies of a worldly courtesy to deny that she had intended to say so. He was pitch to her, and she declared to herself that were she to touch him she would be defiled. But she knew not in what language to explain all this. 'What you call graciousness, Hester, is an obligation of which religion knows nothing,' she said after a pause.

'I don't know why it shouldn't. Are we to be divided, mamma, because of religion?'

'If you were alone——'

'But I am not alone. Oh, mamma, mamma, do you not know that I am going to become a mother?'

'My child!'

'And you will not be with me, because you think that you and John differ as to religious forms.'

'Forms!' she said. 'Forms! Is the spirit there? By their fruits ye shall know them. I ask you yourself whether his life as you have seen it is such as I should think comformable with the Word of God?'

'Whose life is so?'

'But an effort may be made. Do not let us palter with each other, Hester! There are the sheep,—and there are the goats! Of which is he? According to the teaching of your early years, in which flock would he be found if account were taken now?'

There was something so terrible in this that the young wife who was thus called upon to denounce her husband separated herself by some steps from her mother, retreating back to a chair in which she seated herself. 'Do you remember, mamma, the words you said just now? Judge not and ye shall not be judged.'

'Nor do I judge.'

'And how does it go on? Forgive and ye shall be forgiven.'

'Neither do I judge, nor can I forgive.' This she said, putting all·her emphasis on the pronoun, and thereby declaring her own humility. 'But the great truths of my religion are dear to me. I will not trust myself in the way of sinners, because by some worldly alliance to which I myself was no consenting party, I have been brought into worldly contact with them. I at any rate will be firm. I say to you now no more than I said, ah, so many times, when it was still possible that my words should not be vain. They were vain. But not on that account am I to be changed. I will not be wound like a skein of silk round your little finger.' That was it. Was she to give way in everything because they had been successful among them in carrying out this marriage in opposition to her judgment? Was she to assent that this man be treated as a sheep because he had prevailed against her, while she was so well aware that he would still have been a goat to them all had he not prevailed? She at any rate was sincere. She was consistent. She would be true to her principles even at the expense of all her natural yearnings. Of what use to her would be her religious convictions if she were to give them up just because her heartstrings were torn and agonised? The man was a goat though he were ten times told her child's husband. So she looked again away into the garden and resolved that she would not yield in a single point.

'Good-bye, mamma,' said Hester, rising from her chair, and coming up to her mother.

'Good-bye, Hester. God bless you, my child!'

'You will not come to me to Folking?'

'No. I will not go to Folking.'

'I may come to you here?'

'Oh yes;—as often as you will, and for as long as you will.'

'I cannot stay away from home without him, you know,' said the young wife.

'As often as you will, and for as long as you will,' the mother said again, repeating the words with emphasis. 'Would I could have you here as I used to do, so as to look after every want and administer to every wish. My fingers shall work for your baby, and my prayers shall be said for him and for you, morning and night. I am not changed, Hester. I am still and ever shall be, while I am spared, your own loving mother.' So they parted, and Hester was driven back to Folking.

In forming our opinion as to others we are daily brought into difficulty by doubting how much we should allow to their convictions, and how far we are justified in condemning those who do not accede to our own. Mrs. Bolton believed every word that she said. There was no touch of hypocrisy about her. Could she without sting of conscience have gone off to Folking and ate of her son-in-law's bread and drank of his cup, and sat in his presence, no mother living would have enjoyed more thoroughly the delight of waiting upon and caressing and bending over her child. She denied herself all this with an agony of spirit, groaning not only over their earthly separation, thinking not only of her daughter's present dangers, but tormented also by reflections as to dangers and possible separations in another world. But she knew she was right. She knew at least that were she to act otherwise there would be upon her conscience the weight of sin. She did not know that the convictions on which she rested with such confidence had come in truth from her injured pride,—had settled themselves in her mind because she had been beaten in her endeavours to prevent her daughter's marriage. She was not aware that she regarded John Caldigate as a goat,—as one who beyond all doubt was a goat,— simply because John Caldigate had had his way, while she had been debarred from hers. Such no doubt was the case. And yet who can deny her praise for fidelity to her own convictions? When we read of those who have massacred and tortured their opponents in religion, have boiled alive the unfortunates who have differed from themselves as to the meaning of an unintelligible word or two, have vigorously torn the entrails out of those who have been pious with a piety different from their own, how shall we dare to say that they should be punished for their fidelity? Mrs. Bolton spent much of that afternoon with her knees on the hard boards,—thinking that a hassock would have taken something from the sanctity of the action,—wrestling for her child in prayer. And she told herself that her prayer had been heard. She got up more than ever assured that she must not touch pitch lest she should be defiled. Let us pray for what we will with earnestness,—though it be for the destruction of half of a world,—we are sure to think that our prayers have been heard.

CHAPTER XXIII

The New Heir

THINGS went on smoothly at Folking, or with apparent smoothness, for three months, during which John Caldigate surprised both his friends and his enemies by the exemplary manner in which he fulfilled his duties as a parish squire. He was put on the commission, and was in the way to become the most active Justice of the Peace in those parts. He made himself intimate with all the tenants, and was almost worshipped by Mr. Ralph Holt, his nearest neighbour, to whose judgment he submitted himself in all agricultural matters. He shot a little, but moderately, having no inclination to foster what is called a head of game. And he went to church very regularly, having renewed his intimacy with Mr. Bromley, the parson, a gentleman who had unfortunately found it necessary to quarrel with the old squire, because the old squire had been so manifestly a pagan.

There had been unhappiness in the parish on this head, and, especially, unhappiness to Mr. Bromley, who was a good man. That Mr. Caldigate should be what he called a pagan had been represented by Mr. Bromley to his friends as a great misfortune, and especially a misfortune to the squire himself. But he would have ignored that in regard to social life,—so Mr. Bromley said when discussing the matter,— if the pagan would have desisted from arguing the subject. But when Mr. Caldigate insisted on the parson owning the unreasonableness of his own belief, and called upon him to confess himself to be either a fool or a hypocrite, then the parson found himself constrained to drop all further intercourse. 'It is the way with all priests,' said the old squire triumphantly to the first man he could get to hear him. 'The moment you disagree with them they become your enemies at once, and would straightway kill you if they had the power.' He probably did not know how very disagreeable he had made himself to the poor clergyman.

But now matters were on a much better footing, and all the parish rejoiced. The new squire was seen in his pew every Sunday morning, and often entertained the parson at the house. The rumour of this change was indeed so great that more than the truth reached the ears of some of the Boltons, and advantage was taken of it by those who desired to prove to Mrs. Bolton that the man was not a goat. What more would she have? He went regularly to morning and evening service,—here it was that rumour exaggerated our hero's virtues,—did all his duty as a country gentleman, and was kind to his wife. The Daniels, who were but lukewarm people, thought that Mrs. Bolton was bound to give way. Mrs. Robert declared among her friends that the poor woman was becoming mad from religion, and the old banker himself was driven very hard for a reply when Robert asked him whether such a son-in-law as John Caldigate ought to be kept at arms' length. The old man did in truth hate the name of John Caldigate, and regretted bitterly the indiscretion of that day when the spendthrift had been admitted within his gates. Though he had agreed to the marriage, partly from a sense of duty to his child, partly under the influences of his son, he had, since that, been subject to his wife for nine or ten months. She had not been able to prevail against him in action; but no earthly power could stop her tongue. Now when these new praises were dinned into his ears, when he did convince himself that, as far as worldly matters went, his son-in-law was likely to become a prosperous and respected gentleman, he would fain have let the question of hostility drop. There need not have been much intercourse between Puritan Grange and Folking; but then also there need be no quarrel. He was desirous that Caldigate should be allowed to come to the house, and that even visits of ceremony should be made to Folking. But Mrs. Bolton would have nothing to do with such half friendship. In the time that was coming she must be everything or nothing to her daughter. And she could not be brought to think that one who had been so manifestly a goat should cease to be a goat so suddenly. In other words, she could not soften her heart towards the man who had conquered her. Therefore when the time came for the baby to be born there had been no reconciliation between Puritan Grange and Folking.

Mrs. Babington had been somewhat less stern. Immediately on the return of the married couple to their own home she had still been full of wrath, and had predicted every kind of evil; but when she heard that all tongues were saying all good things of this nephew of hers, and when she was reminded by her husband that blood is thicker than water, and when she reflected that it is the duty of Christians to forgive injuries, she wrote to the sinner as follows:—

'BABINGTON HALL, *November* 187–
'My Dear John,—We are all here desirous that bygones should be bygones, and are willing to forgive,—though we may not perhaps be able to forget. I am quite of opinion that resentments should not be lasting, let them have been ever so well justified by circumstances at first.

'Your uncle bids me say that he hopes you will come over and shoot the Puddinghall coverts with Humphrey and John. They propose Thursday next, but would alter the day if that does not suit.

'We have heard of your wife's condition, of course, and trust that everything may go well with her. I shall hope to make her acquaintance some day when she is able to receive visitors.

'I am particularly induced at the present moment to hold out to you once more the right hand of fellowship and family affection by the fact that dear Julia is about to settle herself most advantageously in life. She is engaged to marry the Rev. Augustus Smirkie, the rector of Plum-cum-Pippins near Woodbridge in this county. We all like Mr. Smirkie very much indeed, and think *that Julia has been most fortunate in her choice*.' (These words were underscored doubly by way of showing how very much superior was Mr. Angustus Smirkie to Mr. John Caldigate.) 'I may perhaps as well mention, to avoid anything disagreeable at present, that Julia is at this time staying with Mr. Smirkie's mother at Ipswich.—Your affectionate aunt,

'MARYANNE BABINGTON'

Caldigate was at first inclined to send, in answer to this letter, a reply which would not have been agreeable to his aunt, but was talked into a better state of mind by his wife. 'Telling me that she will forgive me! The question is whether I will forgive her!' 'Let that be the question,' said his wife, 'and do forgive her. She wants to come round, and, of course, she has to make the best of it for herself. Tell her from me that I shall be delighted to see her whenever she choose to come.'

'Poor Julia!' said Caldigate, laughing.

'Of course you think so, John. That's natural enough. Perhaps I think so too. But what has that to do with it?'

'It's rather unfortunate that I know so much about Mr. Smirkie. He is fifty years old, and has five children by his former wife.'

'I don't see why he shouldn't be a good husband for all that.'

'And Plum-cum-Pippins is less than £300 a-year. Poor dear Julia!'

'I believe you are jealous, John.'

'Well; yes. Look at the way she has underscored it. Of course I'm jealous.' Nevertheless he wrote a courteous answer promising to go over and shoot the coverts, and stay for one night.

He did go over and shoot the coverts, and stayed for one night; but the visit was not very successful. Aunt Polly would talk of the glories of the Plum-cum-Pippins rectory in a manner which implied that dear Julia's escape from a fate which once threatened her had been quite providential. When he alluded,—as he did, but should not have done,—

to the young Smirkies, she spoke with almost ecstatic enthusiasm of the 'dear children,' Caldigate knowing the while that the eldest child must be at least sixteen. And then, though Aunt Polly was kind to him, she was kind in an almost insulting manner,—as though he were to be received for the sake of auld lang syne in spite of the step he had taken downwards in the world. He did his best to hear all this with no more than an inward smile, telling himself that it behoved him as a man to allow her to have her little revenge. But the smile was seen, and the more that was seen of it, the more often was he reminded that he had lost that place in the Babington elysium which might have been his, had he not been too foolish to know what was good for him. And a hint was given that the Boltons a short time since had not been aristo-cratic, whereas it was proved to him from Burke's Landed Gentry that the Smirkies had been established in Suffolk ever since Cromwell's time. No doubt their land had gone, but still there had been Smirkies.

'How did you get on with them?' his father asked, as he passed home through Cambridge.

'Much the same as usual. Of course in such a family a son-in-law elect is more thought of than a useless married man.'

'They snubbed you.'

'Aunt Polly snubbed me a little, and I don't think I had quite so good a place for the shooting as in the old days. But all that was to be expected. I quite agree with Aunt Polly that family quarrels are foolish things.'

'I am not so sure. Some people doom themselves to an infinity of annoyance because they won't avoid the society of disagreeable people. I don't know that I have ever quarrelled with any one. I have never intended to do so. But when I find that a man or woman is not sympathetic I think it better to keep out of the way.' That was the squire's account of himself. Those who knew him in the neighbour-hood were accustomed to say that he had quarrelled with everybody about him.

In December the baby was born, just twelve months after the marriage, and there was great demonstrations of joy, and ringing of bells in the parishes of Utterden and Netherden. The baby was a boy, and all was as it ought to be. John Caldigate himself, when he came to look at his position and to understand the feeling of those around him, was astonished to find how strong was the feeling in his own favour, and how thoroughly the tenants had been outraged by the idea that the property might be made over to a more distant member of the family. What was it to them who lived in the house at Folking? Why should they have been solicitous in the matter? They had their leases, and there was no adequate reason for supposing that one Caldigate would be more pleasant in his dealing with them than another. And yet it was evident to him now that this birth of a real heir at the squire's house, with a fair prospect that the acres would descend in a right line, was regarded by them all with almost superstitious satisfaction. The bells were rung as though the church-towers were going to be pulled down, and there was not a farmer or a farmer's wife who did not come to the door of Folking to ask how the young mother and the baby were doing.

'This is as it should be, squoire,' said Ralph Holt, who was going about in his Sunday clothes, as though it was a day much too sacred for muck and work. He had caught hold of Caldigate in the stable yard, and was now walking with him down towards the ferry.

'Yes;—she's doing very well, they tell me,' said the newly-made father.

'In course she'll do well. Why not? A healthy lass like she, if I may make so free? There ain't nothing like having them strong and young, with no town-bred airs about 'em. I never doubted as she wouldn't do well. I can tell from their very walk what sort of mothers they'll be.' Mr. Holt had long been known as the most judicious breeder of stock in that neighbourhood. 'But it ain't only that, squoire.'

'The young'un will do well too, I hope.'

'In course he will. Why not? The foals take after their dams for a time, pretty much always. But what I mean is;—we be all glad you've come back from them out-o'-the-way parts.'

'I had to go there, Holt.'

'Well;—we don't know much about that, sir, and I don't mean nothing about that.'

'To tell the truth, my friend, I should not have done very well here unless I had been able to topdress the English acres with a little Australian gold.'

'Like enough, squoire; like enough. But I wasn't making bold to say nothing about that. For a young gentleman to go out a while and then to come back was all very well. Most of 'em does it. But when there was a talk as you wern't to come back, and that Master George was to take the place;—why then it did seem as things was very wrong.'

'Master George might have been quite as good as I.'

'It wasn't the proper thing, squoire. It wasn't straight. If you hadn't never a' been, sir, or if the Lord Almighty had taken you as he did the others, God bless 'em, nobody wouldn't have had a right to say nothing. But as you was to the fore it wouldn't have been straight, and no one wouldn't have thought it straight.' Instigated by this John

Caldigate looked a good deal into the matter that day, and began to feel that, having been born Squire of Folking, he had, perhaps, no right to deal with himself otherwise. Then various thoughts passed through his mind as to other dealings which had taken place. How great had been the chance against his being Squire of Folking when he started with Dick Shand to look for Australian gold! And how little had been the chance of his calling Hester Bolton his wife when he was pledging his word to Mrs. Smith on board the Goldfinder! But now it had all come round to him just as he would have had it. There was his wife up-stairs in the big bed-room with her baby,—the wife as to whom he had made that romantic resolution when he had hardly spoken to her; and there had been the bells ringing and the tenants congratulating him, and everything had been pleasant. His father who had so scorned him,—who in the days of Davis and Newmarket had been so well justified in scorning him,—was now his closest friend. Thinking of all this, he told himself that he had certainly received better things than he had deserved.

A day or two after the birth of the baby Mrs. Robert came out to see the new prodigy, and on the following day Mrs. Daniel, Mrs. Robert was, of course, very friendly and disposed to be in all respects a good sister-in-law. Hester's great grief was in regard to her mother. She was steadfast enough in her resolution to stand in all respects by her husband, if there must be a separation,—but the idea of the separation robbed her of much of her happiness. Mrs. Robert was aware that a great effort was being made with Mrs. Bolton. The young squire's respectability was so great, and his conduct so good, that not only the Boltons themselves, but neighbours around who knew aught of the Bolton affairs, were loud in denouncing the woman for turning up her nose at such a son-in-law. The great object was to induce her to say that she would allow Caldigate to enter the house at Chesterton. 'You know I never see her now,' said Mrs. Robert; 'I'm too much of a sinner to think of entering the gates.'

'Do not laugh at her, Margaret,' said Hester.

'I do not mean to laugh at her. It is simply the truth. Robert and I have made up our minds that it is better for us all that I should not put myself in her way.'

'Think how different it must be for me!'

'Of course it is. It is dreadful to think that she should be so—prejudiced. But what can I do, dear? If they will go on persevering, she will, of course, have to give way.' The 'they' spoken of were the Daniels, and old Mr. Bolton himself, and latterly the Nicholases, all of whom were of opinion that the separation of the mother from her

171

daughter was very dreadful, especially when it came to be understood that the squire of Folking went regularly to his parish church.

On the next day Mrs. Daniel came out; and though she was much less liked by Hester than her younger sister-in-law, she brought more comfortable tidings. She had been at the Grange a day or two before, and Mrs. Bolton had almost consented to say that she would see John Caldigate. 'You shouldn't be in a hurry, you know, my dear,' said Mrs. Daniel.

'But what has John done that there should be any question about all this?'

'I suppose he was a little—just a little—what they call fast once.'

'He got into debt when he was a boy,' said the wife, 'and then paid off everything and a great deal more by his own industry. It seems to me that everybody ought to be proud of him.'

'I don't think your mother is proud of him, my dear.'

'Poor mamma!'

'I hope he'll go when he's told to do so.'

'John! Of course he'll go if I ask him. There's nothing he wouldn't do to make me happy. But really when I talk to him about it at all, I am ashamed of myself. Poor mamma!' The result of this visit was, however, very comforting. Mrs. Daniel had seen Mrs. Bolton, and had herself been witness to the fact that Mrs. Bolton had mitigated the sternness of her denial when asked to receive her son-in-law at Puritan Grange. It was, said Mrs. Daniel, the settled opinion of the Bolton family that, in the course of another month or so, the woman would be induced to give way under the pressure put upon her by the family generally.

CHAPTER XXIV

News From The Gold Mines

IT was said at the beginning of the last chapter that things had gone on smoothly, or with apparent smoothness, at Folking since the return of the Caldigates from their wedding tour; but there had in truth been a small cloud in the Folking heavens over and beyond that Babington haze which was now vanishing, and the storm at Chesterton as to which hopes were entertained that it would clear itself away. It will perhaps be remembered that Caldigate's offer for the sale of his interest in the Polyeuka mine had been suddenly accepted by certain enterprising persons in Australia, and that the money itself had been absolutely forthcoming. This had been in every way fortunate, as he had been saved from the trouble of another journey to the colony; and his money matters had been put on such a footing as to make him altogether comfortable. But just when he heard that the money had been lodged to his account,—and when the money actually had been so paid,—he received a telegram from Mr. Crinkett, begging that the matter might be for a time postponed. This, of course, was out of the question. His terms had been accepted,—which might have gone for very little had not the money been forthcoming. But the cash was positively in his hands. Who ever heard of a man 'postponing' an arrangement in such circumstances? Let them do what they might with Polyeuka, he was safe! He telegraphed back to say that there could be no postponement. As far as he was concerned the whole thing was settled. Then there came a multiplicity of telegrams, very costly to the Crinkett interest;—costly also and troublesome to himself; for he, though the matter was so pleasantly settled as far as he was concerned, could not altogether ignore the plaints that were made to him. Then there came very long letters, long and loud; letters not only from Crinkett, but from others, telling him that the Polyeuka gold had come to an end, the lode disappearing altogether, as lodes sometimes do disappear. The fact was that the Crinkett Company asked to have back half its money, offering him the Polyeuka mine in its entirety if he chose to accept it.

John Caldigate, though in England he could be and was a liberal gentleman, had been long enough in Australia to know that if he meant to hold his own among such men as Mr. Crinkett, he must make the best of such turns of fortune as chance might give him. Under no circumstances would Crinkett have been generous to him. Had Polyeuka suddenly become more prolific in the precious metal than any mine in the colony the Crinkett Company would have laughed at any claim made by him for further payment. When a bargain has been fairly made, the parties must make the best of it. He was therefore very decided in his refusal to make restitution, though he was at the same time profuse in his expressions of sorrow.

Then there came a threat,—not from Crinkett, but from Mrs. Euphemia Smith. And the letter was not signed Euphemia Smith,—but Euphemia Caldigate. And the letter was as follows:-

'In spite of all your treachery to me I do not wish to ruin you, or to destroy your young wife, by proving myself in England to have been married to you in Ahalala. But I will do so unless you assent to the terms which Crinkett has proposed. He and I are in partnership in the matter with two or three others, and are willing to let all that has gone before be forgotten if we have means given us to make another start. You cannot feel that the money you have received is fairly yours, and I can hardly think you would wish to become rich by taking from me all that I have earned after so many hardships. If you will do as I propose, you had better send out an agent. On paying us the money he shall not only have the marriage-certificate, but shall stand by and see me married to Crinkett, who is now a widower. After that, of course, I can make no claim to you. If you will not do this, both I and Crinkett, and the other man who was present at our marriage, and Anne Young, who has been with me ever since, will go at once to England, and the law must take its course.

'I have no scruple in demanding this as you owe me so much more.

'Allan, the Wesleyan who married us, has gone out of the colony, no one knows where,—but I send you the copy of the certificate; and all the four of us who were there are still together. And there were others who were at Ahalala at the time, and who remember the marriage well. Dick Shand was not in the chapel, but Dick knew all about it. There is quite plenty of evidence.

'Send back by the wire word what you will do, and let your agent come over as soon as possible.

'EUPHEMIA CALDIGATE'

However true or however false the allegations made in the above letter may have been, for a time it stunned him greatly. This letter reached him about a month before the birth of his son, and for a day or two it disturbed him greatly. He did not show it to his wife, but wandered about the place alone thinking whether he would take any notice of it, and what notice. At last he resolved that he would take the letter to his brother-in-law Robert, and ask the attorney's advice. 'How much of it is true?' demanded Robert, when he read the letter twice from beginning to end.

'A good deal,' said Caldigate,—'as much as may be, with the exception that I was never married to the woman.'

'I suppose not that.' Robert Bolton as he spoke was very grave, but did not at first seem disposed to be angry. 'Had you not better tell me everything, do you think?'

'It is for that purpose that I have come and brought you the letter. You understand about the money.'

'I suppose so.'

'There can be no reason why I should return a penny of it?'

'Certainly not, now. You certainly must not return it under a threat,—even though the woman should be starving. There can be no circumstances—' and as he spoke he dashed his hand down upon the table,—'no circumstances in which a man should allow money to be extorted from him by a threat. For Hester's sake you must not do that.'

'No;—no; I must not do that, of course.'

'And now tell me what is true?' There was something of authority in the tone of his voice, something perhaps of censure, something too of doubt, which went much against the grain with Caldigate. He had determined to tell his story feeling that counsel was necessary to him, but he wished so to tell it as to subject himself to no criticism and to admit no fault. He wanted assistance, but he wanted it on friendly and sympathetic terms. He had a great dislike to being—'blown up,' as he would probably have expressed it himself, and he already thought that he saw in his companion's eye a tendency that way. Turning all this in his mind, he paused a moment before he began to tell his tale. 'You say that a good deal in this woman's letter is true. Had you not better tell me what is true?'

'I was very intimate with her.'

'Did she ever live with you?'

'Yes, she did.'

'As your wife?'

'Well; yes. It is of course best that you should know all.' Then he gave a tolerably true account of all that had happened between himself and Mrs. Smith up to the time at which, as the reader knows, he found her performing at the Sydney theatre.

175

'You had made her a distinct promise of marriage on board the ship?'

'I think I had.'

'You think?'

'Yes. I think I did. Can you not understand that a man may be in great doubt as to the exact words that he may have spoken at such a time?'

'Hardly.'

'Then I don't think you realise the man's position. I wish to let you know the truth as exactly as I can. You had better take it for granted that I did make such a promise, though probably no such promise was absolutely uttered. But I did tell her afterwards that I would marry her.'

'Afterwards?'

'Yes, when she followed me up to Ahalala.'

'Did Richard Shand know her?'

'Of course he did,—on board the ship;—and he was with me when she came to Ahalala.'

'And she lived with you?'

'Yes.'

'And you promised to marry her?'

'Yes.'

'And was that all?'

'I did not marry her, of course,' said Caldigate.

'Who heard the promise?'

'It was declared by her in the presence of that Wesleyan minister she speaks of. He went to her to rebuke her, and she told him of the promise. Then he asked me, and I did not deny it. At the moment when he taxed me with it I was almost minded to do as I had promised.'

'You repeated your promise, then, to him?'

'Nothing of the kind. I did not deny it, and I told him at last to mind his own business. Life up there was a little rough at that time.'

'So it seems, indeed. And then, after that?'

'I had given her money and she had some claims in a gold-mine. When she was successful for a time she became so keen about her money that I fancy she hardly wished to get herself married. Then we had some words, and so we parted.'

'Did she call herself—Mrs. Caldigate?'

'I never called her so.'

'Did she herself assume the name?'

'It was a wild kind of life up there, Robert, and this was apparent in nothing more than in the names people used. I daresay some of the people did call her Mrs. Caldigate. But they knew she was not my wife.'

'And this man Crinkett?'

'He knew all about it.'

'He had a wife. Did his wife know her?'

'He had quarrelled with his wife at that time and had sent her away from Nobble. Mrs. Smith was then living at Nobble, and Crinkett knew more about her than I did. She was mad after gold, and it was with Crinkett she was working. I gave her a lot of shares in another mine to leave me.'

'What mine?'

'The Old Stick-in-the-Mud they called it. I had been in partnership with Crinkett and wanted to get out of the thing, and go in altogether for Polyeuka. At that time the woman cared little for husbands or lovers. She had been bitten with the fury of gold-gambling and, like so many of them, filled her mind with an idea of unlimited wealth. And she had a turn of luck. I suppose she was worth at one time eight or ten thousand pounds.'

'But she did not keep it?'

'I knew but little of her afterwards. I kept out of her way; and though I had dealings with Crinkett, I dropped them as soon as I could.' Then he paused;–but Robert Bolton held his peace with anything but a satisfied countenance. 'Now I think you know all about it.'

'It is a most distressing story.'

'All attempts at robbery and imposition are of course distressing.'

'There is so much in it that is—disgraceful.'

'I deny it altogether,–if you mean disgraceful to me.'

'If it had all been known as it is known now,—as it is known even by your own telling, do you think that I should have consented to your marriage with my sister?'

'Why not?' Robert Bolton shrugged his shoulders. 'And I think, moreover, that had you refused your consent I should have married your sister just the same.'

'Then you know very little about the matter.'

'I don't think there can be any good in going into that. It is at any rate the fact that your sister is my wife. As this demand has been made upon me it was natural that I should wish to discuss it with some one whom I can trust. I tell you all the facts, but I am not going to listen to any fault-findings as to my past life.'

'Poor Hester!'

'Why is she poor? She does not think herself so.'

'Because there is a world of sorrow and trouble before her; and

177

because all that you have told to me must probably be made known to her.'

'She knows it already;—that is, she knows what you mean. I have not told her of the woman's lie, nor of this demand for money. But I shall when she is strong enough to hear it and to talk of it. You are very much mistaken if you think that there are secrets between me and Hester.'

'I don't suppose you will be pleased to hear the story of such a life told in all the public papers.'

'Certainly not;—but it will be an annoyance which I can bear. You or any one else would be very much mistaken who would suppose that life out in those places can go on in the same regular way that it does here. Gold beneath the ground is a dangerous thing to touch, and few who have had to do with it have come out much freer from misfortune than myself. As for these people, I don't suppose that I shall hear from them again. I shall send them both word that not a shilling is to be expected from me.'

There was after this a long discussion as to the nature of the messages to be sent. There was no absolute quarrel between the two men, and the attorney acknowledged to himself that it was now his duty to give the best advice in his power to his brother-in-law; but their manner to each other was changed. It was evident that Robert did not quite believe all that Caldigate told him, and evident also that Caldigate resented this want of confidence. But still each knew that he could not do without the other. Their connection was too firm and too close to be shaken off. And, therefore, though their tones were hardly friendly, still they consulted as to what should be done. It was at last decided that two messages should be sent by Caldigate, one to Crinkett and the other to Mrs. Smith, and each in the same words. 'No money will be sent you on behalf of the Polyeuka mine,' and that this should be all. Any letter, Robert Bolton thought, would be inexpedient. Then they parted, and the two messages were at once sent.

After a day or two Caldigate recovered his spirits. We all probably know how some trouble will come upon us and for a period seem to quell all that is joyous in our life, and that then by quick degrees the weight of the trouble will grow less, till the natural spring and vivacity of the mind will recover itself, and make little or nothing of that which a few hours ago was felt to be so grievous a burden. So it had been with John Caldigate. He had been man enough to hold up his head when telling his story to Robert Bolton, and to declare that the annoyance would be one that he could bear easily;—but still for some hours after that he had been unhappy. If by sacrificing some considerable sum of money,—even a large sum of money, say ten thousand pounds,—he could at that moment have insured the silence of Crinkett and the woman, he would have paid his money. He knew the world well enough to be aware that he could insure nothing by any such sacrifice. He must defy these claimants;—and then if they chose to come to England with their story, he must bear it as best he could. Those who saw him did not know that aught ailed him, and Robert Bolton spoke no word of the matter to any one at Cambridge.

But Robert Bolton thought very much of it,—so much that on the following day he ran up to London on purpose to discuss the matter with his brother William. How would it be with them, and what would be his duty, if the statement made by the woman should turn out to be true? What security had they after the story told by Caldigate himself that there had been no marriage? By his own showing he had lived with the woman, had promised to marry her, had acknowledged his promise in the hearing of a clergyman, and had been aware that she had called herself by his name. Then he had given her money to go away. This had been his own story. 'Do you believe him?' he said to his brother William.

'Yes; I do. In the first place, though I can understand from his antecedents and from his surroundings at the time, that he should have lived a loose sort of life when he was out there, I don't think that he is a rascal or even a liar.'

'One wouldn't wish to think so.'

'I do not think so. He doesn't look like it, or talk like it, or act like it.'

'How many cases do we know in which some abominable unexpected villainy has destroyed the happiness and respectability of a family?'

'But what would you do?' asked the barrister. 'She is married to him. You cannot separate them if you would.'

'No,—poor girl. If it be so, her misery is accomplished; but if it be so she should at once be taken away from him. What a triumph it would be to her mother!'

'That is a dreadful thing to say, Robert.'

'But nevertheless true. Think of her warnings and refusals, and of my persistence! But if it be so, not the less must we all insist upon—destroying him. If it be so, he must be punished to the extent of the law.'

William Bolton, however, would not admit that it could be so, and Robert declared that though he suspected,—though in such a case he found himself bound to suspect,—he did not in truth believe that

179

Caldigate had been guilty of so terrible a crime. All probability was against it;—but still it was possible. Then, after much deliberation it was decided that an agent should be sent out by them to New South Wales, to learn the truth, as far as it could be learned, and to bring back whatever evidence might be collected without making too much noise in the collection of it. Then there arose the question whether Caldigate should be told of this;—but it was decided that it should be done at the joint expense of the two brothers without the knowledge of Hester's husband.

CHAPTER XXV

The Baby's Sponsors

'IS there anything wrong between you and Robert?' Hester asked this question of her husband, one morning in January, as he was sitting by the side of her sofa in their bedroom. The baby was in her arms, and at that moment there was a question as to the godfathers and godmother for the baby.

The letter from Mrs. Smith had arrived on the last day of October, nearly two months before the birth of the baby, and the telegrams refusing to send the money demanded had been despatched on the 1st November,—so that, at this time, Caldigate's mind was accustomed to the burden of the idea. From that day to this he had not often spoken of the matter to Robert Bolton,—nor indeed had there been much conversation between them on other matters. Robert had asked him two or three times whether he had received any reply by the wires. No such message had come; and of course he answered his brother-in-law's questions accordingly;—but he had answered them almost with a look of offence. The attorney's manner and tone seemed to him to convey reproach; and he was determined that none of the Boltons should have the liberty to find fault with him. It had been suggested, some weeks since, before the baby was born, that an effort should be made to induce Mrs. Bolton to act as godmother. And, since that, among the names of many other relatives and friends, those of uncle Babington and Robert Bolton had been proposed. Hester had been particularly anxious that her brother should be asked, because,—as she often said to her husband,—he had always been her firm friend in the matter of her marriage. But now, when the question was to be settled, John Caldigate shook his head.

'I was afraid there was something even before baby was born,' said the wife.

'There is something, my pet.'

'What is it, John? You do not mean to keep it secret from me?'

'I have not the slightest objection to your asking him to stand;—but I think it possible that he may refuse.'

'Why should he refuse?'

'Because, as you say, there is something wrong between us. There have been applications for money about the Polyeuka mine. I would not trouble you about it while you were ill.'

'Does he think you ought to give back the money?'

'No,—not that. We are quite agreed about the money. But another question has come up;—and though we are, I believe, agreed about that too, still there has been something a little uncomfortable.'

'Would not baby make all that right?'

'I think if you were to ask your brother William it would be better.'

'May I not know what it is now, John?'

'I have meant you to know always,—from the moment when it occurred,—when you should be well enough.'

'I am well now.'

'I hardly know; and yet I cannot bear to keep it secret from you.'

There was something in his manner which made her feel at once that the subject to which he alluded was of the greatest importance. Whether weak or strong, of course, she must be told now. Let the shock of the tidings be what it might, the doubt would be worse. She felt all that, and she knew that he could feel it. 'I am quite strong,' she said; 'you must tell me now.'

'Is baby asleep? Put him in the cradle.'

'Is it so bad as that?'

'I do not say that it is bad at all. There is nothing bad in it,—except a lie. Let me put him in the cradle.'

Then he took the child very gently and deposited him, fast asleep, among the blankets. He had already assumed for himself the character of being a good male nurse; and she was always delighted when she saw the baby in his arms. Then he came and seated himself close to her on the sofa, and put his arm round her waist. 'There is nothing bad—but a lie.'

'A lie may be so very bad!'

'Yes, indeed; and this lie is very bad. Do you remember my telling you—about a woman?'

'That Mrs. Smith;—the dancing woman?'

'Yes;—her.'

'Of course I remember.'

'She was one of those, it seems, who bought the Polyeuka mine.'

'Oh, indeed!'

'She, with Crinkett and others. Now they want their money back again.'

'But can they make you send it? And would it be very bad—to lose it?'

'They cannot make me send it. They have no claim to a single shilling. And if they could make me pay it, that would not be very bad.'

'What is it, then? You are afraid to tell me?'

'Yes, my darling,—afraid to speak to you of what is so wicked;—afraid to shock you, to disgust you; but not afraid of any injury that can be done to you. No harm will come to you.'

'But to you?'

'Nor to me;—none to you, or to me, or to baby there.' As he said this she clutched his hand with hers. 'No harm, dearest; and yet the thing is so abominable that I can hardly bring myself to wound your ears with it.'

'You must tell now, John.'

'Yes, I must tell you. I have thought about it much, and I know that it is better that you should be told.' He had thought much about it, and had so resolved. But he had not quite known how difficult the telling would be. And now he was aware that he was adding to the horror she would feel by pausing and making much of the thing. And yet he could not tell it as though it were a light matter. If he could have declared it all at once,—at first, with a smile on his face, then expressing his disgust at the woman's falsehood,—it would have been better. 'That woman has written me a letter in which she declares herself to be—my wife!'

'Your wife! John! Your wife?' These exclamations came from her almost with a shriek as she jumped up from his arms and for a moment stood before him.

'Come back to me,' he said. Then again she seated herself. 'You did not leave me then because you doubted me?'

'Oh no,' she cried, throwing herself upon him and smothering him with kisses—'No, no! It was surprise at such horrid words,—not doubt, not doubt of you. I will never doubt you.'

'It was because I was sure of you that I have ventured to tell you this.'

'You may be sure of me,' she said, sobbing violently the while. 'You are sure of me; are you not? And now tell it me all. How did she say so? why did she say so? Is she coming to claim you? Tell me all. Oh, John, tell me everything.'

'The why is soon told. Because she wants money. She had heard no doubt of my marriage and thought to frighten me out of money. I do not think she would do it herself. The man Crinkett has put her up to it.'

'What does she say?'

'Just that,—and then she signs herself,—Euphemia Caldigate.'

'Oh, John!'

'Now you know it all.'

'May I not see the letter?'

'For what good? But you shall see it if you wish it. I have determined that nothing shall be kept back from you. In all that there may ever be to trouble us the best comfort will be in perfect confidence.' He had already learned enough of her nature to be sure that in this way would he best comfort her, and most certainly ensure her trust in himself.

'Oh yes,' she cried. 'If you will tell me all, I will never doubt you.' Then she took the letter from his hand, and attempted to read it. But her excitement was so great that though the words were written very clearly, she could not bring her mind to understand them. 'Treachery! Ruin! Married to you! What is it all? Do you read it to me;—every word of it.' Then he did read it; every word of it. 'She says that she will marry the other man. How can she marry him when she says that she is—your wife?'

'Just so, my pet. But you see what she says. It does not matter much to her whether it be true or false, so that she can get my money from me. But, Hester, I would fain be just even to her. No doubt she wrote the letter.'

'Who else would have written it?'

'She wrote it. I know her hand. And these are her words,—because they are properly expressed. But it is all his doing,—the man's doing. He has got her in his power, and he is using her in this way.'

'If you sent her money——?'

'Not a shilling;—not though she were starving; not now. A man who gives money under a threat is gone. If I were to send her money, everyone would believe this tale that she tells. Your brother Robert would believe it.'

'He knows it?'

'I took the letter to him instantly, but I made up my mind that I would not show it you till baby was born. You can understand that?' She only pressed closer to him as he said this. 'I showed it to Robert, and, altogether we are not quite such friends since as we were before.'

'You do not mean that he believes it?'

'No; not that. He does not believe it. If he did, I do not see how he and I could ever speak to each other again. I don't think he believes it at all. But I had to tell him the whole story, and that, perhaps, offended him.' The 'whole story' had not been told to Hester, nor did he think it necessary that it should be told. There was no reason why these details which Robert had elicited by his questions should be repeated to her,—the promise of marriage, the interference of the Wesleyan minister, the use made of his name,—of all this he said nothing. But she had now been told that which to her had been very dreadful, and she was not surprised that her brother should have been offended when he heard the same sad story. She, of course, had at once pardoned the old offence. A young wife when she is sure of her husband, will readily forgive all offences committed before marriage, and will almost be thankful for the confidence placed in her when offences are confessed. But she could understand that a brother could not be thankful, and she would naturally exaggerate in her own mind the horror which he would feel at such a revelation. Then the husband endeavoured to lighten the effect of what he had said. "Offence, perhaps, is the wrong word. But he was stiff and masterful, if you know what I mean.'

'You would not bear that, certainly, John?::

'No. I have to own that I do not love the assumption of authority,—except from you.'

'You do not like it from anybody, John.'

'You would not wish me to submit myself to your brother?'

'No; but I think I might ask him to be baby's godfather.'

'As you please; only you would be unhappy if he refused.'

Then there came a little wail from the cradle and the baby was taken up, and for some minutes his little necessities occupied the mother to the exclusion even of that terrible letter. But when Caldigate was about to leave the room, she asked him another question. 'Will she do anything more, John?'

'I can hardly say. I should think not.'

'What does Robert think?'

'He has not told me. I sent an immediate refusal by the telegraph wires, and have heard nothing since.'

'Is he—nervous about it?'

'I hardly know. It dwells in his mind, no doubt.'

'Are you nervous?'

'It dwells in my mind. That is all.'

'May I speak to him about it?'

'Why should you? What good would it do? I would rather you did not. Nevertheless, if you feel frightened, if you think that there is anything wrong, it will be natural that you should go to him for assistance. I will not forbid it.' As he said this he stood back away from her. It was but by a foot or two, but still there was a sign of separation which instantly made itself palpable to her.

'Wrong, how wrong?' she said, following him and clinging to him. 'You do not suppose that I would go to him because I think you wrong? Do you not know that whatever might come I should cling to you? What is he compared to you? No; I will never speak to him about it.'

185

He returned her caress with fervour, and stroked her hair, and kissed her forehead. 'My dearest! my own! my darling! But what I mean is that if some other man's opinion on this subject is necessary to your comfort, you may go to him.'

'No other man's opinion shall be necessary to me about anything. I will not speak about it to Robert, or to any one. But if more should come of it, you will tell me?'

'You shall know everything that comes. I have never for a moment had the idea of keeping it back from you. But because of baby, and because baby had to be born, I delayed it.' This was an excuse which, as the mother of her child, she could not but accept with thankfulness.

'I think I will ask him,' she said that night, referring again to the vexed question of godfathers. Uncle Babington had some weeks since very generously offered his services, and, of course, they had been generously accepted. Among the baby's relations he was the man of highest standing in the world; and then this was a mark of absolute forgiveness in reference to the wrongs of poor Julia. And a long letter had been prepared to Mrs. Bolton, written by Hester's own hand, not without much trouble, in which the baby's grandmother was urged to take upon herself the duties of godmother. All this had been discussed in the family, so that the nature of the petition was well known to Mrs. Bolton for some time before she received it. Mrs. Daniel, who had consented to act in the event of a refusal from Puritan Grange, had more than once used her influence with her step-mother-in-law. But no hint had as yet come to Folking as to what the answer might be. It had also been suggested that Robert should be the other godfather,—the proposal having been made to Mrs. Robert. But there had come upon all the Boltons a feeling that Robert was indifferent,—or, perhaps, even unwilling to undertake the task. And yet no one knew why. Mrs. Robert herself did not know why.

The reader, however, will know why, and will understand how it was that Mrs. Robert was in the dark. The attorney, though he was suspicious, though he was frightened, though he was, in truth, very angry with this new brother-in-law, through whose ante-nuptial delinquencies so much sorrow was threatened to the Bolton family, nevertheless kept the secret from all the Cambridge Boltons. It had been necessary to him to seek counsel with some one, but he had mentioned the matter only to his brother William. But he did not wish to add to the bond which now tied him to Folking. If this horror, this possible horror, should fall upon them,—if it should turn out that he had insisted on giving his sister in marriage to a man already married,—then,—then,—then—! Such possible future incidents were too terrible to be considered closely, but with such a possibility he would not add to the bonds. At Puritan Grange they would throw all the responsibility of what had been done upon him. This feeling was mingled with his love for his sister,—with the indignation he would not only feel but show if it should turn out that she had been wronged. 'I will destroy him,—I will destroy him utterly,' he would sometimes say to himself as he thought of it.

And now the godfather question had to be decided. 'No,' he said to his wife, 'I don't care about such things. I won't do it. You write and tell her that I have prejudices, or scruples, or whatever you choose to call it.'

'There is to be a little tarradiddle told, and I am to tell it?'

'I have prejudices and scruples.'

'About the religion of the thing?' She knew,—as, of course, she was bound to know,—that he had at any rate a round dozen of godchildren somewhere about the country. There were the young Williams, and the young Daniels, and her own nephews and nieces, with the parents of all of whom uncle Robert had been regarded as the very man for a godfather. The silversmith in Trumpington Street knew exactly the weight of the silver cup that was to be given to the boy or to a girl. The Bible and prayer-books were equally well regulated. Mrs. Robert could not but smile at the idea of religious scruples. 'I wish I knew what it was that has come over you of late. I fancy you have quarrelled with John Caldigate.'

'If you think that, then you can understand the reason.'

'What is it about?'

'I have not quarrelled with him. It is possible that I may have to do so. But I do not mean to say what it is about.' Then he smiled. 'I don't want you to ask any more questions, but just to write to Hester as kindly as you can, saying I don't mean to be godfather any more. It will be a good excuse in regard to all future babies.' Mrs. Robert was a good wife as did as she was bid. She worked her refusal as cautiously as she could, and,—on that occasion,—asked her husband no further question.

The prayer that was addressed to the lady of Puritan Grange became the subject of much debate, of great consideration, and I may say also of lengthened prayer. To Mrs. Bolton this position of godmother implied much of the old sacred responsibility which was formerly attached to it, and which Robert Bolton, like other godfathers and godmothers of the day, had altogether ignored. She had been already partly brought round, nearly persuaded, in regard to the acceptance of John Caldigate as her son-in-law. It did not occur to her to do other than hate him. How was it possible that such a woman should do other than hate the man who had altogether got the better of her as to the very marrow of her life, the very apple of her eye? But she was alive to her duty towards her daughter; and when she was told that the man was honest in his dealings, well-to-do in the world, a professing Christian who was constant in his parish church, she did not know how to maintain her opinion, that in spite of all this, he was an unregenerate castaway. Therefore, although she was determined still to hate him, she had almost made up her mind to enter his house. With these ideas she wrote a long letter to Hester, in which she promised to have herself taken out to Folking in order that she might be present as godmother at the baby's baptism. She would lunch at Folking, but must return to Chesterton before dinner. Even this was a great thing gained.

Then it was arranged that Daniel Bolton should stand as second godfather in place of his brother Robert.

CHAPTER XXVI

A Stranger In Cambridge

'I AM sorry you will not come out to us tomorrow.' On the day before the christening, which was at last fixed for a certain Tuesday in the middle of February, John Caldigate went into Cambridge, and at once called upon the attorney at his office. This he did partly instigated by his own feelings, and partly in compliance with his wife's wishes. Before that letter had come he and his brother-in-law had been fast friends; and now, though for a day or two he had been angry with what he had thought to be unjustifiable interference, he regretted the loss of such a friend. More than three months had now passed since the letter had come, but his mind was far from being at ease, and he felt that if trouble should come it would be very well for him to have Robert Bolton on his side.

'Margaret is going,' said the attorney.

'Why do you not bring her?'

'Days are days with me, my boy. I can't afford to give up a morning for every baby that is born.'

'That of course may be true, and if that is the reason, I have nothing more to say.' As he spoke he looked in his brother-in-law's face, so as almost to prevent the possibility of continued pretence.

'Well, Caldigate, it isn't the reason altogether,' said the other. 'If you would have allowed it to pass without further explanation so would I. But if the truth must be spoken in so many words, I will confess that I would rather not go out to Folking till I am sure we shall be no more troubled by your friends in Australia.'

'Why not? Why should you not go out to Folking?'

'Simply because I may have to take an active part against you. I do not suppose it will come to that, but it is possible. I need not say that I trust there may be nothing of the kind, but I cannot be sure. It is on the cards.'

'I think that is a hard judgment. Do you mean to say that you believe that woman's statement not only against mine, but against the whole tenor of my life and character?'

'No; I do not believe the woman's statement. If I did, I should not be talking to you now. The woman has probably lied, and is probably a tool in the hands of others for raising money, as you have already suggested. But, according to your own showing, there has been much in your life to authorise the statement. I do not know what does or does not constitute a marriage there.'

'The laws are the same as ours.'

'There at any rate you are wrong. Their marriage laws are not the same as ours, though how they may differ you and I probably do not accurately know. And they may be altered at any time as they may please. Let the laws be what they will, it is quite possible, after what you have told me, that they may bring up evidence which you would find it very difficult to refuse. I don't think it will be so. If I did I should use all my influence to remove my sister at once.'

'You couldn't do it,' said Caldigate, very angrily.

'I tell you what I should endeavour to do. You must excuse me if I stand aloof just at present. I don't suppose you can defend such a condition of things as you described to me the other day.'

'I do not mean to be put upon my defence,—at any rate by you,' said Caldigate, very angrily. And then he left the office.

He had come into Cambridge with the intention of calling at Puritan Grange after he had left the attorney, and when he found himself in the street he walked on in the direction of Chesterton. He had wished to thank his wife's mother for her concession, and had been told by Hester that if he would call, Mrs. Bolton would certainly see him now. Had there been no letter from the woman in Australia, he would probably not have obeyed his wife's behest in this matter. His heart and spirit would then have been without a flaw, and, proud in his own strength, and his own rectitude, he would have declared to himself that the absurd prejudices of a fanatic woman were beneath his notice. But that letter had been a blow, and the blow, though it had not quelled him, had weakened his forces. He could conceal the injury done him even from his wife, but there was an injury. He was not quite the man that he had been before. From day to day, and from hour to hour, he was always remonstrating with himself because it was so. He was conscious that in some degree he had been cowed, and was ever fighting against the feeling. His tenderness to his wife was perhaps increased, because he knew that she still suffered from the letter; but he was almost ashamed of his own tenderness, as being a sign of weakness. He made himself very busy in these days,—busy among his brother magistrates, busy among his farming operations, busy with his tenants, busy among his books, so as to show to those around him that he was one who could perform all the duties of life, and enjoy all the pleasures, with an open brow and a clear conscience. He had been ever bold and self-asserting; but now he was perhaps a little over-bold. But through it all the Australian letter and the Australian woman were present to him day and night.

It was this resolution not to be quelled that had made him call upon the attorney at his office; and when he found himself back in the street he was very angry with the man. 'If it pleases him, let it be so,' he said to himself. 'I can do in the world without him.' And then he thought of that threat,—when the attorney had said that he would remove his sister. 'Remove her! By heavens!' He had a stick in his hand, and as he went he struck it angrily against a post. Remove his wife! All the Boltons in Cambridgeshire could not put a hand upon her, unless by his leave! For some moments his anger supported him; but after a while that gave way to the old feeling of discomfort which pervaded him always. She was his wife, and nobody should touch her. Nevertheless he might find it difficult, as Robert Bolton had said, to prove that that other woman was not his wife.

Robert Bolton's office was in a small street close to Pembroke College, and when he came out of it he had intended to walk direct through Trumpington Street and Trinity Street to Chesterton. But he found it necessary to compose himself and so to arrange his thoughts that he might be able to answer such foolish questions as Mrs. Bolton would probably ask him without being flurried. He was almost sure that she had heard nothing of the woman. He did not suspect Robert Bolton of treachery in that respect; but she would probably talk to him about the iniquity of his past life generally, and he must be prepared to answer her. It was incumbent upon him to shake off, before he reached Chesterton, that mixture of alarm and anger which at present dominated him; and with this object, instead of going straight along the street, he turned into the quadrangle of King's College, and passing through the gardens and over the bridge, wandered for a while slowly under the trees at the back of the college. He accused himself of a lack of manliness in that he allowed himself to be thus cowed. Did he not know that such threats as these were common? Was it not just what might have been expected from such a one as Crinkett, when Crinkett was driven to desperation by failing speculations? As he thought of the woman, he shook his head, looking down upon the ground. The woman had at one time been very dear to him. But it was clearly now his duty to go on as though there were no such woman as Euphemia Smith, and no such man as Thomas Crinkett. And as for Robert Bolton, he would henceforth treat him as though his anger and his suspicions were unworthy of notice. If the man should choose of his own accord to reassume the old friendly relations,—well and good. No overtures should come from him—Caldigate. And if the anger and the suspicions endured, why then, he, Caldigate, could do very well without Robert Bolton.

As he made these resolutions he turned in at a little gate opening into a corner of St. John's Gardens, with the object of passing through the college back into the streets of the town. It was not quite his nearest way, but he loved the old buildings, and the trees, and the river, even in winter. It still was winter, being now the middle of February; but, as it happened, the air was dry and mild, and the sun was shining. Still, he was surprised at such a time of the year to see an elderly man apparently asleep on one of the benches which are placed close to the path. But there he was, asleep, with his two hands on a stick, and his head bent forward over his stick. It was impossible not to look at the man sleeping there in that way; but Caldigate would hardly have looked, would hardly have dared to look, could he have anticipated what he would see. The elderly man was Thomas Crinkett. As he passed he was quite sure that the man was Thomas Crinkett. When he had gone a dozen yards, he paused for a moment to consider what he would do. A dozen different thoughts passed through his mind in that moment of time. Why was the man there? Why, indeed, could he have come to England except with the view of prosecuting the demand which he and the woman had made? His presence even in England was sufficient to declare that this battle would have to be fought. But to Cambridge he could have come with no other object than that of beginning the attack at once. And then, had he already commenced his work? He had not at any rate been to Robert Bolton, to whom any one knowing the family would have first referred him. And why was he sleeping there? Why was he not now at work upon his project? Again, would it be better at the present moment that he should pass by the man as though he had not seen him; or should he go back and ask him his purpose? As the thought passed through his mind, he stayed his step for a moment on the pathway and looked round. The man had moved his position, and was now sitting with his head turned away but evidently not asleep. Then it occurred to Caldigate that Crinkett's slumbers had been only a pretence, that the man had seen and recognised him, and at the moment had not chosen to make himself known. And it occurred to him also that in a matter of such importance as this he should do nothing on the spur of the moment,—nothing without consideration. A word spoken to Crinkett, a word without consideration, might be fatal to him. So he passed on, having stood upon the path hardly more than a second or two.

Before he had got up to the new buildings of St. John's a cold sweat had come out all over him. He was conscious of this, and conscious also that for a time he was so confounded by the apparition of his enemy

192

as to be unable to bring his mind to work properly on the subject. 'Let him do his worst,' he kept on saying to himself; 'let him do his worst.' But he knew that the brave words, though spoken only to himself, were mere braggadocio. No doubt the man would do his worst, and very bad it would be to him. At the moment he was so cowed by fear that he would have given half his fortune to have secured the woman's silence,—and the man's. How much better would it have been had he acceded to the man's first demand as to restitution of a portion of the sum paid for Polyeuka, before the woman's name had been brought into the matter at all?

But reflections such as these were now useless and he must do something. It was for his wife's sake,—he assured himself,—for his wife's sake that he allowed himself to be made thus miserable by the presence of this wretched creature. What would she not be called upon to suffer? The woman no doubt would be brought before magistrates and judges, and would be made to swear that she was his wife. The whole story of his life in Australia would be made public,—and there was so much that could not be made public without overwhelming her with sorrow! His own father, too, who had surrendered the estate to him, must know it all. His father hitherto had not heard the name of Mrs. Smith, and had been told only of Crinkett's dishonest successes and dishonest failures. When Caldigate had spoken of Crinkett to his father, he had done so with a triumph as of a man whom he had weighed and measured and made use of,—whose frauds and cunning he had conquered by his own honesty and better knowledge. Now he could no longer weigh and measure and make use of Crinkett. Crinkett had been a joke to him in talking with his father. But Crinkett was no joke now.

While walking through the college quad, he was half stupefied by his confusion, and was aware that such was his condition. But going out under the gate he paused for a moment and shook himself. He must at any rate summon his own powers to his aid at the moment and resolve what he would do. However bad all this might be, there was a better course and a worse. If he allowed this confusion to master him he would probably be betrayed into the worse course. Now, at this moment, in what way would it become him to act? He drew himself together, shaking his head and shoulders,—so as to shake off his weakness,— pressing his foot for a moment on the earth so as to convince himself of his own firmness, and then he resolved.

He was on the way out to see his mother-in-law, but he thought that nothing now could be gained by going to Chesterton. It was not impossible that Crinkett might have been there. If so the man would have told something of his story; and his wife's mother was the last person in the world whom, under such circumstances, he could hope to satisfy. He must tell no lie to any one; he must at least conceal nothing of the things as they occurred now. He must not allow it to be first told by Crinkett that they two had seen each other in the Gardens. But he could not declare this to Mrs. Bolton. For the present, the less he saw of Mrs. Bolton the better. She would come to the christening to-morrow,—unless indeed Crinkett had already told enough to induce her to change her mind,—but after that any intimacy with the house at Chesterton had better be postponed till this had all been settled.

But how much would have to be endured before that! Robert Bolton had almost threatened to take his wife away from him. No one could take his wife away from him,—unless, indeed, the law were to say that she was not his wife. But how would it be with him if she herself, under the influence of her family, were to wish to leave him! The law no doubt would give him the custody of his own wife, till the law had said that she was not his wife. But could he keep her if she asked him to let her go? And should she be made to doubt,—should her mind be so troubled as it would be should she once be taught to think it possible that she had been betrayed,—would she not then want to go from him? Would it not be probable that she would doubt when she should be told that this woman had been called by her husband's name in Australia, and when he should be unable to deny that he had admitted, or at least had not contradicted, the appellation?

On a sudden, when he turned away from the street leading to Chesterton as he came out of the College, he resolved that he would at once go back to Robert Bolton. The man was offensive, suspicious, and self-willed; but, nevertheless, his good services, if they could be secured, would be all-important. For his wife's sake, as Caldigate said to himself,—for his wife's sake he must bear much. 'I have come to tell you something that has occurred since I was here just now,' said Caldigate, meeting his brother-in-law at the door of the office. 'Would you mind coming back?'

'I am rather in a hurry.'

'It is of importance, and you had better hear it,' said Caldigate, leading the way imperiously to the inner room. 'It is for your sister's sake. That man Crinkett is in Cambridge.'

'In Cambridge?'

'I saw him just now.'

'And spoke to him?' the attorney asked.

'No. I passed him; and I do not know even whether he recognised me. But he is here, in Cambridge.'

'And the woman?'

'I have told you all that I know. He has not come here for nothing.'

'Probably not,' said the attorney, with a scornful smile. 'You will hear of him before long.'

'Of course I shall. I have come to you now to ask a question. I must put my case at once into a lawyer's hands. Crinkett, no doubt, will commit perjury, and I must undergo the annoyance and expense of proving him to be a perjurer. She probably is here also, and will be ready to commit perjury. Of course I must have a lawyer. Will you act for me?'

'I will act for my sister.'

'Your sister and I are one; and I am obliged, therefore, to ask again whether you will act for me? Of course I should prefer it. Though you are, I think, hard to me in this matter, I can trust you implicitly. It will be infinitely better for Hester that it should be so. But I must have some lawyer.'

'And so must she.'

'Hers and mine must be the same. As to that I will not admit any question. Can you undertake to fight this matter on my behalf,—and on hers? If you feel absolutely hostile to me you had better decline. For myself, I cannot understand why there should be such hostility.'

Caldigate had so far conquered his own feelings of abasement as to be able to say this with a determined face, looking straight into the attorney's eyes, at any rate without sign of fear.

'It wants thinking about,' said Robert Bolton.

'To-morrow the baby is to be christened, and for Hester's sake I will endeavour to put this matter aside;—but on Wednesday I must know.'

'On Wednesday morning I will answer your question. But what if this man comes to me in the meantime?'

'Listen to him or speak to him, just as seems good to you. You know everything that there is to tell, and may therefore know whether he lies or speaks the truth.'

Then Caldigate went to the inn, got his horse, and rode back to Folking.

CHAPTER XXVII

The Christening

THE next day was the day of the christening. Caldigate, on his return home from Cambridge, had felt himself doomed to silence. He could not now at this moment tell his wife that the man had come,—the man who would doubtless work her such terrible misery. She was very strong. She had gone through the whole little event of her baby's birth quite as well as could be expected, and had been just what all her friends might have wished her to be. But that this blow had fallen upon her,—but that these ill news had wounded her,—she would now have been triumphant. Her mother was at last coming to her. Her husband was all that a husband should be. Her baby was, to her thinking, sweeter, brighter, more satisfactory than any other baby ever had been. But the first tidings had been told to her. She had seen the letter signed 'Euphemia Caldigate'; and of course she was ill at ease. Knowing how vexatious the matter was to her husband, she had spoken of it but seldom,—having asked but a question now and again when the matter pressed itself too severely on her mind. He understood it all, both her reticence and her sufferings. Her sufferings must of course be increased. She must know before long that Crinkett, and probably the woman also, were in her neighbourhood. But he could not tell her now when she was preparing her baby for his ceremony in the church.

The bells were rung, and the baby was prepared, and Mrs. Bolton came out to Folking according to her promise. Though Robert was not there, many of the Boltons were present, as was also Uncle Babington. He had come over on the preceding evening, making on this occasion his first journey to Folking since his wife's sister had died; and the old squire was there in very good humour, though he excused himself from going to the church by explaining that as he had no duty to perform he would only be in the way amongst them all. Daniel and Mrs. Bolton had also been at Folking that night, and had then for the first time been brought into contact with the Babington grandeur. The party had been almost gay, the old squire having taken some delight in what he thought to be the absurdities of his brother-in-law. Mr. Babington himself was a man who was joyous on most occasions, and always gay on such an occasion as this. He had praised the mother, and praised the baby, and praised the house of Folking generally, graciously declaring that his wife looked forward to the pleasure of making acquaintance with her new niece, till old Mr. Caldigate had been delighted with these manifestations of condescension. 'Folking is a poor place,' said he, 'but Babington is really a country-house.'

'Yes,' replied the other squire, much gratified, 'Babington is what you may call really a good country-house.'

You had to laugh very hard at him before you could offend Uncle Babington. In all this John Caldigate was obliged to assist, knowing all the time, feeling all the time, that Crinkett was in Cambridge; and through all this the young mother had to appear happy, knowing the existence of that letter signed 'Euphemia Caldigate,'–feeling it at every moment. And they both acted their parts well. Caldigate himself,–though when he was alone the thought of what was coming would almost crush him,–could always bear himself bravely when others were present.

On the morning before they went to church, when the bells were ringing, old Mr. Bolton came in a carriage with his wife from Cambridge. She, of course, condescended to give her hand to her son-in-law, but she did it with a look which was full of bitterness. She did not probably intend to be specially bitter, but bitterness of expression was common to her. She was taken, however, at once up to the baby, and then in the presence of her daughter and grandchild it may be presumed that she relaxed a little. At any rate, her presence in the house made her daughter happy for the time.

Then they all went to the church, except the squire, who, as he himself pleaded, had no duty to perform there. Mrs. Bolton, as she was taken through the hall, saw him and recognised him, but would not condescend even to bow her head to him, though she knew how intimate he had been with her husband. She still felt,–though she had yielded for this day, this day which was to make her grandchild a Christian,–that there must be, and should be, a severance between people such as the Boltons and people such as the Caldigates.

As the service went on, and as the water was sprinkled, and as the prayers were said, Caldigate felt thankful that so much had been allowed to be done before the great trouble had disclosed itself. The doubt whether even the ceremony could be performed before the clap of thunder had been heard through all Cambridge had been in itself a distinct sorrow to him. Had Crinkett showed himself at Chesterton, neither Mrs. Bolton nor Daniel Bolton would have been standing then at the font. Had Crinkett been heard of at Babington, Uncle Babington would not now have been at Folking. All this was passing through his mind as he was standing by the font. When the ceremony of making the young Daniel Humphrey Caldigate a Christian was all but completed, he fancied that he saw old Mr. Bolton's eyes fixed on something in the church, and he turned his head suddenly, with no special purpose, but simply looking, as one is apt to look, when another looks. There he saw, on a seat divided from himself by the breadth of the little nave, Thomas Crinkett sitting with another man.

There was not a shadow of a doubt on his mind as to the identity of the Australian—nor as to that of Crinkett's companion. At the moment he did not remember the man's name, but he knew him as a miner with whom he had been familiar at Ahalala, and who had been in partnership both with himself and Crinkett at Nobble,—as one who had, alas! been in his society when Euphemia Smith had been there also. At that instant he remembered the fact that the man had called Euphemia Smith Mrs. Caldigate in his presence, and that he had let the name pass without remonstrance. The memory of that moment flashed across him now as he quickly turned back his face towards his child who was still uttering his little wail in the arms of the clergyman.

Utterden church is not a large building. The seat on which Crinkett had placed himself was one usually occupied by parish boys at the end of the row of appropriated seats and near to the door. Less than half-a-dozen yards from it, at the other side of the way leading up the church, stood the font, so that the stranger was almost close to Caldigate when he turned. They were so near that others there could not but have observed them. Even the clergyman, however absorbed he might have been in his sacred work, could not but have observed them. It was not there as it might have been in a town. Any stranger, even on a Sunday, would be observed by all in Utterden church,—how much then at a ceremony which, as a rule, none but friends attend! And Crinkett was looking on with all his eyes, leaning forward over his stick and watching closely. Caldigate had taken it all in, even in that moment. The other man was sitting back, gazing at nothing as though the matter to him were indifferent. Caldigate could understand it all. The man was there simply to act or to speak when he might be wanted.

As the ceremony was completed John Caldigate stood by and played with all proper words and actions the part of the young father. No one standing there could see by his face that he had been struck violently; that he had for a few moments been almost unable to stand. But he himself was aware that a cold sweat had broken out all over him as before. Though he leaned over the baby lying in his mother's arms and kissed it, and smiled on the young mother, he did so as some great actor will carry out his part before the public when nearly sinking to the ground from sudden suffering. What would it be right that he should do now,—now,—now? No one there had heard of Crinkett except his wife. And even she herself had no idea that the man of whom she had heard was in England. Should he speak to the man, or should he endeavour to pass out of the church as though he had not recognised him? Could he trust himself even to make the endeavour when he should have turned round and when he would find himself face to face with the man?

And then what should he say, and how should he act, if the man addressed him in the church? The man had not come out there to Utterden for nothing, and probably would so address him. He had determined on telling no lie,—no lie, at any rate, as to present circumstances. That life of his in Australia had been necessarily rough; and though successful, had not been quite as it should have been. As to that, he thought that it ought to be permitted to him to be reticent. But as to nothing since his marriage would he lie. If Crinkett spoke to him he must acknowledge the man,—but if Crinkett told his story about Euphemia Smith in the church before them all, how should he then answer? There was but a moment for him to decide it all. The decision had to be made while he was handing back his babe to its mother with his sweetest smile.

As the party at the font was broken up, the eyes of them all were fixed upon the two strangers. A christening in a public church is a public service, and open to the world at large. There was no question to be asked them, but each person as he looked at them would of course think that somebody else would recognise them. They were decently dressed,—dressed probably in such garments as gentlemen generally wear on winter mornings,—but any one would know at a glance that they were not English gentlemen. And they were of an appearance unfamiliar to any one there but Caldigate himself,—clean, but rough, not quite at home in their clothes, which had probably been bought ready-made, with rough, ignoble faces,—faces which you would suspect, but faces, nevertheless, which had in them something of courage. As the little crowd prepared to move from the font, the two men got up and stood in their places.

Caldigate took the opportunity to say a word to Mr. Bromley before he turned round so that he might yet pause before he decided. At that moment he resolved that he would recognise his enemy, and treat him with the courtesy of old friendship. It would be bad to do at the moment, but he thought that in this way he might best prepare himself for the future. Crinkett had appealed to him for money, but Crinkett himself had said nothing to him about Euphemia Smith. The man had not as yet accused him of bigamy. The accusation had come from her, and it still might be that she had used Crinkett's name wrongfully. At any rate, he thought that when the clap of thunder should have come, it would be better for him not to have repudiated a man with whom it would then be known that his relations had once been so intimate.

He addressed himself therefore at once to his old associate. 'I am surprised to see you here, Mr. Crinkett.' This he said with a smile and a pleasant voice, putting out his hand to him. How hard it was to summon up that smile! How hard to get that tone of voice! Even those commonplace words had been so difficult of selection! 'Was it you I saw yesterday in the College gardens?'

'Yes, it was me, no doubt.'

'I turned round, and then thought that it was impossible. We have just been christening my child. Will you come up to our breakfast?'

'You remember Jack Adamson,—eh?'

'Of course I do,' said Caldigate, giving his hand to the second man, who was rougher even than Crinkett. 'I hope he will come up also. This is my uncle, Mr. Babington; and this is my father-in-law, Mr. Bolton.' 'These were two of my partners at Nobble,' he said, turning to the two old gentlemen, who were looking on with astonished eyes. 'They have come over here, I suppose, with reference to the sale I made to them lately of my interests at Polyeuka.'

'That's about it,' said Adamson.

'We won't talk business just at this moment, because we have to eat our breakfast and drink our boy's health. But when that is done, I'll hear what you have to say;—or come into Cambridge to-morrow, just as you please. You'll walk up to the house now, and I'll introduce you to my wife?'

'We don't mind if we do eat a bit,—do we Jack?' said Crinkett. Jack bobbed his head, and so they walked back to Folking, the three of them together, while the two Mr. Boltons and Uncle Babington followed behind. The ladies and the baby had been taken in a carriage.

The distance from the church to the house at Folking was less than half a mile, but Caldigate thought that he would never reach his hall door. How was he to talk to the men,—with what words and after what fashion? And what should he say about them to his wife when he reached home? She had seen him speak to them, had known that he had been obliged to stay behind with them when it would have been so natural that he should have been at her side as she got into the carriage. Of that he was aware, but he could not know how far their presence would have frightened her. 'Yes,' he said, in answer to some question from Crinkett; 'the property round here is not exactly mine, but my father's.'

'They tell me as it's yours now?' said Crinkett.

'You haven't to learn to-day that in regard to other people's concerns men talk more than they know. The land is my father's estate, but I live here.'

'And him?' asked Adamson.

'He lives in Cambridge.'

'That's what we mean,—ain't it, Crinkett?' said Adamson. 'You're boss here?'

'Yes, I'm boss.'

'And a deuced good time you seem to have of it,' said Crinkett.

'I've nothing to complain of,' replied Caldigate, feeling himself at the moment to be the most miserable creature in existence.

It was fearful work,—work so cruel that his physical strength hardly enabled him to support it. He already repented his present conduct, telling himself that it would have been better to have treated the men from the first as spies and enemies;—though in truth his conduct had probably been the wisest he could have adopted. At last he had the men inside the hall door, and, introducing them hurriedly to his father, he left them that he might rush up to his wife's bedroom. The nurse was there and her mother; and, at the moment, she only looked at him. She was too wise to speak to him before them. But at last she succeeded in making an opportunity of being alone with her husband. 'You stay here, nurse; I'll be back directly, mamma,' and then she took him across the passage into his own dressing-room. 'Who are they, John? who are they?'

'They are men from the mines. As they were my partners, I have asked them to come in to breakfast.'

'And the woman?' As she spoke she held on to the back of a chair by which she stood, and only whispered her question.

'No woman is with them.'

'Is it the man,—Crinkett?'

'Yes, it is Crinkett.'

'In this house! And I am to sit at table with him?'

'It will be best so. Listen, dearest; all that I know, all that we know of Crinkett is, that he is asking money of me because the purchase he made of me has turned out badly for him.'

'But he is to marry that woman, who says that she is——' Then she stopped, looking into his face with agony. She could not bring herself to utter the words which would signify that another woman claimed to be her husband's wife.

'You are going too fast, Hester. I cannot condemn the man for what the woman has written until I know that he says the same himself. He was my partner, and I have had his money;—I fear, all his money. He as yet has said nothing about the woman. As it is so, it behoves me to be courteous to him. That I am suffering much, you must be well aware. I am sure you will not make it worse for me.'

'No, no,' she said, embracing him; 'I will not. I will be brave. I will do all that I can. But you will tell me everything?'

'Everything,' he said. Then he kissed her, and went back again to his unwelcome guests. She was not long before she followed him, bringing her baby in her arms. Then she took the child round to be kissed by all its relatives, and afterwards bowed politely to the two men, and told them that she was glad to see her husband's old friends and fellow-workmen.

'Yes, mum,' said Jack Adamson; 'we've been fellow-workmen when the work was hard enough. 'T young squire seems to have got over his difficulties pretty tidy!' Then she smiled again, and nodded to them, and retreated back to her mother.

Mrs. Bolton scowled at them, feeling certain that they were godless persons;—in which she was right. The old banker, drawing his son Daniel out of the room, whispered an inquiry; but Daniel Bolton knew nothing. 'There's been something wrong as to the sale of that mine,' said the banker. Daniel Bolton thought it probable that there had been something wrong.

The breakfast was eaten, and the child's health was drunk, and the hour was passed. It was a bad time for them all, but for Caldigate it was a very bitter hour. To him the effort made was even more difficult than to her;—as was right;—for she at any rate had been blameless. Then the Boltons went away, as had been arranged, and also Uncle Babington, while the men still remained.

'If you don't mind, squire, I'll take a turn with you,' said Crinkett at last; 'while Jack can sit anywhere about the place.'

'Certainly,' said Caldigate. And so they took their hats and went off, and Jack Adamson was left 'sitting anywhere' about the place.

CHAPTER XXVIII

Tom Crinkett At Folking

CALDIGATE thought that he had better take his companion where there would be the least chance of encountering many eyes. He went therefore through the garden into the farmyard and along the road leading back to the dike, and then he walked backwards and forwards between the ferry, over the Wash, and the termination of the private way by which they had come. The spot was not attractive, as far as rural prettiness was concerned. They had, on one hand or the other as they turned, the long, straight, deep dike which had been cut at right angles to the Middle Wash; and around, the fields were flat, plashy, and heavy-looking with the mud of February. But Crinkett for a while did not cease to admire everything. 'And them are all yourn?' he said, pointing to a crowd of cornstacks standing in the haggard.

'Yes, they're mine. I wish they were not.'

'What do you mean by that?'

'As prices are at present, a man doesn't make much by growing corn and keeping it to this time of the year.'

'And where them chimneys is,—is that yourn?' This he said pointing along the straight line of the road to Farmer Holt's homestead, which showed itself on the other side of the Wash.

'It belongs to the estate,' said Caldigate.

'By jingo! And how I remember your a-coming and talking to me across the gate at Polyeuka Hall!'

'I remember it very well.'

'I didn't know as you were an estated gent in those days.'

'I had spent a lot of money when I was young, and the estate, as you call it, was not large enough to bear the loss. So I had to go out and work, and get back what I had squandered.'

'And you did it?'

'Yes, I did it.'

'My word, yes! What a lot of money you took out of the colony, Caldigate!'

'I'm not going to praise myself, but I worked hard for it, and when I got it I didn't run riot.'

'Not with drink.'

'Nor in any other way. I kept my money.'

'Well;—I don't know as you was very much more of a Joseph than

203

anybody else.' Then Crinkett laughed most disagreeably; and Caldigate, turning over various ideas rapidly in his mind, thought that a good deed would be done if a man so void of feeling could be drowned beneath the waters of the black deep dike which was slowly creeping along by their side. 'Any way you was lucky,–infernally lucky.'

'You did not do badly yourself. When I first reached Nobble you had the name of more money than I ever made.'

'Who's got it now? Eh, Caldigate! who's got my money now?'

'It would take a clever man to tell that.'

'It don't take much cleverness for me to tell who has got more of it nor anybody else, and it don't take much cleverness for me to tell that I ain't got none of it left myself;–none of it, Caldigate. Not a d—— hundred pounds!' This he said with terrible energy.

'I'm sorry it's so bad as that with you, Crinkett.'

'Yes;–you is sorry, I daresay. You've acted sorry in all you said and done since I got taken in last by that —— mine;–haven't you? Well;–I have got just a few hundreds; what I could scrape together to bring me and a few others as might be wanted over to England. There's Jack Adamson with me and —— just two more. They may be wanted, squire.'

The attack now was being commenced, and how was he to repel it, or to answer it? Only on one ground had he received from Robert Bolton a decided opinion. Under no circumstances was he to give money to these persons. Were he to be guilty of that weakness he would have delivered himself over into their hands. And not only did he put implicit trust in the sagacity of Robert Bolton, but he himself knew enough of the world's opinion on such a matter to be aware that a man who has allowed himself to be frightened out of money is supposed to have acknowledged some terrible delinquency. He had been very clear in his mind when that letter came from Euphemia Smith that he would not now make any rebate. Till that attack had come, it might have been open to him to be generous;–but not now. And yet when this man spoke of his own loss, and reminded him of his wealth;– when Crinkett threw it in his teeth that by a happy chance he had feathered his nest with the spoils taken from the wretched man himself, –then he wished that it was in his power to give back something.

'Is that said as a threat?' he asked, looking round on his companion, and resolving that he would be brave.

'That's as you take it, squire. We don't want to threaten nothing.'

'Because if you do, you'd better go, and do what you have to do away from here.'

'Don't you be so rough now with an old pal. You won't do no good by being rough. I wasn't rough to you when you came to Polyeuka Hall without very much in your pocket.' This was untrue, for Crinkett had been rough, and Caldigate's pockets had been full of money; but there could be no good got by contradicting him on small trifles. 'I was a good mate to you then. You wouldn't even have got your finger into the "Old Stick-in-the-Mud," nor yet into Polyeuka, but for me. I was the making of your fortin, Caldigate. I was.'

'My fortune, such as it is, was made by my own industry.'

'Industry be blowed! I don't know that you were so much better than anybody else. Wasn't I industrious? Wasn't I thinking of it morning, noon, and night, and nothing else? You was smart. I do allow that, Caldigate. You was very smart.'

'Did you ever know me dishonest?'

'Pooh! what's honesty? There's nothing so smart as honesty. Whatever you got, you got a sure hold of. That's what you mean by honesty. You was clever enough to take care as you had really got it. Now about this Polyeuka business. I'll tell you how it is. I and Jack Adamson and another,'—as he alluded to the 'other' he winked,—'we believed in Polyeuka; we did. D—— the cussed hole! Well;—when you was gone we thought we'd try it. It was not easy to get the money as you wanted, but we got it. One of the banks down at Sydney went shares, but took all the plant as security. Then the cussed place ran out the moment the money was paid. It was just as though fortin had done it a purpose. If you don't believe what I'm a-saying, I've got the documents to show you.'

Caldigate did believe what the man said. It was a matter as to which he had, in the way of business, received intelligence of his own from the colony, and he was aware that he had been singularly lucky as to the circumstances and time of the sale. But there had been nothing 'smart' about it. Those in the colony who understood the matter thought at the time that he was making a sacrifice of his own interests by the terms proposed. He had thought so himself, but had been willing to make it in order that he might rid himself of further trouble. He had believed that the machinery and plant attached to the mine had been nearly worth the money, and he had been quite certain that Crinkett himself, when making the bargain, had considered himself to be in luck's way. But such property, as he well knew, was, by its nature, precarious, and liable to sudden changes. He had been fortunate, and the purchasers had been the reverse. Of that he had no doubt, though probably the man had exaggerated his own misfortune. When he had been given to understand how bad had been the fate of these old companions of his in the matter, with the feelings of a liberal

205

gentleman he was anxious to share with them the loss. Had Crinkett come to him, explaining all that he now explained, without any interference from Euphemia Smith, he would have been anxious to do much. But now;–how could he do anything now? 'I do not at all disbelieve what you tell me about the mine,' he said.

'And yet you won't do anything for us? You ain't above taking all our money and seeing us starve; and that when you have got everything round you here like an estated gentleman, as you are?'

There was a touch of eloquence in this, a soundness of expostulation which moved him much. He could afford to give back half the price he had received for the mine and yet be a well-to-do man. He paid over to his father the rents from Folking, but he had the house and home-farm for nothing. And the sum which he had received for Polyeuka by no means represented all his savings. He did not like to think that he had denuded this man who had been his partner of everything in order that he himself might be unnecessarily rich. It was not pleasant to him to think that the fatness of his opulence had been extracted from Jack Adamson and from—Euphemia Smith. When the application for return of the money had been first made to him from Australia, he hadn't known what he knew now. There had been no eloquence then,– no expostulation. Now he thoroughly wished that he was able to make restitution. 'A threat has been used to me,' he muttered, almost anxious to explain to the man his exact position.

'A threat! I ain't threatened nothing. But I tell you there will be threats and worse than threats. Fair means first and foul means afterwards! That's about it, Caldigate.'

If he could have got this man to say that there was no threat, to be simply piteous, he thought that he might even yet have suggested some compromise. But that was impossible when he was told that worse than threats was in store for him. He was silent for some moments, thinking whether it would not be better for him to rush into that matter of Euphemia Smith himself. But up to this time he had no absolute knowledge that Crinkett was aware of the letter which had been written. No doubt that in speaking of 'another' as being joined with himself and Adamson he had intended that Euphemia Smith should be understood. But till her name had been mentioned, he could not bring himself to mention it. He could not bring himself to betray the fear which would become evident if he spoke of the woman.

'I think you had better go to my lawyer,' he said.

'We don't want no lawyering. The plunder is yours, no doubt. Whether you'll have so much law on your side in other matters,–that's the question.' Crinkett did not in the least understand the state of his companion's mind. To Crinkett it appeared that Caldigate was simply anxious to save his money.

'I do not know that I can say anything else to you just at present. The bargain was a fair bargain, and you have no ground for any claim. You come to me with some mysterious threat—'

'You understand,' said Crinkett.

'I care nothing for your threats. I can only bid you go and do your worst.'

'That's what we intend.'

'That you should have lost money by me is a great sorrow to me.'

'You look sorry, squire.'

'But after what you have said, I can make you no offer. If you will go to my brother-in-law, Mr. Robert Bolton—'

'That's the lady's brother?'

'My wife's brother.'

'I know all about it, Caldigate. I won't go to him at all. What's he to us? It ain't likely that I am going to ask him for money to hold our tongues. Not a bit of it. You've had sixty thousand pounds out of that mine. The bank found twenty and took all the plant. There's forty gone. Will you share the loss? Give us twenty and we'll be off back to Australia by the first ship. And I'll take a wife back with me. You understand? I'll take a wife back with me. Then we shall be all square all round.'

With what delight would he have given the twenty thousand pounds, had he dared! Had there been no question about the woman, he would have given the money to satisfy his own conscience as to the injury he had involuntarily done to his old partners. But he could not do it now. He could make no suggestion towards doing it. To do so would be to own to all the Boltons that Mrs. Euphemia Smith was his wife. And were he to do so, how could he make himself secure that the man and the woman would go back to Australia and trouble him no more? All experience forbade him to hope for such a result. And then the payment of the money would be one of many damning pieces of evidence against him. They had now got back for the second time to the spot at which the way up to the house at Folking turned off from the dike. Here he paused and spoke what were intended to be his last words. 'I have nothing more to say, Crinkett. I will not promise anything myself. A threatened man should never give way. You know that yourself. But if you will go to my brother-in-law I will get him to see you.'

'D— your brother-in-law. He ain't your brother-in-law, no more than I am.'

Now the sword had been drawn and the battle had been declared. 'After that,' said Caldigate, walking on in front, 'I shall decline to speak to you any further.' He went back through the farmyard at a quick pace, while Crinkett kept up with him, but still a few steps behind. In the front of the house they found Jack Adamson, who, in obedience to his friend's suggestion had been sitting anywhere about the place.

'I'm blowed if he don't mean to stick to every lump he's robbed us of!' said Crinkett, in a loud voice.

'He do, do he? Then we know what we've got to be after.'

'I've come across some of 'em precious mean,' continued Crinkett; 'but a meaner skunk nor this estated gent, who is a justice of the peace and a squire and all that, I never did come across, and I don't suppose I never shall.' And then they stood looking at him, jeering at him. And the gardener, who was then in the front of the house, heard it all.

'Darvell,' said the squire, 'open the gate for these gentlemen.' Darvell of course knew that they had been brought from the church to the house, and had been invited in to the christening breakfast.

'If I were Darvell I wouldn't take wages from such a skunk as you.' said Crinkett. 'A man as has robbed his partners of every shilling, and has married a young lady when he has got another wife living out in the colony. At least she was out in the colony. She ain't there now, Darvell. She's somewhere else now. That's what your master is, Darvell. You'll have to look out for a place, because your master'll be in quod before long. How much is it they gets for bigamy, Jack? Three years at the treadmill;—that's about it. But I pities the young lady and the poor little bastard.'

What was he to do? A sense of what was fitting for his wife rather than for himself forbade him to fly at the man and take him by the throat. And now, of course, the wretched story would be told through all Cambridgeshire. Nothing could prevent that now. 'Darvell,' he said, as he turned towards the hall steps, 'you must see these men off the premises. The less you say to them the better.'

'We'll only just tell him all about it as we goes along comfortable,' said Adamson. Darvell, who was a good sort of man in his way,—slow rather than stupid, weighted with the ordinary respect which a servant has for his master,—had heard it all, but showed no particular anxiety to hear more. He accompanied the men down to the Causeway, hardly opening his mouth to them, while they were loud in denouncing the meanness of the man who had deserted a wife in Australia, and had then betrayed a young lady here in England.

'What were they talking about?' said his wife to him when they were alone. 'I heard their voices even here.'

'They were threatening me:—threatening me and you.'

'About that woman?'

'Yes; about that woman. Not that they have dared yet to mention her name,—but it was about that woman.'

'And she?'

'I've heard nothing from her since that letter. I do not know that she is in England, but I suppose that she is with them.'

'Does it make you unhappy, John?'

'Very unhappy.'

'Does it frighten you?'

'Yes. It makes me fear that you for a while will be made miserable,— you whom I thought that I could protect from all sorrow and from all care! O my darling! of course it frightens me; but it is for you.'

'What will they do first, John?'

'They have already said words before the man there which will of course be spread about the country.'

'What words?'

Then he paused, but after pausing he spoke very plainly. 'They said that you were not my wife.'

'But I am.'

'Indeed you are.'

'Tell me all truly. Though I were not, I would still be true to you.'

'But, Hester,—Hester, you are. Do not speak as though that were possible.'

'I know that you love me. I am sure of that. Nothing should ever make me leave you;—nothing. You are all the world to me now. Whatever you may have done I will be true to you. Only tell me everything.'

'I think I have,' he said, hoarsely. Then he remembered that he had told much to Robert Bolton which she had not heard. 'I did tell her that I would marry her.'

'You did.'

'Yes, I did.'

'Is not that a marriage in some countries?'

'I think nowhere,—certainly not there. And the people, hearing of it all, used to call her by my name.'

'O John!—will not that be against us?'

'It will be against me,—in the minds of persons like your mother.'

'I will care nothing for that. I know that you have repented, and are sorry. I know that you love me now.'

'I have always loved you since the first moment that I saw you.'

'Never for a moment believe that I will believe them. Let them do what they will, I will be your wife. Nothing shall take me away from you. But it is sad, is it not; on that the very day that poor baby has been christened?' Then they sat and wept together, and tried to comfort each other. But nothing could comfort him. He was almost prostrated at the prospect of his coming misery,—and of hers.

CHAPTER XXIX

'Just By Telling Me That I Am'

THE thunderbolt had fallen now. Caldigate, when he left his wife that he might stroll about the place after the dusk had fallen, told himself again and again that the thunderbolt had certainly fallen now. There could be no longer a doubt but that this woman would claim him as her husband. A whole world of remorse and regrets oppressed his conscience and his heart. He looked back and remembered the wise counsels which had been given him on board the ship, when the captain and Mrs. Callender and poor Dick Shand had remonstrated with him, and called to mind his own annoyance when he had bidden them mind their own affairs. And then he remembered how he had determined to break away from the woman at Sydney, and to explain to her, as he might then have done without injustice, that they two could be of no service the one to the other, and that they had better part. It seemed now, as he looked back, to have been so easy for him then to have avoided danger, so easy to have kept a straight course! But now,—now, surely he would be overwhelmed.

And then how easy it would have been, had he been more careful at the beginning of these troubles, to have bought these wretches off! He had been, he now acknowledged, too peremptory in his first refusal to refund a portion of the money to Crinkett. The application had, indeed, been made without those proofs as to the condition of the mine which had since reached him, and he had distrusted Crinkett. Crinkett he had known to be a man not to be trusted. But yet, even after receiving the letter from Euphemia Smith, the matter might have been arranged. When he had first become assured that the new Polyueka Company had failed, he should have made an offer, even though Euphemia Smith had then commenced her threats. With skill, might he not have done it on this very day? Might he not have made the man understand that if he would base his claim simply on his losses, and make it openly on that ground, then his claim should be considered? But now it was too late, and the thunderbolt had fallen.

What must he do first? Robert Bolton had promised to tell him on the morrow whether he would act for him as his lawyer. He felt sure now that his brother-in-law would not do so; but it would be necessary that he should have an answer, and that necessity would give him an excuse for going into Cambridge and showing himself among

211

the Boltons. Let his sufferings or his fears be what they might, he would never confess to the world that he suffered or that he was frightened, by shutting himself up. He would be seen about Cambridge, walking openly, as though no reports, no rumours, had been spread about concerning him. He would go to the houses of his wife's relations until he should be told that he was not welcome.

'John,' his wife said to him that night, 'bear it like a man.'

'Am I not bearing it like a man?'

'It is crushing your very heart. I see it in your eyes.'

'Can you bear it?' He asked his question with a stern voice; but as he asked it he turned to her and kissed her.

'Yes,' she said, 'yes. While I have you with me, and baby, I can bear anything. While you will tell me everything that happens, I will bear everything. And, John, when you were out just now, and when I am alone and trying to pray, I told myself that I ought not to be unhappy; for I would sooner have you and baby and all these troubles, than be back at Chesterton—without you.'

'I wish you were back there. I wish you had never seen me.'

'If you say that, then I shall be crushed.'

'For your sake, my darling; for your sake,—for your sake! How shall I comfort you when all those around you are saying that you are not my wife?'

'By telling me that I am,' she said, coming and kneeling at his feet, and looking up into his face. 'If you say so, you may be sure that I shall believe no one who says the contrary.'

It was thus, and only now, that he begun to know the real nature of the woman whom he had succeeded in making his own, and of whom he found now that even her own friends would attempt to rob him. 'I will bear it,' he said, as he embraced her. 'I will bear it, if I can, like a man.'

'Oh, ma'am! those men were saying horrid things,' her nurse said to her that night.

'Yes; very horrid things. I know it all. It is part of a wicked plot to rob Mr. Caldigate of his money. It is astonishing the wickedness that people will contrive. It is very very sad. I don't know how long it may be before Mr. Caldigate can prove it all.'

'But he can prove it all, ma'am?'

'Of course he can. The truth can always be proved at last. I trust there will be no one about the place to doubt him. If there were such a one, I would not speak to him,—though it were my own father; though it were my own mother.' Then she took the baby in her arms, as though fearing that the nurse herself might not be loyal.

'I don't think there will be any as knows master, will be wrong enough for that,' said the nurse, understanding what was expected of her. After that, but not quite readily, the baby was once more trusted to her.

On the following morning Caldigate rode into the town, and as he put his horse up at the inn, he felt that the very ostler had heard the story. As he walked along the street, it seemed to him that everyone he met knew all about it. Robert Bolton would, of course, have heard it; but nevertheless he walked boldly into the attorney's office. His fault at the time was in being too bold in manner, in carrying himself somewhat too erect, in assuming too much confidence in his eye and mouth. To act a part perfectly requires a consummate actor; and there are phases in life in which acting is absolutely demanded. A man cannot always be at his ease, but he should never seem to be discomfited. For petty troubles the amount of acting necessary is so common that habit has made it almost natural. But when great sorrows come it is hard not to show them,—and harder still not to seem to hide them.

When he entered the private room he found that the old man was there with his son. He shook hands, of course, with both of them, and then he stood a moment silent to hear how they would address him. But as they also were silent he was compelled to speak. 'I hope you got home all right, sir, yesterday; and Mrs. Bolton.'

The old man did not answer, but he turned his face round to his son. 'I hear that you had that man Crinkett out at Folking yesterday,' said Robert.

'He was there, certainly, to my sorrow.'

'And another with him?'

'Yes; and another with him, whom I had also known at Nobble.'

'And they were brought in to breakfast?'

'Yes.'

'And then afterwards declared that you had married a wife out there in the colony?'

'That also is true.'

'They have been with my father this morning.'

'I am very, very sorry, sir,' said Caldigate, turning to the old man, 'that you should have been troubled in so disagreeable a business.'

'Now, Caldigate, I will tell you what we propose.' It was still the attorney who was speaking, for the old man had not as yet opened his mouth since his son-in-law had entered the room. 'There can, I think, be no doubt that this woman intends to bring an accusation of bigamy against you.'

213

'She is threatening to do it. I think it very improbable that she will be fool enough to make the attempt.'

'From what I have heard I feel sure that the attempt will be made. Depositions, in fact, will be made before the magistrates some day this week. Crinkett and the woman have been with the mayor this morning, and have been told the way in which they should proceed.' Caldigate, when he heard this, felt that he was trembling, but he looked into the speaker's face without allowing his eyes to turn to the right or left. 'I am not going to say anything now about the case itself. Indeed, as I know nothing, I can say nothing. You must provide yourself with a lawyer.'

'You will not act for me?'

'Certainly not. I must act for my sister. Now what I propose, and what her father proposes, is this,—that she shall return to her home at Puritan Grange while this question is being decided.'

'Certainly not,' said the husband.

'She must,' said the old man, speaking for the first time.

'We shall compel it,' said the attorney.

'Compel! How will you compel it? She is my wife.'

'That has to be proved. Public opinion will compel it, if nothing else. You cannot make a prisoner of her.'

'Oh, she shall go if she wishes it. You shall have free access to her. Bring her mother. Bring your carriage. She shall dispose of herself as she pleases. God forbid that I should keep her, though she be my wife, against her will.'

'I am sure she will do as her friends shall advise her when she hears the story,' said the attorney.

'She has heard the story. She knows it all. And I am sure that she will not stir a foot,' said the husband. 'You know nothing about her.' This he said turning to his wife's half-brother; and then again he turned to the old man. 'You, sir, no doubt, are well aware that she can be firm to her purpose. Nothing but death could take her away from me. If you were to carry her by force to Chesterton she would return to Folking on foot before the day was over. She knows what it is to be a wife. I am not a bit afraid of her leaving me.' This he was able to say with a high spirit and an assured voice.

'It is quite out of the question that she should stay with you while this is going on.'

'Of course she must come away,' said the banker, not looking at the man whom he now hated as thoroughly as did his wife.

'Consult your own friends, and let her consult hers. They will all tell you so. Ask Mrs. Babington. Ask your own father.'

'I shall ask no one—but her.'

'Think what her position will be! All the world will at least doubt whether she be your wife or not.'

'There is one person who will not doubt,—and that is herself.'

'Very good. If it be so, that will be a comfort to you, no doubt. But, for her sake, while other people doubt, will it not be better that she should be with her father and mother? Look at it all round.'

'I think it would be better that she should be with me,' replied Caldigate.

'Even though your former marriage with that other woman were proved?'

'I will not presume that to be possible. Though a jury should so decide, their decision would be wrong. Such an error could not effect us. I will not think of such a thing.'

'And you do not perceive that her troubles will be lighter in her father's house than in yours?'

'Certainly not. To be away from her own house would be such a trouble to her that she would not endure it unless restrained by force.'

'If you press her, she would go. Cannot you see that it would be better for her name?'

'Her name is my name,' he said, clenching his fist in his violence, 'and my name is hers. She can have no good name distinct from me,— no name at all. She is part and parcel of my very self, and under no circumstances will I consent that she shall be torn away from me. No word from any human being shall persuade me to it,—unless it should come from herself.'

'We can make her,' said the old man.

'No doubt we could get an order from the Court,' said the attorney, thinking that anything might be fairly said in such an emergency as this; 'but it will be better that she should come of her own accord, or by his direction. Are you aware how probable it is that you may be in prison within a day or two?'

To this Caldigate made no answer, but turned round to leave the room. He paused a moment at the doorway to think whether another word or two might not be said in behalf of his wife. It seemed hard to him, or hard rather upon her, that all the wide-stretching solid support of her family should be taken away from her at such a crisis as the present. He knew their enmity to himself. He could understand both the old enmity and that which had now been newly engendered. Both the one and the other were natural. He had succeeded in getting the girl away from her parents in opposition to both father and mother. And now, almost within the first year of his marriage, she had been brought to this terrible misery by means of disreputable people with whom he had been closely connected! Was it not natural that Robert Bolton should turn against him! If Hester had been his sister and there had come such an interloper what would he have felt? Was it not his duty to be gentle and to give way, if by any giving way he could lessen the evil which he had occasioned. 'I am sorry to have to leave your presence like this,' he said, turning back to Mr. Bolton.

'Why did you ever come into my presence?'

'What has been done is done. Even if I would give her back, I cannot. For better or for worse she is mine. We cannot make it otherwise now. But understand this, when you ask that she shall come back to you, I do not refuse it on my own account. Though I should be miserable indeed were she to leave me, I will not even ask her to stay. But I know she will stay. Though I should try to drive her out, she would not go. Good-bye, sir.' The old man only shook his head. 'Good-bye, Robert.'

'Good-bye. You had better get some lawyer as soon as you can. If you know any one in London you should send for him. If not, Mr. Seely here is as good a man as you can have. He is no friend of mine, but he is a careful attorney who understands his business.' Then Caldigate left the room with the intention of going at once to Mr. Seely.

But standing patiently at the door, just within the doorway of the house, he met a tall man in dark plain clothes; whom he at once knew to be a policeman. The man, who was aware that Caldigate was a country magistrate, civilly touched his hat, and then, with a few whispered words, expressed his opinion that our hero had better go with him to the mayor's office. Had he a warrant? Yes, he had a warrant, but he thought that probably it might not be necessary for him to show it. 'I will go with you, of course,' said Caldigate. 'I suppose it is on the allegation of a man named Crinkett.'

'A lady, sir, I think,' said the policeman.

'One Mrs. Smith.'

'She called herself—Caldigate, sir,' said the policeman. Then they went together without any further words to the mayor's court, and from thence, before he heard the accusation made against him, he sent both for his father and for Mr. Seely.

He was taken through to a private room, and thither came at once the mayor and another magistrate of the town with whom he was acquainted. 'This is a very sad business, Mr. Caldigate,' said the mayor.

'Very sad, indeed. I suppose I know all about it. Two men were with me yesterday threatening to indict me for bigamy if I did not give them a considerable sum of money. I can quite understand that they should have been here, as I know the nature of the evidence they can use. The policeman tells me the woman is here too.'

'Oh yes;—she is here, and has made her deposition. Indeed, there are two men and another woman who all declare that they were present at her marriage.' Then, after some further conversation, the accusers were brought into the room before him, so that their depositions might be read to him. The woman was closely veiled, so that he could not see a feature of her face; but he knew her figure well, and he remembered the other woman who had been half-companion, half-servant to Euphemia Smith when she had come up to the diggings, and who had been with her both at Ahalala and at Nobble. The woman's name, as he now brought to mind, was Anna Young. Crinkett also and Adamson followed them into the room, each of whom had made a deposition on the matter. 'Is this the Mr. Caldigate,' said the mayor, 'whom you claim as your husband?'

'He is my husband,' said the woman. 'He and I were married at Ahalala in New South Wales.'

'It is false,' said Caldigate.

'Would you wish to see her face?' asked the mayor.

'No; I know her voice well. She is the woman in whose company I went out to the Colony, and whom I knew while I was there. It is not necessary that I should see her. What does she say?'

'That I am your wife, John Caldigate.'

Then the deposition was read to him, which stated on the part of the woman, that on a certain day she was married to him by the Rev. Mr. Allan, a Wesleyan minister, at Ahalala, that the marriage took place in a tent belonging, as she believed, to Mr. Crinkett, and that Crinkett, Adamson, and Anna Young were all present at the marriage. Then the three persons thus named had taken their oaths and made their depositions to the same effect. And a document was produced, purporting to be a copy of the marriage certificate as made out by Mr. Allan,—a copy which she, the woman, stated that she obtained at the time, the register itself, which consisted simply of an entry in a small book, having been carried away by Mr. Allan in his pocket. Crinkett, when asked what had become of Mr. Allan, stated that he knew nothing but that he had left Ahalala. From that day to this none of them had heard of Mr. Allan.

Then the mayor gave Caldigate to understand that he must hold himself as committed to stand his trial for bigamy at the next Assizes for the County.

CHAPTER XXX

The Conclave At Puritan Grange

JOHN CALDIGATE was committed, and liberated on bail. This occurred in Cambridge on the Wednesday after the christening; and before the Saturday night following, all the Boltons were thoroughly convinced that this wretched man, who had taken from them their daughter and their sister, was a bigamist, and that poor Hester, though a mother, was not a wife. The evidence against him, already named, was very strong, but they had been put in possession of other, and as they thought more damning evidence than any to which he had alluded in telling his version of the story to Robert Bolton. The woman had produced, and had shown to Robert Bolton, the envelope of a letter addressed in John Caldigate's handwriting to 'Mrs. Caldigate, Ahalala, Nobble,' which letter had been dated inside from Sydney, and which envelope bore the Sydney post-mark. Caldigate's handwriting was peculiar, and the attorney declared that he could himself swear to it. The letter itself she also produced, but it told less than the envelope. It began as such a letter might begin, 'Dearest Feemy,' and ended 'Yours, ever and always, J.C.' As she herself had pointed out, a man such as Caldigate does not usually call his wife by that most cherished name in writing to her. The letter itself referred almost altogether to money matters, though perhaps hardly to such as a man generally discusses with his wife. Certain phrases seemed to imply a distinct action. She had better sell these shares or those, if she could, for a certain price,— and suchlike. But she explained, that they both when they married had been possessed of mining shares, represented by scrip which passed from hand to hand readily, and that each still retained his or her own property. But among the various small documents which she had treasured up for use, should they be needed for some possible occasion such as this, was a note, which had not, indeed, been posted, but which purported to have been written by the minister, Allan, to Caldigate himself, offering to perform the marriage at Ahalala, but advising him to have the ceremony performed at some more settled place, where an established church community with a permanent church or chapel admitted the proper custody of registers. Nothing could be more sensible, or written in a better spirit than this letter, though the language was not that of an educated man. This letter, Caldigate had, she said, showed to her, and she had retained it. Then she brought forward two handkerchiefs which she herself had marked with her new name, Euphemia Caldigate, and the date of the year. This had been done, she declared, immediately after her marriage, and the handkerchiefs seemed by their appearance to justify the assertion. Caldigate had admitted a promise, admitted that he had lived with the woman, admitted that she had passed by his name, admitted that there had been a conversation with the clergyman in regard to his marriage. And now there were three others, besides the woman herself, who were ready to swear,—who had sworn,—that they had witnessed the ceremony!

A clerk had been sent out early in November by Robert and William Bolton to make inquiry in the colony, and he could not well return before the end of March. And, if the accused man should ask for delay, it would hardly be possible to refuse the request, as it might be necessary for his defence that he, too, should get evidence from the colony. The next assizes would be in April, and it would hardly be possible that the trial should take place so soon. And if not there would be a delay of three or four months more. Even that might hardly suffice should a plea be made on Caldigate's behalf that prolonged inquiry was indispensable. A thousand allegations might be made, as to the characters of these witnesses,—characters which doubtless were open to criticism; as to the probability of forgery; as to the necessity of producing Allan, the clergyman; as to Mrs. Smith's former position,— whether or no she was in truth a widow when she was living at Ahalala. Richard Shand had been at Ahalala, and must have known the truth. Caldigate might well declare that Richard Shand's presence was essential to his defence. There would and must be delay.

But what, in the meantime, would be the condition of Hester,— Hester Bolton, as they feared that they would be bound in duty to call her,—of Hester and her infant. The thing was so full of real tragedy,— the true human nature of them all was so strongly affected, that for a time family jealousies and hatred had to give way. To father and mother and to the brothers, and to the brother's wife, it was equally a catastrophe, terrible, limitless, like an earthquake, or the falling upon them of some ruined tower. One thing was clear to them all,—that she and her child must be taken away from Folking. Her continued residence there would be a continuation of the horror. The man was not her husband. Not one of them was inspired by a feeling of mercy to allege that, in spite of all that they had heard, he still might be her husband. Even Mrs. Robert, who had been most in favour of the Caldigate marriage, did not doubt for an instant. The man had been a gambler at home on racecourses, and then had become a gambler at the gold-mines in the colony. His life then, by his own admission, had been disreputable. Who does not know that vices which may be treated with tenderness, almost with complaisance, while they are kept in the background, became monstrous, prodigious, awe-inspiring when they are made public? A gentleman shall casually let slip some profane word, and even some friendly parson standing by will think but little of it; but let the profane word, through some unfortunate accident, finds its way into the newspapers, and the gentleman will be held to have disgraced himself almost for ever. Had nothing been said of a marriage between Caldigate and Mrs. Smith, little would have been thought by Robert Bolton, little perhaps by Robert Bolton's father, little even by Robert Bolton's wife, of the unfortunate alliance which he had admitted. But now, everything was added to make a pile of wickedness as big as a mountain.

From the conclave which was held on Saturday at Puritan Grange to decide what should be done, it was impossible to exclude Mrs. Bolton. She was the young mother's mother, and how should she be excluded? From the first moment in which something of the truth had reached her ears, it had become impossible to silence her or to exclude her. To her all those former faults would have been black as vice itself, even though there had been no question of a former marriage. Outside active sins, to which it may be presumed no temptation allured herself, were abominable to her. Evil thoughts, hardness of heart, suspicions, unforgivingness, hatred, being too impalpable for denunciation in the Decalogue but lying nearer to the hearts of most men than murder, theft, adultery, and perjury, were not equally abhorrent to her. She had therefore allowed herself to believe all evil of this man, and from the very first had set him down in her heart as a hopeless sinner. The others had opposed her,—because the man had money. In the midst of her shipwreck, in the midst of her misery, through all her maternal agony, there was a certain triumph to her in this. She had been right,—right from first to last, right in everything. Her poor old husband was crushed by the feeling that they had among them, allowed this miscreant to take their darling away from them,—that he himself had assented; but she had not assented; she was not crushed. Before Monday night all Cambridge had heard something of the story, and then it had been impossible to keep her in the dark. And now, when the conclave met, of course she was one. The old man was there, and Robert Bolton, and William the barrister, who had come down from London to give his advice, and both Mr. and Mrs. Daniel. Mrs. Daniel, of all the females of the family, was the readiest to endure the severity of the step-mother, and she was now giving what comfort she

220

could by her attendance at the Grange.

'Of course she should come home,' said the barrister. Up to this moment no one had seen Hester since the evil tidings had been made known; but a messenger had been sent out to Folking with a long letter from her mother, in which the poor nameless one had been implored to come back with her baby to her old home till this matter had been settled. The writer had endeavoured to avoid the saying of hard things against the sinner; but her feelings had been made very clear. 'Your father and brothers and all of us think that you should come away from him while this is pending. Nay; we do not hesitate to say that it is your bounden duty to leave him.'

'I will never, never leave my dearest, dearest husband. If they were to put my husband into gaol I would sit at the door till they had let him out.' That, repeated over and over again, had been the purport of her reply. And that word 'husband', she used in almost every line, having only too clearly observed that her mother had not used it at all. 'Dearest mother,' she said, ending her letter, 'I love you as I have always done. But when I became his wife, I swore to love him best. I did not know then how strong my love could be. I have hardly known till now, when he is troubled, of what devotion I was capable. I will not leave him for a moment,—unless I have to do so at his telling.'

Such being her determination, and so great her obstinacy, it was quite clear that they could not by soft words or persuasive letters bring her to their way of thinking. She would not submit to their authority, but would claim that as a married woman she owed obedience only to her husband. And it would certainly not be within their power to make her believe that she was not Caldigate's wife. They believed it. They felt that they knew the facts. To them any continuation of the alliance between their poor girl and the false traitor was abominable. They would have hung the man without a moment's thought of mercy had it been possible. There was nothing they would not have done to rescue their Hester from his power. But how was she to be rescued till the dilatory law should have claimed its victim? 'Can't she be made to come away by the police?' asked the mother.

The barrister shook his head. 'Couldn't the magistrates give an order?' asked the father. Mr. Bolton had been a magistrate himself,— was one still indeed, although for some years he had not sat upon the bench,—but he had no very clear idea of a magistrate's power. The barrister again shook his head. 'You seemed to think that something of the kind could be done,' he said, turning to Robert. When he wanted advice he would always turn to Robert, especially in the presence of the barrister, intending to show that he thought the lower branch of the profession to be at any rate more accurate than the higher.

'I said something about an order from the Vice-Chancellor. But I fear we should not succeed in getting it.' The barrister again shook his head.

'Do you mean to say that nothing can be done?' exclaimed Mrs. Bolton, rising up from her seat; 'that no steps can be taken?'

'If she were once here, perhaps you could—prevent her return,' whispered the barrister.

'Persuade her not to go back,' suggested Mrs. Daniel.

'Well;—that might come after a time. But I think you would have the feeling of the community with you if you succeeded;—well, not violence, you understand.'

'No; not violence,' said the father.

'I could be violent with him,' said Mrs. Bolton.

'Just do not let her leave the house,' continued the barrister. 'Of course it would be disagreeable.'

'I should not mind that,' said Mrs. Bolton. 'In doing my duty I could bear anything. To separate her from him I could undergo any trouble.'

'But he would have the power to fetch her?' asked the father, doubtfully.

'No doubt;—by law he would have such power. But the magistrates would be very loath to assist him. The feeling of the community, as I said, would be in your favour. She would be cowed, and when once she was away from him he would probably feel averse to increase our enmity by taking strong measures for her recovery.' Mrs. Bolton seemed to declare by her face that it would be quite impossible for him to increase her enmity.

'But we can't lock her up,' said the old man.

'Practically you can. Take her bonnet away,—or whatever she came in. Don't let there be a vehicle to carry her back. Let the keys be turned if it be necessary. The servants must know of course what you are doing, but they will probably be on your side. I don't mean to say that if she be resolute to escape at any cost you can prevent her. But probably she will not be resolute like that. It requires a deal of resolution for a young woman to show herself in the streets alone in so wretched a plight as hers. It depends on her disposition.'

'She is very determined,' said Hester's mother.

'And you can be equally so.' To this assertion Mrs. Bolton assented with a little nod. 'You can only try it. It is one of those cases in which, unfortunately, publicity cannot be avoided. We have to do the best we can for her, poor dear, according to our conscience. I should induce her to come on a visit to her mother, and then I should, if possible, detain her.'

It was thus that William Bolton gave his advice; and as Robert Bolton assented, it was determined that this should be the line of action. Nor can it be said that they were either cruel or unloving in their projected scheme. Believing as they did that the man was not her husband, it must be admitted that it was their duty to take her away from him if possible. But it was not probable that Hester herself would look upon their care of her in the same light. She would beat herself against the bars of her cage; and even should she be prevented from escaping by the motives and reasons which William Bolton had suggested, she would not the less regard her father and mother as wicked tyrants. The mother understood that very well. And she, though she was hard to all the world besides, had never been hard to her girl. No tenderest female bosom that ever panted at injustice done to her offspring was more full than hers of pity, love, and desire. To save her Hester from sin and suffering she would willingly lay down her life. And she knew that in carrying out the scheme that had been proposed she must appear to her girl to be an enemy,—to be the bitterest of all enemies! I have seen a mother force open the convulsively closed jaws of her child in order that some agonising torture might be applied,—which, though agonising, would tend to save her sick infant's life. She did it though the child shrank from her as from some torturing fiend. This mother resolved that she would do the same,—though her child, too, should learn to hate her.

William Bolton undertook to go out to Folking and give the invitation by which she was to be allured to come to Puritan Grange,— only for a day and night if longer absence was objectionable; only for a morning visit, if no more could be achieved. It was all treachery and falsehood;—a doing of certain evil that possible good might come from it. 'She will hate me for ever, but yet it ought to be done,' said William Bolton; who was a good man, an excellent husband and father, regarded in his own profession as an honourable trustworthy man.

'She will never stay,' the old man said to his wife, when the others had gone and they two were left together.

'I don't know.'

'I am sure she will never stay.'

'I will try.'

Mrs. Robert said the same thing when the scheme was explained to her. 'Do you think anybody could keep me a prisoner against my will,— unless they locked me up in a cell? Do you think I would not scream?'

The husband endeavoured to explain that the screaming might depend on the causes which had produced the coercion. 'I think you would scream, and scream till you were let loose, if the person locking you up had nothing to justify him. But if you felt that the world would be all against you, then you would not scream and would not be let out.'

Mrs. Robert, however, seemed to think that no one could keep her in any house against her own will without positive bolts, bars, and chains.

In the meantime much had been settled out at Folking, or had been settled at Cambridge, so that the details were known at Folking. Mr. Seely had taken up the case, and had of course gone into it with much more minuteness than Robert Bolton had done. Caldigate owned to the writing of the envelope, and to the writing of the letter, but declared that that letter had not been sent in that envelope. He had written the envelope in some foolish joke while at Ahalala,—he remembered doing it well; but he was quite sure that it had never passed through the Sydney post-office. The letter itself had been written from Sydney. He remembered writing that also, and he remembered posting it at Sydney in an envelope addressed to Mrs. Smith. When Mr. Seely assured him that he himself had seen the post-office stamp of Sydney on the cover, Caldigate declared that it must have been passed through the post-office for fraudulent purposes after it had left his hands. 'Then,' said Mr. Seely, 'the fraud must have been meditated and prepared three years ago,—which is hardly probable.'

As to the letter from the clergyman, Allan, of which Mr. Seely had procured a copy, Caldigate declared that it had certainly never been addressed to him. He had never received any letter from Mr. Allan,—had never seen the man's handwriting. He was quite sure that if he were in New South Wales he could get a dozen people to swear that there had never been such a marriage at Ahalala. He did name many people, especially Dick Shand. Then Mr. Seely proposed to send out an agent to the colony, who should take the depositions of such witnesses as he could find, and who should if possible bring Dick Shand back with him. And, at whatever cost, search should be made for Mr. Allan; and Mr. Allan should, if found, be brought to England, if money could bring him. If Mr. Allan could not be found, some document written by him might perhaps be obtained with reference to his handwriting. But, through it all, Mr. Seely did believe that there had been some marriage ceremony between his client and Mrs. Euphemia Smith.

All this, down to the smallest detail, was told to Hester,—Hester

Bolton or Hester Caldigate, whichever she might be. And there was no word uttered by the man she claimed as her husband which she did not believe as though it were gospel.

CHAPTER XXXI

Hester Is Lured Back

ON the Monday morning, Mr. William Bolton, the barrister, who had much to his own inconvenience remained at Cambridge for the purpose of carrying out the scheme which he had proposed, went over to Folking in a fly. He had never been at the place before, and was personally less well acquainted with the family into which his sister had married than any other Bolton. Had everything been pleasant, nothing could have been more natural than such a visit; but as things were very far from pleasant Hester was much surprised when he was shown into her room. It had been known to Robert Bolton that Caldigate now came every day into Cambridge to see either his lawyer or his father, and that therefore he would certainly not be found at home about the middle of the day. It was henceforth to be a law with all the Boltons, at any rate till after the trial, that they would not speak to, or if possible see, John Caldigate. Not without very strong cause would William Bolton have entered his house, but that strong cause existed.

'Oh, William! I am so glad to see you,' said Hester, rushing into her brother's arms.

'I too am glad to see you, Hester, though the time is so sad to us all.'

'Yes; yes. It is sad;—oh, so sad! Is it not terrible that there should be people so wicked, and that they should be able to cause so much trouble to innocent persons.'

'With all my heart I feel for you,' said the brother, caressing his young sister.

With quickest instinct she immediately perceived that a slight emphasis given to the word 'you' implied the singular number. She drew herself back a little, still feeling, however, that no offence had as yet been committed against which she could express her indignation. But it was necessary that a protest should be made at once. 'I am so sorry that my husband is not here to welcome you. He has gone into Cambridge to fetch his father. Poor Mr. Caldigate is so troubled by all this that he prefers now to come and stay with us.'

'Ah, indeed! I dare say it will be better that the father and the son should be together.'

'Father and son, or even mother and daughter, are not like husbands and wives, are they?'

'No; they are not,' said the barrister, not quite knowing how to answer so very self-evident a proposition, but understanding accurately the line of thought which had rendered it necessary for the poor creature to reassert at every moment the bond by which she would fain be bound to the father of her child.

'But Mr. Caldigate is so good,—so good and gentle to me and baby, that I am delighted that he should be here with John. You know of all this.'

'Yes, I know, of course.'

'And will feel all that John has to suffer.'

'It is very bad, very bad for everybody concerned. By his own showing, his conduct——'

'William,' said she, 'let this be settled in one word. I will not hear a syllable against my husband from you or any one else. I am delighted to see you,—I cannot tell you how delighted. Oh, if papa would come,— or mamma! Dear, dear mamma! You don't suppose but what I love you all!'

'I am sure you do.'

'But not from papa or mamma even will I hear a word against him. Would Fanny,'—Fanny was the barrister's wife—'let her people come and say things behind your back?'

'I hope not.'

'Then, believe that I can be as stout as Fanny. But we need not quarrel. You will come and see baby, and have some lunch. I am afraid they will not be here till three or four, but they will be so glad to see you if you will wait.'

He would not wait, of course; but he allowed himself to be taken away to see baby, and did eat his lunch. Then he brought forward the purport of his mission. 'Your mother is most anxious to see you, Hester. You will go and visit her?'

'Oh, yes,' said Hester, unaware of any danger. 'But I wish she would come to me.'

'My dear girl, as things are at present that is impossible. You can understand as much as that. There must be a trial.'

'I suppose so.'

'And till that has been held your mother would be wrong to come here. I express no judgment against any one.'

'I should have thought mamma would have been the first to support me,—me and baby,' she said sobbing.

'Certainly, if you were homeless——'

'But I am not. My husband gives me a house to live in, and I want none other.'

227

'What I wish to explain is that if you were in want of anything—'

'I am in want of nothing—but sympathy.'

'You have it from me and from all of us. But pray, listen for a moment. She cannot come to you till the trial be over. I am sure Mr. Caldigate would understand that.'

'He comes to me,' she said, alluding to her father-in-law, and not choosing to understand that her brother should have called her husband 'Mr. Caldigate.'

'But there can be no reason why you should not go to Chesterton.'

'Just to see mamma?'

'For a day or two,' he replied, blushing inwardly at his own lie. 'Could you go to-morrow?'

'Oh, no;—not to stay. Of course I must ask my husband. I'm sure he'll let me go if I ask, but not to-morrow. Why to-morrow?'

'Only that your mother longs to see you.' He had been specially instigated to induce her to come as soon as possible. 'You may imagine how anxious she is.'

'Poor mamma! Yes;—I know she suffers. I know mamma's feelings. Mamma and I must, must, must quarrel if we talk about this. Of course I will go to see her. But will you tell her this,—that if she cannot speak of my husband with affection and respect it will be better that—she should not mention him at all. I will not submit to a word even from her.'

When he took his departure it was settled that she should, with her husband's permission, go over to Chesterton for a couple of nights in the course of the next week; but that she could not fix the day till she had seen him. Then, when he was taking his departure and kissing her once again, she whispered a word to him. 'Try and be charitable, William. I sometimes think that at Chesterton we hardly knew what charity meant.'

That evening the proposed visit to Chesterton was discussed at Folking. The old man had very strongly taken up his son's side, and was of opinion that the Boltons were not only uncharitable, but perversely ill-conditioned in the view which they took. To his thinking, Crinkett, Adamson, and the woman were greedy, fraudulent scoundrels, who had brought forward this charge solely with the view of extorting money. He declared that the very fact that they had begun by asking for money should have barred their evidence before any magistrates. The oaths of the four 'scoundrels' were, according to him, worth nothing. The scrap of paper purporting to be a copy of the marriage certificate, and the clergyman's pretended letter, were mere forgeries, having about them no evidence or probability of truth. Any one could have written them. As to that envelope addressed to Mrs. Caldigate, with the Sydney postmark, he had his own theory. He thought but little of the intercourse which his son acknowledged with the woman, but was of opinion that his son 'had been an ass' in writing those words. But a man does not marry a woman by simply writing his own name with the word mistress prefixed to it on an envelope. Any other woman might have adduced the envelope as evidence of his marriage with her! It was, he said, monstrous that any one should give credence to such bundles of lies. Therefore his words were gospel, and his wishes were laws to Hester. She clung round him, and hovered over him, and patted him like a very daughter, insisting that he should nurse the baby, and talking of him to her husband as though he were manifestly the wisest man in Cambridgeshire. She forgot even that little flaw in his religious belief. To her thinking at the present moment, a man who would believe that her baby was the honest son of an honest father and mother had almost religion enough for all purposes.

'Quite right that you should go,' said the old man.

'I think so,' said the husband, 'though I am afraid they will trouble her.'

'The only question is whether they will let her come back.'

'What!' exclaimed Hester.

'Whether they won't keep you when they've got you.'

'I won't be kept. I will come back. You don't suppose I'd let them talk me over?'

'No, my dear; I don't think they'll be able to do that. But there are such things as bolts and bars.'

'Impossible!' said his son.

'Do you mean that they'll send me to prison?' asked Hester.

'No; they can't do that. They wouldn't take you in at the county jail, but they might make a prison of Puritan Grange. I don't say they will, but they might try it.'

'I should get out, of course.'

'I daresay you would; but there might be trouble.'

'Papa would not allow that,' said Hester. 'Papa understands better than that. I've a right to go where I like, just as anybody else;—that is, if John tells me.' The matter was discussed at some length, but John Caldigate was of opinion that no such attempt as the old man had suggested was probable,—or even possible. The idea that in these days any one should be kept a prisoner in a private house,—any one over whom no one in that house possessed legitimate authority,—seemed to him to be monstrous. That a husband should lock up his wife might be possible, or a father his unmarried and dependent daughter; but that

229

any one should venture to lock up another man's wife was, he declared, out of the question. Mr. Caldigate again said that he should not be surprised if it were attempted; but acknowledged that the attempt could hardly be successful.

As Hester was anxious to make the visit, it was arranged that she should go. It was not that she expected much pleasure even in seeing her mother;—but that it was expedient at such a time to maintain what fellowship might still be possible with her own family. The trial would of course liberate them from all their trouble; and then, when the trial should be over, it would be very sad if an entire rupture between herself and her parents should have been created. She would be true to her husband; as true as a part must to to the whole, as the heart must be to the brain. They two were, and ever would be, one. But if her mother could be spared to her, if she could be saved from a lasting quarrel with her mother, it would be so much to her! Tears came into the eyes even of the old man as he assented; and her husband swore to her that for her sake he would forgive every injury from any one bearing the name of Bolton when all this should be over.

A day was therefore fixed, and a note was written, and on the last day of February she and her baby and her nurse were taken over to Puritan Grange. In the meantime telegrams at a very great cost had been flying backwards and forwards between Cambridge and Sydney. William and Robert Bolton had determined among them that, at whatever expense to the family, the truth must be ascertained; and to this the old banker had assented. So far they were right, no doubt. If the daughter and sister was not in truth a wife,—if by grossest, by most cruel ill-usage she had been lured to a ruin for which there could be no remedy in this world,—it would be better that the fact should be known at once, so that her life might be pure though it could never again be bright. But it was strange that, with all these Boltons, there was a desire, an anxiety, to prove the man's guilt rather than his innocence. Mrs. Bolton had always regarded him as a guilty man,— though guilty of she knew not what. She had always predicted misery from a marriage so distasteful to her; and her husband, though he had been brought to oppose her and to sanction the marriage, had, from the moment in which the sanction was given, been induced by her influence to reject it. Robert Bolton, when the charge was first made, when the letter from the woman was first shown to him, had become aware that he had made a mistake in allowing this trouble to come upon the family; and then, as from point to point the evidence had been opened out to him, he had gradually convinced himself that the son-in-law and brother-in-law, whom he had, as it were, forced into the family, was a bigamist. There was present to them all an intense desire to prove the man's guilt, which was startling to all around who heard anything of the matter. Up to this time the Bolton telegrams and the Caldigate telegrams had elicited two facts,—that Allan the Wesleyan minister had gone to the Fiji Islands and had there died, and that they at Nobble who had last known Dick Shand's address, now knew it no longer. Caldigate had himself gone to Pollington, and had there ascertained that no tidings had been received from Dick by any of the Shand family for the last twelve months. It had been decided that the trial must be postponed at any rate till the summer assizes, which would be held in Cambridge about the last week in August; and it was thought by some that even then the case would not be ready. There was, no doubt, an opinion prevalent in Cambridge that the unfortunate young mother should be taken home to her own family till the matter should be decided; and among the ladies of the town John Caldigate himself was blamed severely for not allowing her to place herself under her father's protection; but the ladies of the town generally were not probably well acquainted with the disposition and temper of the young wife herself.

Things were in this condition when Hester and her baby went to her father's house. Though that suspicion as to some intended durance which Mr. Caldigate had expressed was not credited by her, still, as she was driven up to the house, the idea was in her mind. She looked at the door and she looked at the window, and she could not conceive it possible that such a thing should be attempted. She thought of her own knowledge of the house; how, if it were necessary, she could escape from the back of the garden into the little field running down to the river, and how she could cross the ferry. Of course she knew every outlet and inlet about the place, and was sure that confinement would be impossible. But she did not think of her bonnet nor of her boots, nor of the horror which it would be to her should she be driven to wander forth into the town, and to seek a conveyance back to Folking in the public streets.

She went on a Monday with an understanding that she was to remain there till Wednesday. Mrs. Bolton almost wished that a shorter visit had been arranged in order that she might at once commence her hostile operations without any intermediate and hypocritical pretences. She had planned her campaign thoroughly in her own mind, and had taken the cook into her confidence, the cook being the oldest and most religious servant in the house. When the day of departure should have come the cook was to lock the doors, and the gardener was to close the little gate at the bottom of the garden; and the bonnet and other things were to be removed, and then the mother would declare her purpose. But in the meantime allusions to that intended return to Folking must be accepted, and listened to with false assent. It was very grievous, but so it was arranged. As soon as Hester was in the house the mother felt how much better it would have been to declare to her daughter at once that she was a prisoner;—but it was then too late to alter their proposed plans.

It very nearly came to pass that Hester left her mother on the morning of her arrival. They had both determined to be cautious, reticent, and forbearing, but the difference between them was so vital that reticence was impossible. At first there was a profusion of natural tears, and a profusion of embraces. Each clung to the other for a while as though some feeling might be satisfied by mere contact; and then the woe of the thing, the woe of it, was acknowledged on both sides! They could agree that the wickedness of the wicked was very wicked. Wherever might lie the sin of fraud and falsehood, the unmerited misfortunes of poor Hester were palpable enough. They could weep together over the wrongs inflicted on that darling baby. But by degrees it was impossible to abstain from alluding to the cause of their sorrow;— and such allusion became absolutely necessary when an attempt was made to persuade Hester to remain at her old home with her own consent. This was done by her father on the evening of her arrival, in compliance with the plan that had been arranged. 'No, papa, no; I cannot do that,' she said, with a tone of angry determination.

'It is your duty, Hester. All your friends will tell you so.'

'My duty is to my husband,' she said, 'and in such a matter I can allow myself to listen to no other friend.' She was so firm and fixed in this that he did not even dare to go on with his expostulation.

But afterwards, when they were upstairs together, Mrs. Bolton spoke out more at length and with more energy. 'Mamma, it is of no use,' said Hester.

'It ought to be of use. Do you know the position in which you are?'

'Very well. I am my husband's wife.'

'If it be so, well. But if it be not so, and if you remain with him while there is a doubt upon the matter, then you are his mistress.'

'If I am not his wife, then I will be his mistress,' said Hester, standing up and looking as she spoke much as her mother would look in her most determined moments.

'My child!'

'What is the use of all this, mamma? Nothing shall make me leave him. Others may be ashamed of me; but because of this I shall never be ashamed of myself. You are ashamed of me!'

'If you could mean what you said just now I should be ashamed of you.'

'I do mean it. Though the juries and the judges should say that he was not my husband, though all the judges in England should say it, I would not believe them. They may put him in prison and so divide us; but they never shall divide my bone from his bone, and my flesh from his flesh. As you are ashamed of me, I had better go back to-morrow.'

Then Mrs. Bolton determined that early in the morning she would look to the bolts and bars; but when the morning came matters had softened themselves a little.

CHAPTER XXXII

The Babington Wedding

'IT is your duty,—especially your duty,—to separate them.' This was
said by Mr. Smirkie, the vicar of Plum-cum-Pippin, to Mr. Bromley,
the rector of Utterden, and the words were spoken in the park at
Babington where the two clergymen were taking a walk together. Mr.
Smirkie's first wife had been a Miss Bromley, a sister of the clergyman
at Utterden; and as Julia Babington was anxious to take to her bosom
all her future husband's past belongings, Mr. Bromley had been
invited to Babington. It might be that Aunt Polly was at this time well
inclined to exercise her hospitality in this direction by a feeling that
Mr. Bromley would be able to talk to them about this terrible affair.
Mr. Bromley was intimate with John Caldigate, and of course would
know all about it. There was naturally in Aunt Polly's heart a certain
amount of self-congratulation at the way in which things were going.
Mr. Smirkie, no doubt, had had a former wife, but no one would call
him a bigamist. In what a condition might her poor Julia have been
but for that interposition of Providence! For Aunt Polly regarded poor
Hester Bolton as having been quite a providential incident, furnished
expressly for the salvation of Julia. Hitherto Mr. Bromley had been
very short in his expressions respecting the Folking tragedy, having
simply declared that, judging by character, he could not conceive that
a man such as Caldigate would have been guilty of such a crime. But
now he was being put through his facings more closely by his brother-
in-law.

'Why should I want to separate them?'

'Because the evidence of his guilt is so strong.'

'That is for a jury to judge.'

'Yes; and if a jury should decide that there had been no Australian
marriage,—which I fear we can hardly hope;—but if a jury were to
decide that, then of course she could go back to him. But while there
is a doubt, I should have thought, Tom, you certainly would have seen
it, even though you never have had a wife of your own.'

'I think I see all that there is to see,' said the other. 'If the poor
lady has been deceived and betrayed, no punishment can be too heavy
for the man who has so injured her. But the very enormity of the
iniquity makes me doubt it. As far as I can judge, Caldigate is a high-
spirited, honest gentleman, to whom the perpetration of so great a sin

234

would hardly suggest itself.'

'But if,—but if—! Think of her condition, Tom!'

'You would have to think of your own, if you were to attempt to tell her to leave him.'

'That means you are afraid of her.'

'It certainly means that I should be very much afraid if I thought of taking such a liberty. If I believed it to be my duty, I hope that I would do it.'

'You are her clergyman.'

'Certainly. I christened her child. I preach to her twice every Sunday. And if she were to die I should bury her.'

'Is that all?'

'Pretty nearly;—except that I generally dine at the house once a week.'

'Is there nothing further confided to you than that?'

'If she were to come to me for advice, then it would be my duty to give her what advice I thought to be best; and then——'

'Well, then?'

'Then I should have to make up my mind,—which I have not done at present,—I should have to make up my mind, not as to his guilt, for I believe him to be innocent, but as to the expediency of a separation till a jury should have acquitted him. But I am well aware that she won't come to me; and from little words which constantly drop from her, I am quite sure that nothing would induce her to leave her husband but a direct command from himself.'

'You might do it through him.'

'I am equally sure that nothing would induce him to send her away.'

But such a conviction as this was not sufficient for Mr. Smirkie. He was alive to the fact,—uncomfortably alive to the fact,—that the ordinary life of gentlefolk in England does not admit of direct clerical interference. As a country clergyman, he could bestow his admonitions upon his poorer neighbours; but upon those who were well-to-do he could not intrude himself unasked, unless, as he thought, in cases of great emergency. Here was a case of very great emergency. He was sure that he would have courage for the occasion if Folking were within the bounds of Plum-cum-Pippin. It was just the case in which counsel should be volunteered;—in which so much could be said which would be gross impertinence from others though it might be so manifest a duty to a clergyman. But Mr. Bromley could not be aroused to a sense either of his duty or of his privileges. All this was sad to Mr. Smirkie, who regretted those past days in which, as he believed, the delinquent soul had been as manifestly subject to ecclesiastical interference as the delinquent body has always been to the civil law.

But with Julia, who was to be his wife, he could be more imperative. She was taught to give thanks before the throne of grace because she had been spared the ignominy of being married to a man who could not have made her his wife, and had had an unstained clergyman of the Church of England given to her for her protection. For with that candour which is so delightful, and so common in these days, everything had been told to Mr. Smirkie,—how her young heart had for a time turned itself towards her cousin, how she had been deceived, and then how rejoiced she was that by such deceit she had been reserved for her present more glorious fate. 'And won't Mr. Bromley speak to her?' Julia asked.

'It is a very difficult question,—a very difficult question, indeed,' said Mr. Smirkie, shaking his head. He was quite sure that were Folking in his parish he would perform the duty, though Mr. Caldigate and the unfortunate lady might be as a lion and a lioness in opposition to him; but he was also of opinion that sacerdotal differences of opinion should not be discussed among laymen,—should not be discussed by a clergyman even with the wife of his bosom.

At Babington opinion was somewhat divided. Aunt Polly and Julia were of course certain that John Caldigate had married the woman in Australia. But the two other girls and their father were not at all so sure. Indeed, there had been a little misunderstanding among the Babingtons on the subject, which was perhaps strengthened by the fact that Mr. Smirkie had more endeared himself to Julia's mother than to Julia's father or sisters, and that Mr. Smirkie himself was very clear as to the criminality of the bigamist. 'I suppose you are often there,' Mr. Babington said to his guest, the parson of Utterden.

'Yes; I have seen a good deal of them.'

'Do you think it possible?'

'Not probable,' said the clergyman.

'I don't,' said the Squire. 'I suppose he was a little wild out there, but that is a very different thing from bigamy. Young men, when they get out to those places, are not quite so particular as they ought to be, I daresay. When I was young, perhaps I was not as steady as I ought to have been. But, by George! here is a man comes over and asks for a lot of money; and then the woman asks for money; and then they say that if they don't get it, they'll swear the fellow was married in Australia. I can't fancy that any jury will believe that.'

'I hope not.'

'And yet, Madame,'—the Squire was in the habit of calling his wife Madame when he intended to insinuate anything against her,—

'has got it settled in her head that this young woman isn't his wife at all. I think it's uncommon hard. A man ought to be considered innocent till he has been found guilty. I shall go over and see him one of these days, and say a kind word to her.'

There was at that moment some little difference of opinion, which was coming to a head in reference to a very delicate matter. When the conversations above related took place, the Babington wedding had been fixed to take place in a week's time. Should cousin John be invited, or should he not? Julia was decidedly against it. 'She did not think,' she said, 'that she could stand up at the altar and conduct herself on an occasion so trying if she were aware that he were standing by her.' Mr. Smirkie, of course, was not asked,—was not directly asked. But equally, of course, he was able to convey his own opinion through his future bride. Aunt Polly thought that the county would be shocked if a man charged with bigamy was allowed to be present at the marriage. But the Squire was a man who could have an opinion of his own; and after having elicited that of Mr. Bromley, insisted that the invitation should be sent.

'It will be a pollution,' said Julia, sternly, to her younger sisters.

'You will be a married woman almost before you have seen him,' said Georgiana, the second, 'and so it won't matter so much to you. We must get over it as we can.'

Julia had been thought by her sisters not to bear the Smirkie triumph with sufficient humility; and they, therefore, were sometimes a little harsh to her. 'I don't think you understand it at all,' said Julia. 'You have no conception what should be the feelings of a married woman, especially when she is going to become the wife of one of God's ministers.'

But in spite of all this, Aunt Polly wrote to her nephew as follows:—

'Dear John,—Our dearest Julia is to be married on Tuesday next. You know how anxious we all have been to maintain affectionate family relations with you, and we therefore do not like the idea of our sweet child passing from her present sphere to other duties without your presence. Will you come over on Monday evening, and stay till after the breakfast? It is astonishing how many of our friends from the two counties have expressed their wish to grace the ceremony by their company. I doubt whether there is a clergyman in the diocese of Ely more respected and thought of by all the upper classes than Augustus Smirkie.

'I do not ask Mrs. Caldigate, because, under present circumstances, she would not perhaps wish to go into company, and because Augustus

237

has never yet had an opportunity of making her acquaintance. I will only say that it is the anxious wish of us all here that you and she together may soon see the end of these terrible troubles.—Believe me to be, your affectionate aunt,

'MARYANNE BABINGTON'

The writing of this letter had not been effected without much difficulty. The Squire himself was not good at the writing of letters, and, though he did insist on seeing this epistle, so that he might be satisfied that Caldigate had been asked in good faith, he did not know how to propose alterations. 'That's all my eye,' he said, referring to his son-in-law that was to be. 'He's as good as another, but I don't know that he's any better.'

'That, my dear,' said Aunt Polly, 'is because you do not interest yourself about such matters. If you had heard what the Archdeacon said of him the other day, you would think differently.'

'He's another parson,' said the Squire. 'Of course they butter each other up.' Then he went on to the other paragraph. 'I wouldn't have said anything about his wife.'

'That would not have been civil,' said Aunt Polly; 'and as you insist on my asking him, I do not wish to be rude.' And so the letter was sent as it was written.

It reached Caldigate on the day which Hester was passing with her mother at Chesterton,—on the Tuesday. She had left Folking on the Monday, intending to return on the Wednesday. Caldigate was therefore alone with his father. 'They might as well have left that undone,' said he, throwing the letter over the table.

'It's about the silliest letter I ever read,' said the old Squire; 'but it is intended for civility. She means to show that she does not condemn you. There are many people who do not know when to speak and when to be silent. I shouldn't go.'

'No, I shan't go.'

'But I should take it as meant in kindness.'

Then John Caldigate wrote back as follows:—

'All this that has befallen my wife and me prevents us from going anywhere. She is at the present moment with her own people at Chesterton, but when she returns I shall not leave her. Give my kindest love to Julia, and ask her from me to accept the little present which I send her.'

Julia declared that she would much rather not have accepted the brooch, and that she would never wear it. But animosity against such articles wears itself out quickly, and it may be expected that the little ornament will be seen in the houses of the Suffolk gentry among whom Mr. Smirkie is so popular.

Whether it was Mr. Smirkie's popularity, or the general estimation in which the Babington family were held, or the delight which is taken by the world at large in weddings, there was a very great gathering at Babington church, and in the Squire's house afterwards. Though it was early in March,—a time of the year which, in the eastern counties of England, is not altogether propitious to out-of-doors festivity,—though the roads were muddy, and the park sloppy, and the church abominably open to draughts, still there was a crowd. The young ladies in that part of the world had been slow in marrying lately, and it was felt that the present occasion might give a little fillip to the neighbourhood. This was the second Suffolk young lady that Mr. Smirkie had married, and he was therefore entitled to popularity. He certainly had done as much as he could, and there was probably no one around who had done more.

'I think the dear child will be happy,' said Mrs. Babington to her old friend, Mrs. Munday,—the wife of Archdeacon Munday, the clerical dignitary who had given Mr. Smirkie so good a character.

'Of course she will,' said Mrs. Munday, who had already given three daughters in marriage to three clergymen, and who had, as it were, become used to the transfer.

'And that she will do her duty in it.'

'Why not? There's nothing difficult in it if she only sees that he has his surplice and bands properly got up. He is not, on the whole, a bad-tempered man; and though the children are rough, they'll grow out of that. And she ought to make him take two, or perhaps three, glasses of port wine on Sundays. Mr. Smirkie is not as young as he used to be, and two whole duties, with Sunday school, which must be looked into, do take a good deal out of a man. The archdeacon, of course, has a curate; but I suppose Mr. Smirkie could hardly manage that just at present?'

The views which had hitherto been taken at Babington of the bride's future life had been somewhat loftier than this. The bands and the surplice and the port wine seemed to be small after all that had been said. The mother felt that she was in some degree rebuked,—not having yet learned that nothing will so much lessen the enthusiasm one may feel for the work of a barrister, or a member of Parliament, or a clergyman, as a little domestic conversation with the wife of the one or the other. But Mrs. Munday was a lady possessing much clerical authority, and that which she said had to be endured with equanimity.

Mr. Smirkie seemed to enjoy the occasion, and held his own through the day with much dignity. The archdeacon, and the clergyman of the parish, and Mr. Bromley, all assisted, and nothing was wanting of outward ceremony which a small country church could supply. When his health was drunk at the breakfast he preached quite a little sermon as he returned thanks, holding his bride's hands in his the while, performing his part in the scene in a manner which no one else would have dared to attempt.

Then there was the parting between the mother and daughter, upstairs, before she was taken away for her ten days' wedding-tour to Brighton. 'My darling;—it is not so far but that I can come and see you very often.'

'Pray do, mamma.'

'And I think I can help you with the children.'

'I am not a bit afraid of them, mamma. I intend to have my way with them, and that will be everything. I don't mean to be weak. Of course Augustus will do what he thinks best in the parish, but he quite understands that I am to be mistress at home. As for Mrs. Munday, mamma, I don't suppose that she knows everything. I believe I can manage quite as well as Mrs. Munday.'

Then there was a parting joint congratulation that she had not yielded to the allurements of her cousin, John Caldigate. 'Oh, no, mamma; that would never have done.'

'Think where you might have been now!'

'I am sure I should have found out his character in time and have broken from him, let it have cost what it might. A man that can do such things as that is to me quite horrible. What is to become of her, and her baby;—and, perhaps, two,' she added in a whisper, holding up her hands and shaking her head. The ceremony through which she had just passed had given her courage to hint at such a possibility. 'I suppose she'll have to be called Miss Bolton again.' Of course there was some well-founded triumph in the bosom of the undoubted Mrs. Augustus Smirkie as she remembered what her own fate might have been. Then she was carried away in the family carriage, amidst a deluge of rice and a shower of old shoes.

That same night Mr. Bromley gave an account of the wedding to John Caldigate at Folking, telling him how well all the personages had performed their parts. 'Poor Julia! she at any rate will be safe.'

'Safe enough, I should think,' said the clergyman.

'What I mean is that she has no dangers to fear such as my poor wife has encountered. Whomever I think of now I cannot but compare them to ourselves. No woman surely was ever so ill-used as she, and no man ever so unfortunate as myself.'

'It will be all over in August.'

'And where shall I be? My own lawyer tells me that it is too probable that I shall be in prison. And where will she be then?'

CHAPTER XXXIII

Persuasion

EARLY on the Tuesday morning Hester came down into the break-fast parlour at Puritan Grange, having with difficulty persuaded herself that she would stay the appointed hours in her mother's house. On the previous evening her mother had, she thought, been very hard on her, and she had determined to go. She would not stay even with her mother, if her mother insisted upon telling her that she was not her husband's wife. But during the night she was able to persuade herself to bear what had been already said,—to let it be as though it had been forgotten. Her mother was her mother. But she would bear no more. As to herself and her own conduct, her parents might say what they pleased to her. But of her husband she would endure to hear no evil word spoken. In this spirit she came down into the little parlour.

Mrs. Bolton was also up,—had been up and about for some time previous. She was a woman who never gave way to temptations of ease. A nasty dark morning at six o'clock, with just light enough to enable her to dress without a candle, with no fire and no hot water, with her husband snoring while she went through her operations, was to her thinking the proper condition of things for this world. Not to be cold, not to be uncomfortable, not to strike her toes against the furniture because she could not quite see what she was about, would to her have been to be wicked. When her daughter came into the parlour, she had been about the house for more than an hour, and had had a conference both with the cook and with the gardener. The cook was of opinion that not a word should be said, or an unusual bolt drawn, or a thing removed till the Wednesday. 'She can't carry down her big box herself, ma'am; and the likes of Miss Hester would never think of going without her things;—and then there's the baby.' A look of agony came across the mother's face as she heard her daughter called Miss Hester;—but in truth the woman had used the name from old association, and not with any reference to her late young mistress's present position. 'I should just tell her flat on Wednesday morning that she wasn't to stir out of this, but I wouldn't say nothing at all about any of it till then.' The gardener winked and nodded his head, and promised to put a stake into the ground behind the little wicket-gate which would make the opening of it impossible. 'But take my word for it, ma'am, she'll never try that. She'll be a deal too proud. She'll rampage at the front door, and 'll despise any escaping like.' That was the gardener's idea, and the gardener had long known the young lady. By these arguments Mrs. Bolton was induced to postpone her prison arrangements till the morrow.

When she found her daughter in the small parlour she had settled much in her mind. During the early morning,—that is, till Mr. Bolton should have gone into Cambridge,—not a word should be said about the marriage. Then when they two would be alone together, another attempt should be made to persuade Hester to come and live at Chesterton till after the trial. But even in making that attempt no opinion should be expressed as to John Caldigate's wickedness, and no hint should be given as to the coming incarceration. 'Did you bring baby down with you?' the grandmother asked. No; baby had been awake ever so long, and then had gone to sleep again, and the nurse was now with him to protect him from the sufferings incident to waking. 'Your papa will be down soon, and then we will have breakfast,' said Mrs. Bolton. After that there was silence between them for some time.

A bond of discord, if the phrase may be allowed, is often quite as strong as any bond coming from concord and agreement. There was to both these women a subject of such paramount importance to each that none other could furnish matter of natural conversation. The one was saying to herself ever and always, 'He is my husband. Let the outside world say what it may, he is my husband.' But the other was as constantly denying to herself this assertion, and saying, 'He is not her husband. Certainly he is not her husband.' And as to the one the possession of that which she claimed was all the world, and as to the other the idea of the possession without true possession entailed upon her child pollution, crime, and ignominy, it was impossible but that the mind of each should be too full to admit of aught but forced expressions on other matters. It was in vain for them to attempt to talk of the garden, the house, the church, or of the old man's health. It was in vain even to attempt to talk of the baby. There are people who, however full their hearts may be, full of anger or full of joy, can keep the fulness in abeyance till a chosen time for exhibiting it shall come. But neither of these two was such a person. Every stiff plait in the elder woman's muslin and crape declared her conviction that John Caldigate was not legally married to her daughter. Every glance of Hester's eye, every motion made with her hands, every little shake of her head, declared her purpose of fighting for that one fact, whatever might be the odds against her.

When the banker came down to breakfast things were better for a little time. The pouring out of his tea mitigated somewhat the starchiness of his wife's severity, and Hester when cutting the loaf for him could seem to take an interest in performing an old duty. He said not a word against Caldigate; and when he went out, Hester, as had been her custom, accompanied him to the gate. 'Of course you will be here when I come,' he said.

'Oh, yes; I do not go home till to-morrow.' Then she parted from him, and spent the next hour or two up-stairs with her baby.

'May I come in?' said the mother, knocking at the door.

'Oh yes mamma. Don't you think baby is very like his father?'

'I dare say. I do not know that I am good at tracing likenesses. He certainly is like you.'

'So much more like his father!' said Hester.

After that there was a pause, and then the mother commenced her task in her most serious voice. 'Hester, my child, you can understand that a duty may become so imperious that it must be performed.'

'Yes,' said Hester, pressing her lips close together. 'I can understand that.' There might be a duty very necessary for her to perform, though in the performance of it she should be driven to quarrel absolutely with her own mother.

'So it is with me. Whom do you think I love best in all the world?'

'Papa.'

'I do love your father dearly, and I endeavour, by God's grace, to do my duty by him, though, I fear, it is done imperfectly. But, my child, our hearts, I think, yearn more to those who are younger than ourselves than to our elders. We love best those whom we have cherished and protected, and whom we may perhaps still cherish and protect. When I try to tear my heart away from the things of this vile world, it clings to you—to you—to you!'

Of course this could not be borne without an embrace. 'Oh, mamma!' Hester exclaimed, throwing herself on her knees before her mother's lap.

'If you suffer, must not I suffer? If you rejoice, would I not fain rejoice with you if I could? Did I not bring you into the world, my only one, and nursed you, and prayed for you, and watched you with all a mother's care as you grew up among the troubles of the world? Have you not known that my heart has been too soft towards you even for the due performance of my duties?'

'You have always been good to me, mamma.'

'And am I altered now? Do you think that a mother's heart can be changed to her only child?'

'No, mamma.'

'No, Hester. That, I think, is impossible. Though for the last twelve

months I have not seen you day by day,—though I have not prepared
the food which you eat and the clothes which you wear, as I used to
do,—you have been constantly in my mind. You are still my child,
my only child.'

'Mamma, I know you love me.'

'I so love you as to know that I sin in so loving aught that is
human. And so loving you, must I not do my duty by you? When love
and duty both compel me to speak, how shall I be silent?'

'You have said it, mamma,' said Hester, slowly drawing herself up
from off the ground.

'And is saying it once enough, when, as I think, the very soul, the
immortal soul, of her who is of all the dearest to me depends on what
I may say;—may be saved, or, oh, perhaps lost for ever by the manner
in which I may say it! How am I not to speak when such thoughts as
these are heavy within me?'

'What is it you would say?' This Hester asked with a low hoarse
voice and a stern look, as though she could not resist her mother's
prayer for the privilege of speaking; but at the same time was resolutely
prepared not to be turned a hair's-breadth by anything that might be
said.

'Not a word about him.'

'No, mamma; no. Unless you can tell me that you will love him as
your son-in-law.'

'Not a word about him,' she repeated, in a harsher voice. She felt
that the promise should have been enough, and that in the present
circumstances she should not have been invited to love the man she
hated. 'Your father and I wish you for the next few months to come
and live with us.'

'It is quite impossible,' said Hester, standing very upright, with a
face altogether unlike that she had worn when kneeling at her mother's
knees.

'You should listen to me.'

'Yes, I will listen.'

'There will be a trial.'

'Undoubtedly. John, at least, seems to think so. It is possible that
these wicked people may give it up, or that they may have no money
to go on; but I suppose there will be a trial.'

'The woman has bound herself to prosecute him.'

'Because she wants to get money. But we need not discuss that,
mamma. John thinks that there will be a trial.'

'Till that is over, will you not be better away from him? How will
it be with you if it should be decided that he is not your husband?'

Here Hester of course prepared herself for interruption, but her mother prayed for permission to continue.

'Listen to me for one moment, Hester.'

'Very well, mamma. Go on.'

'How would it be with you in that case? You must be separated then. As that is possible, is it not right that you should obey the ordinances of God and man, and keep yourself apart till they who are in authority shall have spoken?'

'There are no such ordinances.'

'There are indeed. If you were to ask all your friends, all the married women in Cambridgeshire, what would they say? Would they not all tell you that no woman should live with a man while there is a shadow of doubt? And as to the law of God, you know God's law, and can only defend yourself by your own certainty as to a matter respecting which all others are uncertain. You think yourself certain because such certainty is a way to yourself out of your present misery.'

'It is for my child,' she shouted; 'and for him.'

'As for your babe, your darling babe, whether he be yours in joy of heart or in agony of spirit, he is still yours. No one will rob you of him. If it be as we fear, would not I help you to love him, help you to care for him, help you to pray for him? If it were so, would I desert him or you because in your innocence you had been betrayed into misfortune? Do I not feel for your child? But when he grows up and is a man, and will have learned the facts of his early years, let him be able to tell himself that his mother though unfortunate was pure.'

'I am pure,' she said.

'My child, my own one, can I, your mother, think aught else of you? Do I not know your heart? Do not I know the very thoughts within you?'

'I am pure. He has become my husband, and nothing can divide us. I never gave a thought to another man. I never had the faintest liking, as do other girls. When he came and told me that he had seen me and loved me, and would take me for his wife, I felt at once that I was all his,—his to do as he liked with me, his to nourish him, his to worship him, his to obey him, his to love him let father or mother or all the world say what they would to the contrary. Then we were married. Till he was my own, I never even pressed my lips upon his. But I became his wife by a bond that nothing shall break. You tell me of God's law. By God's law I am his wife, let the people say what they will. I have but two to think of.'

'Yourself and him?' asked her mother.

'I have three to think of,—God and him, and my child; and may

God be good to me and them, as in this matter I will put myself away from myself altogether. It is for me to obey him, and I will submit myself to none other. If he bids me go, I will go; if he bids me stay here, I will stay. I have become his so entirely, that no judges—no judges can divide us. Judges! I know but one Judge, and He is there; and He has said that those whom He has joined together, man shall not put asunder. Pure! pure! No one should praise herself, but as a woman I do know that I am pure.'

Then the mother's heart yearned greatly towards her daughter; and yet she was no whit changed. She knew nothing of phrases of logic, but she felt that Hester had begged the whole question. Those whom God had joined together! True, true! If only one could know whether in this or the other case God had joined the couple. As Hester argued the matter, no woman should be taken from the man she had married, though he might have a dozen other wives all living. And she spoke of purity as though it were a virtue which could be created and consecrated simply by the action of her own heart, as though nothing outside,—no ceremony, no ordinance,—could affect it. The same argument would enable her to live with John Caldigate after he should come out of prison, even though, as would then be the case, another woman would have the legal right of calling herself Mrs. John Caldigate! On the previous day she had declared that if she could not be his wife, she would be his mistress. The mother knew what she meant,—that, let people call her by what name they might, she would still be her husband's wife in the eye of God. But she would not be so. And then she would not be pure. And, to Mrs Bolton, the worst of it was that·this cloudiness had come upon her daughter,—this incapacity to reason it out,—because the love of a human being had become so strong within her bosom as to have superseded and choked the love of heavenly things. But how should she explain all this? 'I am not asking you to drop his name.'

'Drop his name! I will never drop it. I cannot drop it. It is mine. I could not make myself anything but Mrs. John Caldigate if I would. And he,' she said, taking the baby up from its cradle and pressing it to her bosom, 'he shall be Daniel Caldigate to the day of his death. Do you think that I will take a step that shall look like robbing my child of his honest name,—that will seem to imply a doubt that he is not his own father's honest boy,—that he is not a fitting heir to the property which his forefathers have owned so long? Never! They may call me what name they will, but I will call myself John Caldigate's wife as long as I have a voice to make myself heard.'

It was the same protest over and over again, and it was vain to

247

answer. 'You will not stay under your father's roof?'

'No; I have to live under my husband's roof.' Then Mrs. Bolton left the room, apparently in anger. Though her heart within might be melting with ruth, still it was necessary that she should assume a look of anger. On the morrow she would have to show herself angry with a vengeance, if she should then still be determined to carry out her plan. And she thought that she was determined. What had pity to do with it, or love, or moving heart-stirring words? Were not all these things temptation from the Evil One, if they were allowed to interfere with the strict line of hard duty? When she left the room, where the young mother was still standing with her baby in her arms, she doubted for some minutes,—perhaps for some half-hour,—then she wrestled with those emanations from the Evil One,—with pity, with love, and suasive tenderness,—and at last overcame them. 'I know I am pure,' the daughter had said. 'I know I am right,' said the mother.

But she spoke a word to her husband when he came home. 'I cannot bend her; I cannot turn her, in the least.'

'She will not stay?'

'Not of her own accord.'

'You have told her?'

'Oh no; not till to-morrow.'

'She ought to stay, certainly,' said the father. There had been very little intercourse between the mother and daughter during the afternoon, and while the three were sitting together, nothing was said about the morrow. The evening would have seemed to be very sad and very silent, had they not all three been used to so many silent evenings in that room. Hester, during her wedding tour and the few weeks of her happiness at Folking, before the trouble had come, had felt a new life and almost an ecstasy of joy in the thorough liveliness of her husband. But the days of her old home were not so long ago that its old manners should seem strange to her. She therefore sat out the hours patiently, stitching some baby's ornament, till her mother told her that the time for prayer had come. After worship her father called her out into the hall as he went up to his room. 'Hester,' he said, 'it is not right that you should leave us to-morrow.'

'I must, papa.'

'I tell you that it is not right. You have a home in which everybody will respect you. For the present you should remain here.'

'I cannot, papa. He told me to go back to-morrow. I would not disobey him now,—not now,—were it ever so.' Then the old man paused as though he were going on with the argument, but finding that he had said all that he had to say, he slowly made his way upstairs.

'Good-night, mamma,' said Hester, returning only to the door of the sitting-room.

'Good-night, my love.' As the words were spoken they both felt that there was something wrong,—much that was wrong. 'I do not think they will do that,' said Hester to herself, as she went up the stairs to her chamber.

CHAPTER XXXIV

Violence

IT had been arranged at Folking, before Hester had started, that Caldigate himself should drive the waggonette into Cambridge to take her back on the Wednesday, but that he would bring a servant with him who should drive the carriage up to the Grange, so that he, personally, should not have to appear at the door of the house. He would remain at Mr. Seely's, and then the waggonette should pick him up. This had been explained to Mrs. Bolton. 'John will remain in town, because he has so much to do with Mr. Seely,' Hester had said; 'and Richard will call here at about twelve.' All her plans had thus been made known, and Mrs. Bolton was aware at what hour the bolts must be drawn and the things removed.

But, as the time drew nearer, her dislike to a sudden commencement of absolute hostilities became stronger,—to hostilities which would seem to have no sanction from Mr. Bolton himself, because he would then be absent. And he too, though as he lay awake through the dreary hours of the long night he said no word about the plan, felt, and felt more strongly as the dawn was breaking, that it would be mean to leave his daughter with a farewell kiss, knowing as he would do that he was leaving her within prison-bars, leaving her to the charge of jailers. The farewell kiss would be given as though he and she were to meet no more in her old home till this terrible trial should be over, and some word appropriate to such a parting would then be spoken. But any such parting word would be false, and the falsehood would be against his own child! 'Does she expect it?' he said, in a low voice, when his wife came up to him as he was dressing.

'She expects nothing. I am thinking that perhaps you would tell her that she could not go to-day.'

'I could not say "to-day." If I tell her anything, I must tell her all.'

'Will not that be best?' Then the old man thought it all over. It would be very much the best for him not to say anything about it if he could reconcile it to his conscience to leave the house without doing so. And he knew well that his wife was more powerful than he,—gifted with greater persistence, more capable of enduring a shower of tears or a storm of anger. The success of the plan would be more probable if the conduct of it were left entirely to his wife, but his conscience was sore within him.

'You will come with me to the gate,' he said to his daughter, after their silent breakfast.

'Oh yes;—to say good-bye.'

Then he took his hat, and his gloves, and his umbrella, very slowly, lingering in the hall as he did so, while his wife kept her seat firm and square at the breakfast table. Hester had her hat and shawl with her; but Mrs. Bolton did not suspect that she would endeavour to escape now without returning for her child. Therefore she sat firm and square, waiting to hear from Hester herself what her father might bring himself to communicate to her. 'Hester,' he said, as he slowly walked round the sweep in front of the house, 'Hester,' he said, 'you would do your duty best to God and man,—best to John Caldigate and to your child,—by remaining here.'

'How can I unless he tells me?'

'You have your father's authority.'

'You surrendered it when you gave me to him as his wife. It is not that I would rebel against you, papa, but that I must obey him. Does not St. Paul say, "Wives, submit yourselves unto your own husbands as unto the Lord"?'

'Certainly; and you cannot suppose that in any ordinary case I would interfere between you and him. It is not that I am anxious to take anything from him that belongs to him.' Then, as they were approaching the gate, he stood still. 'But now, in such an emergency as this, when a question has risen as to his power of making you his wife—'

'I will not hear of that. I am his wife.'

'Then it may become my duty and your mother's to—to—to provide you with a home till the law shall have decided.'

'I cannot leave his home unless he bids me.'

'I am telling you of my duty—of my duty and your mother's.' Then he passed out through the gate, thus having saved his conscience from the shame of a false farewell; and she slowly made her way back to the house, after standing for a moment to look after him as he went. She was almost sure now that something was intended. He would not have spoken in that way of his duty unless he had meant her to suppose that he intended to perform it. 'My duty,' he had said, 'my duty and your mother's!' Of course something was intended, something was to be done or said more than had been done or said already. During the breakfast she had seen in the curves of her mother's mouth the signs of some resolute purpose. During the very prayers she had heard in her mother's voice a sound as of a settled determination. She knew,—she knew that something was to be done, and with that knowledge she went back into her mother's room, and sat herself down firmly and squarely at the table. She had left her cup partly full, and began again to drink her tea. 'What did your papa say to you?' asked her mother.

'Papa bade me stay here, but I told him that most certainly I should go home to Folking.' Then Mrs. Bolton also became aware of fixed will and resolute purpose on her daughter's part.

'Does his word go for nothing?'

'How can two persons' words go for anything when obedience is concerned? It is like God and Mammon.'

'Hester!'

'If two people tell one differently, it must be right to cling to one and leave the other. No man can serve two masters. I have got to obey my husband. Even were I to say that I would stay, he could come and take me away.'

'He could not do that.'

'I shall not be so disobedient as to make it necessary. The carriage will be here at twelve, and I shall go. I had better go and help nurse to put the things up.' So saying she left the room, but Mrs. Bolton remained there a while, sitting square and firm at the table.

It was not yet ten when she slowly followed her daughter up-stairs. She first went into her own room for a moment, to collect her thoughts over again, and then she walked across the passage to her daughter's chamber. She knocked at the door, but entered as she knocked. 'Nurse,' she said, 'will you go into my room for a minute or two? I wish to speak to your mistress. May she take the baby, Hester?' The baby was taken, and then the two were alone. 'Do not pack up your things to-day, Hester.'

'Why not?'

'You are not going to-day.'

'I am going to-day, mamma.'

'That I should seem to be cruel to you,—only seem,—cuts me to the heart. But you cannot go back to Folking to-day.'

'When am I to go?'

'Ah, Hester!'

'Tell me what you mean, mamma. Is it that I am to be a prisoner?'

'If you would be gentle I would explain it.'

'I will not be gentle. You mean to keep me,—by violence; but I mean to go; my husband will come. I will not be kept. Oh, mamma, you would not desire me to quarrel with you openly, before the servants, before all the world! I will not be kept. I will certainly go back to Folking. Would I not go back though I had to get through the windows, to walk the whole way, to call upon the policemen even to help me?'

'No one will help you, Hester. Every one will know that for the present this should be your home.'

'It never shall be my home again,' said Hester, bursting into tears, and rushing after her baby.

Then there were two hours of intense misery in that house,—of misery to all who were concerned. The servants, down to the girl in the scullery and the boy who cleaned the boots, were made aware that master and mistress were both determined to keep their married daughter a prisoner in the house. The servants of the house sided with their mistress generally, having all of them been induced to regard John Caldigate with horror. Hester's nurse, of course, sympathised with her and her baby. During these two hours the packing was completed, but Hester found that her strong walking-boots and her bonnet had been abstracted. Did they really think that at such a time as this boots and bonnets would be anything to her? They could know nothing of her nature. They could not understand the sort of combat she would carry on if an attempt were made to take from her her liberty,—an attempt made by those who had by law no right to control her! When once she had learned what was being done she would not condescend to leave her room till the carriage should have come. That would come punctually at twelve she was sure. Then she would go down without her bonnet and without her boots, and see whether any one would dare to stand in her way, as with her baby in her arms she would attempt to walk forth through the front door.

But it had not occurred to her that other steps might be taken. Just before twelve the gardener stationed himself on the road before the house,—a road which was half lane and half street, belonging to the suburban village of Chesterton,—and there awaited the carriage at a spot some yards away from the gate. It was well that he was early, because Richard was there a few minutes before the time appointed. 'She ain't a-going back to-day,' said the gardener, laying his hands gently on the horse's back.

'Who ain't not a-going back?' asked the coachman.

'Miss Hester ain't.'

'Mrs. John ain't a-going home?'

'No;—I was to come out and tell you, as master don't like wheels on the gravel if it can be helped. We ain't got none of our own.'

'Missus ain't a-going home? Why, master expects her for certain!'

'I was to say she ain't a-going to-day.'

The man who was driving passed the reins into his whip-hand, and raising his hat, began to scratch his head with the other. He knew at once that there was something wrong,—that this prolonged staying away from home was not merely a pleasantly lengthened visit. His master had been very urgent with him as to punctuality, and was evidently intent upon the return of his wife. All the facts of the accusation were known to the man, and the fact also that his master's present wife was entirely in accord with his master. It could not be that she should have determined to prolong her visit, and then have sent him back to her husband with such a message as this! 'If you hold the hosses just a minute,' he said, 'I'll go in and see my missus.'

But the Grange gardener was quite as intent on his side of the question as was the Folking coachman on the other. To him the horrors of bigamy were manifest. He was quite of opinion that 'Miss Hester,'—who never ought to have been married in that way at all,—should now be kept a prisoner in her father's house. 'It ain't no use your going in,—and you can't,' said the gardener. 'I ain't a-going to hold the horses, and there's nobody as will.'

'What's up, mate?'

'I don't know as I'm mate to you, nor yet to no one like you. And as to what's up, I've told you all as I'm bade to tell you; and I ain't a-going to tell you no more. You can't turn your horses there. You'd better drive round into the village, and there you'll get the high-road back to Cambridge.' Then the gardener retreated within a little gate of his own which led from the lane into the precincts close to his own cottage. The man was an honest, loyal old fanatic, who would scruple at nothing in carrying out the orders of his mistress in so good a cause. And personally his feelings had been acerbated in that he had been called 'mate' by a man not half his age.

The coachman did as he was bid, seeing before him no other possible course. He could not leave his horses. But when he was in front of the iron gates he stopped and examined the premises. The gates were old, and were opened and closed at ordinary times by an ordinary ancient lock. But now there was a chain passed in and out with a padlock,—evidently placed there to prevent him from entering in opposition to the gardener's instructions. There was clearly no course open to him but to drive the carriage back to his master.

At a quarter before twelve Hester left her own room,—which looked backwards into the garden, as did all the pleasanter rooms of the house,—with the intention of seating herself in a spare room looking out to the front, from which she could have seen the carriage as it entered the gate. Had she so seen it she would certainly have called to the man from the window when he was standing in the road. But the door of that front room was locked against her; and when she tried the other

254

she found that all the front rooms were locked. She knew the house, of course, as well as did her mother, and she rushed up to the attics where the servants occupied the rooms looking out to the road. But they, too, were locked against her. Then it flashed upon her that the attempt to make her a prisoner was to be carried out through every possible detail.

What should she do? Her husband would come of course; but what if he were unable to force an entrance? And how could he force it? Would the police help him? Would the magistrates help him? She knew that the law was on her side, and on his,—that the law would declare him to be her lord and owner till the law should have separated them. But would the law allow itself to be used readily for this purpose? She, too, could understand that the feeling of the community would be against her, and that in such a case the law might allow itself to become slow, lethargic, and perhaps inoperative, yielding to the popular feeling. She saw the points which were strong against her as clearly as William and Robert Bolton had seen those which were strong on their side. But—! As she stood there beating her foot angrily on the floor of the passage, she made up her mind that there should be more than one 'but' in his favour. If they kept her, they should have to lock her up as in a dungeon; they and all the neighbourhood should hear her voice. They should be driven to do such things that the feeling of the community would be no longer on their side.

Various ideas passed through her mind. She thought for a moment that she would refuse to take any nourishment in that house. Her mother would surely not see her die; and would thus have to see her die or else send her forth to be fed. But that thought stayed with her but for a moment. It was not only for herself that she must eat and drink, but for her baby. Then, finding that she could not get to the front windows, and seeing that the time had come in which the carriage should have been there, she went down into the hall, where she found her mother seated on a high-backed old oak armchair. The windows of the hall looked out on to the sweep before the house; but she was well aware that from these lower windows the plot of shrubs in the centre of the space hindered any view of the gate. Without speaking to her mother she put her hand upon the lock of the door as though to walk forth, but found it barred. 'Am I a prisoner?' she said.

'Yes, Hester; yes. If you will use such a word as to your father's house, you are a prisoner.'

'I will not remain so. You will have to chain me, and to gag me, and to kill me. Oh, my baby,—oh, my child! Nurse, nurse, bring me my boy.' Then with her baby in her arms, she sat down in another high-backed oak armchair, looking at the hall-door. There she would sit till her husband should come. He surely would come. He would make his way up to those windows, and there she could at any rate hear his commands. If he came for her, surely she would be able to escape.

The coachman drove back to the town very quickly, and went to the inn at which his horses were generally put up, thinking it better to go to his master thence on foot. But there he found John Caldigate, who had come across from Mr. Seely's office. 'Where is Mrs. Caldigate?' he said, as the man drove the empty carriage down the entrance to the yard. The man, touching his hat, and with a motion of his hand which was intended to check his master's impetuosity, drove on; and then, when he had freed himself from the charge of his horses, told his story with many whispers.

'The gardener said she wasn't to come!'

'Just that, sir. There's something up more than you think, sir; there is indeed. He was that fractious that he wouldn't hold the hosses for me, not for a minute, till I could go in and see, and then—'

'Well?'

'The gates was chained, sir.'

'Chained?'

'A chain was round the bars, and a padlock. I never see such a thing on a gentleman's gate in my life before. Chained; as nobody wasn't to go in, nor yet nobody wasn't to come out!' The man as he said this wore that air of dignity which is always imparted by the possession of great tidings the truth of which will certainly not be doubted.

The tidings were great. The very thing which his father had suggested, and which he had declared to be impossible, was being done. The old banker himself would not, he thought, have dared to propose and carry out such a project. The whole Bolton family had conspired together to keep his wife from him, and had allured her away by the false promise of a friendly visit! He knew, too, that the law was on his side; but he knew also that he might find it very difficult to make use of the law. If the world of Cambridge chose to think that Hester was not his wife, the world of Cambridge would probably support the Boltons by their opinion. But if she, if his Hester, were true to him, and she certainly would be true to him—and if she were as courageous as he believed her to be,— then, as he thought, no house in Chesterton would be able to hold her.

He stood for a moment turning in his mind what he had better do. Then he gave his orders to the man in a clear natural voice. 'Take the horses out, Richard, and feed them. You had better get your dinner here, so that I may be sure to find you here the moment I want you.'

'I won't stir a step from the place,' said the man.

CHAPTER XXXV

In Prison

WHAT should he do? John Caldigate, as he walked out of the inn-yard, had to decide for himself what he would do at once. His first impulse was to go to the mayor and ask for assistance. He had a right to the custody of his wife. Her father had no right to make her a prisoner. She was entitled to go whither she pleased, so long as she had his sanction; and should she be separated from him by the action of the law, she would be entitled to go whither she pleased without sanction from any one. Whether married or unmarried she was not subject to her father. The husband was sure that he was entitled to the assistance of the police, but he doubted much whether he would be able to get it, and he was most averse to ask for it.

And yet what other step could he take? With no purpose as yet quite fixed, he went to the bank, thinking that he might best commence his work by expostulating with his wife's father. It was Mr. Bolton's habit to walk every morning into the town, unless he was deterred by heat or wet or ill health; and till lately it had been his habit also to walk back, his house being a mile and a half distant from the bank; but latterly the double walk had become too much for him, and, when the time for his return came, he would send out for a cab to take him home. His hours were very various. He would generally lunch at the bank, in his own little dingy room; but if things went badly with him, so as to disturb his mind, he would go back early in the day, and generally pass the afternoon asleep. On this occasion he was very much troubled, so that when Caldigate reached the bank, which he did before one, Mr. Bolton was already getting into his cab. 'Could I speak a few words to you, sir?' said Caldigate in the street.

'I am not very well to-day,' said the banker, hardly looking round, persevering in his effort to get into the vehicle.

'I would not keep you for a minute, sir. I must see you, as you are aware.'

There were already half-a-dozen people collected, all of whom had no doubt heard the story of John Caldigate's wife. There was, indeed, no man or woman in Cambridge whose ears it had not reached. In the hearing of these Mr. Bolton was determined not to speak of his daughter, and he was equally determined not to go back into the house. 'I have nothing to say,' he muttered—'nothing, nothing; drive on.' So the cab was driven on, and John Caldigate was left in the street.

The man's anger now produced a fixed purpose, and with a quick step he walked away from the bank to Robert Bolton's office. There he soon found himself in the attorney's room. 'Are you aware of what they are doing at the Grange?' he asked, in a voice which was not so guarded as it should have been on such an occasion. Anger and the quickness of his walk had combined to make him short of breath, and he asked the question with that flurried, hasty manner which is common to angry people who are hot rather than malicious in their angers.

'I don't think I am,' said the attorney. 'But if I were, I doubt whether I should just at present be willing to discuss their doings with you.'

'My wife has gone there on a visit.'

'I am glad to hear it. It is the best thing that my sister could do.'

'And now it seems some difficulty is made about her returning.'

'That I think very likely. Her father and mother can hardly wish that she should go back to your house at present. I cannot imagine that she should wish it herself. If you have the feelings of a gentleman or the heart of a man you ought not to wish it.'

'I have not come here to be taught what is becoming either to a man or a gentleman.'

'If you will allow me to say so, while things are as they are at present, you ought not to come here at all.'

'I should not have done so but for this violence, this breach of all hospitality at your father's house. My wife went there with the understanding that she was to stay for two days.'

'And now, you say, they detain her. I am not responsible; but in doing so they have my thorough sympathy and approbation. I do not know that I can help them, or that they will want my help; but I shall help them if I can. The fact is, you had better leave her there.'

'Never!'

'I should not have volunteered my advice, but, as you are here, I may perhaps say a word. If you attempt to take her by violence from her father's house you will have all the town, all the county, all England against you.'

'I should;—I own it;—unless she wished to come to me. If she chooses to stay, she shall stay.'

'It must not be left to her. If she be so infatuated, she must not be allowed to judge for herself. Till this trial be over, she and you must live apart. Then, if that woman does not make good her claim,—if you can prove that the woman is lying,—then you will have back your wife. But if, as everybody I find believes at present, it should be proved that you are the husband of that woman, and that you have basely betrayed my poor sister by a mock marriage, then she must be left to the care of her father and her mother, and may Heaven help her in her misery.' All this he said with much dignity, and in a manner with which even Caldigate could not take personal offence. 'You must remember,' he added, 'that this poor injured one is their daughter and my sister.'

'I say that she has been in no wise injured but,—as I also am injured, —by a wicked plot. And I say that she shall come back to me, unless she herself elects to remain with her parents.' Then he left the office and went forth again into the streets.

He now took at once the road to Chesterton, trying as he did so to make for himself in his own mind a plan or map of the premises. It would, he thought, be impossible but that his wife would be able to get out of the house and come to him if he could only make her aware of his presence. But then there was the baby, and it would be necessary not only that she should escape herself but that she should bring her child with her. Would they attempt to hold her? Could it be that they should have already locked her up in some room up-stairs? And if she did escape out of some window, even with her baby in her arms, how would it be with them then as they made their way back into the town? Thinking of this he hurried back to the inn and told Richard to take the carriage into Chesterton and wait there at the turn of the lane, where the lane leads down from the main road to the Grange. He was to wait there, though it might be all the day, till he heard from or saw his master. The man, who was quite as keen for his master as was the old gardener for his mistress on the other side, promised accurate obedience. Then he retraced his steps and walked as fast as he could to the Grange.

During all this time the mother and the daughter kept their weary seats in the hall, Hester having her baby in her arms. She had quite determined that nothing should induce her again to go up-stairs,—lest the key of the room should be turned upon her. For a long time they sat in silence, and then she declared her purpose.

'I shall remain here, mamma.'

'If so, I must remain too.'

'I shall not go up to my bedroom again, you may be sure of that.'

'You will go up to-night, I hope.'

'Certainly not. Nurse shall take baby up to his cradle. I do not suppose you will be cruel enough to separate me from my child.'

'Cruel! Do you not know that I would do anything for you or your child,—that I would die for you or your child?'

'I suppose you will let them bring me food here. You would not wish him to be starved.'

'Hester!'

'Well; what would you have me say? Are you not my jailer?'

'I am your mother. According to my conscience I am acting for you as best I know how. Do you not know that I mean to be good to you?'

'I know you are not good to me. Nobody can be good who tries to separate me from my husband. I shall remain here till he comes and tells me how I am to be taken away.' Then Mr. Bolton returned, and made his way into the house with the assistance of the gardener through the kitchen. He found the two women sitting in the hall, each in the high-backed arm-chair, and his daughter with her baby in her arms,—a most piteous sight, the two of them thus together. 'Papa,' she said, as he came up into the hall from the kitchen, 'you are treating me badly, cruelly, unjustly. You have no right to keep me here against my will. I am my husband's wife, and I must go to my husband.'

'It is for the best, Hester.'

'What is wrong cannot be for the best. Do you suppose that he will let me be kept here in prison? Of course he will come. Why do you not let me go?'

'It is right that you should be here, Hester,' he said, as he passed up-stairs to his own bedroom. It was a terrible job of work for which he had no strength whatever himself, and as to which he was beginning to doubt whether even his wife's strength would suffice. As for her, as for Hester, perhaps it would be well that she should be wearied and broken into submission. But it was fearful to think that his wife should have to sit there the whole day saying nothing, doing nothing, merely watching lest her daughter should attempt to escape through some window.

'It will kill your father, I think,' said the mother.

'Why does he not let me go then? I have to think of my husband and my child.' Then again there was silence. When they had been seated thus for two hours, all the words that had been spoken between them had not spread themselves over ten minutes, and Mrs. Bolton was looking forward to hour after hour of the same kind. It did not seem to her to be possible that Hester should be forced up into her own room. Even she, with all her hardihood, could not ask the men about the place to take her in their arms and carry her with violence up the stairs. Nor would the men have done it, if so required. Nothing but a policeman's garb will seem to justify the laying of a hand upon a woman, and even that will hardly do it unless the woman be odiously disreputable. Mrs. Bolton saw clearly what was before her. Should Hester be strong in her purpose to remain seated as at present, she also must remain seated. Weariness and solicitude for her baby might perhaps drive the young mother to bed. Then she also would go to her bed,—and would rest, with one eye ever open, with her ears always on the alert. She was somewhat sure of herself. Her life had not been so soft but that she could endure much,—and of her purpose she was quite sure. Nothing would trouble her conscience if she could succeed in keeping her daughter separated from John Caldigate.

Caldigate in his hot haste walked up to the iron gates and found them chained. It was in vain that he shook them, and in vain that he looked at them. The gates were fully twelve feet high, and spiked at the top. At each side of the gates ran a wall surmounted by iron railings,—extending to the gardener's cottage on the one side, and to the coach-house on the other. The drive up to the house, which swept round a plot of thick shrubs, lay between the various offices,—the stables and coach-house being on one side, and the laundry and gardener's cottage on the other. From the road there was no mode of ingress for him to this enclosure, unless he could get over the railings. This might perhaps have been possible, but it would have been quite impossible for him to bring his wife back the same way. There was a bell at the gardener's little gate, which he rang loudly; but no one would come to him. At last he made his way round into the kitchen-garden by a corner where access was made by climbing a moderately high gate which gave an entrance to the fields. From thence he had no difficulty in making his way on to the lawn at the back of the house, and up by half-a-dozen stone steps to the terrace which ran along under the windows. Here he found that the lower shut-into any of the rooms. But he could rap at the windows, which he did loudly, and it was in his power to break them if he pleased. He rapped very loudly; but poor Hester, who sat at the front hall, heard nothing of the noise.

He knew that from the back-garden he could make his way to the front, with more or less of violence. Between the gardener's cottage and the laundry there was a covered passage leading to the front, the buildings above being continuous, but leaving a way through for the convenience of the servants. This, however, was guarded by a trellis-work gate. But even on this gate the gardener had managed to fix a lock. When Caldigate reached the spot the man was standing, idle and observant, at his own cottage door. 'You had better open this gate,' said Caldigate, 'or I shall kick it open.'

'You mustn't do that, Mr. Caldigate. It's master's orders as it's to be locked. It's master's orders as you ain't to be in here at all.' Then Caldigate raised his foot, and the trellis-work gate was very soon despatched. 'Very well,' said the man;—'very well, Mr. Caldigate. That'll have to come agin you when the other things come. It's my belief as it's burglorious.' Then Caldigate went up before the house windows, and the gardener followed him.

The front door was approached by half-a-dozen stone steps, which were guarded on each side by a curved iron rail. Along the whole front of the house, passing under the steps, there ran a narrow, shallow area, contrived simply to give light to the kitchen and offices in the basement storey. But this area was, again, guarded by an iron rail, which was so constructed as to make it impossible that any one less expert than a practised house-breaker should get in or out of any of the windows looking that way. From the hall there were no less than four windows looking to the front; but they were all equally unapproachable.

The moment that Caldigate appeared coming round the curve of the gravel road Hester saw him. Jumping from her chair with her baby, she rushed to the window, and called to him aloud, tapping at the window as she did so, 'John, I am here! Come to me! come to me! Take me out! They have shut me in, and will not let me come to you.' Then she held up the baby. 'Mamma, let him in, so that he come to his own baby. You dare not keep the father away from his own child.' At this time the nurse was in the hall, as was also the cook. But the front door was locked as well as chained, and the key was in Mrs. Bolton's own pocket. She sat perfectly silent, rigid, without a motion. She had known that he would come and show himself; and she had determined that she would be rigid, silent, and motionless. She would not move or speak unless Hester should endeavour to make her way down into the kitchen. But just in the passage which led to the top of the kitchen stairs stood the cook,— strong, solid, almost twice the weight of Hester,—a pious, determined woman, on whom her mistress could depend that she would remain there impervious.

They could talk to each other now, Hester and Caldigate, each explaining or suggesting what had been done or should be done; but they could converse only so that their enemies around them should hear every word that was spoken. 'No, John, no; I will not stay,' she said, when her husband told her that he would leave the decision to her. 'Unless it be to do your bidding, I will not stay here willingly. And, John, I will not move upstairs. I will remain here; and if they choose to give me food they may bring it to me. Unless they carry me I will not go to my bedroom. And they shall tear me to pieces before I will let them carry me. Poor baby! poor baby! I know he will be ill,' she said, moaning, but still so that he, standing beyond the railings, should hear her through the window. 'I know he will be ill; but what can I do? They do not care for my baby. If he should die it will be nothing to them.' During all this Mrs. Bolton kept her resolve, and sat there rigid, with her eyes fixed on vacancy, speaking no word, apparently paying no attention to the scene around her. Her back was turned to the front door, so that she could not see John Caldigate. Nor would she attempt to look at him. He could not get in, nor could the other get out. If that were so she would endeavour to bear it all. In the meantime the old man was sitting in his armchair up in his bedroom, reduced almost to inanity of mind by the horror of the occasion. When he could think of it all he would tell himself that he must let her go. He could not keep the mother and her baby a prisoner in such a condition as this.

Then there came dinner. Let misfortunes be what they may, dinner will come. The old man crawled down-stairs, and Hester was invited into the dining-room. 'No,' she said. If you choose to send it to me here because of baby, I will eat.' Then, neither would Mrs. Bolton go to her husband; but both of them, seated in their high-backed arm-chairs, ate their food with their plates upon their laps.

During this time Caldigate still remained outside, but in vain. As circumstances were at present, he had no means of approaching his wife. He could kick down a slight trellis-work gate; but he could bring no adequate force to bear against the stout front door. At last, when the dusk of evening came on he took his departure, assuring his wife that he would be there again on the following morning.

CHAPTER XXXVI

The Escape

DURING the whole of that night Hester kept her position in the hall, holding her baby in her arms as long as the infant would sleep in that position, and then allowing the nurse to take it to its cradle up-stairs. And during the whole night also Mrs. Bolton remained with her daughter. Tea was brought to them, which each of them took, and after that neither spoke a word to the other till the morning. Before he went to bed, Mr. Bolton came down and made an effort for their joint comfort. 'Hester,' he said, 'why should you not go to your room? You can do yourself no good by remaining there.'

'No,' she said, sullenly; 'no, I will stay.'

'You will only make yourself ill,—you and your mother.'

'She can go. Though I should die, I will stay here.'

Nor could he succeed better with his wife. 'If she is obstinate, so must I be,' said Mrs. Bolton. It was in vain that he endeavoured to prove to her that there could be no reason for such obstinacy, that her daughter would not attempt to escape during the hours of the night without her baby.

'You would not do that,' said the old man, turning to his daughter. But to this Hester would make no reply, and Mrs. Bolton simply declared her purpose of remaining. To her mind there was present an idea that she would, at any rate, endure as much actual suffering as her daughter. There they both sat, and in the morning they were objects pitiable to be seen.

Macbeth and Sancho have been equally eloquent in the praise of sleep. 'Sleep that knits up the ravelled sleave of care!' But sleep will knit up effectually no broken stitches unless it be enjoyed in bed. 'Blessings on him who invented sleep,' said Sancho. But the great inventor was he who discovered mattresses and sheets and blankets. These two unfortunates no doubt slept; but in the morning they were weary, comfortless and exhausted. Towels and basins were brought to them, and then they prepared themselves to watch through another day. It seemed to be a trial between them, which could outwatch the other. The mother was, of course, much the older; but with poor Hester there was the baby to add to her troubles. Never was there a woman more determined to carry out her purpose than Mrs. Bolton, or one more determined to thwart the purpose of another than she who still called herself Hester Caldigate. In the morning Mrs. Bolton implored her husband to go into Cambridge as usual; but he felt that he could not leave the house with such inmates. So he sat in his bedroom dozing wretchedly in his arm-chair.

Caldigate appeared before the house at nine o'clock, no further attempt having been made to exclude his entrance by the side gate, and asked to see Mr. Bolton. 'Papa is up-stairs,' said Hester through the window. But the old man would not come down to see his visitor, nor would he send any message. Then Caldigate declared his purpose of going at once to the mayor and demanding assistance from the police. He at any rate would return with the carriage as early as he could after his visit to the magistrates' office. He went to the mayor, and inflicted much trouble on that excellent officer, who, however, at last, with the assistance of his clerk,—and of Robert Bolton, whom he saw on the sly,— came to the decision that his own authority would not suffice for the breaking open of a man's house in order that his married daughter should be taken by violence from his custody. 'No doubt,' he said; 'no doubt,' when Caldigate pleaded that Mr. Bolton's daughter was, at any rate for the present, his own wife; and that a man's right to have his wife is undoubted. Those words 'no doubt' were said very often; but no other words were said. Then the clerk expressed an opinion that the proper course would be for Mr. Caldigate to go up to London and get an order from the Vice-Chancellor; which was, of course, tantamount to saying that his wife was to remain at Chesterton till after the trial,— unless she could effect her own escape.

But not on that account was he inclined to yield. He had felt from the first, as had she also, that she would make her way out of the house, or would not make it, as she might or might not have the courage to be persistent in demanding it. This, indeed, had been felt both by William and Robert Bolton when they had given their counsel. 'She is a woman with a baby, and when in your house will be subject to your influences. She will be very angry at first, but will probably yield after a time to your instructions. She will at last give an unwilling assent to the course you propose. That is what may be expected. But if she should be firmer than we think, if there should be in her bosom a greater power of resistance than we expect, should she dash herself too violently against the cage,—then you must let her go.' That was intended to be the gist of the advice given, though it perhaps was not so accurately expressed. It was in that way understood by the old man; but Mrs. Bolton would not so understand it. She had taken the matter in hand, and as she pressed her lips together she told herself that she intended to go through with it. — And so did Hester. But as this day went on, Hester became at times almost hysterical in her efforts to communicate with her husband through the window, holding up her baby and throwing back her head, and was almost in convulsions in her efforts to get at him. He on the other side thundered at the door with the knocker, till that instrument had been unscrewed from within. But still he could knock with his stick and shout with his voice; while the people outside the iron gates stood looking on in a crowd. In the course of the day Robert Bolton endeavoured to get an order from the magistrates for the removal of Caldigate by the police. But the mayor would not assent either to that. Old Mr. Bolton was the owner of the house, and if there was a nuisance to be complained of, it was he that must complain. The mayor during these days was much tried. The steady married people of the borough,—the shopkeepers and their wives, the doctors and lawyers and clergymen,—were in favour of Mr. and Mrs. Bolton. It was held to be fitting that a poor lady in Hester's unfortunate position should be consigned to the care of her parents till the matter had been settled. But the people generally sympathised with the young husband and young wife, and were loud in denouncing the illegality of the banker's proceedings. And it was already rumoured that among the undergraduates Caldigate's side was favoured. It was generally known that Crinkett and the woman had asked for money before they had brought their accusation, and on that account sympathy ran with the Squire of Folking. The mayor, therefore, did not dare to give an order that Caldigate should be removed from off the premises at Puritan Grange, knowing that he was there in search of a wife who was only anxious to place herself in his custody.

But nothing was done all that day. About four in the afternoon, while Caldigate was still there, and at a moment in which poor Hester had been reduced by the continuance of her efforts to a state of hysterical prostration, the old man summoned his wife upstairs. She, with a motion to the cook, who still guarded the stairs, obeyed the order, and for a moment left her watch.

'You must let her go,' said the old man, with tremulous anxiety, beating with his fingers on his knees as he spoke. 'You must let her go.'

'No; no!'

'It will kill her.'

'If I let her go, I shall kill her soul,' said the determined woman. 'Is not her soul more than her body?'

'They will say we—murdered her.'

'Who will say it? And what would that be but the breath of a man? Does not our Father who is in heaven know that I would die to do her a service, if the service accorded with His will? Does He not know that I am cruel to her here in order that she may be saved from eternal—' She was going to say, in the natural fervour of her speech, 'from eternal cruelty to come,' but she checked herself. To have admitted that such a judgment could be worse than just, worse even than merciful, would be blasphemy to her. 'Oh, He knows! He knows! And if He knows, what matters what men say that I have done to her.'

'I cannot have it go on like this,' said he, still whispering.

'She will be wearied out, and then we will take her to her bed.'

But Mr. Bolton succeeded in demanding that a telegram should be sent up to William requesting him to come down to the Grange as early as possible on the following morning. This was sent, and also a message to Robert Bolton in Cambridge, telling him that William had been summoned. During these two days he had not been seen at the Grange, though he knew much of what was being done there. Had he, however, been aware of all that his sister and step-mother were enduring, he would probably have appeared upon the scene. As it was, he had justified his absence by pleading to himself Mrs. Bolton's personal enmity, and the understanding which existed that he should not visit the house. Then, when it was dark, Caldigate with the carriage again returned to the town, where he slept as he had done on the previous night. Again their food was brought to the two women in the hall, and again each of them swallowed a cup of tea as they prepared themselves for the work of the night.

In the hall there was a gas-stove, which was kept burning, and gave a faint glimmer, so that each could see the outline of the other. Light beyond that there was none. In the weary long hours of nights such as these, nights passed on the seats of railway carriages, or rougher nights, such as some of us remember, on the outside of coaches, or sitting by the side of the sick, sleep will come early and will early go. The weariness of the past day will produce some forgetfulness for an hour or two, and then come the slow, cold, sad hours through which the dawn has to be expected. Between two and three these unfortunates were both awake, the poor baby having been but lately carried back from its mother to its cradle. Then suddenly Mrs. Bolton heard rather than saw her daughter slip down from her chair on to the ground and stretch herself along upon the hard floor. 'Hester,' she said; but Hester did not answer. 'Hester, are you hurt?' When there was still no answer, the mother got up, with limbs so stiff that she could hardly use them, and stood over her child. 'Hester, speak to me.'

'I will never speak to you more,' said the daughter.

'My child, why will you not go to your comfortable wholesome bed?'

'I will not go; I will die here.'

'The door shall not be locked. You shall have the key with you. I will do nothing to hurt you if you will go to your bed.'

'I will not go; leave me alone. You cannot love me, mamma, or you

267

would not treat me like this.'

'Love you! Oh, my child! If you knew! If you could understand! Why am I doing this? Is it not because I feel it to be my duty? Will you let me take you to your bed?'

'No, never. I, too, can do my duty,—my duty to my husband. It is to remain here till I can get to him, even though I should die.' Then she turned her poor limbs on the hard floor, and the mother covered her with a cloak and placed a cushion beneath her head. Then, after standing a while over her child, she returned to her chair, and did not move or speak again till the old cook came, with the first glimmer of the morning, to inquire how the night had been passed.

'I cannot allow this; I cannot allow this,' said Mr. Bolton, when he shuffled down in his slippers. The old servant had been up to him and had warned him that such sufferings as these might have a tragic end,— too probably an end fatal to the infant. If the mother's strength should altogether fail her, would it not go badly with the baby? So the cook had argued, who had been stern enough herself, anxious enough to secure 'Miss Hester' from the wickedness of John Caldigate. But she was now cowed and frightened, and had acknowledged to herself that if 'Miss Hester' would not give way, then she must be allowed to go forth, let the wickedness be what it might.

'There must be an end to this,' said the old man.

'What end?' asked his wife. 'Let her obey her parents.'

'I will obey only my husband.' said Hester.

'Of course there must be an end. Let her go to her bed, and, weary as I am, I will wait upon her as only a mother can wait upon her child. Have I not prayed for her through the watches of the night, that she might be delivered from this calamity, that she might be comforted by Him in her sorrow? What have I done these two last weary days but pray to the Lord God that He might be merciful to her?'

'Let me go,' said Hester.

'I will not let you go,' said the mother, rising from her seat. 'I too can suffer. I too can endure. I will not be conquered by my own child.' There spoke the human being. That was the utterance natural to the woman. 'In this struggle, hard as it is, I will not be beat by one who has been subject to my authority.' In all those prayers,—and she had prayed, —there had been the prayer in her heart, if not in her words, that she might be saved from the humiliation of yielding.

Early in the day Caldigate was again in front of the house, and outside there was a close carriage with a pair of horses, standing at the gardener's little gate. And at the front gate, which was still chained, there was again the crowd. At about one both William and Robert Bolton came

268

upon the scene, and were admitted by the gardener and cook through the kitchen-door into the house. They were close to Caldigate as they entered; neither did they speak to him or he to them. At that moment Hester was standing with the baby at the window, and saw them. 'Now I shall be allowed to go,' she exclaimed. Mrs. Bolton was still seated with her back to the windows; but she had heard the steps on the gravel, and the opening of the kitchen-door; and she understood Hester's words, and was aware that her husband's sons were in the house.

They had agreed as to what should be done, and at once made their way up into the hall. 'William, you will make them let me go. You will make them let me go,' said Hester, rushing at once to the elder of the two, and holding out her baby as though for him to take. She was now in a state so excited, so nervous, so nearly hysterical, that she was hardly able to control herself. 'You will not let them kill me, William,—me and my baby.' He kissed her and said a kind word or two, and then, inquiring after his father, passed on up-stairs. Then Mrs. Bolton followed him, leaving Robert in the hall with Hester. 'I know that you have turned against me,' said Hester.

'Indeed no. I have never turned against you. I have thought that you would be better here than at Folking for the present.'

'That is being against me. A woman should be with her husband. You told them to do this. And they have nearly killed me,—me and my baby.'

In the meantime William Bolton up-stairs was very decided in his opinion that they must at once allow Caldigate to take her back to Folking. She had, as he said, proved herself to be too strong for them. The experiment had been tried and had failed. No doubt it would be better,—so he thought,—that she should remain for the present at the Grange; so much better that a certain show of force had been justified. But as things were going, no further force would be justified. She had proved her power, and must be allowed to go. Mrs. Bolton, however, would not even yet acknowledge that she was beaten. In a few more hours, she thought, Hester would allow herself to be taken to her bed, and then all might be well. But she could not stand against the combined force of her husband and his two sons; and so it was decided that the front door should be opened for the prisoner, and that the chains should be removed from the gate. 'I should be afraid of the people,' William Bolton said to his father.

It was not till this decision had been given that Mrs. Bolton felt that the struggle of the last three days had been too much for her. Now, at last, she threw herself upon her bed, weeping bitter tears, tears of a broken spirit, and there she lay prostrate with fatigue and misery. Nor would she go down to say a word of farewell. How could she say adieu to her daughter, leaving her house in such circumstances? 'I will give her your love,' said William Bolton.

'Say nothing to her. She does not care for my love, nor for the love of her Father in heaven. She cares only for that adulterer.'

The door was opened from within, and the chains were taken away from the gate. 'Oh, John,—oh, my husband,' she exclaimed, as she leaped down the steps into his arms, 'never let me go again; not for a day,—not for an hour!' Then her boxes were brought down, and the nurse came with the child, whom the mother at once took and placed in his father's arms. And the carriage was brought in, and the luggage was placed on it, and the nurse and the baby were seated. 'I will go up to poor mamma for one moment,' she said. She did go to her mother's room, and throwing herself upon the wretched woman, wept over her and kissed her. But the mother, though in some sort she returned the caress, said not a word as her daughter left the room. And she went also to her father and asked his blessing. He muttered a word or two, blessing her, no doubt, with inarticulate words. He also had been thoroughly vanquished.

Then she got into the carriage, and was taken back to Folking lying in John Caldigate's arms.

CHAPTER XXXVII

Again At Folking

THUS Hester prevailed, and was taken back to the house of the man who had married her. By this time very much had been said about the matter publicly. It had been impossible to keep the question,—whether John Caldigate's recent marriage had been true or fraudulent,—out of the newspapers; and now the attempt that had been made to keep them apart by force gave an additional interest to the subject. There was an opinion, very general among elderly educated people, that Hester ought to have allowed herself to be detained at the Grange. 'We do not mean to lean heavily on the unfortunate young lady,' said the 'Isle-of-Ely-Church-Intelligencer'; 'but we think that she would have better shown a becoming sense of her position had she submitted herself to her parents till the trial is over. Then the full sympathy of all classes would have been with her; and whether the law shall restore her to a beloved husband, or shall tell her that she has become the victim of a cruel seducer, she would have been supported by the approval and generous regard of all men.' It was thus for the most part that the elderly and the wise spoke and thought about it. Of course, they pitied her; but they believed all evil of Caldigate, declaring that he too was bound by a feeling of duty to restore the unfortunate one to her father and mother until the matter should have been set at rest by the decision of a jury.

But the people,—especially the people of Utterden and Netherden, and of Chesterton, and even of Cambridge,—were all on the side of Caldigate and Hester as a married couple. They liked the persistency with which he had claimed his wife, and applauded her to the echo for her love and firmness. Of course the scene at Puritan Grange had been much exaggerated. The two nights were prolonged to intervals varying from a week to a fortnight. During that time she was said always to have been at the window holding up her baby. And Mrs. Bolton was accused of cruelties which she certainly had not committed. Some details of the affair made their way into the metropolitan Press,—so that the expected trial became one of those *causes célèbres* by which the public is from time to time kept alive to the value and charm of newspapers.

During all this John Caldigate was specially careful not to seclude himself from public view, or to seem to be afraid of his fellow-creatures. He was constantly in Cambridge, generally riding thither on horseback, and on such occasions was always to be seen in Trumpington Street and

271

Trinity Street. Between him and the Boltons there was, by tacit consent, no intercourse whatever after the attempted imprisonment. He never showed himself at Robert Bolton's office, nor when they met in the street did they speak to each other. Indeed at this time no gentlemen or lady held any intercourse with Caldigate, except his father and Mr. Bromley the clergyman. The Babingtons were strongly of opinion that he should have surrendered the care of his wife; and Aunt Polly went so far as to write to him when she first heard of the affair at Chesterton, recommending him very strongly to leave her at the Grange. Then there was an angry correspondence, ended at last by a request from Aunt Polly that there might be no further intercourse between Babington and Folking till after the trial.

Caldigate, though he bore all this with an assured face, with but little outward sign of inward misgiving, suffered much,—much even from the estrangement of those with whom he had hitherto been familiar. To be 'cut' by any one was a pain to him. Not to be approved of, not to be courted, not to stand well in the eyes of those around him, was to him positive and immediate suffering. He was supported no doubt by the full confidence of his father, by the friendliness of the parson, and by the energetic assurances of partisans who were all on his side,—such as Mr. Ralph Holt, the farmer. While Caldigate had been in Cambridge waiting for his wife's escape, Holt and one or two others were maturing a plan for breaking into Puritan Grange, and restoring the wife to her husband. All this supported him. Without it he could hardly have carried himself as he did. But with all this, still he was very wretched. 'It is that so many people should think me guilty,' he said to Mr. Bromley.

She bore it better—though, of course, now that she was safe at Folking she had but little to do as to outward bearing. In the first place, no doubt as to his truth ever touched her for a moment,—and not much doubt as to the result of the trial. It was to her an assured fact that John Caldigate was her husband, and she could not realise the idea that, such being the fact, a jury should say that he was not. But let all that be as it might, they two were one; and to adhere to him in every word, in every thought, in every little action, was to her the only line of conduct possible. She heard what Mr. Bromley said, she knew what her father-in-law thought, she was aware of the enthusiasm on her side of the folk at Folking. It seemed to her that this opposition to her happiness was but a continuation of that which her mother had always made to her marriage. The Boltons were all against her. It was a terrible sorrow to her. But she knew how to bear it bravely. In the tenderness of her husband, who at this time was very tender to her, she had her great consolation.

On the day of her return she had been very ill,—so ill that Caldigate

and his father had been much frightened. During the journey home in
the carriage, she had wept and laughed hysterically, now clutching her
baby, and then embracing her husband. Before reaching Folking she had
been so worn with fatigue that he had hardly been able to support her on
the seat. But after rest for a day or two, she had rallied completely. And
she herself had taken pleasure and great pride in the fact that through it
all her baby had never really been ill. 'He is a little man,' she said, boasting to the boy's father. 'and knows how to put up with troubles. And
when his mamma was so bad, he didn't peak and pine and cry, so as to
break her heart. Did he, my own, own brave little man? And she could
boast of her own health too. 'Thank God, I am strong, John. I can bear
things which would break down other women. You shall never see me
give way because I am a poor creature.' Certainly she had a right to
boast that she was not a poor creature.

Caldigate no doubt was subject to troubles of which she knew nothing. It was quite clear to him that Mr. Seely, his own lawyer, did in
truth believe that there had been some form of marriage between him
and Euphemia Smith. The attorney had never said so much,—had never
accused him. It would probably have been opposed to all the proprieties
in such a matter that any direct accusation should have been made
against him by his own attorney. But he could understand from the
man's manner that his mind was not free from a strong suspicion. Mr.
Seely was eager enough as to the defence; but seemed to be eager as
against opposing evidence rather than on the strength of evidence on
his own side. He was not apparently desirous of making all the world
know that such a marriage certainly never took place; but that, whether
such a marriage had taken place or not, the jury ought not to trust the
witnesses. He relied, not on the strength of his own client, but on the
weakness of his client's adversaries. It might probably be capable of
proof that Crinkett and Adamson and the woman had conspired together
to get money from John Caldigate; and if so, then their evidence as to
the marriage would be much weakened. And he showed himself not
averse to any tricks of trade which might tend to get a verdict. Could it
be proved that John Caldigate had been dishonest in his mining operation?
Had Euphemia Smith allowed her name to be connected with that of any
other man in Australia? What had been her antecedents? Was it not on
the cards that Allan, the minister, had never undergone any ceremony
of ordination? And, if not, might it not be shown that a marriage service
performed by him would be no marriage service at all? Could not the
jury be made to think,—or at least some of the jury,—that out there, in
that rough lawless wilderness, marriage ceremonies were very little understood? These were the wiles to which he seemed disposed to trust;

whereas Caldigate was anxious that he should instruct some eloquent indignant advocate to declare boldly that no English gentleman could have been guilty of conduct so base, so dastardly, and so cruel! 'You see Mr. Caldigate,' the lawyer said on one occasion, 'to make the best of it, our own hands are not quite clean. You did promise the other lady marriage.'

'No doubt. No doubt I was a fool; and I paid for my folly. I bought her off. Having fallen into the common scrape,—having been pleased by her prettinesses and clevernesses and women's ways,—I did as so many other men have done. I got out of it as best I could without treachery and without dishonour. I bought her off. Had she refused to take my money, I should probably have married her,—and probably have blown my brains out afterwards. All that has to be acknowledged,—much to my shame. Most of us would have to blush if the worst of our actions were brought out before us in a court of law. But there was an end of it. Then they come over here and endeavour to enforce their demand for money by a threat.'

'That envelope is so unfortunate,' said the lawyer.

'Most unfortunate.'

'Perhaps we shall get some one before the day comes who will tell the jury that any marriage up at Ahalala must have been a farce.'

All this was unsatisfactory, and became so more and more as the weeks went by. The confidential clerk whom the Boltons had sent out when the first threat reached them early in November,—the threat conveyed in that letter from the woman which Caldigate had shown to Robert Bolton,—returned about the end of March. The two brothers, Robert and William, decided upon sending him to Mr. Seely, so that any information obtained might be at Caldigate's command, to be used, if of any use, in his defence. But there was in truth very little of it. The clerk had been up to Nobble and Ahalala, and had found no one there who knew enough of the matter to give evidence about it. The population of mining districts in Australia is peculiarly a shifting population, so that the most of those who had known Caldigate and his mode of life there were gone. The old woman who kept Henniker's Hotel at Nobble had certainly heard that they were married; but then she had added that many people there called themselves man and wife from convenience. A woman would often like a respectable name where there was no parson near at hand to entitle her to it. Then the parsons would be dilatory and troublesome and expensive, and a good many people were apt to think that they could do very well without ceremonies. She evidently would have done no good to either side as a witness. This clerk had found Ahalala almost deserted,—occupied chiefly by a few Chinese,

who were contented to search for the specks of gold which more ambitious miners had allowed to slip through their fingers. The woman
had certainly called herself Mrs. Caldigate, and had been called so by
many. But she had afterwards been called Mrs. Crinkett, when she and
Crinkett had combined their means with the view of buying the Polyeuka mine. She was described as an enterprising, greedy woman, upon
whom the love of gold had had almost more than its customary effect.
And she had for a while been noted and courted for her success, having
been the only female miner who was supposed to have realised money
in these parts. She had been known to the banks at Nobble, also even at
Sydney; and had been supposed at one time to have been worth twenty
or thirty thousand pounds. Then she had joined herself with Crinkett,
and all their money had been supposed to vanish in the Polyeuka mine.
No doubt there had been enough in that to create animosity of the most
bitter kind against Caldigate. He in his search for gold had been uniform-
ly successful,—was spoken of among the Nobble miners as the one man
who in gold-digging had never had a reverse. He had gone away just
before the bad time came on Polyeuka; and then had succeeded, after
he had gone, in extracting from these late unfortunate partners of his
every farthing that he had left them! There was ample cause for animosity.

Allan, the minister, who certainly had been at Ahalala, was as certainly dead. He had gone out from Scotland as a Presbyterian clergyman,
and no doubt had ever been felt as to his being that which he called
himself;—and a letter from him was produced, which had undoubtedly
been written by himself. Robert Bolton had procured a photograph of
the note which the woman produced as having been written by Allan
to Caldigate. The handwriting did not appear to him to be the same, but
an expert had given an opinion that they both might have been written
by the same person. Of Dick Shand no tidings had been found. It was
believed that he had gone from Queensland to some of the Islands,—
probably to the Fijis; but he had sunk so low among men as to have left
no trace behind him. In Australia no one cares to know whence a shepherd has come or whither he goes. A miner belongs to a higher class, and
is more considered. The result of all which was, in the opinion of the
Boltons, adverse to John Caldigate. And in discussing this with his client,
Mr. Seely acknowledged that nothing had as yet come to light sufficient
to shake the direct testimony of the woman, corroborated as it was by
three persons, all of whom would swear that they had been present at
the marriage.

'No doubt they endeavoured to get money from you,' said Mr. Seely;
'and I may be well assured in my own mind that money was their sole
object. But then it cannot be denied that their application to you for

money had a sound basis,—one which, though you might fairly refuse
to allow it, takes away from the application all idea of criminality.
Crinkett has never asked for money as a bribe to hold his tongue. In a
matter of trade between them and you, you were very successful; they
were very unfortunate. A man asking for restitution in such circumstances will hardly be regarded as dishonest.'

It was to no purpose that Caldigate declared that he would willingly
have remitted a portion of the money had he known the true circumstances. He had not done so, and now the accusation was made. The
jury, feeling that the application had been justifiable, would probably
keep the two things distinct. That was Mr. Seely's view; and thus, in
these days, Caldigate gradually came to hate Mr. Seely. There was no
comfort to be had from Mr. Seely.

Mr. Bromley was much more comfortable, though, unfortunately, in
such a matter less to be trusted.

'As to the minister's handwriting,' he said, 'that will go for nothing.
Even if he had written the note—'

'Which he didn't,' said Caldigate.

'Exactly. But should it be believed to have been his, it would prove
nothing. And as to the envelope, I cannot think that any jury would
disturb the happiness of a family on such evidence as that. It all depends
on the credibility of the people who swear that they were present; and I
can only say that were I one of the jury, and were the case brought
before me as I see it now, I certainly should not believe them. There is
here one letter to you, declaring that if you will comply with her demands, she will not annoy you, and declaring also her purpose of marrying some one else. How can any juryman believe her after that?'

'Mr. Seely says that twelve men will not be less likely to think me a
bigamist because she has expressed her readiness to commit bigamy;
that, if alone, she would not have a leg to stand upon, but that she is
amply corroborated; whereas I have not been able to find a single witness to support me. It seems to me that in this way any man might be
made the victim of a conspiracy.'

Then Mr. Bromley said that all that would be too patent to a jury to
leave any doubt upon the matter. But John Caldigate himself, though
he took great comfort in the society of the clergyman, did in truth rely
rather on the opinion of the lawyer.

The old squire never doubted his son for a moment, and in his intercourse with Hester showed her all the tenderness and trust of a loving
parent. But he, too, manifestly feared the verdict of a jury. According
to him, things in the world around him generally were very bad. What
was to be expected from an ordinary jury such as Cambridgeshire would

supply but prejudice, thick-headed stupidity, or at the best a strick obe-dience to the dictum of a judge. 'It is a case,' he said, 'in which no jury about here will have sense enough to understand and weigh the facts. There will be on one side the evidence of four people, all swearing the same thing. It may be that one or more of them will break down under cross-examination, and that all will then be straight. But if not, the twelve men in a box will believe them because they are four, not under-standing that in such a case four may conspire as easily as two or three. There will be the Judge, no doubt; but English judges are always favour-able to convictions. The Judge begins with the idea that the man before him would hardly have been brought there had he not been guilty.'

In all this, and very much more that he said both to Mr. Bromley and his son, he was expressing his contempt for the world around him rather than any opinion of his own on this particular matter. 'I often think,' said he, 'that we have to bear more from the stupidity than from the wickedness of the world.'

It should be mentioned that about a week after Hester's escape from Chesterton there came to her a letter from her mother.

'Dearest Hester,—You do not think that I do not love you because I tried to protect you from what I believe to be sin and evil and tempta-tion? You do not think that I am less your mother because I caused you suffering? If your eye offend you, pluck it out. Was I not plucking out my own eye when I caused pain to you? You ought to come back to me and your father. You ought to do so even now. But whether you come back or not, will you not remember that I am the mother who bore you, and have always loved you? And when further distress shall come upon you, will you not return to me?—Your unhappy but most loving Mother,

'MARY BOLTON.'

In answer to this Hester, in a long letter, acknowledged her mother's love, and said that the memory of those two days at Chesterton should lessen neither her affection nor her filial duty; but, she went on to say that, in whatever distress might come upon her, she should turn to her husband for comfort and support, whether he should be with her, or whether he should be away from her. 'But,' she added, concluding her letter, 'beyond my husband and my child, you and papa will always be the dearest to me.'

CHAPTER XXXVIII

Bollum

THERE was not much to enliven the house at Folking during these days. Caldigate would pass much of his time walking about the place, applying his mind as well as he could to the farm, and holding up his head among the tenants, with whom he was very popular. He had begun his reign over them with hands not only full but free. He had drained, and roofed, and put up gates, and repaired roads, and shown himself to be an active man, anxious to do good. And now in his trouble they were very true to him. But their sympathy could not ease the burden at his heart. Though by his words and deeds among them he seemed to occupy himself fully, there was a certain amount of pretence in every effort that he made. He was always affecting a courage in which he felt himself to be deficient. Every smile was false. Every brave word spoken was an attempt at deceit. When alone in his walks,—and he was mostly alone,—his mind would fix itself on his great trouble, and on the crushing sorrow which might only too probably fall upon that loved one whom he had called his wife. Oh, with what regret now did he think of the good advice which the captain had given him on board the Goldfinder, and of the sententious, timid wisdom of Mrs. Callender! Had she, his Hester, ever uttered to him one word of reproach,—had she ever shuddered in his sight when he had acknowledged that the now odious woman had in that distant land been in his own hearing called by his own name,—it would have been almost better. Her absolute faith added a sting to his sufferings.

Then, as he walked alone about the estate, he would endeavour to think whether there might not yet be some mode of escape,—whether something might not be done to prevent his having to stand in the dock and abide the uncertain verdict of a jury. With Mr. Seely he was discontented. Mr. Seely seemed to be opposed to any great effort,—would simply trust to the chance of snatching little advantages in the Court. He had money at command. If fifty thousand pounds,—if double that sum, —would have freed him from this trouble, he thought that he could have raised it, and was sure that he would willingly pay it. Twenty thousand pounds two months since, when Crinkett appeared at the christening, would have sent these people away. The same sum, no doubt, would send them away now. But then the arrangement might have been possible. But now,—how was it now? Could it still be done? Then the whole thing might have been hidden, buried in darkness. Now it was already in the mouths of all men. But still, if these witnesses were made to disappear,—if this woman herself by whom the charge was made would take herself away—then the trial must be abandoned. There would be a whispering of evil,—or, too probably, the saying of evil without whispering. A terrible injury would have been inflicted upon her and his boy; —but the injury would be less than that which he now feared.

And there was present to him through all this a feeling that the money ought to be paid independently of the accusation brought against him. Had he known at first all that he knew now,—how he had taken their all from these people, and how they had failed absolutely in the last great venture they had made,—he would certainly have shared their loss with them. He would have done all that Crinkett had suggested to him when he and Crinkett were walking along the dike. Crinkett had said that on receiving twenty thousand pounds he would have gone back to Australia, and would have taken a wife with him! That offer had been quite intelligible, and if carried out would have put an end to all trouble. But he had mismanaged that interview. He had been too proud, too desirous not to seem to buy off a threatening enemy. Now, as the trouble pressed itself more closely upon him,—upon him and his Hester,—he would so willingly buy off his enemy if it were possible! 'They ought to have the money,' he said to himself; 'if only I could contrive that it should be paid to them.'

One day as he was entering the house by a side door, Darvell the gardener told him that there was a gentleman waiting to see him. The gentleman was very anxious to see him, and had begged to be allowed to sit down. Darvell, when asked whether the gentleman was a gentleman, expressed an affirmative opinion. He had been driven over from Cambridge in a hired gig, which was now standing in the yard, and was dressed, as Darvell expressed it, 'quite accordingly and genteel.' So Caldigate passed into the house and found the man seated in the dining-room.

'Perhaps you will step into my study?' said Caldigate. Thus the two men were seated together in the little room which Caldigate used for his own purposes.

Caldigate, as he looked at the man, distrusted his gardener's judgment. The coat and hat and gloves, even the whiskers and head of hair, might have belonged to a gentleman; but not, as he thought, the mouth or the eyes or the hands. And when the man began to speak there was a mixture of assurance and intended complaisance, an affected familiarity and an attempt at ease, which made the master of the house quite sure that his guest was not all that Darvell had represented. The man soon

told his story. His name was Bollum, Richard Bollum, and he had connections with Australia;—was largely concerned in Australian gold-mines.
When Caldigate heard this, he looked round involuntarily to see whether
the door was closed. 'We're tiled, of course,' said Bollum. Caldigate
with a frown nodded his head, and Bollum went on. He hadn't come
there, he said, to speak of some recent troubles of which he had heard.
He wasn't the man to shove his nose into other people's matters. It was
nothing to him who was married to whom. Caldigate shivered, but sat
and listened in silence. But Mr. Bollum had had dealings,—many dealings,—with Timothy Crinkett. Indeed he was ready to say that Timothy
Crinkett was his uncle. He was not particularly proud of his uncle, but
nevertheless Timothy Crinkett was his uncle. Didn't Mr. Caldigate think
that something ought to be done for Timothy Crinkett?

'Yes, I do,' said Caldigate, finding himself compelled to say something
at the moment, and feeling that he could say so much with positive
truth.

Then Bollum continued his story, showing that he knew all the circumstances of Polyeuka. 'It was hard on them, wasn't it, Mr. Caldigate?'

'I think it was.'

'Every rap they had among them, Mr. Caldigate! You left them as
bare as the palm of my hand!'

'It was not my doing. I simply made him an offer, which every one
at the time believed to be liberal.'

'Just so. We grants all that. But still you got all their money;—old
pals of yours too, as they say out there.'

'It is a matter of most intense regret to me. As soon as I knew the
circumstances, Mr. Bollum, I should have been most happy to have
divided the loss with them—'

'That's it,—that's it. That's what'd be right between man and man,'
said Mr. Bollum, interrupting him.

'Had no other subject been introduced.'

'I know nothing about other subjects. I haven't come here to meddle
with other subjects. I'm, as it were, a partner of Crinkett's. Any way, I
am acting as his agent. I'm quite above board, Mr. Caldigate, and in what
I say I mean to stick to my own business and not go beyond it. Twenty
thousand pounds is what we ask,—so that we and you may share the loss.
You agree to that?'

'I should have agreed to it two months since,' said Caldigate, fearing
that he might be caught in a trap,—anxious to do nothing mean, unfair,
or contrary to the law,—craving in his heart after the bold, upright conduct of a thoroughly honourable English gentleman, and yet desirous
also to use, if it might be used, the instrumentality of this man.

'And why not now? You see,' said Bollum, becoming a little more confidential, 'how difficult it is for me to speak. Things ain't altered. You've got the money. They've lost the money. There isn't any ill-will, Mr. Caldigate. As for Crinkett, he's a rough diamond, of course. What am I to say about the lady?'

'I don't see that you need say anything.'

'That's just it. Of course she's one of them. That's all. If there is to be money, she'll have her share. He's an old fool, and perhaps they'll make a match of it.' As he said this he winked. 'At any rate they'll be off to Australia together. And what I propose is this, Mr. Caldigate—' Then he paused.

'What do you propose?'

'Make the money payable in bills to their joint order at Sydney. They don't want to be wasting any more time here. They'll start at once. This is the 12th April, isn't it? Tuesday the 12th?' Caldigate assented. 'The old Goldfinder leaves Plymouth this day week.' From this he was sure that Bollum had heard all the story from Euphemia Smith herself, or he would not have talked of the 'old' Goldfinder. 'Let them have the bills handed to them on board, and they'll go. Let me have the duplicates here. You can remit the money by July to your agents,—to take up the bills when due. Just let me be with you when the order is given to your banker in London, and everything will be done. It's as easy as kiss.'

Caldigate sat silent, turning it over in his own mind, trying to determine what would be best. Here was another opportunity. But it was one as to which he must come to a decision on the spur of the moment. He must deal with the man now or never. The twenty thousand pounds were nothing. Had there been no question about his wife, he would have paid the money, moved by that argument as to his 'old pals,'—by the conviction that the result of his dealing with them had in truth been to leave them 'as bare as the palm of his hand.' They were welcome to the money; and if by giving the money he could save his Hester, how great a thing it would be! Was it not his duty to make the attempt? And yet there was in his bosom a strong aversion to have any secret dealing with such a man as this,—to have any secret dealing in such a matter. To buy off witnesses in order that his wife's name and his boy's legitimacy might be half,—only half,—established! For even though these people should be made absolutely to vanish, though the sea should swallow them, all that had been said would be known, and too probably believed for ever!

And then, too, he was afraid. If he did this thing alone, without counsel, would he not be putting himself into the hands of these wretches? Might he not be almost sure that when they had gotten his money they would turn upon him and demand more? Would not the payment of the money be evidence against him to any jury? Would it be possible to make judge or jury believe, to make even a friend believe, that in such an emergency he had paid away so large a sum of money because he had felt himself bound to do so by his conscience?

'Well, squire,' said Bollum, 'I think you see your way through it; don't you?'

'I don't regard the money in the least. They would be welcome to the money.'

'That's a great point, anyway.'

'But—'

'Ay; but! You're afraid they wouldn't go. You come down to Plymouth, and don't put the bills into their hands or mine till the vessel is under weigh, with them aboard. Then you and I will step into the boat, and be back ashore. When they know the money's been deposited at a bank in London, they'll trust you as far as that. The Goldfinder won't put back again when she's once off. Won't that make it square?'

'I was thinking of something else.'

'Well, yes; there's that trial a-coming on; isn't there?'

'These people have conspired together to tell the basest lie.'

'I know nothing about that, Mr. Caldigate. I haven't got so much as an opinion. People tell me that all the things look very strong on their side.'

'Liars sometimes are successful.'

'You can be quit of them,—and pay no more than what you say you kind of owes. I should have thought Crinkett might have asked forty thousand; but Crinkett, though he's rough,—I do own he's rough,—but he's honest after a fashion. Crinkett wants to rob no man; but he feels it hard when he's got the better of. Lies, or no lies, can you do better?'

'I should like to see my lawyer first,' said Caldigate, almost panting in his anxiety.

'What lawyer? I hate lawyers.'

'Mr. Seely. My case is in his hands, and I should have to tell him.'

'Tell him when you come back from Plymouth, and hold your peace till that's done. No good can come of lawyers in such a matter as this. You might as well tell the town-crier. Why should he want to put bread out of his own mouth? And if there is a chance of hard words being said, why should he hear them? He'll work for his money, no doubt; but what odds is it to him whether your lady is to be called Mrs. Caldigate or Miss Bolton? He won't have to go to prison. His boy won't be!—you know what.' This was terrible, but yet it was all so true! 'I'll tell you what it is, squire. We can't make it lighter by talking about it all round. I used to do a bit of hunting once; and I never knew any good come of asking what there was the other side of the fence. You've got to have it, or you've got to leave it alone. That's just where you are. Of course it isn't nice.'

'I don't mind the money.'

'Just so. But it isn't nice for a swell like you to have to hand it over to such a one as Crinkett just as the ship's starting, and then to bolt ashore along with me. The odds are, it is all talked about. Let's own all that. But then it's not nice to have to hear a woman swear that she's your wife, when you've got another,—specially when she's got three men as can swear the same. It ain't nice for you to have me sitting here. I'm well aware of that. There's the choice of evils. You know what that means. I'm a-putting it about as fair as a man can put anything. It's a pity you didn't stump up the money before. But it's not altogether quite too late yet.'

'I'll give you an answer tomorrow, Mr. Bollum.'

'I must be in town to-night.'

'I will be with you in London to-morrow if you will give me an address. All that you have said is true; but I cannot do this thing without thinking of it.'

'You'll come alone?'

'Yes,—alone.'

'As a gentleman?'

'On my word as a gentleman I will come alone.'

Then Bollum gave him an address,—not the place at which he resided, but a certain coffee-house in the City, at which he was accustomed to make appointments. 'And don't you see any lawyer,' said Bollum, shaking his finger. 'You can't do any good that way. It stands to reason that no lawyer would let you pay twenty thousand pounds to get out of any scrape. He and you have different legs to stand upon.' Then Mr. Bollum went away, and was driven back in his gig to the Cambridge Hotel.

As soon as the front door was closed Hester hurried down to her husband, whom she found still in the hall. He took her into his own room, and told her everything that had passed,—everything, as accurately as he could. 'And remember,' he said, 'though I do not owe them money, that I feel bound by my conscience to refund them so much. I should do it, now I know the circumstances, if no charge had been brought against me.'

'They have perjured themselves, and have been so wicked.'

'Yes, they have been very wicked.'

'Let them come and speak the truth, and then let them have the money.'

283

'They will not do that, Hester.'

'Prove them to be liars, and then give it to them.'

'My own girl, I am thinking of you.'

'And I of you. Shall it be said of you that you bought off those who had dared to say that your wife was not your wife? I would not do that. What if the people in the Court should believe what they say?'

'It would be bad for you, then, dearest.'

'But I should still be your wife. And baby would still be your own, own honest boy. I am sometimes unhappy, but I am never afraid. Let the devil do his worst, but never speak him fair. I would scorn them till it is all over. Then, if money be due to them, let them have it.' As she said this, she had drawn herself a little apart from him,—a little away from the arm which had been round her waist, and was looking him full in the face. Never before, even during the soft happiness of their bridal tour, had she seemed to him to be so handsome.

But her faith, her courage, and her beauty did not alter the circumstances of the case. Because she trusted him, he was not the less afraid of the jury who would have to decide, or of the judge, who, with stern eyes, would probably find himself compelled to tell the jury that the evidence against the prisoner was overwhelming. In choosing what might be best to be done on her account, he could not allow himself to be guided by her spirit. The possibility that the whole gang of them might be made to vanish was present to his mind. Nor could he satisfy himself that in doing as had been proposed to him he would be speaking the devil fair. He would be paying money which he ought to pay, and would perhaps be securing his wife's happiness.

He had promised, at any rate, that he would see the man in London on the morrow, and that he would see him alone. But he had not promised not to speak to his attorney on the subject. Therefore, after much thought, he wrote to Mr. Seely to make an appointment for the next morning, and then told his wife that he would have to go to London on the following day.

'Not to buy those men off?' she said.

'Whatever is done will be done by the advice of my lawyer,' he said, peevishly. 'You may be sure that I am anxious enough to do the best. When one has to trust to a lawyer, one is bound to trust to him.' This seemed to be so true that Hester could say nothing against it.

CHAPTER XXXIX

Restitution

HE had still the whole night to think about it,—and throughout the whole night he was thinking about it. He had fixed a late hour in the afternoon for his appointment in London, so that he might have an hour or two in Cambridge before he started by the mid-day train. It was during his drive into the town that he at last made up his mind that he would not satisfy himself with discussing the matter with Mr. Seely, but that he would endeavour to explain it all to Robert Bolton. No doubt Robert Bolton was now his enemy, as were all the Boltons. But the brother could not but be anxious for his sister's name and his sister's happiness. If a way out of all this misery could be seen, it would be a way out of misery for the Boltons as well as for the Caldigates. If only he could make the attorney believe that Hester was in truth his wife, still, even yet, there might be assistance on that side. But he went to Mr. Seely first, the hour of his appointment requiring that it should be so.

But Mr. Seely was altogether opposed to any arrangement with Mr. Bollum. 'No good was ever done,' he said, 'by buying off witnesses. The thing itself is disreputable, and would to a certainty be known to every one.'

'I should not buy them off. I regard the money as their own. I will give Crinkett the money and let him go or stay as he pleases. When giving him the money, I will tell him that he may do as he pleases.'

'You would only throw your money away. You would do much worse than throw it away. Their absence would not prevent the trial. The Boltons will take care of that.'

'They cannot want to injure their own side, Mr. Seely.'

'They want to punish you, and to take her away. They will take care that the trial shall go on. And when it was proved, as it would be proved, that you had given these people a large sum of money, and had so secured their absence, do you think that the jury would refuse to believe their sworn depositions, and whatever other evidence would remain? The fact of your having paid them money would secure a verdict against you. The thing would, in my mind, be so disreputable that I should have to throw up the case. I could not defend you.'

It was clear to him that Bollum had understood his own side of the question in deprecating any reference to an attorney. The money should have been paid and the four witnesses sent away without a word to any one,—if any attempt in that direction were made at all. Nevertheless he went to Robert Bolton's office and succeeded in obtaining an interview with his wife's brother. But here, as with the other attorney, he failed to make the man understand the state of his own mind. He had failed in the same way even with his wife. If it were fit that the money should be paid, it could not be right that he should retain it because the people to whom it was due had told lies about him. And if this could be explained to the jury, surely the jury would not give a verdict against him on insufficient evidence, simply because he had done his duty in paying the money!

Robert Bolton listened to him with patience and without any quick expression of hot anger; though before the interview was over he had used some very cruel words. 'We should think ourselves bound to prevent their going, if possible.'

'Of course; I have no idea of going down to Plymouth as the man proposed, or of taking any steps to secure their absence.'

'Your money is your own, and you can do what you like with it. It certainly is not for me to advise you. If you tell me that you are going to pay it, I can only say that I shall look very sharp after them.'

'Why should you want to ruin your sister?'

'You have ruined her. That is our idea. We desire now to rescue her as far as we can from further evil. You have opposed us in every endeavour that we have made. When in the performance of a manifest duty we endeavoured to separate you till after the trial, you succeeded in thwarting us by your influence.'

'I left it to her.'

'Had you been true and honest and upright, you would have known that as long as there was a doubt she ought to have been away from you.'

'I should have sent her away?'

'Certainly.'

'So as to create a doubt in her mind, so as to disturb her peace, so as to make her think that I, having been found out, was willing to be rid of her? It would have killed her.'

'Better so than this.'

'And yet I am truly her husband as you are the husband of your wife. If you would only teach yourself to think that possible, then you would feel differently.'

'Not as to a temporary separation.'

'If you believed me, you would,' said Caldigate.

'But I do not believe you. In a matter like this, as you will come to me, I must be plain. I do not believe you. I think that you have betrayed and seduced my sister. Looking at all the evidence and at your own confession, I can come to no other conclusion. I have discussed the matter with my brother, who is a clear, cool-headed, most judicious man, and he is of the same opinion. In our own private court we have brought you in guilty,—guilty of an offence against us all which necessarily makes us as bitter against you as one man can be against another. You have destroyed our sister, and now you come here and ask me my advice as to buying off witnesses!'

'It is all untrue. As there is a God above me I am her loyal, loving husband. I will buy off no witness.'

'If I were you I would make no such attempt. It will do no good. I do not think that you have a chance of being acquitted,—not a chance; and then how much worse it will be for Hester when she finds herself in your house!'

'She will remain there.'

'Even she will feel that to be impossible. Your influence will then probably be removed, and I presume that for a time you will have no home. But we need not discuss that. As you are here, I should not do my duty were I not to assure you that as far as we are concerned,—Hester's family,—nothing shall be spared either in trouble or money to insure the conviction and punishment of the man whom we believe to have brought upon us so terrible a disgrace.'

Caldigate, when he got out into the street, felt that he was driven almost to despair. At first he declared to himself, most untruly, that there was no one to believe him,—no, not one. Then he remembered how faithful was his wife; and as he did so, in his misery, he told himself that it might have been better for her had she been less faithful. Looking at it all as he now looked at it, after hearing the words of that hard man, he almost thought that it would have been so. Everybody told him that he would be condemned; and if so, what would be the fate of that poor young mother and her child? It was very well for her to declare, with her arms round his neck, that even should he be dragged away to prison, she would still be his true wife, and that she would wait,—in sorrow indeed and mourning, but still with patience,—till the cruel jailers and the harsh laws had restored him to her. If the law declared him a bigamist, she could not then be his wife. The law must decide,— whether rightly or wrongly, still must decide. And then how could they live together? An evil done must be endured, let it be ever so unendurable. But against fresh evils a man may guard. Was it not his duty, his manifest, his chief duty, to save her, as far as she could be saved, from further suffering and increased disgrace? Perhaps, after all, Robert Bolton was right when he told him that he ought to have allowed Hester to remain at Chesterton.

Whatever he might do when he got to London, he felt it to be his duty to go up and keep his appointment with Bollum. And he brought with him from home securities and certificates for stock by which he knew that he could raise the sum named at a moment's warning, should he at last decide upon paying the money. When he got into the train, and when he got out of the train, he was still in doubt. Those to whom he had gone for advice had been so hard to him, that he felt himself compelled to put on one side all that they had said. Bollum had suggested, in his graphic manner, that a lawyer and his client stood upon different legs. Caldigate acknowledged to himself that Bollum was right. His own lawyer had been almost as hard to him as his brother-in-law, who was his declared enemy. But what should he do? As to precautions to be taken in reference to the departure of the gang, all that was quite out of the question. They should go to Australia or stay behind, as they pleased. There should be no understanding that they were to go—or even that they were to hold their tongues because the money was paid to them. It should be fully explained to them that the two things were distinct. Then as he was taken to the inn at which he intended to sleep that night, he made up his mind in the cab that he would pay the money to Crinkett.

He got to London just in time to reach the bank before it was closed, and there made his arrangements. He deposited his documents and securities, and was assured that the necessary sum should be placed to his credit on the following day. Then he walked across a street or two in the city, to the place indicated by Bollum for the appointment. It was at the Jericho Coffee House, in Levant Court,—a silent secluded spot, lying between Lombard Street and Cornhill. Here he found himself ten minutes before the time, and, asking for a cup of coffee, sat down at a table fixed to the ground in a little separate box. The order was given to a young woman at a bar in the room. Then an ancient waiter hobbled up to him and explained that coffee was not quite ready. In truth, coffee was not often asked for at the Jericho Coffee House. The house, said the waiter, was celebrated for its sherry. Would he take half a pint of sherry? So he ordered the sherry, which was afterwards drunk by Bollum.

Bollum came, punctual to the moment, and seated himself at the table with good-humoured alacrity. 'Well, Mr. Caldigate, how is it to be? I think you must have seen that what I have proposed will be for the best.'

'I will tell you what I mean to do, Mr. Bollum,' said Caldigate, very gravely. 'It cannot be said that I owe Mr. Crinkett a shilling.'

'Certainly not. But it comes very near owing, doesn't it?'

'So near that I mean to pay it.'

'That's right.'

'So near that I don't like to feel that I have got his money in my pocket. As far as money goes, I have been a fortunate man.'

'Wonderful!' said Bollum, enthusiastically.

'And as I was once in partnership with your uncle, I do not like to think that I enriched myself by a bargain which impoverished him.'

'It ain't nice, is it,—that you should have it all, and he nothing?'

'Feeling that very strongly,' continued Caldigate, merely shaking his head in token of displeasure at Bollum's interruption, 'I have determined to repay Mr. Crinkett an amount that seems to me to be fair. He shall have back twenty thousand pounds.'

'He's a lucky fellow, and he'll be off like a shot;—like a shot.'

'He and others have conspired to rob me of all my happiness, thinking that they might so most probably get this money from me. They have invented a wicked lie,—a wicked damnable lie,—a damnable lie! They are miscreants,—foul miscreants!'

'Come, come, Mr. Caldigate.'

'Foul miscreants! But they shall have their money, and you shall hear me tell them when I give it to them,—and they must both be here to take it from my hands,—that I do not at all require their absence. There is to be no bargain between us. They are free to remain and swear their false oaths against me. Whether they go or whether they stay will be no affair of mine.'

'They'll go, of course, Mr. Caldigate.'

'Not at my instance. I will take care that that shall be known. They must both come; and into their joint hands will I give the cheque, and they must come prepared with a receipt declaring that they accept the money as restitution of the loss incurred by them in purchasing the Polyeuka mine from me. Do you understand? And I shall bring a witness with me to see them take the money.' Bollum, who was considerably depressed by his companion's manner, said that he did understand.

'I suppose I can have a private room here, at noon to-morrow?' asked Caldigate, turning to the woman at the bar.

When that was settled he assured Bollum that a cheque for the amount should be placed in the joint hands of Timothy Crinkett and Euphemia Smith if he, and they with him, would be there at noon on the following day. Bollum in vain attempted to manage the payment without the personal interview, but at last agreed that the man and the woman should be forthcoming.

That night Caldigate dined at his Club, one of the University Clubs, at which he had been elected just at the time of his marriage. He had seldom been there, but now walked into the dining-room, resolving that he would not be ashamed to show himself. He fancied that everybody looked at him, and probably there were some present who knew that he was about to stand his trial for bigamy. But he got his dinner, and smoked his cigar; and before the evening was over he had met an old College friend. He was in want of a friend, and explained his wants. He told something of his immediate story, and then asked the man to be present at the scene on the morrow.

'I must have a witness, Gray,' said he, 'and you will do me a kindness if you will come.' Then Mr. Gray promised to be present on the occasion.

On the following morning he met Gray at the Club, having the cheque ready in his pocket, and together they proceeded to Levant Court. Again he was a little before his time, and the two sat together in the gloomy little room up-stairs. Bollum was the first to come, and when he saw the stranger, was silent,—thinking whether it might not be best to escape and warn Crinkett and the woman that all might not be safe. But the stranger did not look like a detective; and, as he told himself, why should there be danger? So he waited, and in a few minutes Crinkett entered the room, with the woman veiled.

'Well, Caldigate,' said Crinkett, 'how is it with you?'

'If you please, Mrs. Smith,' said Caldigate, 'I must ask you to remove your veil,—so that I may be sure that it it you.'

She removed her veil very slowly, and then stood looking him in the face,—not full in the face, for she could not quite raise her eyes to meet his. And though she made an effort to brazen it out, she could not quite succeed. She attempted to raise her head, and carry herself with pride; but every now and again there was a slight quiver,—slight, but still visible. The effort, too, was visible. But there she stood, looking at him, and to be looked at,—but without a word. During the whole interview she never once opened her lips.

She had lost all her comeliness. It was now nearly seven years since they two had been on the Goldfinder together, and then he had found her very attractive. There was no attraction now. She was much aged; and her face was coarse, as though she had taken to drinking. But there was still about her something of that look of intellect which had captivated him more, perhaps, than her beauty. Since those days she had become a slave to gold,—and such slavery is hardly compatible with good looks in a woman. There she stood,—ready to listen to him, ready to take his money, but determined not to utter a word.

Then he took the cheque out of his pocket, and holding it in his hand, spoke to them as follows: 'I have explained to Mr. Bollum, and have explained to my friend here, Mr. Gray, the reasons which induce me to pay to you, Timothy Crinkett, and to you, Euphemia Smith, the large sum of twenty thousand pounds. The nature of our transactions has been such that I feel bound in honour to repay so much of the price you paid for the Polyeuka mine.'

'All right, Caldigate; all right,' said Crinkett.

'And I have explained also to both of them that this payment has nothing whatever to do with the base, false, and most wicked charge which you are bringing against me. It is not because that woman, by a vile perjury, claims me as her husband, and because I wish to buy her silence or his, that I make this restitution. I restore the money of my own free will, without any base bargain. You can go on with your perjury or abstain from it, as you may think best.'

'We understand, squire,' said Crinkett, affecting to laugh. 'You hand over the money,—that's all.' Then the woman looked round at her companion, and a frown came across her face; but she said nothing, turning her face again upon Caldigate, and endeavouring to keep her eyes steadfastly fixed upon him.

'Have you brought a receipt signed by both of you?' Then Bollum handed him a receipt signed 'Timothy Crinkett, for self and partners.' But Caldigate demanded that the woman also should sign it.

'There is a difficulty about the name, you see,' said Bollum. There was a difficulty about the name, certainly. It would not be fair, he thought, that he should force her to the use of a name she disowned, and he did not wish to be hindered from what he was doing by her persistency in calling herself by his own name.

'So be it,' said he. 'There is the cheque. Mr. Gray will see that I put it into both their hands.' This he did, each of them stretching out a hand to take it. 'And now you can go where you please and act as you please. You have combined to rob me of all that I value most by the basest of lies; but not on that account have I abstained from doing what I believe to be an act of justice.' Then he left the room, and paying for the use of it to the woman at the bar, walked off with his friend Gray, leaving Crinkett, Bollum, and the woman still within the house.

CHAPTER XL

Waiting for the Trial

AS he returned to Cambridge Caldigate was not altogether contented with himself. He tried to persuade himself, in reference to the money which he had refunded, that in what he had done he had not at all been actuated by the charge made against him. Had there been no such accusation he would have felt himself bound to share the loss with these people as soon as he had learned the real circumstances. The money had been a burden to him. For the satisfaction of his own honour, of his own feelings, it had become necessary that the money should be refunded. And the need of doing so was not lessened by the fact that a base conspiracy had been made by a gang of villains who had thought that the money might thus be most readily extracted from him. That was his argument with himself, and his defence for what he had done. But nevertheless he was aware that he had been driven to do it now,—to pay the money at this special moment,—by an undercurrent of hope that these enemies would think it best for themselves to go as soon as they had his money in their hands. He wished to be honest, he wished to be honourable, he wished that all that he did could be what the world calls 'above board'; but still it was so essential for him and for his wife that they should go! He had been very steady in assuring these wretched ones that they might go or stay, as they pleased. He had been careful that there should be a credible witness of his assurance. He might succeed in making others believe that he had not attempted to purchase their absence; but he could not make himself believe it.

Even though a jury should not convict him, there was so much in his Australian life which would not bear the searching light of cross-examination! The same may probably be said of most of us. In such trials as this that he was anticipating, there is often a special cruelty in the exposure of matters which are for the most part happily kept in the background. A man on some occasion inadvertently takes a little more wine than is good for him. It is an accident most uncommon with him, and nobody thinks much about it. But chance brings the case to the notice of the police courts, and the poor victim is published to the world as a drunkard in the columns of all the newspapers. Some young girl fancies herself in love, and the man is unworthy. The feeling passes away, and none but herself, and perhaps her mother, are the wiser.

But if by some chance, some treachery, a letter should get printed and read, the poor girl's punishment is so severe that she is driven to wish herself in the grave.

He had been foolish, very foolish, as we have seen, on board the Goldfinder,—and wicked too. There could be no doubt about that. When it would all come out in this dreaded trial he would be quite unable to defend himself. There was enough to enable Mrs. Bolton to point at him with a finger of scorn as a degraded sinner. And yet,—yet there had been nothing which he had not dared to own to his wife in the secrecy of their mutual confidence, and which, in secret, she had not been able to condone without a moment's hesitation. He had been in love with the woman,—in love after a fashion. He had promised to marry her. He had done worse than that. And then, when he had found that the passion for gold was strong upon her, he had bought his freedom from her. The story would be very bad as told in Court, and yet he had told it all to his wife! She had admitted his excuse when he had spoken of the savageness of his life, of the craving which a man would feel for some feminine society, of her undoubted cleverness, and then of her avarice. And then when he swore that through it all he had still loved her,—her, Hester Bolton,—whom he had but once seen, but whom, having seen, he had never allowed to pass out of his mind, she still believed him, and thought that the holiness of that love had purified him. She believed him;—but who else would believe him? Of course he was most anxious that those people should go.

Before he left London he wrote both to Mr. Seely and to Robert Bolton, saying what he had done. The letter to his own attorney was long and full. He gave an account in detail of the whole matter, declaring that he would not allow himself to be hindered from paying a debt which he believed to be due, by the wickedness of those to whom it was owing. 'The two things have nothing to do with each other,' he said, 'and if you choose to throw up my defence, of course you can do so. I cannot allow myself to be debarred from exercising my own judgment in another matter because you think that what I decide upon doing may not tally with your views as to my defence.' To Robert Bolton he was much shorter. 'I think you ought to know what I have done,' he said; 'at any rate, I do not choose that you should be left in ignorance.' Mr. Seely took no notice of the communication, not feeling himself bound to carry out his threat by withdrawing his assistance from his client. But Robert and William Bolton agreed to have Crinkett's movements watched by a detective policeman. They were both determined that if possible Crinkett and the woman should be kept in the country.

In these days the old Squire made many changes in his residence, vacillating between his house in Cambridge and the house at Folking. His books were at Cambridge, and he could not have them brought back; and yet he felt that he ought to evince his constancy to his son, his conviction of his son's innocence, by remaining at Folking. And he was aware, too, that his presence there was a comfort both to his son and Hester. When John Caldigate had gone up to London, his father had been in Cambridge, but on his return he found the old Squire at his old house. 'Yes,' he said, telling the story of what he had just done, 'I have paid twenty thousand pounds out of hand to those rascals, simply because I thought I owed it to them!' The Squire shook his head, not being able to approve of the act. 'I don't see why I should have allowed myself to be hindered from doing what I thought to be right because they were doing what they knew to be wrong.'

'They won't go, you know.'

'I daresay not, sir. Why should they?'

'But the jury will believe that you intended to purchase their absence.'

'I think I have made all that clear.'

'I am afraid not, John. The man applied to you for the money, and was refused. That was the beginning of it. Then the application was repeated by the woman with a threat; and you again refused. Then they present themselves to the magistrates, and made the accusation; and, upon that, you pay the money. Of course it will come out at the trial that you paid it immediately after this renewed application from Bollum. It would have been better to have defied them.'

'I did defy them,' said John Caldigate. But all that his father said seemed to him to be true, so that he repented himself of what he had done.

He made no inquiry on the subject, but, early in May he heard from Mr. Seely that Crinkett and the woman were still in London, and that they had abandoned the idea of going at once to Australia. According to Mr. Seely's story,—of the truth of which he declared himself to be by no means certain,—Crinkett had wished to go, but had been retained by the woman. 'As far as I can learn,' said Mr. Seely, 'she is in communication with the Boltons, who will of course keep her if it be possible. He would get off if he could; but she, I take it, has got hold of the money. When you made the cheque payable to her order, you effectually provided for their remaining here. If he could have got the money without her name, he would have gone, and she would have gone with him.'

'But that was not my object,' said Caldigate angrily. Mr. Seely

294

thereupon shrugged his shoulders.

Early in June the man came back who had been sent out to Sydney in February on behalf of Caldigate. He also had been commissioned to seek for evidence, and to bring back with him, almost at any cost, whatever witness or witnesses he might find whose presence in England would serve Caldigate's cause. But he brought no one, and had learned very little. He too had been at Ahalala and at Nobble. At Nobble the people were now very full of the subject, and were very much divided in opinion. There were Crinketters and anti-Crinketters, Caldigatites and anti-Caldigatites. A certain number of persons were ready to swear that there had been a marriage, and an equal number, perhaps, to swear that there had been none. But no new fact had been brought to light. Dick Shand had not been found,—who had been living with Caldigate when the marriage was supposed to have been solemnised. Nor had that register been discovered from which the copy of the certificate was supposed to have been taken. All through the Colony,— so said this agent,—a very great interest was felt in the matter. The newspapers from day to day contained paragraphs about it. But nobody had appeared whom it was worth while to bring home. Mrs. Henniker, of the hotel at Nobble, had offered to swear that there had been no marriage. This offer she made and repeated when she had come to understand accurately on whose behalf this last agent had come to the Colony. But then, before she had understood this, she had offered to swear the reverse; and it became known that she was very anxious to be carried back to the old country free of expense. No credible witness could be found who had heard Caldigate call the woman Mrs. Smith after the date assigned to the marriage. She no doubt had used various names, had called herself sometimes Mrs. Caldigate, sometimes Mrs. Smith, but generally, in such documents as she had to sign in reference to her mining shares, Euphemia Cettini. It was by that name that she had been known in Sydney when performing on the stage, and it was now alleged on her behalf that she had bought and sold shares in that name under the idea that she would thus best secure to herself their separate and undisturbed possession. Proof was brought home that Caldigate himself had made over to her shares in that name; but Mr. Seely did not depend much on this as proof against the marriage.

Mr. Seely seemed to depend very little on anything,—so little that Caldigate almost wished that he had carried out his threat and thrown up the case. 'Does he not believe you when you tell him?' his wife asked. Caldigate was forced to confess that apparently the lawyer did not believe him. In fact, Mr. Seely had even said as much. 'In such cases a lawyer should never believe or disbelieve; or, if he does, he should never speak of his belief. It is with your acquittal or conviction that I am concerned, in which matter I can better assist you by cool judgment than by any fervid assurance.' All this made Caldigate not only angry but unhappy, for he could not fail to perceive that the public around him were in the same mind as Mr. Seely. In his own parish they believed him, but apparently not beyond his parish. It might be possible that he should escape,—that seemed to be the general opinion; but then general opinion went on to declare that there was no reason for supposing that he had not married the woman merely because he said that he had not done so.

Then gradually there fell upon poor Hester's mind a doubt,—and, after that, almost a conviction. Not a doubt as to her husband's truth! No suspicion on that score ever troubled her for a moment. But there came upon her a fear, almost more than a fear, that these terrible enemies would be strong enough to override the truth, and to carry with them both a judge and a jury. As the summer months ran on, they all became aware that for any purpose of removing the witnesses the money had been paid in vain. Crinkett was living in all opulence at a hotel at Brighton; and the woman, calling herself Mrs. Caldigate, had taken furnished apartments in London. Rumour came that she was frequently seen at the theatres, and that she had appeared more than once in an open carriage in the parks. There was no doubt but that Caldigate's money had made them very comfortable for the present. The whole story of the money had been made public, and of course there were various opinions about it. The prevailing idea was, that an attempt had been made to buy off the first wife, and that the first wife had been clever enough to get the money without having to go. Caldigate was thought to have been very foolish; on which subject Bollum once expressed himself strongly to a friend. 'Clever!' he said; 'Caldigate clever! The greatest idiot I ever came across in my life! I'd made it quite straight for him,—so that there couldn't have been a wrinkle. But he wouldn't have it. There are men so soft that one can't understand 'em.' To do Bollum justice it should be said that he was most anxious to induce his uncle and the woman to leave the country when they had got the money.

Though very miserable, Hester was very brave. In the presence of her husband she would never allow herself to seem to doubt. She would speak of their marriage as a thing so holy that nothing within the power of man could disturb it. Of course they were man and wife, and of course the truth would at last prevail. Was not the Lord able, in His own good time, to set all these matters right? And in discussing the matter with him she would always seem to imply that the Lord's good time would be the time of the trial. She would never herself hint to him that there might be a period of separation coming. Though in secrecy she was preparing for what might befall him, turning over in her woman's mind how she might best relieve the agony of his jail, she let no sign escape her that she looked forward to such misery. She let no such sign escape her in her intercourse with him. But with his father she could speak more freely. It had, indeed, come to be understood between her and the old Squire, that it would be best that they should discuss the matter openly. Arrangements must be made for their future life, so that when the blow came they might not be unprepared. Hester declared that nothing but positive want of shelter should induce her to go back to Chesterton. 'They think him to be all that's bad,' she said. 'I know him to be all that's good. How is it possible that we should live together?' The old man had, of course, turned it over much in his mind. If it could be true that that woman had in truth become his son's wife, and that this dear, sweet, young mother had been deceived, betrayed, and cheated out of her very existence, then that house at Folking could be no proper home for her. Her grave would be best, but till that might be reached any home would be better than Folking. But he was almost sure that it was not so, and her confidence,—old as he was, and prone to be suspicious,—made him confident.

When the moment came he could not doubt how he would answer her. He could not crush her spirit by seeming for a moment to have a suspicion. 'Your home, of course, shall be here,' he said. 'It shall be your own house.'

'And you?'

'It shall be my house too. If it should come to that, we will be, at any rate, together. You shall not be left without a friend.'

'It is not for myself,' she said; 'but for his boy and for him;—what will be best for them. I would take a cabin at the prison-gate, so as to be nearest to him,—if it were only myself.' And so it was settled between them, that should that great misery fall upon them, she would remain at Folking and he would remain with her. Nothing that judge or jury could do would deprive her of the right to occupy her husband's house.

In this way the months of May and June and the first fortnight of July wore themselves away, and then the time for the trial had come. Up to the last it had been hoped that tidings might be heard either by letter or telegram from Dick Shand; but it seemed that he had vanished from the face of the earth. No suggestion of news as to his whereabouts was received on which it might have been possible to found an argument for the further postponement of the trial. Mr. Seely had been anxious for such postponement,—perhaps thinking that as the hotel at Brighton and the carriages in the park were expensive, Crinkett and the lady might take their departure for Australia without saying a word to the lawyer who had undertaken the prosecution. But there was no adequate ground for delay, and on Tuesday the 17th July the trial was to be commenced. On the previous day Caldigate, at his own request, was introduced to Sir John Joram, who had been brought down special to Cambridge for his defence. Mr. Seely had advised him not to see the barrister who was to defend him, leaving it, however, quite at his option to do so or not as he pleased. 'Sir John will see you, but I think he had rather not,' said Mr. Seely. But Caldigate had chosen to have the interview. 'I have thought it best to say just one word to you,' said Caldigate.

'I am quite at your service,' said Sir John.

'I want you to hear from my own lips that a falser charge than this was never made against a man.'

'I am glad to hear it,' said Sir John,—and then he paused. 'That is to say, Mr. Caldigate, I am bound in courtesy to you to make some such civil reply as I should have made had I not been employed in your case, and had circumstances then induced you to make such a statement to me. But in truth, as I am so employed, no statement from your lips ought to affect me in the least. For your own sake I will say that no statement will affect me. It is not for me to believe or disbelieve anything in this matter. If, carried away by my feelings, I were to appeal to the jury for their sympathy because of my belief, I should betray your cause. It will be my duty not to make the jury believe you, who, in your position, will not be expected even to tell the truth; but to induce them, if possible, to disbelieve the witnesses against you who will be on their oath. Second-hand protestations from an advocate are never of much avail, and in many cases have been prejudicial. I can only assure you that I understand the importance of the interests confided to me, and that I will endeavour to be true to my trust.'

Caldigate, who wanted sympathy, who wanted an assurance of confidence in his word, was by no means contented with his counsellor; but he was too wise at the present moment to quarrel with him.

CHAPTER XLI

The First Day

THEN came the morning on which Caldigate and Hester must part. Very little had been said about it, but a word or two had been absolutely necessary. The trial would probably take two days, and it would not be well that he should be brought back to Folking for the sad intervening night. And then,—should the verdict be given against him, the prison doors would be closed against her, his wife, more rigidly than against any other friend who might knock at them inquiring after his welfare. Her, at any rate, he would not be allowed to see. All the prison authorities would be bound to regard her as the victim of his crime and as the instrument of his vice. The law would have locked him up to avenge her injuries,—of her, whose only future joy could come from that distant freedom which the fraudulent law would at length allow to him. All this was not put into words between them, but it was understood. It might be that they were to be parted now for a term of years, during which she would be as a widow at Folking while he would be alone in his jail.

There are moments as to which it would be so much better that their coming should never be accomplished! It would have been better for them both had they been separated without that last embrace. He was to start from Folking at eight that he might surrender himself to the hands of justice in due time for the trial at ten. She did not come down with him to the breakfast parlour, having been requested by him not to be there among the servants when he took his departure; but standing there in her own room, with his baby in her arms, she spoke her last word, 'You will keep up your courage, John?'

'I will try, Hester.'

'I will keep up mine. I will never fail, for your sake and his,'—here she held the child a moment away from her bosom,—'I will never allow myself to droop. To be your wife and his mother shall be enough to support me even though you should be torn from both of us for a time.'

'I wish I were as brave as you,' he said.

'You will leave me here,' she continued, 'mistress of your house; and if God spares me, here you will find me. They can't move me from this. Your father says so. They may call me what they will, but they cannot move me. There is the Lord above us, and before Him they cannot make me other than your wife,—your wife,—your wife.' As she repeated the name, she put the boy out to him, and when he had taken the child, she stretched out her hands upwards, and falling on her knees at his feet, prayed to God for his deliverance. 'Let him come back to us, O my God. Deliver him from his enemies, and let him come back to us.'

'One kiss, my own,' he said, as he raised her from the ground.

'Oh yes;—and a thousand shall be in store for you when you come back to us. Yes; kiss him too. Your boy shall hear the praises of his father every day, till at last he shall understand that he may be proud of you even though he should have learned why it is that you are not with him. Now go, my darling. Go; and support yourself by remembering that I have got that within me which will support me.' Then he left her.

The old Squire had expressed his intention of being present throughout the trial, and now was ready for the journey. When counselled to remain at home, both by Mr. Seely and by his son, he had declared that only by his presence could he make the world around him understand how confident he was of his son's innocence. So it was arranged, and a place was kept for him next to the attorney. The servants all came out into the hall and shook hands with their young master; and the cook, wiping her eyes with her apron, declared that she would have dinner ready for him on the following day. At the front door Mr. Holt was standing, having come over the ferry to greet the young squire before his departure. 'They may say what they will there, squire, but they won't make none of us here believe that you've been the man to injure a lady such as she up there.' Then there was another shaking of hands, and the father and son got into the carriage.

The court was full, of course. Mr. Justice Bramber, by whom the case was to be tried, was reputed to be an excellent judge, a man of no softnesses,—able to wear the black cap without convulsive throbbings, anxious also that the law should run its course,—averse to mercy when guilt had been proved, but as clear-sighted and as just as Minos;—a man whom nothing could turn one way or another,—who could hang his friend, but who would certainly not mulct his enemy because he was his enemy. It had reached Caldigate's ears that he was unfortunate in his judge; by which, they who had so said, had intended to imply that this judge's mind would not be perverted by any sentiments as to the prisoner, as to the sweet young woman who called herself his wife at home, or as to want of sweetness on the part of the other woman who claimed him.

The jury was sworn in without more than ordinary delay, and then the trial was commenced. That which had to be done for the prosecution seemed to be simple enough. The first witness called was the woman herself, who was summoned in the names of Euphemia Caldigate *alias* Smith. She gave her evidence very clearly, and with great composure,—saying how she had become acquainted with the man on board the ship; how she had been engaged to him at Melbourne; how he had come down to her at Sydney; how, in compliance with his orders, she had followed him up to Ahalala; and how she had there been married to him by Mr. Allan. Then she brought forth the documents which professed to be the copy of the register of the marriage, made by the minister in his own book; and the envelope,—the damning envelope,—which Caldigate was prepared to admit that he had himself addressed to Mrs. Caldigate; and the letter which purported to have been written by the minister to Caldigate, recommending him to be married in some better established township than that existing at Ahalala. She did it well. She was very correct, and at the same time very determined, giving many details of her early theatrical life, which it was thought better to get from her in the comparative ease of a direct examination than to have them extracted afterwards by an adverse advocate. During her evidence in chief, which was necessarily long, she seemed to be quite at ease; but those around her observed that she never once turned her eyes upon him whom she claimed as her husband except when she was asked whether the man there before her was the man she had married at Ahalala. Then, looking at him for a moment in silence, she replied, very steadily, 'Yes; that is my husband, John Caldigate.'

To Caldigate and his friends,—and indeed to all those collected in the court,—the most interesting person of the day was Sir John Joram. In a sensational cause the leading barrister for the defence is always the hero of the plot,—the actor from whom the best bit of acting is expected,—the person who is most likely to become a personage on the occasion. The prisoners are necessarily mute, and can only be looked at, not heard. The judge is not expected to do much till the time comes for his charge, and even then is supposed to lower the dignity of the bench if he makes his charge with any view to effect on his own behalf. The barrister who prosecutes should be tame, or he will appear to be vindictive. The witnesses, however interesting they may be in detail, are but episodes. Each comes and goes, and there is an end of them. But the part of the defending advocate requires action through the whole of the piece. And he may be impassioned. He is bound to be on the alert. Everything seems to depend on him. They who accuse can have or should have no longing for the condemnation of the accused one. But in regard to the other, an acquittal is a matter of personal prowess, of professional truimph, and possibly of well simulated feeling.

Sir John Joram was at this time a man of considerable dignity, above fifty years of age, having already served the offices of Solicitor and Attorney-General to his party. To his compeers and intimate friends it seemed to be but the other day since he was Jacky Joram, one of the jolliest little fellows ever known at an evening party, up to every kind of fun, always rather short of money, and one of whom it was thought that, because he was good-looking, he might some day achieve the success of marrying a woman with money. On a sudden he married a girl without a shilling, and men shook their heads and sighed as they spoke of poor Jacky Joram. But, again, on a sudden,—quite as suddenly,—there came tidings that Jacky had been found out by the attorneys, and that he was earning his bread. As we grow old things seem to come so quickly! His friends had hardly realised the fact that Jacky was earning his bread before he was in Parliament and had ceased to be Jacky. And the celerity with which he became Sir John was the most astonishing of all. Years no doubt had passed by. But years at fifty are no more than months at thirty,—are less than weeks in boyhood. And now while some tongues, by dint of sheer habit, were still forming themselves into Jacky, Sir John Joram had become the leading advocate of the day, and a man renowned for the dignity of his manners.

In the House,—for he had quite got the ear of the House,—a certain impressive good sense, a habit of saying nothing that was not necessary to the occasion, had chiefly made for him the high character he enjoyed; but in the law courts it was perhaps his complaisance, his peculiar courtesy, of which they who praised him talked the most. His aptitude to get verdicts was of course the cause of his success. But it was observed of him that in perverting the course of justice,—which may be said to be the special work of a successful advocate,—he never condescended to bully anybody. To his own witnesses he was simple and courteous, as are barristers generally. But to adverse witnesses he was more courteous, though no doubt less simple. Even to some perjured comrade of an habitual burglar he would be studiously civil: but to a woman such as Euphemia Caldigate, *alias* Smith, it was certain that he would be so smooth as to make her feel almost pleased with the amenities of her position.

He asked her very many questions, offering to provide her with the comfort of a seat if it were necessary. She said that she was not at all tired, and that she preferred to stand. As to the absolute fact of the marriage she did not hesitate at all. She was married in the tent at

Ahalala in the presence of Crinkett and Adamson, and of her own female companion, Anna Young,—all of whom were there to give evidence of the fact. Whether any one else was in the tent, she could not say, but she knew that there were others at the entrance. The tent was hardly large enough for more than five or six. Dick Shand had not been there, because he had always been her enemy, and had tried to prevent the marriage. And she was quite clear about the letter. There was a great deal said about the letter. She was sure that the envelope with the letter had come to her at Ahalala by post from Sydney when her husband was at the latter place. The Sydney postmark with the date was very plain. There was much said as to the accuracy and clearness of the Sydney postmark, and something as to the absence of any postmark at Nobble. She could not account for the absence of the Nobble postmark. She was aware that letters were stamped at Nobble generally. Mr. Allan, she said, had himself handed to her the copy of the register almost immediately after the marriage, but she could not say by whom it had been copied. The letter purporting to be from Mr. Allan to her husband was no doubt, she said, in the minister's handwriting. Caldigate had showed it to her before their marriage, and she had kept it without any opposition from him. Then she was asked as to her residence after her marriage, and here she was less clear. She had lived with him first at Ahalala and then at Nobble, but she could not say for how long. It had been off and on. There had been quarrels, and after a time they had agreed to part. She had received from him a certain amount of mining shares and of money, and had undertaken in return never to bother him any more. There was a great deal said about times and dates, which left an impression upon those around her in the court that she was less sure of her facts than a woman in such circumstances naturally would have been.

Then Sir John produced the letter which she had written to Caldigate, and in which she had distinctly offered to marry Crinkett if the money demanded were paid. She must have expected the production of this letter, but still, for a few moments, it silenced her. 'Yes,' she said, at last, 'I wrote it.'

'And the money you demanded has been paid?'

'Yes, it has been paid. But not then. It was not paid till we came over.'

'But if it had been paid then you would have—married Mr. Crinkett?' Sir John's manner as he asked the question was so gentle and so soft that it was felt by all to contain an apology for intruding on so delicate a subject. But when she hesitated, he did, after a pause, renew his inquiry in another form. 'Perhaps this was only a threat, and you

303

had no purpose of carrying it out.'

Then she plucked up her courage. 'I have not married him,' she said.

'But did you intend it?'

'I did. What were the laws to me out there? He had left me and had taken another wife. I had to do the best for myself. I did intend it. But I didn't do it. A woman can't be tried for her intentions.'

'No,' said Sir John. 'But she may be judged by her intentions.'

Then she was asked why she had not gone when she had got the money, according to her promise. 'He defied us,' she said, 'and called us bad names,—liars and perjurers. He knew that we were not liars. And then we were watched and told that we might not go. As he said that he was indifferent, I was willing enough to stay and see it out.'

'You cannot give us,' he asked again,—and this was his last question, —'any clearer record of those months which you lived with your husband?'

'No,' she said, 'I cannot. I kept no journal.' Then she was allowed to go, and though she had been under examination for three hours, it was thought she had escaped easily.

Crinkett was next, who swore that he had been Caldigate's partner in sundry mining speculations,—that they had been in every way intimate,—that he had always recommended Caldigate to marry Mrs. Smith, thinking, as he said, 'that respectability paid in the long run,'—and that, having so advised him, he had become Caldigate's special friend at the time, to the exclusion of Dick Shand, who was generally drunk, and who, whether drunk or sober, was opposed to the marriage. He had been selected to stand by his friend at the marriage, and he, thinking that another witness would be beneficial, had taken Adamson with him. His only wonder was that any one should dispute a fact which was at the time so notorious both at Ahalala and at Nobble. He held his head high during his evidence in chief, and more than once called the prisoner 'Caldigate,'—'Caldigate knew this,'—and 'Caldigate did that.' It was past four when he was handed over for cross-examination; but when it was said that another hour would suffice for it, the judge agreed to sit for that other hour.

But it was nearly two hours before the gentleman who was with Sir John had finished his work, during which Mr. Crinkett seemed to suffer much. The gentleman was by no means so complacent as Sir John, and asked some very disagreeable questions. Had Crinkett intended to commit bigamy by marrying the last witness, knowing at the time that she was a married woman? 'I never said that I intended to marry her,' said Crinkett. 'What she wrote to Caldigate was nothing to me.' He could not be made to own, as she had done in a straightforward way, that he had intended to set the law at defiance. His courage failed him, and his presence of mind, and he was made to declare at last that he had only talked about such a marriage, with the view of keeping the woman in good humour, but that he had never intended to marry her. Then he was asked as to Bollum;—had he told Bollum that he intended to marry the woman? At last he owned that he might have done so. Of course he had been anxious to get his money, and he had thought that he might best do so by such an offer. He was reduced to much misery during his cross-examination; but on the one main statement that he had been present at the marriage he was not shaken.

At six o'clock the trial was adjourned till the next day, and the two Caldigates were taken in a fly to a neighbouring inn, at which rooms had been provided for them. Here they were soon joined by Mr. Seely, who explained, however, that he had come merely to make arrangements for the morrow. 'How is it going?' asked Caldigate.

The question was very natural, but it was one which Mr. Seely was not disposed to answer. 'I couldn't give an opinion,' he said. 'In such cases I never do give an opinion. The evidence is very clear, and has not been shaken; but the witnesses are people of a bad character. Character goes a long way with a jury. It will depend a good deal on the judge, I should say. But I cannot give an opinion.'

No opinion one way or the other was expressed to the father or son,—who indeed saw no one else the whole evening; but Robert Bolton, in discussing the matter with his father, expressed a strong conviction that Caldigate would be acquitted. He had heard it all, and understood the nature of such cases. 'I do not in the least doubt that they were married,' said Robert Bolton. 'All the circumstances make me sure of it. But the witnesses are just of that kind which a jury always distrusts. The jury will acquit him, not because they do not believe the marriage, but out of enmity to Crinkett and the woman.'

'What shall we do, then?' asked the old man. To this Robert Bolton could make no answer. He only shook his head and turned away.

CHAPTER XLII

The Second Day

THE court had been very full on the first day of the trial, but on the following morning it was even more crowded, so that outsiders who had no friend connected with justice, had hardly a chance of hearing or seeing anything. Many of the circumstances of the case had long been known to the public, but matters of new and of peculiar interest had been elicited,—the distinct promise made by the woman to marry another man, so as to render her existing husband safe in his bigamy by committing bigamy herself,—the payment to these peoply by Caldigate of an immense sum of money,—the fact that they two had lived together in Australia whether married or not;—all this, which had now been acknowledged on both sides, added to the romance of the occasion. While it could hardly be doubted, on the one side, that Caldigate had married the woman,—so strong was the evidence,—it could not be at all doubted, on the other side, that the accusation had been planned with the view of raising money, and had been the result of a base conspiracy. And then there was the additional marvel, that though the money had been paid,—the whole sum demanded,—yet the trial was carried on. The general feeling was exactly that which Robert Bolton had attributed to the jury. People did believe that there had been a marriage, but trusted nevertheless that Caldigate might be acquitted,— so that his recent marriage might be established. No doubt there was a feeling with many that anything done in the wilds of Australia ought not 'to count' here at home in England.

Caldigate with his father was in court a little before ten, and at that hour punctually the trial was recommenced. The first business was the examination of Adamson, who was quite clear as to the marriage. He had been concerned with Crinkett in money operations for many years, and had been asked by him to be present simply as a witness. He had never been particularly intimate with Caldigate, and had had little or nothing to do with him afterwards. He was cross-examined by the second gentleman, but was not subjected to much annoyance. He had put what little money he possessed into the Polyeuka mine, and had come over to England becuase he had thought that, by so doing, he might perhaps get a portion of his money back. Had there been a conspiracy, and was he one of the conspirators? Well, he rather thought that there had been a conspiracy, and that he was one of the conspirators.

306

But then he had only conspired to get what he thought to be his own. He had lost everything in the Polyeuka mine; and as the gentleman no doubt had married the lady, he thought he might as well come forward,— and that perhaps in that way he would get his money. He did not mind saying that he had received a couple of thousand pounds, which was half what he had put into Polyeuka. He hoped that, after paying all his expenses, he would be able to start again at the diggings with something above a thousand. This was all straight sailing. The purpose which he had in view was so manifest that it had hardly been worth while to ask him the questions.

Anna Young was the next, and she encountered the sweet courtesies of Sir John Joram. These sweet courtesies were prolonged for above an hour, and were not apparently very sweet to Miss Young. Of the witnesses hitherto examined she was the worst. She had been flippantly confident in her memories of the marriage ceremony when questioned on behalf of the prosecution, but had forgotten everything in reference to her friend's subsequent married life. She had forgotten even her own life, and did not quite know where she had lived. And at last she positively refused to answer questions though they were asked with the most engaging civility. She said that, 'Of course a lady had affairs which she could not tell to everybody.' 'No, she didn't mean lovers;—she didn't care for the men at all.' 'Yes; she did mean money. She had done a little mining, and hoped to do a little more.' She was to have a thousand pounds and her expenses, but she hadn't got the money yet,'—and so on. Probably of all the witnesses yet examined Miss Young had amused the court the most.

There were many others, no doubt necessary for the case, but hardly necessary for the telling of the story. Captain Munday was there, the captain of the Goldfinder, who spoke of Caldigate's conduct on board, and of his own belief that they two were engaged when they left the ship. 'As we are prepared to acknowledge that there was an engagement, I do not think that we need trouble you, Captain Munday,' said Sir John. 'We only deny the marriage.' Then the cheque for twenty thousand pounds was produced, and clerks from the bank to prove the payment, and the old waiter from the Jericho Coffee-house,—and others, of whom Sir John Joram refused to take any notice whatever. All that had been acknowledged. Of course the money had been paid. Of course the intimacy had existed. No doubt there had been those interviews both at Folking and up in London. But had there ever been a marriage in that tent at Ahalala? That, and that only, was the point to which Sir John Joram found it necessary to give attention.

A slight interval was allowed for lunch, and then Sir John rose to begin his speech. It was felt on all sides that his speech was to be of the great affair of the trial. Would he be able so to represent these witnesses as to make a jury believe that they had sworn falsely, and that the undoubted and acknowledged conspiracy to raise money had been concocted without any basis of truth? There was a quarter of an hour during which the father remained with his son in the precincts of the prison, and then the judge and the lawyers, and all they whose places were assured to them trooped back into court. They who were less privileged had fed themselves with pocketed sandwiches, not caring to risk the loss of their seats.

Sir John Joram began by holding, extended in his fingers towards the jury, the envelope which had undoubtedly been addressed by Caldigate to 'Mrs. Caldigate, Ahalala, Nobble,' and in which a certain letter had been stated to have been sent by him to her. 'The words written on that envelope,' said he, 'are to my mind the strongest evidence I have ever met of the folly to which a man may be reduced by the softness of feminine intercourse. I acknowledge, on the part of my client, that he wrote these words. I acknowledge, that if a man could make a woman his wife by so describing her on a morsel of paper, this man would have made this woman his wife. I acknowledge so much, though I do not acknowledge, though I deny, that any letter was ever sent to this woman in the envelope which I hold in my hand. His own story is that he wrote those words at a moment of soft and foolish confidence, when they two together were talking of a future marriage,—a marriage which no doubt was contemplated, and which probably had been promised. Then he wrote the address, showing the woman the name which would be hers should they ever be married;—and she has craftily kept the document. That is his story. That is my story. Now I must show you why I think it also should be your story. The woman,—I must describe her in this way lest I should do her an injustice by calling her Mrs. Smith, or do my client an injustice by calling her Mrs. Caldigate,—has told you that this envelope, with an enclosure which she produced, reached her at Nobble through the post from Sydney. To that statement I call upon you to give no credit. A letter so sent would, as you have been informed, bear two postmarks, those of Sydney and of Nobble. This envelope bears one only. But that is not all. I shall call before you two gentlemen experienced in affairs of the post-office, and they will tell you that the post-marks on this envelope, both that of the town, Sydney, and that by which the postage stamp is obliterated, are cleaner, finer, and better perceived than they would have been had it passed in ordinary course through the post-office. Letters in the post-office are hurried quickly through the operation of stamping, so that one passing over the other while the stamping ink is still moist, will to some extent blot and blur that with which it has come in contact. He will produce some dozens taken at random, and will show that with them all such has been the case. This blotting, this smudging, is very slight, but it exists; it is always there. He will tell you that this envelope has been stamped as one and alone,—by itself,—with peculiar care;—and I shall ask you to believe that the impression has been procured by fraud in the Sydney post-office. If that be so; if in such a case as this fraud be once discovered, then I say that the whole case will fall to the ground, and that I shall be justified in telling you that no word that you have heard from these four witnesses is worthy of belief.

'Nothing worthy of belief has been adduced against my client unless that envelope be so. That those four persons have conspired together for the sake of getting money is clear enough. To their evidence I shall come presently, and shall endeavour to show you why you should discredit them. At present I am concerned simply with this envelope, on which I think that the case hangs. As for the copy of the register, it is nothing. It would be odd indeed if in any conspiracy so much as that could not be brought up. Had such a register been found in the archives of any church, however humble, and had an attested copy been produced, that would have been much. But this is nothing. Nor is the alleged letter from Mr. Allan anything. Were the letter genuine it would show that such a marriage had been contemplated, not that it had been solemnised. We have, however, no evidence to make us believe that the letter is genuine. But this envelope,'—and he again stretched it out towards the jury,—'is evidence. The impression of a post-office stamp has often been accepted as evidence. But the evidence may be false evidence, and it is for us to see whether it may not probably be so now.

'In the first place, such evidence requires peculiar sifting, which unfortunately cannot be applied to it in the present case, because it has been brought to us from a great distance. Had the envelope been in our possession from the moment in which the accusation was first made, we might have tested it, either by sending it to Sydney or by obtaining from Sydney other letters or documents bearing the same stamp, affixed undoubtedly on the date here represented. But that has not been within our power. The gentlemen whom I shall bring before you will tell you that these impressions or stamps have a knack of verifying themselves, which makes it very dangerous indeed for fraudulent persons to tamper with them. A stamp used in June will be hardly the same as it will be in July. Some little bruise will have so altered a portion of the surface as to enable detection to be made with a microscope. And the stamp used in 1870 will certainly have varied its form in 1871. Now, I maintain that time and opportunity should have been given to us to verify this impression. Copies of all impressions from day to day are kept in the Sydney post-office, and if it be found that on this day named, the 10th of May, no impression in the Sydney office is an exact facsimile of this impression, then I say that this impression has been subsequently and fraudulently obtained, and that the only morsel of corroborative evidence offered to you will be shown to be false evidence. We have been unable to get impressions of this date. Opportunities have not been given to us. But I do not hesitate to tell you that you should demand such opportunities before you accept that envelope as evidence on which you can send my client to jail, and deprive that young wife, whom he has made his own, of her husband, and afford the damning evidence of your verdict towards robbing his son of his legitimacy.'

He said very much more about the envelope, clearly showing his own appreciation of its importance, and declaring again and again that if he could show that a stain of perjury affected the evidence in any one point all the evidence must fall to the ground, and that if there were ground to suspect that the envelope had been tampered with, then that stain of perjury would exist. After that he went on to the four conspirators, as he called them, justifying the name by their acknowledged object of getting money from his client. 'That they came to this country as conspirators, with a fraudulent purpose, my learned friend will not deny.'

'I acknowledge nothing of the kind,' said the learned friend.

'Then my learned friend must feel that his is a case in which he cannot safely acknowledge anything. I do not doubt, gentlemen, but that you have made up your mind on that point.' He went on to show that they clearly were conspirators;—that they had confessed as much themselves. 'It is no doubt possible that my client may have married this female conspirator, and she is not the less entitled to protection from the law because she is a conspirator. Nor, because she is a conspirator, should he be less amenable to the law for the terrible injury he would then have done to that other lady. But if they be conspirators,—if it be shown to you that they came to this country,—not that the woman might claim her husband, not that the others might give honest testimony against a great delinquent,—but in order that they might frighten him out of money, then I am entitled to tell you that you should not rest on their evidence unless it be supported, and that the fact of their conspiracy gives you a right, nay, makes it your imperative duty, to suspect perjury.

The remainder of the day was taken up with Sir John's speech, and with the witnesses which he called for the defence. He certainly succeeded in strengthening the compassion which was felt for Caldigate and for the unfortunate young mother at Folking. 'It was very well,' he said, 'for my learned friend to tell you of the protection which is due to a married woman when a husband has broken the law, and betrayed his trust by taking another wife to himself, as this man is accused of having done. But there is another aspect in which you will regard the question. Think of that second wife and of her child, and of the protection which is due to her. You well know that she does not suspect her husband, that she fears nothing but a mistaken verdict from you,—that she will be satisfied, much more than satisfied, if you will leave her in possession of her home, her husband, and the unalloyed domestic happiness she has enjoyed since she joined her lot with his. Look at the one woman, and then at the other. Remember their motives, their different lives, their different joys, and what will be the effect of your verdict upon each of them. If you are satisfied that he did marry that woman, that vile woman, the nature of whose life has been sufficiently exposed to you, of course your verdict must be against him. The law is the law, and must be vindicated. In that case it will be your duty, your terrible duty, to create misery, to destroy happiness, to ruin a dear innocent young mother and her child, and to separate a loving couple, every detail of whose life is such as to demand your sympathy. And this you must do at the bidding of four greedy, foul conspirators. Innocent, sweet, excellent in all feminine graces as is the one wife,—unlovely, unfeminine, and abhorrent as is the other, —you must do your duty. God forbid that I should ask you to break an oath, even for the sake of that young mother. But in such a case, I do think, I may ask you to be very careful as to what evidence you accept. I do think that I may again point out to you that those four witnesses, bound as they are together by a bond of avarice, should be regarded but as one,—and as one to whose sworn evidence no credit is due unless it be amply corroborated. I say that there is no corroboration. This envelope would be strong corroboration if it had been itself trustworthy.' When he sat down the feeling in court was certainly in favour of John Caldigate.

Then a cloud of witnesses were brought up for the defence, each of whom, however, was soon despatched. The two clerks from the post-office gave exactly the evidence which Sir John had described, and exposed to the jury their packet of old letters. In their opinion the impression on the envelope was finer and cleaner than that generally produced in the course of business. Each of them thought it not improbable that the impression had been surreptitiously obtained. But each of them acknowledged, on cross-examination, that a stamp so clean and perfect might be given and maintained without special care; and each of them said that it was quite possible that a letter passing through the post-office might escape the stamp of one of the offices in which it would be manipulated.

Then there came the witnesses as to character, and evidence was given as to Hester's determination to remain with the man whom she believed to be her husband. As to this there was no cross-examination. That Caldigate's life had been useful and salutary since his return to Folking no one doubted, —nor that he had been a loving husband. If he had committed bigamy, it was, no doubt, for the public welfare that such a crime should be exposed and punished. But that he should have been a bigamist, would be a pity,—oh, such a pity! The pity of it; oh, the pity of it! For now there had been much talk of Hester and her home at Folking, and her former home at Chesterton; and people everywhere concerned themselves for her peace, for her happiness, for her condition of life.

CHAPTER XLIII

The Last Day

AFTER Sir John Joram's speech, and when the work of the second day had been brought to a close, Caldigate allowed his hopes to rise higher than they had ever mounted since he had first become aware that the accusation would in truth be brought against him. It seemed to be almost impossible that any jury should give a verdict in opposition to arguments so convincing as those Sir John had used. All those details which had appeared to himself to be so damning to his own cause now melted away, and seemed to be of no avail. And even Mr. Seely, when he came to see his client in the evening, was less oppressive than usual. He did not, indeed, venture to express hope, but in his hopelessness he was somewhat more hopeful than before. 'You must remember, Mr. Caldigate,' he said, 'that you have not yet heard the judge, and that with such a jury the Judge will go much further than any advocate. I never knew a Cambridgeshire jury refuse to be led by Judge Bramber.'

'Why a Cambridgeshire jury?' asked old Mr. Caldigate; 'and why Judge Bramber especially?'

'We are a little timid, I think, here in the eastern counties,—a little wanting in self-confidence. An advocate in the north of England has a finer scope, because the people like to move counter to authority. A Lancashire jury will generally be unwilling to do what a judge tells them. And then Judge Bramber has a peculiar way of telling a jury. If he has a strong opinion of his own he never leaves the jury in doubt about it. Some judges are—what I call flabby, Mr. Caldigate. They are a little afraid of responsibility, and leave the jury and the counsel to fight it out among them. Sir John did it very well, no doubt;—very well. He made the best he could of that postage stamp, though I don't know that it will go for much. The point most in our favour is that those Australians are a rough lot to look at. The woman has been drinking, and has lost her good looks,—so that the jurymen won't be soft about her.' Caldigate, when he heard this, thought of Euphemia Smith on board the Goldfinder, when she certainly did not drink, when her personal appearance was certainly such 'as might touch the heart of any juryman. Gold and drink together had so changed the woman that he could hardly persuade himself that she was that forlorn attractive female whom he had once so nearly loved.

Before he went to bed, Caldigate wrote to his wife as he had done

313

also on the preceding evening. 'There is to be another long, tedious, terrible day, and then it may be that I shall be able to write no more. For your sake, almost more than for my own, I am longing for it to be over. It would be vain for me to attempt to tell you all that took place. I do not dare to give you hope which I know may be fallacious. And yet I feel my own heart somewhat higher than it was when I wrote last night.' Then he did tell her something of what had taken place, speaking in high praise of Sir John Joram. 'And now my own, own wife, my real wife, my beloved one, I have to call you so, perhaps for the last time for years. If these men shall choose to think that I married that woman, we shall have to be so parted that it would be better for us to be in our graves. But even then I will not give up all hope. My father has promised that the whole colony shall be ransacked till proof be found of the truth. And then, though I shall have been convicted, I shall be reinstated in my position as your husband. May God Almighty bless you, and our boy, till I may come again to claim my wife and my child without disgrace.'

The old man had made the promise. 'I would go myself,' said he, 'were it not that Hester will want my support here.' For there had been another promise made,—that by no entreaty, no guile, no force, should Hester be taken from Folking to Chesterton.

Early on the third day Judge Bramber began his charge, and in doing so he told the jury that it would occupy him about three hours. And in exactly three hours' time he had completed his task. In summing up the case he certainly was not 'flabby';—so little so, that he left no doubt on the minds of any who heard him of the verdict at which he had himself arrived. He went through the evidence of the four chief witnesses very carefully, and then said that the antecedents of these people, or even their guilt, if they had been guilty, had nothing to do with the case except in so far as it might affect the opinion of the jury as to their veracity. They had been called conspirators. Even though they had conspired to raise money by threats, than which nothing could be more abominable,—even though by doing so they should have subjected themselves to criminal proceedings, and to many penalties,—that would not lessen the criminality of the accused if such a marriage as that described had in truth taken place. 'This,' said the judge, 'is so much a matter of course that I should not insist upon it had it not been implied that the testimony of these four persons is worth nothing because they are conspirators. It is for you to judge what their testimony is worth, and it is for you to remember that they are four distinct witnesses, all swearing to the same thing.' Then he went into the question of the money. There could be no doubt that the four persons had come to England with the

purpose of getting money out of the accused, and that they had succeeded. With their mode of doing this,—whether criminal or innocent,—
the jury had nothing to do, except as it affected their credit. But they
were bound to look to Caldigate's motive in paying so large a sum. It
had been shown that he did not owe them a shilling, and that when the
application for money reached him from Australia he had refused to
give them a shilling. Then, when they had arrived here in England, accusation was made; and when they had offered to desert the case if paid
the money, then the money was paid. The prisoner, when paying it, had
no doubt intimated to those who received it that he made no bargain
with them as to their going away. And he had taken a friend with him
who had given his evidence in court, and this friend had manifestly been
taken to show that the money was not secretly paid. The jury would
give the prisoner the benefit of all that,—if there was benefit to be de-
rived from it. But they were bound to remember, in coming to their
verdict, that a very large sum of money had been paid to the witnesses
by the prisoner, which money certainly was not due to them.

He dwelt, also, at great length on the stamp on the envelope, but contrived at last to leave a feeling on the minds of those who heard him,
that Sir John had shown the weakness of his case by trusting so much
to such allegations as he had made. 'It has been represented,' said Judge
Bramber, 'that the impression which you have seen of the Sydney post-
office stamp has been fraudulently obtained. Some stronger evidence
should, I think, be shown of this before you believe it. Two clerks from
the London post-office have told you that they believed the impression
to be a false one; but I think they were hardly justified in their opinion.
They founded it on the clearness and cleanness of the impression; but
they both of them acknowledged afterwards that such clearness and
cleanness is simply unusual, and by no means impossible,—not indeed
improbable. But how would it have been if the envelope had been
brought to you without any post-office impression, simply directed to
Mrs. Caldigate, by the man who is alleged to have made the woman his
wife shortly before the envelope was written? Would it not in that case
have been strong evidence? If any fraud were proved,—such a fraud as
would be that of getting some post-office official falsely to stamp the
envelope,—then the stain of perjury would be there. But it will be for
you to consider whether you can find such stain of perjury merely
because the impression on the envelope is clear and clean.'

When he came to the present condition of Caldigate's wife and child
at Folking, he was very tender in his speech,—but even his tenderness
seemed to turn itself against the accused.

'Of that poor lady I can only speak with that unfeigned respect which I am sure you all feel. That she was happy in her marriage till this accusation reached her ears, no one can doubt. That he to whom she was given in marriage has done his duty by her, treating her with full affection and confidence, has been proved to us. Who can think that such a condition of things shall be disturbed, that happiness so perfect is to be turned to misery and misfortune, without almost an agony of regret? But not on that account can you be in any way released from your duty. In this case you are not entitled to think of the happiness of individuals. You have to confine yourself to the evidence, and must give your verdict in accordance with that.'

John Caldigate, as he heard the words, told himself at once that the judge had, in fact, desired the jury to find a verdict against him. Not a single point had been made in his favour, and every point had been made to tell against him. The judge had almost said that a man's promise to marry a woman should be taken as evidence of marriage. But the jury, at any rate, did not show immediate alacrity in obeying the judge's behest. They returned once or twice to ask questions; and at three o'clock Caldigate was allowed to go to his inn, with an intimation that he must hold himself in readiness to be brought back and hear the verdict at a moment's notice. 'I wish they would declare it at once,' he said to his father. 'The suspense is worse than all.'

During the afternoon the matter was discussed very freely throughout the borough. 'I thought they would have agreed almost at once,' said the mayor, at about four o'clock, to Mr. Seely, who, at this moment, had retired to his own office where the great magistrate of the borough was closeted with him. The mayor had been seated on the bench throughout the trial, and had taken much interest in the case. 'I never imagined that there could be much doubt after Judge Bramber's summing up.'

'I hear that there's one man holding out,' said the attorney in a low voice.

'Who is it?' whispered the mayor. The mayor and Mr. Seely were very intimate.

'I suppose it's Jones, the tanner at Ely. They say that the Caldigates have had dealings with his family from generation to generation. I knew all about it, and when they passed his name, I wondered that Burder hadn't been sharper.' Mr. Burder was the gentleman who had got up the prosecution on the part of the Crown.

'It must be something of that kind,' said the mayor. 'Nothing else would make a jury hesitate after such a charge as that. I suppose he did marry her.' Mr. Seely shrugged his shoulders. 'I have attended very closely to the case, and I know I should have been against him on a jury.

316

God bless my soul! Did any man ever write to a woman as his wife without having married her?'

'It has been done, I should think.'

'And that nobody should have been got to say that they weren't man and wife.'

'I really have hardly formed an opinion,' said Mr. Seely, still whispering, 'I am inclined to think that there was probably some ceremony, and that Caldigate salved his conscience, when he married Bolton's daughter, by an idea that the ceremony wasn't valid. But they'll convict him at last. When he told me that he had been up to town and paid that money, I knew it was all up with him. How can any juryman believe that a man will pay twenty thousand pounds, which he doesn't owe, to his sworn enemy, merely on a point of conscience?'

At the same time the old banker was sitting in his room at the bank, and Robert Bolton was with him. 'There cannot be a doubt of his guilt,' said Robert Bolton.

'No, no,—not a doubt.'

'But the jury may disagree?'

'What shall we do then?' said the banker.

'There must be another trial. We must go on till we get a verdict.'

'And Hester? What can we do for Hester?'

'She is very obstinate, and I fear we have no power. Even though she is declared not to be his wife, she can choose her own place of living. If he is convicted, I think that she would come back. Of course she ought to come back.'

'Of course, of course.'

'Old Caldigate, too, is very obstinate; but it may be that we should be able to persuade him. He will know that she ought to be with her mother.'

'Her poor mother! Her poor mother! And when he comes out of prison?'

'Her very nature will have been altered by that time,' said the attorney. 'She will, I trust, have consented before that to take up her residence under your roof.'

'I shall be dead,' said the old man. 'Disgrace and years together will have killed me before that time comes.'

The Smirkies were staying at Babington, and the desire for news there was very intent. Mr. Smirkie was full of thought on the matter, but was manifestly in favour of a conviction. 'Yes; the poor young woman is very much to be pitied,' he said, in answer to the squire, who had ventured to utter a word in favour of Hester. 'A young woman who falls into the hands of an evil man must always be pitied; but it is to prevent the evil men from preying upon the weaker sex that examples such as these are needed. When we think what might have been the case here, in this house, we have all of us a peculiar reason to be thankful for the interposition of divine Providence.' Here Mr. Smirkie made a little gesture of thanksgiving, thanking Heaven for its goodness to his wife in having given her himself. 'Julia, my love, you have a very peculiar reason to be thankful, and I trust you are so. Yes,—we must pity the poor young lady; but it will be well that the offender should be made subject to the outraged laws of his country.' Mrs. Smirkie, as she listened to these eloquent words, closed her eyes and hands in token of her thankfulness for all that Providence had done for her.

If she knew how to compare her condition with that of poor Hester at this time, she had indeed cause for thankfulness. Hester was alone with her baby, and with no information but what had been conveyed to her by her husband's letters. As she read the last of the two she acknowledged to herself that too probably she would not even see his handwriting again till the period of his punishment should have expired. And then? What would come then? Sitting alone, at the open window of her bed-room, with her boy on her lap, she endeavoured to realise her own position. She would be a mother, without a husband,—with her bastard child. However innocent he might be, such would be her position under the law. It did not suffice that they too should be man and wife as thoroughly as any whom God had joined together, if twelve men assembled together in a jury-box should say otherwise. She had told him that she would be brave;—but how should she be brave in such a condition as this? What should she do? How should she look forward to the time of his release? Could anything ever again give her back her husband, and make him her own in the eyes of men? Could anything make men believe that he had always been her own, and that there had been no flaw? She had been very brave when they had attempted to confine her, to hold her by force at Chesterton. Then she had been made strong, ahd always been comforted, by opposition. The determination of her purpose to go back had supported her. But now,—how should it be with her now? and with her boy? and with him?

The old man was very good, good and eager in her cause, and would let her live at Folking. But what would they call her? When they wrote to her from Chesterton how would they address her letters? Never, never would she soil her fingers by touching a document that called her by any other name than her own. Yes, her own;—let all the jurymen in all the counties, let all the judges on the bench, say what they would to the contrary. Though it should be for all her life,—though there should never come the day on which they,—they,—the world at large would do him justice and her, though they should call her by what hard name they would, still up there, in the courts of her God, she would be his wife. She would be a pure woman there, and there would her child be without a stain. And here, here in this world, though she could never more be a wife in all things, she would be a wife in love, a wife in care, a wife in obedience, a wife in all godly truth. And though it would never be possible for her to show her face again among mankind, never for her, surely the world would be kinder to her boy! They would not begrudge him his name! And when it should be told how it had come to pass that there was a blot upon his escutcheon, they would not remind him of his mother's misery. But, above all, there should be no shade of doubt as to her husband. 'I know,' she said, speaking aloud, but not knowing that she spoke aloud, 'I know that he is my husband.' Then there was a knock at the door. 'Well; yes—has it come? Do you know?'

No; nothing was known there at that moment, but in another minute all would be known. The wheels of the old Squire's carriage had been heard upon the gravel. 'No, ma'am, no; you shall not leave the room,' said the nurse. 'Stay here and let him come to you.'

'Is he alone?' she asked. But the woman did not know. The wheels of the carriage had only been heard.

Alas, alas! he was alone. His heart too had been almost broken as he bore the news home to the wife who was a wife no longer.

'Father!' she said, when she saw him.

'My daughter;—O my daughter!' And then, with their hands clasped together, they sat speechless and alone, while the news was spread through the household which the old man did not dare to tell to his son's wife.

It was very slowly that the actual tidings reached her ears. Mr. Caldigate, when he tried to tell them, found that the power of words had left him. Old as he was, and prone to cynic indifference as he had shown himself, he was affected almost like a young girl. He sobbed convulsively as he hung over her, embracing her. 'My daughter!' he said, 'my daughter! my daughter!'

But at last it was all told. Caldigate had been declared guilty, and the judge had condemned him to be confined to prison for two years. Judge Bramber had told him that, in his opinion, the jury could have found no other verdict; but he went on to say that, looking for some excuse for so terrible a deed as that which had been done,—so terrible for that poor lady who was now left nameless with a nameless infant,—he could imagine that the marriage, though legally solemnised, had nevertheless been so deficient in the appearances of solemnity as to have imbued the husband with the idea that it had not meant all that a marriage

319

would have meant if celebrated in a church and with more of the outward appurtenances of religion. On that account he refrained from inflicting a severer penalty.

CHAPTER XLIV

After The Verdict

WHEN the verdict was given, Caldigate was at once marched round into the dock, having hitherto been allowed to sit in front of the dock between Mr. Seely and his father. But, standing in the dock, he heard the sentence pronounced upon him. 'I never married the woman, my lord,' he said, in a loud voice. But what he said could be of no avail. And then men looked at him as he disappeared with the jailers down the steps leading to regions below, and away to his prison, and they knew that he would no more be seen or heard of for two years. He had vanished. But there was the lady who was not his wife out at Folking,—the lady whom the jury had declared not to be his wife. What would become of her?

There was an old gentleman there in the court who had known Mr. Caldigate for many years,—one Mr. Ryder, who had been himself a practising barrister, but had now retired. In those days they seldom saw each other; but, nevertheless, they were friends. 'Caldigate,' he said, 'you had better let her go back to her own people.'

'She shall stay with me,' he replied.

'Better not. Believe me, she had better not. If so, how will it be with her when he is released? The two years will soon go by, and then she will be in his house. If that woman should die, he might marry her,—but till then she had better be with her own people.'

'She shall stay with me,' the old man said again, repeating the words angrily, and shaking his head. He was so stunned by the blow that he could not argue the matter, but he knew that he had made the promise, and that he was resolved to abide by it.

She had better go back to her own people! All the world was saying it. She had no husband now. Everybody would respect her misfortune. Everybody would acknowledge her innocence. All would sympathise with her. All would love her. But she must go back to her own people. There was not a dissentient voice. 'Of course she must go back to you now,' Nicholas Bolton said to her father, and Nicholas Bolton seldom interfered in anything. 'The poor lady will of course be restored to her family,' the judge had said in private to his marshal, and the marshal had of course made known what the judge had said. On the next morning there came a letter from William Bolton to Robert. 'Of course Hester must come back now. Nothing else is possible.' Everybody decided that she must come back. It was a matter which admitted of no

321

doubt. But how was she to be brought to Chesterton?

None of them who decided with so much confidence as to her future, understood her ideas of her position as a wife. 'I am bone of his bone and flesh of his flesh,' she said to herself, 'made so by a sacrament which no jury can touch. What matters what the people say? They may make me more unhappy than I am. They may kill me by their cruelty. But they cannot make me believe myself not to be his wife. And while I am his wife, I will obey him, and him only.'

What she called 'their cruelty' manifested itself very soon. The first person who came to her was Mrs. Robert Bolton, and her visit was made on the day after the verdict. When Hester sent down word begging to be permitted in her misery to decline to see even her sister-in-law, Mrs. Robert sent her up a word or two written in pencil—'My darling, whom have you nearer? Who loves you better than I? Then the wretched one gave way, and allowed her brother's wife to be brought to her. She was already dressed from head to foot in black, and her baby was with her.

The arguments which Mrs. Robert Bolton used need not be repeated, but it may be said that the words she used were so tender, and that they were urged with so much love, so much sympathy, and so much personal approval, that Hester's heart was touched. 'But he is my husband,' Hester said. 'The judge cannot alter it; he is my husband.'

'I will not say a word to the contrary. But the law has separated you, and you should obey the law. You should not even eat his bread now, because—because—. Oh, Hester, you understand.'

'I do understand,' she said, rising to her feet in her energy, 'and I will eat his bread though it be hard, and I will drink of his cup though it be bitter. His bread and his cup shall be mine, and none other shall be mine. I do understand. I know that these wicked people have blasted my life. I know that I can be nothing to him now. But his child shall never be made to think that his mother had condemned his father. Yes, Margaret,' she said again, 'I do love you, and I do trust you, and I know that you love me. But you do not love him; you do not believe in him. If they came to you and took Robert away, would you go and live with other people? I do love papa and mamma. But this is his house, and he bids me stay here. The very clothes which I wear are his clothes. I am his; and though they were to cut me apart from him, still I should belong to him. No,—I will not go to mamma. Of course I have forgiven her, because she meant it for the best; but I will never go back to Chesterton.'

Then there came letters from the mother, one letter hot upon the other, all appealing to those texts in Scripture by which the laws of nations are supposed to be supported. 'Give unto Caesar the things which are Caesar's.' It was for the law to declare who were and who were not man and wife, and in this matter the law had declared. After this how could she doubt? Or how could she hesitate as to tearing herself away from the belongings of the man who certainly was not her husband? And there were dreadful words in these letters which added much to the agony of her who received them,—words which were used in order that their strength might prevail. But they had no strength to convert, though they had strength to afflict. Then Mrs. Bolton, who in her anxiety was ready to submit herself to any personal discomfort, prepared to go to Folking. But Hester sent back word that, in her present condition, she would see nobody,—not even her mother.

But it was not only from the family of the Boltons that these applications and entreaties came. Even Mr. Seely took upon himself to tell Mr. Caldigate that under existing circumstances Hester should not be detained at Folking.

'I do not know that either she or I want advice in the matter,' Mr. Caldigate replied. But as a stone will be worn hollow in time by the droppings of many waters, so was it thought that if all Cambridge would continue firm in its purpose, then this stone might at last be made to yield. The world was so anxious that it resolved among itself that it would submit to any amount of snubbing in carrying out its object. Even the mayor wrote. 'Dear Mr. Caldigate, greatly as I object to all interference in families, I think myself bound to appeal to you as to the unfortunate condition of that young lady from Chesterton.' Then followed all the arguments, and some of the texts,—both of which were gradually becoming hackneyed in the matter. Mr. Caldigate's answer to this was very characteristic: 'Dear Mr. Mayor, if you have an objection to interfere in families, why do you do it?' The Mayor took the rebuke with placid good-humour, feeling that his little drop might also have done something towards hollowing the stone.

But of all the counsellors, perhaps Mr. Smirkie was the most zealous and the most trusting. He felt himself to be bound in a peculiar manner to Folking,—by double ties. Was not the clergyman of the parish the brother of his dear departed one? And with whom better could he hold sweet counsel? And then that second dear one, who had just been vouchsafed to him,—had she not as it were by a miracle been rescued from the fate into which the other poor lady had fallen, and obtained her present thoroughly satisfactory position? Mr. Smirkie was a clergyman who understood it to be his duty to be urgent for the good cause, in season and out of season, and who always did his duty. So he travelled over to Utterden and discussed the matter at great length with Mr. Bromley. 'I do believe in my heart,' said Mr. Bromley, 'that the verdict is wrong.' But Mr. Smirkie, with much eloquence, averred that that had nothing to do with the question. Mr. Bromley opened his eyes very wide. 'Nothing at all,' said Mr. Smirkie. 'It is the verdict of the jury, confirmed by the judge, and the verdict itself dissolves the marriage. Whether the verdict be wrong or right, that marriage ceremony is null and void. They are not man and wife;—not now, even if they ever were. Of course you are aware of that.'

Mr. Smirkie was altogether wrong in his law. Such men generally are. Mr. Bromley in vain endeavoured to point out to him that the verdict could have no such power as was here claimed for it, and that if any claim was to be brought up hereafter as to the legitimacy of the child, the fact of the verdict could only be used as evidence, and that that evidence would or would not be regarded as true by another jury, according to the views which that other jury might take. Mr. Smirkie would only repeat his statements with increased solemnity,—'That marriage is no marriage. That poor lady is not Mrs. John Caldigate. She is Miss Hester Bolton, and, therefore, every breath of air which she draws under that roof is a sin.' As he said this out upon the dike-side, he looked about him with manifest regret that he had no other audience than his brother-in-law.

And at last, after much persevering assiduity, Mr. Smirkie succeeded in reaching Mr. Caldigate himself, and expressed himself with boldness. He was a man who had at any rate the courage of his opinions. 'You have to think of her future life in this world and in the next,' he said. 'And in the next,' he repeated with emphasis, when Mr. Caldigate paused.

'As to what will affect her happiness in this world, sir,' said the old man very gravely, 'I think you can hardly be a judge.'

'Good repute,' suggested the clergyman.

'Has she done anything that ought to lessen the fair fame of a woman in the estimation of other women? And as to the next world, in the rewards and punishments of which you presume it to be your peculiar duty to deal, has she done anything which you think will subject her to the special wrath of an offended Deity?' This question he asked with a vehemence of voice which astounded his companion. 'She has loved her husband with a peculiar love,' he continued. 'She has believed herself to be joined to him by ties which you shall call romantic, if you will,—superstitious, if you will.'

'I hope not,—I hope not,' said Mr. Smirkie, holding up both his hands, not at all understanding the old man's meaning, but intending to express horror at 'superstition,' which he supposed to be a peculiar attribute of the Roman Catholic branch of the Christian Church. 'Not that I hope.'

'I cannot fathom, and you, apparently, cannot at all understand, her idea of the sanctity of the marriage vow. But if you knew anything about her, I think you would refrain from threatening her with divine wrath; and as you know nothing about her, I regard such threats, coming from you, as impertinent, unmanly, inhuman, and blaspehmous.' Mr. Caldigate had commenced this conversation, though vehemently, still in so argumentative a manner, and in his allusions to the lady's romantic and superstitious ideas had seemed to yield so much, that the terrible vigour of his last words struck the poor clergyman almost to the ground. One epithet came out after another, very clearly spoken, with a pause between each of them; and the speaker, as he uttered them, looked his victim close in the face. Then he walked slowly away, leaving Mr. Smirkie fixed to the ground. What had he done? He had simply made a gentle allusion to the next world, as, surely, it was his duty to do. Whether this old pagan did or did not believe in a next world himself, he must at any rate be aware that it is the peculiar business of a clergyman to make such references. As to 'impertinent' and 'unmanly', he would let them go by. He was, he conceived, bound by his calling to be what people called impertinent, and manliness had nothing to do with him. But 'inhuman' and 'blasphemous!' Why had he come all the way over from Plum-cum-Pippins, at considerable personal expense, except in furtherance of that highest humanity which concerns itself with eternity? And as for blasphemy, it might, he thought, as well be said that he was blasphemous whenever he read the Bible aloud to his flock! His first idea was to write an exhaustive letter on the subject to Mr. Caldigate, in which he would invite that gentleman to recall the offensive words. But as he drove his gig into the parsonage yard at Plum-cum-Pippins, he made up his mind that this, too, was among the things which a Christian minister should bear with patience.

But the dropping water always does hollow the stone,—hollow it a little though the impression may not be visible to the naked eye. Even when rising in his wrath, Mr. Caldigate had crushed the clergyman by the violence of his language,—having been excited to anger chiefly by the thick-headedness of the man in not having understood the rebuke intended to be conveyed by his earlier and gentler words,—even when leaving the man, with a full conviction that the man was crushed, the old Squire was aware that he, the stone, was being gradually hollowed. Hester was now very dear to him. From the first she had suited his ideas of a wife for his son. And her constancy in her misery had wound itself into his heart. He quite understood that her welfare should now be his great care. There was no one else from whom she would listen to a word of advice. From her husband, whose slightest word would have been a law to her, no word could now come. From her own family she was entirely estranged, having been taught to regard them simply as enemies in this matter. She loved her mother; but in this matter her mother was her declared enemy. His voice, and his voice alone, could now reach her ears. As to that great hereafter to which the clergyman had so flippantly alluded, he was content to leave that to herself. Much as he differed from her as to details of a creed, he felt sure that she was safe there. To his thinking, she was the purest human being that had ever come beneath his notice. Whatever portion of bliss there may be for mankind in a life after this life, the fullest portion of that bliss would be hers, whether by reason of her creed or in spite of it. Accustomed to think much of things, it was thus that he thought of her in reference to the world to come. But as to this world, he was not quite so sure. If she could die and have that other bliss at once, that would be best,—only for the child, only for the child! But he did doubt. Would it do for her to ignore that verdict altogether, when his son should be released from jail, and be to him as though there had been no verdict? Would not the finger of scorn be pointed at her;—and, as he thought of it,—possibly at future children? Might it not be better for her to bow to the cruelty of Fate, and consent to be apart from him at any rate while that woman should be alive? And again, if such would be better, then was it not clear that no time should be lost in beginning that new life? If at last it should be ruled that she must go back to her mother, it would certainly be well that she should do so now, at once, so that people might know that she had yielded to the verdict. In this way the stone was hollowed—though the hollowing had not been made visible to the naked eye of Mr. Smirkie.

He was a man whose conscience did not easily let him rest when he believed that a duty was incumbent on him. It was his duty now, he thought, not to bid her go, not to advise her to go,—but to put before her what reasons there might be for her going.

'I am telling you,' he said, 'what other people say.'

'I do not regard what other people say.'

'That might be possible for a man, Hester, but a woman has to regard what the world says. You are young, and may have a long life before you. We cannot hide from ourselves the fact that a most terrible misfortune has fallen upon you, altogether undeserved, but very grievous.'

'God, when he gave me my husband,' she replied, 'did me more good than any man can do me harm by taking him away. I never cease to tell myself that the blessing is greater than the misfortune.'

'But, my dearest—'

'I know it all father. I know what you would tell me. If I live here after he comes out of prison people will say that I am his mistress.'

'Not that, not that,' he cried, unable to bear the contumely of the word, even from her lips.

'Yes, father; that is what you mean. That is what they all mean. That is what mamma means, and Margaret. Let them call me what they will. It is not what they call me, but what I am. It is bad for a woman to have evil said of her, but it is worse for her to do evil. It is your house, and you, of course, can bid me go.'

'I will never do that.'

'But unless I am turned out homeless on to the roads, I will stay here where he left me. I have only one sure way of doing right, and that is to obey him as closely as I can. He cannot order me now, but he has left his orders. He has told me to remain under this roof, and to call myself by his name, and in no way to derogate from my own honour as his wife. By God's help I will do as he bids me. Nothing that any of them can say shall turn me an inch from the way he has pointed out. You are good to me.'

'I will try to be good to you.'

'You are so good to me that I can hardly understand your goodness. Trusting to that, I will wait here till he shall come again and tell me where and how I am to live.'

After that the old Squire made no further attempt in the same direction, finding that no slightest hollow had been made on that other stone.

CHAPTER XLV

The Boltons Are Much Troubled

THE condition of the inhabitants of Puritan Grange during the six weeks immediately after the verdict was very sad indeed. I have described badly the character of the lady living there, if I have induced my readers to think that her heart was hardened against her daughter. She was a woman of strong convictions and bitter prejudices; but her heart was soft enough. When she married, circumstances had separated her widely from her own family, in which she had never known either a brother or a sister; and the burden of her marriage with an old man had been brightened to her by the possession of an only child,—of one daughter, who had been the lamp of her life, the solitary delight of her heart, the single relief to the otherwise solitary tedium of her monotonous existence. She had, indeed, attended to the religious training of her girl with constant care;—but the yearnings of her maternal heart had softened even her religion, so that the laws, and dogmas, and texts, and exercises by which her husband was oppressed, and her servants afflicted, had been made lighter for Hester,—sometimes not without pangs of conscience on the part of the self-convicted parent. She had known, as well as other mothers, how to gloat over the sweet charms of the one thing which in all the world had been quite her own. She had revelled in kisses and soft touches. Her Hester's garments had been a delight to her, till she had taught herself to think that though sackcloth and ashes were the proper wear for herself and her husband, nothing was too soft, too silken, too delicate for her little girl. The roses in the garden and the goldfish in the bowl, and the pet spaniel, had been there because such surroundings had been needed for the joyousness of her girl. And the theological hardness of the literature of the house had been somewhat mitigated as Hester grew into reading, so that Watt was occasionally relieved by Wordsworth, and Thomson's 'Seasons' was alternated with George Wither's 'Hallelujah.'

Then had come, first the idea of the marriage, and, immediately consequent upon the idea, the marriage itself. The story of that has been told, but the reader has perhaps hardly been made to understand the utter bereavement which it brought on the mother. It is natural that the adult bird should delight to leave the family nest, and that the mother bird should have its heart-strings torn by the separation. It

must be so, alas! even when the divulsions are made in the happiest
manner. But here the tearing away had nothing in it to reconcile the
mother. She was suddenly told that her daughter was to be no longer
her own. Her step-son had interfered, and her husband had become
powerful over her with a sudden obstinacy. She had had no hand in
the choice. She would fain have postponed any choice, and would then
fain have herself made the choice. But a man was brought who was
distasteful to her at all points, and she was told that that man was to
have her daughter! He was thoroughly distasteful! He had been a
spendthrift and a gambler;—then a seeker after gold in wild, godless
countries, and, to her thinking, not at all the better because he had been
a successful seeker. She believed the man to be an atheist. She was told
that his father was an infidel, and was ready to believe the worst of the
son. And yet in this terrible emergency she was powerless. The girl
was allowed to see the man, and declared almost at once that she
would transfer herself from her mother's keeping to the keeping of this
wicked one! She was transferred, and the mother had been left alone.

Then came the blow,—very quickly, the blow which, as she now
told herself morning, noon, and night, was no worse than she had
expected. Another woman claimed the man as her husband, and so
claimed him that the world all around her had declared that the claim
would be made good. And the man himself had owned enough to make
him unfit,—as she thought,—to have the custody of any honest
woman. Then she acknowledged to herself the full weight of the misfortune that had fallen upon them,—the misfortune which never
would have fallen upon them had they listened to her counsel,—and
she had immediately put her shoulders to the wheel with the object
of rescuing her child from the perils, from the sin, from the degradation
of her position. And could she have rescued her, could she have induced
her daughter to remain at Puritan Grange, there would even then have
been consolation. It was one of the tenets of her life,—the strongest,
perhaps, of all those doctrines on which she built her faith,—that this
world is a world of woe; that wailing and suffering, if not gnashing of
teeth, is and should be the condition of mankind preparatory to eternal
bliss. For eternal bliss there could, she thought, be no other preparation.
She did not want to be happy here, or to have those happy around her
whom she loved. She had stumbled and gone astray,—she told herself
hourly now that she had stumbled and gone astray,—in preparing
those roses and ribbons, and other lightnesses, for her young girl. It
should have been all sackcloth and ashes. Had it been all sackcloth and
ashes there would not have been this terrible fall. But if the loved one
would now come back to sackcloth and ashes,—if she would assent to

the blackness of religious asceticism, to penitence and theological gloom, and would lead the life of the godly but comfortless here in order that she might insure the glories and joys of the future life, then there might be consolation;—then it might be felt that this tribulation had been a precious balm by which an erring soul had been brought back to its due humility.

But Wordsworth and Thomson, though upon the whole moral poets, had done their work. Or, if not done altogether by them, the work had been done by the latitude which had admitted them. So that the young wife, when she found herself breathing the free air with which her husband surrounded her, was able to burst asunder the remnants of those cords of fanaticism with which her mother had endeavoured to constrain her. She looked abroad, and soon taught herself to feel that the world was bright and merry, that this mortal life was by no means necessarily a place of gloom, and the companionship of the man to whom Providence had allotted her was to her so happy, so enjoyable, so sufficient, that she found herself to have escaped from a dark prison and to be roaming among shrubs and flowers, and running waters, which were ever green, which never faded, and the music of which was always in her ears. When the first tidings of Euphemia Smith came to Folking she was in all her thoughts and theories of life poles asunder from her mother. There might be suffering and tribulation,—suffering even to death. But her idea of the manner in which the suffering should be endured and death awaited was altogether opposed to that which was hot within her mother's bosom.

But not the less did the mother still pray, still struggle, and still hope. They, neither of them, quite understood each other, but the mother did not at all understand the daughter. She, the mother, knew what the verdict had been, and was taught to believe that by that verdict the very ceremony of her daughter's marriage had been rendered null and void. It was in vain that the truth of the matter came to her from Robert Bolton, diluted through the vague explanations of her husband. 'It does not alter the marriage, Robert says.' So it was that the old man told his tale, not perfectly understanding, not even quite believing, what his son had told him.

'How can he dare to say so?' demanded the indignant mother of the injured woman. 'Not alter the marriage when the jury have declared that the other woman is his wife! In the eyes of God she is not his wife. That cannot be imputed as sin to her,—not that,—because she did it not knowing. She, poor innocent, was betrayed. But now that she knows it, every mouthful that she eats of his bread is a sin.'

'It is the old man's bread,' said this older man, weakly.

'What matter? It is the bread of adultery.' It may certainly be said that at this time Mrs. Bolton herself would have been relieved from none of her sufferings by any new evidence which would have shown that Crinkett and the others had sworn falsely. Though she loved her daughter dearly, though her daughter's misery made her miserable, yet did she not wish to restore the husband to the wife. Any allusion to a possibility that the verdict had been a mistaken verdict was distasteful to her. Her own original opinion respecting Caldigate had been made good by the verdict. The verdict had proved her to be right, and her husband with all his sons to have been wrong. The triumph had been very dark to her; but still it had been a triumph. It was to her an established fact that John Caldigate was not her daughter's husband; and therefore she was anxious, not to rehabilitate her daughter's position, but to receive her own miserable child once more beneath the shelter of her own wing. That they two might pray together, struggle together, together wear their sackcloth and ashes, and together console themselves with their hopes of eternal joys, while they shuddered, not altogether uncomfortably, at the torments prepared for others,—this was now the only outlook in which she could find a gleam of satisfaction; and she was so assured of the reasonableness of her wishes, so convinced that the house of her parents was now the only house in which Hester could live without running counter to the precepts of her own religion, and counter also the rules of the wicked outside world, that she could not bring herself to believe but that she would succeed at last. Merely to ask her child to come, to repeat the invitation, and then to take a refusal, was by no means sufficient for her energy. She had failed grievously when she had endeavoured to make her daughter a prisoner at the Grange. After such an attempt as that, it could hardly be thought that ordinary invitations would be efficacious. But when that attempt had been made, it was possible that Hester should justify herself by the law. According to law she had then been Caldigate's wife. There had been some ground for her to stand upon as a wife, and as a wife she had stood upon it very firmly. But now there was not an inch of ground. The man had been convicted as a bigamist, and the other woman, the first woman, had been proved to be his wife. Mrs. Bolton had got it into her head that the two had been dissevered as though by some supernal power; and no explanation to the contrary, brought to her by her husband from Robert, had any power of shaking her conviction. It was manifest to all men and to all women, that she who had been seduced, betrayed, and sacrificed should now return with her innocent babe to the protection of her father's roof; and no stone must be left unturned till the unfortunate one had been made to understand her duty.

The old banker in these days had not a good time, nor, indeed, had the Boltons generally. Mrs. Bolton, though prone to grasp at power on every side, was apt, like some other women who are equally grasping, to expect almost omnipotence from the men around her when she was desirous that something should be done by them in accordance with her own bidding. Knowing her husband to be weak from age and sorrow, she could still jeer at him because he was not abnormally strong, and though her intercourse with his sons and their families was now scanty and infrequent, still by a word here and a line there she could make her reproaches felt by them all. Robert, who saw his father every day, heard very much of them. Daniel was often stung, and even Nicholas. And the reproaches reached as far as William, the barrister up in London.

'I am sure I don't know what we can do,' said the miserable father, sitting huddled up in his armchair one evening towards the end of August. It was very hot, but the windows were closed because he could not bear a draught, and he was somewhat impatiently waiting for the hour of prayers which were antecedent to bed, where he could be silent even if he could not sleep.

'There are five of you. One should be at the house every day to tell her of her duty.'

'I couldn't go.'

'They could go,—if they cared. If they cared they would go. They are her brothers.'

'Mr. Caldigate would not let them enter the house,' said the old man.

'Do you mean that he would separate her from her brother and her parents?'

'Not if she wished to see them. She is her own mistress, and he will abet her in whatever she may choose to do. That is what Robert says.'

'And what Robert says is to be law?'

'He knows what he is talking about.' Mr. Bolton as he said this shook his head angrily, because he was fatigued.

'And he is to be your guide even when your daughter's soul is in jeopardy?' This was the line of argument in reference to which Mr. Bolton always felt himself to be as weak as water before his wife. He did not dare to rebel against her religious supremacy, not simply because he was a weak old man in presence of a strong woman, but from fear of denunciation. He, too, believed her creed, though he was made miserable by her constant adherence to it. He believed, and would fain have let that suffice. She believed, and endeavoured to live up to her belief. And so it came to pass that when she spoke to him of his own soul, of the souls of those who were dear to him, or even of souls in general, he was frightened and paralysed. He had more than once attempted to reply with worldly arguments, but had suffered so much in the encounter that he had learned to abstain. 'I cannot believe that she would refuse to see us. I shall go myself; but if we all went we should surely persuade her.' In answer to this the poor man only groaned, till the coming in of the old servant to arrange the chairs and put the big Bible on the table relieved him from something of his misery.

'I certainly will not interfere,' Robert Bolton said to his father on the next morning. 'I will not go to Folking, because I am sure that I should do no good. Hester, no doubt, would be better at your house, —much better. There is nothing I would not do to get her back from the Caldigates altogether,—if there was a chance of success. But we have no power,—none whatever.'

'No power at all,' said the banker, shaking his head, and feeling some satisfaction at the possession of an intelligible word which he could quote to his wife.

'She is controller of her own actions as completely as are you and I. We have already seen how inefficacious with her are all attempts at persuasion. And she knows her position. If he were out of prison to-morrow he would be her husband.'

'But he has another wife.'

'Of that the civil law knows nothing. If money were coming to her he could claim it, and the verdict against him would only be evidence, to be taken for what it was worth. It would have been all very well had she wished to sever herself from him; but as she is determined not to do so, any interference would be useless.' The question as to the marriage or no marriage was not made quite clear to the banker's mind, but he did understand that neither he, nor his wife, nor his sons had 'any power,' and of that argument he was determined to make use.

William, the barrister in London, was induced to write a letter, a very lengthy and elaborate epistle having come from Mrs. Bolton to his wife, in which the religious duty of all the Boltons was set forth in strong language, and in which he was incited to do something. It was almost the first letter which Mrs. William Bolton had ever received from her step-mother, whatever trifling correspondence there might have been between them having been of no consequence. They, too, felt that it would be better that Hester should return to her old home, but felt also that they had no power. 'Of course, she won't,' said Mrs. William.

'She has a will of her own,' said the barrister.

'Why should she? Think of the gloom of that home at Chesterton, and her absolute independence at Folking. No doubt it would be better. The position is so frightful that even the gloom would be better. But she won't. We all know that.'

The barrister, however, feeling that it would be better, thought that he should perform his duty by expressing his opinion, and wrote a letter to Hester, which was intended to be if possible persuasive;—and this was the answer:—

'DEAR WILLIAM,—If you were carried away to prison on some horrible false accusation, would Fanny go away from you, and desert your house and your affairs, and return to her parents? You ask her, and ask her whether she would believe anything that anybody could say against you. If they told her that her children were nameless, would she agree to make them so by giving up your name? Wouldn't she cling to you the more, the more all the world was against you?' '(I would,' said Fanny, with tearful energy. 'Fanny' was, of course, Mrs. William Bolton, and was the happy mother of five nearly grown-up sons and daughters, and certainly stood in no peril as to her own or their possession of the name of Bolton. The letter was being read aloud to her by her husband, whose mind was also stirred in his sister's favour by the nature of the arguments used.) 'If so,' continued the writer, 'why shouldn't I be the same? I don't believe a word the people said. I am sure I am his wife. And as, when he was taken away from me, he left a house for his wife and child to live in, I shall continue to live in it.

'All the same, I know you mean to be good to me. Give my best love to Fanny, and believe me your affectionate sister,

'HESTER CALDIGATE'

In every letter and stroke of the name as she wrote it there was an assertion that she claimed it as her own, and that she was not ashamed of it.

'Upon my word,' said Mrs. William Bolton, through her tears, 'I am beginning to think that she is almost right.' There was so much of conjugal proper feeling in this that the husband could only kiss his wife and leave her without further argument on the matter.

CHAPTER XLVI

Burning Words

'NO power at all; none whatever,' the banker said, when he was next compelled to carry on the conversation. This was immediately upon his return home from Cambridge, for his wife never allowed the subject to be forgotten or set aside. Every afternoon and every evening it was being discussed at all hours not devoted to prayers, and every morning it was renewed at the breakfast-table.

'That comes from Robert.' Mr. Bolton was not able to deny the assertion. 'What does he mean by "no power"?'

'We can't make her do it. The magistrates can't interfere.'

'Magistrates! Has it been by the interference of magistrates that men have succeeded in doing great things? Was it by order from the magistrates that the lessons of Christ have been taught over all the world? Is there no such thing as persuasion? Has truth no power? Is she more deaf to argument and eloquence than another?'

'She is very deaf, I think,' said the father, doubting his own eloquence.

'It is because no one has endeavoured to awaken her by burning words to a true sense of her situation.' When she said this she must surely have forgotten much that had occurred during those weary hours which had been passed by her and her daughter outside there in the hall. 'No power!' she repeated. 'It is the answer always made by those who are too sleepy to do the Lord's work. It was because men said that they had no power that the grain fell upon stony places, where they had not much earth. It is that aversion to face difficulties which causes the broad path to be crowded with victims. I, at any rate, will go. I may have no power, but I will make the attempt.'

Soon after that she did make the attempt. Mr. Bolton, though he was assured by Robert that such an attempt would produce no result, could not interfere to prevent it. Had he been far stronger than he was in his own house, he could hardly have forbidden the mother to visit the daughter. Hester had sent word to say that she did not wish to see even her mother. But this had been immediately after the verdict, when she was crushed and almost annihilated by her misery. Some weeks had now passed by, and it could not be that she would refuse to admit the visitor, when such a visitor knocked at her door. They had loved each other as mothers and daughters do love when there is no rival in the affection,—when each has no one else to love. There never had been a more obedient child, or a more loving parent. Much, no doubt, had happened since to estrange the daughter from the mother. A husband had been given to her who was more to her than any parent,—as a husband should be. And then there had been that terrible opposition, that struggle, that battle in the hall. But the mother's love had never waned because of that. She was sure that her child would not refuse to see her.

So the fly was ordered to take her out to Folking, and on the morning fixed she dressed herself in her blackest black. She always wore brown or black,—brown being the colour suitable for the sober and sad domesticities of her week-days, which on ceremonies and Sabbath was changed for a more solemn black. But in her wardrobe there were two such gowns, one of which was apparently blacker than the other, nearer to a guise of widowhood,—more fit, at any rate, for general funereal obsequies. There are women who seem always to be burying someone; and Mrs. Bolton, as she went forth to visit her daughter, was fit to bury any one short of her husband.

It was a hot day in August, and the fly travelled along the dusty road very slowly. She had intended to reach Folking at twelve, so that her interview might be over and that she might return without the need of eating. There is always some idea of festivity connected with food eaten at a friend's table, and she did not wish to be festive. She was, too, most unwilling to partake of John Caldigate's bread. But she did not reach the house till one, and when she knocked at the door Hester's modest lunch was about to be put upon the table.

There was considerable confusion when the servant saw Mrs. Bolton standing in the doorway. It was quite understood by everyone at Folking that for the present there was to be no intercourse between the Boltons and the Caldigates. it was understood that there should be no visitors of any kind at Folking, and it had been thought that Mr. Smirkie had forced an entrance in an impertinent manner. But yet it was not possible to send Mrs. Bolton from her own daughter's door with a mere 'not at home'. Of course she was shown in,—and was taken to the parlour, in which the lunch was prepared, while word was taken up to Hester announcing that her mother was there.

Mr. Caldigate was in the house,—in his own book-room, as it used to be called,—and Hester went to him first. 'Mamma is here,—in the dining-room.'

'Your mother!'

'I long to see mamma.'

'Of course you do.'

'But she will want me to go away with her.'

336

'She cannot take you unless you choose to go.'

'But she will speak of nothing else. I know it. I wish she had not come.'

'Surely, Hester, you can make her understand that your mind is made up.'

'Yes, I shall do that. I must do that. But, father, it will be very painful. You do not know what things she can say. It nearly killed me when I was at the Grange. You will not see her, I suppose?'

'If you wish it, I will. She will not care to see me; and as things are at present, what room is there for friendship?'

'You will come if I send for you?'

'Certainly. If you send for me I will come at once.'

Then she crept slowly out of the room, and very slowly and very silently made her way to the parlour-door. Though she was of a strong nature, unusually strong of heart and fixed of purpose, now her heart misgave her. That terrible struggle, with all its incidents of weariness and agony, was present to her mind. Her mother could not turn the lock on her now; but, as she had said, it would be very dreadful. Her mother would say words to her which would go through her like swords. Then she opened the door, and for a moment there was the sweetness of an embrace. There was a prolonged tenderness in the kiss which, even to Mrs. Bolton, had a charm for the moment to soften her spirit. 'Oh, mamma; my own mamma!'

'My child!'

'Yes, mamma;—every day when I pray for you I tell myself that I am still your child,—I do.'

'My only one! my only one!—all that I have!' Then again they were in each other's arms. Yet, when they had last met, one had been the jailer, and the other the prisoner; and they had fought it out between them with a determined obstinacy which at moments had almost amounted to hatred. But now the very memory of these sad hours increased their tenderness. 'Hester, through it all, do you not know that my heart yearns for you day and night?—that in my prayers I am always remembering you? that my dreams are happy because you are with me? that I am ever longing for you as Ruth longed for Naomi? I am as Rachel weeping for her children, who would not be comforted because they are not. Day and night my heart-strings are torn asunder because my eyes behold you not.'

It was true,—and the daughter knew it to be true. But what could be done? There had grown up something for her, holier, greater, more absorbing even than a mother's love. Happily for most young wives, though the new tie may surmount the old one, it does not crush it or

337

smother it. The mother retains a diminished hold, and knowing what nature has intended, is content. She, too, with some subsidiary worship, kneels at the new altar, and all is well. But here, though there was abundant love, there was no sympathy. The cause of discord was ever present to them both. Unless John Caldigate was acknowledged to be a fitting husband, not even the mother could be received with a full welcome. And unless John Caldigate were repudiated, not even the daughter could be accepted as altogether pure. Parental and filial feelings sufficed for nothing between them beyond the ecstacy of a caress.

As Hester was standing mute, still holding her mother's hand, the servant came to the door, and asked whether she would have her lunch.

'You will stay and eat with me, mamma? But you will come up to my room first?'

'I will go up to your room, Hester.'

'Then we will have our lunch,' Hester said, turning to the servant. So the two went together to the upper chamber, and in a moment the mother had fetched her baby, and placed it in her mother's arms.

'I wish he were at the Grange,' said Mrs. Bolton. Then Hester shook her head; but feeling the security of her position, left the baby with its grandmother. 'I wish he were at the Grange. It is the only fitting home for him at present.'

'No, mamma; that cannot be.'

'It should be so, Hester. It should be so.'

'Pray do not speak of it, dear mamma.'

'Have I not come here on purpose that I might speak of it? Sweet as it is to me to have you in my arms, do you not know that I have come for that purpose,—for that only?'

'It cannot be so.'

'I will not take such an answer, Hester. I am not here to speak of pleasure or delights,—not to speak of sweet companionship, or even of a return to that more godly life which, I think, you would find in your father's house. Had not this ruin come, unhappy though I might have been, and distrustful, I should not have interfered. Those whom God has joined together, let not man put asunder.'

'It is what I say to myself every hour. God has joined us, and no man, no number of men, shall put us asunder.'

'But, my own darling,—God has not joined you! When he pretended to be joined to you, he had a wife then living,—still living.'

'No.'

'Will you set up your own opinion against evidence which the jury has believed, which the judge has believed, which all the world has believed?'

'Yes, I will,' said Hester, the whole nature of whose face was now altered, and who looked as she did when sitting in the hall-chair at Puritan Grange,—'I will. Though I were almost to know that he had been false, I should still believe him to be true.'

'I cannot understand that, Hester.'

'But I know him to be true,—quite true,' she said, wishing to erase the feeling which her unguarded admission had made. 'Not to believe him to have been true would be death to me; and for my boy's sake, I would wish to live. But I have no doubt, and I will listen to no one, —not even to you, when you tell me that God did not join us together.'

'You cannot go behind the law, Hester. As a citizen, you must obey the law.'

'I will live here,—as a citizen,—till he has been restored to me.'

'But he will not then be your husband. People will not call you by his name. He cannot have two wives. She will be his wife. Oh, Hester, have you thought of it?'

'I have thought of it,' she said, raising her face, looking upwards through the open window, out away towards the heavens, and pressing her foot firmly upon the floor. 'I have thought of it,—very much; and I have asked—the Lord—for counsel. And He has given it me. He has told me what to believe, what to know, and how to live. I will never again lie with my head upon his bosom unless all that be altered. But I will serve him as his wife, and obey him; and if I can I will comfort him. I will never desert him. And not all the laws that were ever made, nor all the judges that ever sat in judgment, shall make me call myself by another name than his.'

The mother had come there to speak burning words, and she had in some sort prepared them; but now she found herself almost silenced by the energy of her daughter. And when her girl told her that she had applied to her God for counsel, and that the Lord had answered her prayers—that the Lord had directed her as to her future life,— then the mother hardly knew how to mount to higher ground, so as to seem to speak from a more exalted eminence. And yet she was not at all convinced. That the Lord should give bad counsel she knew to be impossible. That the Lord would certainly give good counsel to such a suppliant, if asked aright, she was quite sure. But they who send others to the throne of heaven for direct advice are apt to think that the asking will not be done aright unless it be done with their spirit and their bias,—with the spirit and bias which they feel when they re-commend the operation. No one has ever thought that direct advice from the Lord was sufficient authority for the doing of that of which he himself disapproved. It was Mrs. Bolton's daily custom to kneel herself and ask for such counsel, and to enjoin such asking upon all those who were subject to her influence. But had she been assured by some young lady to whom she had recommended the practice that heavenly warrant had thus been secured for balls and theatres, she would not have scrupled to declare that the Lord had certainly not been asked aright. She was equally certain of some defalcation now. She did not doubt that Hester had done as she had said. That the prayer had been put up with energetic fervour, she was sure. But energetic fervour in prayer was, she thought, of no use,—nay, was likely to be most dangerous, when used in furtherance of human pre-possessions and desires. Had Hester said her prayers with a proper feeling of self-negation,—in that religious spirit which teaches the poor mortal here on earth to know that darkness and gloom are safer than mirth and comfort,—then the Lord would have told her to leave Folking, to go back to Puritan Grange, and to consent once more to be called Hester Bolton. This other counsel had not come from the Lord, —had come only from Hester's own polluted heart. But she was not at the moment armed with words sufficiently strong to explain all this.

'Hester,' she said, 'does not all this mean that your own proud spirit is to have a stronger dominion over you than the experience and wisdom of all your friends?'

'Perhaps it does. But, at any rate, my proud spirit will retain its pride.'

'You will be obstinate?'

'Certainly I will. Nothing on earth shall make me leave this house till I am told by its owner to go.'

'Who is its owner? Old Mr. Caldigate is its owner.'

'I hardly know. Though John has explained it again and again, I am so bad at such things that I am not sure. But I can do what I please with it. I am the mistress here. As you say that the Grange is your house, I can say that this is mine. It is the abode appointed for me, and here I will abide.'

'Then, Hester, I can only tell you that you are sinning. It is a heavy, grievous, and most obvious sin.'

'Dear mother,—dear mamma; I knew how it would be if you came. It is useless for me to say more. Were I to go away, that to me would be the sin. Why should we discuss it any more? There comes a time to all of us when we must act on our own responsibility. My husband is in prison, and cannot personally direct me. No doubt I could go, were I so pleased. His father would not hinder me, though he is most unwilling that I should go. I must judge a little for myself. But I have his judgment to fall back upon. He told me to stay, and I shall stay.'

Then there was a pause, during which Mrs. Bolton was thinking of her burning words,—was remembering the scorn with which she had treated her husband when he told her that they had 'no power.' She had endeavoured herself not to be sleepy in doing the Lord's work. But her seed, too, had fallen upon stony places. She was powerless to do, or even to say, anything further. 'Then I may go,' she muttered.

'You will come and eat with me, mamma?'

'No, my dear,—no.'

'You do not wish that there should be a quarrel?'

'There is very much, Hester, that I do not wish. I have long ceased to trust much to any wishes. There is a great gulf between us, and I will not attempt to bridge it by the hollow pretence of sitting at table with you. I will still pray that you may be restored to me.' Then she went to the door.

'Mamma, you will kiss me before you go?'

'I will cover you with kisses when you return to your own home.' But in spite of this, Hester went down with her into the hall, holding by her raiment; and as Mrs. Bolton got into the fly, she did succeed in kissing her mother's hand.

'She has gone,' said Hester, going to her father-in-law's room. 'Though I was so glad to see her, I wish she had not come. When people think so very, very differently on a matter which is so very, very important, it is better that they should not meet, let them love each other ever so.'

As far as Hester and Mr. Caldigate were concerned, the visit had in truth been made without much inconvenience. There had been no absolute violence,—no repetition of such outward quarrelling as had made those two days at the Grange so memorable. There was almost a feeling of relief in Hester's bosom when her mother was driven away after that successful grasp at the parting hand. Though they had differed much, they had not hated each other during that last half-hour. Hester had been charged with sin;—which, however, had been a matter of course. But in Mrs. Bolton's heart there was a feeling which made her return home very uncomfortable. Having twitted her husband with his lack of power, she had been altogether powerless herself; and now she was driven to confess to herself that no further step could be taken. 'She is obstinate,' she said to her husband,—'stiff-necked in her sin, as are all determined sinners. I can say no more to her. It may be that the Lord will soften her heart when her sorrows have endured yet for a time.' But she said no more of burning words, or of eloquence, or of the slackness of the work of those who work as though they were not in earnest.

CHAPTER XLVII

Curlydown And Bagwax

THERE had been a sort of pledge given at the trial by Sir John Joram that the matter of the envelope should be further investigated. He had complained in his defence that the trial had been hurried on,—that time had not been allowed for full inquiries, seeing that the character of the deed by which his client had been put in jeopardy depended upon what had been done on the other side of the globe. 'This crime,' he had said, 'if it be a crime, was no doubt committed in the parish church of Utterden in the early part of last year; but all the evidence which has been used or which could be used to prove it to have been a crime, has reference to things done long ago, and far away. Time has not been allowed us for rebutting this evidence by counter-evidence.' And yet much time had been allowed. The trial had been postponed from the spring to the summer assizes; and then the offence was one which, from its very nature, required speedy notice. The Boltons, who became the instigators of the prosecution, demanded that the ill-used woman should be relieved as quickly as possible from her degradation. There had been a general feeling that the trial should not be thrown over to another year; and, as we are aware, it had been brought to judgment, and the convicted criminal was in jail. But Sir John still persevered, and to this perseverance he had been instigated very much by a certain clerk in the post-office.

Two post-office clerks had been used as witnesses at the trial, of whom the elder, Mr. Curlydown, had been by no means a constant or an energetic witness. A witness, when he is brought up for the defence, should not be too scrupulous, or he will be worse than useless. In a matter of fact a man can only say what he saw, or tell what he heard, or declare what he knew. He should at least do no more. Though it be to save his father, he should not commit perjury. But when it comes to opinion, if a man allows himself to waver, he will be taken as thinking the very opposite of what he does think. Such had been the case with Mr. Curlydown. He had intended to be very correct. He had believed that the impression of the Sydney stamp was on the whole adverse to the idea that it had been obtained in the proper way; and yet he had, when cross-examined, acknowledged that it might very probably have been obtained in the proper way. It certainly had not been 'smudged' at all, and such impressions generally did become 'smudged.' But then

343

he was made to say also that impressions very often did not become smudged. And as to the word 'Nobble' which should have been stamped upon the envelope, he thought that in such a case its absence was very suspicious; but still he was brought to acknowledge that post-masters in provincial offices far away from inspection, frequently omit that part of their duty. All this had tended to rob the envelope of those attributes of deceit and conspiracy which Sir John Joram attributed to it, and had justified the judge in his opinion that Mr. Curlydown's evidence had told them little or nothing. But even Mr. Curlydown had found more favour with the judge than Samuel Bagwax, the junior of the two post-office witnesses. Samuel Bagwax had perhaps been a little too energetic. He had made the case his own, and was quite sure that the envelope had been tampered with. I think that the counsel for the Crown pressed his witness unfairly when he asked Mr. Bagwax whether he was absolutely certain that an envelope with such an impression could not have passed through the post-office in the ordinary course of business. 'Nothing is impossible,' Mr. Bagwax had replied. 'Is it not very much within the sphere of possibility?' the learned gentleman had asked. The phrase was misleading, and Mr. Bagwax was induced to say that it might be so. But still his assurance would probably have had weight with the jury but for the overstrained honesty of his companion. The judge had admonished the jury that in reference to such a point they should use their own common-sense rather than the opinion of such a man as Mr. Bagwax. A man of ordinary common-sense would know how the mark made by a die on a letter would be affected by the sort of manipulation to which the letter bearing it would be subjected;— and so on. From all which it came to pass that the judge was understood to have declared that the special envelope might very well have passed in ordinary course through the Sydney post-office.

But Samuel Bagwax was not a man to be put down by the injustice of lawyers. He knew himself to have been ill-treated. He was confident that no man alive was more competent than himself to form an opinion on such a subject; and he was sure, quite sure,—perhaps a little too sure,—that there had been some dishonesty with that envelope. And thus he became a strong partisan of John Caldigate and of Mrs. John Caldigate. If there had been tampering with that envelope, then the whole thing was fraudulent, false, and the outcome of a base conspiracy. Many points were present to his mind which the lawyers between them would not allow him to explain properly to a jury. When had that die been cut, by which so perfect an impression had been formed? If it could be proved that it had been cut since the date it bore, then of course the envelope would be fraudulent. But it was only in

Sydney that this could be ascertained. He was sure that a week's ordinary use would have made the impression less perfect. Some letters must of course be subjected to new dies, and this letter might in due course have been so subjected. But it was more probable that a new stamp should have been selected for a surreptitious purpose. All this could be ascertained by the book of daily impressions kept in the Sydney post-office;–but there had not been time to get this evidence from Sydney since this question of the impression had been ventilated. It was he who had first given importance to the envelope; and being a resolute and almost heroic man, he was determined that no injustice on the part of a Crown prosecutor, no darkness in a judge's mind, no want of intelligence in a jury, should rob him of the delight of showing how important to the world was a proper understanding of post-office details. He still thought that that envelope might be made to prove a conspiracy on the part of Crinkett and the others, and he succeeded in getting Sir John Joram to share that belief.

The envelope itself was still preserved among the sacred archives of the trial. That had not been bodily confided to Samuel Bagwax. But various photographs had been made of the document, which no doubt reproduced exactly every letter, every mark, and every line which was to be seen upon it by the closest inspection. There was the direction, which was admitted to be in Caldigate's handwriting,–the postage-stamp, with its obliterating lines,–and the impression of the Sydney postmark. That was nearly all. The paper of the envelope had no water-marks. Bagwax thought that if he could get hold of the envelope itself something might be done even with that; but here Sir John could not go along with him, as it had been fully acknowledged that the envelope had passed from the possession of Caldigate into the hands of the woman bearing the written address. If anything could be done, it must be done by the postmarks,–and those postmarks Bagwax studied morning, noon, and night.

It had now been decided that Bagwax was to be sent out to Sydney at the expense of the Caldigates. There had been difficulty as to leave of absence for such a purpose. The man having been convicted, the Postmaster-General was bound to regard him as guilty, and hesitated to allow a clerk to be absent so long on behalf of a man who was already in prison. But the Secretary of State overruled this scruple, and the leave was to be given. Bagwax was elate,–first and chiefly because he trusted that he would become the means of putting right a foul and cruel wrong. For in these days Bagwax almost wept over the hardships inflicted on that poor lady at Folking. But he was elated also by the prospect of his travels, and by the godsend of a six months' leave of absence. He was a little proud, too, at having had this personal attention paid to him by the Secretary of State. All this was very gratifying. But that which gratified him was not so charming to his brother clerks. They had never enjoyed the privilege of leaving that weary office for six months. They were not allowed to occupy themselves in contemplating an envelope. They were never specially mentioned by the Secretary of State. Of course there was a little envy, and a somewhat general feeling that Bagwax, having got to the weak side of Sir John Joram, was succeeding in having himself sent out as a first-class overland passenger to Sydney, merely as a job. Paris to be seen, and the tunnel, and the railways through Italy, and the Suez Canal,—all these places, not delightful to the wives of Indian officers coming home or going out, were an Elysium to the post-office mind. His expenses to be paid for six months on the most gentleman-like footing, and his salary going on all the time! Official human nature, good as it generally is, cannot learn that such glories are to be showered on one not specially deserving head without something akin to enmity. The general idea, therefore, in the office, was that Bagwax would do no good in Sydney, that others would have been better than Bagwax,—in fact, that of all the clerks in all the departments, Bagwax was the very last man who ought to have been selected for an enterprise demanding secrecy, discretion, and some judicial severity.

Curlydown and Bagwax occupied the same room at the office in St. Martin's-le-Grand; and there it was their fate in life to arrange, inspect, and generally attend to those apparently unintelligible hieroglyphics with which the outside coverings of our correspondence are generally bedaubed. Curlydown's hair had fallen from his head, and his face had become puckered with wrinkles, through anxiety to make these markings legible and intelligible. The popular newspaper, the popular member of Parliament, and the popular novelist,—the name of Charles Dickens will of course present itself to the reader who remembers the Circumlocution office,—have had it impressed on their several minds,—and have endeavoured to impress the same idea on the minds of the public generally,—that the normal Government clerk is quite indifferent to his work. No greater mistake was ever made, or one showing less observation of human nature. It is the nature of a man to appreciate his own work. The felon who is made simply to move shot, perishes because he knows his work is without aim. The fault lies on the other side. The policeman is ambitious of arresting everybody. The lawyer would rather make your will for you gratis than let you make your own. The General can believe in nothing but in well-trained troops. Curlydown would willingly have expended the whole net revenue of the post-office,—and his own,—in improving the machinery for stamping letters. But he had hardly succeeded in life. He had done his duty, and was respected by all. He lived comfortably in a suburban cottage with a garden, having some private means, and had brought up a happy family in prosperity;—but he had done nothing new. Bagwax, who was twenty years his junior, had with manifest effects, added a happy drop of turpentine to the stamping-oil,—and in doing so had broken Curlydown's heart. The 'Bagwax Stamping Mixture' had absolutely achieved a name, which was printed on the official list of stores. Curlydown's mind was vacillating between the New River and a pension,—between death in the breach and acknowledged defeat,—when a new interest was lent to his life by the Caldigate envelope. It was he who had been first sent by the Postmaster-General to Sir John Joram's chambers. But the matter had become too large for himself alone, and in an ill-fated hour Bagwax had been consulted. Now Bagwax was to be sent to Sydney,— almost with the appointments of a lawyer!

They still occupied the same room,—a fact which infinitely increased the torments of Curlydown's position. They ought to have been moved very far asunder. Curlydown was still engaged in the routine ordinary work of the day, seeing that the proper changes were made in all the stamps used during the various hours of the day,—assuring himself that the crosses and letters and figures upon which so much of the civilisation of Europe depended, were properly altered and arranged. And it may well be that his own labours were made heavier by the devotion of his colleagues to other matters. And yet from time to time Bagwax would ask him questions, never indeed taking his advice, but still demanding his assistance. Curlydown was not naturally a man cf ill-temper or an angry heart. But there were moments in which he could hardly abstain from expressing himself with animosity.

On a certain morning in August, Bagwax was seated at his table, which as usual was laden with the envelopes of many letters. There were some hundreds before him, the marks on which he was perusing with a strong magnifying-glass. It had been arranged that he was to start on his great journey in the first week in September, and he employed his time before he went in scanning all the envelopes bearing the Sydney post-mark which he had been able to procure in England. He spent the entire day with a magnifying-glass in his hand;—but as Curlydown was also always armed in the same fashion, that was not peculiar. They did much of their work with such tools.

The date on the envelope,—the date conveyed by the impression, to which so much attention had been given,—was 10th May, 1873. Bagwax had succeeded in getting covers bearing dates very close to that. The

7th of May had been among his treasures for some time, and now he had acquired an entire letter, envelope and all, which bore the Sydney impression of the 13th May. This was a great triumph. 'I have brought it within a week,' he said to Curlydown, bending down over his glass, and inspecting at the same time the two dates.

'What's the good of that?' asked Curlydown, as he passed rapidly under his own glass the stamps which it was his duty to inspect from day to day.

'All the good in the world,' said Bagwax, brandishing his own magnifier with energy. 'It is almost conclusive.' Now the argument with Bagwax was this,—that if he found in the Sydney post-marks of 7th May, and in those of 13th May, the same deviations or bruises in the die, those deviations must have existed also on the days between these two dates;—and as the impression before him was quite perfect, without any deviation, did it not follow that it must have been obtained in some manner outside the ordinary course of business?

'There are a dozen stamps in use at the Sydney office,' said Curlydown.

'Perhaps so; or, at any rate, three or four. But I can trace as well as possible the times at which new stamps were supplied. Look here.' Then he threw himself over the multitude of envelopes, all of which had been carefully arranged as to dates, and began to point out the periods. 'Here, you see, in 1873, there is nothing that quite tallies with the Caldigate letter. I have measured them to the twentieth part of an inch, and I am sure that early in May '73 there was not a stamp in use in the Sydney office which could have made that impression. I have eighteen Mays '73, and not one of them could have been made by the stamp that did this.' As he spoke thus, he rapped his finger down on the copy of the sacred envelope which he was using. 'Is not that conclusive?'

'If it was not conclusive to keep a man from going to prison,' said Curlydown, remembering the failure of his own examination, 'it will not be conclusive to get him out again.'

'There I differ. No doubt further evidence is necessary, and therefore I must go to Sydney.'

'If it is conclusive, I don't see why you should go to Sydney at all. If your proof is so perfect, why should that fellow be kept in prison while you are running about the world?'

This idea had also occurred to Bagwax, and he had thought whether it would be possible for him to be magnanimous enough to perfect his proof in England, so as to get a pardon from the Secretary of State at once, to his own manifest injury. 'What would satisfy you and me,' said Bagwax, 'wouldn't satisfy the ignorant.' To the conductor of an

348

omnibus on the Surrey side of the river, the man who does not know what 'The Castle' means is ignorant. The outsider who is in a mist as to the 'former question,' or 'the order of the day,' is ignorant to the member of Parliament. To have no definite date conveyed by the term 'Rogation Sunday' is to the clerical mind gross ignorance. The horsey man thinks you have been in bed all your life if the 'near side' is not as descriptive to you as 'the left hand.' To Bagwax and Curlydown, not to distinguish post-marks was to be ignorant. 'I fear it wouldn't satisfy the ignorant,' said Bagwax, thinking of his projected journey to Sydney.

'Proof is proof,' said Curlydown. 'I don't think you'll ever get him out. The time has gone by. But you may do just as much here as there.'

'I'm sure we shall get him out. I'll never rest in my bed till we have got him out.'

'Mr. Justice Bramber won't mind whether you rest in your bed or not,—nor yet the Secretary of State.'

'Sir John Joram—' began Bagwax. In these discussions Sir John Joram was always his main staff.

'Sir John Joram has got other fish to fry before this time. It's a marvel to me, Bagwax, that they should give way to all this nonsense. If anything could be done, it could be done in half the time,—and if anything could be done, it could be done here. By the time you're back from Sydney, Caldigate's time will be half out. Why don't you let Sir John see your proof? You don't want to lose your trip, I suppose.'

Caldigate was languishing in prison, and that poor, nameless lady was separated from her husband, and he had the proof lying there on the table before him,—sufficient proof, as he did in his heart believe! But how often does it fall to the lot of a post-office clerk to be taken round the world free of expense? The way Curlydown put it was ill-natured and full of envy. Bagwax was well aware that Curlydown was instigated solely by envy. But still, these were his own convictions,—and Bagwax was in truth a soft-hearted, conscientious man.

'I do think it ought to be enough for any Secretary of State,' said he, 'and I'll go to Sir John Joram tomorrow. Of course, I should like to see the world;—who wouldn't? But I'd rather be the means of restoring that fellow to his poor wife, than be sent to all the four quarters of the globe with a guinea a-day for personal expenses.' In this way he nobly made up his mind to go at once to Sir John Joram.

CHAPTER XLVIII

Sir John Joram's Chambers

MR. CURLYDOWN'S insinuations had been very cruel, but also very powerful. Bagwax, as he considered the matter that night in his bed, did conscientiously think that a discreet and humane Secretary of State would let the unfortunate husband out of prison on the evidence which he (Bagwax) had already collected. My readers will not perhaps agree with him. The finding of a jury and the sentence of a judge must be regarded seriously by Secretaries of State, and it is probable that Bagwax's theory would not make itself clear to that great functionary. A good many 'ifs' were necessary. If the woman claiming Caldigate as her husband would swear falsely to anything in that matter, then she would swear falsely to everything. If this envelope had never passed through the Sydney post-office, then she would have sworn falsely about the letter,—and therefore her evidence would have been altogether false. If this postmark had not been made in the due course of business, and on the date as now seen, then the envelope had not passed regularly through the Sydney office. So far it was all clear to the mind of Bagwax, and almost clear that the postmark could not have been made on the date it bore. The result for which he was striving with true faith had taken such a hold of his mind, he was so adverse to the Smith-Crinkett interest, and so generously anxious for John Caldigate and the poor lady at Folking, that he could not see obstacles;—he could not even clearly see the very obstacles which made his own going to Sydney seem to others to be necessary. And yet he longed to go to Sydney with all his heart. He would be almost broken-hearted if he were robbed of that delight.

In this frame of mind he packed all his envelopes carefully into a large hand-bag, and started in a cab for Sir John Joram's chambers. 'Where are you going with them now?' Curlydown asked, somewhat disdainfully, just as Bagwax was starting. Curlydown had taken upon himself of late to ridicule the envelopes, and had become almost an anti-Caldigate. Bagwax vouchsafed to make him no reply. On the previous afternoon he had declared his purpose of going at once to Sir John, and had written, as Curlydown well knew, a letter to Sir John's clerk to make an appointment. Sir John was known to be in town though it was the end of August, being a laborious man who contented himself with a little partridge-shooting by way of holiday. It had been understood that he was to see Bagwax before his departure. All this had been known to Curlydown, and the question had been asked only to exasperate. There was a sarcasm in the 'now' which determined Bagwax to start without a word of reply.

As he went down to the Temple in the cab he turned over in his mind a great question which often troubles many of us. How far was he bound to sacrifice himself for the benefit of others? He had done his duty zealously in this matter, and now was under orders to continue the work in a manner which opened up to him a whole paradise of happiness. How grand was this opportunity of seeing something of the world beyond St. Martin's-le-Grand! And then the pecuniary gain would be so great! Hitherto he had received no pay for what he had done. He was a simple post-office clerk, and was paid for his time by the Crown,— very moderately. On this projected journey all his expenses would be paid for him, and still he would have his salary. Sir John Joram had declared the journey to be quite necessary. The Secretary of State had probably not occupied his mind much with the matter; but in the mind of Bagwax there was a fixed idea that the Secretary thought of little else, and that the Secretary had declared that his hands were tied till Bagwax should have been to Sydney. But his conscience told him that the journey was not necessary, and that the delay would be cruel. In that cab Bagwax made up his mind that he would do his duty like an honest man.

Sir John's chambers in Pump Court were gloomy without, though commodious and ample within. Bagwax was now well known to the clerk, and was received almost as a friend. 'I think I've got it all as clear as running water, Mr. Jones,' he said, feeling no doubt that Sir John's clerk, Mr. Jones, must feel that interest in the case which pervaded his mind.

'That will be a good thing for the gentleman in prison, Mr. Bagwax.'

'And for the lady; poor lady! I don't know whether I don't think almost more of her than of him.' Mr. Jones was returning to his work, having sent in word to Sir John of this visitor's arrival. But Bagwax was too full of his subject, and of his own honesty, for that. 'I don't think that I need go out after all, Mr. Jones.'

'Oh indeed!'

'Of course it will be a great sell for me.'

'Will it, now?'

'Sydney, I am told, is an Elysium upon earth.'

'It's much the same as Botany Bay; isn't it?' asked Jones.

'Oh, not at all; quite a different place. I was reading a book the other day which said Sydney harbour is the most beautiful thing God

351

ever made on the face of the globe.'

'I know there used to be convicts there,' said Mr. Jones, very positively.

'Perhaps they had a few once, but never many. They have oranges there, and a Parliament almost as good as our own, and a beautiful new post-office. But I shan't have to go, Mr. Jones. Of course, a man has to do his duty.'

'Some do, and more don't. That's as far as I see, Mr. Bagwax.'

'I'm all for Nelson's motto, Mr. Jones,—"England expects that every man this day shall do his duty." ' In repeating these memorable words Bagwax raised his voice.

'Sir John don't like to hear anything through the partition, Mr. Bagwax.'

'I beg pardon. But whenever I think of that glorious observation I am apt to become a little excited. It'll go a long way, Mr. Jones, in keeping a man straight if he'll only say it to himself often enough.'

'But not to roar it out in an eminent barrister's chambers. He didn't hear you, I daresay; only I thought I'd just caution you.'

'Quite right, Mr. Jones. Now I mean to do mine. I think we can get the party out of prison without any journey to Sydney at all; and I'm not going to stand in the way of it. I have devoted myself to this case and I'm not going to let my own interest stand in the way. Mr. Jones, let a man be ever so humble, England does expect—that he'll do his duty.'

'By George, he'll hear you, Mr. Bagwax;—he will indeed.' But at that moment Sir John's bell was rung, and Bagwax was summoned into the great man's room. Sir John was sitting at a large office-table so completely covered with papers that a whole chaos of legal atoms seemed to have been deposited there by the fortuitous operation of ages. Bagwax, who had his large bag in his hand, looked forlornly round the room for some freer and more fitting board on which he might expose his documents. But there was none. There were bookshelves filled with books, and a large sofa which was covered also with papers, and another table laden with what seemed to be a concrete chaos,—whereas the chaos in front of Sir John was a chaos in solution. Sir John liked Bagwax, though he was generally opposed to zealous co-operators. There was in the man a mixture of intelligence and absurdity, of real feeling and affectation, of genuine humility as to himself personally and of thorough confidence in himself post-officially, which had gratified Sir John; and Sir John had been quite sure that the post-office clerk had intended to speak the absolute truth, with an honest, manly conviction in the innocence of his client, and in the guilt of the witnesses on the other side. He was therefore well disposed towards Bagwax. 'Well, Mr. Bagwax,' he said; 'so I understand you have got a little further in the matter since I saw you last.'

'A good deal further, Sir John.'

'As how? Perhaps you can explain it shortly.'

This was troublesome. Bagwax did not think that he could explain the matter very shortly. He could not explain the matter at all without showing his envelopes; and how was he to show them in the present condition of that room? He immediately dived into his bag and brought forth the first bundle of envelopes. 'Perhaps, Sir John, I had better put them out upon the floor,' he said.

'Must I see all those?'

There were many more bundles within which Bagwax was anxious that the barrister should examine minutely. 'It is very important, Sir John. It is indeed. It is really altogether a case of postmarks,—altogether. We have never in our branch had anything so interesting before. If we can show that that envelope certainly was not stamped with that post-mark in the Sydney post-office on the 10th May 1873, then we shall get him out,—shan't we?'

'It will be very material, Mr. Bagwax,' said Sir John, cautiously.

'They will all have sworn falsely, and then somebody must have obtained the postmark surreptitiously. There must have been a regular plant. The stamp must have been made up and dated on purpose,—so as to give a false date. Some official in the Sydney post-office must have been employed.'

'That's what we want you to find out over there,' said Sir John, who was not quite so zealous, perhaps not quite so conscientious, as his more humble assistant,—whose mind was more occupied with other matters. 'You'll find out all that at Sydney.'

The temptation was very great. Sir John wanted him to go,—told him that he ought to go! Sir John was the man responsible for the whole matter. He, Bagwax, had done his best. Could it be right for him to provoke Sir John by contesting the matter,—contesting it so much to his own disadvantage? Had he not done enough for honesty?—enough to satisfy even that grand idea of duty? As he turned the bundle of documents round in his hand, he made up his mind that he had not done enough. There was a little gurgle in his throat, almost a tear in his eye, as he replied, 'I don't think I should be wanted to go if you would look at these envelopes.'

Sir John understood it all at once,—and there was much to understand. He knew how anxious the man was to go on this projected journey, and he perceived the cause which was inducing him to surrender his own interests. He remembered that the journey must be made at a great expense to his own client. He ran over the case in his mind, and acknowledged to himself that conclusive evidence,—evidence that should be quite conclusive,—of fraud as to the envelope, might possibly suffice to release his client at once from prison. He told himself also that he could not dare to express an opinion on the matter himself without a close inspection of those postmarks,—that a close inspection might probably take two hours, and that the two hours would finally have to be abstracted from the already curtailed period of his nightly slumbers. Then he thought of the state of his tables, and of the difficulties as to space. Perhaps that idea was the one strongest in his mind against the examination.

But then what a hero was Bagwax! What self-abnegation was there! Should he be less ready to devote himself to his client,—he, who was paid for his work,—then this post-office clerk, who was as pure in his honesty as he was zealous in the cause? 'There are a great many of them, I suppose?' he said, almost whining.

'A good many, Sir John.'

'Have at it!' said the Queen's Counsel and late Attorney-General, springing up from his chair. Bagwax almost jumped out of the way, so startled was he by the quick and sudden movement. Sir John rang his bell; but not waiting for the clerk, began to hurl the chaos in solution on to the top of the concrete chaos. Bagwax naturally attempted to assist him. 'For G—'s sake, don't you touch them!' said Sir John, as though avenging himself by a touch of scorn for the evil thing which was being done to him. Then Jones hurried into the room, and with more careful hands assisted his master, trying to preserve some order with the disturbed papers. In this way the large office-table was within three minutes made clear for the Bagwaxian strategy. Mr. Jones declared afterwards that it was seven years since he had seen the entire top of that table. 'Now go ahead!' said Sir John, who seemed, during the operation, to have lost something of his ordinary dignity.

Bagwax, who since that little check had been standing perfectly still, with his open bag in his hands, at once began his work. The plain before him was immense, and he was able to marshall all his forces. In the centre, and nearest to Sir John, as he sat in his usual chair, were exposed all the Mays '73. For it was thus that he denominated the envelopes with which he was so familiar. There were 71's, and 72's, and 74's, and 75's. But the 73's were all arranged in months, and then in days. He began by explaining that he had obtained all these envelopes 'promiscuously,' as he said. There had been no selection, none had been rejected. Then courteously handing his official magnifying-glass to the barrister, he invited him to inspect them all generally,—to make, as it were, a first cursory inspection,—so that he might see that there was not one perfect impression, perfect as that impression on the Caldigate envelope was perfect. 'Not one,' said Bagwax, beating his bosom in triumph.

'That seems perfect,' said Sir John, pointing with the glass to a selected specimen.

'Your eyes are very good, Sir John,—very good indeed. You have found the cleanest and truest of the whole lot. But if you'll examine the tail of the Y, you'll see it's been rubbed a little. And then if you'll follow with your eye the circular line which makes up the round of the postmark, you'll find a dent on the outside bar. I go more on the dents in those bars, Sir John, than I do on the figures. All the bars are dented more or less,—particularly the Mays '73. They don't remain quite true, Sir John,—not after a day's fair use. They've taken a new stamp out of the store to do the Caldigate envelope. They couldn't get at the stamps in use. That's how it has been.'

Sir John listened in silence as he continued to examine one envelope after another through the glass. 'Now, Sir John, if we come to the Mays '73, we shall find that just about that time there has been no new stamp brought into use. There isn't one, either, that is exactly the Caldigate breadth. I've brought a rule by which you can get to the fiftieth of an inch.' Here Bagwax brought out a little ivory instrument marked all over with figures. 'Of course they're intended to be of the same pattern. But gradually, very gradually, the circle has always become smaller. Isn't that conclusive? The Caldigate impression is a little, very little—ever so little—but a little smaller than any of the Mays '73. Isn't that conclusive?'

'If I understand it, Mr. Bagwax, you don't pretend to say that you have got impressions of all the stamps which may have been in use in the Sydney office at that time? But in Sydney, if I understand the matter rightly, they keep daily impressions of all the stamps in a book.'

'Just so—just so, Sir John,' said Bagwax, feeling that every word spoken to the lawyer renewed his own hopes of going out to Sydney,— but feeling also that Sir John would be wrong, very wrong, if he subjected his client to so unnecessarily prolonged a detention in the Cambridge county prison. 'They do keep a book which would be quite conclusive. I could have the pages photographed.'

'Would not that be best? and you might probably find out who it was who gave this fraudulent aid.'

'I could find out everything,' said Bagwax, energetically; 'but—'
'But what?'

'It is all found out there. It is indeed, Sir John. If I could get you to go along with me, you would see that that letter couldn't have gone through the Sydney post-office.'

'I think I do see it. But it is so difficult, Mr. Bagwax, to make others see things.'

'And if it didn't,—and it never did;—but if it didn't, why did they say it did? Why did they swear it did? Isn't that enough to make any Secretary let him go?'

The energy, the zeal, the true faith of the man, were admirable. Sir John was half disposed to rise from his seat to embrace the man, and hail him as his brother,—only that had he done so he would have made himself as ridiculous as Bagwax. Zeal is always ridiculous. 'I think I see it all,' he said.

'And won't they let the man go?'

'There were four persons who swore positively that they were present at the marriage, one of them being the woman who is said to have been married. That is direct evidence. With all our search, we have hitherto found no one to give us any direct evidence to rebut this. Then they brought forward, to corroborate these statements, a certain amount of circumstantial evidence,—and among other things this letter."

'The Caldigate envelope,' said Bagwax, eagerly.

'What you call the Caldigate envelope. It was unnecessary, perhaps; and, if fraudulent, certainly foolish. They would have had their verdict without it.'

'But they did it,' said Bagwax in a tone of triumph.

'It is a pity, Mr. Bagwax, you were not brought up to our profession. You would have made a great lawyer.'

'Oh, Sir John!'

'Yes, they did it. And if it can be proved that they have done it fraudulently, no doubt that fraud will stain their direct evidence. But we have to remember that the verdict has been already obtained. We are not struggling now with a jury, but with an impassive emblem of sovereign justice.'

'And therefore the real facts will go the further, Sir John.'

'Well argued, Mr. Bagwax,—admirably well argued. If you should ever be called, I hope I may not have you against me very often. But I will think of it all. You can take the envelopes away with you because you have impressed me vividly with all that they can tell me. My present impression is, that you had better take the journey. But within the next few days I will give a little more thought to it, and you shall hear from me.' Then he put out his hand, which was a courtesy

Mr. Bagwax had never before enjoyed. 'You may believe me, Mr. Bagwax, when I say that I have come across many remarkable men in many cases which have fallen into my hands,—but that I have rarely encountered a man whom I have more thoroughly respected than I do you.'

Mr. Bagwax went away to his own lodgings exulting,—but more then ever resolved that the journey to Sydney was unnecessary. As usual, he spent a large portion of that afternoon in contemplating the envelopes; and then, as he was doing so, another idea struck him,—an idea which made him tear his hairs with disgust because it had not occurred to him before. There was now opened to him a new scope of inquiry, an altogether different matter of evidence. But the idea was by far too important to be brought in and explained at the fag-end of a chapter.

CHAPTER XLIX

All The Shands

THERE had been something almost approaching to exultation at Babington when the tidings of Caldigate's alleged Australian wife were first heard there. As the anger had been great that Julia should be rejected, so had the family congratulation been almost triumphant when the danger which had been escaped was appreciated. There had been something of the same feeling at Pollington among the Shands— who had no doubt allowed themselves to think that Maria had been ill-treated by John Caldigate. He ought to have married Maria,—at least such was the opinion of the ladies of the family, who were greatly impressed with the importance of the little book which had been carried away. But in regard to the Australian marriage, they had differed among themselves. That Maria should have escaped the terrible doom which had befallen Mrs. Bolton's daughter, was, of course, a source of comfort. But Maria herself would never believe the evil story. John Caldigate had not been——well, perhaps not quite true to her. So much she acknowledged gently with the germ of a tear in her eye. But she was quite sure that he would not have married Hester Bolton while another wife was living in Australia. She arose almost to enthusiasm as she vindicated his character from so base a stain. He had been, perhaps, a little unstable in his affections,—as men are so commonly. But not even when the jury found their verdict, could she be got to believe that the John Caldigate whom she had known would have betrayed a girl whom he loved as he was supposed to have betrayed Hester Bolton. The mother and sisters, who knew the softness of Maria's disposition,—and who had been more angry than their sister with the man who had been wicked enough to carry away Thomson's 'Seasons' in his portmanteau without marrying the girl who had put it there,—would not agree to this. The verdict, at any rate, was a verdict. John Caldigate was in prison. The poor young woman with her infant was a nameless, unfortunate creature. All this might have happened to their Maria. 'I should always have believed him innocent,' said Maria, wiping away the germ of the tear with her knuckle.

The matter was very often discussed in the doctor's house at Pollington,—as it was, indeed, by the public generally, and especially in the eastern counties. But in this house there a double interest attached to it. In the first place, there was Maria's escape,—which the younger

358

girls were accustomed to talk of as having been 'almost miraculous,' and then there was Dick's absolute disappearance. It had been declared at the trial, on behalf of Caldigate, that if Dick could have been put into the witness-box, he would have been able to swear that there had been no such marriage ceremony as that which the four witnesses had elaborately described. On the other hand, the woman and Crinkett had sworn boldly that Dick Shand, though not present at the marriage, had been well aware that it had taken place, and that Dick, could his evidence have been secured, would certainly have been a witness on their side. He had been outside the tent,—so said the woman,—when the marriage was being performed, and had refused to enter, by way of showing his continued hostility to an arrangement which he had always opposed. But when the woman said this, it was known that Dick Shand would not appear, and the opinion was general that Dick had died in his poverty and distress. Men who sink to be shepherds in Australia because they are noted drunkards, generally do die. The constrained abstinence of perhaps six months in the wilderness is agonising at first, and nearly fatal. Then the poor wretch rushes to the joys of any orgy with ten or fifteen pounds in his pocket; and the stuff which is given to him as brandy soon puts an end to his sufferings. There was but little doubt that such had been the fate of Dick,—unless, perhaps, in the bosom of Maria and of his mother.

It was known too at Pollington, as well as elsewhere, in the month of August, that efforts were still to be made with the view of upsetting the verdict. Something had crept out to the public as to the researches made by Bagwax, and allusions had been frequent as to the unfortunate absence of Dick Shand. The betting, had there been betting, would no doubt have been in favour of the verdict. The four witnesses had told their tale in a straightforward way; and though they were, from their characters, not entitled to perfect credit, still their evidence had in no wise been shaken. They were mean, dishonest folk, no doubt. They had taken Caldigate's money, and had still gone on with the prosecution. Even if there had been some sort of a marriage, the woman should have taken herself off when she had received her money, and left poor Hester to enjoy her happiness, her husband, and her home at Folking. That was the general feeling. But it was hardly thought that Bagwax, with his envelope, would prevail over Judge Bramber in the mind of the Secretary of State. Probably there had been a marriage. But it was singular that the two men who could have given unimpeachable evidence on the matter should both have vanished out of the world; Allan, the minister, —and Dick Shand, the miner and shepherd.

'What will she do when he comes out?' Maria asked. Mrs. Rewble,—

Harriet,—the curate's wife, was there. Mr. Rewble, as curate, found it convenient to make frequent visits to his father-in-law's house. And Mrs. Posttlethwaite,—Matilda,—was with them, as Mr. Posttlethwaite's business in the soap line caused him to live at Pollington. And there were two unmarried sisters, Fanny and Jane. Mrs. Rewble was by this time quite the matron, and Mrs. Posttlethwaite was also the happy mother of children. But Maria was still Maria. Fanny already had a string to her bow,—and Jane was expectant of many strings.

'She ought to go back to her father and mother, of course,' said Mrs. Rewble, indignantly.

'I know I wouldn't,' said Jane.

'You know nothing about it, miss, and you ought not to speak of such a thing,' said the curate's wife. Jane at this made a grimace which was intended to be seen only by her sister Fanny.

'It is very hard that two loving hearts should be divided,' said Maria.

'I never thought so much of John Caldigate as you did,' said Mrs. Posttlethwaite. 'He seems to have been able to love a good many young women all at the same time.'

'It's like tasting a lot of cheeses, till you get the one that suits you,' said Jane. This offended the elder sister so grievously that she declared she did not know what their mother was about, to allow such liberty to the girls, and then suggested that the conversation should be changed.

'I'm sure I did not say anything wrong,' said Jane, 'and I suppose it is like that. A gentleman has to find out whom he likes best. And as he liked Miss Bolton best, I think it's a thousand pities they should be parted.'

'Ten thousand pities!' said Maria enthusiastically.

'Particularly as there is a baby,' said Jane,—upon which Mrs. Rewble was again very angry.

'If Dick were to come home, he'd clear it all up at once,' said Mrs. Posttlethwaite.

'Dick will never come home,' said Matilda mournfully.

'Never!' said Mrs. Rewble. 'I am afraid that he has expiated all his indiscretions. It should make us who were born girls thankful that we have not been subjected to the same temptations.'

'I should like to be a man all the same,' said Jane.

'You do not at all know what you are saying,' replied the monitor. 'How little have you realized what poor Dick must have suffered! I wonder when they are going to let us have tea. I'm almost famished.' Mrs. Rewble was known in the family for having a good appetite. They were sitting at this moment round a table on the lawn, at which they intended to partake of their evening meal. The doctor might or might not join them. Mrs. Shand, who did not like the open air, would have hers sent to her in the drawing-room. Mr. Rewble would certainly be there. Mr. Posttlethwaite, who had been home to his dinner, had gone back to the soapworks. 'Don't you think, Jane, if you were to go in, you could hurry them?' Then Jane went in and hurried the servant.

'There's a strange man with papa,' said Jane, as she returned.

'There are always strange men with papa,' said Fanny. 'I daresay he has come to have his tooth out.' For the doctor's practice was altogether general. From a baby to a back-tooth, he attended to everything now, as he had done forty years ago.

'But this man isn't like a patient. The door was half open, and I saw papa holding him by both hands.

'A lunatic!' exclaimed Mrs. Rewble, thinking that Mr. Rewble ought to be sent at once to her father's assistance.

'He was quite quiet, and just for a moment I could see papa's face. It wasn't a patient at all. Oh, Maria!'

'What is it child?' asked Mrs. Rewble.

'I do believe that Dick has come back.'

They all jumped from their seats suddenly. Then Mrs. Rewble re-seated herself. 'Jane is such a fool!' she said.

'I do believe it,' said Jane. 'He had yellow trousers on, as if he had come from a long way off. And I'm sure papa was very glad,—why should he take both his hands?'

'I feel as though my legs were sinking under me,' said Maria.

'I don't think it possible for a moment,' said Mrs. Rewble. 'Maria, you are so romantic! You would believe anything.'

'It is possible.' said Mrs. Posttlethwaite.

'If you will remain here, I will go into the house and inquire,' said Mrs. Rewble. But it did not suit the others to remain there. For a moment the suggestion had been so awful that they had not dared to stir; but when the elder sister slowly moved towards the door which led into the house from the garden, they all followed her. Then suddenly they heard a scream, which they knew to come from their mother. 'I believe it is Dick,' said Mrs. Rewble, standing in the doorway so as to detain the others. 'What ought we to do?'

'Let me go in,' said Jane, impetuously. 'He is my brother.'

Maria was already dissolved in tears. Mrs. Posttlethwaite was struck dumb by the awfulness of the occasion, and clung fast to her sister Harriet.

'It will be like one from the grave,' said Mrs. Rewble solemnly.

'Let me go in,' repeated Jane, impetuously. Then she pushed by her sisters, and was the first to enter the house. They all followed her into the hall, and there they found their mother supported in the arms of the man who wore the yellow trousers. Dick Shand had in truth returned to his father's house.

The first thing to do with a returned prodigal is to kiss him, and the next to feed him; and therefore Dick was led away at once to the table on the lawn. But he gave no sign of requiring the immediate slaughter of a fatted calf. Though he had not exactly the appearance of a well-to-do English gentleman, he did not seem to be in want. The yellow trousers were of strong material, and in good order, made of that colour for colonial use, probably with the idea of expressing some contempt for the dingy hues which prevail among the legs of men at home. He wore a very large checked waistcoat, and a stout square coat of the same material. There was no look of poverty, and no doubt he had that day eaten a substantial dinner; but the anxious mother was desirous of feeding him immediately, and whispered to Jane some instructions as to cold beef, which was to be added to the tea and toast.

As they examined him, holding him by the arms and hands, and gazing up into his face, the same idea occurred to all of them. Though they knew him very well now, they would hardly have known him had they met him suddenly in the streets. He seemed to have grown fifteen years older during the seven years of his absence. His face had become thin and long and almost hollow. His beard went all round under his chin, and was clipped into the appearance of a stiff thick hedge—equally thick, and equally broad, and equally protrusive at all parts. And within this enclosure it was shorn. But his mouth had sunk in, and his eyes. In colour he was almost darker than brown. You would have said that his skin had been tanned black, but for the infusion of red across it here and there. He seemed to be in good present health, but certainly bore the traces of many hardships. 'And here you are all just as I left you,' he said, counting up his sisters.

'Not exactly,' said Mrs. Rewble, remembering her family. 'And Matilda has got two.'

'Not husbands, I hope,' said Dick.

'Oh Dick! that is so like you,' said Jane, getting up and kissing him again in her delight. Then Mr. Rewble came forward, and the brothers-in-law renewed their old acquaintance.

'It seems just like the other day,' said Dick, looking round upon the rose-bushes.

'Oh my boy! my darling, darling boy!' said the mother, who had hurried up-stairs for her shawl, conscious of her rheumatism even amidst the excitement of her son's return. 'Oh, Dick! This is the happiest day of my life. Wouldn't you like something better than tea?' This she said with many memories and many thoughts; but still, with a mother's love, unable to refrain from offering what she thought her son would wish to have.

'There ain't anything better,' said Dick very solemnly.

'Nothing half so good to my thinking,' said Mrs. Rewble, imagining that by a word in season she might help the good work.

The mother's eyes were filled with tears, but she did not dare to speak a word. Then there was a silence for a few moments. 'Tell us all about it, Dick,' said the father. 'There's whisky inside if you like it.' Dick shook his head solemnly,—but, as they all thought, with a certain air of regret. 'Tell us what you have to say,' repeated the doctor.

'I'm sworn off these two years.'

'Touched nothing for two years?' said the mother exultingly, with her arms and shawl again round her son's neck.

'A teetotaller?' said Maria.

'Anything you like to call it. Only, what a gentleman's habits are in that respect needn't be made the subject of general remark.' It was evident he was a little sore, and Jane, therefore, offered him a dish full of gooseberries. He took the plate in his hand and ate them assiduously for a while in silence, as though unconscious of what he was doing. 'You know all about it now, don't you?'

'Oh my dearest boy!' ejaculated the mother.

'You didn't get better gooseberries than those on your travels,' said the doctor, calling him back to the condition of the world around him.

Then he told them of his adventures. For two terrible years he had been a shepherd on different sheep-runs in Queensland. Then he had found employment on a sugar plantation, and had superintended the work of a gang of South Sea Islanders,—Canakers they are called,—men who are brought into the colony from the islands of the Pacific,—and who return thence to their homes generally every three years, much to the regret of their employers. In the transit of these men agents are employed, and to this service Dick had, after a term, found himself promoted. Then it had come to pass that he had remained for a period on one of these islands, with the view of persuading the men to emigrate and re-emigrate; and had thus been resident among them for more than a couple of years. They had used him well, and he had liked the islands, —having lived in one of them without seeing another European for many months. Then the payments which had from time to time been made to him by the Queensland planters were stopped, and his business, such as it had been, came to an end. He had found himself with just sufficient money to bring him home; and here he was.

'My boy, my darling boy!' exclaimed his mother again, as though all their joint troubles were now over.

The doctor remembered the adage of the rolling stone, and felt that the return of a son at the age of thirty, without any means of maintaining himself, was hardly an unalloyed blessing. He was not the man to turn a son out of doors. He had always broadened his back to bear the full burden of his large family. But even at this moment he was a little melancholy as he thought of the difficulty of finding employment for the wearer of those yellow trousers. How was it possible that a man should continue to live an altogether idle life at Pollington and still remain a teetotaller? 'Have you any plans I can help you in now?' he asked.

'Of course he'll remain at home for a while before he thinks of anything,' said the mother.

'I suppose I must look about me,' said Dick. 'By-the-way, what has become of John Caldigate?'

They all at once gazed at each other. It could hardly be that he did not in truth know what had become of John Caldigate.

'Haven't you heard?' asked Maria.

'Of course he has heard,' said Mrs. Rewble.

'You must have heard,' said the mother.

'I don't know in the least what you are talking about. I have heard nothing at all.'

In very truth he had heard nothing of his old friend,—not even that he had returned to England. Then by degrees the whole story was told to him. 'I know that he was putting a lot of money together,' said Dick enviously. 'Married Hester Bolton? I thought he would! Bigamy! Euphemia Smith! Married before! Certainly not at the diggings.'

'He wasn't married up at Ahalala?' asked the doctor.

'To Euphemia Smith? I was there when they quarrelled, and when she went into partnership with Crinkett. I am sure there was no such marriage. John Caldigate in prison for bigamy? And he paid them twenty thousand pounds? The more fool he!'

'They all say that.'

'But it's an infernal plant. As sure as my name is Richard Shand, John Caldigate never married that woman.

CHAPTER L

Again At Sir John's Chambers

AND this was the man as to whom it had been acknowledged that his evidence, if it could be obtained, would be final. The return of Dick himself was to the Shands an affair so much more momentous than the release of John Caldigate from prison, that for some hours or so the latter subject was allowed to pass out of sight. The mother got him upstairs and asked after his linen,—vain inquiry,—and arranged for his bed, turning all the little Rewbles into one small room. In the long run, grandmothers are more tender to their grand-children than their own offspring. But at this moment Dick was predominant. How grand a thing to have her son returned to her, and such a son,—a teetotaller of two years' growth, who had seen all the world of the Pacific Ocean! As he could not take whisky-and-water, would he like ginger-beer before he went to bed,—or arrowroot? Dick decided in favour of ginger-beer, and consented to be embraced again.

It was, I think, to Maria's credit that she was the first to bring back the conversation to John Caldigate's marriage. 'Was she a very horrible woman?' Maria asked, referring to Euphemia Smith.

'There were a good many of 'em out there, greedy after gold,' said Dick; 'but she beat 'em all; and she was awfully clever.'

'In what way, Dick?' asked Mrs. Rewble. 'Because she does not seem to have done very well with herself.'

'She knew more about shares than any man of them all. But I think she just drank a little. It was that which disgusted Caldigate.'

'He had been very fond of her?' suggested Maria.

'I never knew a man so taken with a woman.' Maria blushed, and Mrs. Rewble looked round at her younger sisters as though desirous that they should be sent to bed. 'All that began on board the ship. Then he was fool enough to run after her down to Sydney; and of course she followed him up to the mines.'

'I don't know why of course,' said Mrs. Posttlethwaite, defending her sex generally.

'Well, she did. And he was going to marry her. He did mean to marry her;—there's no doubt of that. But it was a queer kind of life we lived up there.'

'I suppose so,' said the doctor. Mrs. Rewble again looked at the girls and then at her mother; but Mrs. Shand was older and less timid than

365

her married daughter. Mrs. Rewble when a girl herself had never been sent away, and was now a pattern of femal discretion.

'And she,' continued Dick, 'as soon as she had begun to finger the scrip, thought of nothing but gold. She did not care much for marriage just then, because she fancied the stuff wouldn't belong to herself. She became largely concerned in the "Old Stick-in-the-Mud." That was Crinkett's concern, and there were times at which I thought she would marry him. Then Caldigate got rid of her altogether. That was before I went away.'

'He never married her?' asked the doctor.

'He certainly hadn't married her when I left Nobble in June '73.'

'You can swear to that, Dick?'

'Certainly I can. I was with him every day. But there wasn't anyone round there who didn't know how it was. Crinkett himself knew it.'

'Crinkett is one of the gang against him.'

'And there was a man named Adamson. Adamson knew.'

'He's another of the conspirators,' said the doctor.

'They won't dare to say before me,' declared Dick, stoutly, 'that Mrs. Smith and John Caldigate had become man and wife before June '73. And they hated one another so much then that it is impossible they should have come together since. I can swear they were not married up to June '73.'

'You'll have to swear it,' said the doctor, 'and that with as little delay as possible.'

All this took place towards the end of August, about five weeks after the trial, and a day or two subsequent to the interview between Bagwax and the Attorney-General. Bagwax was now vehemently prosecuting his inquiries as to that other idea which had struck him, and was at this very moment glowing with the anticipation of success, and at the same time broken-hearted with the conviction that he never would see the pleasant things of New South Wales.

On the next morning, under the auspices of his father, Dick Shand wrote the following letter to Mr. Seely, the attorney.

'POLLINGTON, 30th August, 187–.

'Sir,—I think it right to tell you that I reached my father's house in this town late yesterday evening. I have come direct from one of the South Sea Islands *via* Honolulu and San Francisco, and have not yet been in England forty-eight hours. I am an old friend of Mr. John Caldigate, and went with him from England to the gold diggings in New South Wales. My name will be known to you, as I am now aware that it was frequently mentioned in the course of the late trial. It will probably seem odd to you that I had never even heard of the trial till I reached my father's house last night. I did not know that Caldigate had married Miss Bolton, nor that Euphemia Smith had claimed him as her husband.

'I am able and willing to swear that they had not become man and wife up to June 1873, and that no one at Ahalala or Nobble conceived them to be man and wife. Of course, they had lived together. But everybody knew all about it. Some time before June,—early, I should say, in that autumn,—there had been a quarrel. I am sure they were at daggers drawn with each other all that April and May in respect to certain mining shares, as to which Euphemia Smith behaved very badly. I don't think it possible that they should ever have come together again; but in May '73,—which is the date I have heard named,—they certainly were not man and wife.

'I have thought it right to inform you of this immediately on my return, and am, your obedient servant,

'RICHARD SHAND.'

Mr. Seely, when he received this letter, found it to be his duty to take it at once to Sir John Joram, up in London. He did not believe Dick Shand. But then he had put no trust in Bagwax, and had been from the first convinced, in his own mind, that Caldigate had married the woman. As soon as it was known to him that his client had paid twenty thousand pounds to Crinkett and the woman, he was quite sure of the guilt of his client. He had done the best for Caldigate at the trial, as he would have done for any other client; but he had never felt any of that enthusiasm which had instigated Sir John. Now that Caldigate was in prison, Mr. Seely thought that he might as well be left there quietly, trusting to the verdict, trusting to Judge Bramber, and trusting still more strongly on his own early impressions. This letter from Dick,—whom he knew to have been a ruined drunkard, a disgrace to his family, and an outcast from society,—was to his thinking just such a letter as would be got up in such a case, in the futile hope of securing the succour of a Secretary of State. He was sure that no Secretary of State would pay the slightest attention to such a letter. But still it would be necessary that he should show it to Sir John, and as a trip to London was not disagreeable to his professional mind, he started with it on the very day of its receipt.

'Of course we must have his deposition on oath,' said Sir John.

'You think it will be worth while?'

'Certainly. I am more convinced than ever that there was no marriage. That post-office clerk has been with me,—Bagwax,—and has altogether convinced me.'

'I didn't think so much of Bagwax, Sir John.'

'I dare say not, Mr. Seely;—an absurdly energetic man,—one of those who destroy by their over-zeal all the credit which their truth and energy ought to produce. But he has, I think, convinced me that that letter could not have passed through the Sydney post-office in May '73.'

'If so, Sir John, even that is not much,—towards upsetting a verdict.'

'A good deal, I think, when the characters of the persons are considered. Now comes this man, whom we all should have believed, had he been present, and tells this story. You had better get hold of him and bring him to me, Mr. Seely.'

Then Mr. Seely hung up his hat in London for three or four days, and sent to Pollington for Dick Shand. Dick Shand obeyed the order, and both of them waited together upon Sir John. 'You have come back at a very critical point of time for your friend,' said the barrister.

Dick had laid aside the coat and waistcoat with the broad checks, and the yellow trousers, and had made himself look as much like an English gentleman as the assistance of a ready-made-clothes shop at Pollington would permit. But still he did not quite look like a man who had spent three years at Cambridge. His experiences among the gold diggings, then his period of maddening desolation as a Queensland shepherd, and after that his life among the savages in a South Sea island, had done much to change him. Sir John and Mr. Seely together almost oppressed him. But still he was minded to speak up for his friend. Caldigate had, upon the whole, been very good to him, and Dick was honest. 'He has been badly used any way,' he said.

'You have had no intercourse with any of his friends since you have been home, I think?' This question Sir John asked because Mr. Seely had suggested that this appearance of the man at this special moment might not improbably be what he called a 'plant'.

'I have had no intercourse with anybody, sir. I came here last Friday, and I hadn't spoken a word to anybody before that. I didn't know that Caldigate had been in trouble at all. My people at Pollington were the first to tell me about it.'

'Then you wrote to Mr. Seely? You have heard of Mr. Seely?'

'The governor,—that's my father,—he had heard of Mr. Seely. I wrote first as he told me. They knew all about it at Pollington as well as you do.'

'You were surprised then, when you heard the story?'

'Knocked off my pins, sir. I never was so much taken aback in my life. To be told that John Caldigate had married Euphemia Smith after all that I had seen,—and that he had been married to her in May '73! I knew of course that it was all a got-up thing. And he's in prison?'

'He is in prison, certainly.'

'For bigamy?'

'Indeed he is, Mr. Shand.'

'And how about his real wife?'

'His real wife, as you call her——'

'She is, as sure as my name is Richard Shand.'

'It is on behalf of that lady that we are almost more anxious than for Mr. Caldigate himself. In this matter she has been perfectly innocent; and whoever may have been the culprit,—or culprits,—she has been cruelly ill-used.'

'She'll have her husband back again, of course,' said Dick.

'That will depend in part upon what faith the judge who tried the case may place in your story. Your deposition shall be taken, and it will be my duty to submit it to the Secretary of State. He will probably be actuated by the weight which this further evidence will have upon the judge who heard the former evidence. You will understand, Mr. Shand, that your word will be opposed to the words of four other persons.'

'Four perjured scoundrels,' said Dick, with energy.

'Just so,—if your story be true.'

'It is true, sir,' said Dick, with much anger in his tone.

'I hope so,—with all my heart. You are on the same side with us, you know. I only want to make you understand how much ground there may be for doubt. It is not easy to upset a verdict. And, I fear, many righteous verdicts would be upset if the testimony of one man could do it. Perhaps you will be able to prove that you only arrived at Liverpool on Saturday night.'

'Certainly I can.'

'You cannot prove that you had not heard of the case before.'

'Certainly I can. I can swear it.' Sir John smiled. 'They all knew that at Pollington. They told me of it. The governor told me about Mr. Seely and made me write the letter.'

'That would not be evidence,' said Sir John.

'Heavens on earth! I tell you I was struck all on a heap when I heard it, just as much as if they had said he'd been hung for murder. You put Crinkett and me together and then you'll know. I suppose you think somebody's paying me for this,—that I've got a regular tip.'

'Not at all, Mr. Shand. And I quite understand that it should be difficult for you to understand. When a man sees a thing clearly himself he cannot always realise the fact that others do not see it also. I think I perceive what you have to tell us, and we are very much obliged to you for coming forward so immediately. Perhaps you would not mind sitting in the other room for five minutes while I say a word to Mr. Seely.'

'I can go away altogether.'

'Mr. Seely will be glad to see you again with reference to the deposition you will have to make. You shall not be kept waiting long.' Then Dick returned, with a sore heart, feeling half inclined to blaze out in wrath against the great advocate. He had come forward to tell a plain story, having nothing to gain, paying his railway fare and other expenses out of his own—or rather out of his father's pocket, and was told he would not be believed! It is always hard to make an honest witness understand that it may be the duty of others to believe him to be a liar, and Dick Shand did not understand it now.

'There was no Australian marriage,' Sir John said as soon as he was alone with Mr. Seely.

'You think not?'

'My mind is clear about it. We must get that man out, if it be only for the sake of the lady.'

'It is so very easy, Sir John, to have a story like that made up.'

'I have had to do with a good many made-up stories, Mr. Seely;—and with a good many true stories.'

'Of course, Sir John;—no man with more.'

'He might be a party to making up a story. There is nothing that I have seen in him to make me sure that he could not come forward with a determined perjury. I shouldn't think it, but it would be possible. But his father and mother and sisters wouldn't join him.' Dick had told the story of the meeting on the lawn at great length. 'And had it been a plot, he couldn't have imposed upon them. He wouldn't have brought them into it. And who would have got at him to arrange the plot?'

'Old Caldigate.'

Sir John shook his head. 'Neither old Caldigate nor young Caldigate knew anything of that kind of work. And then his story tallies altogether with my hero Bagwax. Of Bagwax I am quite sure. And as Shand corroborates Bagwax, I am nearly sure of him also. You must take his deposition, and let me have it. It should be rather full, as it may be necessary to hear the depositions also of the doctor and his wife. We shall have to get him out.'

'You know best, Sir John.'

'We shall have to get him out, Mr. Seely, I think,' said Sir John, rising from his chair. Then Mr. Seely took his leave, as was intended.

Mr. Seely was not at all convinced. He was quite willing that John Caldigate should be released from prison, and that the Australian marriage should be so put out of general credit in England as to allow the young people to live in comfort at Folking as man and wife. But he liked to feel that he knew better himself. He would have been quite content that Mrs. John Caldigate should be Mrs. John Caldigate to all the world,

—that all the world should be imposed on,—so that he was made subject to no imposition. In this matter, Sir John appeared to him to be no wider awake than a mere layman. It was clear to Mr. Seely that Dick Shand's story was 'got up,'—and very well got up. He had no pang of conscience as to using it. But when it came to believing it, that was quite another thing. The man turning up exactly at the moment! And such a man! And then his pretending never to have heard of a case so famous! Never to have heard this story of his most intimate friend! And then his notorious poverty! Old Caldigate would of course be able to buy such a man. And then Sir John's fatuity as to Bagwax! He could hardly bring himself to believe that Sir John was quite in earnest. But he was well aware that Sir John would know,—no one better,—by what arguments such a verdict as had been given might be practically set aside. The verdict would remain. But a pardon, if a pardon could be got from the Secretary of State, would make the condition of the husband and wife the same as though there had been no verdict. The indignities which they had already suffered would simply produce for them the affectionate commendation of all England. Mr. Seely felt all that, and was not at all averse to a pardon. He was not at all disposed to be severe on Caldigate senior if, as he thought, Caldigate senior had bribed this convenient new witness. But it was too much to expect that he should believe it all himself.

'You must come with me, Mr. Shand,' he said, 'and we must take your story down in writing. Then you must swear to it before a magistrate.'

'All right, Mr. Seely.'

'We must be very particular, you know.'

'I needn't be particular at all;—and as to what Sir John Joram said, I felt half inclined to punch his head.'

'That wouldn't have helped us.'

'It was only that I thought of Caldigate in prison that I didn't do it. Because I have been roaming about the world, not always quite as well off as himself, he tells me that he doesn't believe my word.'

'I don't think he said that.'

'He didn't quite dare; but what he said was as bad. He told me that some one else wouldn't believe it. I don't quite understand what it is they're not to believe. All I say is, that they two were not married in May '73.'

'But about your never having heard of the case till you got home?'

'I never had heard a word about it. One would think I had done something wrong in coming forward to tell what I know.' The deposition, however, was drawn out in due form, at considerable length, and was properly attested before one of the London magistrates.

CHAPTER LI

Dick Shand Goes To Cambridgeshire

THE news of Shand's return was soon common in Cambridge. The tidings, of course, were told to Mr. Caldigate, and were then made known by him to Hester. The old man, though he turned the matter much in his mind,—doubting whether the hopes thus raised would not add to Hester's sorrow should they not ultimately be realised,—decided that he could not keep her in the dark. Her belief could not be changed by any statement which Shand might make. Her faith was so strong that no evidence could shake it,—or confirm it. But there would, no doubt, arise in her mind a hope of liberation if any new evidence against the Australian marriage were to reach her; which hope might so probably be delusive! But he knew her to be strong to endure as well as strong to hope, and therefore he told her at once. Then Mr. Seely returned to Cambridge, and all the facts of Shand's deposition were made known at Folking. 'That will get him out at once, of course,' said Hester, triumphantly, as soon as she heard it. But the Squire was older and more cautious, and still doubted. He explained that Dick Shand was not a man who by his simple word would certainly convince a Secretary of State:—that deceit might be suspected;—that a fraudulent plot would be possible; and that very much care was necessary before a convicted prisoner would be released.

'I am quite sure, from Mr. Seely's manner, that he thinks I have bribed the young man,' said Caldigate.

'You!'

'Yes;—I. These are the ideas which naturally come into people's heads. I am not in the least angry with Mr. Seely, and feel that it is only too likely that the Secretary of State and the judge will think the same. If I were Secretary of State I should have to think so.'

'I couldn't suspect people like that.'

'And therefore, my dear, you are hardly fit to be Secretary of State. We must not be too sanguine. That is all.'

But Hester was very sanguine. When it was fully known that Dick had written to Mr. Seely immediately on his arrival at Pollington, and that he had shown himself to be a warm partisan in the Caldigate interests, she could not rest till she saw him herself, and persuaded Mr. Caldigate to invite him down to Folking. To Folking therefore he went, with the full intention of declaring John Caldigate's innocence, not only there, but all through Cambridgeshire. The Boltons, of whom he had now heard something, should be made to know what an honest man had to say on the subject,—an honest man, and who was really on the spot at the time. To Dick's mind it was marvellous that the Boltons should have been anxious to secure a verdict against Caldigate,—which verdict was also against their own daughter and their own sister. Being quite sure himself that Caldigate was innocent, he could not understand the condition of feeling which would be produced by an equally strong conviction of his guilt. Nor was his mind, probably, imbued with much of that religious scruple which made the idea of a feigned marriage so insupportable to all Hester's relations. Nor was he aware that when a man has taken a preconception home to himself, and fastened it and fixed it, as it were, into his bosom, he cannot easily expel it,—even though personal interest should be on the side of such expulsion. It had become a settled belief with the Boltons that John Caldigate was a bigamist, which belief had certainly been strengthened by the pertinacious hostility of Hester's mother. Dick had heard something of all this, and thought that he would be able to open their eyes.

When he arrived at Folking he was received with open arms. Sir John Joram had not quite liked him, because his manner had been rough. Mr. Seely had regarded him from the first as a ruined man, and therefore a willing perjurer. Even at Pollington his 'bush' manners had been a little distasteful to all except his mother. Mr. Caldigate felt some difficulty in making conversation with him. But to Hester he was as an angel from heaven. She was never tired of hearing from him every detail as to her husband's life at Ahalala and Nobble,—particularly as to his life after Euphemia Smith had taken herself to those parts and had quarrelled with him. The fact of the early infatuation had been acknowledged on all sides. Hester was able to refer to that as a mother, boasting of her child's health, may refer to the measles,—which have been bad and are past and gone. Euphemia Smith had been her husband's measles. Men generally have the measles. That was a thing so completely acknowledged, that it was not now the source of discomfort. And the disease had been very bad with him. So bad that he had talked of marriage,—had promised marriage. Crafty women do get hold of innocent men, and drive them sometimes into perdition,—often to the brink of perdition. That was Hester's theory as to her husband. He had been on the brink, but had been wise in time. That was her creed, and as it was supported by Dick, she found no fault with Dick's manner,—not even with the yellow trousers which were brought into use at Folking.

'You were with him on that very day,' she said. This referred to the day in April on which it had been sworn that the marriage was solemnized.

374

'I was with him every day about that time. I can't say about particular days. The truth is,—I don't mind telling you, Mrs. Caldigate,—I was drinking a good deal just then.' His present state of abstinence had of course become known at Folking, not without the expression of much marvel on the part of the old Squire as to the quantity of tea which their visitor was able to swallow. And as this abstinence had of course been admired, Dick had fallen into a way of confessing his past back-slidings to a pretty, sympathetic, friendly woman, who was willing to believe all that he said, and to make much of him.

'But I suppose——' Then she hesitated; and Dick understood the hesitation.

'I was never so bad,' said he, 'but what I knew very well what was going on. I don't believe Caldigate and Mrs. Smith even so much as spoke to each other all that month. She had had a wonderful turn of luck.'

'In getting gold?'

'She had bought and sold shares till she was supposed to have made a pot of money. People up there got an idea that she was one of the lucky ones,—and it did seem so. Then she got it into her head that she didn't want Caldigate to know about her money, and he was downright sick of her. She had been good-looking at one time, Mrs. Caldigate.'

'I daresay. Most of them are so, I suppose.'

'And clever. She'd talk the hind-legs off a dog, as we used to say out there.'

'You had very odd sayings, Mr. Shand.'

'Indeed we had. But when she got in that way about her money, and then took to drinking brandy, Caldigate was only too glad to be rid of her. Crinkett believed in her because she had such a run of luck. She held a lot of his shares,—shares that used to be his. So they got together, and she left Ahalala and went to Polyeuka Hall. I remember it all as if it were yesterday. When I broke away from Caldigate in June, and went to Queensland, they hadn't seen each other for two months. And as for having been married;—you might as well tell me that I had married her!'

If Mr. Caldigate had ever allowed a shade of doubt to cross his mind as to his son's story, Dick Shand's further story removed it. The picture of the life which was led at Ahalala and Nobble was painted for him clearly, so that he could see, or fancy that he saw, what the condition of things had been. And this increased faith trickled through to others. Mr. Bromley, who had always believed, believed more firmly than before, and sent tidings of his belief to Plum-cum-Pippins, and thence to Babington. Mr. Holt, the farmer, became more than ever energetic, and in a loud voice at a Cambridge market ordinary, declared the ill-usage done to Caldigate and his young wife. It had been said over and over again at the trial that Dick Shand's evidence was the one thing wanted, and here was Dick Shand to give his evidence. Then the belief gained ground in Cambridge; and with the belief there arose a feeling as to the egregious wrong which was being done.

But the Boltons were still assured. None of them had as yet given any sign of yielding. Robert Bolton knew very well that Shand was at Folking, but had not asked to see him. He and Mr. Seely were on different sides, and could not discuss the matter; but their ideas were the same. It was incredible to Robert that Dick Shand should appear just at this moment, unless as part of an arranged plan. He could not read the whole plot; but was sure that there was a plot. It was held in his mind as a certain fact, that John Caldigate would not have paid away that large sum of money had he not thought that by doing so he was buying off Crinkett and the other witnesses. Of course there had been a marriage in Australia, and therefore the arrival of Dick Shand was to him only a lifting of the curtain for another act of the play. An attempt was to be made to get Caldigate out of prison, which attempt it was his duty to oppose. Caldigate had, he thought, deceived and inflicted a terrible stain on his family; and therefore Caldigate was an enemy upon whom it behoved him to be revenged. This feeling was the stronger in his bosom, because Caldigate had been brought into the family by him.

But when Dick Shand called upon him at his office, he would not deny himself. 'I have been told by some people that, as I am here in the neighbourhood, I ought to come and speak to you,' said Dick. The 'some people' had been, in the first instance, Mr. Ralph Holt, the farmer. But Dick had discussed the matter with Mr. Bromley, and Mr. Bromley had thought that Shand's story should be told direct to Hester's brother.

'If you have anything to say, Mr. Shand, I am ready to hear it.'

'All this about a marriage at Ahalala between John Caldigate and Mrs. Smith is a got-up plan, Mr. Bolton.'

'The jury did not seem to think so, Mr. Shand.'

'I wasn't here then to let them know the truth.' Robert Bolton raised his eyebrows, marvelling at the simplicity of the man who could fancy that his single word would be able to weigh down the weight of evidence which had sufficed to persuade twelve men and such a judge as Judge Bramber. 'I was with Caldigate all the time, and I'm sure of what I'm saying. The two weren't on speaking terms when they were said to be married.'

'Of course, Mr. Shand, as you have come to me, I will hear what you may have to say. But what is the use of it? The man has been tried and found guilty.'

'They can let him out again if he's innocent.'

'The Queen can pardon him, no doubt,—but even the Queen cannot quash the conviction. The evidence was as clear as noonday. The judge and the jury and the public were all in one mind.'

'But I wasn't here, then,' said Dick Shand with perfect confidence. Robert Bolton could only look at him and raise his eyebrows. He could not tell him to his face that no unprejudiced person would believe the evidence of such a witness. 'He's your brother-in-law,' said Dick, 'and I supposed you'd be glad to know that he was innocent.'

'I can't go into that question, Mr. Shand. As I believe him to have been guilty of as wicked a crime as any man can well commit, I cannot concern myself in asking for a pardon for him. My own impression is that he should have been sent to penal servitude.'

'By George!' exclaimed Dick. 'I tell you that it is all a lie from beginning to end.'

'I fear we cannot do any good by talking about it, Mr. Shand.'

'By George!' Dick hitched up his yellow trousers as though he were preparing for a fight. He wore his yellow trousers without braces, and in all moments of energy hitched them up.

'If you please I will say good morning to you.'

'By George! when I tell you that I was there all the time, and that Caldigate never spoke to the woman, or so much as saw her all that month, and that therefore your own sister is in honest truth Caldigate's wife, you won't listen to me! Do you mean to say that I'm lying?'

'Mr. Shand, I must ask you to leave my office.'

,By George! I wish I had you, Mr. Bolton, out at Ahalala, where there are not quite so many policemen as there are here at Cambridge.'

'I shall have to send for one of them if you don't go away, Mr. Shand.'

'Here's a man who, even for the sake of his own sister, won't hear the truth, just because he hates his sister's husband! What have I got to get by lying?'

'That I cannot tell.' Bolton, as he said this, prepared himself for a sudden attack; but Shand had sense enough to know that he would injure the cause in which he was interested, as well as himself, by any exhibition of violence, and therefore left the office.

'No,' said Mr. Bromley, when all this was told him; 'he is not a cruel man, nor dishonest, nor even untrue to his sister. But having quite made up his mind that Caldigate had been married in Australia, he cannot release himself from the idea. And, as he thinks so, he feels it to be his duty to keep his sister and Caldigate apart.'

'But why does he not believe me?' demanded Dick.

'In answer to that, I can only say that I do believe you.'

Then there came a request from Babington that Dick Shand would go over to them there for a day. At Babington opinion was divided. Aunt Polly and her eldest daughter, and with them Mr. Smirkie, still thought that John Caldigate was a wicked bigamist; but the Squire and the rest of the family had gradually gone over to the other side. The Squire had never been hot against the offender, having been one of those who fancied that a marriage at a very out-of-the-way place such as Ahalala did not signify much. And now when he heard of Dick Shand's return and proffered evidence, he declared that Dick Shand having been born a gentleman, though he had been ever so much a sinner, and ever so much a drunkard, was entitled to credence before a host of Crinketts. But with Aunt Polly and Julia there remained the sense of the old injury, robbing Shand of all his attributes of birth, and endowing even Crinkett with truth. Then there had been a few words, and the Squire had asserted himself, and insisted upon asking Shand to Babington.

'Did you ever see such trousers?' said Julia to her mother. 'I would not believe him on his oath.'

'Certainly not,' said Mr. Smirkie, who of the three was by far the most vehement in his adherence to the verdict. 'The man is a notorious drunkard. And he has that look of wildness which bad characters always bring with them from the colonies.'

'He didn't drink anything but water at lunch,' said one of the younger girls.

'They never do when they're eating,' said Mr. Smirkie. For the great teetotal triumph had not as yet been made known to the family at Babington. 'These regular drunkards take it at all times by themselves, in their own rooms. He has delirium tremens in his face. I don't believe a word that he says.'

'He certainly does wear the oddest trousers I ever saw,' said Aunt Polly.

At the same time Dick himself was closeted with the Squire, and was convincing him that there had been no Australian marriage at all. 'They didn't jump over a broomstick, or anything of that kind?' asked the Squire, intending to be jocose.

'They did nothing at all,' said Dick, who had worked himself up to a state of great earnestness. 'Caldigate wouldn't as much as look at her at that time;—and then to come home here and find him in prison because he had married her! How any one should have believed it!'

'They did believe it. The women here believe it now, as you perceive'.

'It's an awful shame, Mr. Babington. Think of her, Mr. Babington.

It's harder on her even than him, for he was,—well, fond of the woman once.'

'It is hard. But we must do what we can to get him out. I'll write to our member. Sir George supports the Government, and I'll get him to see the Secretary. It is hard upon a young fellow just when he has got married and come into a nice property.'

'And her, Mr. Babington!'

'Very bad, indeed. I'll see Sir George myself. The odd part of it is, the Boltons are all against him. Old Bolton never quite liked the marriage, and his wife is a regular Tartar.'

Thus the Squire was gained, and the younger daughter. But Mr. Smirkie was as obdurate as ever. Something of his ground was cut from under his feet when Dick's peculiar habits were observed at dinner. Mr. Smirkie did indeed cling to his doctrine that your real drunkard never drinks at his meals; but when Dick, on being pressed in regard to wine, apologised by saying that he had become so used to tea in the colonies as not to be able to take anything else at dinner, the peculiarity was discussed till he was driven to own that he had drank nothing stronger for the last two years. Then it became plain that delirium tremens was not written on his face quite so plainly as Mr. Smirkie had at first thought, and there was nothing left but his trousers to condemn him. But Mr. Smirkie was still confident. 'I don't think you can go beyond the verdict,' he said. 'There may be a pardon, of course;—though I shall never believe it till I see it. But though there were twenty pardons she ought not to go back to him. The pardon does not alter the crime,— and whether he was married in Australia, or whether he was not, she ought to think that he was, because the jury has said so. If she had any feeling of feminine propriety she would shut herself up and call herself Miss Bolton.

'I don't agree with you in the least,' said the Squire; 'and I hope I may live to see a dozen little Caldigates running about on that lawn.'

And there were a few words upstairs on the subject between Mr. Smirkie and his wife—for even Mrs. Smirkie and Aunt Polly at last submitted themselves to Dick's energy. 'Indeed, then, if he comes out,' said the wife, 'I shall be very glad to see him at Plum-cum-Pippins.' This was said in a voice which did not admit of contradiction, and was evidence at any rate that Dick's visit to Babington had been successful in spite of the yellow trousers.

CHAPTER LII

The Fortunes Of Bagwax

AN altogether new idea had occurred to Bagwax as he sat in his office after his interview with Sir John Joram;—and it was an idea of such a nature that he thought that he saw his way quite plain to a complete manifestation of the innocence of Caldigate, to a certainty of a pardon, and to an immediate end of the whole complication. By a sudden glance at the evidence his eye had caught an object which in all his glances he had never before observed. Then at once he went to work, and finding that certain little marks were distinctly legible, he became on a sudden violently hot,—so that the sweat broke out on his forehead. Here was the whole thing disclosed at once,—disclosed to all the world if he chose to disclose it. But if he did so, then there could not be any need for that journey to Sydney, which Sir John still thought to be expedient. And this thing which he had now seen was not one within his own branch of work,—was not a matter with which he was bound to be conversant. Somebody else ought to have found it out. His own knowledge was purely accidental. There would be no disgrace to him in not finding it out. But he had found it out.

Bagwax was a man who, in his official zeal and official capacity, had exercised his intellect far beyond the matters to which he was bound to apply himself in the mere performance of his duties. Post-marks were his business; and had he given all his mind to post-marks, he would have sufficiently carried out that great doctrine of doing the duty which England expects from every man. But he had travelled beyond post-marks, and had looked into many things. Among other matters he had looked into penny stamps, twopenny stamps, and other stamps. In post-office phraseology there is sometimes a confusion because the affixed effigy of her Majesty's head, which represents the postage paid, is called a stamp, and the post-marks or impressions indicating the names of towns are also called stamps. Those postmarks or impressions had been the work of Bagwax's life; but his zeal, his joy in his office, and the general energy of his disposition, had opened up to him also all the mysteries of the queen's heads. That stamp, that effigy, that twopenny queen's-head, which by its presence on the corner of the envelope purported to have been the price of conveying the letter from Sydney to Nobble, on 10th May, 1873, had certainly been manufactured and sent out to the colony since that date!

There are signs invisible to ordinary eyes which are plain as the sun at noonday to the initiated. It is so in all arts, in all sciences. Bagwax was at once sure of his fact. To his instructed gaze the little receipt for twopence was as clearly dated as though the figures were written on it. And yet he had never looked at it before. In the absorbing interest which the post-mark had created,—that fraudulent postmark, as it certainly was,—he had never condescended to examine the postage-stamp. But now he saw and was certain.

If it was so,—and he had no doubt,—then would Caldigate surely be released. It is hoped that the reader will follow the mind of Bagwax, which was in this matter very clear. This envelope had been brought up at the trial as evidence that, on a certain day, Caldigate had written to the woman as his wife, and had sent the letter through the post-office. For such sending the postage-stamp was necessary. The postage-stamp had certainly been put on when the envelope was prepared for its intended purpose. But if it could be proved by the stamp itself that it had not been in existence on the date impressed on the envelope, then the fraud would be quite apparent. And if there had been such fraud, then would the testimony of all those four witnesses be crushed into arrant perjury. They had produced the fraudulent document, and by it would be thoroughly condemned. There could be no necessity for a journey to Sydney.

As it all became clear to his mind, he thumped his table partly in triumph,—partly in despair. 'What's the matter with you now?' said Mr. Curlydown. It was a quarter past four, and Curlydown had not completed his daily inspections. Had Bagwax been doing his proper share of work, Curlydown would have already washed his hands and changed his coat, and have been ready to start for the 4.30 train. As it was, he had an hour of labour before him, and would be unable to count the plums upon his wall, as was usual with him before dinner.

'It becomes more wonderful every day,' said Bagwax, solemnly,— almost awfully.

'It is very wonderful to me that a man should be able to sit so many hours looking at one dirty bit of paper.'

'Every moment that I pass with that envelope before my eyes I see the innocent husband in jail, and the poor afflicted wife weeping in her solitude.'

'You'll be going on to the stage, Bagwax, before this is done.'

'I have sometimes thought that it was the career for which I was best adapted. But, as to the envelope, the facts are now certain.'

'Any new facts?' asked Curlydown. But he asked the question in a jeering tone, not at all as though desiring confidence or offering sympathy.

'Yes,' replied Bagwax, slowly. 'The facts are certainly new,—and most convincing; but as you have not given attention to the particular branch concerned, there can be no good in my mentioning them. You would not understand me.' It was thus that he revenged himself on Curlydown. Then there was again silence between them for a quarter of an hour, during which Curlydown was hurrying through his work, and Bagwax was meditating whether it was certainly his duty to make known the facts as to the postage-stamp. 'You are so unkind,' said Bagwax at last, in a tone of injured friendship, burning to tell his new discovery.

'You have got it all your way,' said Curlydown, without lifting his head. 'And then, as you said just now,—I don't understand.'

'I'd tell you everything if you'd only be a little less hard.'

Curlydown was envious. He had, of course, been told of the civil things which Sir John Joram had said; and though he did not quite believe all, he was convinced that Bagwax was supposed to have distinguished himself. If there was anything to be known he would like to know it. Nor was he naturally quarrelsome. Bagwax was his old friend. 'I don't mean to be hard,' he said. 'Of course one does feel oneself fretted when one has been obliged to miss two trains.'

'Can I lend a hand?' said Bagwax.

'It doesn't signify now. I can't catch anything before the 5.20. One does expect to get away a little earlier than that on a Saturday. What is it that you've found out?'

'Do you really care to know?'

'Of course I do,—if it's anything in earnest. I took quite as much interest as you in the matter when we were down at Cambridge.'

'You see that postage-stamp?' Bagwax stretched out the envelope,—or rather the photograph of the envelope, for it was no more. But the Queen's head, with all its obliterating smudges, and all its marks and peculiarities, was to be seen quite as plainly as on the original, which was tied up carefully among the archives of the trial. 'You see that postage-stamp?' Curlydown took his glass, and looked at the document, and declared that he saw the postage-stamp very plainly.

'But it does not tell you anything particular?'

'Nothing very particular—at the first glance,' said Curlydown, gazing through the glass with all his eyes.

'Look again.'

'I see that they obliterate out there with a kind of star.'

'That has nothing to do with it.'

'The bunch of hair at the back of the head isn't quite like our bunch of hair.'

'Just the same;—taken from the same die,' said Bagwax.

'The little holes for dividing the stamps are bigger.'

'It isn't that.'

'Then what the d— is it?'

'There are letters at every corner,' said Bagwax.

'That's of course,' said Curlydown.

'Can you read those letters?' Curlydown owned that he never had quite understood what those letters meant. 'Those two P's in the two bottom corners tell me that that stamp wasn't printed before '74. It was all explained to me not long ago. Now the postmark is dated '73.' There was an air of triumph about Bagwax as he said this which almost drove Curlydown back to hostility. But he checked himself, merely shaking his head, and continued to look at the stamp. 'What do you think of that?' asked Bagwax.

'You'd have to prove it.'

'Of course I should. But the stamps are made here and are sent out to the colony. I shall see Smithers at the stamp-office on Monday of course.' Mr. Smithers was a gentleman concerned in the manufacture of stamps. 'But I know my facts. I am as well aware of the meaning of those letters as though I had made postage-stamps my own peculiar duty. Now what ought I to do?'

'You wouldn't have to go, I suppose?'

'Not a foot.'

'And yet it ought to be found out how that date got there.' And Curlydown put his finger upon the impression—10th May, 1873.

'Not a doubt about it. I should do a deal of good by going if they'd give me proper authority to overhaul everything in the office out there. They had the letter stamped fraudulently;—fraudulently, Mr. Curlydown! Perhaps if I stayed at home to give evidence, they'd send you to Sydney to find all that out.'

There was a courtesy in this suggestion which induced Curlydown to ask his junior to come down and take pot-luck at Apricot Villa. Bagwax was delighted, for his heart had been sore at the coolness which had grown up between him and the man under whose wing he had worked for so many years. He had been devoted to Curlydown till growing ambition had taught him to think himself able to strike out a line for himself. Mr. Curlydown had two daughters, of whom the younger, Jemima, had found much favour in the eyes of Bagwax. But since the jealousy had sprung up between the two men he had never seen Jemima, nor tasted the fruits of Curlydown's garden. Mrs. Curlydown, who approved of Bagwax, had been angry, and Jemima herself had become sullen and unloving to her father. On that very morning Mrs. Curlydown had declared that she hated quarrels like poison. 'So do I, mamma,' said Jemima, breaking her silence emphatically. 'Not that Mr. Bagwax is anything to anybody.'

'That does look like something,' said Curlydown, whispering to his friend in the railway carriage. They were sitting opposite to each other, with their knees together,—and were of course discussing the envelope.

'It is everything. When they were making up their case in Australia, and when the woman brought out the cover with his writing upon it, with the very name, Mrs. Caldigate, written by himself,—Crinkett wasn't contented with that. So they put their heads together, and said that if the letter could be got to look like a posted letter,—a letter sent regularly by the post,—that would be real evidence. The idea wasn't bad.'

'Nothing has ever been considered better evidence than post-marks,' said Curlydown, with authority.

'It was a good idea. Then they had to get a postage-stamp. They little knew how they might put their foot into it there. And they got hold of some young man at the post-office who knew how to fix a date-stamp with a past date. How these things become clear when one looks at them long enough!'

'Only one has to have an eye in one's head.'

'Yes,' said Bagwax, as modestly as he could at such a moment. 'A fellow has to have his wits about him before he can do anything out of the common way in any line. You'd tell Sir John everything at once;— wouldn't you?' Curlydown raised his hat and scratched his head. 'Duty first, you know. Duty first,' said Bagwax.

'In a man's own line,—yes,' said Curlydown. 'Somebody else ought to have found that out. That's not post-office. It's stamps and taxes. It's very hard that a man should have to cut the nose off his own face by knowing more than he need know.'

'Duty! Duty!' said Bagwax as he opened the carriage-door and jumped out on to the platform.

When he got up to the cottage, Mrs. Curlydown assured him that it was quite a cure for sore eyes to see him. Sophia, the elder of the two daughters at home, told him that he was a false truant; and Jemima surmised that the great attractions of the London season had prevented him from coming down to Enfield. 'It isn't that, indeed,' he said. 'I am always delighted in running down. But the Caldigate affair has been so important!'

'You mean the trial,' said Mrs. Curlydown. 'But the man has been in prison ever so long.'

'Unjustly! Most unjustly!'

'Is it so, really?' asked Jemima. 'And the poor young bride?'

'Not so much of a bride,' said Sophia. 'She's got one, I know.'

'And papa says you're to go out to Botany Bay,' said Jemima. 'It'll be years and years before you are back again.' Then he explained it was not Botany Bay, and he would be back in six months. And, after all, he wasn't going at all. 'Well, I declare, if papa isn't down the walk already,' said Jemima, looking out of the window.

'I don't think I shall go at all,' said Bagwax in a melancholy tone as he went up-stairs to wash his hands.

The dinner was very pleasant; and as Curlydown and his guest drank their bottle of port together at the open window, it was definitely settled that Bagwax should reveal the mystery of the postage-stamp to Sir John Joram at once. 'I should have it like a lump of lead on my conscience all the time I was on the deep,' said Bagwax, solemnly.

'Conscience is conscience, to be sure,' said Curlydown.

'I don't think that I'm given to be afraid,' said Bagwax. 'The ocean, if I know myself, would have no terrors for me,—not if I was doing my duty. But I should hear the ship's sides cracking with every blast if that secret were lodged within my breast.'

'Take another glass of port, old boy.'

Bagwax did take another glass, finishing the bottle, and continued. 'Farewell to those smiling shores. Farewell Sydney, and all her charms. Farewell to her orange groves, her blue mountains, and her rich goldfields.'

'Take a drop of whitewash to wind up, and then we'll join the ladies.' Curlydown was a strictly hospitable man, and in his own house would not appear to take amiss anything his guest might say. But when Bagwax became too poetical over his wine, Curlydown waxed impatient. Bagwax took his drop of whitewash, and then hurried on to the lawn to join Jemima.

'And you really are not going to those distant parts?'

'No,' said Bagwax, with all that melancholy which wine and love combined with sorrow can produce. 'That dream is over.'

'I am so glad.'

'Why should you be glad? Why should a resolve which it almost breaks my heart to make be a source of joy to you?'

'Of course you would have nothing to regret at leaving, Mr. Bagwax.'

'Very much,—if I were going for ever. No;—I could never do that, unless I were to take some dear one with me. But as I said, that dream is over. It has ever been my desire to see foreign climes, and the chance so seldom comes in a man's way.'

'You've been to Ostend, I know, Mr. Bagwax.'

'Oh yes, and to Boulogne,' said Bagwax, proudly. 'But the desire of travel grows with the thing it feeds on. I long to overcome great distances,—to feel that I have put illimitable space behind me. To set my foot on shores divided from these by the thickness of all the earth would give me a sense of grandeur which I—which,—which,—would be magnificent.'

'I suppose that is natural in a man.'

'In some men,' said Bagwax, not liking to be told that his heroic instincts were shared by all his brethren.

'But women, of course, think of the dangers. Suppose you were to be cast away!'

'What matter? With a father of a family of course it would be different. But a lone man should never think of such things.' Jemima shook her head and walked silently by his side. 'If I had some dear one who cared for me I suppose it would be different with me.'

'I don't know,' said Jemima. 'Gentlemen like to amuse themselves sometimes, but it doesn't often go very deep.'

'Things always go deep with me,' said Bagwax. 'I panted for that journey to the Antipodes;—panted for it! Now that it is over, perhaps some day I may tell you under what circumstances it has been relinquished. In the meantime my mind passes to other things; or perhaps I should say my heart—Jemima!' Then Bagwax stopped on the path.

'Go on, Mr. Bagwax. Papa will be looking at you.'

'Jemima,' he said, 'will you recompense me by your love for what I have lost on the other side of the globe?' She recompensed him, and he was happy.

The future father and son-in-law sat and discussed their joint affairs for an hour after the ladies had retired. As to Jemima and his love, Bagwax was allowed to be altogether truimphant. Mrs. Curlydown kissed him, and he kissed Sophia. That was in public. What passed between him and Jemima no human eye saw. The old post-office clerk took the younger one to his heart, and declared that he was perfectly satisfied with his girl's choice. 'I've always known that you were steady,' he said, 'and that's what I look to. She has had her admirers, and perhaps might have looked higher; but what's rank or money if a man's fond of pleasure?' But when that was settled they returned again to the Caldigate envelope. Curlydown was not quite so sure as to that question of duty. The proposed journey to Sydney, with a pound a-day allowed for expenses, and the traveller's salary going on all the time, would put a nice sum of ready-money into Bagwax's pocket. 'It wouldn't be less than two hundred towards furnishing, my boy,' said Curlydown. 'You'll want it. And as for the delay, what's six months? Girls like to have a little time to boast about it.'

But Bagwax had made up his mind, and nothing would shake him.

'If they'll let me go out all the same, to set matters right, of course I'd take the job. I should think it a duty, and would bear the delay as well as I could. If Jemima thought it right I'm sure she wouldn't complain. But since I saw that letter on that stamp my conscience has told me that I must reveal it all. It might be me as was in prison, and Jemima who was told that I had a wife in Australia. Since I've looked at it in that light I've been more determined than ever to go to Sir John Joram's chambers on Monday. Good-night, Mr. Curlydown. I am very glad you asked me down to the cottage to-day; more glad than anything.'

At half-past eleven, by the last train, Bagwax returned to town, and spent the night with mingled dreams, in which Sydney, Jemima, and the envelope were all in their turns eluding him, and all in their turns within his grasp.

CHAPTER LIII

Sir John Backs His Opinion

'WELL, Mr. Bagwax, I'm glad that it's only one envelope this time.' This was said by Sir John Joram to the honest and energetic post-office clerk on the morning of Wednesday the 3rd September, when the lawyer would have been among the partridges down in Suffolk but for the vicissitudes of John Caldigate's case. It was hard upon Sir John, and went something against the grain with him. He was past the time of life at which men are enthusiastic as to the wrongs of others,—as was Bagwax; and had, in truth, much less to gain from the cause, or to expect, than Bagwax. He thought that the pertinacity of Bagwax, and the coming of Dick Shand at the moment of his holidays, were circumstances which justified the use of a little internal strong language,—such as he had occasionally used externally before he had become Attorney-General. In fact he had——damned Dick Shand and Bagwax, and in doing so had considered that Jones his clerk was internal. 'I wish he had gone to Sydney a month ago,' he said to Jones. But when Jones suggested that Bagwax might be sent to Sydney without further trouble, Sir John's conscience pricked him. Not to be able to shoot a Suffolk partridge on the 1st of September was very cruel, but to be detained wrongfully in Cambridge jail was worse; and he was of opinion that such cruelty had been inflicted on Caldigate. On the Saturday Dick Shand had been with him. He had remained in town on the Monday and Tuesday by agreement with Mr. Seely. Early on the Tuesday intimation was given to him that Bagwax would come on the Wednesday with further evidence,—with evidence which should be positively conclusive. Bagwax had, in the meantime, been with his friend Smithers at the stamp-office, and was now fully prepared. By the help of Smithers he had arrived at the fact that the postage-stamp had certainly been fabricated in 1874, some months after the date imprinted on the cover of the letter to which it was affixed.

'No, Sir John;—only one this time. We needn't move anything.' All the chaos had been restored to its normal place, and looked as though it had never been moved since it was collected.

'And we can prove that this queen's-head did not exist before the 1st January, 1874.'

'Here's the deposition,' said Bagwax, who, by his frequent intercourse with Mr. Jones, had become almost as good as a lawyer himself,

—'at least, it isn't a deposition, of course,—because it's not sworn.'

'A statement of what can be proved on oath.'

'Just that, Sir John. It's Mr. Smithers! Mr. Smithers has been at the work for the last twenty years. I knew it just as well as he from the first, because I attend to these sort of things; but I thought it best to go to the fountain-head.'

'Quite right.'

'Sir John will want to hear it from the fountain-head, I said to myself; and therefore I went to Smithers. Smithers is perhaps a little conceited, but his word is—gospel. In a matter of postage-stamps Smithers is gospel.'

Then Sir John read the statement and though he may not have taken it for gospel, still to him it was credible. 'It seems clear,' he said.

'Clear as the running stream,' said Bagwax.

'I should like to have all that gang up for perjury, Mr. Bagwax.'

'So should I, Sir John;—so should I. When I think of that poor dear lady and her infant babe without a name, and that young father torn from his paternal acres and cast into a vile prison, my blood boils within my veins, and all my passion to see foreign climes fades into the distance.'

'No foreign climes now, Mr. Bagwax.'

'I suppose not, Sir John,' said the hero, mournfully.

'Not if this be true.'

'It's gospel, Sir John;—gospel. They might send me out to set that office to rights. Things must be very wrong when they could get hold of a date-stamp and use it in that way. There must be one of the gang in the office.'

'A bribe did it, I should say.'

'I could find it out, Sir John. Let me alone for that. You could say that you have found me—quick-like, in this matter;—couldn't you, Sir John?' Bagwax was truly happy in the love of Jemima Curlydown; but the idea of earning two hundred pounds for furniture, and of seeing distant climes at the same time, had taken a strong hold of his imagination.

'I am afraid I should have no voice in the matter,—unless with the view of getting evidence.'

'And we've got that;—haven't we, Sir John?'

'I think so.'

'Duty, Sir John, duty!' said Bagwax, almost sobbing through his triumph.

'That's it, Mr. Bagwax.' Sir John too had given up his partridges,—for a day or two.

'And that gentleman will now be restored to his wife?'

'It isn't for me to say. As you and I have been engaged on the same side——'To be told that he had been on the same side with the late Attorney-General, was almost compensation to Bagwax for the loss of his journey. 'As you and I have been on the same side, I don't mind telling you that I think that he ought to be released. The matter remains with the Secretary of State, who will probably be guided by the judge who tried the case.'

'A stern man, Sir John.'

'Not soft-hearted, Mr. Bagwax,—but as conscientious a man as you'll be able to put your hand upon. The young wife with her nameless baby won't move him at all. But were he moved by such consideration, he would be so far unfit for his office.'

'Mercy is divine,' said Bagwax.

'And therefore unfit to be used by a merely human judge. You know, I suppose, that Richard Shand has come home?'

'No!'

'Indeed he has, and was with me a day or two since.'

'Can he say anything?' Bagwax was not rejoiced at Dick's opportune return. He thoroughly wished that Caldigate should be liberated, but he wished himself to monopolise the glory of the work.

'He says a great deal. He has sworn point-blank that there was no such marriage at the time named. He and Caldigate were living together then, and for some weeks afterwards, and the woman was never near them during the time.'

'To think of his coming just now!'

'It will be a great help, Mr. Bagwax; but it wouldn't be enough alone. He might possibly—tell an untruth.'

'Perjury on the other side, as it were.'

'Just that. But this little queen's-head here can't be untrue.'

'No, Sir John, no; that can't be,' said Bagwax, comforted; 'and the dated impression can't lie either. The envelope is what'll do it after all.'

'I hope so. You and Mr. Jones will prepare the statement for the Secretary of State, and I will send it myself.' With that Mr. Bagwax took his leave, and remained closeted with Mr. Jones for much of the remainder of the day.

The moment Sir John was alone he wrote an almost angry note to his friend Honybun, in conjunction with whom and another Member of Parliament he had the shooting in Suffolk. Honybun, who was also a lawyer, though less successful than his friend, was a much better shot, and was already taking the cream off the milk of the shooting. 'I cannot conceive,' he said at the end of his letter, 'that, after all my experience,

I should have put myself so much out of my way to serve a client. A man should do what he's paid to do, and what it is presumed that he will do, and nothing more. But here I have been instigated by an insane ambition to emulate the good-natured zeal of a fellow who is absolutely willing to sacrifice himself for the good of a stranger.' Then he went on to say that he could not leave London till the Friday.

On the Thursday morning he put all the details together, and himself drew out a paper for the perusal of the Secretary of State. As he looked at the matter all round, it seemed to him that the question was so clear that even Judge Bramber could not hesitate. The evidence of Dick Shand was quite conclusive,—if credible. It was open, of course, to strong doubt, in that it could not be sifted by cross-examination. Alone, it certainly would not have sufficed to extort a pardon from any Secretary of State,—as any Secretary of State would have been alive to the fact that Dick might have been suborned. Dick's life had not been such that his single word would have been regarded as certainly true. But in corroboration it was worth much. And then if the Secretary or the judge could be got to go into that very complicated question of the dated stamp, it would, Sir John thought, become evident to him that the impression had not been made at the time indicated. This had gradually been borne in upon Sir John's mind, till he was almost as confident in his facts as Bagwax himself. But this operation had required much time and much attention. Would the Secretary, or would the judge, clear his table, and give himself time to inspect and to measure two or three hundred post-marks? The date of the fabrication of the postage-stamp would of course require to be verified by official report;—but if the facts as stated by Bagwax were thus confirmed, then the fraudulent nature of the envelope would be put beyond doubt. It would be so manifest that this morsel of evidence had been falsely concocted, that no clear-headed man, let his prepossessions be what they might, could doubt it. Judge Bramber would no doubt begin to sift the case with a strong bias in favour of the jury. It was for a jury to ascertain the facts; and in this case the jury had done so. In his opinion,—in Judge Bramber's opinion, as the judge had often declared it,—a judge should not be required to determine facts. A new trial, were that possible, would be the proper remedy, if remedy were wanted; but as that was impossible, he would be driven to investigate such new evidence as was brought before him, and to pronounce what would, in truth, be another verdict. All this was clear to Sir John; and he told himself that even Judge Bramber would not be able to deny that false evidence had been submitted to the jury.

Sir John, as he occupied his mind with the matter on the Thursday morning, did wake himself up to some generous energy on his client's behalf,—so that in sending the written statements of the case to the Home Secretary, he himself wrote a short but strongly-worded note. 'As it is quite manifest,' he said, 'that a certain amount of false and fraudulent circumstantial evidence has been brought into court by the witnesses who proved the alleged marriage, and as direct evidence has now come to hand on the other side which is very clear, and as far as we know trustworthy, I feel myself justified in demanding her Majesty's pardon for my client.'

On the next day he went down to Birdseye Lodge, near Ipswich, and was quite enthusiastic on the matter with his friend Honybun. 'I never knew Bramber go beyond a jury in my life,' said Honybun.

'He'll have to do it now. They can't keep him in prison when they find that the chief witness was manifestly perjured. The woman swore on her oath that the letter reached her by post in May, 1873. It certainly did not do so. The cover, as we see it, has been fabricated since that date.'

'I never thought the cover went for much,' said Honybun.

'For very little,—for nothing at all perhaps,—till proved to be fraudulent. If they had left the letter alone their case would have been strong enough for a conviction. As it was, they were fools enough to go into a business of this sort; but they have done so, and as they have been found out, the falsehood which has been detected covers every word of their spoken evidence with suspicion. It will be like losing so much of the heart's blood, but the old fellow will have to give way.'

'He never gave way in his life.'

'We'll make him begin.'

'I'll bet you a pony he don't.'

'I'll take the bet,' said the late Attorney-General. But as he did so he looked round to see that not even a gamekeeper was near enough to hear him.

On that Friday Bagwax was in a very melancholy state of mind at his office, in spite of the brilliancy of his prospects with Miss Curlydown. 'I'll just come back to my old work,' he said to his future father-in-law. 'There's nothing else for me to do.'

This was all as it should be, and would have been regarded a day or two ago by Curlydown as simple justice. There had been quite enough of that pottering over an old envelope, to the manifest inconvenience of himself and others. But now the matter was altered. His was a paternal and an affectionate heart, and he saw very plainly the pecuniary advantage of a journey to Sydney. And he knew too that, in official life as well as elsewhere, to those who have much, more is given. Now that

Bagwax was to him in the light of a son, he wished Bagwax to rise in the world. 'I wouldn't give it up,' said he.

'But what would you do?'

'I'd stick to it like wax till they did something for me.'

'There's nothing to stick to.'

'I'd take it for granted I was going at once to Sydney. I'd get my out-fit, and, by George! I'd take my place.'

'I've told Sir John I wasn't going; and he said it wasn't necessary.' As Bagwax told his sad tale he almost wept.

'I wouldn't mind that. I'd have it out of them somehow. Why is he to have all the pay? No doubt it's been hundreds to him; and you've done the work and got nothing.'

'When I asked him to get me sent, he said he'd no power;—not now it's all so plain.' He turned his face down towards the desk to hide the tear that now was, in truth, running down his face. 'But duty!' he said, looking up again. 'Duty! England expects——. D——n it, who's going to whimper? When I lay my head on my pillow at night and think that I, I, Thomas Bagwax, have restored that nameless one to her babe and her lord, I shall sleep even though that pillow be no better than a hard bolster.'

'Jemima will look after that,' said the father, laughing. 'But still I wouldn't give it up. Never give a chance up,—they come so seldom. I'll tell you what I should do;—I should apply to the Secretary for leave to go to Sydney at once.'

'At my own expense?' said Bagwax, horrified.

'Certainly not;—but that you might have an opportunity of investigating all this for the public service. It'll get referred round in some way to the Secretary of State, who can't but say all that you've done. When it gets out of a man's own office he don't so much mind doing a little job. It sounds good-natured. And then if they don't do anything for you, you'll get a grievance. Next to a sum of money down, a grievance is the best thing you can have. A man who can stick to a grievance year after year will always make money of it at last.'

On the Saturday, Bagwax went down to Apricot Lodge, having been invited to stay with his beloved till the Monday. In the smiles of his beloved he did find much consolation, especially as it had already been assured to him that sixty pounds a-year. would be settled on Jemima on and from her wedding-day. And then they made very much of him. 'You do love me, Tom; don't you?' said Jemima. They were sitting on camp-stools behind the grotto, and Bagwax answered by pressing the loved one's waist. 'Better than going to Sydney, Tom,—don't you?'

'It is so very different,' said Bagwax,—which was true.

'If you don't like me better than anything else in all the world, however different, I will never stand at the altar with you.' And she moved her camp-stool perhaps an inch away.

'In the way of loving, of course I do.'

'Then why do you grieve when you've got what you like best?'

'You don't understand, Jemima, what a spirit of adventure means.'

'I think I do, or I shouldn't be going to marry you. That's quite as great an adventure as a journey to Sydney. You ought to be very glad to get off, now you're going to settle down as a married man.'

'Think what two hundred pounds would be, Jemima;—in the way of furniture.'

'That's papa's putting in, I know. I hate all that hankering after filthy lucre. You ought to be ashamed of wanting to go so far away just when you're engaged. You wouldn't care about leaving me, I suppose;—not the least.'

'I should always be thinking of you.'

'Yes, you would! But suppose I wasn't thinking of you. Suppose I took to thinking of somebody else. How would it be then?'

'You wouldn't do that, Jemima.'

'You ought to know when you're well off, Tom.' By this time he had recovered the inch and perhaps a little more. 'You ought to feel that you've plenty to console you.'

'So I do. Duty! duty! England expects that every man—'

'That's your idea of consolation, is it?' And away went the camp-stool half a yard.

'You believe in duty, don't you, Jemima?'

'In a husband's duty to his wife, I do;—and in a young man's duty to his sweetheart.'

'And in a father's to his children.'

'That's as may be,' said she, getting up and walking away into the kitchen-garden. He of course accompanied her, and before they got to the house had promised her not to sigh for the delights of Sydney, nor for the perils of adventure any more.

CHAPTER LIV

Judge Bramber

A SECRETARY of State who has to look after the police and the magistrates, to answer questions in the House of Commons, and occasionally to make a telling speech in defence of his colleagues, and, in addition to this, is expected to perform the duties of a practical court of appeal in criminal cases, must have something to do. To have to decide whether or no some poor wretch shall be hanged, when, in spite of the clearest evidence, humanitarian petitions by the dozen overwhelm him with claims for mercy, must be a terrible responsibility. 'No, your Majesty, I think we won't hang him. I think we'll send him to penal servitude for life;—if your Majesty pleases.' That is so easy, and would be so pleasant. Why should any one grumble at so right royal a decision? But there are the newspapers, always so prone to complain;— and the Secretary has to acknowledge that he must be strong enough to hang his culprits in spite of petitions, or else he must give up that office. But when the evidence is not clear, the case is twice more difficult. The jury have found their verdict, and the law intends that the verdict of a jury shall be conclusive. When a man has been declared to be guilty by twelve of his countrymen,—he is guilty, let the facts have been what they may, and let the twelve have been ever so much in error. Majesty, however, can pardon guilt, and hence arises some awkward remedy for the mistakes of jurymen. But an unassisted Majesty cannot itself investigate all things,—is not, in fact, in this country supposed to perform any duties of that sort,—a Secretary of State is invested with the privilege of what is called mercy. It is justice rather that is wanted. If Bagwax were in the right about that envelope,—and the reader will by this time think that he was right; and if Dick Shand had sworn truly, then certainly our friend John Caldigate was not in want of mercy. It was instant justice that he required,—with such compensation as might come to him from the indignant sympathy of all good men.

I remember to have seen a man at Bermuda whose fate was peculiar. He was sleek, fat, and apparently comfortable, mixing pills when I saw him, he himself a convict and administering to the wants of his brother convicts. He remonstrated with me on the hardness of his position. 'Either I did do it, or I didn't,' he said. 'It was because they thought I didn't that they sent me here. And if I didn't, what right had they to keep me here at all?' I passed on in silence, not daring to argue the matter with the man in face of the warder. But the man was right. He had murdered his wife;—so at least the jury had said,—and had been sentenced to be hanged. He had taken the poor woman to a little island, and while she was bathing had drowned her. Her screams had been heard on the mainland, and the jury had found the evidence sufficient. Some newspaper had thought the reverse, and had mooted the question;—was not the distance too great for such screams to have been heard, or, at any rate, understood? So the man was again brought to trial in the Court of the Home Office, and was,—not pardoned, but sent to grow fat and make pills at Bermuda. He had, or he had not, murdered his wife. If he did the deed he should have been hanged;—and if not, he should not have been forced to make extorted pills.

What was a Secretary of State to do in such a case? No doubt he believed that the wretch had murdered his wife. No doubt the judge believed it. All the world believed it. But the newspaper was probably right in saying that the evidence was hardly conclusive,—probably right because it produced its desired effect. If the argument had been successfully used with the jury, the jury would have acquitted the man. Then surely the Secretary of State should have sent him out as though acquitted; and, not daring to hang him, should have treated him as innocent. Another trial was, in truth, demanded.

And so it was in Caldigate's case. The Secretary of State, getting up early in the morning after a remarkable speech, in which he vindicated his Ministry from the attacks of all Europe, did read all the papers, and took home to himself the great Bagwaxian theory. He mastered Dick's evidence;—and managed to master something also as to Dick's character. He quite understood the argument as to the postage-stamps,—which went further with him than the other arguments. And he understood the perplexity of his own position. If Bagwax was right, not a moment should be lost in releasing the ill-used man. To think of pardon, to mention pardon, would be an insult. Instant justice, with infinite regrets that the injuries inflicted admitted of no compensation,—that, and that only, was impressively demanded. How grossly would that man have been ill-used!—how cruelly would that woman have been injured! But then, again,—if Bagwax was wrong;—if the cunning fraud had been concocted over here and not in Sydney;—if the plot had been made, but to liberate a guilty man, then how unfit would he show himself for his position were he to be taken in by such guile! What crime could be worse than that committed by Caldigate against the young lady he had betrayed, if Caldigate were guilty? Upon the whole, he thought it would be safer to trust to the jury; but comforted himself by the reflection that he could for a while transfer the responsibility.

It would perhaps be expedient to transfer it altogether. So he sent all the papers on to Judge Bramber.

Judge Bramber was a great man. Never popular, he had been wise enough to disregard popularity. He had forced himself into practice, in opposition to the attorneys, by industry and perspicuity. He had attended exclusively to his profession, never having attempted to set his foot on the quicker stepping-stones of political life. It was said of him that no one knew whether he called himself Liberal or Conservative. At fifty-five he was put upon the bench, simply because he was supposed to possess a judicial mind. Here he amply justified that opinion,—but not without the sneer and ill-words of many. He was now seventy, and it was declared that years had had no effect on him. He was supposed to be absolutely merciless,—as hard as a nether millstone, a judge who could put on the black cap without a feeling of inward disgust. But it may be surmised that they who said so knew nothing of him,—for he was a man not apt to betray the secrets of his inner life. He was noted for his reverence for a jury, and for his silence on the bench. The older he grew the shorter became his charges; nor were there wanting those who declared that his conduct in this respect was intended as a reproach to some who are desirous of adorning the bench by their eloquence. To sit there listening to everything, and subordinating himself to others till his interposition was necessary, was his idea of a judge's duty. But when the law had declared itself, he was always strong in supporting the law. A man condemned for murder ought to be hanged,—so thought Judge Bramber,—and not released, in accordance with the phantasy of philanthropists. Such were the requirements of the law. If the law were cruel, let the legislators look to that. He was once heard to confess that the position of a judge who had condemned an innocent man might be hard to bear; but, he added, that a country would be unfortunate which did not possess judges capable of bearing even that sorrow. In his heart he disapproved of the attribute of mercy as belonging to the Crown. It was opposed to his idea of English law, and apt to do harm rather than good.

He had been quite convinced of Caldigate's guilt,—not only by the direct evidence, but by the concurrent circumstances. To his thinking, it was not in human nature that a man should pay such a sum as twenty thousand pounds to such people as Crinkett and Euphemia Smith,—a sum of money which was not due either legally or morally,—except with an improper object. I have said that he was a great man; but he did not rise to any appreciation of the motives which had unquestionably operated with Caldigate. Had Caldigate been quite assured, when he paid the money, that his enemies would remain and bear witness against him, still he would have paid it. In that matter he had endeavoured to act as he would have acted had the circumstances of the mining transaction been made known to him when no threat was hanging over his head. But all that Judge Bramber did not understand. He understood, however, quite clearly, that under no circumstances should money have been paid by an accused person to witnesses while that person's guilt and innocence were in question. In his summing-up he had simply told the jury to consider the matter;–but he had so spoken the word as to make the jury fully perceive what had been the result of his own consideration.

And then Caldigate and the woman had lived together, and a distinct and repeated promise of marriage had been acknowledged. It was acknowledged that the man had given his name to the woman, so far as himself to write it. Whatever might be the facts as to the post-mark and postage-stamp, the words 'Mrs. Caldigate' had been written by the man now in prison.

Four persons had given direct evidence; and in opposition to them there had been nothing. Till Dick Shand had come, no voice had been brought forward to throw even a doubt upon the marriage. That two false witnesses should adhere well together in a story was uncommon; that three should do so, most rare; with four it would be almost a miracle. But these four had adhered. They were people, probably of bad character,–whose lives had perhaps been lawless. But if so, it would have been so much easier to prove them false if they were false. Thus Judge Bramber, when he passed sentence on Caldigate, had not in the least doubted that the verdict was a true verdict.

And now the case was sent to him for reconsideration. He hated such reconsiderations. He first read Sir John Joram's letter, and declared to himself that it was unfit to have come from any one calling himself a lawyer. There was an enthusiasm about it altogether beneath a great advocate,–certainly beneath any forensic advocate employed otherwise than in addressing a jury. He, Judge Bramber, had never himself talked of 'demanding' a verdict even from a jury. He had only endeavoured to win it. But that a man who had been Attorney-General,–who had been the head of the bar,–should thus write to a Secretary of State, was to him disgusting. To his thinking, a great lawyer, even a good lawyer, would be incapable of enthusiasm as to any case in which he was employed. The ignorant childish world outside would indulge in zeal and hot feelings,–but for an advocate to do so was to show that he was no lawyer,–that he was no better than the outside world. Even spoken eloquence was, in his mind, almost beneath a lawyer,–studied eloquence certainly was so. But such written words as these disgusted him. And then he came across allusions to the condition of the poor lady at Folking. What could the condition of the lady at Folking have to do with the matter? Though the poor lady at Folking should die in her sorrow, that could not alter the facts as they had occurred in Australia! It was not for him, or for the Secretary of State, to endeavour to make things pleasant all round here in England. It had been the jury's duty to find out whether that crime had been committed, and his duty to see that all due facilities were given to the jury. It had been Sir John Joram's duty to make out what best case he could for his client,—and then to rest contented. Had all things been as they should be, the Secretary of State would have had no duty at all in the matter. It was in this frame of mind that Judge Bramber applied himself to the consideration of the case. No juster man ever lived;—and yet in his mind there was a bias against the prisoner.

Nevertheless he went to his work with great patience, and a resolve to sift everything that was to be sifted. The Secretary of State had done no more than his required duty in sending the case to him, and he would now do his. He took the counter-evidence as it came in the papers. In order that the two Bagwaxian theories, each founded on the same small document, might be expounded, one consecutively after the other, Dick Shand and his deposition were produced first. The judge declared to himself that Dick's single oath, which could not now be tested by cross-examination, amounted to nothing. He had been a drunkard and a pauper,—had descended to the lowest occupation which the country afforded, and had more than once nearly died from delirium tremens. He had then come home penniless, and had—produced his story. If such evidence could avail to rescue a prisoner from his sentence, and to upset a verdict, what verdict or what sentence could stand? Poor Dick's sworn testimony, in Judge Bramber's mind, told rather against Caldigate than for him.

Then came the post-marks,—as to which the Bagwaxian theory was quite distinct from that as to the postage-stamp. Here the judge found the facts to be somewhat complicated and mazy. It was long before he could understand the full purport of the argument used, and even at last he hardly understood the whole of it. But he could see nothing in it to justify him in upsetting the verdict;—nothing even to convince him that the envelope had been fraudulently handled. There was no evidence that such a dated stamp had not been in use at Sydney on the day named. Copies from the records kept daily at Sydney,—photographed copies,— should have been submitted before that argument had been used.

But when it came to the postage-stamp, then he told himself very quickly that the envelope had been fraudulently handled. The evidence as to the date of the manufacture of the stamp was conclusive. It could not have served to pay the postage on a letter from Sydney to Nobble in May 1873, seeing that it had not then been in existence. And thus any necessity there might otherwise have been for further inquiry as to the post-marks was dissipated. The envelope was a declared fraud, and the fraud required no further proof. That morsel of evidence had been fabricated, and laid, at any rate, one of the witnesses in the last trial open to a charge of perjury. So resolving, Judge Bramber pushed the papers away from him, and began to think the case over in his mind.

There was certainly something in the entire case as it now stood to excuse Sir John. That was the first line which his thoughts took. An advocate having clearly seen into a morsel of evidence on the side opposed to him, and having proved to himself beyond all doubt that it was maliciously false, must be held to be justified in holding more than a mere advocate's conviction as to the innocence of his client. Sir John had of course felt that a foul plot had been contrived. A foul plot no doubt had been contrived. Had the discovery taken place before the case had been submitted to the jury, the detection of that plot would doubtless have saved the prisoner, whether guilty or innocent. So much Judge Bramber admitted.

But should it necessarily serve to save him now? Before a jury it would have saved him, whether guilty or innocent. But the law had got hold of him, and had made him guilty, and the law need not now subject itself to the normal human weakness of a jury. The case was now in his hands,—in his, and those of the Secretary, and there need be no weakness. If the man was innocent, in God's name let him go;—though, as the judge observed to himself, he had deserved all he had got for his folly and vice. But this discovered plot by no means proved the man's innocence. It only proved the determination of certain persons to secure his conviction, whether by foul means or fair. Then he recapitulated to himself various cases in which he had known false evidence to have been added to true, with the object of convincing a jury as to a real fact.

It might well be that this gang of ruffians,—for it was manifest that there had been such a gang,—finding the envelope addressed by the man to his wife, had fraudulently,—and as foolishly as fraudulently,—endeavoured to bolster up their case by the postage-stamp and the post-mark. Looking back at all the facts, remembering that fatal twenty thousand pounds, remembering that though the post-marks were forged on that envelope the writing was true, remembering the acknowledged promise and the combined testimony of the four persons,—he was inclined to think that something of the kind had been done in this case.

If it were so, though he would fain see the perpetrators of that fraud on their trial for perjury, their fraud in no way diminished Caldigate's guilt. That a guilty man should escape out of the hands of justice by any fraud was wormwood to Judge Bramber. Caldigate was guilty. The jury had found him so. Could he take upon himself to say that the finding of the jury was wrong because the prosecuting party had concocted a fraud which had not been found out before the verdict was given? Sir John Joram, whom he had known almost as a boy, had 'demanded' the release of his client. The word stuck in Judge Bramber's throat. The word had been injudicious. The more he thought of the word the more he thought that the verdict had been a true verdict, in spite of the fraud. A very honest man was Judge Bramber;—but human.

He almost made up his mind,—but then was obliged to confess to himself that he had not quite done so. 'It taints the entire evidence with perjury,' Sir John had said. The woman's evidence was absolutely so tainted,—was defiled with perjury. And the man Crinkett had been so near the woman that it was impossible to disconnect them. Who had concocted the fraud? The woman could hardly have done so without the man's connivance. It took him all the morning to think the matter out, and then he had not made up his mind. To reverse the verdict would certainly be a thorn in his side,—a pernicious thorn,—but one which, if necessary, he would endure. Thorns, however, such as these are very persuasive.

At last he determined to have inquiry made as to the woman by the police. She had laid herself open to an indictment for perjury, and in making inquiry on that head something further might probably be learned.

CHAPTER LV

How The Conspirators Throve

THERE had been some indiscretion among Caldigate's friends from which it resulted that, while Judge Bramber was considering the matter, and before the police intelligence of Scotland Yard even had stirred itself in obedience to the judge's orders, nearly all the circumstances which had been submitted to the judge had become public. Shand knew all that Bagwax had done. Bagwax was acquainted with the whole of Dick's evidence. And Hester down at Folking understood perfectly what had been revealed by each of those enthusiastic allies. Dick, as we know, had been staying at Folking, and had made his presence notable throughout the county. He had succeeded in convincing uncle Babington, and had been judged to be a false witness by all the Boltons. In that there had perhaps been no great indiscretion. But when Bagwax opened a correspondence with Mrs. John Caldigate and explained to her at great length all the circumstances of the post-mark and the postage-stamps, and when at her instance he got a day's holiday and rushed down to Folking, then, as he felt himself, he was doing that of which Sir John Joram and Mr. Jones would not approve. But he could not restrain himself. And why should he restrain himself when he had lost all hope of his journey to Sydney? When the prospect of that delight no longer illumined his days, why should he not enjoy the other delight of communicating his tidings,—his own discoveries,—to the afflicted lady? Unless he did so it would appear to her that Joram had done it all, and there would be no reward,—absolutely none! So he told his tale,—at first by letter and then with his own natural eloquence. 'Yes, Mrs. Caldigate; the post-marks are difficult. It takes a lifetime of study to understand all the ins and outs of post-marks. To me it is A B C of course. When I had spent a week or two looking into it I was sure that impression had never been made in the way of business.' Bagwax was sitting out on the lawn at Folking, and the bereaved wife, dressed in black, was near him, holding in her hand one of the photographed copies of the envelope. 'It's A B C to me; but I don't wonder you shouldn't see it.'

'I think I do see a good deal,' said Hester.

'But any babe may understand that,' said Bagwax, pressing forward and putting his forefinger on the obliteration of the postage-stamp. 'You see the date in the post-mark.'

402

'I know the date very well.'

'We've had it proved that on the date given there, this identical postage-stamp had not yet been manufactured. The Secretary of State can't get over that, I'll defy him.'

'Why don't they release him at once, then?'

'Between you and me, Mrs. Caldigate, I think it's Judge Bramber.'

'He can't want to injure an innocent man.'

'From what I've heard Sir John say, I fancy he doesn't like to have the verdict upset. But they must do it. I'll defy them to get over that.' And again he tapped the queen's-head. Then he told the story of his love for Jemima, and of his engagement. Of course he was praised and petted,—as indeed he deserved; and thus, though the house at Folking was a sad house, he enjoyed himself,—as men do when much is made of them by pretty women.

But the result of all this was that every detail of the story became known to the public, and was quite common down at Cambridge. The old squire was urgent with Mr. Seely, asking why it was that when those things were known an instant order had not come from the Secretary of State for the liberation of his son. Mr. Seely had not been altogether pleased at the way in which Sir John had gone to work, and was still convinced of the guilt of his own client. His answer was therefore unsatisfactory, and the old squire proclaimed his intention of proceeding himself to London and demanding an interview with the Secretary of State. Then the Cambridge newspapers took up the subject,—generally in the Caldigate interest,—and from thence the matter was transferred to the metropolitan columns,—which, with one exception, were strong in favour of such a reversal of the verdict as could be effected by a pardon from the Queen. The one exception was very pellucid, very unanswerable, and very cold-blooded. It might have been written by Judge Bramber himself, but that Judge Bramber would sooner have cut his hand off than have defiled it by making public aught that had come before him judicially or officially. But all Judge Bramber's arguments were there set forth. Dick wished his father at once to proceed against the paper for libel because the paper said that his word could not be taken for much. The post-mark theory was exposed to derision. There was no doubt much in the postage-stamp, but not enough to upset the overwhelming weight of evidence by which the verdict had been obtained. And so the case became really public, and the newspapers were bought and read with the avidity which marks those festive periods in which some popular criminal is being discussed at every breakfast-table.

Much of this had occurred before the intelligence of Scotland Yard had been set to work in obedience to Judge Bramber. The papers had been a day or two in the Home Office, and three or four days in the judge's hands before he could look at them. To Hester and the old squire at Folking the incarceration of that injured darling was the one thing in all the world which now required attention. To redress that terrible grievance, judges, secretaries, thrones, and parliaments, should have left their wonted tracks and thought of nothing till it had been accomplished. But Judge Bramber, in the performance of his duties, was never hurried; and at the Home Office a delay but of three or four days amounted to official haste. Thus it came to pass that all that Bagwax had done and all that Shand had said were known to the public at large before the intelligence of Scotland Yard was at work,— before anybody had as yet done anything.

Among the public were Euphemia Smith and Mr. Crinkett,— Adamson also, and Anna Young, the other witness. Since the trial, this confraternity had not passed an altogether fraternal life. When the money had been paid, the woman had insisted on having the half. She, indeed, had carried the cheque for the amount away from the Jericho Coffee-house. It had been given into her hands and those of Crinkett conjointly, and she had secured the document. The amount was payable to their joint order, and each had felt that it would be better to divide the spoil in peace. Crinkett had taken his half with many grumblings, because he had, in truth, arranged the matter and hitherto paid the expenses. Then the woman had wished to start at once for Australia, taking the other female with her. But to this Crinkett had objected. They would certainly, he said, be arrested for breaking their bail at whatever port they might reach,—and why should they go, seeing that the money had been paid to them on the distinct understanding that they were not pledged to abandon the prosecution. Most unwillingly the woman remained;—but did so fearing lest worse evil might betide her. Then there had arisen quarrels about the money between the two females, and between Crinkett and Adamson. It was in vain that Crinkett showed that, were he to share with Adamson, there would be very little of the plunder left to him. Adamson demanded a quarter of the whole, short of a quarter of the expenses, declaring that were it not paid to him, he would divulge everything to the police. The woman, who had got her money in her hand, and who was, in truth, spending it very quickly, would give back nothing for expenses, unless her expenses in England also were considered. Nor would she give a shilling to Anna Young, beyond an allowance of £2 a week, till, as she said, they were both back in the colony again. But Anna Young did not wish to go back to the colony. And so they quarrelled till the trial came and was over.

The verdict had been given on the 20th July, and it was about the middle of September when the newspapers made public all that Shand and Bagwax between them had said and done. At that time the four conspirators were still in England. The two men were living a wretched life in London, and the women were probably not less wretched at Brighton. Mrs. Smith, when she learned that Dick Shand was alive and in England, immediately understood her danger,—understood her danger, but did not at all measure the security which might come to her from the nature of Dick's character. She would have flown instantly without a word to any one, but that the other woman watched her day and night. They did not live under the same roof, nor in similar style. Euphemia Smith wore silk, and endeavoured to make the best of what female charms her ill mode of life had left to her; while Young was content with poor apparel and poor living,—but spent her time in keeping guard on the other. The woman in silk knew that were she to leave her lodgings for half a day without the knowledge of the woman in calico, the woman in calico would at once reveal everything to the police. But when she understood the point which had been raised and made as to the post-mark,—which she did understand thoroughly,—then she comprehended also her own jeopardy, and hurried up to London to see Crinkett. And she settled matters with Young. If Young would go back with her to Australia, everything there should be made pleasant. Terms were made at the Brighton station. Anna Young was to receive two thousand pounds in London, and would then remain as companion with her old mistress.

In London there was a close conference, at first between the two principals only. Crinkett thought that he was comparatively safe. He had sworn to nothing about the letter; and though he himself had prepared the envelope, no proof of his handiwork was forthcoming that he had done so. But he was quite ready to start again to some distant portion of the earth's surface,—to almost any distant portion of the earth's surface,—if she would consent to a joining of purses. 'And who is to keep the joint purse?' asked Mrs. Smith, not without a touch of grand irony.

'Me, of course,' said Crinkett. 'A man always must have the money.'

'I'd sooner have fourteen years for perjury, like the Claimant,' said Mrs. Smith, with a grand resolve that, come what might, she would stick to her own money.

But at last it was decided. Adamson would not stir a step, but consented to remain with two thousand pounds, which Crinkett was compelled to pay him. Crinkett handed him the money within the precincts of one of the city banks not an hour before the sailing of the

Julius Vogel from the London Docks for Auckland in New Zealand. At that moment both the women were on board the Julius Vogel, and the gang was so far safe. Crinkett was there in time, and they were carried safely down the river. New Zealand had been chosen because there they would be further from their persecutors than at any other spot they could reach. And the journey would occupy long, and they were pervaded by an idea that as they had been hitherto brought in question as to no crime, the officers of justice would hardly bring them back from so great a distance.

The Julius Vogel touched at Plymouth on her outward voyage. How terribly inconvenient must be this habit of touching to passengers going from home, such as Euphemia Smith and Thomas Crinkett! And the wretched vessel, which had made a quick passage round from the Thames, lay two days and two nights at Dartmouth, before it went on to Plymouth. Our friends, of course, did not go on shore. Our friends, who were known as Mr. Catley and his two widowed sisters, Mrs. Salmon and Mrs. York, kept themselves very quiet, and were altogether well-behaved. But the women could not restrain some manifestation of their impatience. Why did not the vessel start? Why were they to be delayed? Then the captain made known to them that the time for starting had not yet come. Three o'clock on that day was the time fixed for starting. As the slow moments wore themselves away, the women trembled, huddled together on the poop of the vessel; while Crinkett, never letting the pipe out of his mouth, stood leaning against the taffrail, looking towards the port, gazing across the waters to see whether anything was coming towards the ship which might bode evil to his journey. Then there came the bustle preparatory to starting, and Crinkett thought that he was free, at any rate, for that journey. But such bustle spreads itself over many minutes. Quarter of a hour succeeded quarter of an hour, and still they were not off. The last passenger came on board, and yet they were not off. Then Crinkett with his sharp eyes saw another boat pushed off from the shore, and heard a voice declare that the Julius Vogel had received a signal not to start. Then Crinkett knew that a time of desperate trouble had come upon him, and he bethought himself what he would do. Were he to jump overboard, they would simply pick him up. Nor was he quite sure that he wished to die. The money which he had kept had not been obtained fraudulently, and would be left to him, he thought, after that term of imprisonment which it might be his fate to endure. But then, again, it might be that no such fate was in store for him. He had sworn only to the marriage and not to the letter. It might still be possible that he should be acquitted, while the woman was condemned. So he stood perfectly still, and said not a word to either of his companions as to the boat which was coming. He could soon see two men in the guise of policemen, and another who was certainly a policeman, though not in that guise. He stood there very quiet, and determined that he would tell his own name and those of the two women at the first question that was asked him. On the day but one following, Crinkett and Euphemia Smith were committed in London to take their trial for perjury.

Adamson, when he had read the reports in the newspapers, and had learned that the postage-stamp had been detected, and that Shand was at home, also looked about him a little. He talked over the matter at great length with Crinkett, but he did not tell Crinkett all his own ideas. Some of them he did make known to Crinkett. He would not himself go to the colonies with Crinkett, nor would he let Crinkett go till some share of the plunder had been made over to him. This, after many words, had been fixed at two thousand pounds; and the money, as we have seen, had been paid. Crinkett had been careful to make the payment at as late a moment as possible. He had paid the amount,– very much to his own regret when he saw that boat coming,–because he was quite sure that Adamson would at once have denounced him to the police, had he not done so. Adamson might denounce him in spite of the payment,–but the payment appeared to him to be his best chance. When he saw the boat coming, he knew that he had simply thrown away his two thousand pounds.

In truth, he had simply thrown it away. There is no comfort in having kept one's word honestly, when one would fain have broken it dishonestly. Adamson, with the large roll of bank-notes still in his pocket, had gone at once to Scotland Yard and told his story. At that time all the details had been sent by the judge to the police-office, and it was understood that a great inquiry was to be made. In the first place, Crinkett and Euphemia Smith were wanted. Adamson soon made his bargain. He could tell something,–could certainly tell where Crinkett and the women were to be found; but he must be assured that any little peccadillo of which he himself might have been guilty would be overlooked. The peccadillo on his part had been very small, but he must be assured. Then he was assured, and told the police at once that they could stop the two travellers at Plymouth.

And of course he told more than that. There had been no marriage,– no real marriage. He had been induced to swear that there had been a marriage, because he had regarded the promise and the cohabitation as making a marriage,–'in heaven.' So he had expressed himself, and so excused himself. But now his eyes had been opened to the error of his ways, and he was free to acknowledge that he had committed

407

perjury. There had been no marriage;—certainly none at all. He made his deposition, and bound himself down, and submitted to live under the surveillance of the police till the affair should be settled. Then he would be able to go where he listed, with two thousand pounds in his pocket. He was a humble, silent, and generally obedient man, but in this affair he had managed to thrive better than any of the others. Anna Young was afterwards allowed to fill the same position; but she failed in getting any of the money. While the women were in London together, and as they were starting, Euphemia Smith had been too strong for her companion. She had declared that she would not pay the money till they were afloat, and then that she would not pay it till they had left Plymouth. When the police came on board the Julius Vogel, Anna Young had as yet received nothing.

CHAPTER LVI

The Boltons Are Very Firm

WHILE all this was going on, as the general opinion in favour of Caldigate was becoming stronger every day, when even Judge Bramber had begun to doubt, the feeling which had always prevailed at Puritan Grange was growing in intensity and converting itself from a conviction into a passion. That the wicked bigamist had falsely and fraudulently robbed her of her daughter was a religion to Mrs. Bolton;—and, as the matter had proceeded, the old banker had become ever more and more submissive to his wife's feelings. All the Cambridge Boltons were in accord on this subject,—who had never before been in accord on any subject. Robert Bolton, who understood thoroughly each point as it was raised on behalf of Caldigate, was quite sure that the old squire was spending his money freely, his own money and his son's, with the view of getting the verdict set aside. What was so clear as that Dick Shand and Bagwax, and probably also Smithers from the Stamps and Taxes, were all in the pay of old Caldigate? At this time the defection of Adamson was not known to him, but he did know that a strong case was being made with the Secretary of State. 'If it costs me all I have in the world I will expose them,' he said up in London to his brother William, the London barrister.

The barrister was not quite in accord with the other Boltons. He had been disposed to think that Dick Shand and Bagwax might have been bribed by the squire. It was at any rate possible. And the twenty thousand pounds paid to the accusing witnesses had always stuck in his throat when he had endeavoured to believe that Caldigate might be innocent. It seemed to him still that the balance of evidence was against the man who had taken his sister away from her home. But he was willing to leave that to the Secretary of State and to the judge. He did not see why his sister should not have her husband and be restored to the world,—if Judge Bramber should at last decide that so it ought to be. No money could bribe Judge Bramber. No undue persuasion could weaken him. If that Rhadamanthus should at last say that the verdict had been a wrong verdict, then,—for pity's sake, for love's sake, in the name of humanity, and for the sake of all Boltons present and to come,— let the man be considered innocent.

But Robert Bolton was more intent on his purpose, and was a man of stronger passion. Perhaps some real religious scruple told him that a woman should not live with a man who was not her true husband,—let any judge say what he might. But hatred, probably, had more to do with it than religion. It was he who had first favoured Caldigate's claim on Hester's hand, and he who had been most grievously deceived. From the moment in which the conviction had come upon him that Caldigate had even promised his hand in marriage to Euphemia Smith, he had become Caldigate's enemy,—his bitter enemy; and now he could not endure the thought that he should be called upon again to receive Caldigate as his brother-in-law. Caldigate's guilt was an idea fixed in his mind which no Secretary of State, no Judge Bramber, no brother could expel.

And so it came to pass that there were hard words between him and his brother. 'You are wrong,' said William.

'How wrong? You cannot say that you believe him to be innocent.'

'If he receives the Queen's pardon he is to be considered as innocent.'

'Even though you should know him to have been guilty?'

'Well,—yes,' said William, slowly, and perhaps indiscreetly. 'It is a matter in which a man's guilt or innocence must be held to depend upon what persons in due authority have declared. As he is now guilty of bigamy in consequence of the verdict, even though he should never have committed the offence, so should he be presumed to be innocent, when the verdict has been set aside by the Queen's pardon on the advice of her proper officers,—even though he committed the offence.'

'You would have your sister live with a man who has another wife alive? It comes to that.'

'For all legal purposes he would have no other wife alive.'

'The children would be illegitimate.'

'There you are decidedly wrong,' said the barrister. 'The children would be legitimate. Even at this moment, without any pardon, the child could claim and would enter in upon his inheritance.'

'The next of kin would claim,' said the attorney.

'The burden of proving the former marriage would then be on him,' said the barrister.

'The verdict would be evidence,' said the attorney.

'Certainly,' said the barrister; 'but such evidence would not be worth a straw after a Queen's pardon, given on the advice of the judge who had tried the former case. As yet we know not what the judge may say,—we do not know the facts as they have been expounded to him. But if Caldigate be regarded as innocent by the world at large, it will be our duty so to regard him.'

'I will never look on him as Hester's husband,' said the attorney.

'I and Fanny have already made up our minds that we would at

410

once ask them to come to us for a month,' said the barrister.

'Nothing on earth will induce me to speak to him,' said the attorney.

'Then you will be very cruel to Hester,' said the barrister.

'It is dreadful to me,' said the attorney, 'that you should care so little for your sister's reputation.'

And so they quarrelled. Robert, leaving the house in great dudgeon, went down on the following morning to Cambridge.

At Puritan Grange the matter was argued rather by rules of religion than of law; but as the rules of law were made by those interested to fit themselves to expediency, so were the rules of religion fitted to prejudice. No hatred could be more bitter than that which Mrs. Bolton felt for the man whom she would permit no one to call her son-in-law. Something as to the postage-stamp and the post-marks was told her; but with a woman's indomitable obstinacy she closed her mind against all that,—as indeed did also the banker. 'Is her position in the world to depend upon a postage-stamp?' said the banker, intending to support his wife. Then she arose in her wrath, and was very eloquent. 'Her position in the world!' she said. 'What does it matter? It is her soul! Though all men and all women should call her a castaway, it would be nothing if the Lord knew her to be guiltless. But she will be living as an adulteress with an adulterer. The law has told her that it is so. She will feel every day and every night that she is a transgressor, and will vainly seek consolation by telling herself that men have pardoned that which God has condemned.' And again she broke forth. 'The Queen's pardon! What right has the Queen to pardon an adulterer who has crept into the bosom of a family and destroyed all that he found there? What sense of justice can any Queen have in her bosom who will send such a one back, to heap sin upon sin, to fasten the bonds of iniquity on the soul of my child?' Postage-stamps and post-marks and an old envelope! The triviality of the things as compared with the importance of everlasting life made her feel that they were unworthy to be even noticed. It did not occur to her that the presence of a bodkin might be ample evidence of murder. Post-marks indeed,—when her daughter's everlasting life was the matter in question! Then they told her of Dick Shand. She, too, had heard of Dick Shand. He had been a gambler. So she said,—without much truth. He was known for a drunkard, a spendthrift, a penniless idle ne'er-do-well who had wandered back home without clothes to his back;—which was certainly untrue, as the yellow trousers had been bought at San Francisco;—and now she was told that the hated miscreant was to be released from prison because such a one as this was ready to take an oath! She had a knack of looking on such men,—ne'er-do-wells like Dick Shand and Caldigate,—as human beings who had, as it were, lost their souls before death, so that it was useless to think of them otherwise than as already damned. That Caldigate should become a good, honest, loving husband, or Dick Shand a truth-speaking witness, was to her thinking much more improbable than that a camel should go through the eye of a needle. She would press her lips together and grind her teeth and shake her head when any one about her spoke of a doubt. The man was in prison, at any rate for two years,—locked up safe for so much time, as it might be a wild beast which with infinite trouble had been caged. And now they were talking of undoing the bars and allowing the monster to gorge himself again with his prey!

'If the Queen were told the truth she would never do it,' she said to her amazed husband. 'The Queen is a mother and a woman who kneels in prayer before her Maker. Something should be done, so that the truth may be made known to her.'

To illuminate all the darkness which was betrayed by this appeal to him was altogether beyond Mr. Bolton's power. He appreciated the depth of the darkness. He knew, for instance, that the Queen herself would in such a matter act so simply in accordance with the advice of some one else, that the pardon, if given, would not in the least depend on her Majesty's sentiments. To call it the Queen's pardon was a simple figure of speech. This was manifest to him, and he was driven to endeavour to make it manifest to her. She spoke of a petition to be sent direct to the Queen, and insinuated that Robert Bolton, if he were anything like a real brother, would force himself into her Majesty's presence. 'It isn't the Queen,' said her husband.

'It is the Queen. Mercy is the prerogative of the Crown. Even I know as much as that. And she is to be made to believe that this is mercy!'

'Her Majesty does what her Ministers tell her.'

'But she wouldn't if she was told the truth. I do not for a moment believe that she would allow such a man as that to be let loose about the world like a roaring lion if she knew all that you and I know. Mercy indeed!'

'It won't be meant for mercy, my dear.'

'What then? Do you not know that the man has another wife alive,—a wife much more suited to him than our poor darling? Nobody would hear my voice while there was yet time. And so my child, my only one, was taken away from me by her own father and her own brothers, and no one now will exert himself to bring her back to her home!' The poor old man had had but little comfort in his home since his daughter's marriage, and was now more miserable than ever.

Then there came a letter from Hester to her mother. Since Mrs. Bolton's last visit to Folking there had been some correspondence maintained.

A few letters had passed, very sad on each side, in which the daughter had assured the mother of her undying love, and in which the mother had declared that day and night she prayed for her child. But of Caldigate, neither on one side nor on the other had mention been made. Now Hester, who was full of hope, and sick with hope deferred, endeavoured to convince her mother that the entire charge against her husband had been proved by new evidence to be false. She recapitulated all the little details with which the diligent reader must by this time be too well acquainted. She made quite clear, as she thought, the infamous plot by which the envelope had been made to give false evidence, and she added the assurance that certainly before long her dear, dearest, ill-used husband would be restored to her. Then she went on to implore her mother's renewed affection both for herself and him and her boy, promising that bygones should all be bygones; and then she ended by declaring that though the return of her husband would make her very happy, she could not be altogether happy unless her parents also should be restored to her.

To this there came a crushing answer, as follows:—

'PURITAN GRANGE, *28th September.*'

'Dearest Hester,—It was unnecessary that you should ask for a renewal of your mother's love. There has never been a moment in which she has not loved you,—more dearly, I fear, than one human creature should ever love another. When I was strongest in opposing you, I did so from love. When I watched you in the hall all those hours, endeavouring to save you from further contact with the man who had injured you, I did it from love. You need not doubt my love.

'But as to all the rest, I cannot agree to a word that you say. They are plotting with false evidence to rescue the man from prison. I will not give way to it when my soul tells me that it is untrue. As your mother, I can only implore you to come back to me, and to save yourself from the further evil which is coming upon you. It may be that he will be enabled to escape, and then you will again have to live with a husband that is no husband,—unless you will listen to your mother's words.

'You are thinking of the good things of this world,—of a home with all luxuries and ease, and of triumph over those who, for the good of your soul, have hitherto marred your worldly joys. Is it thus that you hope to win that crown of everlasting life which you have been taught to regard as the one thing worthy of a Christian's struggles? Is it not true that, since that wretched day on which you were taken away from me, you have allowed your mind to pass from thoughts of eternity to longings after vain joys in this bitter, fruitless vale of tears? If that be so, can he who has so encouraged you have been good to you? Do you remember David's words; "Some trust in chariots, and some in horses; but we will remember the name of the Lord our God"? And then, again; "They are brought down and fallen; but we are risen and stand upright." Ask yourself whether you have stood upright or have fallen, since you left your father's house; whether you have trusted in the Lord your God, or in horses and chariots,—that is, in the vain comforts of an easy life? If it be so, can it be for your good that you have left your father's house? And should you not accept this scourge that has fallen upon you as a healing balm from the hands of the Lord?

'My child, I have no other answer to send you. That I love you till my very bowels yearn after you is most true. But I cannot profess to believe a lie, or declare that to be good which I know to be evil.

'May the Lord bless you, and turn your feet aright, and restore you to your loving mother,

'MARY BOLTON.'

When Hester read this she was almost crushed. The delay since the new tidings had come to her had not, in truth, been very great. It was not yet quite a month since Shand had been at Folking, and a shorter period since the discoveries of Bagwax had been explained to her. But the days seemed to her to be very long, and day after day she thought that on that day at least the news of his promised release would be brought to her. And now, instead of these news, there came this letter from her mother, harder almost in its words than any words which had hitherto been either written or spoken in the matter. Even when all the world should have declared him innocent,—when the Queen, and the great officer of State, and that stern judge, should have said that he was innocent,—even then her cruel mother would refuse to receive him! She had been invited to ask herself certain questions as to the state of her soul, and as to the teaching she had received since her marriage. The subject is one on which there is no possible means of convergence between persons who have learned to differ. Her mother's allusion to chariots and horses was to her the enthusiasm of a fanatic. No doubt, teaching had come to her from her husband, but it had come at the period of life at which such lessons are easily learned. 'Brought down and fallen!' she said to herself. 'Yes, we are all brought down and fallen;' for she had not at all discarded the principles of her religious faith;—'but a woman will hardly raise herself by being untrue to her husband.' She, too, yearned for her mother;—but there was never a moment's doubt in her mind to which she would cling if at last it should become necessary that one should be cast off.

Mrs. Bolton, when the letter had been despatched, sat brooding over it in deep regret mixed with deeper anger. She was preparing for herself an awful tragedy. She must be severed for ever from her daughter, and so severed with the opinion of all her neighbours against her! But what was all that if she had done right? Or of what service to her would be the contrary if she were herself to think,—nay, to know,—that she had done wrong?

CHAPTER LVII

Squire Caldigate At The Home Office

WHEN October came no information from the Secretary of State's office had yet reached Folking, and the two inhabitants there were becoming almost despondent as well as impatient. There was nobody with whom they could communicate. Sir John Joram had been obliged to answer a letter from the squire by saying that, as soon as there was anything to tell the tidings would assuredly be communicated to him from the Home Office. The letter had seemed to be cold and almost uncivil; but Sir John had in truth said all that he could say. To raise hopes which, after all, might be fallacious, would have been, on his part, a great fault. Nor, in spite of his bet, was he very sanguine, sharing his friend Honybun's opinion as to Judge Bramber's obstinacy. And there was a correspondence between the elder Caldigate and the Home Office, in which the letters from the squire were long and well argued, whereas the replies, which always came by return of post, were short and altogether formal. Some assistant under-secretary would sign his name at the end of three lines, in which the correspondent was informed that as soon as the matter was settled the result would be communicated.

Who does not know the sense of aggravated injustice which comes upon a sufferer when redress for an acknowledged evil is delayed? The wronged one feels that the whole world must be out of joint in that all the world does not rise up in indignation. So it was with the old squire, who watched Hester's cheek becoming paler day by day, and who knew by her silence that the strong hopes which in his presence had been almost convictions were gradually giving way to a new despair. Then he would abuse the Secretary of State, say hard things of the Queen, express his scorn as to the fatuous absurdities of the English law, and would make her understand by his anger that he also was losing hope.

During these days preparations were being made for the committal of Crinkett and Euphemia Smith, nor would Judge Bramber report to the Secretary till he was convinced that there was sufficient evidence for their prosecution. It was not much to him that Caldigate should spend another week in prison. The condition of Hester did not even come beneath his ken. When he found allusion to it in the papers before him, he treated it as a matter which should not have been adduced,—in bringing which under his notice there had been something akin to contempt of court, as though an endeavour had been made to talk him over in private. He knew his own character, and was indignant that such an argument should have been used with himself. He was perhaps a little more slow,—something was added to his deliberation,— because he was told that a young wife and an infant child were anxiously expecting the liberation of the husband and father. It was not as yet clear to Judge Bramber that the woman had any such husband, or that the child could claim his father.

At this crisis, when the first weeks in October had dragged themselves tediously along, Mr. Caldigate, in a fit which was half rage and half moodiness, took himself off to London. He did not tell Hester that he was going till the morning on which he started, and then simply assured her that she should hear from him by every post till he returned.

'You will tell me the truth, father.'

'If I know it myself, I will tell you.'

'But you will conceal nothing?'

'No;—I will conceal nothing. If I find that they are all utterly unjust, altogether hard-hearted, absolutely indifferent to the wrong they have done, I will tell you even that.' And thus he went.

He had hardly any fixed purpose in going. He knew that Sir John Joram was not in London, and that if he were in town he ought not to be made subject to visits on behalf of clients. To call upon any judge in such a matter would be altogether out of place, but to call upon such a judge as Judge Bramber, would be very vain indeed. He had in his head some hazy idea of forcing an answer from the officials in Downing Street; but in his heart he did not believe that he should be able to get beyond the messengers. He was of a class, not very small in numbers, who, from cultivating within their bosom a certain tendency towards suspicion, have come to think that all Government servants are idle, dilatory, supercilious, and incompetent. That some of these faults may have existed among those who took wages from the Crown in the time of George III is perhaps true. And the memory of those times has kept alive the accusation. The vitality of these prejudices calls to mind the story of the Nottinghamshire farmer who, when told of the return of Charles II, asked what had become of Charles I. Naseby, Worcester, and the fatal day at Whitehall had not yet reached him. Tidings of these things had only been approaching him during these twelve years. The true character of the Civil Service is only now approaching the intelligence of those who are still shaking their heads over the delinquencies of the last century. But old Mr. Caldigate was a man peculiarly susceptible to such hard judgments. From the crown down to the black helmet worn by the policeman who was occasionally to be seen on Folking causeway, he thought that all such headpieces were coverings for malpractices. The bishop's wig had, he thought, disappeared as being too ridiculous for the times; but even for the judge's wig he had no respect. Judge Bramber was to him simply pretentious, and a Secretary of State no better than any other man. In this frame of mind how was it probable that he should do any good at the Home Office?

But in this frame of mind he went to the Home Office, and asked boldly for the great man. It was then eleven o'clock in the morning and neither had the great man, nor even any of the deputy great men, as yet made their appearance. Mr. Caldigate of course fell back upon his old opinion as to public functionaries, and, mentally, applied opprobrious epithets to men who, taking the public pay, could not be at their posts an hour before mid-day. He was not aware that the great man and the first deputy great man were sitting in the House of Commons at 2 a.m. on that morning, and the office generally was driven by the necessity of things to accommodate itself to Parliamentary exigencies.

Then he was asked his business. How could he explain to a messenger that his son had been unjustly convicted of bigamy and was now in prison as a criminal? So he left his card and said that he would call again at two.

At that hour precisely he appeared again and was told that the great man himself would not see him. Then he nearly boiled over in his wrath, while the messenger, with all possible courtesy, went on to explain that one of the deputies was ready to receive him. The deputy was the Honourable Septimus Brown, of whom it may be said that the Home Office was so proud that it considered itself to be superior to all other public offices whatever simply because it possessed Brown. He had been there for forty years, and for many sessions past had been the salvation of Parliamentary secretaries and under-secretaries. He was the uncle of an earl, and the brother-in-law of a duke and a marquis. Not to know Brown was, at the West End, simply to be unknown. Brooks's was proud of him; and without him the Travellers' would not have been such a Travellers' as it is. But Mr. Caldigate, when he was told that Mr. Brown would see him, almost left the lobby in instant disgust. When he asked who was Mr. Brown, there came a muttered reply in which 'permanent' was the only word audible to him. He felt that were he to go away in dudgeon simply because Brown was the name of the man whom he was called upon to see, he would put himself in the wrong. He would by so doing close his own mouth against complaint, which to Mr. Caldigate, would indeed have been a cutting of his own nose off his own face. With a scowl, therefore, he consented to be taken away to Mr. Brown.

He was, in the first place, somewhat scared by the room into which he was shown, which was very large and very high. There were two clerks with Mr. Brown, who vanished, however, as soon as the squire entered the room. It seemed that Mr. Brown was certainly of some standing in the office, or he would not have had two arm-chairs and a sofa in his room. Mr. Caldigate, when he first consented to see Mr. Brown, had expected to be led into an uncarpeted chamber where there would have been half-a-dozen other clerks.

'I have your card, Mr. Caldigate,' said the official. 'No doubt you have called in reference to your son.'

The squire had determined to be very indignant,—very indignant even with the Secretary of State himself, to whose indifference be attributed the delay which had occurred;—but almost more than indignant when he found that he was to be fobbed off with Mr. Brown. But there was something in the gentleman's voice which checked his indignation. There was something in Mr. Brown's eye, a mixture of good-humour and authority, which made him feel that he ought not to be angry with the gentleman till he was quite sure of the occasion. Mr. Brown was a handsome hale old man with grey whiskers and greyish hair, with a well-formed nose and a broad forehead, carefully dressed with a light waistcoat and a checked linen cravat, wearing a dark-blue frockcoat, and very well made boots,—an old man, certainly, but who looked as though old age must naturally be the happiest time of life. When a man's digestion is thoroughly good and his pockets adequately filled, it probably is so. Such were the circumstances of Mr. Brown, who, as the squire looked at him, seemed to partake more of the nature of his nephew and brothers-in-law than of the Browns generally.

'Yes, sir,' said Mr. Caldigate; 'I have called about my son who, I think I may undertake to say, has been wrongly condemned, and is now wrongly retained in prison.'

'You beg all the questions, Mr. Caldigate,' said the permanent under-secretary, with a smile.

'I maintain that what you call the questions are now so clearly proved as not to admit of controversy. No one can deny that a conspiracy was got up against my son.'

'I shall not deny it, certainly, Mr. Caldigate. But in truth I know very little or nothing about it.' The squire, who had been seated, rose from his chair,—as in wrath,—about to pour forth his indignation. Why was he treated in this way,—he who was there on a subject of such tragic interest to him? When all the prospects, reputation, and condition of his son were at stake, he was referred to a gentleman who began by telling him that he knew nothing about the matter! 'If you will sit down for a moment, Mr. Caldigate, I will explain all that can be explained,' said Mr. Brown, who was weather-wise in such matters, and had seen the signs of a coming storm.

'Certainly I will sit down.'

'In such cases as this the Secretary of State never sees those who are interested. It is not right that he should do so.'

'There might be somebody to do so.'

'But not somebody who has been concerned in the inquiry. The Secretary of State, if he saw you, could only refuse to impart to you any portion of the information which he himself may possess, because it cannot be right that he should give an opinion in the matter while he himself is in doubt. You may be sure that he will open his mouth to no one except to those from whom he may seek assistance, till he has been enabled to advise her Majesty that her Majesty's pardon should be given or refused.'

'When will that be?'

'I am afraid that I cannot name a day. You, Mr. Caldigate, are, I know, a gentleman of position in your county and a magistrate. Cannot you understand how minutely facts must be investigated when a Minister of the Crown is called upon to accept the responsibility of either upsetting or confirming the verdict of a jury?'

'The facts are as clear as daylight.'

'If they be so, your son will soon be a free man.'

'If you could feel what his wife suffers in the meantime!'

'Though I did feel it,—though we all felt it; as probably we do, for though we be officials still we are men,—how should that help us? You would not have a man pardoned because his wife suffers!'

'Knowing how she suffered, I do not think I should let much grass grow under my feet while I was making the inquiry.'

'I hope there is no such grass grows here. The truth is, Mr. Caldigate, that, as a rule, no person coming here on such an errand as yours is received at all. The Secretary of State cannot, either in his own person or in that of those who are under him, put himself in communication with the friends of individuals who are under sentence. I am sure that you, as a man conversant with the laws, must see the propriety of such a rule.'

'I think I have a right to express my natural anxiety.'

'I will not deny it. The post is open to you, and though I fear that our replies may not be considered altogether satisfactory, we do give our full attention to the letters we receive. When I heard that you had been here, and had expressed an intention of returning, from respect to yourself personally, I desired that you might be shown into my room. But I could not have done that had it not been that I myself have not been concerned in this matter.' Then he got up from his seat, and Mr. Caldigate found himself compelled to leave the room with thanks rather than with indignation.

He walked out of the big building into Downing Street, and down the steps into the park. And going into the gardens, he wandered about them for more than an hour, sometimes walking slowly along the water-side, and then seating himself for a while on one of the benches. What must he say to Hester in the letter which he must write as soon as he was back at his hotel? He tried to sift some wheat out of what he was pleased to call the chaff of Mr. Brown's courtesy. Was there not some indication to be found in it of what the result might be? If there were any such indication, it was, he thought, certainly adverse to his son. In whose bosom might be the ultimate decision,—whether in that of the Secretary, or the judge, or of some experienced clerk in the Secretary's office,—it was manifest that the facts which had now been proven to the world at large for many days, had none of the effects on that bosom which they had on his own. Could it be that Shand was false, that Bagwax was false, that the postage-stamp was false,—and that he only believed them to be true? Was it possible that after all his son had married the woman? He crept back to his hotel in Jermyn Street, and there he wrote his letter.

'I think I shall be home to-morrow, but I will not say so for certain. I have been at the Home Office, but they would tell me nothing. A man was very civil to me, but explained that he was civil only because he knew nothing about the case. I think I shall call on Mr. Bagwax at the Post-office to-morrow, and after that return to Folking. Send in for the day-mail letters, and then you will hear from me again if I mean to stay.'

At ten o'clock on the following day he was at the Post-office, and there he found Bagwax prepared to take his seat exactly at that hour. Thereupon he resolved with true radical impetuosity, that Bagwax was a much better public servant than Mr. Brown. 'Well, Mr. Caldigate,—so we've got it all clear at last,' said Bagwax.

There was a triumph in the tone of the clerk's voice which was not intelligible to the despondent old squire. 'It is not at all clear to me,' he said.

'Of course you've heard?'

'Heard what? I know all about the postage-stamp, of course.'

'If Secretaries of State and judges of the Court of Queen's Bench only had their wits about them, the postage-stamp ought to have been quite sufficient,' said Bagwax, sententiously.

'What more is there?'

'For the sake of letting the world know what can be done in our department, it is a pity that there should be anything more.'

'But there is something. For God's sake tell me, Mr. Bagwax.'

'You haven't heard that they caught Crinkett just as he was leaving Plymouth?'

'Not a word.'

'And the woman. They've got the lot of 'em, Mr. Caldigate. Adamson and the other woman have agreed to give evidence, and are to be let go.'

'When did you hear it?'

'Well;—it is in the "Daily Tell-tale." But I knew it last night,—from a particular source. I have been a good deal thrown in with Scotland Yard since this began, Mr. Caldigate, and, of course, I hear things.' Then it occurred to the squire that perhaps he had flown a little too high in going at once to the Home Office. They might have told him more, perhaps, in Scotland Yard. 'But it's all true. The depositions have already been made. Adamson and Young have sworn that they were present at no marriage. Crinkett, they say, means to plead guilty; but the woman sticks to it like wax.'

The squire had written a letter by the day-mail to say that he would remain in London that further day. He now wrote again, at the Post-office, telling Hester all that Bagwax had told him, and declaring his purpose of going at once to Scotland Yard.

If this story were true, then certainly his son would soon be liberated.

CHAPTER LVIII

Mr. Smirkie Is Ill-used

IT was on a Tuesday that Mr. Caldigate made his visit to the Home Office, and on the Thursday he returned to Cambridge. On the platform whom should he meet but his brother-in-law Squire Babington, who had come into Cambridge that morning intent of hearing something further about his nephew. He, too, had read a paragraph in his newspaper, 'The Snapper,' as to Crinkett and Euphemia Smith.

'Thomas Crinkett, and Euphemia Smith, who gave evidence against Mr. John Caldigate, in the well-known trial at the last Cambridge assizes, have been arrested at Plymouth just as they were about to leave the country for New Zealand. These are the persons to whom it was proved that Caldigate had paid the enormous sum of twenty thousand pounds a few days before the trial. It is alleged that they are to be indicted for perjury. If this be true, it implies the innocence of Mr. Caldigate, who, as our readers will remember, was convicted of bigamy. There will be much in the whole case for Mr. Caldigate to regret, but nothing so much as the loss of that very serious sum of money. It would be idle to deny that it was regarded by the jury, and the judge, and the public as a bribe to the witnesses. Why it should have been paid will now probably remain for ever a mystery.'

The squire read this over three times before he could quite understand the gist of it, and at last perceived,—or thought that he perceived, —that if this were true the innocence of his nephew was incontestable. But Julia, who seemed to prefer the paternal mansion at Babington to her own peculiar comforts and privileges at Plum-cum-Pippins, declared that she didn't believe a word of it; and aunt Polly, whose animosity to her nephew had somewhat subsided, was not quite inclined to accept the statement at once. Aunt Polly expressed an opinion that newspapers were only born to lie, but added that had she seen the news anywhere else she would not have been a bit surprised. The squire was prepared to swear by the tidings. If such a thing was not to be put into a newspaper, where was it to be put? Aunt Polly could not answer this question, but assisted in persuading her husband to go into Cambridge for further information.

'I hope this is true,' said the Suffolk squire, tendering his hand cordially to his brother-in-law. He was a man who could throw all his heart into an internecine quarrel on a Monday and forget the circumstance altogether on the Tuesday.

423

'Of what are you speaking?' asked the squire of Folking, with his usual placid look, partly indifferent and partly sarcastic, covering so much contempt of which the squire from Suffolk was able to read nothing at all.

'About the man and the woman, the witnesses who are to be put in prison at Plymouth, and who now say just the contrary to what they said before.'

'I do not think that can be true.' said Mr. Caldigate.

'Then you haven't seen the "Snapper"?' asked Mr. Babington, dragging the paper out of his pocket. 'Look at that.'

They were now in a cab together, going towards the town, and Mr. Caldigate did not find it convenient to read the paragraph. But of course he knew the contents. 'It is quite true,' he said, 'that the persons you allude to have been arrested, and that they are up in London. They will, I presume, be tried for perjury.'

'It is true?'

'There is no doubt of it.'

'And the party are splitting against each other?' asked Mr. Babington eagerly.

'Two of them have already sworn that what they swore before was false.'

'Then why don't they let him out?'

'Why not, indeed?' said Mr. Caldigate.

'I should have thought they wouldn't have lost a moment in such a case. They've got one of the best fellows in the world at the Home Office. His name is Brown. If you could have seen Brown I'm sure he wouldn't have let them delay a minute. The Home Office has the reputation of being so very quick.'

In answer to this the squire of Folking only shook his head. He would not even condescend to say that he had seen Brown, and certainly not to explain that Brown had seemed to him to be the most absurdly-cautious and courteously-dilatory man that he had ever met in his life. In Trumpington Street they parted, Mr. Caldigate proceeding at once to Folking, and Mr. Babington going to the office of Mr. Seely the attorney. 'He'll be out in a day or two,' said the man of Suffolk, again shaking his brother-in-law's hand; 'and do you tell him from me that I hope it won't be long before we see him at Babington. I've been true to him almost from the first, and his aunt has come over now. There is no one against him but Julia, and these are things of course which young women won't forget.'

Mr. Caldigate almost became genial as he accepted this assurance, telling himself that his brother magistrate was as honest as he was silly.

Mr. Babington, who was well known in Cambridge, asked many questions of many persons. From Mr. Seely he heard but little. Mr. Seely had heard of the arrest made at Plymouth, but did not quite know what to think about it. If it was all square, then he supposed his client must after all be innocent. But this went altogether against the grain with Mr. Seely. 'If it be so, Mr. Babington,' he said, 'I shall always think the paying away of that twenty thousand pounds the greatest miracle I ever came across.' Nevertheless, Mr. Seely did believe that the two witnesses had been arrested on a charge of perjury.

The squire then went to the governor of the jail, who had been connected with him many years as a county magistrate. The governor had heard nothing, received no information as to his prisoner from any one in authority; but quite believed the story as to Crinkett and the woman. 'Perhaps you had better not see him, Mr. Babington,' said the governor, 'as he has heard nothing as yet of all this. It would not be right to tell him till we know what it will come to.' Assenting to this, Mr. Babington took his leave with the conviction on his mind that the governor was quite prepared to receive an order for the liberation of his prisoner.

He did not dare to go to Robert Bolton's office, but he did call at the bank. 'We have heard nothing about it, Mr. Babington,' said the old clerk over the counter. But then the old clerk added in a whisper, 'None of the family take to the news, sir; but everybody else seems to think there is a great deal in it. If he didn't marry her I suppose he ought to be let out.'

'I should think he ought,' said the squire, indignantly, as he left the bank.

Thus fortified by what he considered to be the general voice of Cambridge, he returned the same evening to Babington. Cambridge, including Mr. Caldigate, had been unanimous in believing the report. And if the report were true, then, certainly, was his nephew innocent. As he thought of this, some appropriate idea of the injustice of the evil done to the man and to the man's wife came upon him. If such were the treatment to which he and she had been subjected,—if he, innocent, had been torn away from her and sent to the common jail, and if she, certainly innocent, had been wrongly deprived for a time of the name which he had honestly given her,—then would it not have been right to open to her the hearts and the doors at Babington during the period of her great distress? As he thought of this he was so melted by ruth that a tear came into each of his old eyes. Then he remembered the attempt which had been made to catch this man for Julia—as to which he certainly had been innocent,—and his daughter's continued wrath. That a woman should be wrathful in such a matter was natural to him. He conceived that it behoved a woman to be weak, irascible, affectionate, irrational, and soft-hearted. When Julia would be loud in condemnation of her cousin, and would pretend to commiserate the woes of the poor wife who had been left in Australia, though he knew the source of these feelings, he could not be in the least angry with her. But that was not at all the state of his mind in reference to his son-in-law Augustus Smirkie. Sometimes, as he had heard Mr. Smirkie inveigh against the enormity of bigamy and of this bigamist in particular, he had determined that some 'odd-come-shortly,' as he would call it, he would give the vicar of Plum-cum-Pippins a moral pat on the head which should silence him for a time. At the present moment when he got into his carriage at the station to be taken home, he was not sure whether or no he should find the vicar at Babington. Since their marriage, Mr. Smirkie had spent much of his time at Babington, and seemed to like the Babington claret. He would come about the middle of the week and return on the Saturday evening, in a manner which the squire could hardly reconcile with all that he had heard as to Mr. Smirkie's exemplary conduct in his own parish. The squire was hospitality itself, and certainly would never have said a word to make his house other than pleasant to his own girl's husband. But a host expects that his corns should be respected, whereas Mr. Smirkie was always treading on Mr. Babington's toes. Hints had been given to him as to his personal conduct which he did not take altogether in good part. His absence from afternoon service had been alluded to, and it had been suggested to him that he ought sometimes to be more careful as to his language. He was not, therefore, ill-disposed to resent on the part of Mr. Smirkie the spirit of persecution with which that gentleman seemed to regard his nephew. 'Is Mr. Smirkie in the house,' he asked the coachman. 'He came by the 3.40, as usual,' said the man. It was very much 'as usual,' thought the squire.

'There isn't a doubt about it,' said the squire to his wife as he was dressing. 'The poor fellow is as innocent as you.'

'He can't be,—innocent,' said aunt Polly.

'If he never married the woman whom they say he married he can't be guilty.'

'I don't know about that, my dear.'

'He either did marry her or he didn't, I suppose.'

'I don't say he married her, but,—he did worse.'

'No, he didn't,' said the squire.

'That may be your way of thinking of it. According to my idea of what is right and what is wrong, he did a great deal worse.'

'But if he didn't marry that woman he didn't commit bigamy when he married this one,' argued he, energetically.

'Still he may have deserved all he got.'

'No; he mayn't. You wouldn't punish a man for murder because he doesn't pay his debts.'

'I won't have it that he's innocent.' said Mrs. Babington.

'Who the devil is, if you come to that?'

'You are not, or you wouldn't talk in that way. I'm not saying anything now against John. If he didn't marry the woman I suppose they'll let him out of prison, and I for one shall be willing to take him by the hand; but to say he's innocent is what I won't put up with!'

'He has sown his wild oats, and he's none the worse for that. He's as good as the rest of us, I dare say.'

'Speak for yourself,' said the wife. 'I don't suppose you mean to tell me that in the eyes of the Creator he is as good a man as Augustus.'

'Augustus be——,' The word was spoken with great energy. Mrs. Babington at the moment was employed in sewing a button on the wristband of her husband's shirt, and in the start which she gave stuck the needle into his arm.

'Humphrey!' exclaimed the agitated lady.

'I beg your pardon, but not his,' said the squire, rubbing the wound. 'If he says a word more about John Caldigate in my presence, I shall tell him what I think about it. He has got his wife, and that ought to be enough for him.'

After that they went down-stairs and dinner was at once announced. There was Mr. Smirkie to give an arm to his mother-in-law. The squire took his married daughter while the other two followed. As they crossed the hall Julia whispered her cousin's name, but her father bade her be silent for the present. 'I was sure it was not true,' said Mrs. Smirkie.

'Then you're quite wrong,' said the squire, 'for it's as true as the Gospel.' Then there was no more said about John Caldigate till the servants had left the room.

Mr. Smirkie's general appreciation of the good things provided, did not on this occasion give the owner of them that gratification which a host should feel in the pleasures of his guests. He ate a very good dinner and took his wine with a full appreciation of its merits. Such an appetite on the part of his friends was generally much esteemed by the squire of Babington, who was apt to press the bottle upon those who sat with him, in the old-fashioned manner. At the present moment he eyed his son-in-law's enjoyments with a feeling akin to disappointment. There was a habit at Babington with the ladies of sitting with the squire when he was the only man present till he had finished his wine, and, at Mrs. Smirkie's instance, this custom was continued when she and her husband were at the house. Fires had been commenced, and when the dinner-things had been taken away they clustered round the hearth. The squire himself sat silent in his place, out of humour, knowing that the peculiar subject would be introduced, and determined to make himself disagreeable.

'Papa, won't you bring your chair round?' said one of the girls who was next to him. Whereupon he did move his chair an inch or two.

'Did you hear anything about John?' said the other unmarried sister.

'Yes, I heard about him. You can't help hearing about him at Cambridge now. All the world is talking about him.'

'And what does all the world say?' asked Julia, flippantly. To this question her father at first made no answer. 'Whatever the world may say, I cannot alter my opinion,' continued Julia. 'I shall never be able to look upon John Caldigate and Hester Bolton as man and wife in the sight of God.'

'I might just as well take upon myself to say that I didn't look upon you and Smirkie as man and wife in the sight of God.'

'Papa!' screamed the married daughter.

'Sir!' ejaculated the married son-in-law.

'My dear, that is a strange thing to say of your own child,' whispered the mother.

'Most strange!' said Julia, lifting both her hands up in an agony.

'But it's true,' roared the squire. 'She says that, let the law say what it may, these people are not to be regarded as man and wife.'

'Not by me,' said Julia.

'Who are you that you are to set up a tribunal of your own?' And if you judge of another couple in that way, why isn't some one to judge of you after the same fashion?'

'There is the verdict,' said Mr. Smirkie. 'No verdict has pronounced me a bigamist.'

'But it might for anything I know,' said the squire, angrily. 'Some woman might come up in Plum-cum-Pippins and say you had married her before your first wife.'

'Papa, you are very disagreeable,' said Julia.

'Why should'nt there be a wicked lie told in one place as well as in another? There has been a wicked lie told here; and when the lie is proved to have been a lie, as plain as the nose on your face, he is to tell me that he won't believe the young folk to be man and wife because of an untrue verdict! I say they are man and wife;—as good a man and wife as you and he;—and let me see who'll refuse to meet them as such in my house?'

Mr. Smirkie had not, in truth, made the offensive remark. It had been made by Mrs. Smirkie. But it had suited the squire to attribute it to the clergyman. Mr. Smirkie was now put upon his mettle, and was obliged either to agree or to disagree. He would have preferred the former, had he not been somewhat in awe of his wife. As it was, he fell back upon the indiscreet assertion which his father-in-law had made some time back. 'I, at any rate, sir, have not had a verdict against me.'

'What does that signify?'

'A great deal, I should say. A verdict, no doubt, is human, and therefore may be wrong.'

'So is a marriage human.'

'I beg your pardon, sir;—a marriage is divine.'

'Not if it isn't a marriage. Your marriage in our church wouldn't have been divine if you'd had another wife alive.'

'Papa, I wish you wouldn't.'

'But I shall. I've got to hammer it into his head somehow.'

Mr. Smirkie drew himself up and grinned bravely. But the squire did not care for his frowns. That last backhander at the claret-jug had determined him. 'John Caldigate's marriage with his wife was not in the least interfered with by the verdict.'

'It took away the lady's name from her at once,' said the indignant clergyman.

'That's just what it didn't do,' said the squire, rising from his chair;— 'of itself it didn't affect her name at all. And now that it is shown to have been a mistaken verdict, it doesn't affect her position. The long and the short of it is this, that anybody who doesn't like to meet him and his wife as honoured guests in my house had better stay away. Do you hear that Julia?' Then without waiting for an answer he walked out before them all into the drawing-room, and not another word was said that night about the matter. Mr. Smirkie, indeed, did not utter a word on any subject, till at an early hour he wished them all good-night with dignified composure.

CHAPTER LIX

How The Big-wigs Doubted

'IT'S what I call an awful shame.' Mr. Holt and parson Bromley were standing together on the causeway at Folking, and the former was speaking. The subject under discussion was, of course, the continued detention of John Caldigate in the county prison.

'I cannot at all understand it,' said Mr. Bromley.

'There's no understanding nothing about it, sir. Every man, woman, and child in the county knows as there wasn't no other marriage, and yet they won't let 'un out. It's sheer spite, because he wouldn't vote for their man last 'lection.'

'I hardly think that, Mr. Holt.'

'I'm as sure of it as I stands here,' said Mr. Holt, slapping his thigh. 'What else'd they keep 'un in for? It's just like their ways.'

Mr. Holt was one of a rare class, being a liberal farmer,—a Liberal, that is, in politics; as was also Mr. Bromley, a Liberal among parsons,— *rara avis.* The Caldigates had always been Liberal, and Mr. Holt had been brought up to agree with his landlord. He was now beyond measure acerbated, because John Caldigate had not been as yet declared innocent on evidence which was altogether conclusive to himself. The Conservatives were now in power, and nothing seemed so natural to Mr. Holt as that the Home Secretary should keep his landlord in jail because the Caldigates were Liberals. Mr. Bromley could not quite agree to this, but he also was of opinion that a great injustice was being done. He was in the habit of seeing the young wife almost daily, and knew the havoc which hope turned into despair was making with her. Another week had now gone by since the old squire had been up in town, and nothing yet had been heard from the Secretary of State. All the world knew that Crinkett and Euphemia Smith were in custody, and still no tidings came, —yet the husband, convicted on the evidence of these perjurers, was detained in prison!

Hope deferred maketh the heart sick, and Hester's heart was very sick within her. 'Why do they not tell me something?' she said when her father-in-law vainly endeavoured to comfort her. Why not, indeed? He could only say hard things of the whole system under which the perpetration of so great a cruelty was possible, and reiterate his opinion that, in spite of that system, they must, before long, let his son go free.

The delay in truth was not at the Home Office. Judge Bramber could not as yet quite make up his mind. It is hoped that the reader has made up his, but the reader knows somewhat more than the judge knew. Crinkett had confessed nothing,—though a rumour had got abroad that he intended to plead guilty. Euphemia Smith was constant in her assertion to all those who came near her, that she had positively been married to the man at Ahalala. Adamson and Anna Young were ready now to swear that all which they had sworn before was false; but it was known to the police that they had quarrelled bitterly as to the division of the spoil ever since the money had been paid to the ring-leaders. It was known that Anna Young had succeeded in getting nothing from the other woman, and that the man had unwillingly accepted his small share, fearing that otherwise he might get nothing. They were not trustworthy witnesses, and it was very doubtful whether the other two could be convicted on their evidence. The judge, as he turned it all over in his mind, was by no means sure that the verdict was a mistaken verdict. It was at any rate a verdict. It was a decision constitutionally arrived at from a jury. This sending back of the matter to him hardly was constitutional.

It was abhorrent to his nature,—not that a guilty man should escape, which he knew to be an affair occurring every day,—but that a guilty man, who had been found to be guilty, should creep back through the meshes of the law. He knew how many chances were given by the practice of British courts to an offender on his trial, and he was quite in favour of those chances. He would be urgent in telling a jury to give the prisoner the benefit of a doubt. But when the transgressor, with all those loopholes stopped, stood before him convicted, then he felt a delight in the tightness of the grip with which he held the wretch, and would tell himself that the world in which he lived was not as yet all astray, in that a guilty man could still be made to endure the proper reward of his guilt.

It was with him as when a hunter has hunted a fox after the approved laws of venery. There have been a dozen ways of killing the animal of which he has scorned to avail himself. He has been careful to let him break from his covert, regarding all who would stop him as enemies to himself. It has been a point of honour with him that the animal should suffer no undue impediment. Any ill-treatment shown to the favoured one in his course, is an injury done to the hunter himself. Let no man head the fox, let no man strive to drive him back upon the hounds. Let all be done by hunting law,—in accordance with those laws which give so many chances of escape. But when the hounds have run into their quarry, not all the eloquence of all the gods should serve to save that doomed one's life.

So it was with Judge Bramber and a convicted prisoner. He would

431

give the man the full benefit of every quibble of the law till he was convicted. He would be severe on witnesses, harsh to the police, apparently
a very friend to the man standing at the bar,—till the time came for him
to array the evidence before the jury. Then he was inexorable; and when
the verdict had been once pronounced, the prisoner was but as a fox
about to be thrown to the hounds.

And now there was a demand that this particular fox should be put
back into his covert! The Secretary of State could put him back, if he
thought fit. But in these matters there was so often a touch of cowardice. Why did not the Secretary do it without asking him? There had
arisen no question of law. There was no question as to the propriety of
the verdict as found upon the evidence given at the trial. The doubt which
had arisen since had come from further evidence, of which the Secretary was as well able to judge as he. No doubt the case was difficult.
There had been gross misdoing on both sides. But if Caldigate had not
married the woman, why had he paid those twenty thousands? Why had
he written those words on the envelope? There was doubt enough now,
but the time for giving the prisoner the benefit of the doubt was gone.
The fox had been fairly hunted, and Judge Bramber thought that he had
better die.

But he hesitated;—and while he was hesitating there came to him a
little reminder, a most gentle hint, in the shape of a note from the Secretary of State's private secretary. The old squire's visit to the office had
not seemed to himself to be satisfactory, but he had made a friend for
himself in Mr. Brown. Mr. Brown looked into the matter, and was of
opinion that it would be well to pardon the young man. Even though
there had been some jumping over a broomstick at Ahalala, why should
things not be made comfortable here at home? What harm would a
pardon do to any one?—whereas there were so many whom it would
make happy. So he asked the Secretary whether that wasn't a hard case
of young Caldigate. The Secretary whispered that it was in Bramber's
hands, upon which Mr. Brown observed that, if so, is was certainly hard.
But the conversation was not altogether thrown away, for on that afternoon the private secretary wrote his note.

Judge Bramber when he received the note immediately burned it,—
and this he did with considerable energy of action. If they would send
him such cases as that, what right had they to remind him of his duty?
He was not going to allow any private secretary, or any Secretary of
State, to hurry him! There was no life or death in this matter. Of what
importance was it that so manifest an evil-doer as this young Caldigate
should remain in prison a day or two more,—a man who had attempted
to bribe four witnesses by twenty thousand pounds? It was an

additional evil that such a one should have such a sum for such a purpose. But still he felt that there was a duty thrown upon him; and he sat down with all the papers before him, determined to make up his mind before he rose from his chair.

He did make up his mind, but did so at last by referring back the responsibility to the Secretary of State. 'The question is one altogether of evidence,' he said, 'and not of law. Any clear-headed man is as able to reach a true decision as I am. It is such a question as should be left to a jury,—and would justify a trial on appeal if that were practicable. It would be well that the case should stand over till Thomas Crinkett and Euphemia Smith shall have been tried for perjury, which, as I understand, will take place at the next winter assizes. If the Secretary of State thinks that the delay would be too long, I would humbly suggest that he should take her Majesty's pleasure in accordance with his own opinion as to the evidence.'

When that document was read at the Home Office by the few who were privileged to read it, they knew that Judge Bramber had been in a very ill humour. But there was no help for that. The judge had been asked for advice and had refused to give it; or had advised,—if his remark on that subject was to be taken for advice,—that the consideration of the matter should be postponed for another three months. The case, if there was any case in favour of the prisoner, was not one for pardon but for such redress as might now be given for a most gross injustice. The man had been put to a very great expense, and had been already in prison for ten or eleven weeks, and his further detention would be held to have been very cruel if it should appear at last that the verdict had been wrong. The public press was already using strong language on the subject, and the Secretary of State was not indifferent to the public press. Judge Bramber thoroughly despised the press,—though he would have been very angry if his 'Times' had not been ready for him at breakfast every morning. And two or three questions had already been asked in the House of Commons. The Secretary of State, with that habitual strategy, without which any Secretary of State must be held to be unfit for the position which he holds, contrived to answer the questions so as to show that, while the gentlemen who asked them were the most indiscreet of individuals, he was the most discreet of Secretaries. And he did this, though he was strongly of opinion that Judge Bramber's delay was unjustifiable. But what would be thought of a Secretary of State who would impute blame in the House of Commons to one of the judges of the land before public opinion had expressed itself so strongly on the matter as to make such expression indispensable? He did not think that he was in the least untrue in throwing blame back upon the questioners, and in implying that on the side of the Crown there had been no undue delay, though, at the moment, he was inwardly provoked at the dilatoriness of the judge.

Public opinion was expressing itself very strongly in the press. 'The Daily Tell-Tale' had a beautifully sensational article, written by their very best artist. The whole picture was drawn with a cunning hand. The young wife in her lonely house down in Cambridge, which the artist not inaptly called The Moated Grange! The noble, innocent, high-souled husband, eating his heart out within the bars of a county prison, and with very little else to eat! The indignant father, driven almost to madness by the wrongs done to his son and heir! Had the son not been an heir this point would have been much less touching. And then the old evidence was dissected, and the new evidence against the new culprits explained. In regard to the new culprits, the writer was very loud in expressing his purpose to say not a word against persons who were still to be tried;—but immediately upon that he went on and said a great many words against them. Assuming all that was said about them to be true, he asked whether the country would for a moment endure the idea that a man in Mr. Caldigate's position should be kept in prison on the evidence of such miscreants. When he came to Bagwax and the post-marks, he explained the whole matter with almost more than accuracy. He showed that the impression could not possibly have been made till after the date it conveyed. He fell into some little error as to the fabrication of the postage-stamp in the colony, not having quite seized Bagwax's great point. But it was a most telling article. And the writer, as he turned it off at his club, and sent it down to the office of the paper, was ready to bet a five-pound note that Caldigate would be out before a week was over. The Secretary of State saw the article, and acknowledged its power. And then even the 'Slipper' turned round and cautiously expressed an opinion that the time had come for mercy.

There could be no doubt that public opinion was running very high in Caldigate's favour, and that the case had become thoroughly popular. People were again beginning to give dinner-parties in London, and at every party the matter was discussed. It was a peculiarly interesting case because the man had thrown away so large a sum of money! People like to have a nut to crack which is 'uncrackable,'—a Gordian knot to undo which cannot even be cut. Nobody could understand the twenty thousand pounds. Would any man pay such a sum with the object of buying false witnesses,—and do it in such a manner that all the facts muct be brought to light when he was tried? It was said here and there that he had paid the money because he owed it;—but then it had been shown so clearly that he had not owed any one a penny! Nevertheless the men were all certain that he was not guilty, and the ladies thought that whether he were guilty or not did not matter much. He certainly ought to be released from prison.

But yet the Secretary doubted. In that unspoken but heartfelt accusation of cowardice which the judge had made against the great officer of State there had been some truth. How would it be if it should be made to appear at the approaching trial that the two reprobates, who had turned Queen's evidence against their associates, were to break down altogether in their assertions? It might possibly then become quite apparent that Caldigate had married the woman, and had committed bigamy, when he would already have been pardoned for the last three months! The pardon in that case would not do away with the verdict,— and the pardoned man would be a convicted bigamist. What, then, would be the condition of his wife and child? If subsequent question should arise as to the boy's legitimacy, as might so probably be the case, in what light would he appear, he who had taken upon himself, on his own responsibility, to extort from her Majesty a pardon in opposition to a righteous and just verdict,—in opposition to the judge who had tried the case? He had been angry with Judge Bramber for not deciding, and was now frightened at the necessity of deciding himself.

In this emergency he sent for the gentleman who had managed the prosecution on the part of the Crown, and asked him to read up the case again. 'I never was convinced of the prisoner's guilt,' said the barrister.

'No!'

'It was one of those cases in which we cannot be convinced. The strongest point against him was the payment of the money. It is possible that he paid it from a Quixotic feeling of honour.'

'To false witnesses, and that before the trial!' said the Secretary.

'And there may have been a hope that, in spite of what he said himself as to their staying, they would take themselves off when they had got the money. In that way he may have persuaded himself that, as an honest man, he ought to make the payment. Then as to the witnesses, there can be little doubt that they were willing to lie. Even if their main story were true, they were lying as to details.'

'Then you would advise a pardon?'

'I think so,' said the barrister, who was not responsible for his advice.

'Without waiting for the other trial?'

'If the perjury be then proved,—or even so nearly proved as to satisfy the outside world,—the man's detention will be thought to have been a hardship.' The Secretary of State thanked the barrister and let him go. He then went down to the House, and amidst the turmoil of a strong party conflict at last made up his mind. It was unjust that such responsibility should be thrown upon any one person. There ought to be some Court of Appeal for such cases. He was sure of that now. But at last he made up his mind. Early on the next morning the Queen should be advised to allow John Caldigate to go free.

CHAPTER LX

How Mrs. Bolton Was Nearly Conquered

ONE morning about the middle of October, Robert Bolton walked out from Cambridge to Puritan Grange with a letter in his pocket,—a very long and a very serious letter. The day was that on which the Secretary of State was closeted with the barrister, and on the evening of which he at length determined that Caldigate should be allowed to go free. There had, therefore, been no pardon granted,—as yet. But in the letter the writer stated that such pardon would, almost certainly, be awarded.

It was from William Bolton, in London, to his brother the attorney, and was written with the view of proving to all the Boltons at Cambridge, that it was their duty to acknowledge Hester as the undoubted wife of John Caldigate; and recommended also that, for Hester's sake, they should receive him as her husband. The letter had been written with very great care, and had been powerful enough to persuade Robert Bolton of the truth of the first proposition.

It was very long, and as it repeated all the details of the evidence for and against the verdict, it shall not be repeated here at its full length. Its intention was to show that, looking at probabilities, and judging from all that was known, there was much more reason to suppose that there had been no marriage at Ahalala than that there had been one. The writer acknowledged that, while the verdict stood confirmed against the man, Hester's family were bound to regard it, and to act as though they did not doubt its justice;—but that when that verdict should be set aside,—as far as any criminal verdict can be set aside,—by the Queen's pardon, then the family would be bound to suppose that they who advised her Majesty had exercised a sound discretion.

'I am sure you will all agree with me,' he said, 'that no personal feeling in regard to Caldigate should influence your judgment. For myself, I like the man. But that, I think, has had nothing to do with my opinion. If it had been the case that, having a wife living, he had betrayed my sister into all the misery of a false marriage, and had made her the mother of a nameless child, I should have felt myself bound to punish him to every extent within my power. I do not think it unchristian to say that in such a case I could not have forgiven him. But presuming it to be otherwise,—as we all shall be bound to do if he be pardoned,—then, for Hester's sake, we should receive the man with whom her lot in life is so closely connected. She, poor dear, has suffered enough, and should not

437

be subjected to the further trouble of our estrangement.

'Nor, if we acknowledge the charge against him to be untrue, is there any reason for a quarrel. If he has not been bad to our sister in that matter, he has been altogether good to her. She has for him that devotion which is the best evidence that a marriage has been well chosen. Presuming him to be innocent, we must confess, as to her, that she has been simply loyal to her husband,—with such loyalty as every married man would desire. For this she should be rewarded rather than punished.

'I write to you thinking that in this way I may best reach my father and Mrs. Bolton. I would go down and see them did I not know that your words would be more efficacious with them than my own. And I do it as a duty to my sister, which I feel myself bound to perform. Pray forgive me if I remind you that in this respect she has a peculiar right to a performance of your duty in the matter. You counselled and carried out the marriage,—not at all unfortunately if the man be, as I think, innocent. But you are bound at any rate to sift the evidence very closely, and not to mar her happiness by refusing to acknowledge him if there be reasonable ground for supposing the verdict to have been incorrect.'

Sift the evidence, indeed! Robert Bolton had done that already very closely. Bagwax and the stamps had not moved him, nor the direct assurance of Dick Shand. But the incarceration by Government of Crinkett and Euphemia Smith had shaken him, and the fact that they had endeavoured to escape the moment they heard of Shand's arrival. But not the less had he hated Caldigate. The feeling which had been impressed on his mind when the first facts were made known to him remained. Caldigate had been engaged to marry the woman, and had lived with her, and had addressed her as his wife! The man had in a way got the better of him. And then the twenty thousand pounds! And then, again, Caldigate's manner to himself! He could not get over his personal aversion, and therefore unconsciously wished that his brother-in-law should be guilty,—wished at any rate that he should be kept in prison. Gradually had fallen upon him the conviction that Caldigate would be pardoned. And then of course there had come much consideration as to his sister's condition. He, too, was a conscientious and an affectionate man. He was well aware of his duty to his sister. While he was able to assure himself that Caldigate was not her husband, he could satisfy himself by a conviction that it was his duty to keep them apart. Thus he could hate the man, advocate all severity against the man, and believe the while that he was doing his duty to his sister as an affectionate brother. But now there was a revulsion. It was three weeks since he and his brother had parted, not with the kindest feelings, up in London, and during that time the sifting of the evidence had been going on within his own breast from hour to hour. And now this letter had come,—a letter which he could not put away in anger, a letter which he could not ignore. To quarrel permanently with his brother William was quite out of the question. He knew the value of such a friend too well, and had been too often guided by his advice. So he sifted the evidence once again, and then walked off to Puritan Grange with the letter in his pocket.

In these latter days old Mr. Bolton did not go often into Cambridge. Men said that his daughter's misfortune had broken him very much. It was perhaps the violence of his wife's religion rather than the weight of his daughter's sufferings which cowed him. Since Hester's awful obstinacy had become hopeless to Mrs. Bolton, an atmosphere of sackcloth and ashes had made itself more than ever predominant at Puritan Grange. If any one hated papistry Mrs. Bolton did so; but from a similar action of religious fanaticism she had fallen into worse that papistical self-persecution. That men and women were all worms to be trodden under foot, and grass of the field to be thrown into the oven, was borne in so often on poor Mr. Bolton that he had not strength left to go to the bank. And they were nearer akin to worms and more like grass of the field than ever, because Hester would stay at Folking instead of returning to her own home.

She was in this frame of mind when Robert Bolton was shown into the morning sitting-room. She was sitting with the Bible before her, but with some domestic needlework in her lap. He was doing nothing,—not even having a book ready to his hand. Thus he would sit the greater part of the day, listening to her when she would read to him, but much preferring to be left alone. His life had been active and prosperous, but the evening of his days was certainly not happy.

His son Robert had been anxious to discuss the matter with him first, but found himself unable to separate them without an amount of ceremony which would have filled her with suspicion. 'I have received a letter this morning from William,' he said, addressing himself to his father.

'William Bolton is, I fear, of the world worldly,' said the stepmother. 'His words always savour to me of the huge ungodly city in which he dwells.'

But that this was not a time for such an exercise he would have endeavoured to expose the prejudice of the lady. As it was he was very gentle. 'William is a man who understands his duty well,' he said.

'Many do that, but few act up to their understanding,' she rejoined.

'I think, sir, I had better read his letter to you. It has been written with that intention, and I am bound to let you know the contents.

Perhaps Mrs. Bolton will let me go to the end so that we may discuss it afterwards.'

But Mrs. Bolton would not let him go to the end. He had not probably expected such forbearance. At every point as to the evidence she interrupted him, striving to show that the arguments used were of no real weight. She was altogether irrational, but still she argued her case well. She withered Bagwax and Dick with her scorn; she ridiculed the quarrels of the male and female witnesses; she reviled the Secretary of State, and declared it to be a shame that the Queen should have no better advisers. But when William Bolton spoke of Hester's happiness, and of the concessions which should be made to secure that, she burst out into eloquence. What did he know of her happiness? Was it not manifest that he was alluding to this world without a thought of the next? 'Not a reflection as to her soul's welfare has once come across his mind,' she said; —'not an idea as to the sin with which her soul would be laden were she to continue to live with the man when knowing that he was not her husband.'

'She would know nothing of the kind,' said the attorney.

'She ought to know it,' said Mrs. Bolton, again begging the whole question.

But he persevered, as he had resolved to do when he left his house upon this difficult mission. 'I am sure my father will acknowledge,' he said, 'that however strong our own feelings have been, we should bow to the conviction of others who—'

But he was promulgating a doctrine which her conscience required her to stop at once. 'The conviction of others shall never have weight with me when the welfare of my eternal soul is at stake.'

'I am speaking of those who have had better means of getting at the truth than have come within our reach. The Secretary of State can have no bias of his own in the matter.'

'He is, I fear, a godless man, living and dealing with the godless. Did I not hear the other day that the great Ministers of State will not even give a moment to attend to the short meaningless prayers which are read in the House of Commons?'

'No one,' continued Robert Bolton, trying to get away from sentiment into real argument,—'no one can have been more intent on separating them than William was when he thought that the evidence was against him. Now he thinks the evidence in his favour. I know no man whose head is clearer than my brother's. I am not very fond of John Caldigate.'

'Nor am I,' said the woman with an energy which betrayed much of her true feeling.

'But if it be the case that they are in truth man and wife—'

'In the sight of God they are not so,' she said.

'Then,' he continued, trying to put aside her interruption, and to go on with the assertion he had commenced, 'it must be our duty to acknowledge him for her sake. Were we not to do so, we should stand condemned in the opinion of all the world.'

'Who cares for the opinion of the world?'

'And we should destroy her happiness.'

'Her happiness here on earth! What does it matter? There is no such happiness.'

It was a very hard fight, but perhaps not harder than he had expected. He had known that she would not listen to reason,—that she would not even attempt to understand it. And he had learned before this how impregnable was that will of fanaticism in which she would entrench herself,—how improbable it was that she would capitulate under the force of any argument. But he thought it possible that he might move his father to assert himself. He was well aware that, in the midst of that apparent lethargy, his father's mind was at work with much of its old energy. He understood the physical infirmities and religious vacillation which, combined, had brought the old man into his present state of apparent submission. It was hardly two years since the same thing had been done in regard to Hester's marriage. Then Mr. Bolton had asserted himself, and declared his will in opposition to his wife. There had indeed been much change in him since that time, but still something of the old fire remained. 'I have thought it to be my duty, sir,' he said, 'to make known to you William's opinion and my own. I say nothing as to social intercourse. That must be left to yourself. But if this pardon be granted, you will, I think, be bound to acknowledge John Caldigate to be your son-in-law.'

'Your father agrees with me,' said Mrs. Bolton, rising from her chair, and speaking in an angry tone.

'I hope you both will agree with me. As soon as tidings of the pardon reach you, you should, I think, intimate to Hester that you accept her marriage as having been true and legal. I shall do so, even though I should never see him in my house again.'

'You of course will do as you please.'

'And you, sir?' he said, appealing to the old man.

'You have no right to dictate to your father,' said the wife angrily.

'He has always encouraged me to offer him my advice.' Then Mr. Bolton shuffled in his chair, as though collecting himself for an effort,— and at last sat up, with his head, however, bent forward, and with both his arms resting on the arms of his chair. Though he looked to be old, much older than he was, still there was a gleam of fire in his eye. He was

441

thin, almost emaciated, and his head hung forward as though there were not strength left in his spine for him to sit erect. 'I hope, sir, you do not think that I have gone beyond my duty in what I have said.'

'She shall come here,' muttered the old man.

'Certainly, she shall,' said Mrs. Bolton, 'if she will. Do you suppose that I do not long to have my own child in my arms?'

'She shall come here, and be called by her name,' said the father.

'She shall be Hester,—my own Hester,' said the mother, not feeling herself as yet called upon to contradict her husband.

'And John Caldigate shall come,' he said.

'Never!' exclaimed Mrs. Bolton.

'He shall be asked to come. I say he shall. Am I to be harder on my own child than are all the others? Shall I call her a castaway, when others say that she is an honest married woman?'

'Who has called her a castaway?'

'I took the verdict of the jury, though it broke my heart,' he continued. 'It broke my heart to be told that my girl and her child were nameless,—but I believed it because the jury said so, and because the judge declared it. When they tell me the contrary, why shall I not believe that? I do believe it; and she shall come here, if she will, and he shall come.' Then he got up and slowly moved out of the room, so that there might be no further argument on the subject.

She had reseated herself with her arms crossed, and there sat perfectly mute. Robert Bolton stood up and repeated all his arguments, appealing even to her maternal love,—but she answered him never a word. She had not even yet succeeded in making the companion of her life submissive to her! That was the feeling which was now uppermost in her mind. He had said that Caldigate should be asked to the house, and should be acknowledged throughout all Cambridge as his son-in-law. And having said it, he would be as good as his word. She was sure of that. Of what avail had been all the labour of her life with such a result?

'I hope you will think that I have done no more than my duty,' said Robert Bolton, offering her his hand. But there she sat perfectly silent, with her arms still folded, and would take no notice of him. 'Good-bye,' said he, striving to put something of the softness of affection into his voice. But she would not even bend her head to him;—and thus he left her.

She remained motionless for the best part of an hour. Then she got up, and according to her daily custom walked a certain number of times round the garden. Her mind was so full that she did not as usual observe every twig, almost every leaf, as she passed. Nor, now that she was alone, was that religious bias, which had so much to do with her daily life, very strong within her. There was no taint of hypocrisy in her character; but yet, with the force of human disappointment heavy upon her, her heart was now hot with human anger, and mutinous with human resolves. She had proposed to herself to revenge herself upon the men of her husband's family,—upon the men who had contrived that marriage for her daughter, —by devoting herself to the care of that daughter and her nameless grandson, and by letting it be known to all that the misery of their condition would have been spared had her word prevailed. That they should live together a stern, dark, but still sympathetic life, secluded within the high walls of that lonely abode, and that she should thus be able to prove how right she had been, how wicked and calamitous their interference with her child,—that had been the scheme of her life. And now her scheme was knocked on the head, and Hester was to become a prosperous ordinary married woman amidst the fatness of the land at Folking! It was all wormwood to her. But still, as she walked, she acknowledged to herself, that as that old man had said so,—so it must be. With all her labour, with all her care, and with all her strength, she had not succeeded in becoming the master of that weak old man.

CHAPTER LXI

The News Reaches Cambridge

THE tidings of John Caldigate's pardon reached Cambridge on the Saturday morning, and was communicated in various shapes. Official letters from the Home Office were written to the governor of the jail and to the sub-sheriff, to Mr. Seely who was still acting as attorney on behalf of the prisoner, and to Caldigate himself. The latter was longer than the others, and contained a gracious expression of Her Majesty's regret that he as an innocent person should have been subjected to imprisonment. The Secretary of State also was described as being keenly sensible of the injustice which had been perpetrated by the unfortunate and most unusual circumstances of the case. As the Home Office had decided that the man was to be considered innocent, it decided also on the expression of its opinion without a shadow of remaining doubt. And the news reached Cambridge in other ways by the same post. William Bolton wrote both to his father and brother, and Mr. Brown the Under-Secretary sent a private letter to the old squire at Folking, of which further mention shall be made. Before church time on the Sunday morning, the fact that John Caldigate was to be released, or had been released from prison, was known to all Cambridge.

Caldigate himself had borne his imprisonment on the whole well. He had complained but little to those around him, and had at once resolved to endure the slowly passing two years with silent fortitude,—as a brave man will resolve to bear any evil for which there is no remedy. But a more wretched man than he was after the first week of bitterness could hardly be found. Fortitude has no effect in abating such misery other than what may come from an absence of fretful impatience. The man who endures all that the tormentors can do to him without a sign, simply refuses to acknowledge the agonies inflicted. So it was with Caldigate. Though he obeyed with placid readiness all the prison instructions, and composed his features and seemed almost to smile when that which was to be exacted from him was explained, he ate his heart in dismay as he counted the days, the hours, the minutes, and then calculated the amount of misery that was in store for him. And there was so much more for him to think of than his own condition. He knew of course that he was innocent of the crime imputed to him;—but would it not be the same to his wife and child as though he had been in truth guilty? Would not his boy to his dying day be regarded as illegitimate? And though he had

444

been wrongly condemned, had not all this come in truth from his own fault? And when that eternity of misery within the prison walls should have come to an end,—if he could live through it so as to see the end of it, what would then be his fate, and what his duty? He had perfect trust in his wife; but who could say what two years might do,—two years during which she would be subjected to the pressure of all her friends? Where should he find her when the months had passed? And if she were no longer at Folking, would she come back to him? He was sure, nearly sure, that he could not claim her as his wife. And were she still minded to share her future lot with him, in what way should he treat her? If that horrid woman was his wife in the eye of the law,—and he feared though hardly knew that it would be so,—then could not that other one, who was to him as a part of his own soul, be his wife also? What would become of his child, who, as far as he could see, would not be his child at all in the eye of the law? Even while he was still a free man, still uncondemned, an effort had been made to rob him of his wife and boy,—an effort which for a time had seemed to be successful. How would Hester be able to withstand such attempts when they would be justified by a legal decision that she was not his wife,—and could not become his wife while that other woman was alive? Such thoughts as these did not tend to relieve the weariness of his days.

The only person from the outside world whom he was allowed to see during the three months of his incarceration was Mr. Seely, and with him he had two interviews. From the time of the verdict Mr. Seely was still engaged in making those enquiries as to the evidence of which we have heard so much, and though he was altogether unsympathetic and incredulous, still he did his duty. He had told his client that these enquiries were being made, and had, on his second visit, informed him of the arrival of Dick Shand. But he had never spoken with hope, and had almost ridiculed Bagwax with his postage-stamps and post-marks. When Caldigate first heard that Dick was in England,—for a minute or two,—he allowed himself to be full of hope. But the attorney had dashed his hopes. What was Shand's evidence against the testimony of four witnesses who had borne the fire of cross-examination? Their character was not very good, but Dick's was, if possible, worse. Mr. Seely did not think that Dick's word would go for much. He could simply say that, as far as he knew, there had been no marriage. And in this Mr. Seely had been right, for Dick's word had not gone for much. Then, when Crinkett and Mrs. Smith had been arrested, no tidings had reached him of that further event. It had been thought best that nothing as to that should be communicated to him till the result should be known.

Thus it had come to pass that when the tidings reached the prison he was not in a state of expectation. The governor of the prison knew what was going on, and had for days been looking for the order of release. But he had not held himself to be justified in acquainting his prisoner with the facts. The despatches to him and to Caldigate from the Home Office were marked immediate, and by the courtesy of the postmaster were given in at the prison gates before daylight. Caldigate was still asleep when the door of the cell was opened by the governor in person, and the communication was made to him as he lay for the last time stretched on his prison pallet. 'You can get up a free man, Mr. Caldigate,' said the governor, with his hand on his prisoner's shoulder. 'I have here the Queen's pardon. It has reached me this morning.' Caldigate got up and looked at the man as though he did not at first understand the words that had been spoken. 'It is true, Mr. Caldigate. Here is my authority,— and this, no doubt, is a communication of the same nature to yourself.' Then Caldigate took the letter, and, with his mind still bewildered, made himself acquainted with the gratifying fact that all the big-wigs were very sorry for the misfortune which had befallen him.

In his state of mind, as it then was, he was by no means disposed to think much of the injustice done to him. He had in store for him, for immediate use, a whole world of glorious bliss. There was his house, his property, his farm, his garden, and the free air. And there would be the knowledge of all those around him that he had not done the treacherous thing of which those wretches had accused him. And added to all this, and above all this, there would be his wife and his child! It was odd enough that a word from the mouth of an exalted Parliamentary personage should be able to give him back one wife and release him from another,—in opposition to the decision of the law,—should avail to restore to his boy the name and birthright of which he had been practically deprived, and should, by a stroke of his pen, undo all that had been done by the combined efforts of jury, judge, and prosecutor! But he found that so it was. He was pardoned, forsooth, as though he were still a guilty man! Yet he would have back his wife and child, and no one could gainsay him.

'When can I go?' he said, jumping from his bed.

'When you please;—now, at once. But you had better come into the house and breakfast with me first.'

'If I may I would rather go instantly. Can you send for a carriage for me?' Then the governor endeavoured to explain to him that it would be better for his wife, and more comfortable for everybody concerned, that she should have been enabled to expect him, if it were only for an hour or two, before his arrival. A communication would doubtless have been made from the Home Office to some one at Folking, and as that would be sent out by the foot-postman it would not be received before nine in the morning.

But Caldigate would not allow himself to be persuaded. As for eating before he had seen the dear ones at home, that he declared to be impossible. A vision of what that breakfast might be to him with his own wife at his side came before his eyes, and therefore a messenger was at once sent for the vehicle.

But the postmaster, who from the beginning had never been a believer in the Australian wife, and, being a Liberal, was staunch to the Caldigate side of the question, would not allow the letter addressed to the old squire to be retained for the slow operations of the regular messenger, but sent it off manfully, by horse express, before the dawn of day, so that it reached the old squire almost as soon as the other letters reached the prison. The squire, who was an early man, was shaving himself when the despatch was brought into his room with an intimation that the boy on horseback wanted to know what he was to do next. The boy of course got his breakfast, and Mr. Caldigate read his letter, which was as follows:—

'HOME OFFICE,—*October,* 187—.

'My Dear Sir,—When you did me the honour of calling upon me here I was able to do no more than express my sympathy as to the misfortune which had fallen upon your family, and to explain to you, I fear not very efficiently, that at that moment the mouths of all of us here were stopped by official prudence as to the matter which was naturally so near your heart. I have now the very great pleasure of informing you that the Secretary of State has this morning received her Majesty's command to issue a pardon for your son. The official intimation will be sent to him and to the county authorities by this post, and by the time that this reaches you he will be a free man.

'In writing to you, I need hardly explain that the form of a pardon from the Throne is the only mode allowed by the laws of the country for setting aside a verdict which has been found in error upon false evidence. Unfortunately, perhaps, we have not the means of annulling a criminal conviction by a second trial; and therefore, on such occasions as this,—occasions which are very rare,—we have but this lame way of redressing a great grievance. I am happy to think that in this case the future effect will be as complete as though the verdict had been reversed. As to the suffering which has been already endured by your son, by his much-injured wife, and by yourself, I am aware that no redress can be given. It is one of those cases in which the honest and good have to endure a portion of the evil produced by the dishonesty of the wicked. I

447

can only add to this my best wishes for your son's happiness on his
return to his home, and express a hope that you will understand that I
would most willingly have made your visit to the Home Office more
satisfactory had it been within my power to do so.—Believe me, very
faithfully yours,

'SEPTIMUS BROWN.'

He had not read this letter to the end, and had hardly washed the
soap from his face, before he was in his daughter-in-law's room. She was
there with her child, still in bed,—thinking, thinking, thinking whether
there would ever come an end to her misery. 'It has come,' said the old
man.

'What has come?' she asked, jumping up with the baby in her arms.
But she knew what had come, for he had the letter open in his hands.

'They have pardoned him. The absurdity of the thing! Pardoning a
man whom they know to be innocent, and to have been injured!'

But the 'absurdity of the thing,' as the old squire very naturally
called it, was nothing to her now. He was to come back to her. She
would be in his arms that day. On that very day she would once again
hold up her boy to be kissed by his father.

'Where is he? When will he come? Of course I will go to him! You
will make them have the waggonnette at once; will you not? I will be
dressed in five minutes if you will go. Of course I will go to fetch him.'

But this the squire would not allow. The carriage should be sent, of
course, and if it met his son on the road, as was probable, there would be
no harm done. But it would not be well that the greeting between the
husband and the wife should be in public. So he went out to order the
carriage and to prepare himself to accompany it, leaving her to think of
her happiness and to make herself ready for the meeting. But when left
to herself she could hardly compose herself so as to brush her hair and
give herself those little graces which should be pleasant to his eye. 'Papa
is coming,' she said to her boy over and over again. 'Papa is coming back.
Papa will be here; your own, own, own papa.' Then she threw aside the
black gown, which she had worn since he left her, and chose for her
wear one which he himself had taken pride in buying for her,—the first
article of her dress in the choice of which he had been consulted as her
husband; and with quick unsteady hand she pulled out some gay ribbon
for her baby. Yes;—she and her boy would once again be bright for his
sake;—for his sake there should again be gay ribbons and soft silks. 'Papa
is coming, my own one; your own, own papa!' and then she smothered
the child with kisses.

While they were sitting at breakfast at Puritan Grange, the same news reached Mr. and Mrs. Bolton. The letter to the old man from his son in town was very short, merely stating that the authorities at the Home Office had at last decided that Caldigate should be released from prison. The writer knew that his father would be prepared for this news by his brother; and all that could be said in the way of argument had been said already. The letters which came to Puritan Grange were few in number, and were generally addressed to the lady. The banker's letters were all received at the house of business in the town. 'What is it?' asked the wife, as soon as she saw the long official envelope. But he read it to the end very slowly before he vouchsafed her any reply. 'It has to do with that wretched man in prison,' she said. 'What is it?'

'He is in prison no longer.'

'They have let him escape?'

'The Queen has pardoned him because he was not guilty.'

'The Queen! As though she could know whether he be guilty or innocent. What can the Queen know of the manner of his life in foreign parts,—before he had taken my girl away from me?'

'He never married the woman. Let there be no more said about it. He never married her.'

But Mrs. Bolton, though she was not victorious, was not to be silenced by a single word. No more about it, indeed! There must be very much more about it. 'If she was not his wife, she was worse,' she said.

'He has repented of that.'

'Repented!' she said, with scorn. What very righteous person ever believed in the repentance of an enemy?

'Why should he not repent?'

'He has had leisure in jail.'

'Let us hope that he has used it. At any rate he is her husband. There are not many days left to me here. Let me at least see my daughter during the few that remain to me.'

'Do I not want to see my own child?'

'I will see her and her boy;—and I will have them called by the name which is theirs. And he shall come,—if he will. Who are you, or who am I, that we shall throw in his teeth the sins of his youth?' Then she became sullen and there was not a word more said between them that morning. But after breakfast the old gardener was sent into town for a fly, and Mr. Bolton was taken to the bank.

'And what are we to do now?' asked Mrs. Robert Bolton of her husband, when the tidings were made known to her also at her breakfast-table.

'We must take it as a fact that she is his wife.'

'Of course, my dear. If the Secretary of State were to say that I was

449

his wife, I suppose I should have to take it as a fact.'

'If he said that you were a goose it might be nearer the mark.'

'Really! But a goose must know what she is to do.'

'You must write her a letter and call her Mrs. Caldigate. That will be an acknowledgment.'

'And what shall I say to her?'

'Ask her to come here, if you will.'

'And him?'

'And him, too. The fact is we have got to swallow it all. I was sure that he had married that woman, and then of course I wanted to get Hester away from him. Now I believe that he never married her, and therefore, we must make the best of him as Hester's husband.'

'You used to like him.'

'Yes;—and perhaps I shall again. But why on earth did he pay twenty thousand pounds to those miscreants? That is what I could not get over. It was that which made me sure he was guilty. It is that which still puzzles me so that I can hardly make up my mind to be quite sure that he is innocent. But still we have to be sure. Perhaps the miracle will be explained some day.'

CHAPTER LXII

John Caldigate's Return

THE carriage started with the old man in it as soon as the horses could be harnessed; but on the Folking causeway it met the fly which was bringing John Caldigate to his home,—so that the father and son greeted each other in the street amidst the eyes of the villagers. To them it did not much matter, but the squire had certainly been right in saving Hester from so public a demonstration of her feelings. The two men said hardly a word when they met, but stood there for a moment grasping each other's hands. Then the driver of the fly was paid, and the carriage was turned back to the house. 'Is she well?' asked Caldigate.

'She will be well now.'

'Has she been ill?'

'She has not been very happy, John, while you have been away from her.'

'And the boy?'

'He is all right. He has been spared the heart-breaking knowledge of the injury done to him. It has been very bad with you, I suppose.'

'I do not like being in jail, sir. It was the length of the time before me that seemed to crush me. I could not bring myself to believe that I should live to see the end of it.'

'The end has come, my boy,' said his father, again taking him by the hand, 'but the cruelty of the thing remains. Had there been another trial as soon as the other evidence was obtained, the struggle would have kept your heart up. It is damnable that a man in an office up in London should have to decide on such a matter, and should be able to take his own time about it!' The grievance was still at the old squire's heart in spite of the amenity of Mr. Brown's letter; but John Caldigate, who was approaching his house and his wife, and to whom, after his imprisonment, even the flat fields and dykes were beautiful, did not at the moment much regard the anomaly of the machinery by which he had been liberated.

Hester in the meantime had donned her silk dress, and had tied the gay bow round her baby's frock, who was quite old enough to be astonished and charmed by the unusual finery in which he was apparelled. Then she sat herself at the window of a bedroom which looked out on to the gravel sweep, with her boy on her lap, and there she was determined to wait till the carriage should come.

But she had hardly seated herself before she heard the wheels. 'He is here. He is coming. There he is!' she said to the child. 'Look! look! It is papa.' But she stood back from the window that she might not be seen. She had thought it out with many fluctuations as to the very spot in which she would meet him. At one moment she had intended to go down to the gate, then to the hall-door, and again she had determined that she would wait for him in the room in which his breakfast was prepared for him. But she had ordered it otherwise at last. When she saw the carriage approaching, she retreated back from the window, so that he should not even catch a glimpse of her; but she had seen him as he sat, still holding his father's hand. Then she ran back to her own chamber and gave her orders as she passed across the passage. 'Go down, nurse, and tell him that I am here. Run quick, nurse; tell him to come at once.'

But he needed no telling. Whether he had divined her purpose, or whether it was natural to him to fly like a bird to his nest, he rushed upstairs and was in the room almost before his father had left the carriage. She had the child in her hands when she heard him turn the lock of the door; but before he entered the boy had been laid in his cradle,—and then she was in his arms.

For the first few minutes she was quite collected, not saying much, but answering his questions by a word or two. Oh yes; she was well; and baby was well,—quite well. He, too, looked well, she said, though there was something of sadness in his face. 'But I will kiss that away,—so soon so soon.' She had always expected that he would come back long, long before the time that had been named. She had been sure of it, she declared, because that it was impossible that so great injustice should be done. But the last fortnight had been very long. When those wicked people had been put in prison she had thought that then surely he would come. But now he was there, with his arms round her, safe in his own home, and everything was well. Then she lifted the baby up to be kissed again and again, and began to dance and spring in her joy. Then, suddenly, she almost threw the child into his arms, and seated herself, covered her face with her hands and began to sob with violence. When he asked her, with much embracing, to compose herself, sitting close to her, kissing her again and again, she shook her head as it lay upon his shoulder, and then burst out into a fit of laughter. 'What does it matter,' she said after a while, as he knelt at her knees;—'what does it matter? My boy's father has come back to him. My boy has got his own name, and he is an honest true Caldigate; and no one again will tell me that another woman owns my husband, my own husband, the father of my boy. It almost killed me, John, when they said that you were not mine. And yet I knew that they said it falsely. I never doubted for a moment.

I knew that you were my own, and that my boy had a right to his father's name. But it was hard to hear them say so, John. It was hard to bear when my mother swore that it was so!'

At last they went down and found the old squire waiting for his breakfast. 'I should think,' said he, 'that you would be glad to see a loaf of bread on a clean board again, and to know that you may cut it as you please. Did they give you enough where you were?'

'I didn't think much about it, sir.'

'But you must think about it now,' said Hester. 'To please me you must like everything; your tea, and your fresh eggs, and the butter and the cream. You must let yourself be spoilt for a time just to compensate me for your absence.'

'You have made yourself smart to receive him at any rate,' said the squire, who had become thoroughly used to the black gown which she had worn morning, noon, and evening while her husband was away.

'Why should I not be smart,' she said, 'when my man has come to me? For whose eyes shall I put on the raiment that is his own but for his? I was much lower than a widow in the eyes of all men; but now I have got my husband back again. And my boy shall wear the very best that he has, so that his father may see him smile at his own gaudiness. Yes, father, I may be smart now. There were moments in which I thought I might never wear more the pretty things which he had given me.' Then she rose from her seat again, and hung on his neck, and wept and sobbed till he feared that her heartstrings would break with joy.

So the morning passed away among them till about eleven o'clock, when the servant brought in word that Mr. Holt and one or two other of the tenants wanted to see the young master. The squire had been sitting alone in the back room so that the husband and wife might be left together; but he had heard voices with which he was familiar, and he now came through to ask Hester whether the visitors should be sent away for the present. But Hester would not have turned a dog from the door which had been true to her husband through his troubles. 'Let them come,' she said. 'They have been so good to me, John, through it all! They have always known that baby was a true Caldigate.'

Holt and the other farmers were shown into the room, and Holt as a matter of course became the spokesman. When Caldigate had shaken hands with them all round, each muttering his word of welcome, then Holt began: 'We wish you to know, squoire, that we, none of us, ain't been comfortable in our minds here at Folking since that crawling villain Crinkett came and showed himself at our young squire's christening.'

'That we ain't,' said Timothy Purvidge, another Netherden farmer.

'I haven't had much comfort since that day myself, Mr. Purvidge,' said Caldigate,—'not till this morning.'

'Nor yet haven't none of us,' continued Mr. Holt, very impressively. 'We knowed as you had done all right. We was as sure as the church tower. Lord love you, sir, when it was between our young missus,—who'll excuse me for noticing these bright colours, and for saying how glad I am to see her come out once again as our squire's wife should come out,—between her and that bedangled woman as I seed in the court, it didn't take no one long to know what was the truth!' The eloquence here was no doubt better than the argument, as Caldigate must have felt when he remembered how fond he had once been of that 'bedangled woman.' Hester, who, though she knew the whole story, did not at this moment join two and two together, thought that Mr. Holt put the case uncommonly well. 'No! we knew,' he continued, with a wave of his hand. 'But the jury weren't Netherden men,—nor yet Utterden, Mr. Halfacre,' he added, turning to a tenant from the other parish. 'And they couldn't tell how it all was as we could. And there was that judge, who would have believed any miscreant as could be got anywhere, to swear away a man's liberty,—or his wife and family, which is a'most worse. We saw how it was to be when he first looked out of his eye at the two post-office gents, and others who spoke up for the young squoire. It was to be guilty. We know'd it. But it didn't any way change our minds. As to Crinkett and Smith and them others, we saw that they were ruffians. We never doubted that. But we saw as there was a bad time coming to you, Mr. John. Then we was unhappy; unhappy along of you, Mr. John,—but a'most worse as to this dear lady and the boy.'

'My missus cried that you wouldn't have believed,' said Mr. Purvidge. ' "If that's true," said my missus, "she ain't nobody; and it's my belief she's as true a wife as ever stretched herself aside her husband." ' Then Hester bethought herself what present, of all presents, would be most acceptable to Mrs. Purvidge, who was a red-faced, red-armed, hardworking old woman, peculiarly famous for making cheeses.

'We all knew it,' said Mr. Holt, slapping his thigh with great energy. 'And now, in spite of 'em all, judge, jury, and lying witnesses,—the king has got his own again.' At this piece of triumphant rhetoric there was a cheer from all the farmers. 'And so we have come to wish you all joy, and particularly you, ma'am, with your boy. Things have been said of you, ma'am, hard to bear, no doubt. But not a word of the kind at Folking, nor yet in Netherden;—nor yet at Utterden, Mr. Halfacre. But all this is over, and we do hope that you, ma'am, and the young squoire 'll live long, and the young 'un of all long after we are gone to our rest, —and that you'll be as fond of Folking as Folking is of you. I can't say no fairer.' Then the tray was brought in with wine, and everybody drank everybody's health, and there was another shaking of hands all round. Mr. Purvidge, it was observed, drank the health of every separate member of the family in a separate bumper, pressing the edge of the glass securely to his lips, and then sending the whole contents down his throat at one throw with a chuck from his little finger.

The two Caldigates went out to see their friends as far as the gate, and while they were still within the grounds there came a merry peal from the bells of Netherden church-tower. 'I knew they'd be at it,' said Mr. Holt.

'And quite right too,' said Mr. Halfacre. 'We'd rung over at Utterden, only we've got nothing but that little tinkling thing as is more fitter to swing round a bullock's neck than on a church-top.'

'I told 'em as they should have beer,' said Mr. Brownby, whose house stood on Folking Causeway, 'and they shall have beer!' Mr. Brownby was a silent man, and added nothing to this one pertinent remark.

'As to beer,' said Mr. Halfacre, 'we'd 'ave found the beer at Utterden. There wouldn't have been no grudging the beer, Mr. Brownby, no more than there is in the lower parish; but you can't get up a peal merely on beer. You've got to have bells.'

While they were still standing at the gate, Mr. Bromley the clergyman joined them, and walked back towards the house with the two Caldigates. He, too, had come to offer his congratulations, and to assure the released prisoner that he never believed the imputed guilt. But he would not go into the house, surmising that on such a day the happy wife would not care to see many visitors. But Caldigate asked him to take a turn about the grounds, being anxious to learn something from the outside world. 'What do they say to it all at Babington?'

'I think they're a little divided.'

'My aunt has been against me, of course.'

'At first she was, I fancy. It was natural that people should believe till Shand came back.'

'Poor, dear old Dick. I must look after Dick. What about Julia?'

'*Spretæ injuria formæ*!' said Mr. Bromley. 'What were you to expect?'

'I'll forgive her. And Mr. Smirkie? I don't think Smirkie ever looked on me with favourable eyes.'

Then the clergyman was forced to own that Smirkie too had been among those who had believed the woman's story. 'But you have to remember how natural it is that a man should think a verdict to be right. In our country a wrong verdict is an uncommon occurrence. It requires close personal acquaintance and much personal confidence to justify a man in supposing that twelve jurymen should come to an erroneous decision. I thought that they were wrong. But still I knew that I could hardly defend my opinion before the outside world.'

'It is all true,' said Caldigate; 'and I have made up my mind that I will be angry with no one who will begin to believe me innocent from this day.'

His mind, however, was considerably exercised in regard to the Boltons, as to whom he feared that they would not even yet allow themselves to be convinced. For his wife's happiness their conversion was of infinitely more importance than that of all the outside world beyond. When the gloom of the evening had come, she too came out and walked with him about the garden and grounds with the professed object of showing him whatever little changes might have been made. But the conversation soon fell back upon the last great incident of their joint lives.

'But your mother cannot refuse to believe what everybody now declares to be true,' he argued.

'Mamma is so strong in her feelings.'

'She must know they would not have let me out of prison in opposition to the verdict until they were very sure of what they were doing.'

Then she told him all that had occurred between her and her mother since the trial,—how her mother had come out to Folking and had implored her to return to Chesterton, and had then taken herself away in dudgeon because she had not prevailed. 'But nothing,—nothing would have made me leave the place,' she said, 'after what they tried to do when I was there before. Except to go to church, I have not once been outside the gate.'

'Your brothers will come round, I suppose. Robert has been very angry with me, I know. But he is a man of the world and a man of sense.'

'We must take it as it will come, John. Of course it would be very much to me to have my father and mother restored to me. It would be very much to know that my brothers were again my friends. But when I remember how I prayed yesterday but for one thing, and that now, to-day, that one thing has come to me;—how I have got that which, when I waked this morning, seemed to me to be all the world to me, the want of which made my heart so sick that even my baby could not make me glad, I feel that nothing ought now to make me unhappy. I have got you, John, and everything else is nothing.' As he stopped in the dark to kiss her again among the rose-bushes, he felt that it was almost worth his while to have been in prison.

After dinner there came a message to them across the ferry from Mr. Holt. Would they be so good as to walk down to the edge of the great dike, opposite to Twopenny Farm, at nine o'clock? As a part of the message, Mr. Holt sent word that at that hour the moon would be rising.

456

Of course they went down to the dike,—Mr. Caldigate, John Caldigate, and Hester;—and there, outside Mr. Holt's farmyard, just far enough to avoid danger to the hay-ricks and corn-stacks, there was blazing an enormous bonfire. All the rotten timber about the place and two or three tar-barrels had been got together, and there were collected all the inhabitants of the two parishes. The figures of the boys and girls and of the slow rustics with their wives could be seen moving about indistinctly across the water by the fluttering flame of the bonfire. And their own figures, too, were observed in the moonlight, and John Caldigate was welcomed back to his home by a loud cheer from all his neighbours.

'I did not see much of it myself,' Mr. Holt said afterwards, 'because me and my missus was busy among the stacks all the time, looking after the sparks. The bonfire might a' been too big, you know.'

CHAPTER LXIII

How Mrs. Bolton Was Quite Conquered

NEARLY a week passed over their heads at Puritan Grange before anything further was either done or said, or even written, as to the return of John Caldigate to his own home and to his own wife. In the meantime, both Mrs. Robert and Mrs. Daniel had gone out to Folking and made visits of ceremony,—visits which were intended to signify their acknowledgement that Mrs. John Caldigate was Mrs. John Caldigate. With Mrs. Daniel the matter was quite ceremonious and short. Mrs. Robert suggested something as to a visit into Cambridge, saying that her husband would be delighted if Hester and Mr. Caldigate would come and dine and sleep. Hester immediately felt that something had been gained, but she declined the proposed visit for the present. 'We have both of us,' she said, 'gone through so much, that we are not quite fit to go out anywhere yet.' Mrs. Robert had hardly expected them to come, but she had observed her husband's behests. So far there had been a family reconciliation during the first few days after the prisoner's release; but no sign came from Mrs. Bolton; and Mr. Bolton, though he had given his orders, was not at first urgent in requiring obedience to them. Then she received a letter from Hester.

'Dearest, Dearest Mamma,—Of course you know that my darling husband has come back to me. All I want now to make me quite happy is to have you once again as my own, own mother. Will you not send me a line to say that it shall all be as though these last long dreary months had never been;—so that I may go to you and show you my baby once again? And, dear mamma, say one word to me to let me know that you know that he is my husband. Tell papa to say so also.—Your most affectionate daughter,

'HESTER CALDIGATE.'

Mrs. Bolton found this letter on the breakfast-table, lying, as was usual with her letters, close to her plate, and she read it without saying a word to her husband. Then she put it in her pocket, and still did not say a word. Before the middle of the day she had almost made up her mind that she would keep the letter entirely to herself. It was well, she thought, that he had not seen it, and no good could be done by showing it to him. But he had been in the breakfast-parlour before her, had seen the envelope, and had recognised the handwriting. They were sitting together after lunch, and she was just about to open the book of sermons with which, at that time, she was regaling him, when he stopped her with a question. 'What did Hester say in her letter?'

Even those who intend to be truthful are sometimes surprised into a lie. 'What letter?' she said. But she remembered herself at once, and knew that she could not afford to be detected in a falsehood. 'That note from Hester? Yes;–I had a note this morning.'

'I know you had a note. What does she say?'

'She tells me that he–he has come back.'

'And what else? She was well aware that we knew that without her telling us.'

'She wants to come here.'

'Bid her come.'

'Of course she shall come.'

'And him.' To this she made no answer, except with the muscles of her face, which involuntarily showed her antagonism to the order she had received. 'Bid her bring her husband with her,' said the banker.

'He would not come,–though I were to ask him.'

'Then let it be on his own head.'

'I will not ask him,' she said at last, looking away across the room at the blank wall. 'I will not belie my own heart. I do not want to see him here. He has so far got the better of me; but I will not put my neck beneath his feet for him to tread on me.'

Then there was a pause;–not that he intended to allow her disobedience to pass, but that he was driven to bethink himself how he might best oppose her. 'Woman,' he said, 'you can neither forgive nor forget.'

'He has got my child from me,–my only child.'

'Does he persecute your child? Is she not happy in his love? Even if he have trespassed against you, who are you that you should not forgive a trespass? I say that he shall be asked to come here, that men may know that in her own father's house she is regarded as his true and honest wife.'

'Men!' she murmured. 'That men may know!' But she did not again tell him that she would not obey his command.

She sat all the remainder of the day alone in her room, hardly touching the work which she had beside her, not opening the book which lay by her hand on the table. She was thinking of the letter which she knew that she must write, but she did not rise to get pen and ink, nor did she even propose to herself that the letter should be written then. Not a word was said about it all the evening. On the next morning the banker pronounced his intention of going into town, but before he started he referred to the order he had given. 'Have you written to Hester?' he asked. She merely shook her head. 'Then write to-day.' So saying, he tottered down the steps with his stick and got into the fly.

About noon she did get her paper and ink, and very slowly wrote her letter. Though her heart was, in truth, yearning towards her daughter,—though at that moment she could have made any possible sacrifice for her child and her child been apart from the man she hated,—she could not in her sullenness force her words into a form of affection.

'Dear Hester,' she said. 'Of course I shall be glad to see you and your boy. On what day would it suit you to come, and how long would you like to stay? I fear you will find me and your father but dull companions after the life you are now used to. If Mr. Caldigate would like to come with you, your father bids me say that he will be glad to see him.—Your loving mother,

'MARY BOLTON.'

She endeavoured, in writing her letter, to obey the commands that had been left with her, but she could not go nearer to it than this. She could not so far belie her heart as to tell her daughter that she herself would be glad to see the man. Then it took her long to write the address. She did write it at last;

Mrs. John Caldigate,
Folking.

But as she wrote it she told herself that she believed it to be a lie.

When the letter reached Hester there was a consultation over it, to which old Mr. Caldigate was admitted. It was acknowledged on all sides that anything would be better than a family quarrel. The spirit in which the invitation had been written was to be found in every word of it. There was not a word to show that Mrs. Bolton had herself accepted the decision to which everyone else had come in the matter;—everything, rather, to show that she had not done so. But, as the squire said, it does not do to inquire too closely into all people's inner beliefs. 'If everybody were to say what he thinks about everybody, nobody would ever go to see anybody.' It was soon decided that Hester, with her baby, should go on an early day to Puritan Grange, and should stay there for a couple of nights. But there was a difficulty as to Caldigate himself. He was naturally enough anxious to send Hester without him, but she was as anxious to take him. 'It isn't for my own sake,' she said,—'because I shall like to have you there with me. Of course it will be very dull for you, but it will be so much better that we should all be reconciled, and that everyone should know that we are so.'

'It would only be a pretence,' said he.

'People must pretend sometimes, John,' she answered. At last it was decided that he should take her, reaching the place about the hour of lunch, so that he might again break bread in her father's house,—that he should then leave her there, and that at the end of the two days she should return to Folking.

On the day named they reached Puritan Grange at the hour fixed. Both Caldigate and Hester were very nervous as to their reception, and got out of the carriage almost without a word to each other. The old gardener, who had been so busy during Hester's imprisonment, was there to take the luggage; and Hester's maid carried the child as Caldigate, with his wife behind him, walked up the steps and rang the bell. There was no coming out to meet them, no greeting them even in the hall. Mr. Bolton was perhaps too old and too infirm for such running out, and it was hardly within his nature to do so. They were shown into the well-known morning sitting-room, and there they found Hester's father in his chair, and Mrs. Bolton standing up to receive them.

Hester, after kissing her father, threw herself into her mother's arms before a word had been said to Caldigate. Then the banker addressed him with a set speech, which no doubt had been prepared in the old man's mind. 'I am very glad,' he said, 'that you have brought this unhappy matter to so good a conclusion, Mr. Caldigate.'

'It has been a great trouble,—worse almost for Hester than for me.'

'Yes, it has been sad enough for Hester,—and the more so because it was natural that others should believe that which the jury and the judge declared to have been proved. How should any one know otherwise?'

'Just so, Mr. Bolton. If they will accept the truth now, I shall be satisfied.'

'It will come, but perhaps slowly to some folk. You should in justice remember that your own early follies have tended to bring this all about.'

It was a grim welcome, and the last speech was one which Caldigate found it difficult to answer. It was so absolutely true that it admitted of no answer. He thought that it might have been spared, and shrugged his shoulders as though to say that that part of the subject was one which he did not care to discuss. Hester heard it, and quivered with anger even in her mother's arms. Mrs. Bolton heard it, and in the midst of her kisses made an inward protest against the word used. Follies indeed! Why had he not spoken out the truth as he knew it, and told the man of his vices?

But it was necessary that she too should address him. 'I hope I see you quite well, Mr. Caldigate,' she said, giving him her hand.

461

'The prison has not disagreed with me,' he said, with an attempt at a smile, 'though it was not an agreeable residence.'

'If you used your leisure there to meditate on your soul's welfare, it may have been of service to you.'

It was very grim. But the banker having made his one severe speech, became kind in his manner, and almost genial. He asked after his son-in-law's future intentions, and when he was told that they thought of spending some months abroad so as to rid themselves in that way of the immediate record of their past misery, he was gracious enough to express his approval of the plan; and then when the lunch was announced, and the two ladies had passed out of the room, he said a word to his son-in-law in private. 'As I was convinced, Mr. Caldigate, when I first heard the evidence, that that other woman was your wife, and was therefore very anxious to separate my daughter from you, so am I satisfied now that the whole thing was a wicked plot.'

'I am very glad to hear you say that, sir.'

'Now, if you please, we will go in to lunch.'

As long as Caldigate remained in the house Mrs. Bolton was almost silent. The duties of a hostess she performed in a stiff ungainly way. She asked him whether he would have hashed mutton or cold beef, and allowed him to pour a little sherry into her wine-glass. But beyond this there was not much conversation. Mr. Bolton had said what he had to say, and sat leaning forward with his chin over his plate perfectly silent. It is to be supposed that he had some pleasure in having his daughter once more beneath his roof, especially as he had implored his wife not to deprive him of that happiness during the small remainder of his days. But he sat there with no look of joy upon his face. That she should be stern, sullen, and black-browed was to be expected. She had been compelled to entertain their guest; and was not at all the woman to bear such compulsion meekly.

The hour at last wore itself away, and the carriage which was to take Caldigate back to Folking was again at the door. It was a Tuesday. 'You will send for me on Thursday,' she said to him in a whisper.

'Certainly.'

'Early? After breakfast, you know. I suppose you will not come yourself.'

'Not here, I think. I have done all the good that I can do, and it is pleasant to no one. But you shall pick me up in the town. I shall go in and see your brother Robert.' Then he went, and Hester was left with her parents.

As she turned back from the hall-door she found her mother standing at the foot of the stairs, waiting for her. 'Shall I come with you, mamma?' she said. Holding each other's arms they went up, and so passed into Hester's room, where the nurse was sitting with the boy. 'Let her go into my room,' said the elder lady. So the nurse took the baby away, and they were alone together. 'Oh, Hester, Hester, my child!' said the mother, flinging her arms wildly round her daughter.

The whole tenor of her face was changed at that moment. Even to Hester she had been stern, forbidding, and sullen. There had not been a gracious movement about her lips or eyes since the visitors had come. A stranger, could a stranger have seen it all, would have said that the mother did not love her child, that there was no touch of tenderness about the woman's heart. But now, when she was alone, with the one thing on earth that was dear to her, she melted at once. In a moment Hester found herself seated on the sofa, with her mother kneeling before her, sobbing, and burying her face in the loved one's lap. 'You love me, Hester,—still.'

'Love you, mamma! You know I love you.'

'Not as it used to be. I am nothing to you now. I can do nothing for you now. You turn away from me, because—because—because—'

'I have never turned away from you, mamma.'

'Because I could not bear that you should be taken away from me and given to him.'

'He is good, mamma. If you would only believe that he is good!'

'He is not good. God only is good, my child.'

'He is good to me.'

'Ah, yes;—he has taken you from me. When I thought you were coming back, in trouble, in disgrace from the world, nameless, a poor injured thing, with your nameless babe, then I comforted myself because I thought that I could be all and everything to you. I would have poured balm into the hurt wounds. I would have prayed with you, and you and I would have been as one before the Lord.'

'You are not sorry, mamma, that I have got my husband again?'

'Oh, I have tried,—I have tried not to be sorry.'

'You do not believe now that that woman was his wife?'

Then the old colour came back upon her face, and something of the old look, and the tenderness was quenched in her eyes, and the softness of her voice was gone. 'I do not know,' she said.

'Mamma, you must know. Get up and sit by me till I tell you. You must teach yourself to know this,—to be quite sure of it. You must not think that your daughter is,—is living in adultery with the husband of another woman. To me who knew him there has never been a shadow of doubt, not a taint of fear to darken the certainty of my faith. It could not have been so, perhaps, with you who have not known his nature. But now, now, when all of them, from the Queen downwards, have declared that this charge has been a libel, when even the miscreants themselves have told against themselves, when the very judge has gone back from the word in which he was so confident, shall my mother,— and my mother only,—think that I am a wretched, miserable, nameless outcast, with a poor nameless, fatherless baby? I am John Caldigate's wife before God's throne, and my child is his child, and his lawful heir, and owns his father's name. My husband is to me before all the world, —first, best, dearest,—my king, my man, my master, and my lover. Above all things, he is my husband.' She had got up, and was standing before her mother with her arms folded before her breast, and the fire glanced from her eyes as she spoke. 'But, mamma, because I love him more, I do not love you less.'

'Oh yes, oh yes; so much less.'

'No, mamma. It is given to us, of God, so to love our husband; "For the husband is head of the wife, even as Christ is head of the Church." You would not have me forget such teaching as that?'

'No,—my child; no.'

'When I went out and had him given to me for my husband, of course I loved him best. The Lord do so to me and more also if aught but death part him and me! But shall that make my mother think that her girl's heart is turned away from her? Mamma, say that he is my husband.' The frown came back, and the woman sat silent and sullen, but there was something of vacillating indecision in her face. 'Mamma,' repeated Hester, 'say that he is my husband.'

'I suppose so,' said the woman, very slowly.

'Mamma, say that it is so, and bless your child.'

'God bless you, my child.'

'And you know that it is so?'

'Yes.' The word was hardly spoken, but the lips of the one were close to the ear of the other, and the sound was heard, and the assent was acknowledged.

CHAPTER LXIV

Conclusion

THE web of our story has now been woven, the piece is finished, and it is only necessary that the loose threads should be collected, so that there may be no unravelling. In such chronicles as this, something no doubt might be left to the imagination without serious injury to the story; but the reader, I think, feels a deficiency when, through tedium or coldness, the writer omits to give all the information which he possesses.

Among the male personages of my story, Bagwax should perhaps be allowed to stand first. It was his energy and devotion to his peculiar duties which, after the verdict, served to keep alive the idea that that verdict had been unjust. It was through his ingenuity that Judge Bramber was induced to refer the inquiry back to Scotland Yard, and in this way to prevent the escape of Crinkett and Euphemia Smith. Therefore we will first say a word as to Bagwax and his history.

It was rumoured at the time that Sir John Joram and Mr. Brown, having met each other at the club after the order for Caldigate's release had been given, and discussing the matter with great interest, united in giving praise to Bagwax. Then Sir John told the story of those broken hopes, of the man's desire to travel, and of the faith and honesty with which he sacrificed his own aspirations for the good of the poor lady whose husband had been so cruelly taken from her. Then,—as it was said at the time,—an important letter was sent from the Home Office to the Postmaster-General, giving Mr. Bagwax much praise, and suggesting that a very good thing would be done to the colony of New South Wales if that ingenious and skilful master of post-marks could be sent out to Sydney with the view of setting matters straight in the Sydney office.[1] There was then much correspondence with the Colonial Office, which did not at first care very much about Bagwax; but at last the order was given by the Treasury, and Bagwax went. There were many tears shed on the occasion at Apricot Villa. Jemima Curlydown thought that she also should be allowed to see Sydney, and was in favour of an immediate marriage with this object. But Bagwax felt that the boisterous ocean might be unpropitious to the delights of a honeymoon; and Mr.

[1] I hope my friends in the Sydney post-office will take no offence should this story ever reach their ears. I know how well the duties are done in that office, and, between ourselves, I think that Mr. Bagwax's journey was quite unnecessary.

Curlydown reminded his daughter of all the furniture which would thus be lost. Bagwax went as a gay bachelor, and spent six happy months in the bright colony. He did not effect much, as the delinquent who had served Crinkett in his base purposes had already been detected and punished before his arrival; but he was treated with extreme courtesy by the Sydney officials, and was able to bring home with him a treasure in the shape of a newly-discovered manner of tying mail-bags. So that when the 'Sydney Intelligencer' boasted that the great English professor who had come to instruct them all had gone home instructed, there was some truth in it. He was married immediately after his return, and Jemima his wife has the advantage, in her very pretty drawing-room, of every shilling that he made by the voyage. My readers will be glad to hear that soon afterwards he was appointed Inspector-General of Post-marks, to the great satisfaction of all the post-office.

One of the few things which Caldigate did before he took his wife abroad was to 'look after Dick Shand.' It was manifest to all concerned that Dick could do no good in England. His yellow trousers and the manners which accompanied them were not generally acceptable in merchants' offices and suchlike places. He knew nothing about English farming, which, for those who have not learned the work early, is an expensive amusement rather than a trade by which bread can be earned. There seemed to be hardly a hope for Dick in England. But he had done some good among the South Sea Islanders. He knew their ways and could manage them. He was sent out, therefore, with a small capital to be junior partner on a sugar estate in Queensland. It need hardly be said that the small capital was lent to him by John Caldigate. There he took steadily to work, and it is hoped by his friends that he will soon begin to repay the loan.

The uncle, aunt, and cousins at Babington soon renewed their intimacy with John Caldigate, and became intimate with Hester. The old squire still turned up his nose at them, as he had done all his life, calling them Bœotians, and reminding his son that Suffolk had always been a silly county. But the Babingtons, one and all, knew this, and had no objection to be accounted thick-headed as long as they were acknowledged to be prosperous, happy, and comfortable. It had always been considered at Babington that young Caldigate was brighter and more clever than themselves; and yet he had been popular with them as a cousin of whom they ought to be proud. He was soon restored to his former favour, and after his return from the Continent spent a fortnight at the Hall, with his wife, very comfortably. Julia, indeed, was not there, nor Mr. Smirkie. Among all their neighbours and acquaintances Mr. Smirkie was the last to drop the idea that there must have been something in that story of an

Australian marriage. His theory of the law on the subject was still incorrect. The Queen's pardon, he said, could not do away with the verdict, and therefore he doubted whether the couple could be regarded as man and wife. He was very anxious that they should be married again, and with great good-nature offered to perform the ceremony himself either at Plum-cum-Pippins or even in the drawing-room at Folking.

'Suffolk to the very backbone!' was the remark of the Cambridgeshire squire when he heard of this very kind offer. But even he at last came round, under his wife's persuasion, when he found that the paternal mansion was likely to be shut against him unless he yielded.

Hester's second tour with her husband was postponed for some weeks, because it was necessary that her husband should appear as a witness against Crinkett and Euphemia Smith. They were tried also at Cambridge, but not before Judge Bramber. The woman never yielded an inch. When she found how it was going with her, she made fast her money, and with infinite pluck resolved that she would endure with patience whatever might be in store for her, and wait for better times. When put into the dock she pleaded not guilty with a voice that was audible only to the jailer standing beside her, and after that did not open her mouth during the trial. Crinkett made a great effort to be admitted as an additional witness against his comrade, but, having failed in that, pleaded guilty at last. He felt that there was no hope for him with such a weight of evidence against him, and calculated that his punishment might thus be lighter, and that he would save himself the cost of an expensive defence. In the former hope he was deceived, as the two were condemned to the same term of imprisonment. When the woman heard that she was to be confined for three years with hard labour her spirit was almost broken. But she made no outward sign; and as she was led away out of the dock she looked round for Caldigate, to wither him with the last glance of her reproach. But Caldigate, who had not beheld her misery without some pang at his heart, had already left the court.

Judge Bramber never opened his mouth upon the matter to a single human being. He was a man who, in the bosom of his family, did not say much about the daily work of his life, and who had but few friends sufficiently intimate to be trusted with his judicial feelings. The Secretary of State was enabled to triumph in the correctness of his decision, but it may be a question whether Judge Bramber enjoyed the triumph. The matter had gone luckily for the Secretary; but how would it have been had Crinkett and the woman been acquitted?—how would it have been had Caldigate broken down in his evidence, and been forced to admit that there had been a marriage of some kind? No doubt the accusation had been false. No doubt the verdict had been erroneous. But the man had brought it upon himself by his own egregious folly, and would have had no just cause for complaint had he been kept in prison till the second case had been tried. It was thus that Judge Bramber regarded the matter;—but he said not a word about it to any one.

When the second trial was over, Caldigate and his wife started for Paris, but stayed a few days on their way with William Bolton in London. He and his wife were quite ready to receive Hester and her husband with open arms. 'I tell you fairly,' said he to Caldigate, 'that when there was a doubt, I thought it better that you and Hester should be apart. You would have thought the same had she been your sister. Now I am only too happy to congratulate both of you that the truth has been brought to light.'

On their return Mrs. Robert Bolton was very friendly,—and Robert Bolton himself was at last brought round to acknowledge that his convictions had been wrong. But there was still much that stuck in his throat. 'Why did John Caldigate pay twenty thousand pounds to those persons when he knew that they had hatched a conspiracy against himself?' This question he asked his brother William over and over again, and never could be satisfied with any answer which his brother could give him.

Once he asked the question of Caldigate himself. 'Because I felt that, in honour, I owed it to them,' said Caldigate; 'and, perhaps, a little too because I felt that, if they took themselves off at once, your sister might be spared something of the pain which she has suffered.' But still it was unintelligible to Robert Bolton that any man in his senses should give away so large a sum of money with so slight a prospect of any substantial return.

Hester often goes to see her mother, but Mrs. Bolton has never been at Folking, and probably never will again visit that house. She is a woman whose heart is not capable of many changes, and who cannot readily give herself to new affections. But having once owned that John Caldigate is her daughter's husband, she now alleges no further doubt on the matter. She writes the words 'Mrs. John Caldigate' without a struggle, and does take delight in her daughter's visits.

When last I heard from Folking, Mrs. John Caldigate's second boy had just been born.